Praise for

STEPHEN KING

and the blockbuster
New York Times bestseller

NEEDFUL THINGS

"A master storyteller."

—*Los Angeles Times*

"America's greatest living novelist."

—Lee Child

"Sharply realized . . . Juicy . . . Every word King writes is worth reading. . . . A read in the tradition of *The Stand*."

—*Booklist*

"Demonic . . . Tremendous . . . The horrormaster in top form . . . One of his best!"

—*Kirkus Reviews*

"An undisputed master of suspense and terror."

—*The Washington Post*

STEPHEN KING

NEEDFUL THINGS

A NOVEL

G

GALLERY BOOKS

New York   London   Toronto   Sydney   New Delhi

G

Gallery Books
An Imprint of Simon & Schuster, Inc.
1230 Avenue of the Americas
New York, NY 10020

Copyright © 1992 by Stephen King

First Gallery Books trade paperback edition March 2018

GALLERY BOOKS and colophon are registered trademarks of Simon & Schuster, Inc.

For information about special discounts for bulk purchases, please contact Simon & Schuster Special Sales at 1-866-506-1949 or business@simonandschuster.com.

The Simon & Schuster Speakers Bureau can bring authors to your live event. For more information or to book an event, contact the Simon & Schuster Speakers Bureau at 1-866-248-3049 or visit our website at www.simonspeakers.com.

Manufactured in the United States of America

10   9   8   7   6   5

ISBN 978-1-5011-4741-8
ISBN 978-1-5011-4127-0 (ebook)

This is for Chris Lavin, who doesn't have all the answers—just the ones that matter.

Ladies and gentlemen, attention, please!
Come in close where everyone can see!
I got a tale to tell, it isn't gonna cost a dime!
(And if you believe that,
we're gonna get along just fine.)
—Steve Earle, "Snake Oil"

I have heard of many going astray even in
the village streets, when the darkness was
so thick you could cut it with a knife, as the
saying is . . .
—Henry David Thoreau, *Walden*

YOU'VE BEEN HERE BEFORE.

Sure you have. Sure. I never forget a face.

Come on over here, let me shake your hand! Tell you somethin: I recognized you by the way you walk even before I saw your face good. You couldn't have picked a better day to come back to Castle Rock. Ain't she a corker? Hunting season will be starting up soon, fools out in the woods bangin away at anything that moves and don't wear blaze orange, and then comes the snow and sleet, but all that's for later. Right now it's October, and in The Rock we let October stay just as long as she wants to.

As far as I'm concerned, it's the best time of year. Spring's nice here, but I'll take October over May every time. Western Maine's a part of the state that's mostly forgotten once the summer has run away and all those people with their cottages on the lake and up on the View have gone back to New York and Massachusetts. People here watch them come and go every year—hello, hello, hello; goodbye, goodbye, goodbye. It's good when they come, because they bring their city dollars, but it's good when they go, because they bring their city aggravations, too.

It's aggravations I mostly want to talk about—can you sit a spell with me? Over here on the steps of the bandstand will be fine. The sun's warm and from here, spang in the middle of the Town Common, we can see just about all of downtown. You want to mind the splinters, that's all. The steps need to be sanded off and then repainted. It's Hugh Priest's job, but Hugh ain't got around to it yet. He drinks, you know. It ain't much of a secret. Secrets can and are kept in Castle Rock, but you have to work mighty hard to do it, and most of us know it's been a long time since Hugh Priest and hard work were on good terms.

What was that?

Oh! *That!* Say, boy—ain't that a piece of work? Them fliers is up all over town! I think Wanda Hemphill (her husband, Don, runs Hemphill's Market) put most of em up all by herself. Pull it off the post and hand it to me. Don't be shy—no one's got any business stickin up fliers on the Town Common bandstand in the first place.

Hot damn! Just *look* at this thing, will you? DICE AND THE DEVIL printed right up at the top. In big red letters with *smoke* comin off em, like these things was mailed special delivery from Tophet! Ha! Someone who didn't know what a sleepy little place this town is would think we're really goin to the dogs, I guess. But you know how things sometimes get blown out of proportion in a town this size. And the Reverend Willie's got a bee under his blanket for sure this time. No question about it. Churches in small towns . . . well, I guess I don't have to tell you how *that* is. They get along with each other—sort of—but they ain't never really *happy* with each other. Everything will go along peaceful for a while, and then a squabble will break out.

Pretty big squabble this time, though, and a lot of hard feelings. The Catholics, you see, are planning something they call Casino Nite at the Knights of Columbus Hall on the other side of town. Last Thursday of the month, I understand, with the profits to help pay for repairs on the church roof. That's Our Lady of Serene Waters—you must have passed it on your way into town, if you came by way of Castle View. Pretty little church, ain't it?

Casino Nite was Father Brigham's idea, but the Daughters

of Isabella are the ones who really picked up the ball and ran with it. Betsy Vigue in particular. I think she likes the idea of dollin up in her slinkiest black dress and dealin blackjack or spinnin a roulette wheel and sayin, "Place your bets, ladies and gentlemen, please place your bets." Aw, but they all kind of like the idea, I guess. It's only nickel-dime stuff, harmless, but it seems a wee bit wicked to em just the same.

Except it don't seem harmless to Reverend Willie, and it seems a lot more than a wee bit wicked to him and his congregation. He's actually the Reverend William Rose, and he ain't never liked Father Brigham much, nor does the Father have much use for him. (In fact, it was Father Brigham who started calling Reverend Rose "Steamboat Willie," and the Reverend Willie knows it.)

Sparks has flown between those two particular witch-doctors before, but this Casino Nite business is a little more than sparks; I guess you could call it a brushfire. When Willie heard that the Catholics meant to spend a night gamblin at the K of C Hall, he just about hit the roof with the top of his pointy little head. He paid for those DICE AND THE DEVIL fliers out of his own pocket, and Wanda Hemphill and her sewing circle buddies put em up everywhere. Since then, the only place the Catholics and the Baptists talk to each other is in the Letters column of our little weekly paper, where they rave and rant and tell each other they're goin to hell.

Looka down there, you'll see what I mean. That's Nan Roberts who just came out of the bank. She owns Nan's Luncheonette, and I guess she's just about the richest person in town now that old Pop Merrill's gone to that big flea-market in the sky. Also, she's been a Baptist since Hector was a pup. And comin the other way is big Al Gendron. He's so Catholic he makes the Pope look kosher, and his best friend is Irish Johnny Brigham. Now, watch close! See their noses go up? Ha! Ain't that a sketch? I'll bet you dollars to doughnuts that the temperature dropped twenty degrees where they passed each other by. It's like my mother used to say—people have more fun than anybody, except for horses, and they can't.

Now lookit over there. See that Sheriff's cruiser parked by the curb near the video shop? That's John LaPointe inside. He's supposed to be keepin an eye out for speeders—downtown's a go-slow zone, you know, especially when school lets out—but if you shade your eyes and look close, you'll see that what he's *really* doin is starin at a picture he took out of his wallet. I can't see it from here, but I know what it is just as well as I know my mother's maiden name. That's the snapshot Andy Clutterbuck took of John and Sally Ratcliffe at the Fryeburg State Fair, just about a year ago. John's got his arm around her in that picture, and she's holdin the stuffed bear he won her in the shootin gallery, and they both look so happy they could just about split. But that was then and this is now, as they say; these days Sally is engaged to Lester Pratt, the high school Phys Ed coach. He's a true-blue Baptist, just like herself. John hasn't got over the shock of losin her yet. See him fetch that sigh? He's worked himself into a pretty good case of the blues. Only a man who's still in love (or thinks he is) can fetch a sigh that deep.

Trouble and aggravation's mostly made up of ordinary things, did you ever notice that? Undramatic things. Let me give you a for-instance. Do you see the fellow just going up the courthouse steps? No, not the man in the suit; that's Dan Keeton, our Head Selectman. I mean the other one—the black guy in the work fatigues. That's Eddie Warburton, the night-shift janitor in the Municipal Building. Keep your eye on him for a few seconds, and watch what he does. There! See him pause on the top step and look upstreet? I'd bet you more dollars to more doughnuts that he's looking at the Sunoco station. The Sunoco's owned and operated by Sonny Jackett, and there's been bad blood between the two of em ever since Eddie took his car there two years ago to get the drive-train looked at.

I remember that car quite well. It was a Honda Civic, noth-ing special about it, except it was special to Eddie, because it was the first and only brand-new car he'd ever owned in his life. And Sonny not only did a bad job, he overcharged for it in the bargain. That's *Eddie's* side of the story. Warburton's just usin his color to see if he can beat me out of the repair-bill—that's *Sonny's* side of the story. You know how it goes, don't you?

Well, so Sonny Jackett took Eddie Warburton to small claims court, and there was some shouting first in the courtroom and then in the hall outside. Eddie said Sonny called him a stupid nigger and Sonny said Well, I didn't call him a nigger but the rest is true enough. In the end, neither of them was satisfied. Judge made Eddie cough up fifty bucks, which Eddie said was fifty bucks too much and Sonny said wasn't anywhere near enough. Then, the next thing you know, there was an electrical fire in Eddie's new car and the way it ended was that Eddie's Civic went off to the junkyard out on Town Road #5, and now Eddie's driving an '89 Oldsmobile which blows oil. Eddie has never quite gotten over the idea that Sonny Jackett knows a lot more about that electrical fire than he's ever told.

Boy, people have more fun than anybody, except horses, and they can't. Ain't it all just about more than you can take on a hot day?

It's just small-town life, though—call it Peyton Place or Grover's Corners or Castle Rock, it's just folks eatin pie and drinkin coffee and talkin about each other behind their hands. There's Slopey Dodd, all by his lonesome because the other kids make fun of his stutter. There's Myrtle Keeton, and if she looks a little lonely and bewildered, as if she's not really sure where she is or what's goin on, it's because her husband (fella you just saw comin up the courthouse steps behind Eddie) hasn't seemed himself for the last six months or so. See how puffy her eyes are? I think she's been cryin, or not sleepin well, or both, don't you?

And there goes Lenore Potter, lookin like she just stepped out of a bandbox. Goin to the Western Auto, no doubt, to see if her special organic fertilizer came in yet. That woman has got more kinds of flowers growin around her house than Carter has liver pills. Awful proud of em, she is. She ain't a great favorite with the ladies of this town—they think she's snooty, with her flowers and her mood-beads and her seventy-dollar Boston perms. They think she's snooty, and I'll tell you a secret, since we're just sittin here side by side on this splintery bandstand step. I think they're right.

All ordinary enough, I guess you'd say, but not all our troubles in Castle Rock are ordinary; I got to set you straight on that. No one has forgotten Frank Dodd, the crossing guard who went crazy here twelve years ago and killed those women, and they haven't forgotten the dog, either, the one that came down with rabies and killed Joe Camber and the old rummy down the road from him. The dog killed good old Sheriff George Bannerman, too. Alan Pangborn is doing that job these days, and he's a good man, but he won't never stack up to Big George in the eyes of the town.

Wasn't nothing ordinary about what happened to Reginald "Pop" Merrill, either—Pop was the old miser who used to run the town junk shop. The Emporium Galorium, it was called. Stood right where that vacant lot is across the street. The place burned down awhile ago, but there are people in town who saw it (or claim they did, anyway) who'll tell you after a few beers down at The Mellow Tiger that it was a lot more than a simple fire that destroyed the Emporium Galorium and took Pop Merrill's life.

His nephew Ace says somethin spooky happened to his uncle before that fire—somethin like on *The Twilight Zone.* Of course, Ace wasn't even around when his uncle bit the dust; he was finishing a four-year stretch in Shawshank Prison for breaking and entering in the nighttime. (People always knew Ace Merrill would come to a bad end; when he was in school he was one of the worst bullies this town has ever seen, and there must have been a hundred kids who crossed to the far side of the street when they saw Ace comin toward em with the buckles and zippers on his motorcycle jacket jingling and the cleats on his engineer boots clockin along the sidewalk.) Yet people believe him, you know; maybe there really was somethin strange about what happened to Pop that day, or maybe it's just more talk in Nan's over those cups of coffee and slabs of apple pie.

It's the same here as where you grew up, most likely. People gettin het up over religion, people carryin torches, people carryin secrets, people carryin grudges . . . and even a spooky story every now and then, like what might or might not have happened on the day Pop died in his junk shop, to liven up the occasional dull day. Castle Rock is still a pretty nice place to live and grow, as the sign you see when you come into town says. The sun shines pretty on the lake and on the leaves of the trees, and on a clear day you can see all the way into Vermont from the top of Castle View. The summer people argue over the Sunday newspapers, and there is the occasional fight in the parkin lot of The Mellow Tiger on Friday or Saturday night (sometimes both), but the summer people always go home and the fights always end. The Rock has always been one of the *good* places, and when people get scratchy, you know what we say? We say *He'll get over it* or *She'll get over it.*

Henry Beaufort, for instance, is sick of Hugh Priest kickin the Rock-Ola when he's drunk . . . but Henry will get over it. Wilma Jerzyck and Nettie Cobb are mad at each other . . . but Nettie will get over it (probably) and bein mad's just a way of life for Wilma. Sheriff Pangborn's still mourning his wife and younger child, who died untimely, and it was a sure-enough tragedy, but he'll get over it in time. Polly Chalmers's arthritis isn't gettin any better—in fact, it's gettin worse, a little at a time—and she may not get over it, but she'll learn to live with it. Millions have.

We bump up against each other every now and then, but mostly things go along all right. Or always have, until now. But I have to tell you a *real* secret, my friend; it's mostly why I called

you over once I saw you were back in town. I think trouble—
real trouble—is on its way. I smell it, just over the horizon, like
an out-of-season storm full of lightning. The argument between
the Baptists and the Catholics over Casino Nite, the kids who
tease poor Slopey about his stutter, John LaPointe's torch,
Sheriff Pangborn's grief . . . I think those things are going to
look like pretty small potatoes next to what is coming.

See that building across Main Street? The one three doors
up from the vacant lot where the Emporium Galorium used to
stand? Got a green canopy in front of it? Yup, that's the one.
The windows are all soaped over because it's not quite open yet.
NEEDFUL THINGS, the sign says—now just what the dog does
that mean? I dunno, either, but that's where the bad feeling
seems to come from.

Right there.

Look up the street one more time. You see that boy, don't
you? The one who's walking his bike and looks like he's havin
the sweetest daydream any boy ever had? Keep your eye on him,
friend. I think he's the one who's gonna get it started.

No, I told you, I dunno what . . . not exactly. But watch
that kid. And stick around town for a little while, would you?
Things just feel *wrong,* and if somethin happens, it might be
just as well if there was a witness.

I know that kid—the one who's pushin his bike. Maybe you
do, too. His name's Brian-something. His dad installs siding
and doors over in Oxford or South Paris, I think.

Keep an eye on him, I tell you. Keep an eye on *everything.*
You've been here before, but things are about to change.

I know it.

I *feel* it.

There's a storm on the way.

PART ONE

GRAND OPENING
CELEBRATION

CHAPTER ONE

1

In a small town, the opening of a new store is big news.

It wasn't as big a deal to Brian Rusk as it was to some; his mother, for instance. He had heard her discussing it (he wasn't supposed to call it gossiping, she had told him, because gossiping was a dirty habit and she didn't do it) at some length on the telephone with her best friend, Myra Evans, over the last month or so. The first workmen had arrived at the old building which had last housed Western Maine Realty and Insurance right around the time school let in again, and they had been busily at work ever since. Not that anyone had much idea what they were up to in there; their first act had been to put in a large display window, and their second had been to soap it opaque.

Two weeks ago a sign had appeared in the doorway, hung on a string over a plastic see-through suction-cup.

OPENING SOON!

the sign read.

NEEDFUL THINGS

A NEW KIND OF STORE

"You won't believe your eyes!"

"It'll be just another antique shop," Brian's mother said to Myra. Cora Rusk had been reclining on the sofa at the time, holding the telephone with one hand and eating chocolate-covered cherries with the other while she watched *Santa Barbara* on the TV. "Just another antique shop with a lot of phony early American furniture and moldy old crank telephones. You wait and see."

That had been shortly after the new display window had been first installed and then soaped over, and his mother spoke with such assurance that Brian should have felt sure the subject was closed. Only with his mother, no subject ever seemed to be completely closed. Her speculations and suppositions seemed as endless as the problems of the characters on *Santa Barbara* and *General Hospital.*

Last week the first line of the sign hanging in the door was changed to read:

GRAND OPENING OCTOBER 9TH—
BRING YOUR FRIENDS!

Brian was not as interested in the new store as his mother (and some of the teachers; he had heard them talking about it in the teachers' room at Castle Rock Middle School when it was his turn to be Office Mailman), but he was eleven, and a healthy eleven-year-old boy is interested in anything new. Besides, the name of the place fascinated him. Needful Things: what, exactly, did that mean?

He had read the changed first line last Tuesday, on his way home from school. Tuesday afternoons were his late days. Brian had been born with a harelip, and although it had been surgically corrected when he was seven, he still had to go to speech therapy. He maintained stoutly to everyone who asked that he hated this, but he did not. He was deeply and hopelessly in love with Miss Ratcliffe, and he waited all week for his special ed class to come around. The Tuesday schoolday seemed to last a thousand years, and he always spent the last two hours of it with pleasant butterflies in his stomach.

There were only four other kids in the class, and none of them came from Brian's end of town. He was glad. After an hour in the same room with Miss Ratcliffe, he felt too exalted for company. He liked to make his way home slowly in the late afternoon, usually pushing his bike instead of riding it, dreaming of her as yellow and gold leaves fell around him in the slanting bars of October sunlight.

His way took him along the three-block section of Main Street across from the Town Common, and on the day he saw the sign announcing the grand opening, he had pushed his nose up to the glass of the door, hoping to see what had replaced the stodgy desks and industrial yellow walls of the departed Western Maine Realtors and Insurance Agents. His curiosity was defeated. A shade had been installed and was pulled all the way down. Brian saw nothing but his own reflected face and cupped hands.

On Friday the 4th, there had been an ad for the new store in Castle Rock's weekly newspaper, the *Call*. It was surrounded by a ruffled border, and below the printed matter was a drawing of angels standing back to back and blowing long trumpets. The ad really said nothing that could not be read on the sign dangling from the suction cup: the name of the store was Needful Things, it would open for business at ten o'clock in the morning on October 9th, and, of course, "You won't believe your eyes." There was not the slightest hint of what goods the proprietor or proprietors of Needful Things intended to dispense.

This seemed to irritate Cora Rusk a great deal—enough, anyway, for her to put in a rare Saturday-morning call to Myra.

"I'll believe *my* eyes, all right," she said. "When I see those *spool beds* that are supposed to be *two hundred years old* but have Rochester, *New York,* stamped on the *frames* for anybody who cares to bend down their *heads* and look under the *bedspread* flounces to see, I'll believe my eyes just *fine.*"

Myra said something. Cora listened, fishing Planter's Peanuts out of the can by ones and twos and munching them rapidly. Brian and his little brother, Sean, sat on the living-room floor watching cartoons on TV. Sean was completely immersed in the world of the Smurfs, and Brian was not totally uninvolved with that community of small blue people, but he kept one ear cocked toward the conversation.

"Ri-iiight!" Cora Rusk had exclaimed with even more assurance and emphasis than usual as Myra made some particularly trenchant point. "High prices and moldy antique telephones!"

Yesterday, Monday, Brian had ridden through downtown right after school with two or three friends. They were across the street from the new shop, and he saw that during the day someone had put up a dark-green awning. Written across the front in white letters were the words NEEDFUL THINGS. Polly Chalmers, the lady who ran the sewing shop, was standing out on the sidewalk, hands on her admirably slim hips, looking at the awning with an expression that seemed to be equally puzzled and admiring.

Brian, who knew a bit about awnings, admired it himself. It was the only *real* awning on Main Street, and it gave the new store its own special look. The word "sophisticated" was not a part of his working vocabulary, but he knew at once there was no other shop in Castle Rock which looked like this. The awning made it look like a store you might see in a television show. The Western Auto across the street looked dowdy and countrified by comparison.

When he got home, his mother was on the sofa, watching *Santa Barbara,* eating a Little Debbie Creme Pie, and drinking Diet Coke. His mother always drank diet soda while she watched the afternoon shows. Brian was not sure why, considering what she was using it to wash down, but thought it would probably be dangerous to ask. It might even get her shouting at him, and when his mother started shouting, it was wise to seek shelter.

"Hey, Ma!" he said, throwing his books on the counter and getting the milk out of the refrigerator. "Guess what? There's an awnin on the new store."

"Who's yawning?" Her voice drifted out of the living room.

He poured his milk and came into the doorway. *"Awning,"* he said. "On the new store downstreet."

She sat up, found the remote control, and pushed the mute button. On the screen, Al and Corinne went on talking over their Santa Barbara problems in their favorite Santa Barbara restaurant, but now only a lip-reader could have told exactly what those problems were. "What?" she said. "That Needful Things place?"

"Uh-huh," he said, and drank some milk.

"Don't *slurp,*" she said, tucking the rest of her snack into her mouth. "It sounds *gruesome.* How many times have I told you that?"

About as many times as you've told me not to talk with my mouth full, Brian thought, but said nothing. He had learned verbal restraint at an early age.

"Sorry, Mom."

"What kind of awning?"

"Green one."

"Pressed or aluminum?"

Brian, whose father was a siding salesman for the Dick Perry Siding and Door Company in South Paris, knew exactly what she was talking about, but if it had been *that* kind of awning, he hardly would have noticed it. Aluminum and pressed-metal awnings were a dime a dozen. Half the homes in The Rock had them sticking out over their windows.

"Neither one," he said. "It's cloth. Canvas, I think. It sticks out, so there's shade right underneath. And it's round, like this." He curved his hands (carefully, so as not to spill his milk) in a semi-circle. "The name is printed on the end. It's most sincerely awesome."

"Well, I'll be butched!"

This was the phrase with which Cora most commonly expressed excitement or exasperation. Brian took a cautious step backward, in case it should be the latter.

"What do you think it is, Ma? A restaurant, maybe?"

"I don't know," she said, and reached for the Princess phone on the endtable. She had to move Squeebles the cat, the *TV Guide,* and a quart of Diet Coke to get it. "But it sounds sneaky."

"Mom, what does Needful Things mean? Is it like—"

"Don't bother me now, Brian, Mummy's busy. There are Devil Dogs in the breadbox if you want one. Just one, though, or you'll spoil your supper." She was already dialling Myra, and they were soon discussing the green awning with great enthusiasm.

Brian, who didn't want a Devil Dog (he loved his Ma a great deal, but sometimes watching her eat took away his appetite), sat down at the kitchen table, opened his math book, and started to do the assigned problems—he was a bright, conscientious boy, and his math was the only homework he hadn't finished at school. As he methodically moved decimal points and then divided, he listened to his mother's end of the conversation. She was again telling Myra that soon they would have *another* store selling stinky old *perfume* bottles and pictures of someone's dead *relatives,* and it was really a shame the way these things came and went. There were just too many people out there, Cora said, whose motto in life was take the money and run. When she spoke of the awning, she sounded as if someone had deliberately set out to offend her, and had succeeded splendidly at the task.

I think she thinks someone was supposed to tell her, Brian had thought as his pencil moved sturdily along, carrying down and rounding off. Yeah, that was it. She was curious, that was number one. And she was pissed off, that was number two. The combination was just about killing her. Well, she would find out soon enough. When she did, maybe she would let him in on the big secret. And if she was too busy, he could get it just by listening in on one of her afternoon conversations with Myra.

But as it turned out, Brian found out quite a lot about Needful Things before his mother or Myra or anyone else in Castle Rock.

2

He hardly rode his bike at all on his way home from school on the afternoon before Needful Things was scheduled to open; he was lost in a warm daydream (which would not have passed his lips had he been coaxed with hot coals or bristly tarantula spiders) where he asked Miss Ratcliffe to go with him to the Castle County Fair and she agreed.

"Thank you, Brian," Miss Ratcliffe says, and Brian sees little tears of gratitude in the corners of her blue eyes—eyes so dark in color that they look almost stormy. "I've been . . . well, very sad lately. You see, I've lost my love."

"I'll help you forget him," Brian says, his voice tough and tender at the same time, "if you'll call me . . . Bri."

"Thank you," she whispers, and then, leaning close enough so he can smell her perfume—a dreamy scent of wildflowers—she says, "Thank you . . . Bri. And since, for tonight at least, we will be girl and boy instead of teacher and student, you may call me . . . Sally."

He takes her hands. Looks into her eyes. "I'm not just a kid," he says. "I can help you forget him . . . Sally."

She seems almost hypnotized by this unexpected understanding, this unexpected manliness; he may only be eleven, she thinks, but he is more of a man than Lester ever was! Her hands tighten on his. Their faces draw closer . . . closer . . .

"No," she murmurs, and now her eyes are so wide and so close that he seems almost to drown in them, "you mustn't, Bri . . . it's wrong . . ."

"It's right, baby," he says, and presses his lips to hers.

She draws away after a few moments and whispers tenderly

"Hey, kid, watch out where the fuck you're goin!"

Jerked out of his daydream, Brian saw that he had just walked in front of Hugh Priest's pick-up truck.

"Sorry, Mr. Priest," he said, blushing madly. Hugh Priest was nobody to get mad at you. He worked for the Public Works Department and was reputed to have the worst temper in Castle Rock. Brian watched him narrowly. If he started to get out of his truck, Brian planned to jump on his bike and be gone down Main Street at roughly the speed of light. He had no interest in spending the next month or so in the hospital just because he'd been daydreaming about going to the County Fair with Miss Ratcliffe.

But Hugh Priest had a bottle of beer in the fork of his legs, Hank Williams, Jr., was on the radio singing "High and Pressurized," and it was all just a little too comfy for anything so radical as beating the shit out of a little kid on Tuesday afternoon.

"You want to keep your eyes open," he said, taking a pull from the neck of his bottle and looking at Brian balefully, "because next time I won't bother to stop. I'll just run you down in the road. Make you squeak, little buddy."

He put the truck in gear and drove off. Brian felt an insane (and mercifully brief) urge to scream *Well I'll be butched!* after him. He waited until the orange road-crew truck had turned off onto Linden Street and then went on his way. The daydream about Miss Ratcliffe, alas, was spoiled for the day. Hugh Priest had let in reality again. Miss Ratcliffe hadn't had a fight with her fiancé, Lester Pratt; she was still wearing her small diamond engagement ring and was still driving his blue Mustang while she waited for her own car to come back from the shop.

Brian had seen Miss Ratcliffe and Mr. Pratt only last evening, stapling those dice and the devil posters to the telephone poles on Lower Main Street along with a bunch of other people. They had been singing hymns. The only thing was, the Catholics went around as soon as they were done and took them down again. It was pretty funny in a way . . . but if he had been bigger, Brian would have tried his best to protect any posters Miss Ratcliffe put up with her hallowed hands.

Brian thought of her dark blue eyes, her long dancer's legs, and felt the same glum amazement he always felt when he realized that, come January, she intended to change Sally Ratcliffe, which was lovely, to Sally Pratt, which sounded to Brian like a fat lady falling down a short hard flight of stairs.

Well, he thought, fetching the other curb and starting slowly down Main Street, maybe she'll change her mind. It's not impossible. Or maybe Lester Pratt will get in a car accident or come down with a brain tumor or something like that. It might even turn out that he's a dope addict. Miss Ratcliffe would never marry a dope addict.

Such thoughts offered Brian a bizarre sort of comfort, but they did not change the fact that Hugh Priest had aborted the daydream just short of its apogee (kissing Miss Ratcliffe and actually *touching her right breast* while they were in the Tunnel of Love at the fair). It was a pretty wild idea anyway, an eleven-year-old kid taking a teacher to the County Fair. Miss Ratcliffe was pretty, but she was also old. She had told the speech kids once that she would be twenty-four in November.

So Brian carefully re-folded his daydream along its creases, as a man will carefully fold a well-read and much-valued document, and tucked it on the shelf at the back of his mind where it belonged. He prepared to mount his bike and pedal the rest of the way home.

But he was passing the new shop at just that moment, and the sign in the doorway caught his eye. Something about it had changed. He stopped his bike and looked at it.

GRAND OPENING OCTOBER 9TH—
BRING YOUR FRIENDS!

at the top was gone. It had been replaced by a small square sign, red letters on a white background.

OPEN

it said, and

OPEN

was *all* it said. Brian stood with his bike between his legs, looking at this, and his heart began to beat a little faster.

You're not going in there, are you? he asked himself. I mean, even if it really *is* opening a day early, you're not going in there, right?

Why not? he answered himself.

Well . . . because the window's still soaped over. The shade on the door's still drawn. You go in there, anything could happen to you. *Anything.*

Sure. Like the guy who runs it is Norman Bates or something, he dresses up in his mother's clothes and stabs his customers. *Ri-iight.*

Well, forget it, the timid part of his mind said, although that part sounded as if it already knew it had lost. There's *something* funny about it.

But then Brian thought of telling his mother. Just saying nonchalantly, "By the way, Ma, you know that new store, Needful Things? Well, it opened a day early. I went in and took a look around."

She'd push the mute button on the remote control in a hurry then, you better believe it! She'd want to hear all about it!

This thought was too much for Brian. He put down his bike's kickstand and passed slowly into the shade of the awning—it felt at least ten degrees cooler beneath its canopy—and approached the door of Needful Things.

As he put his hand on the big old-fashioned brass doorknob, it occurred to him that the sign must be a mistake. It had probably been sitting there, just inside the door, for tomorrow, and someone had put it up by accident. He couldn't hear a single sound from behind the drawn shade; the place had a deserted feel.

But since he had come this far, he tried the knob . . . and it turned easily under his hand. The latch clicked back and the door of Needful Things swung open.

3

It was dim inside, but not dark. Brian could see that track lighting (a specialty of the Dick Perry Siding and Door Company) had been installed, and a few of the spots mounted on the tracks were lit. They were trained on a number of glass display cases which were arranged around the large room. The cases were, for the most part, empty. The spots highlighted the few objects which *were* in the cases.

The floor, which had been bare wood when this was Western Maine Realty and Insurance, had been covered in a rich wall-to-wall carpet the color of burgundy wine. The walls had been painted eggshell white. A thin light, as white as the walls, filtered in through the soaped display window.

Well, it's a mistake, just the same, Brian thought. He hasn't even got his stock in yet. Whoever put the OPEN sign in the door by mistake left the door unlocked by mistake, too. The polite thing to do in these circumstances would be to close the door again, get on his bike, and ride away.

Yet he was loath to leave. He was, after all, actually *seeing* the inside of the new store. His mother would talk to him the rest of the afternoon when she heard that. The maddening part was this: he wasn't sure exactly what he was seeing. There were half a dozen

(*exhibits*)

items in the display cases, and the spotlights were trained on them—a kind of trial run, probably—but he couldn't tell what they were. He could, however, tell what they *weren't*: spool beds and moldy crank telephones.

"Hello?" he asked uncertainly, still standing in the doorway. "Is anybody here?"

He was about to grasp the doorknob and pull the door shut again when a voice replied, "*I'm* here."

A tall figure—what at first seemed to be an *impossibly* tall figure—came through a doorway behind one of the display cases. The doorway was masked with a dark velvet curtain. Brian felt a momentary and quite monstrous cramp of fear. Then the glow thrown by one of the spots slanted across the man's face, and Brian's fear was allayed. The guy was quite old, and his face was very kind. He looked at Brian with interest and pleasure.

"Your door was unlocked," Brian began, "so I thought—"

"Of *course* it's unlocked," the tall man said. "I decided to open for a little while this afternoon as a kind of . . . of preview. And you are my very first customer. Come in, my friend. Enter freely, and leave some of the happiness you bring!"

He smiled and stuck out his hand. The smile was infectious. Brian felt an instant liking for the proprietor of Needful Things. He had to step over the threshold and into the shop to clasp the tall man's hand, and he did so without a single qualm. The door swung shut behind him and latched of its own accord. Brian did not notice. He was too busy noticing that the tall man's eyes were dark blue—exactly the same shade as Miss Sally Ratcliffe's eyes. They could have been father and daughter.

The tall man's grip was strong and sure, but not painful. All the same, there was something unpleasant about it. Something . . . *smooth.* Too hard, somehow.

"I'm pleased to meet you," Brian said,

Those dark-blue eyes fastened on his face like hooded railroad lanterns.

"I am equally pleased to make your acquaintance," the tall

man said, and that was how Brian Rusk met the proprietor of Needful Things before anyone else in Castle Rock.

4

"My name is Leland Gaunt," the tall man said, "and you are—?"

"Brian. Brian Rusk."

"Very good, Mr. Rusk. And since you are my first customer, I think I can offer you a very special price on any item that catches your fancy."

"Well, thank you," Brian said, "but I don't really think I could buy anything in a place like this. I don't get my allowance until Friday, and—" He looked doubtfully at the glass display cases again. "Well, you don't look like you've got all your stock in yet."

Gaunt smiled. His teeth were crooked, and they looked rather yellow in the dim light, but Brian found the smile entirely charming just the same. Once more he found himself almost forced to answer it. "No," Leland Gaunt said, "no, I don't. The majority of my—stock, as you put it—will arrive later this evening. But I still have a few interesting items. Take a look around, young Mr. Rusk. I'd love to have your opinion, if nothing else . . . and I imagine you have a mother, don't you? Of course you do. A fine young man like yourself is certainly no orphan. Am I right?"

Brian nodded, still smiling. "Sure. Ma's home right now." An idea struck him. "Would you like me to bring her down?" But the moment the proposal was out of his mouth, he was sorry. He didn't *want* to bring his mother down. Tomorrow, Mr. Leland Gaunt would belong to the whole town. Tomorrow, his Ma and Myra Evans would start pawing him over, along with all the other ladies in Castle Rock. Brian supposed that Mr. Gaunt would have ceased to seem so strange and different by the end of the month, heck, maybe even by the end of the *week,* but right now he still *was,* right now he belonged to Brian Rusk and Brian Rusk alone, and Brian wanted to keep it that way.

So he was pleased when Mr. Gaunt raised one hand (the fingers were extremely narrow and extremely long, and Brian noticed that the first and second were of exactly the same length) and shook his head. "Not at all," he said. "That's exactly what I *don't* want. She would undoubtedly want to bring a friend, wouldn't she?"

"Yeah," Brian said, thinking of Myra.

"Perhaps even *two* friends, or three. No, this is better, Brian—may I call you Brian?"

"Sure," Brian said, amused.

"Thank you. And you will call me Mr. Gaunt, since I am your elder, if not necessarily your better—agreed?"

"Sure." Brian wasn't sure what Mr. Gaunt meant by elders and betters, but he *loved* to listen to this guy talk. And his eyes were really something—Brian could hardly take his own eyes off them.

"Yes, this is much better." Mr. Gaunt rubbed his long hands together and they made a hissing sound. This was one thing Brian was less than crazy about. Mr. Gaunt's hands rubbing together that way sounded like a snake which is upset and thinking of biting. "You will tell your mother, perhaps even show her what you bought, should you buy something—"

Brian considered telling Mr. Gaunt that he had a grand total of ninety-one cents in his pocket and decided not to.

"—and she will tell *her* friends, and they will tell *their* friends . . . you see, Brian? You will be a better advertisement than the local paper could ever *think* of being! I could not do better if I hired you to walk the streets of the town wearing a sandwich board!"

"Well, if you say so," Brian agreed. He had no idea what a sandwich board was, but he was quite sure he would never allow himself to be caught dead wearing one. "It *would* be sort of fun to look around." *At what little there is to look at,* he was too polite to add.

"Then start looking!" Mr. Gaunt said, gesturing toward the cases. Brian noticed that he was wearing a long red-velvet jacket. He thought it might actually be a smoking jacket, like in the Sherlock Holmes stories he had read. It was neat. "Be my guest, Brian!"

Brian walked slowly over to the case nearest the door. He glanced over his shoulder, sure that Mr. Gaunt would be trailing along right behind him, but Mr. Gaunt was still standing by the door, looking at him with wry amusement. It was as if he had read Brian's mind and had discovered how much Brian disliked having the owner of a store trailing around after him while he was looking at stuff. He supposed most storekeepers were afraid that you'd break something, or hawk something, or both.

"Take your time," Mr. Gaunt said. "Shopping is a joy when one takes one's time, Brian, and a pain in the nether quarters when one doesn't."

"Say, are you from overseas somewhere?" Brian asked. Mr. Gaunt's use of "one" instead of "you" interested him. It reminded him of the old stud-muffin who hosted *Masterpiece Theatre,* which his mother sometimes watched if the *TV Guide* said it was a love-story.

"I," Gaunt said, "am from Akron."

"Is that in England?"

"That is in Ohio," Leland Gaunt said gravely, and then revealed his strong, irregular teeth in a sunny grin.

It struck Brian as funny, the way lines in TV shows like *Cheers* often struck him funny. In fact, this whole *thing* made him feel as if he had wandered into a TV show, one that was a little mysterious but not really threatening. He burst out laughing.

He had a moment to worry that Mr. Gaunt might think he

was rude (perhaps because his mother was always accusing him of rudeness, and as a result Brian had come to believe he lived in a huge and nearly invisible spider's web of social etiquette), and then the tall man joined him. The two of them laughed together, and all in all, Brian could not remember when he had had such a pleasant afternoon as this one was turning out to be.

"Go on, look," Mr. Gaunt said, waving his hand. "We will exchange histories another time, Brian."

So Brian looked. There were only five items in the biggest glass case, which looked as if it might comfortably hold twenty or thirty more. One was a pipe. Another was a picture of Elvis Presley wearing his red scarf and his white jump-suit with the tiger on the back. The King (this was how his mother always referred to him) was holding a microphone to his pouty lips. The third item was a Polaroid camera. The fourth was a piece of polished rock with a hollow full of crystal chips in its center. They caught and flashed gorgeously in the overhead spot. The fifth was a splinter of wood about as long and as thick as one of Brian's forefingers.

He pointed to the crystal. "That's a geode, isn't it?"

"You're a well-educated young man, Brian. That's just what it is. I have little plaques for most of my items, but they're not unpacked yet—like most of the stock. I'll have to work like the very devil if I'm going to be ready to open tomorrow." But he didn't sound worried at all, and seemed perfectly content to remain where he was.

"What's that one?" Brian asked, pointing at the splinter. He was thinking to himself that this was very odd stock indeed for a small-town store. He had taken a strong and instant liking to Leland Gaunt, but if the rest of his stuff was like this, Brian didn't think he'd be doing business in Castle Rock for long. If you wanted to sell stuff like pipes and pictures of The King and splinters of wood, New York was the place where you wanted to set up shop . . . or so he had come to believe from the movies he'd seen, anyway.

"Ah!" Mr. Gaunt said. "*That's* an interesting item! Let me show it to you!"

He crossed the room, went around the end of the case, pulled a fat ring of keys from his pocket, and selected one with hardly a glance. He opened the case and took the splinter out carefully. "Hold out your hand, Brian."

"Gee, maybe I better not," Brian said. As a native of a state where tourism is a major industry, he had been in quite a few gift shops in his time, and he had seen a great many signs with this little poem printed on them: *"Lovely to look at / delightful to hold, / but if you break it, / then it's sold."* He could imagine his mother's horrified reaction if he broke the splinter—or whatever it was—and Mr. Gaunt's no longer so friendly, told him that its price was five hundred dollars.

"Why ever not?" Mr. Gaunt asked, raising his eyebrows—but there was really only one brow; it was bushy and grew across the top of his nose in an unbroken line.

"Well, I'm pretty clumsy."

"Nonsense," Mr. Gaunt replied. "I know clumsy boys when I see them. You're not one of *that* breed." He dropped the splinter into Brian's palm. Brian looked at it resting there in some surprise; he hadn't even been aware his palm was open until he saw the splinter resting on it.

It certainly didn't *feel* like a splinter; it felt more like—

"It feels like stone," he said dubiously, and raised his eyes to look at Mr. Gaunt.

"Both wood *and* stone," Mr. Gaunt said. "It's petrified."

"Petrified," Brian marvelled. He looked at the splinter closely, then ran one finger along its side. It was smooth and bumpy at the same time. It was somehow not an entirely pleasant feeling. "It must be old."

"Over two thousand years old," Mr. Gaunt agreed gravely.

"*Cripes!*" Brian said. He jumped and almost dropped the splinter. He closed his hand around it in a fist to keep it from falling to the floor . . . and at once a feeling of oddness and distortion swept over him. He suddenly felt—what? Dizzy? No; not dizzy but *far*. As if part of him had been lifted out of his body and swept away.

He could see Mr. Gaunt looking at him with interest and amusement, and Mr. Gaunt's eyes suddenly seemed to grow to the size of tea-saucers. Yet this feeling of disorientation was not frightening; it was rather exciting, and certainly more pleasant than the slick feel of the wood had been to his exploring finger.

"Close your eyes!" Mr. Gaunt invited. "Close your eyes, Brian, and tell me what you feel!"

Brian closed his eyes and stood there for a moment without moving, his right arm held out, the fist at the end of it enclosing the splinter. He did not see Mr. Gaunt's upper lip lift, doglike, over his large, crooked teeth for a moment in what might have been a grimace of pleasure or anticipation. He had a vague sensation of movement—a corkscrewing kind of movement. A sound, quick and light: *thudthud . . . thudthud . . . thudthud.* He knew that sound. It was—

"A boat!" he cried, delighted, without opening his eyes. "I feel like I'm on a boat!"

"Do you indeed," Mr. Gaunt said, and to Brian's ears he sounded impossibly distant.

The sensations intensified; now he felt as if he were going up and down across long, slow waves. He could hear the distant cry of birds, and, closer, the sounds of many animals—cows lowing, roosters crowing, the low, snarling cry of a very big cat—not a sound of rage but an expression of boredom. In that one second he could almost feel wood (the wood of which this splinter had once been a part, he was sure) under his feet, and knew that the feet themselves were not wearing Converse sneakers but some sort of sandals, and—

Then it was going, dwindling to a tiny bright point, like the light of a TV screen when the power cuts out, and then it was gone. He opened his eyes, shaken and exhilarated.

His hand had curled into such a tight fist around the splinter that he actually had to will his fingers to open, and the joints creaked like rusty door-hinges.

"Hey, *boy*," he said softly.

"Neat, isn't it?" Mr. Gaunt asked cheerily, and plucked the splinter from Brian's palm with the absent skill of a doctor drawing a splinter from flesh. He returned it to its place and re-locked the cabinet with a flourish.

"Neat," Brian agreed in a long outrush of breath which was almost a sigh. He bent to look at the splinter. His hand still tingled a little where he had held it. Those feelings: the up-tilt and downslant of the deck, the thudding of the waves on the hull, the feel of the wood under his feet . . . those things lingered with him, although he guessed (with a feeling of real sorrow) that they would pass, as dreams pass.

"Are you familiar with the story of Noah and the Ark?" Mr. Gaunt inquired.

Brian frowned. He was pretty sure it was a Bible story, but he had a tendency to zone out during Sunday sermons and Thursday night Bible classes. "Was that like a boat that went around the world in eighty days?" he asked.

Mr. Gaunt grinned again. "Something like that, Brian. Something very like that. Well, that splinter is supposed to be from Noah's Ark. Of course I can't say it *is* from Noah's Ark, because people would think I was the most outrageous sort of fake. There must be four thousand people in the world today trying to sell pieces of wood which they claim to be from Noah's Ark—and probably four *hundred* thousand trying to peddle pieces of the One True Cross—but I *can* say it's over two thousand years old, because it's been carbon-dated, and I *can* say it came from the Holy Land, although it was found not on Mount Ararat, but on Mount Boram."

Most of this was lost on Brian, but the most salient fact was not. "Two thousand years," he breathed. "Wow! You're really sure?"

"I am indeed," Mr. Gaunt said. "I have a certificate from

M.I.T., where it was carbon-dated, and that goes with the item, of course. But, you know, I really believe it *might* be from the Ark." He looked at the splinter speculatively for a moment, and then raised his dazzling blue eyes to Brian's hazel ones. Brian was again transfixed by that gaze. "After all, Mount Boram is less than thirty kilometers, as the crow flies, from Mount Ararat, and greater mistakes than the final resting place of a boat, even a big one, have been made in the many histories of the world, especially when stories are handed down from mouth to ear for generations before they are finally committed to paper. Am I right?"

"Yeah," Brian said. "Sounds logical."

"And, besides—it produces an odd sensation when it's held. Wouldn't you say so?"

"I *guess!*"

Mr. Gaunt smiled and ruffled the boy's hair, breaking the spell. "I like you, Brian. I wish all my customers could be as full of wonder as you are. Life would be much easier for a humble tradesman such as myself if that were the way of the world."

"How much . . . how much would you sell something like that for?" Brian asked. He pointed toward the splinter with a finger which was not quite steady. He was only now beginning to realize how deeply the experience had affected him. It had been like holding a conch shell to your ear and hearing the sound of the ocean . . . only in 3-D and Sensurround. He dearly wished Mr. Gaunt would let him hold it again, perhaps even a little longer, but he didn't know how to ask and Mr. Gaunt did not offer.

"Oh now," Mr. Gaunt said, steepling his fingers below his chin and looking at Brian roguishly. "With an item like that—and with most of the *good* things I sell, the really *interesting* things—that would depend on the buyer. What the *buyer* would be willing to pay. What would *you* be willing to pay, Brian?"

"I don't know," Brian said, thinking of the ninety-one cents in his pocket, and then gulped: "A *lot!*"

Mr. Gaunt threw back his head and laughed heartily. Brian noticed when he did that he'd made a mistake about the man. When he first came in, he had thought Mr. Gaunt's hair was gray. Now he saw that it was only silver at the temples. He must have been standing in one of the spotlights, Brian thought.

"Well, this has been terribly interesting, Brian, but I really *do* have a lot of work ahead of me before ten tomorrow, and so—"

"Sure," Brian said, startled back into a consideration of good manners. "I have to go, too. Sorry to have kept you so long—"

"No, no, no! You misunderstand me!" Mr. Gaunt laid one of his long hands on Brian's arm. Brian pulled his arm away. He hoped the gesture didn't seem impolite, but he couldn't help it even if it did. Mr. Gaunt's hand was hard and dry and somehow unpleasant. It did not feel that different, in fact, from the chunk of petrified wood that was supposed to be from Nora's Ark, or whatever it was. But Mr. Gaunt was too much in earnest to notice Brian's instinctive shrinking away. He acted as if he, not Brian, had committed a breach of etiquette. "I just thought we should get down to business. There's no sense, really, in your looking at the few other things I've managed to unpack; there aren't very many of them, and you've seen the most interesting of those which *are* out. Yet I have a pretty good knowledge of my own stock, even without an inventory sheet in my hand, and I might have something that you'd fancy, Brian. What *would* you fancy?"

"Jeepers," Brian said. There were a *thousand* things he would fancy, and that was part of the problem—when the question was put as baldly as that, he couldn't say just which of the thousand he would fancy the most.

"It's best not to think too deeply about these things," Mr. Gaunt said. He spoke idly, but there was nothing idle about his eyes, which were studying Brian's face closely. "When I say, 'Brian Rusk, what do you want more than anything else in the world at this moment?' what is your response? Quick!"

"Sandy Koufax," Brian responded promptly. He had not been aware that his palm was open to receive the splinter from Noah's Ark until he had seen it resting there, and he hadn't been aware of what he was going to say in response to Mr. Gaunt's question until he heard the words tumbling from his mouth. But the moment he heard them he knew they were exactly and completely right.

5

"Sandy Koufax," Mr. Gaunt said thoughtfully. "How interesting."

"Well, not Sandy Koufax *himself*," Brian said, "but his baseball card."

"Topps or Fleers?" Mr. Gaunt asked.

Brian hadn't believed the afternoon could get any better, but suddenly it had. Mr. Gaunt knew about baseball cards as well as splinters and geodes. It was amazing, really amazing.

"Topps."

"I suppose it's his rookie card you'd be interested in," Mr. Gaunt said regretfully. "I don't think I could help you there, but—"

"No," Brian said. "Not 1954. That's the one I'd like to have. I've got a collection of 1956 baseball cards. My dad got me going on it. It's fun, and there are only a few of them that are really expensive—Al Kaline, Mel Parnell, Roy Campanella, guys like that. I've got over fifty already. Including Al Kaline. He was thirty-eight bucks. I mowed a lot of lawns to get Al."

"I bet you did," Mr. Gaunt said with a smile.

"Well, like I say, most '56 cards aren't really expensive—they cost five dollars, seven dollars, sometimes ten. But a Sandy

Koufax in good condition costs ninety or even a hundred bucks. He wasn't a big star *that* year, but of course he turned out to be great, and that was when the Dodgers were still in Brooklyn. Everybody called them Da Bums back then. That's what my dad says, at least."

"Your dad is two hundred per cent correct," said Mr. Gaunt. "I believe I have something that's going to make you very happy, Brian. Wait right here."

He brushed back through the curtained doorway and left Brian standing by the case with the splinter and the Polaroid and the picture of The King in it. Brian was almost dancing from one foot to the other in hope and anticipation. He told himself to stop being such a wuss; even if Mr. Gaunt *did* have a Sandy Koufax card, and even if it *was* a Topps card from the fifties, it would probably turn out to be a '55 or a '57. And suppose it really was a '56? What good was that going to do him, with less than a buck in his pocket?

Well, I can look at it, can't I? Brian thought. It doesn't cost anything to *look,* does it? This was also another of his mother's favorite sayings.

From the room behind the curtain there came the sounds of boxes being shifted and mild thuds as they were set on the floor. "Just a minute, Brian," Mr. Gaunt called. He sounded a little out of breath. "I'm sure there's a shoebox here some-place . . ."

"Don't go to any trouble on my account, Mr. Gaunt!" Brian called back, hoping like mad that Mr. Gaunt would go to as much trouble as was necessary.

"Maybe that box is in one of the shipments still en route," Mr. Gaunt said dubiously.

Brian's heart sank.

Then: "But I was sure . . . wait! Here it is! Right here!"

Brian's heart rose—did more than rise. It soared and did a backover flip.

Mr. Gaunt came back through the curtain. His hair was a

trifle disarrayed, and there was a smudge of dust on one lapel of his smoking jacket. In his hands he held a box which had once contained a pair of Air Jordan sneakers. He set it on the counter and took off the top. Brian stood by his left arm, looking in. The box was full of baseball cards, each inserted in its own plastic envelope, just like the ones Brian sometimes bought at The Baseball Card Shop in North Conway, New Hampshire.

"I thought there might be an inventory sheet in here, but no such luck," Mr. Gaunt said. "Still, I have a pretty good idea of what I have in stock, as I told you—it's the key to running a business where you sell a little bit of everything—and I'm quite sure I saw . . ."

He trailed off and began flipping rapidly through the cards.

Brian watched the cards flash by, speechless with astonishment. The guy who ran The Baseball Card Shop had what his dad called "a pretty country-fair" selection of old cards, but the contents of the whole store couldn't hold a candle to the treasures tucked away in this one sneaker box. There were chewing-tobacco cards with pictures of Ty Cobb and Pie Traynor on them. There were cigarette cards with pictures of Babe Ruth and Dom DiMaggio and Big George Keller and even Hiram Dissen, the one-armed pitcher who had chucked for the White Sox during the forties. LUCKY STRIKE HAS GONE TO WAR! many of the cigarette cards proclaimed. And there, just glimpsed, a broad, solemn face above a Pittsburgh uniform shirt—

"My God, wasn't that Honus Wagner?" Brian gasped. His heart felt like a very small bird which had blundered into his throat and now fluttered there, trapped. "That's the rarest baseball card in the *universe!*"

"Yes, yes," Mr. Gaunt said absently. His long fingers shuttled speedily through the cards, faces from another age trapped under transparent plastic coverings, men who had whacked the pill and chucked the apple and covered the anchors, heroes of a grand and bygone golden age, an age of which this boy still harbored cheerful and lively dreams. "A little of everything, that's what a successful business is all about, Brian. Diversity, pleasure, amazement, fulfillment . . . what a successful *life* is all about, for that matter . . . I don't give advice, but if I did, you could do worse than to remember that . . . now let me see . . . somewhere . . . somewhere . . . *ah!*"

He pulled a card from the middle of the box like a magician doing a trick and placed it triumphantly in Brian's hand.

It was Sandy Koufax.

It was a '56 Topps card.

And it was *signed*.

"To my good friend Brian, with best wishes, Sandy Koufax," Brian read in a hoarse whisper.

And then found he could say nothing at all.

6

He looked up at Mr. Gaunt, his mouth working. Mr. Gaunt smiled. "I didn't plant it or plan it, Brian. It's just a coincidence . . . but a *nice* sort of coincidence, don't you think?"

Brian still couldn't talk, and so settled for a single nod of his head. The plastic envelope with its precious cargo felt weirdly heavy in his hand.

"Take it out," Mr. Gaunt invited.

When Brian's voice finally emerged from his mouth again, it was the croak of a very old invalid. "I don't dare."

"Well, *I* do," Mr. Gaunt said. He took the envelope from Brian, reached inside with the carefully manicured nail of one finger, and slid the card out. He put it in Brian's hand.

He could see tiny dents in the surface—they had been made by the point of the pen Sandy Koufax had used to sign his name . . . *their* names. Koufax's signature was almost the same as the printed one, except the printed signature said Sanford Koufax and the autograph said *Sandy* Koufax. Also, it was a thousand times better because it was *real*. Sandy Koufax had held this card in his hand and had imposed his mark upon it, the mark of his living hand and magic name.

But there was *another* name on it, as well—Brian's own. Some boy with his name had been standing by the Ebbets Field bullpen before the game and Sandy Koufax, *the real Sandy Koufax,* young and strong, his glory years just ahead of him, had taken the offered card, probably still smelling of sweet pink bubblegum, and had set his mark upon it . . . *and mine, too,* Brian thought.

Suddenly it came again, the feeling which had swept over him when he held the splinter of petrified wood. Only this time it was much, much stronger.

Smell of grass, sweet and fresh-cut.

Heavy smack of ash on horsehide.

Yells and laughter from the batting cage.

"Hello, Mr. Koufax, could you sign your card for me?"

A narrow face. Brown eyes. Darkish hair. The cap comes off briefly, he scratches his head just above the hairline, then puts the cap back on.

"Sure, kid." He takes the card. "What's your name?"

"Brian, sir—Brian Seguin."

Scratch, scratch, scratch on the card. The magic: the inscribed fire.

"You want to be a ballplayer when you grow up, Brian?" The question has the feel of rote recital, and he speaks without raising his face from the card he holds in his large right hand so he can write on it with his soon-to-be-magic left hand.

"Yes, sir."

"Practice your fundamentals." And hands the card back.

"Yes, sir!"

But he's already walking away, then he's breaking into a lazy run on the fresh-cut grass as he jogs toward the bullpen with his shadow jogging along beside him—

"Brian? *Brian?"*

Long fingers were snapping under his nose—Mr. Gaunt's fingers. Brian came out of his daze and saw Mr. Gaunt looking at him, amused.

"Are you there, Brian?"

"Sorry," Brian said, and blushed. He knew he should hand the card back, hand it back and get out of here, but he couldn't seem to let it go. Mr. Gaunt was staring into his eyes—right into his *head,* it seemed—again, and once more he found it impossible to look away.

"So," Mr. Gaunt said softly. "Let us say, Brian, that *you* are the buyer. Let us say that. How much would you pay for that card?"

Brian felt despair like a rockslide weight his heart.

"All I've got is—"

Mr. Gaunt's left hand flew up. "Shhh!" he said sternly. "Bite your tongue! The buyer must never tell the seller how much he has! You might as well hand the vendor your wallet, and turn the contents of your pockets out on the floor in the bargain! If you can't tell a lie, then be still! It's the first rule of fair trade, Brian my boy."

His eyes—so large and dark. Brian felt that he was swimming in them.

"There are two prices for this card, Brian. Half . . . and half. One half is cash. The other is a deed. Do you understand?"

"Yes," Brian said. He felt *far* again—far away from Castle Rock, far away from Needful Things, even far away from himself. The only things which were real in this far place were Mr. Gaunt's wide, dark eyes.

"The cash price for that 1956 autographed Sandy Koufax card is eighty-five cents," Mr. Gaunt said. "Does that seem fair?"

"Yes," Brian said. His voice was far and wee. He felt himself dwindling, dwindling away . . . and approaching the point where any clear memory would cease.

"Good," Mr. Gaunt's caressing voice said. "Our trading has progressed well thus far. As for the deed . . . do you know a woman named Wilma Jerzyck, Brian?"

"Wilma, sure," Brian said out of his growing darkness. "She lives on the other side of the block from us."

"Yes, I believe she does," Mr. Gaunt agreed. "Listen carefully, Brian." So he must have gone on speaking, but Brian did not remember what he said.

7

The next thing he was aware of was Mr. Gaunt shooing him gently out onto Main Street, telling him how much he had enjoyed meeting him, and asking him to tell his mother and all his friends that he had been well treated and fairly dealt with.

"Sure," Brian said. He felt bewildered . . . but he also felt very good, as if he had just awakened from a refreshing early-afternoon nap.

"And come again," Mr. Gaunt said, just before he shut the door. Brian looked at it. The sign hanging there now read

CLOSED.

8

It seemed to Brian that he had been in Needful Things for hours, but the clock outside the bank said it was only ten of four. It had been less than twenty minutes. He prepared to mount his bike, then leaned the handlebars against his belly while he reached in his pants pockets.

From one he drew six bright copper pennies.

From the other he drew the autographed Sandy Koufax card.

They apparently *had* made some sort of deal, although Brian could not for the life of him remember exactly what it had been—only that Wilma Jerzyck's name had been mentioned.

To my good friend Brian, with best wishes, Sandy Koufax.

Whatever deal they had made, this was worth it.

A card like this was worth practically anything.

Brian tucked it carefully into his knapsack so it wouldn't get bent, mounted his bike, and began to pedal home fast. He grinned all the way.

CHAPTER TWO

1

When a new shop opens in a small New England town, the residents—hicks though they may be in many other things—display a cosmopolitan attitude which their city cousins can rarely match. In New York or Los Angeles, a new gallery may attract a little knot of might-be patrons and simple lookers-on before the doors are opened for the first time; a new club may even garner a line, and police barricades with *paparazzi,* armed with gadget bags and telephoto lenses, standing expectantly beyond them. There is an excited hum of conversation, as among theatergoers on Broadway before the opening of a new play which, smash hit or drop-dead flop, is sure to cause comment.

When a new shop opens in a small New England town, there is rarely a crowd before the doors open, and never a line. When the shades are drawn up, the doors unlocked, and the new concern declared open for business, customers come and go in a trickle which would undoubtedly strike an outsider as apathetic . . . and probably as an ill omen for the shopkeeper's future prosperity.

What seems like lack of interest often masks keen anticipation and even keener observation (Cora Rusk and Myra Evans were not the only two women in Castle Rock who had kept the telephone lines buzzing about Needful Things in the weeks before it opened). That interest and anticipation do not change the small-town shopper's conservative code of conduct, however. Certain things are simply Not Done, particularly not in the tight Yankee enclaves north of Boston. These are societies which exist for nine months of every year mostly sufficient unto themselves, and it is considered bad form to show too much interest too soon, or in any way to indicate that one has felt more than a passing interest, so to speak.

Investigating a new shop in a small town and attending a socially prestigious party in a large city are both activities which cause a fair amount of excitement among those likely to participate, and there are rules for both—rules which are unspoken, immutable, and strangely similar. The chief among these is that *one must not arrive first.* Of course, someone has to break this cardinal rule, or no one would arrive at all, but a new shop is apt to stand empty for at least twenty minutes after the CLOSED sign in the window has been turned over to read OPEN for the first time, and a knowledgeable observer would feel safe in wagering that the first arrivals would come in a group—a pair, a trio, but more likely a foursome of ladies.

The second rule is that the investigating shoppers display a politeness so complete that it verges on iciness. The third is that no one must ask (on the first visit, at least) for the new shop-keeper's history or *bona fides.* The fourth is that no one should bring a welcome-to-town present, especially one as tacky as a home-made cake or a pie. The last rule is as immutable as the first: *one must not depart last.*

This stately gavotte—which might be called The Dance of Female Investigation—lasts anywhere from two weeks to two months, and does not apply when someone from town opens a business. *That* sort of opening is apt to be like an Old Home Week church supper—informal, cheery, and quite dull. But when the new tradesman is From Away (it is always said that way, so one can hear the capital letters), The Dance of Female Investigation is as sure as the fact of death and the force of gravity. When the trial period is over (no one takes out an ad in the paper to say that it is, but somehow everyone knows), one of two things happens: either the flow of trade becomes more normal and satisfied customers bring in belated welcome gifts and invitations to Come and Visit, or the new business fails. In towns like Castle Rock, small businesses are sometimes spoken of as "broke down" weeks or even months before the hapless owners discover the fact for themselves.

There was at least one woman in Castle Rock who did not play by the accepted rules, immutable as they might seem to others. This was Polly Chalmers, who ran You Sew and Sew. Ordinary behavior was not expected of her by most; Polly Chalmers was considered by the ladies of Castle Rock (and many of the gentlemen) to be Eccentric.

Polly presented all sorts of problems for the self-appointed social arbiters of Castle Rock. For one thing, no one could quite decide on the most basic fact of all: was Polly From Town, or was she From Away? She had been born and mostly raised in Castle Rock, true enough, but she had left with Duke Sheehan's bun in her oven at the age of eighteen. That had been in 1970, and she had only returned once before moving back for good in 1987.

That brief return call had begun in late 1975, when her father had been dying from cancer of the bowel. Following his death, Lorraine Chalmers had suffered a heart attack, and Polly had stayed on to nurse her mother. Lorraine had suffered a second heart attack—this one fatal—in the early spring of 1976, and after her mother had been buried away in Homeland, Polly (who had by then attained a genuine Air of Mystery, as far as the ladies of the town were concerned) had left again.

Gone for good this time had been the general consensus, and when the last remaining Chalmers, old Aunt Evvie, died in 1981 and Polly did not attend the funeral, the consensus seemed a proven fact. Yet four years ago she *had* returned, and had opened her sewing shop. Although no one knew for certain, it seemed likely that she had used Aunt Evvie Chalmers's money to fund the new venture. Who else would that crazy old rip have left it to?

The town's more avid followers of *la comédie humaine* (this was most of them) felt sure that, if Polly made a success of her little business and stuck around, most of the things they were curious about would be revealed to them in the fullness of time. But in Polly's case, many matters remained dark. It was really quite exasperating.

She had spent *some* of the intervening years in San Francisco, that much was known, but little more—Lorraine Chalmers had been as close as the devil about her wayward daughter. Had Polly gone to school there, or somewhere? She ran her business as if she had taken business courses, and learned a right smart from them, too, but no one could say for sure. She was single when she returned, but had she ever been married, either in San Francisco or in one of those places where she might (or might not) have spent some of her time between Then and Now? No one knew that, either, only that she had never married the Sheehan boy—he had joined the Marines, had done a few turns there, and was now selling real estate someplace in New Hampshire. And why had she come back here to stay after all the years?

Most of all they wondered what had become of the baby. Had pretty Polly gotten an abortion? Had she given it up for adoption? Had she kept it? If so, had it died? Was it (maddening pronoun, that) alive now, at school somewhere, and writing the occasional letter home to its mother? No one knew these things, either, and in many ways the unanswered questions about "it" were the most galling. The girl who had left on a Greyhound with a bun in her oven was now a woman of almost forty and had been back, living and doing business in town, for four years, and no one even knew the sex of the child that had caused her to leave.

Just lately Polly Chalmers had given the town a fresh demonstration of her eccentricity, if one was needed: she had been keeping company with Alan Pangborn, Castle County's Sheriff, and Sheriff Pangborn had buried his wife and younger son only a year and a half ago. This behavior was not quite a Scandal, but it was certainly Eccentric, and so no one was really surprised to see Polly Chalmers go marching down the sidewalk of Main Street from her door to that of Needful Things at two minutes past ten on the morning of October 9th. They were not even surprised at what she was carrying in her gloved hands: a Tupperware container which could only contain a cake.

It was, the locals said when discussing it later, just like her.

2

The display window of Needful Things had been cleansed of soap, and a dozen or so items had been set out there—clocks, a silver setting, a painting, a lovely triptych just waiting for someone to fill it with well-loved photographs. Polly glanced at these items with approval, then went to the door. The sign hanging there read OPEN. As she did what the sign suggested, a small bell jingled over her head—this had been installed since Brian Rusk's preview.

The shop smelled of new carpeting and fresh paint. It was filled with sunshine, and as she stepped in, looking around with interest, a clear thought came to her: *This is a success. Not a customer has stepped through the door yet—unless I'm one—and it's already a success. Remarkable.* Such hasty judgments were not like her, and neither was her feeling of instant approval, but they were undeniable.

A tall man was bending over one of the glass display cases. He looked up when the bell jingled and smiled at her. "Hello," he said.

Polly was a practical woman who knew her own mind and generally liked what she found there, and so the instant of confusion which struck her when she first met this stranger's eyes was confusing in and of itself.

I know him, was the first clear thought to come through that unexpected cloud. *I've met this man before. Where?*

She hadn't, though, and that knowledge—that surety—came a moment later. It was *déjà vu,* she supposed, that sense of false recollection which strikes almost everyone from time to time, a feeling which is disorienting because it is at once so dreamy and so prosaic.

She was put off her stride for a moment or two, and could only smile at him lamely. Then she moved her left hand to get a better grip on the cake container she held, and a harsh bolt of pain shot up the back of it and out toward the wrist in two bright spikes. The tines of a large chrome fork seemed to be planted deep in her flesh. It was arthritis, and it hurt like a son of a bitch, but at least it focused her attention again, and she spoke without a noticeable lag . . . only she thought that the man *might* have noticed, just the same. He had bright hazel eyes which looked as if they might notice a great deal.

"Hi," she said. "My name is Polly Chalmers. I own the little dress and sewing shop two doors down from you. I thought that, since we're neighbors, I'd come over and welcome you to Castle Rock before the rush."

He smiled, and his entire face lit up. She felt an answering smile lift her own lips, even though her left hand was still hurting like a bastard. If I weren't already in love with Alan, she thought, I think I'd fall at this man's feet without a whimper. "Show me to the bedroom, Master, I will go quietly." With a quirk of amusement, she wondered how many of the ladies who would pop in here for a quick peek before the end of the day would go home with ravening crushes on him. She saw he was wearing no wedding band; more fuel to the fire.

"I'm delighted to meet you, Ms. Chalmers," he said, coming forward. "I'm Leland Gaunt." He put out his right hand as he approached her, then frowned slightly as she took a small step backward.

"I'm sorry," she said, "I don't shake hands. Don't think me

impolite, please. I have arthritis." She set the Tupperware container on the nearest glass case and raised her hands, which were encased in kid-leather gloves. There was nothing freakish about them, but they were clearly misshapen, the left a little more than the right.

There were women in town who thought that Polly was actually proud of her disease; why else, they reasoned, would she be so quick to show it off? The truth was the exact opposite. Though not a vain woman, she was concerned enough about her looks that the ugliness of her hands embarrassed her. She showed them as quickly as she could, and the same thought surfaced briefly—so briefly it almost always went unrecognized—in her mind each time she did: *There. That's over. Now we can get on with whatever else there is.*

People usually registered some discomposure or embarrassment of their own when she showed them her hands. Gaunt did not. He grasped her upper arm in hands that felt extraordinarily strong and shook *that* instead. It might have struck her as an inappropriately intimate thing to have done on first acquaintance, but it did not. The gesture was friendly, brief, even rather amusing. All the same, she was glad it was quick. His hands had a dry, unpleasant feel even through the light fall coat she was wearing.

"It must be difficult to run a sewing shop with that particular disability, Ms. Chalmers. How ever do you manage?"

It was a question very few people put to her, and, with the exception of Alan, she couldn't remember anyone's ever asking her in such a straightforward way.

"I went right on sewing full-time as long as I could," she said. "Grinned and bore it, I suppose you'd say. Now I have half a dozen girls working for me part-time, and I stick mostly to designing. But I still have my good days." This was a lie, but she felt it did no harm, since she told it mostly for her own benefit.

"Well, I'm delighted that you came over. I'll tell you the truth—I've got a bad case of stage fright."

"Really? Why?" She was even less hasty about judging people than she was of judging places and events, and she was startled—even a little alarmed—at how rapidly and naturally she felt at home with this man she had met less than a minute ago.

"I keep wondering what I'll do if no one comes in. No one at all, all day long."

"They'll come," she said. "They'll want a look at your stock—no one seems to have any idea what a store called Needful Things sells—but even more important, they'll want a look at you. It's just that, in a little place like Castle Rock—"

"—no one wants to seem too eager," he finished for her. "I know—I've had experience of small towns. My rational mind assures me that what you've just said is the absolute truth, but there's another voice that just goes on saying, 'They won't come, Leland, oohhh, no, they won't come, they'll stay away in *droves,* you just wait and see.' "

She laughed, remembering suddenly that she had felt exactly the same way when she opened You Sew and Sew.

"But what's this?" he asked, touching the Tupperware container with one hand. And she noticed what Brian Rusk had already seen: the first and second fingers of that hand were exactly the same length.

"It's a cake. And if I know this town half as well as I think I do, I can assure you it will be the only one you'll get today."

He smiled at her, clearly delighted. "Thank you! Thank you very much, Ms. Chalmers—I'm touched."

And she, who never asked anyone to use her first name on first or even short acquaintance (and who was suspicious of anyone—realtors, insurance agents, car salesmen—who appropriated that privilege unasked), was bemused to hear herself saying, "If we're going to be neighbors, shouldn't you call me Polly?"

3

The cake was devil's food, as Leland Gaunt ascertained merely by lifting the lid and sniffing. He asked her to stay and have a slice with him. Polly demurred. Gaunt insisted.

"You'll have someone to run your shop," he said, "and no one will dare set foot in mine for at least half an hour—that should satisfy the protocols. And I have a thousand questions about the town."

So she agreed. He disappeared through the curtained doorway at the back of the shop and she heard him climbing stairs—the upstairs area, she supposed, must be his living quarters, if only temporarily—to get plates and forks. While she waited for him to come back, Polly wandered around looking at things.

A framed sign on the wall by the door through which she had entered said that the shop would be open from ten in the morning until five in the afternoon on Mondays, Wednesdays, Fridays, and Saturdays. It would be closed "except by appointment" on Tuesdays and Thursdays until late spring—or, Polly thought with an interior grin, until those wild and crazy tourists and vacationers arrived again, waving their fistfuls of dollars.

Needful Things, she decided, was a curio shop. An upscale curio shop, she would have said after a single glance, but a closer examination of the items for sale suggested it was not that easily categorized.

The items which had been placed out when Brian stopped in the afternoon before—geode, Polaroid camera, picture of Elvis Presley, the few others—were still there, but perhaps four dozen more had been added. A small rug probably worth a small fortune hung on one of the off-white walls—it was Turkish, and old. There was a collection of lead soldiers in one of the cases, possibly antiques, but Polly knew that all lead soldiers, even those cast in Hong Kong a week ago last Monday, have an antique-y look.

The goods were wildly varied. Between the picture of Elvis, which looked to her like the sort of thing that would retail on any carnival midway in America for $4.99, and a singularly uninteresting American eagle weathervane, was a carnival glass lampshade which was certainly worth eight hundred dollars and might be worth as much as five thousand. A battered and charmless teapot stood flanked by a pair of gorgeous *poupées,* and she could not even begin to guess what those beautiful French dollies with their rouged cheeks and gartered gams might be worth.

There was a selection of baseball and tobacco cards, a fan of pulp magazines from the thirties (*Weird Tales, Astounding Tales, Thrilling Wonder Stories*), a table-radio from the fifties which was that disgusting shade of pale pink which the people of that time had seemed to approve of when it came to appliances, if not to politics.

Most—although not all—of the items had small plaques standing in front of them: TRI-CRYSTAL GEODE, ARIZONA, read one. CUSTOM SOCKET-WRENCH KIT, read another. The one in front of the splinter which had so amazed Brian announced it was PETRIFIED WOOD FROM THE HOLY LAND. The plaques in front of the trading cards and the pulp magazines read: OTHERS AVAILABLE UPON REQUEST.

All the items, whether trash or treasure, had one thing in common, she observed: there were no price-tags on any of them.

4

Gaunt arrived back with two small plates—plain old Corning Ware, nothing fancy—a cake-knife, and a couple of forks. "Everything's helter-skelter up there," he confided, removing the top of the container and setting it aside (he turned it upside down so it would not imprint a ring of frosting on the top of the cabinet he was serving from). "I'll be looking for a house as soon as I get things set to rights here, but for the time being I'm going to live over the store. Everything's in cardboard cartons. God, I hate cardboard cartons. Who would you say—"

"Not *that* big," Polly protested. "My goodness!"

"Okay," Gaunt said cheerfully, putting the thick slab of chocolate cake on one of the plates. "This one will be mine. Eat, Rowf, eat, I say! Like this for you?"

"Even thinner."

"I can't cut it any thinner than this," he said, and sliced off a narrow piece of cake. "It smells heavenly. Thank you again, Polly."

"You're more than welcome."

It *did* smell good, and she wasn't on a diet, but her initial refusal had been more than first-meeting politeness. The last three weeks had been a stretch of gorgeous Indian summer weather in Castle Rock, but on Monday the weather had turned cool, and her hands were miserable with the change. The pain would probably abate a little once her joints got used to the cooler temperatures (or so she prayed, and so it always had been, but she was not blind to the progressive nature of the disease), but since early this morning it had been very bad. When it was like this, she was never sure what she would or would not be able to do with her traitor hands, and her initial refusal had been out of worry and potential embarrassment.

Now she stripped off her gloves, flexed her right hand experimentally. A spear of hungry pain bolted up her forearm to the elbow. She flexed again, her lips compressed in anticipation. The pain came, but it wasn't as intense this time. She relaxed a little. It was going to be all right. Not great, not as pleasant as eating cake should be, but all right. She picked up her fork carefully, bending her fingers as little as possible when she grasped it. As she conveyed the first bite to her mouth, she saw Gaunt looking at her sympathetically. *Now he'll commiserate,* she thought glumly, *and tell me how bad his grandfather's arthritis was. Or his ex-wife's. Or somebody's.*

But Gaunt did not commiserate. He took a bite of cake and rolled his eyes comically. "Never mind sewing and patterns," he said, "you should have opened a restaurant."

"Oh, I didn't make it," she said, "but I'll convey the compliment to Nettie Cobb. She's my housekeeper."

"Nettie Cobb," he said thoughtfully, cutting another bite from his slice of cake.

"Yes—do you know her?"

"Oh, I doubt it." He spoke with the air of a man who is suddenly recalled to the present moment. "I don't know *anyone* in Castle Rock." He looked at her slyly from the corners of his eyes. "Any chance she could be hired away?"

"None," Polly said, laughing.

"I was going to ask you about real-estate agents," he said. "Who would you say is the most trustworthy around here?"

"Oh, they're all thieves, but Mark Hopewell's probably as safe as any."

He choked back laughter and put a hand to his mouth to stifle a spray of crumbs. Then he began to cough, and if her hands hadn't been so painful, she would have thumped him companionably on the back a few times. First acquaintance or not, she *did* like him.

"Sorry," he said, still chuckling a little. "They *are* all thieves, though, aren't they?"

"Oh, absolutely."

Had she been another sort of woman—one who kept the facts of her own past less completely to herself—Polly would then have begun asking Leland Gaunt leading questions. Why had he come to Castle Rock? Where had he been before coming here? Would he stay long? Did he have family? But she wasn't that other sort of woman, and so she was content to answer his questions . . . was delighted to, in fact, since none of them were about herself. He wanted to know about the town, and what the flow of traffic was like on Main Street during the winter, and if there was a place nearby where he could shop for a nice little Jøtul stove, and insurance rates, and a hundred other things. He produced a narrow black leather notebook from the pocket of the blue blazer he wore and gravely noted down each name she mentioned.

She looked down at her plate and saw that she had finished all of her cake. Her hands still hurt, but they felt better than they had when she arrived. She recalled that she had almost decided against coming by, because they were so miserable. Now she was glad she'd done it, anyway.

"I have to go," she said, looking at her watch. "Rosalie will think I died."

They had eaten standing up. Now Gaunt stacked their plates neatly, put the forks on top, and replaced the top on the cake container. "I'll return this as soon as the cake is gone," he said. "Is that all right?"

"Perfectly."

"You'll probably have it by mid-afternoon, then," he said gravely.

"You don't have to be *that* prompt," she said as Gaunt walked her to the door. "It's been very nice to meet you."

"Thanks for coming by," he said. For a moment she thought he meant to take her arm, and she felt a sense of dismay at the thought of his touch—silly, of course—but he didn't. "You've made what I expected to be a scary day something of a treat instead."

"You'll be fine." Polly opened the door, then paused. She had asked him nothing at all about himself, but she *was* curious about one thing, too curious to leave without asking. "You've got all sorts of interesting things—"

"Thank you."

"—but nothing is priced. Why is that?"

He smiled. "That's a little eccentricity of mine, Polly. I've always believed that a sale worth making is worth dickering over a little. I think I must have been a Middle Eastern rug merchant in my last incarnation. Probably from Iraq, although I probably shouldn't say so these days."

"So you charge whatever the market will bear?" she asked, teasing just a little.

"You could say so," he agreed seriously, and again she was struck by how deep his hazel eyes were—how oddly beautiful. "I'd rather think of it as defining worth by need."

"I see."

"Do you really?"

"Well . . . I *think* so. It explains the name of the shop."

He smiled. "It might," he said. "I suppose it might, at that."

"Well, I'll wish you a very good day, Mr. Gaunt—"

"Leland, please. Or just Lee."

"Leland, then. And you're not to worry about customers. I think by Friday, you'll have to hire a security guard to shoo them out at the end of the day."

"Do you? That would be lovely."

"Goodbye."

"*Ciao,*" he said, and closed the door after her.

He stood there a moment, watching as Polly Chalmers walked down the street, smoothing her gloves over her hands, so misshapen and in such startling contrast to the rest of her, which was trim and pretty, if not terribly remarkable. Gaunt's smile grew. As his lips drew back, exposing his uneven teeth, it became unpleasantly predatory.

"You'll do," he said softly in the empty shop. "You'll do just fine."

5

Polly's prediction proved quite correct. By closing time that day, almost all of the women in Castle Rock—those who mattered, anyway—and several men had stopped by Needful Things for a quick browse. Almost all of them were at some pains to assure Gaunt that they had only a moment, because they were on their way to someplace else.

Stephanie Bonsaint, Cynthia Rose Martin, Barbara Miller, and Francine Pelletier were the first; Steffie, Cyndi Rose, Babs, and Francie arrived in a protective bunch not ten minutes after Polly was observed leaving the new shop (the news of her departure spread quickly and thoroughly by telephone and the efficient bush telegraph which runs through New England back yards).

Steffie and her friends looked. They ooohed and ahhhed. They assured Gaunt they could not stay long because this was their bridge day (neglecting to tell him that the weekly rubber usually did not start until about two in the afternoon). Francie asked him where he came from. Gaunt told her Akron, Ohio. Steffie asked him if he had been in the antiques business for long. Gaunt told her he did not consider it to be the antiques business . . . exactly. Cyndi wanted to know if Mr. Gaunt had been in New England long. Awhile, Gaunt replied; awhile.

All four agreed later that the shop was interesting—so many odd things!—but it had been a very unsuccessful interview. The man was as close-mouthed as Polly Chalmers, perhaps more. Babs then pointed out what they all knew (or thought they knew): that Polly had been the first person in town to actually enter the new shop, and that she had *brought a cake*. Perhaps, Babs speculated, she knew Mr. Gaunt . . . from that Time Before, that time she had spent Away.

Cyndi Rose expressed interest in a Lalique vase, and asked

Mr. Gaunt (who was nearby but did not hover, all noted with approval) how much it was.

"How much do you think?" he asked, smiling.

She smiled back at him, rather coquettishly. *"Oh,"* she said. "Is *that* the way you do things, Mr. Gaunt?"

"That's the way I do them," he agreed.

"Well, you're apt to lose more than you gain, dickering with Yankees," Cyndi Rose said, while her friends looked on with the bright interest of spectators at a Wimbledon Championship match.

"That," he said, "remains to be seen." His voice was still friendly, but now it was mildly challenging, as well.

Cyndi Rose looked more closely at the vase this time. Steffie Bonsaint whispered something in her ear. Cyndi Rose nodded.

"Seventeen dollars," she said. The vase actually looked as if it might be worth fifty, and she guessed that in a Boston antiques shop, it would be priced at one hundred and eighty.

Gaunt steepled his fingers under his chin in a gesture Brian Rusk would have recognized. "I think I'd have to have at least forty-five," he said with some regret.

Cyndi Rose's eyes brightened; there were possibilities here. She had originally seen the Lalique vase as something only mildly interesting, really not much more than another conversational crowbar to use on the mysterious Mr. Gaunt. Now she looked at it more closely and saw that it really *was* a nice piece of work, one which would look right at home in her living room. The border of flowers around the long neck of the vase was the exact color of her wallpaper. Until Gaunt had responded to her suggestion with a price which was only a finger's length out of her reach, she hadn't realized that she wanted the vase as badly as she now felt she did.

She consulted with her friends.

Gaunt watched them, smiling gently.

The bell over the door rang and two more ladies came in.

At Needful Things, the first full day of business had begun.

6

When the Ash Street Bridge Club left Needful Things ten minutes later, Cyndi Rose Martin carried a shopping bag by the handles. Inside was the Lalique vase, wrapped in tissue paper. She had purchased it for thirty-one dollars plus tax, almost all of her pin money, but she was so delighted with it that she was almost purring.

Usually she felt doubtful and a little ashamed of herself after such an impulse buy, certain that she had been cozened a little if not cheated outright, but not today. This was *one* deal where she had come out on top. Mr. Gaunt had even asked her to come back, saying he had the twin of this vase, and it would be arriving in a shipment later in the week—perhaps even tomorrow! This one would look lovely on the little table in her living room, but if she had two, she could put one on each end of the mantel, and that would be *smashing.*

Her three friends also felt that she had done well, and although they were a little frustrated at having gotten so little of Mr. Gaunt's background, their opinion of him was, on the whole, quite high.

"He's got the most beautiful green eyes," Francie Pelletier said, a little dreamily.

"*Were* they green?" Cyndi Rose asked, a little startled. She herself had thought they were gray. "I didn't notice."

7

Late that afternoon, Rosalie Drake from You Sew and Sew stopped in Needful Things on her coffee break, accompanied by Polly's housekeeper, Nettie Cobb. There were several women browsing in the store, and in the rear corner two boys from Castle County High were leafing through a cardboard

carton of comic books and muttering excitedly to each other—
it was amazing, they both agreed, how many of the items they
needed to fill their respective collections were here. They only
hoped the prices would not prove too high. It was impossible
to tell without asking, because there were no price-stickers on
the plastic bags which held the comics.

Rosalie and Nettie said hello to Mr. Gaunt, and Gaunt
asked Rosalie to thank Polly again for the cake. His eyes followed Nettie, who had wandered away after the introductions
and was looking rather wistfully at a small collection of carnival glass. He left Rosalie studying the picture of Elvis next
to the splinter of PETRIFIED WOOD FROM THE HOLY LAND and
walked over to Nettie.

"Do you like carnival glass, Ms. Cobb?" he asked softly.

She jumped a little—Nettie Cobb had the face and almost
painfully shy manner of a woman made to jump at voices, no
matter how soft and friendly, when they spoke from the general area of her elbow—and smiled at him nervously.

"It's Missus Cobb, Mr. Gaunt, although my husband's been
passed on for some time now."

"I'm sorry to hear it."

"No need to be. It's been fourteen years. A long time. Yes, I
have a little collection of carnival glass." She seemed almost to
quiver, as a mouse might quiver at the approach of a cat. "Not
that I could afford anything so nice as these pieces. Lovely, they
are. Like things must look in heaven."

"Well, I'll tell you something," he said. "I bought quite
a lot of carnival glass when I got these, and they're not as
expensive as you might think. And the others are *much* nicer.
Would you like to come by tomorrow and have a look at
them?"

She jumped again and sidled away a step, as if he had suggested she might like to come by the next day so he could
pinch her bottom a few times . . . perhaps until she cried.

"Oh, I don't think . . . Thursday's my busy day, you know . . .

at Polly's . . . we have to really turn the place out on Thursdays, you know . . ."

"Are you sure you can't drop by?" he coaxed. "Polly told me that you made the cake she brought this morning—"

"Was it all right?" Nettie asked nervously. Her eyes said she expected him to say, No, it was *not* all right, Nettie, it gave me *cramps,* it gave me the backdoor *trots,* in fact, and so I am going to hurt you, Nettie, I'm going to drag you into the back room and twist your nipples until you holler uncle.

"It was wonderful," he said soothingly. "It made me think of cakes my mother used to make . . . and that was a very long time ago."

This was the right note to strike with Nettie, who had loved her own mother dearly in spite of the beatings that lady had administered after her frequent nights out in the juke-joints and ginmills. She relaxed a little.

"Well, that's fine, then," she said. "I'm awfully glad it was good. Of course, it was Polly's idea. She's just about the sweetest woman in the world."

"Yes," he said. "After meeting her, I can believe that." He glanced at Rosalie Drake, but Rosalie was still browsing. He looked back at Nettie and said, "I just felt I owed you a little something—"

"Oh no!" Nettie said, alarmed all over again. "You don't owe me a thing. Not a single solitary thing, Mr. Gaunt."

"Please come by. I can see you have an eye for carnival glass . . . and I could give you back Polly's cake-box."

"Well . . . I suppose I *could* drop by on my break . . ." Nettie's eyes said she could not believe what she was hearing from her own mouth.

"Wonderful," he said, and left her quickly, before she could change her mind again. He walked over to the boys and asked them how they were doing. They hesitantly showed him several old issues of *The Incredible Hulk* and *The X-Men.* Five minutes later they went out with most of the comic books in their hands and expressions of stunned joy on their faces.

The door had barely shut behind them when it opened again. Cora Rusk and Myra Evans strode in. They looked around, eyes as bright and avid as those of squirrels in nut-gathering season, and went immediately to the glass case containing the picture of Elvis. Cora and Myra bent over, cooing with interest, displaying bottoms which were easily two axe-handles wide.

Gaunt watched them, smiling.

The bell over the door jingled again. The new arrival was as large as Cora Rusk, but Cora was fat and this woman looked *strong*—the way a lumberjack with a beer belly looks strong. A large white button had been pinned to her blouse. The red letters proclaimed:

CASINO NITE——JUST FOR FUN!

The lady's face had all the charm of a snowshovel. Her hair, an unremarkable and lifeless shade of brown, was mostly covered by a kerchief which was knotted severely under her wide chin. She surveyed the interior of the store for a moment or two, her small, deepset eyes flicking here and there like the eyes of a gunslinger who surveys the interior of a saloon before pushing all the way through the batwing doors and starting to raise hell. Then she came in.

Few of the women circulating among the displays gave her more than a glance, but Nettie Cobb looked at the newcomer with an extraordinary expression of mingled dismay and hate. Then she scuttled away from the carnival glass. Her movement caught the newcomer's eye. She glanced at Nettie with a kind of massive contempt, then dismissed her.

The bell over the door jingled as Nettie left the shop. Mr. Gaunt observed all of this with great interest.

He walked over to Rosalie and said, "Mrs. Cobb has left without you, I'm afraid."

Rosalie looked startled. "Why—" she began, and then her eyes settled on the newcomer with the Casino Nite button pinned adamantly between her breasts. She was studying the Turkish rug hung on the wall with the fixed interest of an art student in a gallery. Her hands were planted on her vast hips. *"Oh,"* Rosalie said. "Excuse me, I really ought to go along."

"No love lost between those two, I'd say," Mr. Gaunt remarked.

Rosalie smiled distractedly.

Gaunt glanced at the woman in the kerchief again. "Who is she?"

Rosalie wrinkled her nose. "Wilma Jerzyck," she said. "Excuse me . . . I really ought to catch up with Nettie. She's high-strung, you know."

"Of course," he said, and watched Rosalie out the door. To himself he added, "Aren't we all."

Then Cora Rusk was tapping him on the shoulder. "How much is that picture of The King?" she demanded.

Leland Gaunt turned his dazzling smile upon her. "Well, let's talk about it," he said. "How much do you think it's worth?"

CHAPTER THREE

1

Castle Rock's newest port of commerce had been closed for nearly two hours when Alan Pangborn rolled slowly down Main Street toward the Municipal Building, which housed the Sheriff's Office and Castle Rock Police Department. He was behind the wheel of the ultimate unmarked car: a 1986 Ford station wagon. The family car. He felt low and half-drunk. He'd only had three beers, but they had hit him hard.

He glanced at Needful Things as he drove past, approving of the dark-green canopy which jutted out over the street, just as Brian Rusk had done. He knew less about such things (having no relations who worked for the Dick Perry Siding and Door Company in South Paris), but he thought it *did* lend a certain touch of class to Main Street, where most shopowners had added false fronts and called it good. He didn't know yet what the new place sold—Polly would, if she had gone over this morning as she had planned—but it looked to Alan like one of those cozy French restaurants where you took the girl of your dreams before trying to sweet-talk her into bed.

The place slipped from his mind as soon as he passed it. He signalled right two blocks farther down, and turned up the narrow passage between the squat brick block of the Municipal Building and the white clapboard Water District building. This lane was marked OFFICIAL VEHICLES ONLY.

The Municipal Building was shaped like an upside down L, and there was a small parking lot in the angle formed by the two wings. Three of the slots were marked SHERIFF'S OFFICE. Norris Ridgewick's bumbling old VW Beetle was parked in one of them. Alan parked in another, cut the headlights and the motor, reached for the door-handle.

The depression which had been circling him ever since he left The Blue Door in Portland circling the way wolves often circled campfires in the adventure stories he had read as a boy, suddenly fell upon him. He let go of the door-handle and just sat behind the wheel of the station wagon, hoping it would pass.

He had spent the day in Portland's District Court, testifying for the prosecution in four straight trials. The district encompassed four counties—York, Cumberland, Oxford, Castle—and of all the lawmen who served in those counties, Alan Pangborn had the farthest to travel. The three District Judges therefore tried as best they could to schedule his court cases in bunches, so he would have to make the trip only once or twice a month. This made it possible for him to actually spend some time in the county which he had sworn to protect, instead of on the roads between Castle Rock and Portland, but it also meant that, after one of his court days, he felt like a high school kid stumbling out of the auditorium where he has just taken the Scholastic Aptitude Tests. He should have known better than to drink on top of that, but Harry Cross and George Crompton had just been on their way down to The Blue Door, and they had insisted that Alan join them. There had been a good enough reason to do so: a string of clearly related burglaries which had occurred in all of their areas. But the real reason he'd gone was the one most bad decisions have in common: it had seemed like a good idea at the time.

Now he sat behind the wheel of what had been the family car, reaping what he had sown of his own free will. His head ached gently. He felt more than a touch of nausea. But the depression was the worst—it was back with a vengeance.

Hello! it cried merrily from its stronghold inside his head.

Here I am, Alan! Good to see you! Guess what? Here it is, end of a long hard day, and Annie and Todd are still dead! Remember the Saturday afternoon when Todd spilled his milkshake on the front seat? Right under where your briefcase is now, wasn't it? And you shouted at him? Wow! Didn't forget that, did you? You did? Well, that's okay, Alan, because I'm here to remind you! And remind you! And remind you!

He lifted his briefcase and looked fixedly at the seat. Yes, the stain was there, and yes, he had shouted at Todd. *Todd, why do you always have to be so clumsy?* Something like that, no big deal, but not the sort of thing you would ever say if you knew your kid had less than a month left to live.

It occurred to him that the beers weren't the real problem; it was this car, which had never been properly cleaned out. He had spent the day riding with the ghosts of his wife and his younger son.

He leaned over and popped the glove compartment to get his citation book—carrying that, even when he was headed down to Portland to spend the day testifying in court, was an unbreakable habit—and reached inside. His hand struck some tubular object, and it fell out onto the floor of the station wagon with a little thump. He put his citation book on top of his briefcase and then bent over to get whatever it was he had knocked out of the glove compartment. He held it up so it caught the glow of the arc-sodium light and stared at it a long time, feeling the old dreadful ache of loss and sorrow steal into him. Polly's arthritis was in her hands; his, it seemed, was in his heart, and who could say which of them had gotten the worst of it?

The can had belonged to Todd, of course—Todd, who would have undoubtedly *lived* in the Auburn Novelty Shop if he had been allowed. The boy had been entranced with the cheap-jack arcana sold there: joy buzzers, sneezing powder, dribble glasses, soap that turned the user's hands the color of volcanic ash, plastic dog turds.

This thing is still here. Nineteen months they've been dead, and it's still here. How in the hell did I miss it? Christ.

Alan turned the round can over in his hands, remembering how the boy had pleaded to be allowed to buy this particular item with his allowance money, how Alan himself had demurred, quoting his own father's proverb: the fool and his money soon parted. And how Annie had overruled him in her gentle way.

Listen to you, Mr. Amateur Magician, sounding like a Puritan. I love it! Where do you think he got this insane love of gags and tricks in the first place? No one in my *family ever kept a framed picture of Houdini on the wall, believe me. Do you want to tell me you didn't buy a dribble glass or two in the hot, wild days of your youth? That you wouldn't have just about died to own the old snake-in-the-can-of-nuts trick if you'd come across one in a display case somewhere?*

He, hemming and hawing, sounding more and more like a pompous stuffed-shirt windbag. Finally he'd had to raise a hand to his mouth to hide a grin of embarrassment. Annie had seen it, however. Annie always did. That had been her gift . . . and more than once it had been his salvation. Her sense of humor—and her sense of perspective as well—had always been better than his. Sharper.

Let him have it, Alan—he'll only be young once. And it is *sort of funny.*

So he had. And—

—*and three weeks after that he spilled his milkshake on the seat and four weeks after* that *he was dead! They were* both *dead! Wow! Imagine that! Time surely does fly by, doesn't it, Alan? But don't worry! Don't worry, because I'll keep reminding you! Yes, sir! I'll keep reminding you, because that's my job and I mean to* do *it!*

The can was labeled TASTEE-MUNCH MIXED NUTS. Alan twisted off the top and five feet of compressed green snake leaped out, struck the windshield, and rebounded into his lap. Alan looked at it, heard his dead son's laughter inside his head, and began to cry. His weeping was undramatic, silent and exhausted. It seemed that his tears had a lot in common with the possessions of his dead loved ones; you never got to the end of them. There were too many, and just when you started to relax and think that it was finally over, the joint was clean, you found one more. And one more. And one more.

Why had he let Todd buy the goddam thing? Why was it still in the goddam glove compartment? And why had he taken the goddam wagon in the first place?

He pulled his handkerchief out of his back pocket and mopped the tears from his face. Then, slowly, he jammed the snake—just cheap green crepe-paper with a metal spring wound up inside it—back into the bogus mixed-nuts can. He screwed on the top and bounced the can thoughtfully on his hand.

Throw the goddam thing away.

But he didn't think he could do that. Not tonight, at least. He tossed the joke—the last one Todd had ever bought in what he considered the world's finest store—back into the glove compartment and slammed the hatch shut. Then he took hold of the door-handle again, grabbed his briefcase, and got out.

He breathed deeply of the early-evening air, hoping it would help. It didn't. He could smell decomposed wood and chemicals, a charmless odor which drifted down regularly from the paper mills in Rumford, some thirty miles north. He would call Polly and ask her if he could come over, he decided—that would help a little.

A truer thought was never thunk! the voice of depression agreed energetically. *And by the way, Alan, do you remember how happy that snake made him? He tried it on everyone! Just about scared Norris Ridgewick into a heart attack, and you laughed until you almost wet your pants! Remember? Wasn't he lively? Wasn't he great? And Annie—remember how she laughed when you told her? She was lively and great, too, wasn't she? Of course, she wasn't quite as lively at the very end, not quite as great, either, but you didn't really*

*notice, did you? Because you had your own fish to fry. The business
with Thad Beaumont, for instance—you really couldn't get that off
your mind. What happened at their house by the lake, and how, after
it was all over, he used to get drunk and call you. And then his wife
took the twins and left him . . . all of that added to the usual around-
town stuff kept you pretty busy, didn't it? Too busy to see what was
happening right at home. Too bad you* didn't *see it. If you had, why,
they might still be alive! That's something you shouldn't forget, either,
and so I'll just keep reminding you . . . and reminding you . . . and
reminding you. Okay? Okay!*

There was a foot-long scratch along the side of the wagon,
just above the gasoline port. Had that happened since Annie
and Todd died? He couldn't really remember, and it didn't
matter much, anyway. He traced his fingers along it and reminded himself again to take the car to Sonny's Sunoco and
get it fixed. On the other hand, why bother? Why not just take
the damned thing down to Harrie Ford in Oxford and trade it
in on something smaller? The mileage on it was still relatively
low; he could probably get a decent trade-in—

But Todd spilled his milkshake on the front seat! the voice in his
head piped up indignantly. *He did that when he was alive, Alan
old buddy! And Annie—*

"Oh, shut up," he said.

He reached the building, then paused. Parked close by, so
close that the office door would have dented in its side if pulled
all the way open, was a large red Cadillac Seville. He didn't
need to look at the license plates to know what they were:
KEETON 1. He ran a hand thoughtfully over the car's smooth
hide, then went in.

2

Sheila Brigham was sitting in the glass-walled dispatcher's
cubicle, reading *People* magazine and drinking a Yoo-Hoo. The

combined Sheriff's Office/Castle Rock Police Department was otherwise deserted except for Norris Ridgewick.

Norris sat behind an old IBM electric typewriter, working on a report with the agonized, breathless concentration only Norris could bring to paperwork. He would stare fixedly at the machine, then abruptly lean forward like a man who has been punched in the belly, and hit the keys in a rattling burst. He remained in his hunched position long enough to read what he had written, then groaned softly. There was the *click-rap! click-rap! click-rap!* sound of Norris using the IBM's CorrecTape to back over some error (he used one CorrecTape per week, on the average), and then Norris would straighten up. There would be a pregnant pause, and then the cycle would repeat itself. After an hour or so of this, Norris would drop the finished report into Sheila's IN basket. Once or twice a week these reports were even intelligible.

Norris looked up and smiled as Alan crossed the small bull-pen area. "Hi, boss, how's it going?"

"Well, Portland's out of the way for another two or three weeks. Anything happen here?"

"Nah, just the usual. You know, Alan, your eyes are red as hell. Have you been smoking that wacky tobaccy again?"

"Ha ha," Alan said sourly. "I stopped for a couple of drinks with a couple of cops, then stared at people's high beams for thirty miles. Have you got your aspirin handy?"

"Always," Norris said. "You know that." Norris's bottom desk drawer contained his own private pharmacy. He opened it, rummaged, produced a giant-sized bottle of strawberry-flavored Kaopectate, stared at the label for a moment, shook his head, dropped it back into the drawer, and rummaged some more. At last he produced a bottle of generic aspirin.

"I've got a little job for you," Alan said, taking the bottle and shaking two aspirins into his hand. A lot of white dust fell out with the pills, and he found himself wondering why generic aspirin always produced more dust than brand-name aspirin. He wondered further if he might be losing his mind.

"Aw, Alan, I've got two more of these E-9 boogers to do, and—"

"Cool your jets." Alan went to the water-cooler and pulled a paper cup from the cylinder screwed to the wall. *Blub-blub-blub* went the water-cooler as he filled the cup. "All you've got to do is cross the room and open the door I just came through. So simple even a child could do it, right?"

"What—"

"Only don't forget to take your citation book," Alan said, and gulped the aspirin down.

Norris Ridgewick immediately looked wary. "Yours is right there on the desk, next to your briefcase."

"I know. And that's where it's going to stay, at least for to-night."

Norris looked at him for a long time. Finally he asked. "Buster?"

Alan nodded. "Buster. He's parked in the crip space again. I told him last time I was through warning him about it."

Castle Rock's Head Selectman, Danforth Keeton III, was referred to as Buster by all who knew him . . . but municipal employees who wanted to hold onto their jobs made sure to call him Dan or Mr. Keeton when he was around. Only Alan, who was an elected official, dared call him Buster to his face, and he had done it only twice, both times when he was very angry. He supposed he would do it again, however. Dan "Buster" Keeton was a man Alan Pangborn found it very easy to get angry at.

"Come *on!*" Norris said. "*You* do it, Alan, okay?"

"Can't. I've got that appropriations meeting with the select-men next week."

"He hates me already," Norris said morbidly. "I know he does."

"Buster hates everyone except his wife and his mother," Alan said, "and I'm not so sure about his wife. But the fact remains that I have warned him at least half a dozen times in the last month about parking in our one and only handicapped space, and now I'm going to put my money where my mouth is."

"No, I'm going to put my *job* where your mouth is. This is really mean, Alan. I'm sincere." Norris Ridgewick looked like an ad for *When Bad Things Happen to Good People.*

"Relax," Alan said. "You put a five-dollar parking ticket on his windshield. He comes to me, and first he tells me to fire you."

Norris moaned.

"I refuse. Then he tells me to tear up the ticket. I refuse that, too. Then, tomorrow noon, after he's had a chance to froth at the mouth about it for a while, I relent. And when I go into the next appropriations meeting, he owes me a favor."

"Yeah, but what does he owe me?"

"Norris, do you want a new pulse radar gun or not?"

"Well—"

"And what about a fax machine? We've been talking about a fax machine for at least two years."

Yes! the falsely cheerful voice in his mind cried. *You started talking about it when Annie and Todd were still alive, Alan! Remember that? Remember when they were alive?*

"I guess," Norris said. He reached for his citation book with sadness and resignation writ large upon his face.

"Good man," Alan said with a heartiness he didn't feel. "I'll be in my office for a while."

3

He closed the door and dialled Polly's number.

"Hello?" she asked, and he knew immediately that he would not tell her about the depression which had come over him with such smooth completeness. Polly had her own problems tonight. It had taken only that single word to tell him how it was with her. The *l*-sounds in hello were lightly slurred. That only happened when she had taken a Percodan—or perhaps more than one—and she took a Percodan only when the pain was very bad. Although she had never come right out and said so, Alan had an idea she lived in terror of the day when the Percs would stop working.

"How are you, pretty lady?" he asked, leaning back in his chair and putting a hand over his eyes. The aspirin didn't seem to be doing much for his head. *Maybe I should ask her for a Perc*, he thought.

"I'm all right." He heard the careful way she was speaking, going from one word to the next like a woman using stepping-stones to cross a small stream. "How about you? You sound tired."

"Lawyers do that to me every time." He shelved the idea of going over to see her. She would say, *Of course, Alan*, and she would be glad to see him—almost as glad as he would be to see her—but it would put more strain on her than she needed this evening. "I think I'll go home and turn in early. Do you mind if I don't come by?"

"No, honey. It might be a little better if you didn't, actually."

"Is it bad tonight?"

"It's been worse," she said carefully.

"That's not what I asked."

"Not too bad, no."

Your own voice says you're a liar, my dear, he thought.

"Good. What's the deal on that ultrasonic therapy you told me about? Find anything out?"

"Well, it would be great if I could afford a month and a half in the Mayo Clinic—on spec—but I can't. And don't tell me you can, Alan, because I'm feeling a little too tired to call you a liar."

"I thought you said Boston Hospital—"

"Next year," Polly said. "They're going to run a clinic using ultrasound therapy next year. Maybe."

There was a moment of silence and he was about to say

goodbye when she spoke again. This time her tone was a little brighter. "I dropped by the new shop this morning. I had Nettie make a cake and took that. Pure orneriness, of course— ladies don't take baked goods to openings. It's practically graven in stone."

"What's it like? What does he sell?"

"A little bit of everything. If you put a gun to my head, I'd say it's a curios-and-collectibles shop, but it really defies description. You'll have to see for yourself."

"Did you meet the owner?"

"Mr. Leland Gaunt, from Akron, Ohio," Polly said, and now Alan could actually hear the hint of a smile in her voice. "He's going to be quite the heartthrob in Castle Rock's smart set this year—that's my prediction, anyway."

"What did *you* make of him?"

When she spoke again, the smile in her voice came through even more clearly. "Well, Alan, let me be honest—you're my darling, and I hope I'm yours, but—"

"You are," he said. His headache was lifting a little. He doubted if it was Norris Ridgewick's aspirin working this small miracle.

"—but he made *my* heart go pitty-pat, too. And you should have seen Rosalie and Nettie when they came back . . ."

"*Nettie?*" He took his feet off the desk and sat up. "Nettie's scared of her own shadow!"

"Yes. But since Rosalie persuaded her to go down with her—you know the poor old dear won't go *anywhere* alone—I asked Nettie what *she* thought of Mr. Gaunt after I got home this afternoon. Alan, her poor old muddy eyes just lit up. 'He's got carnival glass!' she said. 'Beautiful carnival glass! He even invited me to come back tomorrow and look at some more!' I think it's the most she's said to me all at once in about four years. So I said, 'Wasn't that kind of him, Nettie?' And she said, 'Yes, and do you know what?' I asked her what, of course, and Nettie said, '*And I just might go!*'"

Alan laughed loud and heartily. "If Nettie's willing to go see him without a *duenna,* I *ought* to check him out. The guy must really be a charmer."

"Well, it's funny—he's not handsome, at least not in a movie-star way, but he's got the most *gorgeous* hazel eyes. They light up his whole face."

"Watch it, lady," Alan growled. "My jealous muscle is starting to twitch."

She laughed a little. "I don't think you have to worry. There's one other thing, though."

"What's that?"

"Rosalie said Wilma Jerzyck came in while Nettie was there."

"Did anything happen? Were words passed?"

"No. Nettie glared at the Jerzyck woman, and *she* kind of curled her lip at Nettie—that's how Rosalie put it—and then Nettie scurried out. Has Wilma Jerzyck called you about Nettie's dog lately?"

"No," Alan said. "No reason to. I've cruised past Nettie's house after ten half a dozen nights over the last six weeks or so. The dog doesn't bark anymore. It was just the kind of thing puppies do, Polly. It's grown up a little, and it has a good mistress. Nettie may be short a little furniture on the top floor, but she's done her duty by that dog—what does she call it?"

"Raider."

"Well, Wilma Jerzyck will just have to find something else to bitch about, because Raider is squared away. She will, though. Ladies like Wilma always do. It was never the dog, anyway, not really; Wilma was the only person in the whole neighborhood who complained. It was Nettie. People like Wilma have noses for weakness. And there's a lot to smell on Nettie Cobb."

"Yes." Polly sounded sad and thoughtful. "You know that Wilma Jerzyck called her up one night and told her that if Nettie didn't shut the dog up, she'd come over and cut his throat?"

"Well," Alan said evenly, "I know that Nettie told you so. But I also know that Wilma frightened Nettie very badly, and that Nettie has had . . . problems. I'm not saying Wilma Jerzyck isn't capable of making a call like that, because she is. But it *might* have only been in Nettie's mind."

That Nettie had had problems was understating by quite a little bit, but there was no need to say more; they both knew what they were talking about. After years of hell, married to a brute who abused her in every way a man can abuse a woman, Nettie Cobb had put a meat-fork in her husband's throat as he slept. She had spent five years in Juniper Hill, a mental institution near Augusta. She had come to work for Polly as part of a work-release program. As far as Alan was concerned, she could not possibly have fallen in with better company, and Nettie's steadily improving state of mind confirmed his opinion. Two years ago, Nettie had moved into her own little place on Ford Street, six blocks from downtown.

"Nettie's got problems, all right," Polly said, "but her reaction to Mr. Gaunt was nothing short of amazing. It really was awfully sweet."

"I have to see this guy for myself," Alan said.

"Tell me what you think. And check out those hazel eyes."

"I doubt if they'll cause the same reaction in me they seem to have caused in you," Alan said dryly.

She laughed again, but this time he thought it sounded slightly forced.

"Try to get some sleep," he said.

"I will. Thanks for calling, Alan."

"Welcome." He paused. "I love you, pretty lady."

"Thank you, Alan—I love you, too. Goodnight."

"Goodnight."

He racked the telephone, twisted the gooseneck of the desk lamp so it threw a spot of light on the wall, put his feet up on his desk, and brought his hands together in front of his chest, as if praying. He extended his index fingers. On the wall, a shadow-rabbit poked up its ears. Alan slipped his thumbs between his extended fingers, and the shadow-rabbit wiggled its nose. Alan made the rabbit hop across the makeshift spotlight. What lumbered back was an elephant, wagging its trunk. Alan's hands moved with a dextrous, eerie ease. He barely noticed the animals he was creating; this was an old habit with him, his way of looking at the tip of his nose and saying "Om."

He was thinking about Polly; Polly and her poor hands. What to do about Polly?

If it had been just a matter of money, he would have had her checked into a room at the Mayo Clinic by tomorrow afternoon—signed, sealed, and delivered. He would have done it even if it meant wrapping her in a straitjacket and shooting her full of sedative to get her out there.

But it *wasn't* just a matter of money. Ultrasound as a treatment for degenerative arthritis was in its infancy. It might eventually turn out to be as effective as the Salk vaccine, or as bogus as the science of phrenology. Either way, it didn't make sense right now. The chances were a thousand to one that it was a dry hole. It was not the loss of money he dreaded, but Polly's dashed hopes.

A crow—as limber and lifelike as a crow in a Disney animated cartoon—flapped slowly across his framed Albany Police Academy graduation certificate. Its wings lengthened and it became a prehistoric pterodactyl, triangular head cocked as it cruised toward the filing cabinets in the corner and out of the spotlight.

The door opened. The doleful basset-hound face of Norris Ridgewick poked through. "I did it, Alan," he said, sounding like a man confessing to the murder of several small children.

"Good, Norris," Alan said. "You're not going to get hit with the shit on this, either. I promise."

Norris looked at him for a moment longer with his moist

eyes, then nodded doubtfully. He glanced at the wall. "Do Buster, Alan."

Alan grinned, shook his head, and reached for the lamp.

"Come on," Norris coaxed. "I ticketed his damn car—I deserve it. Do Buster, Alan. *Please.* That wipes me out."

Alan glanced over Norris's shoulder, saw no one, and curled one hand against the other. On the wall, a stout shadow-man stalked across the spotlight, belly swinging. He paused once to hitch up his shadow-pants in the back and then stalked on, head turning truculently from side to side.

Norris's laughter was high and happy—the laughter of a child. For one moment Alan was reminded forcibly of Todd, and then he shoved that away. There had been enough of that for one night, please God.

"Jeez, that *slays* me," Norris said, still laughing. "You were born too late, Alan—you coulda had a career on *The Ed Sullivan Show.*"

"Go on," Alan said. "Get out of here."

Still laughing, Norris pulled the door closed.

Alan made Norris—skinny and a little self-important—walk across the wall, then snapped off the lamp and took a battered notebook from his back pocket. He thumbed through it until he found a blank page, and wrote *Needful Things.* Below that he jotted: *Leland Gaunt, Cleveland, Ohio.* Was that right? No. He scratched out *Cleveland* and wrote *Akron.* Maybe I really am losing my mind, he thought. On a third line he printed: *Check it out.*

He put his notebook back in his pocket, thought about going home, and turned on the lamp again instead. Soon the shadow-parade was marching across the wall once more: lions and tigers and bears, oh my. Like Sandburg's fog, the depression crept back on small feline feet. The voice began speaking about Annie and Todd again. After a while, Alan Pangborn began to listen to it. He did it against his will . . . but with growing absorption.

4

Polly was lying on her bed, and when she finished talking with Alan, she turned over on her left side to hang up the telephone. It fell out of her hand and crashed to the floor instead. The Princess phone's base slid slowly across the nighttable, obviously meaning to join its other half. She reached for it and her hand struck the edge of the table instead. A monstrous bolt of pain broke through the thin web the painkiller had stretched over her nerves and raced all the way up to her shoulder. She had to bite down on her lips to stifle a cry.

The telephone base fell off the edge of the table and crashed with a single *cling!* of the bell inside. She could hear the steady idiot buzz of the open line drifting up. It sounded like a hive of insects being broadcast via shortwave.

She thought of picking the telephone up with the claws which were now cradled on her chest, having to do it not by grasping—tonight her fingers would not bend at all—but by *pressing,* like a woman playing the accordion, and suddenly it was too much, even something as simple as picking up a telephone which had fallen on the floor was too much, and she began to cry.

The pain was fully awake again, awake and raving, turning her hands—especially the one she had bumped—into feverpits. She lay on her bed, looking up at the ceiling through her blurry eyes, and wept.

Oh I would give anything to be free of this, she thought. *I would give anything, anything, anything at all.*

5

By ten o'clock on an autumn weeknight, Castle Rock's Main Street was as tightly locked up as a Chubb safe. The streetlamps threw circles of white light on the sidewalk and the fronts of the business buildings in diminishing perspective, making downtown look like a deserted stage-set. Soon, you might think, a lone figure dressed in tails and a top-hat—Fred Astaire, or maybe Gene Kelly—would appear and dance his way from one of those spots to the next, singing about how lonely a fellow could be when his best girl had given him the air and all the bars were closed. Then, from the other end of Main Street, another figure would appear—Ginger Rogers or maybe Cyd Charisse—dressed in an evening gown. She would dance toward Fred (or Gene), singing about how lonely a gal could be when her best guy had stood her up. They would see each other, pause artistically, and then dance together in front of the bank or maybe You Sew and Sew.

Instead, Hugh Priest hove into view.

He did not look like either Fred Astaire or Gene Kelly, there was no girl at the far end of Main Street advancing toward a romantic chance meeting with him, and he most definitely did not dance. He did drink, however, and he had been drinking steadily in The Mellow Tiger since four that afternoon. At this point in the festivities just walking was a trick, and never mind any fancy dance-steps. He walked slowly, passing through one pool of light after another, his shadow running tall across the fronts of the barber shop, the Western Auto, the video-rental shop. He was weaving slightly, his reddish eyes fixed stolidly in front of him, his large belly pushing out his sweaty blue tee-shirt (on the front was a drawing of a huge mosquito above the words, MAINE STATE BIRD) in a long, sloping curve.

The Castle Rock Public Works pick-up truck he had been driving was still sitting at the rear of the Tiger's dirt parking lot. Hugh Priest was the not-so-proud possessor of several OUI driving violations, and following the last one—which had resulted in a six-month suspension of his privilege to drive—that bastard Keeton, his co-bastards Fullerton and Samuels, and their co-bitch Williams had made it clear that they had reached the end of their patience with him. The next OUI would probably result in the permanent loss of his license, and would certainly result in the loss of his job.

This did not cause Hugh to stop drinking—no power on earth could do that—but it did cause him to form a firm resolution: no more drinking and driving. He was fifty-one years old, and that was a little late in life to be changing jobs, especially with a long drunk-driving rap-sheet following him around like a tin can tied to a dog's tail.

That was why he was walking home tonight, and one fuck of a long walk it was, and there was a certain Public Works employee named Bobby Dugas who was going to have some tall explaining to do tomorrow, unless he wanted to go home with a few less teeth than he had come to work with.

As Hugh passed Nan's Luncheonette, a light drizzle began to mist down. This did not improve his temper.

He had asked Bobby, who had to drive right past Hugh's place on his way home every night, if he was going to drop down to the Tiger that evening for a few brewskis. Bobby Dugas had said, Why shore, Hubert—Bobby always called him Hubert, which was not his fucking *name,* and you could bet *that* shit was going to change, too, and soon. *Why shore, Hubert, I'll prob'ly be down around seven, same as always.*

So Hugh, confident of a ride if he got a little too pixillated to drive, had pulled into the Tiger at just about five minutes of four (he'd knocked off a little early, almost an hour and a half early, actually, but what the hell, Deke Bradford hadn't been around), and had waded right in. And come seven o'clock, guess what? No Bobby Dugas! Golly-gosh-wow! Come eight and nine and nine-thirty, guess *further* what? More of the same, by God!

At twenty to ten, Henry Beaufort, bartender and owner of The Mellow Tiger, had invited Hugh to put an egg in his shoe and beat it, to make like a tree and leave, to imitate an amoeba and split—in other words, to get the fuck out. Hugh had been outraged. It was true he had kicked the jukebox, but the goddam Rodney Crowell record had been skipping again.

"What was I supposed to do, just sit here and listen to it?" he demanded of Henry. "You oughtta take that record off, that's all. Guy sounds like he's havin a fuckin pepileptic fit."

"You haven't had enough, I can see that," Henry said, "but you've had all you're going to get here. You'll have to get the rest out of your own refrigerator."

"What if I say no?" Hugh demanded.

"Then I call Sheriff Pangborn," Henry said evenly.

The other patrons of the Tiger—there weren't many this late on a weeknight—were watching this exchange with interest. Men were careful to be polite around Hugh Priest, especially when he was in his cups, but he was never going to win Castle Rock's Most Popular Fella contest.

"I wouldn't like to," Henry continued, "but I *will* do it, Hugh. I'm sick and tired of you kicking my Rock-Ola."

Hugh considered saying, *Then I guess I'll just have to kick YOU a few times instead, you frog son of a bitch.* Then he thought of that fat bastard Keeton, handing him a pink slip for kicking up dickens in the local tavern. Of course, if he really got fired the pink would come in the mail, it always did, pigs like Keeton never dirtied their hands (or risked a fat lip) by doing it in person, but it helped to think of that—it turned the dials down a little. And he *did* have a couple of six-packs at home, one in the fridge and the other in the woodshed.

"Okay," he said. "I don't need this action, anyway. Gimme my keys." For he had turned them over to Henry, as a precaution, when he sat down at the bar six hours and eighteen beers ago.

"Nope." Henry wiped his hands on a piece of towel and stared at Hugh unflinchingly.

"*Nope?* What the hell do you mean, *nope?*"

"I mean you're too drunk to drive. I know it, and when you wake up tomorrow morning, you're going to know it, too."

"Listen," Hugh said patiently. "When I gave you the goddam keys, I thought I had a ride home. Bobby Dugas said he was coming down for a few beers. It's not my fault the numb fuck never showed."

Henry sighed. "I sympathize with that, but it's not my problem. I could get sued if you wiped someone out. I doubt if that means much to you, but it does to me. I got to cover my ass, buddy. In this world, nobody else does it for you."

Hugh felt resentment, self-pity, and an odd, inchoate wretchedness well to the surface of his mind like some foul liquid seeping up from a long-buried canister of toxic waste. He looked from his keys, hanging behind the bar next to the plaque which read IF YOU DON'T LIKE OUR TOWN LOOK FOR A TIME-TABLE, back to Henry. He was alarmed to find he was on the verge of tears.

Henry glanced past him at the few other customers currently in attendance. "Hey! Any of you yo-yos headed up Castle Hill?"

Men looked down at their tables and said nothing. One or two cracked their knuckles. Charlie Fortin sauntered toward the men's room with elaborate slowness. No one answered.

"See?" Hugh said. "Come on, Henry, gimme my keys."

Henry had shaken his head with slow finality. "If you want to come in here and do some drinking another time, you want to take a hike."

"Okay, I will!" Hugh said. His voice was that of a pouty child on the verge of a temper tantrum. He crossed the floor with his head down and his hands balled into tight fists. He waited for someone to laugh. He almost hoped someone would. He would clean some house then, and fuck the job. But the place was silent except for Reba McEntire, who was whining something about Alabama.

"You can pick up your keys tomorrow!" Henry called after him.

Hugh said nothing. With a mighty effort he had restrained

himself from putting one scuffed yellow workboot right through Henry Beaufort's damned old Rock-Ola as he went by. Then, with his head down, he had passed out into darkness.

6

Now the mist had become a proper drizzle, and Hugh guessed the drizzle would develop into a steady, drenching rain by the time he reached home. It was just his luck. He walked steadily onward, not weaving quite so much now (the air had had a sobering effect on him), eyes moving restlessly from side to side. His mind was troubled, and he wished someone would come along and give him some lip. Even a little lip would do tonight. He thought briefly of the kid who had stepped in front of his truck yesterday afternoon, and wished sulkily that he had knocked the brat all the way across the street. It wouldn't have been his fault, no way. In his day, kids had looked where they were going.

He passed the vacant lot where the Emporium Galorium had stood before it burned down, You Sew and Sew, Castle Rock Hardware . . . and then he was passing Needful Things. He glanced into the display window, looked back up Main Street (only a mile and a half to go, now, and maybe he would beat the rain before it really started to pelt down, after all), and then came to a sudden halt.

His feet had carried him past the new store, and he had to go back. There was a single light on above the window display, casting its soft glow down over the three items arranged there. The light also spilled out onto his face, and it worked a wondrous transformation there. Suddenly Hugh looked like a tired little boy up long past his bedtime, a little boy who has just seen what he wants for Christmas—what he *must* have for Christmas, because all at once nothing else on God's green earth would do. The central object in the window was flanked by two fluted vases (Nettie Cobb's beloved carnival glass, although Hugh didn't know this and would not have cared if he did).

It was a fox-tail.

Suddenly it was 1955 again, he had just gotten his license, and he was driving to the Western Maine Schoolboy Championship game—Castle Rock vs. Greenspark—in his dad's '53 Ford convertible. It was an unseasonably warm November day, warm enough to pull that old ragtop down and tack the tarp over it (if you were a bunch of hot-blooded kids ready, willing, and able to raise some hell, that was), and there were six of them in the car. Peter Doyon had brought a flask of Log Cabin whiskey, Perry Como was on the radio, Hugh Priest was sitting behind the white wheel, and fluttering from the radio antenna had been a long, luxuriant fox-tail, just like the one he was now looking at in the window of this store.

He remembered looking up at that fluttering fox-tail and thinking that, when he owned a convertible of his own, he was going to have one just like that.

He remembered refusing the flask when it came around to him. He was driving, and you didn't drink while you were driving, because you were responsible for the lives of others. And he remembered one other thing, as well: the certainty that he was living the best hour of the best day of his life.

The memory surprised and hurt him in its clarity and total sensory recall—smoky aroma of burning leaves, November sun twinkling on guardrail reflectors, and now, looking at the fox-tail in the display window of Needful Things, it struck him that it *had* been the best day of his life, one of the last days before the booze had caught him firmly in its rubbery, pliant grip, turning him into a weird variation of King Midas: everything he had touched since then, it seemed, had turned to shit.

He suddenly thought: *I could change.*

This idea had its own arresting clarity.

I could start over.

Were such things possible?

Yes, I think sometimes they are. I could buy that fox-tail and tie it on the antenna of my Buick.

They'd laugh, though. The guys'd laugh.

What guys? Henry Beaufort? That little pissant Bobby Dugas? So what? Fuck em. Buy that fox-tail, tie it to the antenna, and drive—

Drive where?

Well, how about that Thursday-night A.A. meeting over in Greenspark for a start?

For a moment the possibility stunned and excited him, the way a long-term prisoner might be stunned and excited by the sight of the key left in the lock of his jail cell by a careless warder. For a moment he could actually see himself doing it, picking up a white chip, then a red chip, then a blue chip, getting sober day by day and month by month. No more Mellow Tiger. Too bad. But also no more paydays spent in terror that he would find a pink slip in his envelope along with his check, and that was not so too bad.

In that moment, as he stood looking at the fox-tail in the display window of Needful Things, Hugh could see a future. For the first time in years he could see a future, and that beautiful orange fox-brush with its white tip floated through it like a battle-flag.

Then reality crashed back in, and reality smelled like rain and damp, dirty clothes. There would be no fox-tail for him, no A.A. meetings, no chips, no future. He was *fifty-one fucking years old,* and fifty-one was too old for dreams of the future. At fifty-one you had to keep running just to escape the avalanche of your own past.

If it had been business hours, though, he would have taken a shot at it, anyway. Damned if he wouldn't. He'd walk in there, just as big as billy-be-damned, and ask how much was that fox-tail in the window. But it was ten o'clock, Main Street was locked up as tight as an ice-queen's chastity belt, and when he woke up tomorrow morning, feeling as if someone had planted an icepick between his eyes, he would have forgotten all about that lovely fox-tail, with its vibrant russet color.

Still, he lingered a moment longer, trailing dirty, callused fingers over the glass like a kid looking into a toyshop window. A little smile had touched the corners of his mouth. It was a gentle smile, and it looked out of place on Hugh Priest's face. Then, somewhere up on Castle View, a car backed off several times, sounds as sharp as shotgun blasts on the rainy air, and Hugh was startled back to himself.

Fuck it. What the hell are you thinking of?

He turned away from the window and pointed his face toward home again—if you wanted to call the two-room shack with the tacked-on woodshed where he lived home. As he passed under the canopy, he looked at the door . . . and stopped again.

The sign there, of course, read

OPEN.

Like a man in a dream, Hugh put his hand out and tried the knob. It turned freely under his hand. Overhead, a small silver bell tinkled. The sound seemed to come from an impossible distance away.

A man was standing in the middle of the shop. He was running a feather-duster over the top of a display case and humming. He turned toward Hugh when the bell rang. He didn't seem a bit surprised to see someone standing in his doorway at ten minutes past ten on a Wednesday night. The only thing that struck Hugh about the man in that confused moment was his eyes—they were as black as an Indian's.

"You forgot to turn your sign over, buddy," Hugh heard himself say.

"No, indeed," the man replied politely. "I don't sleep very well, I'm afraid, and some nights I take a fancy to open late. One never knows when a fellow such as yourself may stop by . . . and take a fancy to something. Would you like to come in and look around?"

Hugh Priest came in and closed the door behind him.

7

"There's a fox-tail—" Hugh began, then had to stop, clear his throat, and start again. The words had come out in a husky, unintelligible mutter. "There's a fox-tail in the window."

"Yes," the proprietor said. "Beauty, isn't it?" He held the duster in front of him now, and his Indian-black eyes looked at Hugh with interest from above the bouquet of feathers which hid his lower face. Hugh couldn't see the guy's mouth, but he had an idea he was smiling. It usually made him uneasy when people—especially people he didn't know—smiled at him. It made him feel like he wanted to fight. Tonight, however, it didn't seem to bother him at all. Maybe because he was still half-shot.

"It is," Hugh agreed. "It is a beauty. My dad had a convertible with a fox-tail just like that tied to the antenna, back when I was a kid. There's a lot of people in this crummy little burg wouldn't believe I ever *was* a kid, but I was. Same as everyone else."

"Of course." The man's eyes remained fixed on Hugh's, and the strangest thing was happening—they seemed to be *growing*. Hugh couldn't seem to pull his own eyes away from them. Too much direct eye-contact was another thing which usually made him feel like he wanted to fight. But this also seemed perfectly okay tonight.

"I used to think that fox-tail was just about the coolest thing in the world."

"Of course."

"Cool—that was the word we used back then. None of this *rad* shit. And *gnarly*—I don't have the slightest fuckin idea what that means, do you?"

But the proprietor of Needful Things was silent, simply

standing there, watching Hugh Priest with his black Indian eyes over the foliage of his feather-duster.

"Anyway, I want to buy it. Will you sell it to me?"

"Of course," Leland Gaunt said for the third time.

Hugh felt relief and a sudden, sprawling happiness. He was suddenly sure everything was going to be all right—everything. This was utterly crazy; he owed money to just about everyone in Castle Rock and the surrounding three towns, he had been on the ragged edge of losing his job for the last six months, his Buick was running on a wing and a prayer—but it was also undeniable.

"How much?" he asked. He suddenly wondered if he would be able to afford such a fine brush, and felt a touch of panic. What if it was out of his reach? Worse, what if he scrounged up the money somehow tomorrow, or the day after that, only to find the guy had sold it?

"Well, that depends."

"Depends? Depends on what?"

"On how much you're willing to pay."

Like a man in a dream, Hugh pulled his battered Lord Buxton out of his back pocket.

"Put that away, Hugh."

Did I tell him my name?

Hugh couldn't remember, but he put the wallet away. "Turn out your pockets. Right here, on top of this case."

Hugh turned out his pockets. He put his pocket-knife, a roll of Certs, his Zippo lighter, and about a dollar-fifty in tobacco-sprinkled change on top of the case. The coins clicked on the glass.

The man bent forward and studied the pile. "That looks about right," he remarked, and brushed the feather-duster over the meager collection. When he removed it again, the knife, the lighter, and the Certs were still there. The coins were gone.

Hugh observed this with no surprise at all. He stood as silently as a toy with dead batteries while the tall man went to the display window and came back with the fox-brush. He laid it on top of the cabinet beside Hugh's shrunken pile of pocket paraphernalia.

Slowly, Hugh stretched out one hand and stroked the fur. It felt cold and rich; it crackled with silky static electricity. Stroking it was like stroking a clear autumn night.

"Nice?" the tall man asked.

"Nice," Hugh agreed distantly, and made to pick up the fox-tail.

"Don't do that," the tall man said sharply, and Hugh's hand fell away at once. He looked at Gaunt with a hurt so deep it was grief. "We're not done dickering yet."

"No," Hugh agreed. *I'm hypnotized,* he thought. *Damned if the guy hasn't hypnotized me.* But it didn't matter. It was, in fact, sort of . . . nice.

He reached for his wallet again, moving as slowly as a man under water.

"Leave that alone, you ass," Mr. Gaunt said impatiently, and laid his feather-duster aside.

Hugh's hand dropped to his side again.

"Why *is* it that so many people think all the answers are in their wallets?" the man asked querulously.

"I don't know," Hugh said. He had never considered the idea before. "It does seem a little silly."

"*Worse,*" Gaunt snapped. His voice had taken on the nagging, slightly uneven cadences of a man who is either very tired or very angry. He *was* tired; it had been a long, demanding day. Much had been accomplished, but the work was still just barely begun. "It's *much* worse. It's criminally *stupid!* Do you know something, Hugh? The world is full of needy people who don't understand that everything, *everything,* is for sale . . . if you're willing to pay the price. They give lip-service to the concept, that's all, and pride themselves on their healthy cynicism. Well, lip-service is bushwah! Absolute . . . *bushwah!*"

"Bushwah," Hugh agreed mechanically.

"For the things people *really* need, Hugh, the wallet is no answer. The fattest wallet in this town isn't worth the sweat from a working man's armpit. Absolute *bushwah!* And souls! If I had a nickel, Hugh, for every time I ever heard someone say 'I'd sell my soul for thus-and-such,' I could buy the Empire State Building!" He leaned closer and now his lips stretched back from his uneven teeth in a huge unhealthy grin. "Tell me this, Hugh: what in the name of all the beasts crawling under the earth would I want with your soul?"

"Probably nothing." His voice seemed far away. His voice seemed to be coming from the bottom of a deep, dark cave. "I don't think it's in very good shape these days."

Mr. Gaunt suddenly relaxed and straightened up. "Enough of these lies and half-truths. Hugh, do you know a woman named Nettie Cobb?"

"Crazy Nettie? Everyone in town knows Crazy Nettie. She killed her husband."

"So they say. Now listen to me, Hugh. Listen carefully. Then you can take your fox-tail and go home."

Hugh Priest listened carefully.

Outside it was raining harder, and the wind had begun to blow.

8

"Brian!" Miss Ratcliffe said sharply. "Why, Brian Rusk! I wouldn't have believed it of you! Come up here! Right now!"

He was sitting in the back row of the basement room where the speech therapy classes were held, and he had done something wrong—terribly wrong, by the sound of Miss Ratcliffe's voice—but he didn't know what it was until he stood up. Then he saw that he was naked. A horrible wave of shame swept over him, but he felt excited, too. When he looked down at his penis and saw it starting to stiffen, he felt both alarmed and thrilled.

"Come up here, I said!"

He advanced slowly to the front of the room while the others—Sally Meyers, Donny Frankel, Nonie Martin, and poor old half-bright Slopey Dodd—goggled at him.

Miss Ratcliffe stood in front of her desk, hands on hips, eyes blazing, a gorgeous cloud of dark-auburn hair floating around her head.

"You're a bad boy, Brian—a very bad boy."

He nodded his head dumbly, but his penis was raising ITS *head, and so it seemed there was at least one part of him that did not mind being bad at all. That in fact* RELISHED *being bad.*

She put a piece of chalk in his hand. He felt a small bolt of electricity when their hands touched. "Now," Miss Ratcliffe said severely, "You must write I WILL FINISH PAYING FOR MY SANDY KOU- FAX CARD *five hundred times on the blackboard."*

"Yes, Miss Ratcliffe."

He began to write, standing on tiptoe to reach the top of the board, aware of warm air on his naked buttocks. He had finished I WILL FINISH PAYING *when he felt Miss Ratcliffe's smooth, soft hand encircle his stiff penis and begin to tug on it gently. For a moment he thought he would faint dead away, it felt so good.*

"Keep writing," she said grimly from behind him, "and I'll keep on doing this."

"M-Miss Ruh-Ruh-Ratcliffe, what about my t-tongue exercises?" asked Slopey Dodd.

"Shut up or I'll run you over in the parking lot, Slopey," Miss Ratcliffe said. "I'll make you squeak, little buddy."

She went on pulling Brian's pudding while she spoke. He was moaning now. It was wrong, he knew that, but it felt good. It felt most sincerely awesome. It felt like what he needed. Just the thing.

Then he turned around and it wasn't Miss Ratcliffe standing at his shoulder but Wilma Jerzyck with her large round pallid face and her deep brown eyes, like two raisins pounded deep into a wad of dough.

"He'll take it back if you don't pay," Wilma said. "And that's not all, little buddy. He'll—"

9

Brian Rusk woke up with such a jerk that he almost fell out of bed and onto the floor. His body was covered with sweat, his heart was pounding like a jackhammer, and his penis was a small, hard branch inside his pajama trousers.

He sat up, shivering all over. His first impulse was to open his mouth and yell for his mother, as he had done when he was small and a nightmare had invaded his sleep. Then he realized that he *wasn't* small anymore, he was eleven . . . and it wasn't exactly the sort of dream you told your mother about, anyway, was it?

He lay back, eyes wide and staring into the dark. He glanced at the digital clock on the table next to the bed and saw it was four minutes past midnight. He could hear the sound of rain, hard now, pelting against his bedroom window, driven by huge, whooping gasps of wind. It sounded almost like sleet.

My card. My Sandy Koufax card is gone.

It wasn't. He knew it wasn't, but he also knew he would not be able to go back to sleep until he'd checked to make sure it was still there, in the looseleaf binder where he kept his growing collection of Topps cards from 1956. He had checked it before leaving for school yesterday, had done so again when he got home, and last night, after supper, he had broken off playing pass in the back yard with Stanley Dawson to check on it once more. He had told Stanley he had to go to the bathroom. He had peeked at it one final time before crawling into bed and turning out the light. He recognized that it had become a kind of obsession with him, but recognition did not put a stop to it.

He slipped out of bed, barely noticing the way the cool air brought out goosebumps on his hot body and made his penis wilt. He walked quietly across to his dresser. He left the shape of his own body behind him on the sheet which covered his mattress, printed in sweat. The big book lay on top of the dresser in a pool of white light thrown by the streetlamp outside.

He took it down, opened it, and paged rapidly through the sheets of clear plastic with the pockets you put the cards in. He passed Mel Parnell, Whitey Ford, and Warren Spahn—treasures over which he had once crowed mightily—with hardly a glance. He had a moment of terrible panic when he reached the sheets at the back of the book, the ones which were still empty, without seeing Sandy Koufax. Then he realized he had turned several pages at once in his hurry. He turned back, and yes, there he was—that narrow face, those faintly smiling, dedicated eyes looking out from beneath the bill of the cap.

To my good friend Brian, with best wishes, Sandy Koufax.

His fingers traced over the sloping lines of the inscription. His lips moved. He felt at peace again . . . or *almost* at peace. The card wasn't really his yet. This was just sort of a . . . a trial run. There was something he had to do before it would really be his. Brian wasn't completely sure what it was, but he knew it had something to do with the dream from which he had just wakened, and he was confident that he would know when the time

(*tomorrow? later today?*)

came.

He closed the looseleaf binder—BRIAN'S COLLECTION DO NOT TOUCH! carefully printed on the file card Scotch-taped to the front—and returned it to the dresser. Then he went back to bed.

Only one thing about having the Sandy Koufax card was troubling. He had wanted to show it to his father. Coming home from Needful Things, he had imagined just how it would be when he showed it to him. He, Brian, elaborately casual: *Hey, Dad, I picked up a '56 today at the new store. Want to check it out?* His dad would say okay, not really interested, just going along with Brian to his room to keep Brian happy—but how his eyes would light up when he saw what Brian had lucked into! And when he saw the inscription—!

Yes, he would be amazed and delighted, all right. He'd probably clap Brian on the back and give him a high-five.

But *then* what?

Then the questions would start, that was what . . . and that was the problem. His father would want to know, first, where he had gotten the card, and second, where he had gotten the money to buy such a card, which was (a.) rare, (b.) in excellent condition, and (c.) autographed. The *printed* signature on the card read Sanford Koufax, which was the fabled fastball pitcher's real name. The *autographed* signature read *Sandy* Koufax, and in the weird and sometimes high-priced world of baseball trading-card collectors, that meant fair market value might be as much as a hundred and fifty dollars.

In his mind, Brian tried out one possible answer.

I got it at the new store, Dad—Needful Things. The guy gave it to me at a really WICKED discount . . . he said it would make people more interested in coming to his store if they knew he kept his prices down.

This was good as far as it went, but even a kid still a year too young to pay the full adult price of admission at the movies knew it didn't go far enough. When you said somebody had given you a really good deal on something, people were always interested. *Too* interested.

Oh yeah? How much did he knock off? Thirty per cent? Forty? Did he give it to you for half price? That'd still be sixty or seventy bucks, Brian, and I KNOW you don't have that kind of money just laying around in your piggy-bank.

Well . . . actually it was a little less than that, Dad.

Okay, tell me. How much did you pay?

Well . . . eighty-five cents.

He sold you a 1956 autographed Sandy Koufax baseball card, in uncirculated condition, for eighty-five cents?

Yeah, that's where the real trouble would start, all right.

What *kind* of trouble? He didn't know, exactly, but there

would be a stink, he was sure of that. Somehow he would get blamed—maybe by his dad, but by his mom for sure.

They might even try to make him give it back, and there was no *way* he was going to give it back. It wasn't just signed; it was signed *to Brian.*

No *way.*

Hell, he hadn't even been able to show Stan Dawson when Stan came over to play pass, although he'd wanted to—Stan would have fudged his Jockeys. But Stan was going to sleep over on Friday night, and it was all too easy for Brian to imagine him saying to Brian's dad: *So how'd you like Brian's Sandy Koufax card, Mr. Rusk? Pretty rad, huh?* The same went for his other friends. Brian had uncovered one of the great truths of small towns: many secrets—in fact, all the really *important* secrets—cannot be shared. Because word has a way of getting around, and getting around fast.

He found himself in a strange and uncomfortable position. He had come by a great thing and could not show or share it. This should have vitiated his pleasure in his new acquisition, and it did, to some extent, but it also afforded him a furtive, niggardly satisfaction. He found himself not so much enjoying the card as *gloating* over it, and so he had uncovered another great truth: gloating in private provides its own peculiar pleasure. It was as if one corner of his mostly open and goodhearted nature had been walled off and then lit with a special black light that both distorted and enhanced what was hidden there.

And he was not going to give it up.

No way, uh-uh, *negatory.*

Then you better finish paying for it, a voice deep in his mind whispered.

He would. No problem there. He didn't think the thing he was supposed to do was exactly nice, but he was pretty sure it wasn't anything totally gross, either. Just a . . . a . . .

Just a prank, a voice whispered in his mind, and he saw the eyes of Mr. Gaunt—dark blue, like the sea on a clear day, and strangely soothing. *That's all. Just a little prank.*

Yeah, just a prank, whatever it was.

No problem.

He settled deeper under his goosedown quilt, turned over on his side, closed his eyes, and immediately began to doze.

Something occurred to him as he and his brother sleep drew closer to each other. Something Mr. Gaunt had said. *You will be a better advertisement than the local paper could ever THINK of being!* Only he couldn't show the wonderful card he had bought. If a little thought had made that obvious to him, an eleven-year-old kid who wasn't even bright enough to keep out of Hugh Priest's way when he was crossing the street, shouldn't a smart guy like Mr. Gaunt have seen it, too?

Well, maybe. But maybe not. Grownups didn't think the same as normal people, and besides, he had the card, didn't he? And it was in his book, right where it should be, wasn't it?

The answer to both questions was yes, and so Brian let go of the whole thing and went back to sleep as the rain pelted against his window and the restless fall wind screamed in the angles beneath the eaves.

CHAPTER FOUR

1

The rain had stopped by daylight on Thursday, and by ten-thirty, when Polly looked out the front window of You Sew and Sew and saw Nettie Cobb, the clouds were beginning to break up. Nettie was carrying a rolled-up umbrella, and went scuttling along Main Street with her purse clamped under her arm as if she sensed the jaws of some new storm opening just behind her.

"How are your hands this morning, Polly?" Rosalie Drake asked.

Polly sighed inwardly. She would have to field the same question, but more insistently put, from Alan that afternoon, she supposed—she had promised to meet him for coffee at Nan's Luncheonette around three. You couldn't fool the people who had known you for a long time. They saw the pallor of your face and the dark crescents below your eyes. More important, they saw the haunted look *in* the eyes.

"Much better today, thanks," she said. This was overstating the truth by more than a little; they were better, but *much* better? Huh-uh.

"I thought with the rain and all—"

"It's unpredictable, what makes them hurt. That's the pure devil of it. But never mind that, Rosalie, come quick and look out the window. I think we're about to witness a minor miracle."

Rosalie joined Polly at the window in time to see the small, scuttling figure with the umbrella clutched tightly in one hand—possibly for use as a bludgeon, judging from the way it was now being held—approach the awning of Needful Things.

"Is that Nettie? Is it really?" Rosalie almost gasped.

"It really is."

"My God, she's going in!"

But for a moment it seemed that Rosalie's prediction had queered the deal. Nettie approached the door . . . then pulled back. She shifted the umbrella from hand to hand and looked at the façade of Needful Things as if it were a snake which might bite her.

"Go on, Nettie," Polly said softly. "Go for it, sweetie!"

"The CLOSED sign must be in the window," Rosalie said.

"No, he's got another one that says TUESDAYS AND THURS-DAYS BY APPOINTMENT ONLY. I saw it when I came in this morning."

Nettie was approaching the door again. She reached for the knob, then drew back again.

"God, this is *killing* me," Rosalie said. "She told me she might come back, and I know how much she likes carnival glass, but I never really thought she'd go through with it."

"She asked me if it would be all right for her to leave the house on her break so she could come down to what she called 'that new place' and pick up my cake-box," Polly murmured.

Rosalie nodded. "That's our Nettie. She used to ask me for permission to use the john."

"I got an idea part of her was hoping I'd say no, there was too much to do. But I think part of her wanted me to say yes, too."

Polly's eyes never left the fierce, small-scale struggle going on less than forty yards away, a mini-war between Nettie Cobb and Nettie Cobb. If she actually *did* go in, what a step forward that would be for her!

Polly felt dull, hot pain in her hands, looked down, and saw she had been twisting them together. She forced them down to her sides.

"It's not the cake-box and it's not the carnival glass," Rosalie said. "It's *him.*"

Polly glanced at her.

Rosalie laughed and blushed a little. "Oh, I don't mean Nettie's got the hots for him, or anything like that, although she *did* look a little starry-eyed when I caught up with her outside. He was *nice* to her, Polly. That's all. Honest and nice."

"Lots of people are nice to her," Polly said. "Alan goes out of his way to be kind to her, and she still shies away from him."

"Our Mr. Gaunt has got a special kind of nice," Rosalie said simply, and as if to prove this, they saw Nettie grasp the knob and turn it. She opened the door and then only stood there on the sidewalk clutching her umbrella, as if the shallow well of her resolve had been utterly exhausted. Polly felt a sudden certainty that Nettie would now pull the door closed again and hurry away. Her hands, arthritis or no arthritis, closed into loose fists.

Go on, Nettie. Go on in. Take a chance. Rejoin the world.

Then Nettie smiled, obviously in response to someone neither Polly nor Rosalie could see. She lowered the umbrella from its position across her chest . . . and went inside.

The door closed behind her.

Polly turned to Rosalie, and was touched to see that there were tears in her eyes. The two women looked at each other for a moment, and then embraced, laughing.

"Way to go, Nettie!" Rosalie said.

"Two points for our side!" Polly agreed, and the sun broke free of the clouds inside her head a good two hours before it would finally do so in the sky above Castle Rock.

2

Five minutes later, Nettie Cobb sat in one of the plush, high-backed chairs Gaunt had installed along one wall of his shop.

Her umbrella and purse lay on the floor beside her, forgotten. Gaunt sat next to her, his hands holding hers, his sharp eyes locked on her vague ones. A carnival glass lampshade stood beside Polly Chalmers's cake container on one of the glass display cases. The lampshade was a moderately gorgeous thing, and might have sold for three hundred dollars or better in a Boston antiques shop; Nettie Cobb had, nevertheless, just purchased it for ten dollars and forty cents, all the money she had had in her purse when she entered the shop. Beautiful or not, it was, for the moment, as forgotten as her umbrella.

"A deed," she was saying now. She sounded like a woman talking in her sleep. She moved her hands slightly, so as to grip Mr. Gaunt's more tightly. He returned her grip, and a little smile of pleasure touched her face.

"Yes, that's right. It's really just a small matter. You know Mr. Keeton, don't you?"

"Oh yes," Nettie said. "Ronald and his son, Danforth. I know them both. Which do you mean?"

"The younger," Mr. Gaunt said, stroking her palms with his long thumbs. The nails were slightly yellow and quite long. "The Head Selectman."

"They call him Buster behind his back," Nettie said, and giggled. It was a harsh sound, a little hysterical, but Leland Gaunt did not seem alarmed. On the contrary; the sound of Nettie's not-quite-right laughter seemed to please him. "They have ever since he was a little boy."

"I want you to finish paying for your lampshade by playing a trick on Buster."

"Trick?" Nettie looked vaguely alarmed.

Gaunt smiled. "Just a harmless prank. And he'll never know it was you. He'll think it was someone else."

"Oh." Nettie looked past Gaunt at the carnival glass lampshade, and for a moment something sharpened her gaze—greed, perhaps, or just simple longing and pleasure. "Well . . ."

"It will be all right, Nettie. No one will ever know . . . and you'll have the lampshade."

Nettie spoke slowly and thoughtfully. "My husband used to play tricks on me a lot. It might be fun to play one on someone else." She looked back at him, and now the thing sharpening her gaze was alarm. "If it doesn't *hurt* him. I don't want to *hurt* him. I hurt my husband, you know."

"It won't hurt him," Gaunt said softly, stroking Nettie's hands. "It won't hurt him a bit. I just want you to put some things in his house."

"How could I get in Buster's—"

"Here."

He put something into her hand. A key. She closed her hand over it.

"When?" Nettie asked. Her dreaming eyes had returned to the lampshade again.

"Soon." He released her hands and stood up. "And now, Nettie, I really ought to put that beautiful lampshade into a box for you. Mrs. Martin is coming to look at some Lalique in—" He glanced at his watch. "Goodness, in fifteen minutes! But I can't begin to tell you how glad I am that you decided to come in. Very few people appreciate the beauty of carnival glass these days—most people are just dealers, with cash registers for hearts."

Nettie also stood, and looked at the lampshade with the soft eyes of a woman who is in love. The agonized nervousness with which she had approached the shop had entirely disappeared. "It *is* lovely, isn't it?"

"Very lovely," Mr. Gaunt agreed warmly. "And I can't tell you . . . can't even begin to express . . . how happy it makes me to know it will have a good home, a place where someone will do more than dust it on Wednesday afternoons and then, after years of that, break it in a careless moment and sweep the pieces up and then drop them into the trash without a second thought."

"I'd never do that!" Nettie cried.

"I know you wouldn't," Mr. Gaunt said. "It's one of your charms, Netitia."

Nettie looked at him, amazed. "How did you know my name?"

"I have a flair for them. I never forget a name or a face."

He went through the curtain at the back of his shop. When he returned, he held a flat sheet of white cardboard in one hand and a large fluff of tissue paper in the other. He set the tissue paper down beside the cake container (it began at once to expand, with secret little ticks and snaps, into something which looked like a giant corsage) and began to fold the cardboard into a box exactly the right size for the lampshade. "I know you'll be a fine custodian of the item you have purchased. That's why I sold it to you."

"Really? I thought . . . Mr. Keeton . . . and the trick . . ."

"No, no, no!" Mr. Gaunt said, half-laughing and half-exasperated. "*Anyone* will play a trick! People love to play tricks! But to place objects with people who love them and need them . . . that is a different kettle of fish altogether. Sometimes, Netitia, I think that what I *really* sell is happiness . . . what do you think?"

"Well," Nettie said earnestly, "I know you've made *me* happy, Mr. Gaunt. Very happy."

He exposed his crooked, jostling teeth in a wide smile. "Good! That's good!" Mr. Gaunt pushed the tissue-paper corsage into the box, cradled the lampshade in its ticking whiteness, closed the box, and taped it shut with a flourish. "And here we are! Another satisfied customer has found her needful thing!"

He held the box out to her. Nettie took it. And as her fingers touched his she felt a shiver of revulsion, although she had gripped them with great strength—even ardor—a few moments ago. But that interlude had already begun to seem hazy and unreal. He put the Tupperware cake container on top of the white box. She saw something inside the former.

"What's that?"

"A note for your employer," Gaunt said.

Alarm rose to Nettie's face at once. "Not about *me?*"

"Good heavens, no!" Gaunt said, laughing, and Nettie relaxed at once. When he was laughing, Mr. Gaunt was impossible to resist or distrust. "Take care of your lampshade, Netitia, and do come again."

"I will," Nettie said, and this could have been an answer to both admonitions, but she felt in her heart (that secret repository where needs and fears elbowed each other continuously like uncomfortable passengers in a crowded subway car) that, while she might come here again, the lampshade was the only thing she would ever buy in Needful Things.

Yet what of that? It was a *beautiful* thing, the sort of thing she had always wanted, the only thing she needed to complete her modest collection. She considered telling Mr. Gaunt that her husband might still be alive if he had not smashed a carnival glass lampshade much like this one fourteen years ago, that it had been the last straw, the one which finally drove her over the edge. He had broken many of her bones during their years together, and she had let him live. Finally he had broken something she *really* needed, and she had taken his life.

She decided she did not have to tell Mr. Gaunt this.

He looked like the sort of man who might already know.

3

"Polly! Polly, she's coming out!"

Polly left the dressmaker's dummy where she had been slowly and carefully pinning up a hem, and hurried to the window. She and Rosalie stood side by side, watching as Nettie left Needful Things in a state which could only be described as heavily laden. Her purse was under one arm, her umbrella was under the other, and in her hands she held Polly's Tupperware cake container balanced atop a square white box.

"Maybe I better go help her," Rosalie said.

"No." Polly put out a hand and restrained her gently. "Better not. I think she'd only be embarrassed and fluttery."

They watched Nettie walk up the street. She no longer scuttled, as if before the jaws of a storm; now she seemed almost to drift.

No, Polly thought. *No, that isn't right. It's more like . . . floating.*

Her mind suddenly made one of those odd connections which were almost like cross-references, and she burst out laughing.

Rosalie looked at her, eyebrows raised. "Share?"

"It's the look on her face," Polly said, watching Nettie cross Linden Street in slow, dreamy steps.

"What do you mean?"

"She looks like a woman who just got laid . . . and had about three orgasms."

Rosalie turned pink, looked at Nettie once more, and then screamed with laughter. Polly joined in. The two of them held each other and rocked back and forth, laughing wildly.

"Gee," Alan Pangborn said from the front of the store. "Ladies laughing well before noon! It's too early for champagne, so what is it?"

"Four!" Rosalie said, giggling madly. Tears were streaming down her cheeks. "It looked more like four to me!"

Then they were off again, rocking back and forth in each other's arms, howling with laughter while Alan stood watching them with his hands in the pockets of his uniform pants, smiling quizzically.

4

Norris Ridgewick arrived at the Sheriff's Office in his street clothes about ten minutes before the noon whistle blew at the mill. He had the mid-shift, from twelve until nine p.m., right through the weekend, and that was just the way he liked it. Let somebody else clean up the messes on the highways and byways of Castle County after the bars closed at one o'clock; he could do it, *had* done it on many occasions, but he almost always puked his guts. He sometimes puked his guts even if the victims were up, walking around, and yelling that they didn't have to take any fucking breathalyzer test, they knew their Constipational rights. Norris just had that kind of a stomach. Sheila Brigham liked to tease him by saying he was like Deputy Andy on that TV show *Twin Peaks,* but Norris knew he wasn't. Deputy Andy cried when he saw dead people. Norris didn't cry, but he was apt to puke on them, the way he had almost puked on Homer Gamache that time when he had found Homer sprawled in a ditch out by Homeland Cemetery, beaten to death with his own artificial arm.

Norris glanced at the roster, saw that both Andy Clutter-buck and John LaPointe were out on patrol, then at the day-watch board. Nothing there for him, which was also just the way he liked it. To make his day complete—this end of it, at least—his second uniform had come back from the cleaners . . . on the day promised, for once. That would save him a trip home to change.

A note pinned to the plastic dry-cleaning bag read, "Hey Barney—you owe me $5.25. Do not stiff me this time or you will be a sadder & wiser man when the sun goes down." It was signed *Clut.*

Norris's good mood was unbroken even by the note's saluta-tion. Sheila Brigham was the only person in the Castle Rock Sheriff's Office who thought of Norris as a *Twin Peaks* kind of guy (Norris had an idea that she was the only person in the department—besides himself, that was—who even watched the show). The other deputies—John LaPointe, Seat Thomas, Andy Clutterbuck—called him Barney, after the Don Knotts character on the old *Andy Griffith Show.* This sometimes irritated him, but not today. Four days of mid-shift, then three days off. A whole week of silk laid out before him. Life could sometimes be grand.

He pulled a five and a one from his wallet and laid them on Clut's desk. "Hey, Clut, live a little," he jotted on the back of a report form, signed his name with a flourish, and left it by the money. Then he stripped the dry-cleaning bag off the uniform and took it into the men's room. He whistled as he changed clothes, then waggled his eyebrows approvingly as he stared at his reflection in the mirror. He was Squared Away, by God. One hundred per cent Squared Away. The evildoers of Castle Rock had damned well better be on the lookout today, or—

He caught movement behind him in the mirror, but before he could do more than begin to turn his head he had been grabbed, spun around, and slammed into the tiles beside the urinals. His head bonked the wall, his cap fell off, and then he was looking into the round, flushed face of Danforth Keeton.

"What in the hell do you think you're doing, Ridgewick?" he asked.

Norris had forgotten all about the ticket he had slipped under the windshield wiper of Keeton's Cadillac the night before. Now it all came back to him.

"Let go of me!" he said. He tried for a tone of indignation, but his voice came out in a worried squeak. He felt his cheeks growing hot. Whenever he was angry or scared—and right now he was both—he blushed like a girl.

Keeton, who overtopped Norris by five inches and outweighed him by a hundred pounds, gave the deputy a harsh little shake and then did let go. He pulled the ticket out of his pocket and brandished it under Norris's nose. "Is this your name on this goddam thing or isn't it?" he demanded, as though Norris had already denied it.

Norris Ridgewick knew perfectly well that it was his signature, rubber-stamped but perfectly recognizable, and that the ticket had been pulled from his citation book.

"You were parked in the crip space," he said, stepping away from the wall and rubbing the back of his head. Damned if he didn't think there was going to be a knot there. As his initial surprise (and Buster had jumped the living Jesus out of him, he couldn't deny that) abated, his anger grew.

"The *what?*"

"The *handicap* space!" Norris shouted. *And furthermore, it was Alan himself who told me to write that ticket!* he was about to continue, and then didn't. Why give this fat pig the satisfaction of passing the buck? "You've been told about it before, Buh . . . Danforth, and you know it."

"*What* did you call me?" Danforth Keeton asked ominously. Red splotches the size of cabbage roses had grown on his cheeks and jowls.

"That's a valid ticket," Norris said, ignoring this last, "and as far as I'm concerned, you better pay it. Why, you're lucky I don't cite you for assaulting a police officer as well!"

Danforth laughed. The sound banged flatly off the walls. "I don't see any police officer," he said. "I see a narrow piece of shit packaged to look like beef jerky."

Norris bent over and picked up his hat. His guts were a roil of fear—Danforth Keeton was a bad enemy for a man to have—and his anger had deepened into fury. His hands trembled. He took a moment, nonetheless, to set his hat squarely on his head.

"You can take this up with Alan, if you want—"

"I'm taking it up with *you!*"

"—but I'm done talking about it. Make sure you pay that within thirty days, Danforth, or we'll have to come and get you." Norris drew himself up to his full five-foot-six and added: "We know where to find you."

He started out. Keeton, his face now looking a little like sunset in a nuclear blast area, stepped forward to block his escape route. Norris stopped and levelled a finger at him.

"If you touch me I'll throw you in a cell, Buster. I mean it."

"Okay, that's it," Keeton said in a queer, toneless voice. "*That* is it. You're fired. Take off that uniform and start looking for another j—"

"No," a voice said from behind them, and they both looked around. Alan Pangborn was standing in the men's-room doorway.

Keeton rolled his hands into fat white fists. "You keep out of this."

Alan walked in, letting the door swoosh slowly shut behind him. "No," he said. "I was the one who told Norris to write that ticket. I also told him I was going to forgive it before the appropriations meeting. It's a five-dollar ticket, Dan. What the hell got into you?"

Alan's voice was puzzled. He *felt* puzzled. Buster had never been a sweet-natured man, not even at the best of times, but an outburst like this was overboard even for him. Since the end of the summer, the man had seemed ragged and always on edge—Alan had often heard the distant bellow of his voice when the selectmen were in committee meetings—and his eyes had taken on a look which was almost haunted. He wondered briefly if Keeton might be sick, and decided that was a consideration for some later time. Right now he had a moderately ugly situation on his hands.

"Nothing got into me," Keeton said sulkily, and smoothed back his hair. Norris took some satisfaction in noticing that Keeton's hands were also trembling. "I'm just good and goddam tired of self-important pricks like this man here . . . I try to do a lot for this town . . . hell, I *accomplish* a lot for this town . . . and I'm sick of the constant persecution . . ." He paused a moment, his fat throat working, and then burst out: "He called me Buster! You know how I feel about that!"

"He'll apologize," Alan said calmly. "Won't you, Norris?"

"I don't know that I will," Norris said. His voice was trembly and his gut was rolling, but he was still angry. "I know he doesn't like it, but the truth is, he surprised it out of me. I was just standing here, looking in the mirror to make sure my tie was straight, when he grabbed me and threw me against the wall. I smacked my head a pretty good one. Jeez, Alan, I don't know *what* I said."

Alan's eyes shifted back to Keeton. "Is that true?"

Keeton dropped his own eyes. "I was mad," he said, and Alan supposed it was as close as a man like him could get to a spontaneous and undirected apology. He glanced back at Norris to see if the deputy understood this. It looked as if maybe Norris did. That was good; it was a long step toward defusing this nasty little stinkbomb. Alan relaxed a little.

"Can we consider this incident closed?" he asked both men. "Just kind of chalk it up to experience and go on from here?"

"All right by me," Norris said after a moment. Alan was touched. Norris was scrawny, he had a habit of leaving half-full cans of Jolt and Nehi in the cruisers he used, and his reports were horrors . . . but he had yards of heart. He was backing down, but not because he was afraid of Keeton. If the burly Head Selectman thought that was it, he was making a very bad mistake.

"I'm sorry I called you Buster," Norris said. He wasn't, not a bit, but it didn't hurt to *say* he was. He supposed.

Alan looked at the heavy-set man in the loud sport-coat and open-necked golfer's shirt. "Danforth?"

"All right, it never happened," Keeton said. He spoke in a tone of overblown magnanimity, and Alan felt a familiar wave of dislike wash over him. A voice buried somewhere deep in his mind, the primitive crocodile-voice of the subconscious, spoke up briefly but clearly: *Why don't you have a heart attack, Buster? Why don't you do us all a favor and die?*

"All right," he said. "Good dea—"

"*If,*" Keeton said, raising one finger.

Alan raised his eyebrows. "If?"

"If we can do something about this ticket." He held it out toward Alan, tweezed between two fingers, as if it were a rag which had been used to clean up some dubious spill.

Alan sighed. "Come on in the office, Danforth. We'll talk about it." He looked at Norris. "You've got the duty, right?"

"Right," Norris said. His stomach was still in a ball. His good feelings were gone, probably for the rest of the day, it was that fat pig's fault, and Alan was going to forgive the ticket. He understood it—politics—but that didn't mean he had to like it.

"Do you want to hang around?" Alan asked. It was as close as he could come to asking, *Do you need to talk this out?* with Keeton standing right there and glowering at both of them.

"No," Norris said. "Places to go and things to do. Talk to you later, Alan." He left the men's room, brushing past Keeton without a glance. And although Norris did not know it, Keeton restrained, with a great—almost heroic—effort, an irrational but mighty urge to plant a foot in his ass to help him on his way.

Alan made a business of checking his own reflection in the mirror, giving Norris time to make a clean getaway, while Keeton stood by the door, watching him impatiently. Then Alan pushed out into the bullpen area again with Keeton at his heels.

A small, dapper man in a cream-colored suit was sitting in one of the two chairs outside the door to his office, ostentatiously reading a large leather-bound book which could only have been a Bible. Alan's heart sank. He had been fairly sure nothing else *too* unpleasant could happen this morning—it would be noon in only two or three minutes, so the idea seemed a reasonable one—but he had been wrong.

The Rev. William Rose closed his Bible (the binding of which almost matched his suit) and bounced to his feet. "Chief-uh Pangborn," he said. The Rev. Rose was one of those deep-thicket Baptists who begin to twist the tails of their words when they are emotionally cranked up. "May I please speak to you?"

"Give me five minutes, please, Reverend Rose. I have a matter to attend to."

"This is-uh extremely important."

I bet, Alan thought. "So is this. Five minutes."

He opened the door and ushered Keeton into his office before the Reverend Willie, as Father Brigham liked to call him, could say anything else.

5

"It'll be about Casino Nite," Keeton said after Alan had closed the office door. "You mark my words. Father John Brigham is a bull-headed Irishman, but I'll take him over that fellow any-time. Rose is an incredibly arrogant prick."

There goes the pot, calling the kettle black, Alan thought.

"Have a seat, Danforth."

Keeton did. Alan went around his desk, held the parking ticket up, and tore it into small fragments. These he tossed into the wastebasket. "There. Okay?"

"Okay," Keeton said, and moved to rise.

"No, sit down a moment longer."

Keeton's bushy eyebrows drew together below his high, pink forehead in a thundercloud.

"Please," Alan added. He dropped into his own swivel chair. His hands came together and tried to make a blackbird; Alan caught them at it and folded them firmly together on the blotter.

"We're having an appropriations committee meeting next

week dealing with budgetary matters for Town Meeting in February—" Alan began.

"Damn right," Keeton rumbled.

"—and that's a political thing," Alan went on. "I recognize it and you recognize it. I just tore up a perfectly valid parking ticket because of a political consideration."

Keeton smiled a little. "You've been in town long enough to know how things work, Alan. One hand washes the other."

Alan shifted in his chair. It made its little creakings and squeakings—sounds he sometimes heard in his dreams after long, hard days. The kind of day this one was turning out to be.

"Yes," he said. "One hand washes the other. But only for so long."

The eyebrows drew together again. "What does *that* mean?"

"It means that there's a place, even in small towns, where politics have to end. You need to remember that I'm not an appointed official. The selectmen may control the purse strings, but the voters elect me. And what they elect me to do is to protect them, and to preserve and uphold the law. I took the oath, and I try to hold to it."

"Are you threatening me? Because if you are—"

Just then the mill-whistle went off. It was muted in here, but Danforth Keeton still jumped as if he had been stung by a wasp. His eyes widened momentarily, and his hands clamped down to white claws on the arms of his chair.

Alan felt that puzzlement again. *He's as skittish as a mare in heat. What the hell's wrong with him?*

For the first time he found himself wondering if maybe Mr. Danforth Keeton, who had been Castle Rock's Head Selectman since long before Alan himself ever heard of the place, had been up to something that was not strictly kosher.

"I'm not threatening you," he said. Keeton was beginning to relax again, but warily . . . as if he were afraid the mill-whistle might go off again, just to goose him.

"That's good. Because it isn't just a question of purse strings,

NEEDFUL THINGS   113

Sheriff Pangborn. The Board of Selectmen, along with the three County Commissioners, holds right of approval over the hiring—and the firing—of Sheriff's Deputies. Among many other rights of approval I'm sure you know about."

"That's just a rubber stamp."

"So it has always been," Keeton agreed. From his inside pocket he produced a Roi-Tan cigar. He pulled it between his fingers, making the cellophane crackle. "That doesn't mean it has to stay that way."

Now who is threatening whom? Alan thought, but did not say. Instead he leaned back in his chair and looked at Keeton. Keeton met his eyes for a few seconds, then dropped his gaze to the cigar and began picking at the wrapper.

"The next time you park in the handicap space, I'm going to ticket you myself, and *that* citation will stand," Alan said. "And if you ever lay your hands on one of my deputies again, I'll book you on a charge of third-degree assault. That will happen no matter how many so-called rights of approval the selectmen hold. Because politics only stretches so far with me. Do you understand?"

Keeton looked down at the cigar for a long moment, as if meditating. When he looked up at Alan again, his eyes had turned to small, hard flints. "If you want to find out just how hard my ass is, Sheriff Pangborn, just go on pushing me." There was anger written on Keeton's face—yes, most assuredly—but Alan thought there was something else written there, as well. He thought it was fear. Did he see that? Smell it? He didn't know, and it didn't matter. But what Keeton was afraid of . . . *that* might matter. That might matter a lot.

"Do you understand?" he repeated.

"Yes," Keeton said. He stripped the cellophane from his cigar with a sudden hard gesture and dropped it on the floor. He stuck the cigar in his mouth and spoke around it. "Do *you* understand *me?*"

The chair creaked and croaked as Alan rocked forward

again. He looked at Keeton earnestly. "I understand what you're saying, but I sure as hell don't understand how you're *acting,* Danforth. We've never been best buddies, you and I—"

"*That's* for sure," Keeton said, and bit off the end of his cigar. For a moment Alan thought that was going to end up on the floor, too, and he was prepared to let it go if it did—politics—but Keeton spat it into the palm of his hand and then deposited it in the clean ashtray on the desk. It sat there like a small dog-turd.

"—but we've always had a pretty good working relationship. Now this. Is there something wrong? If there is, and I can help—"

"Nothing is wrong," Keeton said, rising abruptly. He was angry again—more than just angry. Alan could almost see the steam coming out of his ears. "It's just that I'm so tired of this . . . *persecution.*"

It was the second time he had used the word. Alan found it an odd word, an unsettling word. In fact, he found this whole conversation unsettling.

"Well, you know where I am," Alan said.

"God, *yes!*" Keeton said, and went to the door.

"And, please, Danforth—remember about the handicap space."

"*Fuck* the handicap space!" Keeton said, and slammed out.

Alan sat behind his desk and looked at the closed door for a long time, a troubled expression on his face. Then he went around the desk, picked up the crumpled cellophane cylinder lying on the floor, dropped it into the wastebasket, and went to the door to invite Steamboat Willie in.

6

"Mr. Keeton looked rather upset," Rose said. He seated himself carefully in the chair the Head Selectman had just vacated, looked with distaste at the cigar-end sitting in the ashtray, and then placed his white Bible carefully in the center of his ungenerous lap.

"Lots of appropriations meetings in the next month or so," Alan said vaguely. "I'm sure it's a strain for all the selectmen."

"Yes," Rev. Rose agreed. "For Jesus-uh told us: 'Render unto Caesar those things which are Caesar's, and render unto God those things which are God's.'"

"Uh-huh," Alan said. He suddenly wished he had a cigarette, something like a Lucky or a Pall Mall that was absolutely stuffed with tar and nicotine. "What can I render unto you this afternoon, R . . . Reverend Rose?" He was horrified to realize he had just come extremely close to calling the man Reverend Willie.

Rose took off his round rimless spectacles, polished them, and then settled them back in place, hiding the two small red spots high up on his nose. His black hair, plastered in place with some sort of hair potion Alan could smell but not identify, gleamed in the light of the fluorescent grid set into the ceiling.

"It's about the abomination Father John Brigham chooses to call Casino Nite," the Rev. Rose announced at last. "If you recall, Chief Pangborn, I came to you not long after I first heard of this dreadful idea to demand that you refuse to sanction such an event in the name-uh of decency."

"Reverend Rose, if *you'll* recall——"

Rose held up one hand imperiously and dipped the other into his jacket pocket. He came out with a pamphlet which was almost the size of a paperback book. It was, Alan saw with a sinking heart (but no real surprise), the abridged version of the State of Maine's Code of Laws.

"I now come again," Rev. Rose said in ringing tones, "to demand that you forbid this event not only in the name of decency *but in the name of the law!*"

"Reverend Rose——"

"This is Section 24, subsection 9, paragraph 2 of the Maine State Code of Laws," Rev. Rose overrode him. His cheeks now flared with color, and Alan realized that the only thing he'd managed to do in the last few minutes was swap one crazy for another. " 'Except where noted-uh,' " Rev. Rose read, his voice now taking on the pulpit chant with which his mostly adoring congregation was so familiar, " 'games of chance, as previously defined in Section 23 of the Code-uh, where wagers of money are induced as a condition of play, shall be deemed illegal.' " He snapped the Code closed and looked at Alan. His eyes were blazing. *Shall be deemed-uh illegal!*" he cried.

Alan felt a brief urge to throw his arms in the air and yell *Praise-uh Jeesus!* When it had passed he said: "I'm aware of those sections of the Code which pertain to gambling, Reverend Rose. I looked them up after your earlier visit to me, and I showed them to Albert Martin, who does a lot of the town's legal work. His opinion was that Section 24 does not apply to such functions as Casino Nite." He paused, then added: "I have to tell you that was my opinion, as well."

"Impossible!" Rose spat. "They propose to turn a house of the Lord into a gambler's lair, and you tell me *that* is *legal?*"

"It's every bit as legal as the bingo games that have been going on at the Daughters of Isabella Hall since 1931."

"This-uh is not bingo! This is roulette-uh! This is playing cards for money! This is"—Rev. Rose's voice trembled—"*dice-uh!*"

Alan caught his hands trying to make another bird, and this time he locked them together on the desk blotter. "I had Albert write a letter of inquiry to Jim Tierney, the State's Attorney General. The answer was the same. I'm sorry, Reverend Rose. I know it offends you. Me, I've got a thing about kids on skateboards. I'd outlaw them if I could, but I can't. In a democracy we sometimes have to put up with things we don't like or approve of."

"But this is *gambling!*" Rev. Rose said, and there was real anguish in his voice. "This is *gambling for money!* How can such a thing be legal, when the Code specifically says—"

"The way they do it, it's really not gambling for money. Each . . . participant . . . pays a donation at the door. In return, the participant is given an equal amount of play money. At the end of the night, a number of prizes—not money but *prizes*— are auctioned off. A VCR, a toaster-oven, a Dirt Devil, a set of china, things like that." And some dancing, interior imp made him add: "I believe the initial donation may even be tax deductible."

"It is a sinful abomination," Rev. Rose said. The color had faded from his cheeks. His nostrils flared.

"That's a moral judgment, not a legal one. It's done this way all over the country."

"Yes," Rev. Rose said. He got to his feet, clutching his Bible before him like a shield. "By the *Catholics.* The Catholics *love* gambling. I intend to put a stop to this, Chief-uh Pangborn. With your help or without it."

Alan also got up. "A couple of things, Reverend Rose. It's *Sheriff* Pangborn, not Chief. And I can't tell you what to say from your pulpit any more than I can tell Father Brigham what sort of events he can run in his church, or the Daughters of Isabella Hall, or the K of C Hall—as long as they're not expressly forbidden by the State's laws, that is—but I *can* warn you to be careful, and I think I *have* to warn you to be careful."

Rose looked at him coldly. "What do you mean?"

"I mean that you're upset. The posters your people have been putting up around town are okay, and the letters to the paper are okay, but there's a line of infringement you must not cross. My advice is to let this one go by."

"When-uh Jesus saw the whores and the moneylenders in-uh the Temple, He did not consult any written Code of

Laws, Sheriff. When-uh Jesus saw those evil men and women defiling the house of the Lord-uh, He looked for no line of infringement. *Our Lord did what He-uh knew to be right!*"

"Yes," Alan said calmly, "but you're not Him."

Rose looked at him for a long moment, eyes blazing like gas-jets, and Alan thought: Uh-oh. This guy's just as mad as a hatter.

"Good day, Chief Pangborn," Rose said coldly.

This time Alan did not bother to correct him. He only nodded and held out his hand, knowing perfectly well it would not be shaken. Rose turned and stalked toward the door, Bible still held against his chest.

"Let this one go by, Reverend Rose, okay?" Alan called after him.

Rose neither turned nor spoke. He strode out the door and slammed it shut behind him hard enough to rattle the glass in the frame. Alan sat down behind his desk and pressed the heels of his palms to his temples.

A few moments later, Sheila Brigham poked her head timidly in through the door. "Alan?"

"Is he gone?" Alan asked without looking up.

"The preacher? Yes. He slammed out of here like a March wind."

"Elvis has left the building," Alan said hollowly.

"What?"

"Never mind." He looked up. "I'd like some hard drugs, please. Would you check the evidence locker, Sheila, and see what we have?"

She smiled. "Already have. The cupboard's bare, I'm afraid. Would a cup of coffee do?"

He smiled back. The afternoon had begun, and it had to be better than this morning—*had* to. "Sold."

"Good deal." She closed the door, and Alan at last let his hands out of jail. Soon a series of blackbirds was flying through a band of sunshine on the wall across from the window.

7

On Thursdays, the last period of the day at Castle Rock Middle School was set aside for activities. Because he was an honor student and would not be enrolled in a school activity until casting for the Winter Play took place, Brian Rusk was allowed to leave early on that day—it balanced out his late Tuesdays very nicely.

This Thursday afternoon he was out the side door almost before the sixth-period bell had stopped ringing. His packsack contained not only his books but the rain-slicker his mother had made him wear that morning, and it bulged comically on his back.

He rode away fast, his heart beating hard in his chest. He had something

(*a deed*)

to do. A little chore to get out of the way. Sort of a fun chore, actually. He now knew what it was. It had come to him clearly as he had been daydreaming his way through math class.

As Brian descended Castle Hill by way of School Street, the sun came out from behind the tattering clouds for the first time that day. He looked to his left and saw a shadow-boy on a shadow-bike keeping pace with him on the wet pavement.

You'll have to go fast to keep up with me today, shadow-kid, he thought. *I got places to go and things to do.*

Brian pedaled through the business district without looking across Main Street at Needful Things, pausing briefly at intersections for a perfunctory glance each way before hurrying on again. When he reached the intersection of Pond (which was *his* street) and Ford streets, he turned right instead of continuing up Pond Street to his house. At the intersection of Ford and Willow, he turned left. Willow Street paralleled Pond Street; the back yards of the houses on the two streets backed up against each other, divided in most cases by board fences.

Pete and Wilma Jerzyck lived on Willow Street.

Got to be a little careful here.

But he knew *how* to be careful; he had worked all that out in his mind on the ride from school, and it had come easily, almost as though it had also been there all along, like his knowledge of the thing he was supposed to do.

The Jerzyck house was quiet and the driveway was empty, but that didn't necessarily make everything safe and okay. Brian knew that Wilma worked at least part of the time at Hemphill's Market out on Route 117, because he had seen her there, running a cash-register with the ever-present scarf tied over her head, but that didn't mean she was there now. The beat-up little Yugo she drove might be parked in the Jerzyck garage, where he couldn't see.

Brian pedaled his bike up the driveway, got off, and put down the kickstand. He could feel his heartbeat in his ears and his throat now. It sounded like the ruffle of drums. He walked to the front door, rehearsing the lines he would speak if it turned out Mrs. Jerzyck was there after all.

Hi, Mrs. Jerzyck, I'm Brian Rusk, from the other side of the block? I go to the Middle School and pretty soon we're going to be selling magazine subscriptions, so the band can get new uniforms, and I've been asking people if they want magazines. So I can come back later when I've got my sales kit. We get prizes if we sell a lot.

It had sounded good when he was working it out in his head, and it still sounded good, but he felt tense all the same. He stood on the doorstep for a minute, listening for sounds inside the house—a radio, a TV tuned to one of the stories (not *Santa Barbara,* though; it wouldn't be *Santa Barbara* time for another couple of hours), maybe a vacuum. He heard nothing, but that didn't mean any more than the empty driveway.

Brian rang the doorbell. Faintly, somewhere in the depths of the house, he heard it: *Bing-Bong!*

He stood on the stoop, waiting, looking around occasionally to see if anyone had noticed him, but Willow Street seemed fast asleep. And there was a hedge in front of the Jerzyck house. That was good. When you were up to

(*a deed*)

something that people—your Ma and Pa, for instance—wouldn't exactly approve of, a hedge was about the best thing in the world.

It had been half a minute, and nobody was coming. So far so good . . . but it was also better to be safe than sorry. He rang the doorbell again, thumbing it twice this time, so the sound from the belly of the house was *BingBong! BingBong!*

Still nothing.

Okay, then. Everything was perfectly okay. Everything was, in fact, most sincerely awesome and utterly radical.

Sincerely awesome and utterly radical or not, Brian could not resist another look around—a rather furtive one this time—as he trundled his bike, with the kickstand still down, between the house and the garage. In this area, which the friendly folks at the Dick Perry Siding and Door Company in South Paris called a breezeway, Brian parked his bike again. Then he walked on into the back yard. His heart was pounding harder than ever. Sometimes his voice shook when his heart was pounding hard like this. He hoped that if Mrs. Jerzyck was out back, planting bulbs or something, his voice wouldn't shake when he told her about the magazine subscriptions. If it did, she might suspect he wasn't telling the truth. And that could lead to kinds of trouble he didn't even want to think about.

He halted near the back of the house. He could see part of the Jerzyck back yard, but not all of it. And suddenly this didn't seem like so much fun anymore. Suddenly it seemed like a mean trick—no more than that, but certainly no less. An apprehensive voice suddenly spoke up in his mind. *Why not just climb back on your bike again, Brian? Go on back home. Have a glass of milk and think this over.*

Yes. That seemed like a very good—a very *sane*—idea. He

actually began to turn around . . . and then a picture came to him, one which was a great deal more powerful than the voice. He saw a long black car—a Cadillac or maybe a Lincoln Mark IV—pulling up in front of his house. The driver's door opened and Mr. Leland Gaunt stepped out. Only Mr. Gaunt was no longer wearing a smoking jacket like the one Sherlock Holmes wore in some of the stories. The Mr. Gaunt who now strode across the landscape of Brian's imagination wore a formidable black suit—the suit of a funeral director—and his face was no longer friendly. His dark-blue eyes were even darker in anger, and his lips had pulled back from his crooked teeth . . . but not in a smile. His long, thin legs went scissoring up the walk to the Rusk front door, and the shadow-man attached to his heels looked like a hangman in a horror movie. When he got to the door he would not pause to ring the bell, oh no. He would simply barge in. If Brian's Ma tried to get in his way he would push her aside. If Brian's Pa tried to get in his way he would knock him down. And if Brian's little brother, Sean, tried to get in his way he would heave him the length of the house, like a quarterback throwing a Hail Mary. He would stride upstairs, bellowing Brian's name, and the roses on the wallpaper would wilt when that hangman's shadow passed over them.

He'd find me, too, Brian thought. His face as he stood by the side of the Jerzyck house was a study in dismay. *It wouldn't matter if I tried to hide. It wouldn't matter if I went all the way to* BOMBAY. *He'd find me. And when he did—*

He tried to block the picture, to turn it off, and couldn't. He saw Mr. Gaunt's eyes growing, turning into blue chasms which went down and down into some horrid indigo eternity. He saw Mr. Gaunt's long hands, with their queerly even fingers, turning into claws as they descended upon his shoulders. He felt his skin crawl at that loathsome touch. He heard Mr. Gaunt bellowing: *You have something of mine, Brian, and you haven't paid for it!*

I'll give it back! he heard himself screaming at that twisted, burning face. *Please oh please I'll give it back I'll give it back, just don't hurt me!*

Brian returned to himself, as dazed as he had been when he came out of Needful Things on Tuesday afternoon. The feeling now wasn't as pleasant as it had been then.

He didn't *want* to give back the Sandy Koufax card, that was the thing.

He didn't want to, because it was *his*.

8

Myra Evans stepped under the awning of Needful Things just as her best friend's son was finally walking into Wilma Jerzyck's back yard. Myra's glance, first behind her and then across Main Street, was even more furtive than Brian's glance across Willow Street had been.

If Cora—who really *was* her best friend—knew she was here, and, more important, *why* she was here, she would probably never speak to Myra again. Because *Cora* wanted the picture, too.

Never mind that, Myra thought. Two sayings occurred to her, and both seemed to fit this situation. *First come, first served* was one. *What she doesn't know won't hurt her* was the other.

All the same, Myra had donned a large pair of Foster Grant sunglasses before coming downtown. *Better safe than sorry* was another worthwhile piece of advice.

Now she advanced slowly on the door and studied the sign which hung there:

TUESDAYS AND THURSDAYS
BY APPOINTMENT ONLY

Myra did not have an appointment. She had come down here on the spur of the moment, galvanized into action by a call from Cora not twenty minutes ago.

"I've been thinking about it all day! I've simply got to have it, Myra—I should have bought it on Wednesday, but I only had four dollars in my purse and I wasn't sure if he'd take a personal check. You know how *embarrassing* it is when people won't. I've been kicking myself ever since. Why, I hardly slept a *wink* last night. I know you'll think it's silly, but it's *true.*"

Myra didn't think it was silly at all, and she knew it was true, because *she* had hardly slept a wink last night, either. And it was wrong of Cora to assume that picture should be hers simply because she had seen it first—as if that gave her some sort of divine right, or something.

"I don't believe she saw it first, anyway," Myra said in a small, sulky voice. "I think *I* saw it first."

The question of who had seen that absolutely delicious picture first was really moot, anyway. What *wasn't* moot was how Myra felt when she thought of coming into Cora's house and seeing that picture of Elvis hung above the mantel, right between Cora's ceramic Elvis figure and Cora's porcelain Elvis beer-stein. When she thought of that, Myra's stomach rose to somewhere just under her heart and hung there, knotted like a wet rag. It was the way she'd felt during the first week of the war against Iraq.

It wasn't *right.* Cora had all sorts of nice Elvis things, had even seen Elvis in concert once. That had been at the Portland Civic Center, a year or so before The King was called to heaven to be with his beloved mother.

"That picture should be *mine,*" she muttered, and, summoning all her courage, she knocked on the door.

It was opened almost before she could lower her hand, and a narrow-shouldered man almost bowled her over on his way out.

"Excuse me," he muttered, not raising his head, and she barely had time to register the fact that it was Mr. Constantine, the pharmacist at LaVerdiere's Super Drug. He hurried across the street and then onto the Town Common, holding a small wrapped package in his hands, looking neither to the right nor to the left.

When she looked back, Mr. Gaunt was in the doorway, smiling at her with his cheery brown eyes.

"I don't have an appointment . . ." she said in a small voice. Brian Rusk, who had grown used to hearing Myra pronouncing on things in a tone of total authority and assurance, would not have recognized that voice in a million years.

"You do now, dear lady," Mr. Gaunt said, smiling and standing aside. "Welcome back! Enter freely, and leave some of the happiness you bring!"

After one final quick look around that showed her no one she knew, Myra Evans scurried into Needful Things.

The door swung shut behind her.

A long-fingered hand, as white as the hand of a corpse, reached up in the gloom, found the ring-pull which hung down, and drew the shade.

9

Brian didn't realize he had been holding his breath until he let it out in a long, whistling sigh.

There was no one in the Jerzyck back yard.

Wilma, undoubtedly encouraged by the improving weather, had hung out her wash before leaving for work or wherever she had gone. It flapped on three lines in the sunshine and freshening breeze. Brian went to the back door and peered in, shading the sides of his face with his hands to cut the glare. He was looking into a deserted kitchen. He thought of knocking and decided it was just another way to keep from doing what he had come to do. No one was here. The best thing was to complete his business and then get the hell out.

He walked slowly down the steps and into the Jerzyck back yard. The clotheslines, with their freight of shirts, pants, underwear, sheets, and pillow-cases, were to the left. To the right was a small garden from which all the vegetables, with the exception of a few puny pumpkins, had been harvested. At the far end was a fence of pine boards. On the other side, Brian knew, was the Haverhills' place, only four houses down from his own.

The heavy rain of the night before had turned the garden into a swamp; most of the remaining pumpkins sat half-submerged in puddles. Brian bent, picked up a handful of dark-brown garden muck in each hand, and then advanced on the clothesline with dribbles of brown water running between his fingers.

The clothesline closest to the garden was hung with sheets along its entire length. They were still damp, but drying quickly in the breeze. They made lazy flapping sounds. They were pure, pristine white.

Go on, Mr. Gaunt's voice whispered in his mind. *Go for it, Brian—just like Sandy Koufax. Go for it!*

Brian drew his hands back over his shoulders, palms up to the sky. He was not entirely surprised to find he had a hard-on again, as in his dream. He was glad he hadn't chickened out. This was going to be *fun.*

He brought his hands forward, hard. The mud slung off his palms in long brown swoops that spread into fans before strik-ing the billowing sheets. It splattered across them in runny, ropy parabolas.

He went back to the garden, got two more handfuls, threw them at the sheets, went back, got more, and threw that, too. A kind of frenzy descended on him. He trundled busily back and forth, first getting the mud, then throwing it.

He might have gone on all afternoon if someone hadn't yelled. At first he thought it was *him* the someone was yelling at. He hunched his shoulders and a terrified little squeal es-caped him. Then he realized it was just Mrs. Haverhill, calling her dog from the other side of the fence.

Just the same, he had to get out of here. And quick.

He paused for a moment, though, looking at what he had done, and he felt a momentary quiver of shame and unease.

The sheets had protected most of the clothes, but the sheets themselves were plastered with muck. There were only a few isolated white patches left to show what color they had originally been.

Brian looked at his hands, which were caked with mud. Then he hurried over to the corner of the house, where there was a faucet bib. It hadn't been turned off yet; when he turned the handle, a cold stream of water poured from the spigot. He thrust his hands into it and rubbed them together hard. He washed until all the mud was gone, including the goo under his fingernails, unmindful of the spreading numbness. He even held his shirt-cuffs under the spigot.

He turned off the faucet, went back to his bike, put up the kickstand, and walked it back down the driveway. He had a very bad moment when he saw a small yellow compact car coming, but it was a Civic, not a Yugo. It went past without slowing, its driver unmindful of the little boy with the red, chapped hands frozen beside his bike in the Jerzyck driveway, the little boy whose face was nearly a billboard with one word—GUILTY!—screaming across it.

When the car was gone, Brian mounted his bike and began to pedal, hellbent for leather. He didn't stop until he was coasting up his own driveway. The numbness was leaving his hands by then, but they itched and smarted . . . and they were still red.

When he went in, his mother called, "That you, Brian?" from the living room.

"Yes, Ma." What he had done in the Jerzyck back yard already seemed like something he might have dreamed. Surely the boy standing here in this sunny, sane kitchen, the boy who was now going to the refrigerator and taking out the milk, could not be the same boy who had plunged his hands up to the wrists in the mud of Wilma Jerzyck's garden and then flung that mud at Wilma Jerzyck's clean sheets again and again and again.

Surely not.

He poured himself a glass of milk, studying his hands as he did. They were clean. Red, but clean. He put the milk back. His heart had returned to its normal rhythm.

"Did you have a good day at school, Brian?" Cora's voice floated out.

"It was okay."

"Want to come in and watch TV with me? *Santa Barbara* will be on pretty soon, and there's Hershey's Kisses."

"Sure," he said, "but I'm going upstairs for a few minutes first."

"Don't you leave a milk-glass up there! It goes all sour and stinks and it *never* comes off in the dishwasher!"

"I'll bring it down, Ma."

"You better!"

Brian went upstairs and spent half an hour sitting at his desk, dreaming over his Sandy Koufax card. When Sean came in to ask if he wanted to go down to the corner store with him, Brian shut his baseball-card book with a snap and told Sean to get out of his room and not to come back until he learned how to knock on a door when it was shut. He heard Sean standing out in the hallway, crying, and felt no sympathy at all.

There *was,* after all, such a thing as manners.

10

Warden threw a party in the county jail,
Prison band was there and they began to wail,
The band was jumpin and the joint began to swing,
Y'oughtta heard those knocked-out jailbirds sing!

The King stands with his legs apart, his blue eyes blazing, the bell bottoms of his white jumpsuit shaking. Rhinestones glitter and flash in the overhead spotlights. A sheaf of blue-black hair falls across his forehead. The mike is near his mouth, but not so near Myra cannot see the pouty curl of his upper lip.

She can see everything. She is in the first row.

And suddenly, as the rhythm section blasts off, he is holding a hand out, holding it out to HER, *the way Bruce Springsteen (who will never be The King in a million years, no matter how hard he tries) holds his hand out to that girl in his "Dancing in the Dark" video.*

For a moment she's too stunned to do anything, too stunned to move, and then hands from behind push her forward, and his hand has closed over her wrist, his hand is pulling her up on stage. She can smell him, a mixture of sweat, English Leather, and hot, clean flesh.

A bare moment later, Myra Evans is in Elvis Presley's arms.

The satin of his jumpsuit is slick under her hands. The arms around her are muscular. That face, his face, the face of The King, is inches from hers. He is dancing with her—they are a couple, Myra Josephine Evans from Castle Rock, Maine, and Elvis Aron Presley, from Memphis, Tennessee! They dirty-dance their way across a wide stage in front of four thousand screaming fans as the Jordanaires chant that funky old fifties refrain: "Let's rock . . . everybody let's rock . . ."

His hips move in against hers; she can feel the coiled tension at the center of him nudging against her belly. Then he twirls her, her skirt flares out flat, showing her legs all the way to the lace of her Victoria's Secret panties, her hand spins inside his like an axle inside a hub, and then he is drawing her to him again, and his hand slides down the small of her back to the swell of her buttocks, cupping her tightly to him. For a moment she looks down and there, beyond and below the glare of the footlights, she sees Cora Rusk staring up. Cora's face is baleful with hate and witchy with envy.

Then Elvis turns her head toward him and speaks in that syrupy mid-South drawl: "Ain't we supposed to be lookin at each othah, honeh?"

Before she can reply, his full lips are on hers; the smell of him and the feel of him fill the world. Then, suddenly, his tongue is in her mouth—the King of Rock and Roll is french-kissing her in front of Cora and the whole damned world! He draws her tight against him again and as the horns kick in with a syncopated shriek, she feels ecstatic heat begin to uncoil in her loins. Oh, it has never been like this, not even down at Castle Lake with Ace Merrill all those years ago. She wants to scream, but his tongue is buried in her mouth and she can only claw into his smooth satin back, pumping her hips as the horns thunder into "My Way."

11

Mr. Gaunt sat in one of the plush chairs, watching Myra Evans with clinical detachment as her orgasm ripped through her. She was shaking like a woman experiencing a total neural breakdown, the picture of Elvis clutched tightly in her hands, eyes closed, bosom heaving, legs tightening, loosening, tightening, loosening. Her hair had lost its beauty-shop curl and lay against her head in a not-too-charming helmet. Her double chins ran with sweat much as Elvis's own had done as he gyrated ponderously across the stage during his last few concerts.

"Ooohh!" Myra cried, shaking like a bowl of jelly on a plate. "Ooooh! Oooooooh my *God!* Ooooooooooooh my *Gahhhhhhhhd! OOOOHHHHHH—*"

Mr. Gaunt idly tweezed the crease of his dark slacks between his thumb and forefinger, shook it out to its former razor sharpness, then leaned forward and snatched the picture from Myra's hands. Her eyes, full of dismay, flew open at once. She grabbed for the picture, but it was already out of her reach. She started to get up.

"Sit down," Mr. Gaunt said.

Myra remained where she was, as if she had been turned to stone during the act of rising.

"If you ever want to see this picture again, Myra, *sit . . . down.*"

She sat, staring at him in dumb agony. Large patches of sweat were creeping out from under her arms and along the sides of her breasts.

"Please," she said. The word came out in a croak so dusty that it was like a puff of wind in the desert. She held her hands out.

"Name me a price," Gaunt invited.

She thought. Her eyes rolled in her sweaty face. Her Adam's apple went up and down.

"Forty dollars!" she cried.

He laughed and shook his head.

"Fifty!"

"Ridiculous. You must not want this picture very badly, Myra."

"I do!" Tears began to seep from the corners of her eyes. They ran down her cheeks, mixing with the sweat there. "*I doooooo!*"

"All right," he said. "You want it. I accept the fact that you want it. But do you need it, Myra? Do you really *need* it?"

"Sixty! That's all I've got! That's every red cent!"

"Myra, do I look like a child to you?"

"No—"

"I think I must. I'm an old man—older than you would believe, I've aged very well, if I do say so myself—but I really think I must look like a child to you, a child who will believe a woman who lives in a brand-new duplex less than three blocks from Castle View has only sixty dollars to her name."

"You don't understand! My husband—"

Mr. Gaunt rose, still holding the picture. The smiling man who had stood aside to grant her admittance was no longer in this room. "You didn't have an appointment, Myra, did you? No. I saw you out of the goodness of my heart. But now I'm afraid I'll have to ask you to leave."

"Seventy! Seventy dollars!"

"You insult my intelligence. Please go."

Myra fell on her knees before, him. She was weeping in hoarse, panicky sobs. She clutched his calves as she grovelled before him. "Please! Please, Mr. Gaunt! I have to have that picture! I have to! It does . . . you wouldn't *believe* what it does!"

Mr. Gaunt looked at the picture of Elvis and a momentary moue of distaste crossed his face. "I don't think I'd want to know," he said. "It looked extremely . . . sweaty."

"But if it was more than seventy dollars, I'd have to write a check. Chuck would know. He'd want to know what I spent it for. And if I told him, he'd . . . he'd . . ."

"That," Mr. Gaunt said, "is not my problem. I am a shop-keeper, not a marriage counsellor." He was looking down at her, speaking to the top of her sweaty head. "I'm sure that someone else—Mrs. Rusk, for instance—will be able to afford this rather unique likeness of the late Mr. Presley."

At the mention of Cora, Myra's head snapped up. Her eyes were sunken, glittering points in deep brown sockets. Her teeth were revealed in a snarl. She looked, in that instant, quite insane.

"You'd sell it to *her?*" she hissed.

"I believe in free trade," Mr. Gaunt said. "It's what made this country great. I really wish you'd let go of me, Myra. Your hands are positively *running* with sweat. I'm going to have these pants dry-cleaned, and even then I'm not sure—"

"Eighty! Eighty dollars!"

"I'll sell it to you for exactly twice that," Mr. Gaunt said. "One hundred and sixty dollars." He grinned, revealing his large, crooked teeth. "And Myra—your personal check is good with me."

She uttered a howl of despair. "I can't! Chuck will *kill* me!"

"Maybe," Mr. Gaunt said, "but you would be dying for a hunka-hunka burning love, would you not?"

"A hundred," Myra whined, grabbing his calves again as he tried to step away from her. "Please, a hundred dollars."

"A hundred and forty," Gaunt countered. "It's as low as I can go. It is my final offer."

"All right," Myra panted. "All right, that's all right, I'll pay it—"

"And you'll have to throw in a blowjob, of course," Gaunt said, grinning down at her.

She looked up at him, her mouth a perfect O. "What did you say?" she whispered.

"*Blow* me!" he shouted down at her. "Fel*late* me! Open that gorgeous metal-filled mouth of yours and *gobble my crank!*"

"Oh my God," Myra moaned.

"As you wish," Mr. Gaunt said, beginning to turn away.

She grabbed him before he could leave her. A moment later her shaking hands were scrabbling at his fly.

He let her scrabble for a few moments, his face amused, and then he slapped her hands away. "Forget it," he said. "Oral sex gives me amnesia."

"What—"

"Never *mind,* Myra." He tossed her the picture. She flailed her hands at it, caught it somehow, and clutched it to her bosom. "There *is* one other thing, however."

"What?" she hissed at him.

"Do you know the man who tends the bar on the other side of the Tin Bridge?"

She was beginning to shake her head, her eyes filling with alarm again, then realized who he must mean, "Henry Beaufort?"

"Yes. I believe he also owns the establishment which is called The Mellow Tiger. A rather interesting name."

"Well, I don't *know* him, but I know who he *is,* I guess." She had never been in The Mellow Tiger in her life, but she knew as well as anyone who owned and ran the place.

"Yes. Him. I want you to play a little trick on Mr. Beaufort."

"What . . . what kind of a trick?"

Gaunt reached down, grasped one of Myra's sweat-slimy hands, and helped her to her feet.

"That," he said, "is something we can talk about while you write your check, Myra." He smiled then, and all his charm flooded back into his face. His brown eyes sparkled and danced. "And by the way, would you like your picture gift-wrapped?"

CHAPTER FIVE

1

Alan slid into a booth in Nan's Luncheonette across from Polly and saw at once that the pain was still bad—bad enough for her to have taken a Percodan in the afternoon, which was rare. He knew it even before she opened her mouth—it was something in the eyes. A sort of shine. He had come to know it . . . but not to like it. He didn't think he would ever like it. He wondered, not for the first time, if she was addicted to the stuff yet. In Polly's case, he supposed that addiction was just another side-effect, something to be expected, noted, and then sublimated to the main problem—which was, simply put, the fact that she was living with pain he probably couldn't even comprehend.

His voice showed none of this as he asked, "How's it going, pretty lady?"

She smiled. "Well, it's been an interesting day. *Verrrrry . . . inderesting,* as that guy used to say on *Laugh-In*."

"You're not old enough to remember that."

"I am so. Alan, who's that?"

He turned in the direction of her gaze just in time to spot a woman with a rectangular package cradled in her arms drift past Nan's wide plate-glass window. Her eyes were fixed straight ahead, and a man coming the other way had to jig rapidly out of her way to avoid a collision. Alan flicked rapidly through the huge file of names and faces he kept in his head and came up with what Norris, who was deeply in love with police language, would undoubtedly have called "a partial."

"Evans. Mabel or Mavis or something like that. Her husband's Chuck Evans."

"She looks like she just smoked some very good Panamanian Red," Polly said. "I envy her."

Nan Roberts herself came over to wait on them. She was one of William Rose's Baptist Christian Soldiers, and today she wore a small yellow button above her left breast. It was the third one Alan had seen this afternoon, and he guessed he would see a great many more in the weeks ahead. It showed a slot machine inside a black circle with a red diagonal line drawn through it. There were no words on the button; it made the wearer's feelings about Casino Nite perfectly clear without them.

Nan was a middle-aged woman with a huge bosom and a sweetly pretty face that made you think of Mom and apple pie. The apple pie at Nan's was, as Alan and all his deputies knew, very good, too—especially with a large scoop of vanilla ice cream melting on top. It was easy to take Nan at face value, but a good many business people—realtors, for the most part—had discovered that doing so was a bad idea. Behind the sweet face there was a clicking computer of a mind, and beneath the motherly swell of bosom there was a pile of account books where the heart should have been. Nan owned a very large chunk of Castle Rock, including at least five of the business buildings on Main Street, and now that Pop Merrill was in the ground, Alan suspected she was probably the wealthiest person in town.

She reminded him of a whorehouse madam he had once arrested in Utica. The woman had offered him a bribe, and when he turned that down, she had tried very earnestly to knock his brains out with a birdcage. The tenant, a scrofulous parrot who sometimes said "I fucked your mamma, Frank" in a morose and thoughtful voice, had still been in the cage at the time. Sometimes, when Alan saw the vertical frown-line between Nan Roberts's eyes deepen down, he felt she would be perfectly capable of doing the same thing. And he found it perfectly natural that Nan, who did little these days but sit at the cash register, would come over to serve the County Sheriff herself. It was the personal touch that means so much.

"Hullo, Alan," she said, "I haven't seen you in a dog's age! Where you been?"

"Here and there," he said. "I get around, Nan."

"Well, don't forget your old friends while you're doing it," she said, giving him her shining, motherly smile. You had to spend quite awhile around Nan, Alan reflected, before you started to notice how rarely that smile made it all the way to her eyes. "Come see us once in a while."

"And, lo! Here I be!" Alan said.

Nan pealed laughter so loud and lusty that the men at the counter—loggers, for the most part—craned briefly around. And later, Alan thought, they'll tell their friends that they saw Nan Roberts and the Sheriff yukking it up together. Best of friends.

"Coffee, Alan?"

"Please."

"How about some pie to go with that? Home-made—apples from McSherry's Orchard over in Sweden. Picked yesterday." At least she didn't try to tell us she picked them herself, Alan thought.

"No, thanks."

"Sure? What about you, Polly?" Polly shook her head.

Nan went to get the coffee. "You don't like her much, do you?" Polly asked him in a low voice.

He considered this, a little surprised—likes and dislikes had not really entered his thoughts. "Nan? She's all right. It's just that I like to know who people really are, if I can."

"And what they really want?"

"That's too damn hard," he said, laughing. "I'll settle for knowing what they're up to."

She smiled—he loved to make her smile—and said, "We'll turn you into a Yankee philosopher yet, Alan Pangborn."

He touched the back of her gloved hand and smiled back.

Nan returned with a cup of black coffee in a thick white mug and left at once. One thing you can say for her, Alan thought, she knows when the amenities have been performed and the flesh has been pressed to a sufficiency. It wasn't something everyone with Nan's interests and ambitions *did* know.

"Now," Alan said, sipping his coffee. "Spill the tale of your very interesting day."

She told him in greater detail about how she and Rosalie Drake had seen Nettie Cobb that morning, how Nettie had agonized in front of Needful Things, and how she had finally summoned up enough courage to go in.

"That's wonderful," he said, and meant it.

"Yes—but that's not all. When she came out, she'd *bought* something! I've never seen her so cheerful and so . . . so buoyant as she was today. That's it, *buoyant.* You know how sallow she usually is?"

Alan nodded.

"Well, she had roses in her cheeks and her hair was sort of mussed and she actually laughed a few times."

"Are you sure business was all they were doing?" he asked, and rolled his eyes.

"Don't be silly." She spoke as if she hadn't suggested the same thing to Rosalie herself. "Anyway, she waited outside until you'd left—I knew she would—and then she came in and showed us what she bought. You know that little collection of carnival glass she has?"

"Nope. There are a few things in this town which have escaped my notice. Believe it or not."

"She has half a dozen pieces. Most of them came to her from her mother. She told me once that there used to be more, but some of them got broken. Anyway, she loves the few things she has, and he sold her the most gorgeous carnival glass lampshade I've seen in years. At first glance I thought it was Tiffany.

Of course it isn't—couldn't be, Nettie could never afford a piece of real Tiffany glass—but it's awfully good."

"How much *did* she pay?"

"I didn't ask her. But I'll bet whatever sock she keeps her mad-money in is flat this afternoon."

He frowned a little. "Are you sure she didn't get horn-swoggled?"

"Oh, Alan—do you have to be so suspicious all the time? Nettie may be vague about some things, but she knows her carnival glass. She said it was a bargain, and that means it probably was. It's made her *so* happy."

"Well, that's great. Just The Ticket."

"Pardon?"

"That was the name of a shop in Utica," he said. "A long time ago. I was only a kid. Just The Ticket."

"And did it have *your* Ticket?" she teased.

"I don't know. I never went in."

"Well," she said, "apparently our Mr. Gaunt thinks he might have mine."

"What do you mean?"

"Nettie got my cake-box, and there was a note inside it. From Mr. Gaunt." She pushed her handbag across the table to him. "Take a look—I don't feel up to the clasp this afternoon."

He ignored the handbag for the moment. "How bad is it, Polly?"

"Bad," she said simply. "It's been worse, but I'm not going to lie to you; it's never been *much* worse. All this week, since the weather changed."

"Are you going to see Dr. Van Allen?"

She sighed. "Not yet. I'm due for a respite. Every time it gets bad like this, it lets up just when I feel like I'm going to go crazy any minute. At least, it always has. I suppose that one of these times the respite just won't come. If it's not better by Monday, I'll go see him. But all he can do is write prescriptions. I don't want to be a junkie if I can help it, Alan."

"But—"

"Enough," she said softly. "Enough for now, okay?"

"Okay," he said, a little unwillingly.

"Look at the note. It's very sweet . . . and sort of cute."

He undid the clasp of her handbag and saw a slim envelope lying on top of her billfold. He took it out. The paper had a rich, creamy feel. Written across the front, in a hand so perfectly old-fashioned it looked like something from an antique diary, was *Ms. Polly Chalmers.*

"That style is called copperplate," she said, amused. "I think they stopped teaching it not long after the Age of the Dinosaurs."

He took a single sheet of deckle-edged stationery from the envelope. Printed across the top was

NEEDFUL THINGS
Castle Rock, Maine
Leland Gaunt, Proprietor

The handwriting here was not as formally fancy as that on the envelope, but both it and the language itself still had a pleasingly old-fashioned quality.

Dear Polly,

    Thank you once again for the devil's-food cake. It is my favorite, and it was delicious! I also want to thank you for your kindness and thoughtfulness—I suppose you knew how nervous I must be on my opening day, and in the off-season as well.

    I have an item, not yet in stock but coming with a number of other things via air freight, which I believe might interest you a great deal. I don't want to say more; I'd rather you viewed it yourself. It's actually not much more than a knick-knack, but I thought of it almost the

moment you left, and over the years I've rarely
been wrong in my intuitions. I expect it to come
in either Friday or Saturday. If you have a chance,
why not stop in Sunday afternoon? I'll be in all
day, cataloguing stock, and would be delighted
to show it to you. I don't want to say more just
now; the item either will or will not explain
itself. At least let me repay your kindness with
a cup of tea!

I hope Nettie enjoys her new lampshade. She
is a very dear lady, and it seemed to please her
very much.

Yours sincerely,

LG.

Leland Gaunt

"Mysterious!" Alan said, folding the note back into the envelope and putting the envelope back in her purse. "Are you going to check it out, as we say in the police biz?"

"With a build-up like that—and after seeing Nettie's lampshade—how could I refuse? Yes, I think I'll drop by . . . if my hands feel better. Want to come, Alan? Maybe he'll have something for you, too."

"Maybe. But maybe I'll just stick with the Patriots. They're bound to win one eventually."

"You look tired, Alan. Dark circles under the eyes."

"It's been one of those days. It started with me just barely keeping the Head Selectman and one of my deputies from beating each other to a bloody pulp in the little boys' room."

She leaned forward, concerned. "What are you talking about?"

He told her about the dust-up between Keeton and Norris Ridgewick, finishing with how odd Keeton had seemed—his use of that word *persecution* had kept recurring to him at odd moments all day. When he finished, Polly was quiet for a long time.

"So?" he asked her finally. "What do you think?"

"I was thinking that it's still going to be a lot of years before you know everything about Castle Rock that you need to know. That probably goes for me, too—I was away a long time, and I don't talk about where I was or what became of my 'little problem,' and I think there are a lot of people in town who don't trust me. But you pick things up, Alan, and you remember things. When I came back to The Rock, do you know what it felt like?"

He shook his head, interested. Polly was not a woman to dwell on the past, even with him.

"It was like tuning into a soap opera you've fallen out of the habit of watching. Even if you haven't watched in a couple of years, you recognize the people and their problems at once, because they never really change. Watching a show like that again is like slipping into a comfortable old pair of shoes."

"What are you saying?"

"That there's a lot of soap-opera history here you haven't caught up on yet. Did you know that Danforth Keeton's uncle was in Juniper Hill at the same time Nettie was?"

"No."

She nodded. "Around the age of forty he started to have mental problems. My mother used to say Bill Keeton was a schizophrenic. I don't know if that's the proper term or just the one Mom heard most often on TV, but there sure as hell was *something* wrong with him. I remember seeing him grab people on the street and start to hector them on one thing or another—the national debt, how John Kennedy was a Communist, I don't know whatall else. I was only a little girl. It frightened me, though, Alan—I knew *that*."

"Well, of course it did."

"Or sometimes he'd walk along the street with his head

down, talking to himself in a voice that was loud and muttery at the same time. My mother told me I was never to speak to him when he was behaving like that, not even if we were on our way to church and he was, too. Finally he tried to shoot his wife. Or so I heard, but you know how long-time gossip distorts things. Maybe all he did was wave his service pistol at her. Whatever he did, it was enough to get him carted off to county jail. There was some sort of competency hearing, and when it was over they parked him at Juniper Hill."

"Is he still there?"

"Dead now. His state of mind degenerated pretty fast, once they had him institutionalized. He was catatonic when he finally went. Or so I've heard."

"Jesus."

"But that's not all. Ronnie Keeton, Danforth's father and Bill Keeton's brother, spent four years in the mental wing at the VA hospital in Togus during the mid-seventies. Now he's in a nursing home. Alzheimer's. And there was a great-aunt or a cousin—I'm not sure which—who killed herself in the fifties after some sort of scandal. I'm not sure what it was, but I heard once she liked the ladies a little better than she liked the men."

"It runs in the family, is that what you're saying?"

"No," she said. "There's no moral to this, no theme. I know a little town history you don't, that's all—the kind they don't recount during the Town Common speechmaking on the Fourth of July. I'm just passing it on. Drawing conclusions is a job for the police."

She said this last so primly that Alan laughed a little—but he felt uneasy, just the same. *Did* insanity run in families? He had been taught in high school psychology that the idea was an old wives' tale. Years later, at Albany Police Academy, a lecturer had said it *was* true, or could be, at least, in certain cases: that some mental diseases could be traced through family trees as clearly as physical traits like blue eyes and double-jointedness. One of the examples he'd used had been alcoholism. Had he said something about schizophrenia as well? Alan couldn't remember. His academy days had been a good many years ago.

"I guess I better start asking around about Buster," Alan said heavily. "I'll tell you, Polly, the idea that Castle Rock's Head Selectman could be turning into a human hand grenade does not exactly make my day."

"Of course not. And it's probably not the case. I just thought you ought to know. People around here will answer questions . . . *if* you know what questions to ask. If you don't, they'll cheerfully watch you stumble around in great big circles and never say a word."

Alan grinned. It was the truth. "You haven't heard it all yet, Polly—after Buster left, I had a visit from the Reverend Willie. He—"

"Shhh!" Polly said, so fiercely that Alan was startled to silence. She looked around, seemed to decide no one had been eavesdropping on their conversation, and turned back to Alan again. "Sometimes I despair of you, Alan. If you don't learn some discretion, you're apt to get swept out at the polls two years from now . . . and you'll stand there with a big, puzzled grin on your face and say 'Wha hoppen?' You have to be careful. If Danforth Keeton's a hand grenade, that man's a rocket launcher."

He leaned closer to her and said, "He's not a rocket launcher. A self-righteous, pompous little prick is what *he* is."

"Casino Nite?"

He nodded.

She put her hands over his. "Poor baby. And it looks like such a sleepy little town from the outside, doesn't it?"

"Usually it is."

"Did he go away mad?"

"Oh yeah," Alan said. "This was my second conversation with the good Reverend about the legality of Casino Nite. I expect to have several more before the Catholics finally do the damned thing and get it over with."

"He *is* a self-righteous little prick, isn't he?" she asked in an even lower voice. Her face was serious, but her eyes were sparkling.

"Yes. Now there's the buttons. They're a new wrinkle."

"Buttons?"

"Slot machines with lines drawn through them instead of smiley faces. Nan's wearing one. I wonder whose idea *that* was."

"Probably Don Hemphill. He's not only a good Baptist, he's on the Republican State Committee. Don knows a thing or three about campaigning, but I bet he's finding out that it's a lot harder to swing public opinion where religion is involved." She stroked his hands. "Take it easy, Alan. Be patient. Wait. That's most of what life in The Rock is about—taking it easy, being patient, and waiting for the occasional stink to blow over. Yeah?"

He smiled at her, turned his hands over, and grasped hers . . . but gently. Oh so gently. "Yeah," he said. "Want some company tonight, pretty lady?"

"Oh, Alan, I don't know—"

"No slap and tickle," he assured her. "I'll make a fire, we'll sit in front of it, and you can pull a few more bodies out of the town closet for my amusement."

Polly smiled wanly. "I think you've gotten a look at all the bodies I know about over the last six or seven months, Alan, including mine own. If you want to further your Castle Rock education, you ought to make friends either with old Lenny Partridge . . . or with *her.*" She nodded toward Nan, and then lowered her voice a trifle. "The difference between Lenny and Nan," she said, "is that Lenny is content to know things. Nan Roberts likes to use what she knows."

"Meaning?"

"Meaning the lady didn't pay fair market value for *all* the property she owns," Polly said.

Alan looked at her thoughtfully. He had never seen Polly in a mood quite like this one—introspective, talkative, and depressed all at the same time. He wondered for the first time since becoming her friend and then her lover if he was listening to Polly Chalmers . . . or the drugs.

"I think tonight would be a good night to stay away," she said with sudden decision. "I'm not good company when I feel like I do now. I can see that in your face."

"Polly, that's not true."

"I'm going to go home and take a long, hot bath. I'm not going to drink any more coffee. I'm going to unplug the phone, go to bed early, and the chances are that when I wake up tomorrow, I'll feel like a new woman. *Then* maybe we can . . . you know. No slap, a lot of tickle."

"I worry about you," he said.

Her hands moved gently, delicately, in his. "I know," she said. "It does no good, but I appreciate it, Alan. More than you know."

2

Hugh Priest slowed as he passed The Mellow Tiger on his way home from the Castle Rock motor pool . . . then sped up again. He drove home, parked his Buick in the driveway, and went inside.

His place had two rooms: the one where he slept and the one where he did everything else. A chipped Formica table, covered with aluminum frozen dinner trays (cigarette butts had been crushed in congealing gravy in most of them) stood in the center of this latter room. He went to the open closet, stood on tiptoe, and felt along the top shelf. For a moment he thought the fox-tail was gone, that somebody had come in and stolen it, and panic ignited a ball of heat in his belly. Then his hand encountered that silky softness, and he let out his breath in a long sigh.

He had spent most of the day thinking about the fox-tail, thinking about how he was going to tie it to the Buick's antenna, thinking about how it would look, fluttering cheerfully up there. He had almost tied it on that morning, but it had still been raining then, and he didn't like the idea of the dampness turning it into a soggy fur rope that just hung there like a carcass. Now he took it back outside, absently kicking an empty juice can out of his way as he went, stroking the rich fur through his fingers. God, it felt good!

He entered the garage (which had been too full of junk to admit his car since 1984 or so) and found a sturdy piece of wire after some hunting about. He had made up his mind: first he would wire the fox-tail to the antenna, then he would have some supper, and afterward he would finally drive over to Greenspark. A.A. met at the American Legion Hall there at seven o'clock. Maybe it *was* too late to start a new life . . . but it wasn't too late to find out for sure, one way or another.

He made a sturdy little slip loop in the wire and fastened it around the thick end of the brush. He started to wrap the other end of the wire around the antenna, but his fingers, which had moved with rapid surety at first, began to slow down. He felt his confidence slipping away and, filling the hole it left behind, doubt began to seep in.

He saw himself parking in the American Legion parking lot, and that was okay. He saw himself going in to the meeting, and *that* was okay, too. But then he saw some little kid, like the asshole who had stepped in front of his truck the other day, walking past the Legion Hall while he was inside saying his name was Hugh P. and he was powerless over alcohol. Something catches the kid's eye—a flash of bright orange in the blue-white glare thrown by the arc-sodiums which light the parking lot. The kid approaches his Buick and examines the fox-tail . . . first touching, then stroking. He looks around, sees no one, and yanks on the fox-tail, breaking the wire. Hugh saw this kid going down to the local video-game arcade and telling one of his buddies: *Hey, look what I hawked out of the Legion parking lot. Not bad, huh?*

Hugh felt a frustrated anger creep into his chest, as if this were not simply speculation but something which had already happened. He stroked the fox-tail, then looked around in the growing gloom of five o'clock, as if he expected to see a crowd of light-fingered kids gathering already on the far side of Castle Hill Road, just waiting for him to go back inside and stuff a couple of Hungry Man dinners into the oven so they could take his fox-tail.

No. It was better not to go. Kids had no respect these days. Kids would steal anything, just for the joy of stealing it. Keep it for a day or two, then lose interest and toss it in a ditch or a vacant lot. The picture—and it was a very clear picture, almost a vision—of his lovely brush lying abandoned in a trashy gully, growing sodden in the rain, losing its color amid the Big Mac wrappers and discarded beer cans, filled Hugh with a feeling of angry agony.

It would be *crazy* to take a risk like that.

He untwisted the wire which held the tail to the antenna, took the brush into the house again, and put it back on the high shelf in the closet. This time he closed the closet door, but it wouldn't latch tightly.

Have to get a lock for that, he thought. *Kids'll break in anyplace. There's no respect for authority these days. None at all.*

He went to the refrigerator, got a can of beer, looked at it for a moment, then put it back. A beer—even four or five beers—wouldn't do much to put him back on an even keel. Not the way he felt tonight. He opened one of the lower cupboards, pawed past the assortment of rummage-sale pots and pans stacked there, and found the half-full bottle of Black Velvet he kept for emergencies. He filled a jelly-glass to the halfway mark, considered for a moment, then filled it all the way to the top. He took a swallow or two, felt the heat explode in his belly, and filled the glass again. He started to feel a little better, a little more relaxed. He looked toward the closet and smiled. It was safe up there, and would be safer as soon as he got a good strong Kreig padlock at the Western Auto and put it on. Safe. It was good when you had something you really wanted and needed, but it was even better when that thing was safe. That was the best of all.

Then the smile faded a little.

Is that what you bought it for? To keep it on a high shelf behind a locked door?

He drank again, slowly. All right, he thought, maybe that's not so good. But it's better than losing it to some light-fingered kid.

"After all," he said aloud, "it's not 1955 anymore. This is modern days."

He nodded for emphasis. Still, the thought lingered. What good was the fox-tail doing in there? What good for him, or anyone else?

But two or three drinks took care of that thought. Two or three drinks made putting the fox-tail back seem like the most reasonable, rational decision in the world. He decided to put off dinner; such a sensible decision deserved to be rewarded by another drink or two.

He filled the jelly-glass again, sat down in one of the kitchen chairs with its tubular steel legs, and lit a cigarette. And as he sat there, drinking and tapping curls of ash into one of the frozen dinner trays, he forgot about the fox-tail and started thinking about Nettie Cobb. Crazy Nettie. He was going to play a trick on Crazy Nettie. Maybe next week, maybe the week after that . . . but this week seemed most likely. Mr. Gaunt had told him he was a man who didn't like to waste time, and Hugh was willing to take his word for it.

He looked forward to it.

It would break up the monotony.

He drank, he smoked, and when he finally passed out on the

filthy sheets of the narrow bed in the other room at quarter of
ten, he did it with a smile on his face.

3

Wilma Jerzyck's shift at Hemphill's Market ended when the
store closed at seven. She pulled into her own driveway at
seven-fifteen. Soft light spilled out through the drawn drapes
across the living-room window. She went in and sniffed. She
could smell macaroni and cheese. Good enough . . . at least,
so far.

Pete was sprawled on the couch with his shoes off, watching
Wheel of Fortune. The Portland *Press-Herald* was in his lap.

"I read your note," he said, sitting up quickly and putting
the paper aside. "I put in the casserole. It'll be ready by seven-
thirty." He looked at her with earnest and slightly anxious
brown eyes. Like a dog with a strong urge to please, Pete
Jerzyck had been house trained early and quite well. He had
his lapses, but it had been a long time since she'd come in and
found him lying on the couch with his shoes on, a longer one
since he'd dared to light up his pipe in the house, and it would
be a snowy day in August when he took a piss without remembering to put the ring back down after he was through.

"Did you bring in the wash?"

An expression of mingled guilt and surprise troubled his
round, open face. "Jeez! I was reading the newspaper and forgot. I'll go right out." He was already fumbling for his shoes.

"Never mind," she said, starting for the kitchen.

"Wilma, I'll get it!"

"Don't bother," she said sweetly. "I wouldn't want you to
leave your paper or Vanna White just because I've been on my
feet behind a cash register for the last six hours. Sit right there,
Peter. Enjoy yourself."

She didn't have to look around and check his reaction; after

seven years of marriage, she honestly believed Peter Michael
Jerzyck held no more surprises for her. His expression would
be a mixture of hurt and weak chagrin. He would stand there
for a few moments after she had gone out, looking like a man
who just came out of the crapper and can't quite remember if
he's wiped himself, and then he would go to work setting the
table and dishing up the casserole. He would ask her many
questions about her shift at the market, listen attentively to
her answers, and not interrupt once with the details of his own
day at Williams-Brown, the large real-estate agency in Oxford
where he worked. Which was just as fine as paint with Wilma,
since she found real estate the world's most boring subject.
After dinner, he would clear up without being asked, and *she*
would read the paper. All of these services would be performed
by him because he had forgotten one minor chore. She didn't
mind taking in the wash at all—in fact, she was *fond* of the feel
and smell of clothes which had spent a happy afternoon drying
in the sun—but she had no intention of letting Pete in on that.
It was her little secret.

She had many such secrets, and kept them all for the same
reason: in a war, you held onto every advantage. Some nights
she would come home and there might be an hour or even two
hours of skirmishing before she was finally able to prod Peter
into a full-scale retreat, replacing his white pins on her interior
battle-map with her red ones. Tonight the engagement had
been won less than two minutes after she stepped inside the
door, and that was just fine with Wilma.

She believed in her heart that marriage was a lifetime adventure in aggression, and in such a long campaign, where
ultimately no prisoners could be taken, no quarter given, no
patch of marital landscape left unscorched, such easy victories
might eventually lose their savor. But that time had not yet
come, and so she went out to the clotheslines with the basket
under her left arm and her heart light beneath the swell of her
bosom.

She was halfway across the yard before coming to a puzzled stop. Where in the hell were the sheets?

She should have seen them easily, big rectangular white shapes floating in the dark, but they weren't there. Had they blown away? Ridiculous! There had been a breeze that afternoon, but hardly a *gale.* Had someone stolen them?

Then a gust of wind kicked through the air and she heard a large, lazy flapping sound. Okay, they were there . . . *somewhere.* When you were the oldest daughter in a sprawling Catholic clan of thirteen children, you knew what a sheet sounded like when it flapped on the line. But it still wasn't right, that sound. It was too heavy.

Wilma took another step forward. Her face, which always wore the faintly shadowed look of a woman who expects trouble, grew darker. Now she could see the sheets . . . or shapes that *should* have been the sheets. But they were *dark.*

She took another, smaller step forward, and the breeze whisked through the yard again. The shapes flapped toward her this time, belling out, and before she could get her hand up, something heavy and slimy struck her. Something gooey splattered her cheeks; something thick and soggy pressed against her. It was almost as if a cold, sticky hand were trying to grasp her.

She was not a woman who cried out easily or often, but she cried out now, and dropped the laundry-basket. That sloppy flapping sound came again and she tried to twist away from the shape looming before her. Her left ankle struck the wicker laundry-basket and she stumbled to one knee, missing a full-length tumble only by a combination of luck and quick reflexes.

A heavy, wet thing slobbered its way up her back; thick wetness drooled down the sides of her neck. Wilma cried out again and crawled away from the lines on her hands and knees. Some of her hair had escaped the kerchief she wore and hung against her cheeks, tickling. She hated that feeling . . . but she hated that drooling, clammy caress from the dark shape hung on her clothesline even more.

The kitchen door banged open, and Pete's alarmed voice carried across the yard: "Wilma? Wilma, are you all right?"

Flapping from behind her—a nasty sound, like a chuckle from vocal cords clotted with dirt. In the next yard the Haverhills' mutt began to bellow hysterically in its high, unpleasant voice—*yark! yark! yark!*—and this did nothing to improve Wilma's state of mind.

She got to her feet and saw Pete cautiously descending the back steps. "Wilma? Did you fall down? Are you okay?"

"Yes!" she shouted furiously. "Yes, I fell down! Yes, I'm okay! Turn on the goddam light!"

"Did you hurt yourse—"

"Just turn on the goddam LIGHT!" she screamed at him, and rubbed a hand across the front of her coat. It came away covered with cold goo. She was now so angry she could see her own pulse as bright points of light before her eyes . . . and angriest of all at herself, for being scared. Even for a second.

Yark! Yark! Yark!

The goddam mutt in the next yard was going ape. Christ, she hated dogs, especially the mouthy ones.

Pete's shape retreated to the top of the kitchen steps. The door opened, his hand snaked inside, and then the floodlight came on, bathing the rear yard with bright light.

Wilma looked down at herself and saw a wide swath of dark brown across the front of her new fall coat. She wiped furiously at her face, held out her hand, and saw it had also turned brown. She could feel a slow, syrupy trickle running down the middle of her back.

"Mud!" She was stupefied with disbelief—so much so that she was unaware she had spoken aloud. Who could have done this to her? Who would have *dared?*

"What did you say, honey?" Pete asked. He had been coming toward her; now he stopped a prudent distance away. Wilma's face was working in a way Pete Jerzyck found extremely alarming: it was as if a nest of baby snakes had hatched just beneath her skin.

"*Mud!*" she screamed, holding her hands out toward him . . . *at* him. Flecks of brown flew from her fingertips. "*Mud, I say! Mud!*"

Pete looked past her, finally understanding. His mouth dropped open. Wilma whirled in the direction of his gaze. The floodlight mounted above the kitchen door lit the clotheslines and the garden with merciless clarity, revealing everything that needed to be revealed. The sheets which she had hung out clean were now drooping from their pins in dispirited, soggy clots. They were not just spattered with mud; they were coated with it, *plated* with it.

Wilma looked at the garden and saw deep divots where the mud had been scooped out. She saw a beaten track in the grass where the mudslinger had gone back and forth, first loading up, then walking to the lines, then throwing, then going back to reload.

"God *damn* it!" she screamed.

"Wilma . . . come on in the house, honey, and I'll . . ." Pete groped, then looked relieved as an idea actually dawned. "I'll make us some tea."

"*Fuck* the tea!" Wilma howled at the top, the very tippy-top, of her vocal range, and from next door the Haverhills' mutt went for broke, *yarkyarkyark,* oh she hated dogs, it was going to drive her crazy, fucking loudmouth *dog!*

Her rage overflowed and she charged the sheets, clawed at them, began pulling them down. Her fingers caught over the first line and it snapped like a guitar string. The sheets hung from it dropped in a sodden, meaty swoop. Fists clenched, eyes squinched like a child doing a tantrum, Wilma took a single large, froggy leap and landed on top of one. It made a weary *flooosh* sound and billowed up, splattering gobbets of mud on her nylons. It was the final touch. She opened her mouth and *shrieked* her rage. Oh, she would find who had done this. Yes-indeedy-doodad. You better believe it. And when she did—

"Is everything all right over there, Mrs. Jerzyck?" It was Mrs. Haverhill's voice, wavering with alarm.

"Yes goddammit, we're drinking Sterno and watching Lawrence Welk, can't you shut that mutt of yours up?" Wilma screamed.

She backed off the muddy sheet, panting, her hair hanging all around her flushed face. She swiped at it savagely. Fucking dog was going to drive her crazy. Fucking loudmouth do—

Her thoughts broke off with an almost audible snap.

Dogs.

Fucking loudmouth dogs.

Who lived almost right around the corner from here, on Ford Street?

Correction: What crazy lady with a fucking loudmouth dog named Raider lived right around the corner from here?

Why, Nettie Cobb, that was who.

The dog had barked all spring, those high-pitched puppy yaps that really got under your skin, and finally Wilma had called Nettie and told her that if she couldn't get her dog to shut up, she ought to get rid of it. A week later, when there had still been no improvement (at least none that Wilma was willing to admit), she had called Nettie again and told her that if she couldn't keep the dog quiet, she, Wilma, would have to call the police. The next night, when the goddamned mutt started up its yarking and barking once more, she had.

A week or so after *that,* Nettie had shown up at the market (unlike Wilma, Nettie seemed to be the sort of person who had to turn things over in her mind for a while—brood on them, even—before she was able to act). She stood in line at Wilma's register, although she didn't have a single solitary item. When her turn came, she had said in a squeaky, breathless little voice: "You stop making trouble for me and my Raider, Wilma Jer-zyck. He's a good little doggy, and you just better stop making trouble."

Wilma, always ready for a fight, had not been in the least disconcerted at being confronted in the workplace.

In fact, she rather liked it. "Lady, you don't know what trouble is. But if you can't get your damn dog to shut up, you will."

The Cobb woman had been as pale as milk, but she drew herself up, clutching her purse so tightly that the tendons on her scrawny forearms showed all the way from her wrists to her elbows. She said: "I'm warning you," then hurried out.

"Oh-oh, I think I just peed my panties!" Wilma had called boisterously after her (a taste of battle always put her in good spirits), but Nettie never turned—only hurried on her way a little faster.

After that, the dog had quieted down. This had rather disappointed Wilma, because it had been a boring spring. Pete was showing no signs of rebellion, and Wilma had been feeling an end-of-winter dullness that the new green in the trees and grass couldn't seem to touch. What she really needed to add color and spice to her life was a good feud. For a while it had seemed that crazy Nettie Cobb would fill the bill admirably, but with the dog minding its manners, it seemed to Wilma that she would have to look elsewhere for diversion.

Then one night in May the dog had started barking again. The mutt had only gone on for a while, but Wilma hurried to the telephone and called Nettie anyway—she had marked the number in the book just in case such an occasion offered.

She did not waste time on the niceties but got right to the point. "This is Wilma Jerzyck, dear. I called to tell you that if you don't shut that dog up, I'll shut him up myself."

"He's already stopped!" Nettie had cried. "I brought him in as soon as I got home and heard him! You just leave me and Raider alone! I warned you! If you don't, you'll be sorry!"

"Just remember what I said," Wilma told her. "I've had enough. The next time he starts up that ruckus, I won't bother complaining to the cops. I'll come over and cut his goddam throat."

She had hung up before Nettie could reply. The cardinal rule governing engagements with the enemy (relatives, neighbors, spouses) was that the aggressor *must* have the last word.

The dog hadn't popped off since then. Well, maybe it had, but Wilma hadn't noticed it if so; it had never been that bothersome in the first place, not *really*, and besides, Wilma had inaugurated a more productive wrangle with the woman who ran the beauty parlor in Castle View. Wilma had almost forgotten Nettie and Raider.

But maybe Nettie hadn't forgotten *her*. Wilma had seen Nettie just yesterday, in the new shop. And if looks could kill, Wilma thought, I would have been laid out dead on the floor right there.

Standing here now by her muddied, ruined sheets, she remembered the look of fear and defiance that had come over the nutty bitch's face, the way her lip had curled back, showing her teeth for a second. Wilma was very familiar with the look of hate, and she had seen it on Nettie Cobb's face yesterday.

I warned you . . . you'll be sorry.

"Wilma, come on inside," Pete said. He put a tentative hand on her shoulder.

She shrugged it off briskly. "Leave me alone."

Pete withdrew a step. He looked like he wanted to wring his hands but didn't quite dare.

Maybe she forgot, too, Wilma thought. *At least until she saw me yesterday, in that new store. Or maybe she's been planning something*

(I warned you)

all along in that half-stewed head of hers, and seeing me finally set her off.

Somewhere in the last few moments she had become sure that Nettie was the one—who else had she crossed glances with in the last couple of days who might hold a grudge? There were other people in town who didn't like her, but this kind of trick— this kind of sneaking, cowardly trick—went with the way Nettie had looked at her yesterday. That sneer of mingled fear

(*you'll be sorry*)

and hate. She had looked like a dog herself, one brave enough to bite only when its victim's back is turned.

Yes, it had been Nettie Cobb, all right. The more Wilma thought about it, the surer she became. And the act was unforgivable. Not because the sheets were ruined. Not because it was a cowardly trick. Not even because it was the act of someone with a cracked brain.

It was unforgivable because Wilma had been frightened.

Only for a second, true, that second when the slimy brown thing had flapped out of the darkness and into her face, caressing her coldly like some monster's hand . . . but even one single second of fear was a second too much.

"Wilma?" Pete asked as she turned her flat face toward him. He did not like the expression the porch light showed him, all shiny white surfaces and black, dimpled shadows. He did not like that flat look in her eyes. "Honey? Are you all right?"

She strode past him, taking no notice of him at all. Pete scurried after her as she headed for the house . . . and the telephone.

4

Nettie was sitting in her living room with Raider at her feet and her new carnival glass lampshade on her lap when the telephone rang. It was twenty minutes of eight. She jumped and clutched the lampshade tighter, looking at the telephone with fear and distrust. She had a momentary certainty—silly, of course, but she couldn't seem to rid herself of such feelings—that it would be Some Person in Authority, calling to tell her she must give the beautiful lampshade back, that it belonged to someone else, that such a lovely object could not possibly have accrued to Nettie's little store of possessions in any case, the very idea was ridiculous.

Raider looked up at her briefly, as if to ask if she was going to answer that or not, then put his muzzle back down on his paws.

Nettie set the lampshade carefully aside and picked up the telephone. It was probably just Polly, calling to ask if she'd pick up something for dinner at Hemphill's Market before she came to work tomorrow morning.

"Hello, Cobb residence," she said crisply. All her life she had been terrified of Some Person in Authority, and she had discovered that the best way to handle such a fear was to sound like a person in authority yourself. It didn't make the fear go away, but at least it held the fear in check.

"I know what you did, you crazy bitch!" a voice spat at her. It was as sudden and as gruesome as the stab of an icepick.

Nettie's breath caught as if on a thorn; an expression of trapped horror froze her face and her heart tried to cram its way up into her throat. Raider looked up at her again, questioningly.

"Who . . . who . . ."

"You know goddam well who," the voice said, and of course Nettie did. It was Wilma Jerzyck. It was that evil, evil woman.

"He hasn't been barking!" Nettie's voice was high and thin and screamy, the voice of someone who has just inhaled the entire contents of a helium balloon. "He's all grown up and he's not barking! He's right here at my feet!"

"Did you have a good time throwing mud at my sheets, you numb cunt?" Wilma was furious. The woman was actually trying to pretend this was still about the *dog*.

"Sheets? What sheets? I . . . I . . ." Nettie looked toward the carnival glass lampshade and seemed to draw strength from it. "You leave me alone! *You're* the one that's crazy, not me!"

"I'm going to get you for this. Nobody comes into my yard and throws mud at my sheets while I'm gone. Nobody. NO-BODY! Understand? Is this getting through that cracked skull of yours? You won't know where, and you won't know when, and most of all you won't know *how,* but I . . . am going . . . to GET you. Do you understand?"

Nettie held the phone tightly screwed against her ear. Her face had gone dead pale except for a single bright streak of red which ran across her forehead between her eyebrows and hairline. Her teeth were clenched and her cheeks puffed in and out like a bellows as she panted from the sides of her mouth.

"You leave me alone or you'll be sorry!" she screamed in her high, fainting, helium voice. Raider was standing now, his ears up, his eyes bright and anxious. He sensed menace in the room. He barked once, severely. Nettie didn't hear him. "You'll be very sorry! I . . . I *know* people! People in Authority! I know them *very well!* I don't have to put up with this!"

Speaking slowly in a voice which was low and sincere and utterly furious, Wilma said: "Fucking with me is the worst mistake you ever made in your life. You won't see me coming."

There was a click.

"You don't dare!" Nettie wailed. Tears were running down her cheeks now, tears of terror and abysmal, impotent rage. "You don't dare, you bad thing! I . . . I'll . . ."

There was a second click. It was followed by the buzz of an open line.

Nettie hung up the phone and sat bolt upright in her chair for almost three minutes, staring into space. Then she began to weep. Raider barked again and put his paws up on the edge of her chair. Nettie hugged him and wept against his fur. Raider licked her neck.

"I won't let her hurt you, Raider," she said. She inhaled the sweet and clean doggy warmth of him, trying to take comfort from it. "I won't let that bad, bad woman hurt you. She's not a Person in Authority, not at all. She's just a bad old thing and if she tries to hurt you . . . or me . . . she'll be sorry."

She straightened at last, found a Kleenex tucked down between the side of her chair and the cushion, and used it to wipe her eyes. She was terrified . . . but she could also feel anger buzzing and drilling through her. It was the way she'd felt before she'd taken the meat-fork from the drawer under the sink and stuck it in her husband's throat.

She took the carnival glass lampshade off the table and hugged it gently to her. "If she starts something, she will be very, very sorry," Nettie said.

She sat that way, with Raider at her feet and the lampshade in her lap, for a very long time.

5

Norris Ridgewick cruised slowly down Main Street in his police cruiser, eyeballing the buildings on the west side of the street. His shift would be over soon, and he was glad. He could remember how good he had felt this morning before that idiot had grabbed him; could remember standing at the mirror in the men's room, adjusting his hat and thinking with satisfaction that he looked Squared Away. He could remember it, but the memory seemed very old and sepia-toned, like a photograph from the nineteenth century. From the moment that idiot Keeton had grabbed him up to right now, nothing had gone right.

He'd gotten lunch at Cluck-Cluck Tonite, the chicken shack out on Route 119. The food there was usually good, but this time it had given him a roaring case of acid indigestion followed by a case of the dribbling shits. Around three o'clock he had run over a nail out on Town Road #7 near the old Camber place and had to change the tire. He'd wiped his fingers on the front of his freshly dry-cleaned uniform blouse, not thinking about what he was doing, only wanting to dry the tips so they would provide a better grip on the loosened lug-nuts, and he had rubbed grease across the shirt in four glaring dark-gray stripes. While he was looking at this with dismay, the cramps had turned his bowels to water again and he'd had to hurry off into the puckerbrush. It had been a race to see if he could manage to drop his trousers before he filled them. *That* race Norris managed to win . . . but he hadn't liked the look of the little stand of bushes he had chosen to take a squat in. It had looked like poison sumac, and the way his day had gone so far, it probably had been.

Norris crept slowly past the buildings which made up Castle Rock's downtown: the Norway Bank and Trust, the Western Auto, Nan's Luncheonette, the black hole where Pop Merrill's rickrack palace had once stood, You Sew and Sew, Needful Things, Castle Rock Hardware—

Norris suddenly applied the brakes and came to a stop. He had seen something amazing in the window of Needful Things—or *thought* he had, anyway.

He checked the rearview mirror, but Main Street was deserted. The stop-and-go light at the lower end of the business district abruptly went out, and remained dark for a few seconds while relays clicked thoughtfully inside. Then the yellow light in the center began to flash off and on. Nine o'clock, then. Nine o'clock on the button.

Norris reversed back up the street, then pulled in at the curb. He looked down at the radio, thought of calling in 10-22— officer leaving the vehicle—and decided not to. He only wanted a quick look in the shop window. He turned up the gain on the radio a little and rolled down the window before getting out. That ought to do it.

You didn't see what you thought you saw, he cautioned himself, hitching up his trousers as he walked across the sidewalk. *No way. Today was made for disappointment, not discovery. That was just someone's old Zebco rod and reel—*

Except it wasn't. The fishing rod in the window of Needful Things was arranged in a cute little display with a net and a pair of bright yellow gum-rubber boots, and it was definitely not a Zebco. It was a Bazun. He hadn't seen one since his father died sixteen years before. Norris had been fourteen then, and he had loved the Bazun for two reasons: what it was and what it stood for.

What was it? Just the best damned lake-and-stream fishing rod in the world, that was all.

What had it stood for? Good times. As simple as that. The good times a skinny little boy named Norris Ridgewick had had with his old man. Good times ploughing through the woods beside some stream out on the edge of town, good times in their little boat, sitting in the middle of Castle Lake while everything around them was white with the mist that rose off the lake in steamy little columns and enclosed them in their own private world. A world made only for guys. In some other world moms would soon be making breakfast, and that was a good world, too, but not as good as this one. No world had been as good as that one, before or since.

After his father's fatal coronary, the Bazun rod and reel had disappeared. He remembered looking for it in the garage after the funeral and it was just gone. He had hunted in the cellar, had even looked in the closet of his mom and dad's bedroom (although he knew his mom would have been more likely to let Henry Ridgewick store an elephant in there than a fishing pole), but the Bazun was gone. Norris had always suspected his Uncle Phil. Several times he had gathered his courage to ask, but each time it came to the sticking point, he had backed down.

Now, looking at this rod and reel, which could have been that very one, he forgot about Buster Keeton for the first time that day. He was overwhelmed with a simple, perfect memory: his father sitting in the stern of the boat, his tackle-box between his feet, handing the Bazun to Norris so he could pour himself a cup of coffee from his big red Thermos with the gray stripes. He could smell the coffee, hot and good, and he could smell his father's aftershave lotion: Southern Gentleman, it had been called.

Suddenly the old grief rose up and folded him in its gray

embrace and he wanted his father. After all these years that old pain was gnawing his bones again, as fresh and as hungry as it had been on the day when his mother had come home from the hospital and taken his hands and said *We have to be very brave now, Norris.*

The spotlight high in the display window pricked bright beams of light off the steel casing of the reel and all the old love, that dark and golden love, swept through him again. Norris stared in at the Bazun rod and thought of the smell of fresh coffee rising from a big red Thermos with gray stripes and the calm, wide sweep of the lake. In his mind he felt again the rough texture of the rod's cork handle, and slowly raised one hand to wipe his eyes.

"Officer?" a quiet voice asked.

Norris gave a little cry and leaped back from the window. For one wild moment he thought he was going to fill his pants after all—the perfect end to a perfect day. Then the cramp passed and he looked around. A tall man in a tweed jacket was standing in the open door of the shop, looking at him with a little smile.

"Did I startle you?" he asked. "I'm very sorry."

"No," Norris said, and then managed a smile of his own. His heart was still beating like a triphammer. "Well . . . maybe just a little. I was looking at that rod and thinking about old times."

"That just came in today," the man said. "It's old, but it's in awfully good condition. It's a Bazun, you know. Not a well-known brand, but well-regarded among serious fishermen. It's—"

"—Japanese," Norris said. "I know. My dad used to have one."

"Did he?" The man's smile broadened. The teeth it revealed were crooked, but Norris found it a pleasant smile just the same. "That *is* a coincidence, isn't it?"

"It sure is," Norris agreed.

"I'm Leland Gaunt. This is my shop." He held out his hand.

A momentary revulsion swept over Norris as those long fingers wrapped themselves around his hand. Gaunt's handshake was the matter of a moment, however, and when he let go, the feeling passed at once. Norris decided it was just his stomach, still queasy over those bad clams he'd eaten for lunch. Next time he was out that way, he'd stick to the chicken, which was, after all, the house specialty.

"I could give you an extremely fair deal on that rod," Mr. Gaunt said. "Why not step in, Officer Ridgewick? We'll talk about it."

Norris started a little. He hadn't told this old bird his name, he was sure of it. He opened his mouth to ask how Gaunt had known, then closed it again. He wore a little name-tag above his badge. That was it, of course.

"I really shouldn't," he said, and hoisted a thumb back over his shoulder at the cruiser. He could still hear the radio, although static was all it was putting out; he hadn't had a call all night. "On duty, you know. Well, I'm off at nine, but technically, until I turn in my car—"

"This would only take a minute or so," Gaunt coaxed. His eyes regarded Norris merrily. "When I make up my mind to deal with a man, Officer Ridgewick, I don't waste time. Especially when the man in question is out in the middle of the night protecting my business."

Norris thought of telling Gaunt that nine o'clock was hardly the middle of the night, and in a sleepy little place like Castle Rock, protecting the investments of the local business people was rarely much of a chore. Then he looked back at the Bazun rod and reel and that old longing, so surprisingly strong and fresh, washed over him again. He thought of going out on the lake with such a rod this weekend, going out early in the morning with a box of worms and a big Thermos of fresh coffee from Nan's. It would almost be like being with the old man again.

"Well . . ."

"Oh, come on," Gaunt coaxed. "If I can do a little selling after hours, you can do a little buying on the town's time. And, really, Officer Ridgewick—I don't think anyone is going to rob the bank tonight, do you?"

Norris looked toward the bank, which flicked first yellow and then black in the measured stutter of the blinker-light, and laughed. "I doubt it."

"Well?"

"Okay," Norris said. "But if we can't make a deal in a couple of minutes, I'll really have to split."

Leland Gaunt groaned and laughed at the same time. "I think I hear the soft sound of my pockets being turned out," he said. "Come along, Officer Ridgewick—a couple of minutes it shall be."

"I sure would like to have that rod," Norris blurted. It was a bad way to start a trade and he knew it, but he couldn't help it.

"And so you shall," Mr. Gaunt said. "I'm going to offer you the best deal of your life, Officer Ridgewick."

He led Norris inside Needful Things and closed the door.

CHAPTER SIX

1

Wilma Jerzyck did not know her husband, Pete, quite as well as she thought she did.

She went to bed that Thursday night planning to go over to Nettie Cobb's first thing Friday morning and Take Care of Things. Her frequent wrangles sometimes simply faded away, but on those occasions when they came to a head, it was Wilma who picked the duelling ground and chose the weapons. The first rule of her confrontational life-style was *Always get the last word.* The second was *Always make the first move.* Making this first move was what she thought of as Taking Care of Things, and she meant to take care of Nettie in a hurry. She told Pete she just might see how many times she could turn the crazy bitch's head around before it popped off the stem.

She fully expected to spend most of the night awake and steaming, taut as a drawn bowstring; it wouldn't have been the first time. Instead, she slipped off to sleep less than ten minutes after lying down, and when she woke up she felt refreshed and oddly calm. Sitting at the kitchen table in her housecoat on Friday morning, it came to her that maybe it was too early to Take Care of Things Permanently. She had scared the living Jesus out of Nettie on the phone last night; as mad as Wilma had been, she hadn't been mad enough to miss that. Only a person as deaf as a stone post could have missed it.

Why not just let Ms. Mental Illness of 1991 swing in the wind for a little while? Let *her* be the one to lie awake nights, wondering from which direction the Wrath of Wilma would fall. Do a few drive-bys, perhaps make a few more phone calls. As she sipped her coffee (Pete sat across the table, watching her apprehensively from above the sports section of the paper), it occurred to her that, if Nettie was as cracked as everyone said, she might not have to Take Care of Things at all. This might be one of those rare occasions when Things Took Care of Themselves. She found this thought so cheering that she actually allowed Pete to kiss her as he gathered up his briefcase and made ready to leave for work. .

The idea that her frightened mouse of a husband might have drugged her never crossed Wilma's mind. Nevertheless, that was just what Pete Jerzyck had done, and not for the first time, either.

Wilma knew that she had cowed her husband, but she had no idea to how great an extent. He did not just live in fear of her; he lived in *awe* of her, as natives in certain tropical climes once supposedly lived in awe and superstitious dread of the Great God Thunder Mountain, which might brood silently over their sunny lives for years or even generations before suddenly exploding in a murderous tirade of burning lava.

Such natives, whether real or hypothetical, undoubtedly had their own rituals of propitiation. These may not have helped much when the mountain awoke and cast its bolts of thunder and rivers of fire at their villages, but they surely improved everyone's peace of mind when the mountain was quiet. Pete Jerzyck had no high rituals with which he could worship Wilma; it seemed that more prosaic measures would have to serve. Prescription drugs instead of Communion wafers, for instance.

He made an appointment with Ray Van Allen, Castle Rock's only family practitioner, and told him that he wanted something which would relieve his feelings of anxiety. His work-schedule was a bitch, he told Ray, and as his commission-rate rose, he found it harder and harder to leave his work-related problems at the office. He had finally decided it was time to see if the doctor could prescribe something that would smooth off some of the rough edges.

Ray Van Allen knew nothing about the pressures of the real-estate game, but he had a fair idea of what the pressures of living with Wilma must be like. He suspected that Pete Jerzyck would have a lot less anxiety if he never left the office at all, but of course it was not his place to say so. He wrote a prescription for Xanax, cited the usual cautions, and wished the man good luck and God speed. He believed that, as Pete went down the road of life in tandem with that particular mare, he would need a lot of both.

Pete used the Xanax but did not abuse it. Neither did he tell Wilma about it—she would have had a cow if she knew he was USING DRUGS. He was careful to keep his Xanax prescription in his briefcase, which contained papers in which Wilma had no interest at all. He took five or six pills a month, most of them on the days before Wilma started her period.

Then, last summer, Wilma had gotten into a wrangle with Henrietta Longman, who owned and operated The Beauty Rest up on Castle Hill. The subject was a botched perm. Following the initial shouting match, there was an exchange between them at Hemphill's Market the next day, then a yelling match on Main Street a week later. That one almost degenerated into a brawl.

In the aftermath, Wilma had paced back and forth through the house like a caged lioness, swearing she was going to *get* that bitch, that she was going to put her in the hospital. "She'll need a Beauty Rest when *I* get through with her," Wilma had grated through clenched teeth. "You can count on it. I'm going up there tomorrow. I'm going to go up there and Take Care of Things."

Pete had realized, with mounting alarm, that this was not just talk; Wilma meant it. God knew what wild stunt she might pull. He'd had visions of Wilma ducking Henrietta's head in a vat of corrosive goo that would leave the woman as bald as Sinead O'Connor for the rest of her life.

He'd hoped for some modulation of temperament overnight, but when Wilma got up the next morning, she was even angrier. He wouldn't have believed it possible, but it seemed it was. The dark circles under her eyes were a proclamation of the sleepless night she had spent.

"Wilma," he'd said weakly, "I really don't think it's such a good idea for you to go up there to The Beauty Rest today. I'm sure, if you think this over—"

"I thought it over last night," Wilma had replied, turning that frighteningly flat gaze of hers on him, "and I decided that when I finish with her, she's never going to burn the roots of anyone else's hair. When I finish with her, she's going to need a Seeing Eye dog just to find her way to the john. And if you fuck around with me, Pete, you and her can buy your goddam dogs from the same litter of German shepherds."

Desperate, not sure it would work but unable to think of any other way to stave off the approaching catastrophe, Pete Jerzyck had removed the bottle from the inside pocket of his briefcase and had dropped a Xanax tablet into Wilma's coffee. He then went to his office.

In a very real sense, that had been Pete Jerzyck's First Communion.

He had spent the day in an agony of suspense and had come home terrified of what he might find (Henrietta Longman dead and Wilma in jail was his most recurrent fantasy). He was delighted to find Wilma in the kitchen, singing.

Pete took a deep breath, lowered his emotional blast-shield, and asked her what had happened with the Longman woman.

"She doesn't open until noon, and by then I just didn't feel so angry," Wilma said. "I went up there to have it out with her just the same, though—I'd promised myself I was going to, after all. And do you know, she offered me a glass of sherry and said she wanted to give me my money back!"

"Wow! Great!" Pete had said, relieved and gladdened . . . and that had been the end of *l'affaire* Henrietta. He had spent days waiting for Wilma's rage to return, but it hadn't—at least not aimed in that direction.

He had considered suggesting that Wilma go to Dr. Van Allen and obtain a tranquilizer prescription of her own, but discarded the idea after long and careful consideration. Wilma would blow him out of the water—maybe right into orbit— if he suggested that she TAKE DRUGS. TAKING DRUGS was for junkies, and tranquilizers were for weak-sister junkies. *She* would face life on life's terms, thank you very much. And besides, Pete concluded reluctantly, the truth was too plain to deny: Wilma *liked* being mad. Wilma in a red rage was Wilma fulfilled, Wilma imbued with high purpose.

And he loved her—just as the natives of that hypothetical tropic isle undoubtedly love their Great God Thunder Mountain. His awe and dread actually enhanced his love; she was WILMA, a force unto herself, and he attempted to deflect her from her course only when he was afraid she might injure herself . . . which, through the mystic transubstantiations of love, would also injure him.

He had slipped her the Xanax on just three occasions since then. The third—and the scariest by far—was The Night of the Muddy Sheets. He had been frantic to get her to take a cup of tea, and when she at last consented to drink one (after her short but extremely satisfactory dialogue with Crazy Nettie Cobb), he brewed it strong and dropped in not one Xanax but two. He was greatly relieved at how much her thermostat had dropped the next morning.

These were the things that Wilma Jerzyck, confident in her power over her husband's mind, did not know; they were also the things which kept Wilma from simply driving her Yugo through Nettie's door and snatching her bald-headed (or trying to) on Friday morning.

2

Not that Wilma had forgotten Nettie, or forgiven her, or come to entertain the slightest doubt as to who had vandalized her bed-linen; no medicine on earth would have done those things.

Shortly after Pete left for work, Wilma got into her car and cruised slowly down Willow Street (plastered to the back bumper of the little yellow Yugo was a bumper sticker which told the world IF YOU DON'T LIKE MY DRIVING DIAL 1-800-EAT-SHIT). She turned right, onto Ford Street, and slowed to a crawl as she approached Nettie Cobb's neat little house. She thought she saw one of the curtains twitch, and that was a good start . . . but only a start.

She went around the block (passing the Rusk home on Pond Street without a glance), past her own home on Willow, and around to Ford Street for the second time. This time she honked the Yugo's horn twice as she approached Nettie's house and then parked out front with the engine idling.

The curtain twitched again. No mistake this time. The woman was peering out at her. Wilma thought of her behind the curtain, trembling with guilt and terror, and found she enjoyed the image even more than she enjoyed the one she had gone to bed with—the one where she was twisting the crazy bitch's noodle until it spun like that little girl's head in *The Exorcist.*

"Peekaboo, I see you," she said grimly as the curtain fell back in place. "Don't think I don't."

She circled the block again and stopped in front of Nettie's a second time, honking the horn to notify her prey of her arrival. This time she sat out front for almost five minutes. The curtain twitched twice. At last she drove on again, satisfied.

Crazy broad will spend the rest of the day looking for me, she thought as she parked in her own driveway and got out. *She'll be afraid to set foot out of her door.*

Wilma went inside, light of foot and heart, and plunked

down on the sofa with a catalogue. Soon she was happily ordering three new sets of sheets—white, yellow, and paisley.

3

Raider sat in the middle of the living-room carpet, looking at
his mistress. At last he whined uneasily, as if to remind Nettie
that this was a working day and she was already half an hour
late. Today was the day she was supposed to vacuum the upstairs at Polly's, and the telephone man was coming with the
new phones, the ones with the great big touch-tone pads. They
were supposed to be easier for people who had the arthritis so
terrible, like Polly did, to use.

But how could she go out?

That crazy Polish woman was out there someplace, cruising
around in her little car.

Nettie sat in her chair, holding her lampshade in her lap.
She had been holding it in her lap ever since the crazy Polish
woman had driven past her house the first time. Then she had
come again, parking and honking her horn. When she left,
Nettie thought it might be over, but no—the woman had come
back yet a third time. Nettie had been sure the crazy Polish
woman would try to come in. She had sat in her chair, hugging
the lampshade with one arm and Raider with the other, wondering what she would do when and if the crazy Polish woman
did try—how she would defend herself. She didn't know.

At last she had mustered enough courage to take another peek
out the window, and the crazy Polish woman had been gone.
Her first feeling of relief had been superseded by dread. She was
afraid that the crazy Polish woman was patrolling the streets,
waiting for her to come out; she was even more afraid that the
crazy Polish woman would come here after she was gone.

That she would break in and see her beautiful lampshade
and shatter it to a thousand fragments on the floor.

Raider whined again.

"I know," she said in a voice which was almost a groan. "I *know*."

She had to leave. She had a responsibility, and she knew what it was and to whom she owed it. Polly Chalmers had been good to her. It had been Polly who wrote the recommendation that had gotten her out of Juniper Hill for good, and it had been Polly who had co-signed for her home loan at the bank. If not for Polly, whose father had been *her* father's best friend, she would still be living in a rented room on the other side of the Tin Bridge.

But what if she left and the crazy Polish woman came back?

Raider couldn't protect her lampshade; he was brave, but he was just a little dog. The crazy Polish woman might hurt him if he tried to stop her. Nettie felt her mind, caught in the vise of this horrible dilemma, beginning to slip. She groaned again.

And suddenly, mercifully, an idea occurred to her.

She got up, still cradling the lampshade in her arms, and crossed the living room, which was very gloomy with the shades drawn. She walked through the kitchen and opened the door in its far corner. There was a shed tacked onto this end of the house. The shadows of the woodpile and a great many stored objects bulked in the gloom.

A single lightbulb hung down from the ceiling on a cord. There was no switch or chain; you turned it on by screwing it firmly into its socket. She reached for this . . . then hesitated. If the crazy Polish woman was lurking in the back yard, she would *see* the light go on. And if she saw the light go on, she would know exactly where to look for Nettie's carnival glass lampshade, wouldn't she?

"Oh no, you don't get me that easy," she said under her breath, feeling her way past her mother's armoire and her mother's old Dutch bookcase to the woodpile. "Oh no you don't, Wilma Jerzyck. I'm not *stupid,* you know. I'm warning you of that."

Holding the lampshade against her belly with her left hand, Nettie used her right to pull down the tangle of old, dirty cobwebs in front of the shed's single window. Then she peered out into the back yard, her eyes jerking brightly from one spot to another. She remained so for almost a minute. Nothing in the back yard moved. Once she thought she saw the crazy Polish woman crouching in the far left corner of the yard, but closer study convinced her it was only the shade of the oak at the back of the Fearons' yard. The tree's lower branches overhung her own yard. They were moving a little in the wind, and that was why the patch of shade back there had looked like a crazy woman (a crazy *Polish* woman, to be exact) for a second.

Raider whined from behind her. She looked around and saw him standing in the shed door, a black silhouette with his head cocked.

"I know," she said. "I know, boy—but we're going to fool her. She thinks I'm stupid. Well, I can teach her better news than that."

She felt her way back. Her eyes were adjusting to the gloom and she decided she would not need to screw in the lightbulb after all. She stood on tiptoe and felt along the top of the armoire until her fingers encountered the key which locked and unlocked the long cupboard on the left-hand side. The key which worked on the drawers had been missing for years, but that was all right—Nettie had the one she needed.

She opened the long cupboard and deposited the carnival glass lampshade inside, amid the dust bunnies and mouse-turds.

"It deserves to be in a better place and I know it," she said softly to Raider. "But it's *safe,* and that's the important thing."

She put the key back in the lock, turned it, then tried the cupboard door. It was tight, tight as a tick, and she felt suddenly as if a huge boulder had rolled off her heart. She tried the cupboard door again, nodded briskly, and slipped the key into the pocket of her housedress. When she got to Polly's house, she would put it on a piece of string and hang it around her neck. She would do it first thing.

"There!" she told Raider, who had begun wagging his tail. Perhaps he sensed that the crisis was past. "*That's* taken care of, big boy, and I must get to work! I'm late!"

As she was slipping into her coat, the telephone began to ring. Nettie took two steps toward it and then stopped.

Raider uttered his single, severe bark and looked at her. Don't you know what you're supposed to do when the telephone rings? his eyes asked her. Even I know that, and I'm only the *dog.*

"I won't," Nettie said.

I know what you did, you crazy bitch, I know what you did, I know what you did, and I . . . am going to . . . GET you!

"I won't answer it. I'm going to work. *She's* the one who's crazy, not me. I never did a *thing* to her! Not one solitary *thing!*"

Raider barked agreement.

The telephone stopped ringing.

Nettie relaxed a little . . . but her heart was still pounding hard.

"You be a good boy," she told Raider, stroking him. "I'll be back late, because I'm going in late. But I love you, and if you remember that, you will be a good doggy all day long."

This was a going-to-work incantation which Raider knew well, and he wagged his tail. Nettie opened the front door and peered both ways before stepping out. She had a bad moment when she saw a bright flash of yellow, but it wasn't the crazy Polish woman's car; the Pollard boy had left his Fisher-Price tricycle out on the sidewalk, that was all.

Nettie used her housekey to lock the door behind her, then walked around to the rear of the house to make sure the shed door was locked. It was. She set off for Polly's house, her purse over her arm and her eyes searching for the crazy Polish woman's car (she was trying to decide if she should hide behind a hedge or simply stand her ground if she saw it). She was almost to the end of the block when it came to her that she had not checked the front door as carefully as she should have done. She glanced anxiously at her watch and then retraced her steps. She checked the front door. It was locked tight. Nettie sighed with relief, and then decided she ought to check the lock on the woodshed door, too, just to be safe.

"Better safe than sorry," she muttered under her breath, and went around to the back of the house.

Her hand froze in the act of pulling on the handle of the woodshed door.

Inside, the telephone was ringing again.

"She's crazy," Nettie moaned. "I didn't do *anything!*"

The shed door was locked, but she stood there until the telephone fell silent. Then she set sail for work again with her purse hanging over her arm.

4

This time she had gone almost two blocks before the conviction that she still might not have locked the front door recurred, gnawing at her. She knew she *had,* but she was afraid she *hadn't.*

She stood by the blue U.S. mailbox at the corner of Ford and Deaconess Way, indecisive. She had almost made up her mind to push on when she saw a yellow car drift through the intersection a block down. It wasn't the crazy Polish woman's car, it was a Ford, but she thought it might be an omen. She walked rapidly back to her house and checked both doors again. Locked. She got to the end of her walk before it occurred to her that she ought to double-check the cupboard door of the armoire as well, and make sure it was also locked.

She knew that it *was,* but she was afraid that it *wasn't.*

She unlocked the front door and went inside. Raider jumped up on her, tail wagging wildly, and she petted him for a moment—but only a moment. She had to close the front door, because the crazy Polish woman might come by anytime. Any-time at all.

She slammed it, turned the thumb-bolt, and went back out to the woodshed. The cupboard door was locked, of course. She went back into the house and stood in the kitchen for a min-ute. Already she was beginning to worry, beginning to think she had made a mistake and the cupboard door really *wasn't* locked. Maybe she hadn't tugged on the pull hard enough to be really absolutely one hundred per cent sure. It might only be stuck.

She went back to check it again, and while she was check-ing, the telephone began to ring. She hurried back into the house with the key to the armoire clutched in her sweaty right hand. She barked her shin on a footstool and cried out in pain.

By the time she got to the living room, the telephone had stopped again.

"I can't go to work today," she muttered. "I have to . . . to . . ."

(*stand guard*)

That was it. She had to stand guard.

She picked up the phone and dialled quickly before her mind could start to gnaw at itself again, the way Raider gnawed at his rawhide chewy toys.

"Hello?" Polly said. "This is You Sew and Sew."

"Hi, Polly. It's me."

"Nettie? Is everything all right?"

"Yes, but I'm calling from home, Polly. My stomach is upset." By now this was no lie. "I wonder if I could have the day off. I know about vacuuming the upstairs . . . and the telephone man is coming . . . but. . ."

"That's all right," Polly said at once. "The phone man isn't coming until two, and I meant to leave early today, anyway. My hands still hurt too much to work for long. I'll let him in."

"If you really need me, I could—"

"No, really," Polly assured her warmly, and Nettie felt tears prick her eyes. Polly was so *kind*.

"Are they sharp pains, Nettie? Shall I call Dr. Van Allen for you?"

"No—just kind of crampy. I'll be all right. If I can come in this afternoon, I will."

"Nonsense," Polly said briskly. "You haven't asked for a day off since you came to work for me. Just crawl into bed and go back to sleep. Fair warning: if you try to come in, I'll just send you home."

"Thank you, Polly," Nettie said. She was on the verge of tears. "You're very good to me."

"You deserve goodness. I've got to go, Nettie—customers. Lie down. I'll call this afternoon to see how you're doing."

"Thank you."

"You're more than welcome. Bye-bye."

"Toodle-oo," Nettie said, and hung up.

She went at once to the window and twitched the curtain aside. The street was empty—for now. She went back into the shed, used the key to open the armoire, and took out the lampshade. A feeling of calm and ease settled over her as soon as she had it cradled in her arms. She took it into the kitchen, washed it in warm, soapy water, rinsed it, and dried it carefully.

She opened one of the kitchen drawers and removed her butcher knife. She took this and the lampshade back into the living room and sat down in the gloom. She sat that way all morning, bolt upright in her chair, the lampshade in her lap and the butcher knife clenched in her right hand.

The phone rang twice.

Nettie didn't answer it.

CHAPTER SEVEN

1

Friday, the eleventh of October, was a banner day at Castle Rock's newest shop, particularly as morning gave way to afternoon and people began to cash their paychecks. Money in the hand was an incentive to shop; so was the good word of mouth sent around by those who had stopped in on Wednesday. There were a number of people, of course, who believed the judgments of people crude enough to visit a new store *on the very first day it was open* could not be trusted, but they were a minority, and the small silver bell over the front door of Needful Things jingled prettily all day long.

More stock had been either unpacked or delivered since Wednesday. It was hard for those interested in such things to believe there had been a delivery—no one had seen a truck—but it really didn't matter much, one way or the other. There was a lot more merchandise in Needful Things on Friday; that was the important thing.

Dolls, for instance. And beautifully crafted wooden jigsaw puzzles, some of them double-sided. There was a unique chess set: the pieces were chunks of rock crystal carved into African animals by some primitive but fabulously talented hand—loping giraffes for knights, rhinos with their heads combatively lowered for castles, jackals for pawns, lion kings, sinuous leopard queens. There was a necklace of black pearls which was clearly expensive—how expensive nobody quite dared to ask (at least not *that* day)—but their beauty made them almost painful to look at, and several visitors to Needful Things went home feeling melancholy and oddly distraught, with the image of that pearl necklace dancing in the darkness just behind their eyes, black on black. Nor were all of these women.

There was a pair of dancing jester-puppets. There was a music box, old and ornately carved—Mr. Gaunt said he was sure it played something unusual when it was opened, but he couldn't remember just what, and it was locked shut. He reckoned a buyer would have to find someone to make a key for it; there were still a few old-timers around, he said, who had such skills. He was asked a few times if the music box could be returned if the buyer *did* get the lid to open and discovered that the tune was not to his or her taste. Mr. Gaunt smiled and pointed to a new sign on the wall. It read:

I DO NOT ISSUE REFUNDS OR MAKE EXCHANGES
CAVEAT EMPTOR!

"What does *that* mean?" Lucille Dunham asked. Lucille was a waitress at Nan's who had stopped in with her friend Rose Ellen Myers on her coffee break.

"It means that if you buy a pig in a poke, you keep the pig and he keeps your poke," Rose Ellen said. She saw that Mr. Gaunt had overheard her (and she could have sworn she'd seen him on the other side of the shop only a moment before), and she blushed bright red.

Mr. Gaunt, however, only laughed. "That's right," he told her. "That's *exactly* what it means!"

An old long-barreled revolver in one case with a card in front of it which read NED BUNTLINE SPECIAL; a boy puppet with wooden red hair, freckles, and a fixed friendly grin (HOWDY DOODY PROTOTYPE, read the card); boxes of stationery, very nice but not remarkable; a selection of antique post-cards; pen-and-pencil sets; linen handkerchiefs; stuffed animals. There was, it seemed, an item for every taste and—even though there was not a single price-tag in the entire store—for every budget.

Mr. Gaunt did a fine business that day. Most of the items he sold were nice but in no way unique. He did, however, make a number of "special" deals, and all of these sales took place during those lulls when there was only a single customer in the store.

"When things get slow, I get restless," he told Sally Ratcliffe, Brian Rusk's speech teacher, with his friendly grin, "and when I get restless, I sometimes get reckless. Bad for the seller but *awfully* good for the buyer."

Miss Ratcliffe was a devout member of Rev. Rose's Baptist flock, had met her fiancé Lester Pratt there, and in addition to her No Casino Nite button, she wore one which said I'M ONE OF THE SAVED! HOW 'BOUT YOU? The splinter labelled PETRIFIED WOOD FROM THE HOLY LAND caught her attention at once, and she did not object when Mr. Gaunt took it from its case and dropped it into her hand. She bought it for seventeen dollars and a promise to play a harmless little prank on Frank Jewett, the principal at Castle Rock Middle School. She left the shop five minutes after she had entered, looking dreamy and abstracted. Mr. Gaunt had offered to wrap her purchase for her, but Miss Ratcliffe refused, saying she wanted to hold it. Looking at her as she went out the door, you would have been hard-put to tell if her feet were on the floor or drifting just above it.

2

The silver bell jingled.

Cora Rusk came in determined to buy the picture of The King, and was extremely upset when Mr. Gaunt told her it had been sold. Cora wanted to know who had bought it. "I'm sorry," Mr. Gaunt said, "but the lady was from out of state. There was an Oklahoma plate on the car she was driving."

"Well, I'll be *butched!*" Cora cried in tones of anger and real distress. She hadn't realized just how badly she wanted that picture until Mr. Gaunt informed her that it was gone.

Henry Gendron and his wife, Yvette, were in the shop at that time, and Mr. Gaunt asked Cora to wait a minute while he saw to them. He believed he had something else, he told her, which she would find of equal or perhaps even greater interest. After he had sold the Gendrons a stuffed teddy bear—a present for their daughter—and seen them out, he asked Cora if she could wait a moment longer while he looked for something in the back room. Cora waited, but not with any real interest or expectation. A deep gray depression had settled over her. She had seen hundreds of pictures of The King, maybe *thousands,* and owned half a dozen herself, but this one had seemed . . . special, somehow. She hated the woman from Oklahoma.

Then Mr. Gaunt came back with a small lizard-skin spectacles case. He opened it and showed Cora a pair of aviator glasses with lenses of a deep smoky gray. Her breath caught in her throat; her right hand rose to her quivering neck.

"Are those—" she began, and could say no more.

"The King's sunglasses," Mr. Gaunt agreed gravely. "One of sixty pairs. But I'm told these were his favorites."

Cora bought the sunglasses for nineteen dollars and fifty cents.

"I'd like a little information, as well." Mr. Gaunt looked at Cora with twinkling eyes. "Let's call it a surcharge, shall we?"

"Information?" Cora asked doubtfully. "What sort of information?"

"Look out the window, Cora."

Cora did as she was asked, but her hands never left the sunglasses. Across the street, Castle Rock's Unit I was parked in front of The Clip Joint. Alan Pangborn stood on the sidewalk, talking to Bill Fullerton.

"Do you see that fellow?" Gaunt asked.

"Who? Bill Ful—"

"No, you dummy," Gaunt said. "The *other* one."

"Sheriff Pangborn?"

"Right."

"Yes, I see him." Cora felt dull and dazed. Gaunt's voice seemed to be coming from a great distance. She could not stop thinking about her purchase—the wonderful sunglasses. She wanted to get home and try them on right away . . . but of course she couldn't leave until she was allowed to leave, because the dealing wasn't done until Mr. Gaunt *said* the dealing was done.

"He looks like what folks in my line of work call a tough sell," Mr. Gaunt said. "What do *you* think about him, Cora?"

"He's smart," Cora said. "He'll never be the Sheriff old George Bannerman was—that's what my husband says—but he's smart as a whip."

"Is he?" Mr. Gaunt's voice had taken on that nagging, tired edge again. His eyes had narrowed to slits, and they never left Alan Pangborn. "Well, do you want to know a secret, Cora? I don't much care for smart people, and I *hate* a tough sell. In fact, I *loathe* a tough sell. I don't trust people who always want to turn things over and look for cracks before they buy them, do you?"

Cora said nothing. She only stood with The King's sunglasses case in her left hand and stared blankly out the window.

"If I wanted someone to keep an eye on smart old Sheriff Pangborn, Cora, who would be a good choice?"

"Polly Chalmers," Cora said in her drugged voice. "She's awful sweet on him."

Gaunt shook his head at once. His eyes never left the Sheriff as Alan walked to his cruiser, glanced briefly across the street at Needful Things, then got in and drove away. "Won't do."

"Sheila Brigham?" Cora asked doubtfully. "She's the dispatcher down at the Sheriff's Office."

"A good idea, but she won't do, either. Another tough sell. There are a few in every town, Cora—unfortunate, but true."

Cora thought it over in her dim, distant way. "Eddie Warburton?" she asked at last. "He's the head custodian at the Municipal Building."

Gaunt's face lit up. "The janitor!" he said. "Yes! Excellent! Fifth Business! Really *excellent!*" He leaned over the counter and planted a kiss on Cora's cheek.

She drew away, grimacing and rubbing frantically at the spot. A brief gagging noise came from her throat, but Gaunt appeared not to notice. His face was wreathed in a large, shining smile.

Cora left (still rubbing her cheek with the heel of her hand) as Stephanie Bonsaint and Cyndi Rose Martin of the Ash Street Bridge Club came in. Cora almost bowled Steffie Bonsaint over in her hurry; she felt a deep desire to get home as fast as she could. To get home and actually try those glasses on. But before she did, she wanted to wash her face and rid herself of that loathsome kiss. She could feel it burning in her skin like a low fever.

Over the door, the silver bell tinkled.

3

While Steffie stood by the window, absorbed in the shifting patterns of the old-fashioned kaleidoscope she had found, Cyndi Rose approached Mr. Gaunt and reminded him of what he had told her on Wednesday: that he might have a Lalique vase to match the one she had already bought.

"Well," Mr. Gaunt said, smiling at her in a can-you-keep-a-secret sort of way, "I just might. Can you get rid of your friend for a minute or two?"

Cyndi Rose asked Steffie to go on ahead to Nan's and order coffee for her; she would be right along, she said. Steffie went, but with a puzzled look on her face.

Mr. Gaunt went into the back room and came out with a Lalique vase. It did not just match the other; it was an identical twin.

"How much?" Cyndi Rose asked, and caressed the sweet curve of the vase with a finger which was not quite steady. She remembered her satisfaction at the bargain she had struck on Wednesday with some rue. He had only been planting the hook, it seemed. Now he would reel her in. *This* vase would be no thirty-one-dollar bargain; this time he would really sock it to her. But she wanted it to balance off the other on the mantelpiece in the living room; she wanted it very badly.

She could hardly believe her ears at Leland Gaunt's reply. "Because this is my first week, why don't we call it two for the price of one? Here you are, my dear—enjoy it."

Her shock was so great that she almost dropped the vase on the floor when he put it in her hand.

"What . . . I thought you said . . ."

"You heard me correctly," he said, and she suddenly found she could not take her eyes away from his. *Francie was wrong about them,* she thought in a distant, preoccupied sort of way. *They're not green at all. They're gray. Dark gray.* "There *is* one other thing, though."

"Is there?"

"Yes—do you know a Sheriff's Deputy named Norris Ridgewick?"

The little silver bell tinkled.

Everett Frankel, the Physician's Assistant who worked with Dr. Van Allen, bought the pipe Brian Rusk had noticed on his advance visit to Needful Things for twelve dollars and a prank to be played on Sally Ratcliffe. Poor old Slopey Dodd, the stutterer who attended speech therapy on Tuesday afternoons with Brian, bought a pewter teapot for his mom's birthday. It cost him seventy-one cents . . . and a promise, freely given, that he would play a funny trick on Sally's boyfriend, Lester Pratt. Mr. Gaunt told Slopey he would supply him the few items he would need to play this trick when the time came, and Slopey said that would be ruh-ruh-real g-g-g-good. June Gavineaux, wife of the town's most prosperous dairy farmer, bought a cloisonné vase for ninety-seven dollars and a promise to play a funny trick on Father Brigham of Our Lady of Serene Waters. Not long after she left, Mr. Gaunt arranged for a somewhat similar trick to be played on the Reverend Willie.

It was a busy, fruitful day, and when Gaunt finally hung the CLOSED sign in the window and pulled the shade, he was tired but pleased. Business had been great, and he had even taken a step toward assuring himself he would not be interrupted by Sheriff Pangborn. That was good. Opening was always the most delightful part of his operation, but it was always stressful and could sometimes be risky, as well. He might be wrong about Pangborn, of course, but Gaunt had learned to trust his feelings in such matters, and Pangborn felt like a man he would do well to steer clear of . . . at least until he was ready to deal with the Sheriff on his own terms. Mr. Gaunt reckoned it was going to be an extremely full week, and there would be fireworks before it was over.

Lots of them.

4

It was quarter past six on Friday evening when Alan turned into Polly's driveway and cut the motor. She was standing at the door, waiting for him, and kissed him warmly. He saw she had donned her gloves for even this brief foray into the cold and frowned.

"Now stop," she said. "They're a little better tonight. Did you bring the chicken?"

He held up the white grease-spotted bags. "Your servant, dear lady."

She dropped him a little curtsey. "And yours."

She took the bags from him and led him into the kitchen. He pulled a chair out from the table, swung it around, and sat on it backwards to watch her as she pulled off her gloves and arranged the chicken on a glass plate. He had gotten it from Cluck-Cluck Tonite. The name was country-horrible, but the chicken was just fine (according to Norris, the clams were a different story). The only problem with take-out when you lived twenty miles away was the cooling factor . . . and that, he thought, was what microwave ovens had been made for. In fact, he believed the only three valid purposes microwaves served were reheating coffee, making popcorn, and putting a buzz under take-out from places like Cluck-Cluck Tonite.

"*Are* they better?" he asked as she popped the chicken into the oven and pressed the appropriate buttons. There was no need to be more specific; both of them knew what they were talking about.

"Only a little," she admitted, "but I'm pretty sure they're going to be a *lot* better soon. I'm starting to feel tingles of heat in the palms, and that's the way the improvement usually starts."

She held them up. She had been painfully embarrassed by her twisted, misshapen hands at first, and the embarrassment was still there, but she had come a long way toward accepting his interest as a part of his love. He still thought her hands looked stiff and awkward, as if she were wearing invisible gloves—gloves sewn by a crude and uncaring maker who had pulled them on her and then stapled them to her wrists forever.

"Have you had to take any pills today?"

"Only one. This morning,"

She had actually taken three—two in the morning, one in the early afternoon—and the pain was not much better today than it had been yesterday. She was afraid that the tingle of which she had spoken was mostly a figment of her own wistful imagination. She didn't like lying to Alan; she believed that lies and love rarely went together, and never for long. But she had been on her own for a long time, and a part of her was still terrified by his relentless concern. She trusted him, but was afraid to let him know too much.

He had grown steadily more insistent about the Mayo Clinic, and she knew that, if he really understood how bad the pain was this time, he would grow more insistent still. She did not want her goddamned *hands* to become the most important component of their love . . . and she was also afraid of what a consultation at a place like the Mayo might show. She could live with pain; she was not sure if she could live without hope.

"Will you take the potatoes out of the oven?" she asked. "I want to call Nettie before we eat."

"What's with Nettie?"

"Upset tum. She didn't come in today. I want to make sure it's not intestinal flu. Rosalie says there's a lot of it going around, and Nettie's terrified of doctors."

And Alan, who knew more of how and what Polly Chalmers thought than Polly ever would have guessed, thought, *Look who's talking, love,* as she went to the telephone. He was a cop, and he could not put away his habits of observation when he was off duty; they were automatic. He no longer even tried. If he had been a little more observant during the last few months of Annie's life, she and Todd might still be alive.

He had noted the gloves when Polly came to the door. He had noted the fact that she had pulled them off with her teeth rather than simply stripping them off hand-for-hand. He had watched her arrange the chicken on the plate, and noted the slight grimace which tightened her mouth when she lifted the plate and put it in the microwave. These were bad signs. He walked to the door between the kitchen and the living room, wanting to watch how confidently or tentatively she would use the telephone. It was one of the most important ways he had of measuring her pain. And here, at last, he was able to note a good sign—or what he took for one.

She punched Nettie's telephone number quickly and confidently, and because she was on the far side of the room, he was unable to see that this phone—and all the others—had been changed earlier that day to the type with the oversized finger-pads. He went back into the kitchen, keeping one ear cocked toward the living room as he did so.

"Hello, Nettie? . . . I was about to give up. Did I wake you? . . . Yes . . . Uh-huh . . . Well, how is it? . . . Oh, good. I've been thinking of you . . . No, I'm fine for supper, Alan brought fried chicken from that Cluck-Cluck place in Oxford . . . Yes, it was, wasn't it?"

Alan got a platter from one of the cabinets above the kitchen counter and thought: She is lying about her hands. It doesn't matter how well she handles the phone—they're as bad as they've been in the last year, and maybe worse.

The idea that she had lied to him did not much dismay him; his view of truth-bending was a good deal more lenient than Polly's. Take the child, for instance. She had borne it in early 1971, seven months or so after leaving Castle Rock on a Greyhound bus. She had told Alan the baby—a boy she'd named Kelton—had died in Denver, at the age of three months. Sudden Infant Death Syndrome—SIDS, the young mother's worst nightmare. It was a perfectly plausible story, and Alan had no doubt whatever that Kelton Chalmers was indeed dead. There was only one problem with Polly's version: it wasn't true. Alan was a cop, and he knew a lie when he heard one.

(*except when it was Annie doing it*)

Yeah, he thought. Except when it was Annie doing it. Your exception is duly noted for the record.

What had told him Polly was lying? The rapid flicker of her eyelids over her too-wide, too-direct gaze? The way her left hand kept rising to tug at her left earlobe? The crossing and uncrossing of her legs, that child's game signal which meant *I'm fibbing?*

All of those things and none of them. Mostly it was just a buzzer that had gone off inside, the way a buzzer in an airport metal-detector goes off when a guy with a steel plate in his skull steps through.

The lie neither angered nor worried him. There were people

who lied for gain, people who lied from pain, people who lied simply because the concept of telling the truth was utterly alien to them . . . and then there were people who lied because they were waiting for it to be time to tell the truth. He thought that Polly's lie about Kelton was of this last kind, and he was content to wait. In time, she would decide to show him her secrets. There was no hurry.

No hurry: the thought itself seemed a luxury.

Her voice—rich and calm and somehow just right as it drifted out of the living room—also seemed a luxury. He was not yet over the guilt of just being here and knowing where all the dishes and utensils were stored, of knowing which bedroom drawer she kept her nylon hose in, or exactly where her summer tan-lines stopped, but none of it mattered when he heard her voice. There was really only one fact that applied here, one simple fact which ruled all others: the sound of her voice was becoming the sound of home.

"I could come over later if you wanted, Nettie . . . You are? . . . Well, rest *is* probably the best thing . . . *Tomorrow?*"

Polly laughed. It was a free, pleasing sound that always made Alan feel as if the world had been somehow freshened. He thought he could wait a long time for her secrets to disclose themselves if she would just laugh like that every now and then.

"Gosh, no! Tomorrow's *Saturday!* I'm just going to lie around and be sinful!"

Alan smiled. He pulled out the drawer under the stove, found a pair of pot holders, and opened the conventional oven. One potato, two potato, three potato, four. How in God's name were the two of them supposed to eat four big baked potatoes? But of course he had known there would be too many, because that was the way Polly cooked. There was surely another secret buried in the fact of those four big potatoes, and someday, when he knew all the whys—or most of them, or even some of them—his feelings of guilt and strangeness might pass.

He took the potatoes out. The microwave beeped a moment later.

"I've got to go, Nettie—"

"That's okay!" Alan yelled. "I've got this under control! I'm a policeman, lady!"

"—but you call me if you need anything. You're sure you're okay, now? . . . And you'd tell me if you weren't, Nettie, right? . . . Okay . . . What? . . . No, just asking . . . You too . . . Goodnight, Nettie."

When she came out, he had set the chicken on the table and was busy turning one of the potatoes inside-out on her plate.

"Alan, you sweetheart! You didn't need to do that!"

"All part of the service, pretty lady." Another thing he understood was that, when Polly's hands were bad, life became a series of small, hellacious combats for her; the ordinary events of an ordinary life transformed themselves into a series of gruelling obstacles to be surmounted, and the penalty for failure was embarrassment as well as pain. Loading the dishwasher. Stacking kindling in the fireplace. Manipulating a knife and fork to get a hot potato out of its jacket.

"Sit down," he said. "Let's cluck."

She burst out laughing and then hugged him. She squeezed his back with her inner forearms instead of her hands, the relentless observer inside noted. But a less dispassionate part of him took notice of the way her trim body pressed against his, and the sweet smell of the shampoo she used.

"You are the dearest man," she said quietly.

He kissed her, gently at first, then with more force. His hands slid down from the small of her back to the swell of her buttocks. The fabric of her old jeans was as smooth and soft as moleskin under his hands.

"Down, big fella," she said at last. "Food now, snuggle later."

"Is that an invitation?" If her hands really weren't better, he thought, she would fudge.

But she said, "Gilt-edged," and Alan sat down satisfied. Provisionally.

5

"Is Al coming home for the weekend?" Polly asked as they cleared away the supper things. Alan's surviving son attended Milton Academy, south of Boston.

"Huh-uh," Alan said, scraping plates.

Polly said, a little too casually: "I just thought, with no classes Monday because of Columbus Day—"

"He's going to Dorf's place on Cape Cod," Alan said. "Dorf is Carl Dorfman, his roomie. Al called last Tuesday and asked if he could go down for the three-day weekend. I said okay, fine."

She touched him on the arm and he turned to look at her. "How much of this is my fault, Alan?"

"How much of *what's* your fault?" he asked, honestly surprised.

"You know what I'm talking about; you're a good father, and you're not stupid. How many times has Al been home since school started again?"

Suddenly Alan understood what she was driving at, and he grinned at her, relieved. "Only once," he said, "and that was because he needed to talk to Jimmy Catlin, his old computer-hacking buddy from junior high. Some of his choicest programs wouldn't run on the new Commodore 64 I got him for his birthday."

"You see? That's my point, Alan. He sees me as trying to step into his mother's place too soon, and—"

"Oh, jeez," Alan said. "How long have you been brooding over the idea that Al sees you as the Wicked Stepmother?"

Her brows drew together in a frown. "I hope you'll pardon me if I don't find the idea as funny as you apparently do."

He took her gently by the upper arms and kissed the corner of her mouth. "I don't find it funny at all. There are times— I was just thinking about this—when I feel a little strange, being with you. It seems too soon. It isn't, but sometimes it seems that way. Do you know what I mean?"

She nodded. Her frown smoothed out a little but did not disappear. "Of course I do. Characters in movies and TV shows always get to spend a little more time pining dramatically, don't they?"

"You put your finger on it. In the movies you get a lot of pining and precious little grief. Because grief is too real. Grief is . . ." He let go of her arms, slowly picked up a dish and began to wipe it dry. "Grief is *brutal*."

"Yes."

"So sometimes I feel a little guilty, yeah." He was sourly amused by the defensiveness he heard lurking in his voice. "Partly because it seems too early, even though it isn't, and partly because it seems I got off too easy, even though I didn't. This idea that I owe more grief is still there part of the time, I can't deny that, but to my credit I know that it's nuts . . . because part of me—a *lot* of me, in fact—is *still* grieving."

"You must be human," she said softly. "How weirdly exotic and excitingly perverse."

"Yeah, I guess so. As for Al, he's dealing with this in his own way. It's a good way, too—good enough for me to be proud of him. He still misses his mother, but if he's still *grieving*—and I guess I'm not completely sure he is—then it's Todd he's grieving for. But your idea that he's staying away because he doesn't approve of you . . . or us . . . that's way off the beam."

"I'm glad it is. You don't know how much you've relieved my mind. But it still seems . . ."

"Not quite right, somehow?"

She nodded.

"I know what you mean. But kids' behavior, even when it's as normal as ninety-eight-point-six, never seems quite right to adults. We forget how easy they heal, sometimes, and we almost always forget how fast they change. Al is pulling away. From me, from his old buddies like Jimmy Catlin, from The Rock itself. Pulling away, that's all. Like a rocket when the third-stage booster kicks in. Kids always do it, and I guess it's always kind of a sad surprise to their parents."

"It seems early, though," Polly said quietly. "Seventeen seems early to pull away."

"It *is* early," Alan said. He spoke in a tone which was not quite angry. "He lost his mother and his brother in a stupid accident. His life blew apart, my life blew apart, and we got together the way I guess fathers and sons almost always do in those situations to see if we could find most of the pieces again. We managed pretty well, I think, but I'd be blind not to know that things have changed. My life is here, Polly, in The Rock. His isn't, not anymore. I thought maybe it was going to be again, but the look that came into his eyes when I suggested that he might like to transfer to Castle Rock High this fall set me right on that in a hurry. He doesn't *like* to come back here because there are too many memories. I think that might change . . . in time . . . and for now I'm not going to push him. But it has nothing to do with you and me. Okay?"

"Okay. Alan?"

"Hmmm?"

"You miss him, don't you?"

"Yeah," Alan agreed simply. "Every day." He was appalled to find himself suddenly on the verge of tears. He turned away and opened a cupboard at random, trying to get himself under control. The easiest way to do it would be to re-route the conversation, and fast. "How's Nettie?" he asked, and was relieved to hear that his voice sounded normal.

"She says she's better tonight, but it took her an awfully long time to answer the phone—I had visions of her lying on the floor, unconscious."

"Probably she was asleep."

"She said not, and she didn't *sound* like it. You know how people sound when the phone wakes them up?"

He nodded. It was another cop thing. He had been on both the giving and receiving end of a lot of telephone calls that broke someone's sleep.

"She said she was sorting through some of her mother's old stuff in the woodshed, but—"

"If she has intestinal flu, you probably called while she was on the throne and she didn't want to admit it," Alan said dryly.

She considered this, then burst out laughing. "I'll bet that was it. It's just like her."

"Sure," he said. Alan peered into the sink, then pulled the plug. "Honey, we're all washed up."

"Thank you, Alan." She pecked his cheek.

"Oh, say, look what I found," Alan said. He reached behind her ear and pulled out a fifty-cent piece. "Do you always keep those back there, pretty lady?"

"How do you do that?" she asked, looking at the half-buck with real fascination.

"Do what?" he asked. The fifty-cent piece seemed to float over the gently shuttling knuckles of his right hand. He pinched the coin between his third and fourth fingers and turned his hand over. When he turned it back the other way again, the coin was gone. "Think I ought to run away and join the circus?" he asked her.

She smiled. "No—stay here with me. Alan, do you think I'm silly to worry about Nettie so much?"

"Nope," Alan said. He stuck his left hand—the one to which he had transferred the fifty-cent piece—into his pants pocket, pulled it out empty, and grabbed a dishtowel. "You got her out of the funny-farm, you gave her a job, and you helped buy her a house. You feel responsible for her, and I suppose to some degree you are. If you didn't worry about her, I think I'd worry about you."

She took the last glass from the dish-drainer. Alan saw the

sudden dismay on her face and knew she wasn't going to be able to hold it, although the glass was already almost dry. He moved quickly, bending his knees and sticking out his hand. The move was so gracefully executed that it looked to Polly almost like a dance-step. The glass fell and plunked neatly into his hand, which hung palm up less than eighteen inches from the floor.

The pain which had nagged her all night—and the attendant fear that Alan would tumble to just how bad it was—was suddenly buried under a wave of desire so hard and unexpected that it did more than startle her; it frightened her. And desire was a little too coy, wasn't it? What she felt was simpler, an emotion whose hue was utterly primary. It was lust.

"You move like a damned cat," she said as he straightened. Her voice was thick, a little slurred. She kept seeing the graceful way his legs had bent, the flex of the long muscles in his thighs. The smooth curve of one calf. "How does a man as big as you move that fast?"

"I don't know," he said, and looked at her with surprise and puzzlement. "What's wrong, Polly? You look funny. Do you feel faint?"

"I feel," she said, "like I'm going to come in my pants."

It came to him, too, then. Just like that. There was no wrong about it, no right. It just *was*. "Let's see if you are," he said, and moved forward with that same grace, that weird speed you would never suspect if you saw him ambling down Main Street. "Let's just see about that." He set the glass on the counter with his left hand and slipped his right between her legs before she knew what was happening.

"Alan what are you do—" And then, as his thumb pressed with gentle force against her clitoris, *doing* turned to *do-ooooh!-ing* and he lifted her with his easy, amazing strength.

She put her arms around his neck, being careful even at this warm moment to hold with her forearms; her hands stuck off behind him like stiff bundles of sticks, but they were suddenly

the only parts of her which were stiff. The rest of her seemed to
be melting. "Alan, put me *down!*"

"I don't think so," he said, and lifted her higher. He slid his
free hand between her shoulder-blades as she started to slip
and pressed her forward. And suddenly she was rocking back
and forth on the hand between her legs like a girl on a hobby-
horse, and he was *helping* her rock, and she felt as if she were in
some wonderful swing with her feet in the wind and her hair
in the stars.

"Alan—"

"Hold tight, pretty lady," he said, and he was *laughing,* as if
she weighed no more than a bag of feathers. She leaned back,
almost unaware of his steadying hand in her growing excitement, only knowing he would not let her fall, and then he
brought her forward again, and one hand was rubbing her back,
and the thumb of his other hand was doing things to her down
there, things she had never even *considered,* and she rocked back
again, calling his name out deliriously.

Her orgasm hit like a sweet exploding bullet, rushing both
ways from the center of her. Her legs swung back and forth
six inches above the kitchen floor (one of her loafers flew off
and sailed all the way into the living room), her head fell back
so her dark hair trailed over his forearm in a small tickling
torrent, and at the height of her pleasure he kissed the sweet
white line of her throat.

He set her down . . . then reached out quickly to steady her
as her knees buckled.

"Oh my God," she said, beginning to laugh weakly. "Oh my
God, Alan, I'll never wash these jeans again."

That struck him as hilarious, and he bellowed laughter. He
collapsed into one of the kitchen chairs with his legs stuck out
straight in front of him and howled, holding his stomach. She
took a step toward him. He grasped her, pulled her onto his lap
for a moment, and then stood with her in his arms.

She felt that fainting wave of emotion and need sweep her

again, but it was clearer now, better defined. *Now,* she thought, *now it is desire. I desire this man so much.*

"Take me upstairs," she said. "If you can't make it that far, take me to the couch. And if you can't make it to the couch, do me right here on the kitchen floor."

"I think I can make it at least as far as the living room," he said. "How are your hands, pretty lady?"

"What hands?" she asked dreamily, and closed her eyes. She concentrated on the clear joy of this moment, moving through space and time in his arms, moving in darkness and circled by his strength. She pressed her face against his chest, and when he put her on the couch she pulled him down . . . and this time she used her hands to do it.

6

They were on the couch for nearly an hour, then in the shower for she didn't know how long—until the hot water started to fail and drove them out, anyway. Then she took him into her bed, where she lay too exhausted and too content to do anything but bundle.

She had expected to make love to him tonight, but more to allay his concern than out of any real desire on her own part. She had certainly not expected such a series of explosions as had resulted . . . but she was glad. She could feel the pain in her hands beginning to assert itself again, but she would not need a Percodan to sleep tonight.

"You are one fantastic lover, Alan."

"So are you."

"It's unanimous," she said, and put her head against his chest. She could hear his heart lub-dubbing calmly away in there, as if to say ho-hum, stuff like this is all in a night's work for me and the boss. She thought again—and not without a faint echo of her earlier fierce passion—of how quick he was, how strong . . . but mostly how quick. She had known him ever since Annie had come to work for her, had been his lover for the last five months, and she had never known how quickly he could move until tonight. It had been like a whole-body version of the coin tricks, the card tricks, and the shadow-animals that almost every kid in town knew about and begged for when they saw him. It was spooky . . . but it was also wonderful.

She could feel herself drifting off now. She should ask him if he meant to stay the night, and tell him to put his car in the garage if he did—Castle Rock was a small town where many tongues wagged—but it seemed like too much trouble. Alan would take care. Alan, she was beginning to think, always did.

"Any fresh outbursts from Buster or the Reverend Willie?" she asked sleepily.

Alan smiled. "Quiet on both fronts, at least for the time being. I appreciate Mr. Keeton and Reverend Rose the most when I see them the least, and by that standard today was great."

"That's good," she murmured.

"Yeah, but I know something even better."

"What?"

"Norris is back in a good mood. He bought a rod and reel from your friend Mr. Gaunt, and all he can talk about is going fishing this weekend. I think he'll freeze his butt off—what little butt he has—but if Norris is happy, I'm happy. I was sorry as hell when Keeton rained on his parade yesterday. People make fun of Norris because he's skinny and sort of ditzy, but he's developed into a pretty good small-town peace officer over the past three years. And his feelings are as sensitive as anyone else's. It's not his fault that he looks like Don Knotts's half-brother."

"Ummmmm . . ."

Drifting. Drifting into some sweet darkness where there was no pain. Polly let herself go, and as sleep took her there was a small and catlike expression of satisfaction on her face.

7

For Alan, sleep was longer coming.

The interior voice had returned, but its tone of false glee was gone. Now it sounded questioning, plaintive, almost lost. *Where are we, Alan?* it asked. *Isn't this the wrong room? The wrong bed? The wrong woman? I don't seem to understand anything anymore.*

Alan suddenly found himself feeling pity for that voice. It was not self-pity, because the voice had never seemed so unlike his own as it did now. It occurred to him that the voice wanted to speak as little as he—the rest of him, the Alan existing in the present and the Alan planning for the future—wanted to hear it. It was the voice of duty, the voice of grief. And it was still the voice of guilt.

A little over two years ago, Annie Pangborn had begun having headaches. They weren't bad, or so she said; she was as loath to talk about them as Polly was to talk about her arthritis. Then, one day when he was shaving—very early in 1990, that must have been—Alan noticed that the cap had been left off the family-size bottle of Anacin 3 standing beside the bathroom sink. He started to put the cap back on . . . then stopped. He had taken a couple of aspirin from that bottle, which held two hundred and twenty-five caplets, late the week before. It had been almost full then. Now it was almost empty. He had wiped the remains of shaving cream from his face and gone down to You Sew and Sew, where Annie had worked since Polly Chalmers opened. He took his wife out for coffee . . . and a few questions. He asked her about the aspirin. He remembered being a little frightened.

(*only a little,* the interior voice agreed mournfully)

but only a little, because *nobody* takes a hundred and ninety aspirin caplets in a single week; *nobody.* Annie told him he was being silly. She had been wiping the counter beside the sink, she said, and had knocked the bottle over. The top hadn't been on tight and most of the caplets had poured into the sink. They'd started to melt, and she'd thrown them away.

She said.

But he was a cop, and even when he was off-duty he could not put away the automatic habits of observation which came with the territory. He could not turn off the lie detector. If you watched people when they answered the questions you asked, really *watched* them, you almost always knew when they were lying. Alan had once questioned a man who signalled every lie he told by picking at his eyetooth with his thumbnail. The mouth articulated the lies; the body, it seemed, was doomed to signal the truth. So he had stretched his hand across the table of the booth in Nan's where they had been sitting, had grasped Annie's hands in his own, and had asked her to tell the truth. And when, after a moment's hesitation, she told him that, yes, the headaches *were* a little worse, and yes, she *had* been taking quite a few aspirin, but no, she hadn't taken all the caplets which were missing, that the bottle really *had* spilled in the sink, he had believed her. He had fallen for the oldest trick in the book, the one con-men called bait-and-switch: if you tell a lie and get caught, back up and tell *half* the truth. If he had watched her more closely, he would have known Annie still wasn't being straight with him. He would have forced her to admit something which seemed nearly impossible to him, but which he now believed to be the truth: that the headaches were bad enough for her to be taking at least twenty aspirin a day. And if she had admitted *that,* he would have had her in a Portland or Boston neurologist's office before the week was out. But she was his wife, and in those days he had been less observant when he was off-duty.

He had contented himself with making an appointment for her with Ray Van Allen, and she had kept the appointment. Ray had found nothing, and Alan had never held that against him. Ray had run through the usual reflex tests, had looked into her eyes with his trusty ophthalmoscope, had tested her vision to see if there was any doubling, and had sent her to Oxford Regional for an X-ray. He had not, however, ordered a CAT scan, and when Annie said the headaches were gone, Ray had believed her. Alan suspected he might have been right to believe her. He knew that doctors are almost as attuned to the body's language of lies as cops. Patients are almost as apt to lie as suspects, and from the same motive: simple fear. And when Ray saw Annie, he had not been off-duty. So maybe, between the time Alan had made his discovery and the time Annie went to see Dr. Van Allen, the headaches had gone away. *Probably* they had gone away. Ray had told Alan later, in a long conversation over glasses of brandy at the doctor's Castle View home, that the symptoms often came and went in cases where the tumor was located high on the stem of the brain. "Seizures are often associated with stem tumors," he told Alan. "If she'd had a seizure, maybe . . ." And he had shrugged. Yes. Maybe. And maybe a man named Thad Beaumont was an unindicted co-conspirator in the deaths of his wife and son, but Alan could not find blame in his heart for Thad, either.

Not all the things which happen in small towns are known to the residents, no matter how sharp their ears are or how energetically their tongues wag. In Castle Rock they knew about Frank Dodd, the cop who went crazy and killed the women back in Sheriff Bannerman's day, and they knew about Cujo, the Saint Bernard who had gone rabid out on Town Road #3, and they knew that the lakeside home of Thad Beaumont, novelist and local Famous Person, had burned to the ground during the summer of 1989, but they did not know the circumstances of that burning, or that Beaumont had been haunted by a man who was really not a man at all, but a creature for which there may be no name. Alan Pangborn knew these things, however, and they still haunted his sleep from time to time. All that was over by the time Alan became fully aware of Annie's headaches . . . except it really *wasn't* over. By virtue of Thad's drunken phonecalls, Alan had become an unwilling witness to the crash of Thad's marriage and the steady erosion of the man's sanity. And there was the matter of his own sanity, as well. Alan had read an article in some doctor's office about black holes—great celestial empty places that seemed to be whirl-pools of anti-matter, voraciously sucking up everything within their reach. In the late summer and fall of 1989, the Beaumont affair had become Alan's own personal black hole. There were days when he found himself questioning the most elementary concepts of reality, and wondering if any of it had actually hap-pened. There were nights when he lay awake until dawn stained the east, afraid to go to sleep, afraid the dream would come: a black Toronado bearing down on him, a black Toronado with a decaying monster behind the wheel and a sticker reading HIGH-TONED SON OF A BITCH on the rear bumper. In those days, the sight of a single sparrow perched on the porch railing or hopping about on the lawn had made him feel like scream-ing. If asked, Alan would have said, "When Annie's trouble began, I was distracted." But it wasn't a matter of distraction; somewhere deep down inside of his mind he had been fighting a desperate battle to hold onto his sanity, HIGH-TONED SON OF A BITCH—how that came back to him. How it haunted him. That, and the sparrows.

He had still been distracted on the day in March when Annie and Todd had gotten into the old Scout they kept for around-town errands and had headed off to Hemphill's Mar-ket. Alan had gone over and over her behavior that morning, and could find nothing unusual about it, nothing out of the ordinary. He had been in his study when they left. He had looked out the window by his desk and waved goodbye. Todd had waved back before getting in the Scout. It was the last time he saw them alive. Three miles down Route 117 and less than a mile from Hemphill's, the Scout had veered off the road at high speed and had struck a tree. The State Police estimated from the wreckage that Annie, ordinarily the most careful of drivers, had been doing at least seventy. Todd had been wearing his seatbelt. Annie had not. She had probably been dead as soon as she went through the windshield, leaving one leg and half an arm behind. Todd might still have been alive when the ruptured gas-tank exploded. That preyed on Alan more than anything else. That his ten-year-old son, who wrote a joke astrology column for the school paper and lived for Little League, might have been alive. That he might have burned to death trying to work the clasp on his seatbelt.

There had been an autopsy. The autopsy revealed the brain tumor. It was, Van Allen told him, a small one. About the size of a peanut-cluster was how he put it. He did not tell Alan it would have been operable if it had been diagnosed; this was information Alan gleaned from Ray's miserable face and downcast eyes. Van Allen said he believed she had finally had the seizure which would have alerted them to the real problem if it had come sooner. It could have galvanized her body like a strong electric shock, causing her to jam the gas pedal to the floor and lose control. He did not tell Alan these things of his own free will; he told them because Alan interrogated him mercilessly, and because Van Allen saw that, grief or no grief, Alan meant to have the truth . . . or as much of it as he, or anyone who hadn't actually been in the car that day, could ever know. "Please," Van Allen had said, and touched Alan's hand briefly and kindly. "It was a terrible accident, but that's *all* it was. You have to let it go. You have another son, and he needs you now as much as you need him. You have to let it go and get on with your affairs." He had tried. The irrational horror of the business with Thad Beaumont, the business with the

(*sparrows the sparrows are flying*)

birds, had begun to fade, and he had honestly tried to put his life back together—widower, small-town cop, father of a teenaged boy who was growing up and growing away too fast . . . not because of Polly but because of the accident. Because of that horrible, numbing trauma: *Son, I've got some awful news; you've got to brace yourself* . . . And then, of course, he had begun to cry, and before long, Al had been crying, too.

Nonetheless, they had gone about the business of reconstruction, and were *still* going about it. Things were better these days . . . but two things refused to go away.

One was that huge bottle of aspirin, almost empty after only a week.

The other was the fact that Annie hadn't been wearing her seatbelt.

But Annie *always* wore her seatbelt.

After three weeks of agonizing and sleepless nights, he made an appointment with a neurologist in Portland after all, thinking of stolen horses and barn doors locked after the fact as he did it. He went because the man might have better answers to the questions Alan needed to ask, and because he was tired of dragging answers out of Ray Van Allen with a chainfall. The doctor's name was Scopes, and for the first time in his life, Alan hid behind his job: he told Scopes that his questions were related to an ongoing police investigation. The doctor confirmed Alan's central suspicions: yes, people with brain tumors sometimes suffered bursts of irrationality, and they sometimes became suicidal. When a person with a brain tumor committed suicide, Scopes said, the act was often committed on impulse, after a period of consideration which might last a minute or even seconds. Might such a person take someone with them? Alan asked.

Scopes was seated, behind his desk, cocked back in his chair with his hands laced behind his neck, and could not see Alan's own hands, which were clasped so tightly together between his knees that the fingers were dead white. Oh yes, Scopes said. That was a not uncommon pattern in such cases; tumors of the brain stem often caused behaviors the layman might think of as psychotic. One was a conclusion that the misery which the sufferer feels is a misery which is shared by either his loved ones or the whole human race; another was the idea

that the sufferer's loved ones would not want to live if he was
dead. Scopes mentioned Charles Whitman, the Eagle Scout
who had climbed to the top of the Texas Tower and killed more
than two dozen people before making an end to himself, and
a substitute grammar-school teacher in Illinois who had killed
several of her students before going home and putting a bullet
in her own brain. Autopsies had revealed brain tumors in both
cases. It was a pattern, but not one which held true in all cases,
or even most of them. Brain tumors sometimes caused odd,
even exotic symptoms; sometimes they caused no symptoms at
all. It was impossible to say for sure.

Impossible. So let it alone.

Good advice, but hard to swallow. Because of the aspirin
bottle. And the seatbelt.

Mostly it was the seatbelt that hung in the back of Alan's
mind—a small black cloud that simply wouldn't go away. She
never drove without buckling it. Not even down to the end of
the block and back. Todd had been wearing his, just like always, though. Didn't that mean something? If she had decided,
sometime after she had backed down the driveway for the
last time, to kill herself and take Todd with her, wouldn't she
have insisted that Todd unbuckle his belt as well? Even hurt,
depressed, confused, she wouldn't have wanted Todd to suffer,
would she?

Impossible to say for sure. Let it alone.

Yet even now, lying here in Polly's bed with Polly sleeping
beside him, he found it hard advice to take. His mind went
back to work on it, like a puppy worrying an old and ragged
strip of rawhide with its sharp little teeth.

An image had always come to him at this point, a nightmar-
ish image which had finally driven him to Polly Chalmers,
because Polly was the woman Annie had been closest to in
town—and, considering the Beaumont business and the psychic toll it had taken on Alan, Polly had probably been there for
Annie more than he had during the last few months of her life.

The image was of Annie unbuckling her own seatbelt, jamming the gas pedal to the floor, and taking her hands off the wheel. Taking them off the wheel because she had another job for them in those last few seconds.

Taking them off so she could unbuckle Todd's belt, as well.

That was the image: the Scout roaring down the road at seventy, veering to the right, veering toward the trees under a white March sky that promised rain, while Annie struggled to unbuckle Todd's belt and Todd, screaming and afraid, struggled to beat her hands away. He saw Annie's well-loved face transformed into the haglike mask of a witch, saw Todd's drawn long with terror. Sometimes he woke in the middle of the night, his body dressed in a clammy jacket of sweat, with Todd's voice ringing in his ears: *The trees, Mommy! Look out for the* TREEEES!

So he had gone to see Polly one day at closing time, and asked her if she would come up to the house for a drink, or, if she felt uncomfortable about doing that, if he could come over to her house.

Seated in his kitchen (*the right kitchen,* the interior voice asserted) with a mug of tea for her and coffee for him, he had begun to speak, slowly and stumblingly, of his nightmare.

"I need to know, if I can, if she was going through periods of depression or irrationality that I either didn't know about or didn't notice," he said. "I need to know if . . ." He stopped, momentarily helpless. He knew what words he needed to say, but it was becoming harder and harder to bring them out. It was as if the channel of communication between his unhappy, confused mind and his mouth was growing smaller and shallower, and would soon be entirely closed to shipping.

He made a great effort and went on.

"I need to know if she was suicidal. Because, you see, it wasn't just Annie who died. Todd died with her, and if there were sighs . . . signs, I mean, *signs* . . . that I didn't notice, then I am responsible for his death, too. And that's something I feel I have to know."

He had stopped there, his heart pounding dully in his chest. He wiped a hand over his forehead and was mildly surprised when it came away wet with sweat.

"Alan," she said, and put a hand on his wrist. Her light-blue eyes looked steadily into his. "If I had seen such signs and hadn't told anyone, I would be as guilty as you seem to want to be."

He had gaped at her, he remembered that. Polly might have seen something in Annie's behavior which he had missed; he had gotten that far in his reasoning. The idea that noticing strange behavior conveyed a responsibility to do something about it had never occurred to him until now.

"You didn't?" he asked at last.

"No. I've gone over it and over it in my mind. I don't mean to belittle your grief and loss, but you're not the only one who feels those things, and you're not the only one who has done a fair amount of soul-searching since Annie's accident. I went over those last few weeks until I was dizzy, replaying scenes and conversations in light of what the autopsy showed. I'm doing it again now, in light of what you've told me about that aspirin bottle. And do you know what I find?"

"What?"

"Zilch." She said it with a lack of emphasis which was oddly convincing. "Nothing at all. There were times when I thought she looked a little pale. I can remember a couple of occasions when I heard her talking to herself while she was hemming skirts or unpacking fabric. That's the most eccentric behavior I can recall, and I've been guilty of it myself many times. How about you?"

Alan nodded.

"Mostly she was the way she was ever since I first met her: cheerful, friendly, helpful . . . a good friend."

"But—"

Her hand was still on his wrist; it tightened a little. "No, Alan. No buts. Ray Van Allen is doing it, too, you know—

Monday-morning quarterbacking, I believe it's called. Do you blame *him?* Do you feel *Ray's* to blame for missing the tumor?"

"No, but—"

"What about me? I worked with her every day, side by side most of the time; we drank coffee together at ten, ate lunch together at noon, and drank coffee again at three. We talked very frankly as time went on and we got to know and like each other, Alan. I know you pleased her, both as a friend and as a lover, and I know she loved the boys. But if she was drifting toward suicide as the result of her illness . . . that I didn't know. So tell me—do you blame *me?*" And her clear blue eyes had looked frankly and curiously into his own.

"No, but—"

The hand squeezed again, light but commanding.

"I want to ask you something. It's important, so think carefully."

He nodded.

"Ray was her doctor, and if it was there, he didn't see it. I was her friend, and if it was there, I didn't see it. You were her husband, and if it was there, *you* didn't see it, either. And you think that's all, that's the end of the line, but it's not."

"I don't understand what you're getting at."

"Someone else was close to her," Polly had said. "Someone closer than either of us, I imagine."

"Who are you talking ab—"

"Alan, what did *Todd* say?"

He could only gaze at her, not understanding. He felt as if she had spoken a word in a foreign tongue.

"*Todd,*" she said, sounding impatient. "Todd, your *son.* The one who keeps you awake nights. It *is* him, isn't it? Not her, but him."

"Yes," he said. "Him." His voice came out high and unsteady, not like his own voice at all, and he felt something starting to shift inside him, something large and fundamental. Now, lying here in Polly's bed, he could remember that moment at his kitchen table with almost supernatural clarity: her hand on his wrist in a slanting bar of late-afternoon sun, the hairs a fine spun gold; her light eyes; her gentle relentlessness.

"Did she force Todd into the car, Alan? Was he kicking? Screaming? Fighting her?"

"No, of course not, but she was his m—"

"Whose idea was it for Todd to go with her to the market that day? Hers or his? Can you remember?"

He started to say no, but suddenly he did. Their voices, floating in from the living room, as he sat at his desk, going through county warrant-orders:

Gotta run down to the market, Todd—you want to come?

Can I look at the new video-tapes?

I guess so. Ask your father if he wants anything.

"It was her idea," he told Polly.

"Are you sure?"

"Yes. But she *asked* him. She didn't *tell* him."

That thing inside, that fundamental thing, was still moving. It was going to fall, he thought, and it would rip almighty hell out of the ground when it did, for its roots were planted both deep and wide.

"Was he scared of her?"

Now she was almost cross-examining him, the way he had cross-examined Ray Van Allen, but he seemed helpless to make her stop. Nor was he sure he wanted to. There was something here, all right, something that had never occurred to him on his long nights. Something that was still alive.

"Todd scared of Annie? God, no!"

"Not in the last few months they were alive?"

"No."

"In the last few weeks?"

"Polly, I wasn't in much condition to observe things then. There was this thing that happened with Thad Beaumont, the writer . . . this crazy thing—"

"Are you saying you were so out of it you never noticed

Annie and Todd when they were around, or that you weren't at home much, anyway?"

"No . . . yes . . . I mean of *course* I was home, but—"

It was an odd feeling, being on the receiving end of these rapid-fire questions. It was as if Polly had doped him with Novocain and then started using him for a punching bag. And that fundamental thing, whatever it was, was still in motion, still rolling out toward the boundary where gravitation would begin working not to hold it up but to pull it down.

"Did Todd ever come to you and say 'I'm scared of Mommy'?"

"No—"

"Did he ever come and say 'Daddy, I think Mommy's planning to kill herself, and take me along for company'?"

"Polly, that's ridiculous! I—"

"*Did* he?"

"*No!*"

"Did he ever even say she was acting or talking funny?"

"No—"

"And Al was away at school, right?"

"What does that have to do with—"

"She had one child left in the nest. When you were gone, working, it was just the two of them in that nest. She ate supper with him, helped him with his homework, watched TV with him—"

"Read to him—" he said. His voice was blurred, strange. He hardly recognized it.

"She was probably the first person Todd saw each morning and the last person he saw at night," Polly said. Her hand lay on his wrist. Her eyes looked earnestly into his. "If anyone was in a position to see it coming, it was the person who died with her. *And that person never said a word.*"

Suddenly the thing inside fell. His face began to work. He could feel it happening—it was as if strings had been attached to it in a score of different places, and each was now being tugged by a gentle but insistent hand. Heat flooded his throat and tried to close it. Heat flooded his face. His eyes filled with tears; Polly Chalmers doubled, trebled, and then broke into prisms of light and image. His chest heaved but his lungs seemed to find no air. His hand turned over with that scary quickness he had and clamped on hers—it must have hurt her terribly, but she made no sound.

"*I miss her!*" he cried out at Polly, and a great, painful sob broke the words into a pair of gasps. "*I miss them both, ah, God, how I miss them both!*"

"I know," Polly said calmly. "I know. That's what this is really all about, isn't it? How you miss them both."

He began to weep. Al had wept every night for two weeks, and Alan had been there to hold him and offer what comfort he could, but Alan had not cried himself. Now he did. The sobs took him and carried him just as they would; he had no power to stop or stay them. He could not moderate his grief, and at last found, with deep incoherent relief, that he had no urge to do so.

He pushed the coffee cup blindly aside, heard it hit the floor in some other world and shatter there. He laid his overheated, throbbing head on the table and wrapped his arms around it and wept.

At some point, he had felt her raise his head with her cool hands, her misshapen, kindly hands, and place it against her stomach. She held it there and he wept for a long, long time.

8

Her arm was slipping off his chest. Alan moved it gently, aware that if he bumped her hand even lightly, he would wake her. Looking at the ceiling, he wondered if Polly had deliberately provoked his grief that day. He rather thought she had, either knowing or intuiting that he needed to express his grief much more than he needed to find answers which were almost certainly not there anyway.

That had been the beginning between them, even though he had not recognized it as a beginning; it had felt more like the end of something. Between then and the day when he had finally mustered up enough courage to ask Polly to have dinner with him, he had thought often of the look of her blue eyes and the feel of her hand lying on his wrist. He thought of the gentle relentlessness with which she had forced him toward ideas he had either ignored or overlooked. And during that time he tried to deal with a new set of feelings about Annie's death; once the roadblock between him and his grief had been removed, these other feelings had poured out in a flood. Chief and most distressing among them had been a terrible rage at her for concealing a disease that could have been treated and cured . . . and for having taken their son with her that day. He had talked about some of these feelings with Polly at The Birches on a chilly, rain-swept night last April.

"You've stopped thinking about suicide and started thinking about murder," she'd said. "That's why you're angry, Alan."

He shook his head and started to speak, but she had leaned over the table and put one of her crooked fingers firmly against his lips for a moment. Shush, you. And the gesture so startled him that he *did* shush.

"Yes," she said. "I'm not going to catechize you this time, Alan—it's been a long time since I've been out to dinner with a man, and I'm enjoying it too much to play Ms. Chief Prosecutor. But people don't get angry at other people—not the way you're angry, at least—for being in accidents, unless there has been a big piece of carelessness involved. If Annie and Todd had died because the brakes in the Scout failed, you might blame yourself for not having had them checked, or you might sue Sonny Jackett for having done a sloppy job the last time you took it in for maintenance, but you wouldn't blame *her*. Isn't that true?"

"I guess it is."

"I *know* it is. Maybe there *was* an accident of some kind,

Alan. You know she might have had a seizure while she was driving, because Dr. Van Allen told you so. But has it ever occurred to you that she might have swerved to avoid a deer? That it might have been something as simple as that?"

It had. A deer, a bird, even an oncoming car that had wandered into her lane.

"Yes. But her seatbelt—"

"Oh, *forget* the goddam seatbelt!" she had said with such spirited vehemence that some of the diners close to them looked around briefly. "Maybe she had a headache, and it caused her to forget her seatbelt that one time, but that still doesn't mean she deliberately crashed the car. And a headache—one of her bad ones—would explain why Todd's belt *was* fastened. And it still isn't the point."

"What is, then?"

"That there are too many maybes here to support your anger. And even if the worst things you suspect are true, you'll never know, will you?"

"No."

"And if you *did* know . . ." She looked at him steadily. There was a candle on the table between them. Her eyes were a darker blue in its flame, and he could see a tiny spark of light in each one. "Well, a brain tumor is an accident, too. There is no culprit here, Alan, no—what do you call them in your line of work?—no perpetrator. Until you accept that, there will be no chance."

"What chance?"

"*Our* chance," she said calmly. "I like you very much, Alan, and I'm not too old to take a risk, but I'm old enough to have had some sad experience of where my emotions can lead me when they get out of control. I won't let them get anywhere close to that point until you're able to put Annie and Todd to rest."

He looked at her, speechless. She regarded him gravely over her dinner in the old country inn, firelight flickering orange on one of her smooth cheeks and the left side of her brow. Outside, the wind played a long trombone note under the eaves.

"Have I said too much?" Polly asked. "If I have, I'd like you to take me home, Alan. I hate to be embarrassed almost as much as I hate not speaking my mind."

He reached across the table and touched her hand briefly. "No, you haven't said too much. I like to listen to you, Polly."

She had smiled then. It lit up her whole face. "You'll get your chance, then," she said.

So it began for them. They had not felt guilty about seeing each other, but they had recognized the need to be careful—not just because it was a small town where he was an elected official and she needed the good will of the community to keep her business afloat, but because both of them recognized the possibility of guilt. Neither of them was too old to take a risk, it seemed, but they were both a little too old to be reckless. Care needed to be taken.

Then, in May, he had taken her to bed for the first time, and she had told him about all the years between Then and Now . . . the story he did not completely believe, the one he was convinced she would someday tell him again, without the too-direct eyes and the left hand that tugged too often at the left earlobe. He recognized how difficult it had been for her to tell him as much as she had, and was content to wait for the rest. *Had* to be content. Because care had to be taken. It was enough—quite enough—to fall in love with her as the long Maine summer drowsed past them.

Now, looking up at the pressed-tin ceiling of her bedroom in the dimness, he wondered if the time had come to talk about marriage again. He had tried once, in August, and she had made that gesture with her finger again. Shush, you. He supposed . . .

But his conscious train of thought began to break up then, and Alan slipped easily into sleep.

9

In his dream he was shopping in some mammoth store, wandering down an aisle so long it dwindled to a point in the distance. Everything was here, everything he had ever wanted but could not afford—a pressure-sensitive watch, a genuine felt fedora from Abercrombie & Fitch, a Bell and Howell eight-millimeter movie camera, hundreds of other items—but someone was behind him, just behind his shoulder where he couldn't see.

"Down here we call these things fool's stuffing, old hoss," a voice remarked.

It was one Alan knew. It belonged to that high-toned, Toronado-driving son of a bitch George Stark.

"We call this store Endsville," the voice said, "because it's the place where all goods and services terminate."

Alan saw a large snake—it looked like a python with the head of a rattler—come sliding out of a huge selection of Apple computers marked FREE TO THE PUBLIC. He turned to flee, but a hand with no lines on the palm gripped his arm and stopped him.

"Go on," the voice said persuasively. "Take what you want, hoss. Take *everything* you want . . . and pay for it."

But every item he picked up turned out to be his son's charred and melted beltbuckle.

CHAPTER EIGHT

1

Danforth Keeton did not have a brain tumor, but he *did* have a terrible headache as he sat in his office early Saturday morning. Spread out on his desk beside a stack of red-bound town tax ledgers for the years 1982 to 1989 was a sprawl of correspondence—letters from the State of Maine Bureau of Taxation and Xeroxes of letters he had written in reply.

Everything was starting to come down around his ears. He knew it, but he was helpless to do anything about it.

Keeton had made a trip to Lewiston late yesterday, had returned to The Rock around twelve-thirty in the morning, and had spent the rest of the night pacing his study restlessly while his wife slept the sleep of tranquilizers upstairs. He had found his gaze turning more and more often to the small closet in the corner of his study. There was a high shelf in the closet, stacked with sweaters. Most of the sweaters were old and motheaten. Under them was a carved wooden box his father had made long before the Alzheimer's had stolen over him like a shadow, robbing him of all his considerable skills and memories. There was a revolver in the box.

Keeton found himself thinking about the revolver more and more frequently. Not for himself, no; at least not at first. For Them. The Persecutors.

At quarter to six he had left the house and had driven the dawn-silent streets between his house and the Municipal Building. Eddie Warburton, a broom in his hand and a Chesterfield in his mouth (the solid-gold Saint Christopher's medal he had purchased at Needful Things the day before was safely hidden under his blue chambray shirt), had watched him trudge up the stairs to the second floor. Not a word passed between the two men. Eddie had become used to Keeton's appearances at odd hours over the last year or so, and Keeton had long ago ceased seeing Eddie at all.

Now Keeton swept the papers together, fought an impulse to simply rip them to shreds and fling the pieces everywhere, and began to sort through them. Bureau of Taxation correspondence in one pile, his own replies in another. He kept these letters in the bottom drawer of his filing cabinet—a drawer to which only he had the key.

At the bottom of most of the letters was this notation: DK/sl. DK was, of course, Danforth Keeton. sl was Shirley Laurence, his secretary, who took dictation and typed correspondence. Shirley had typed none of his responses to the Bureau's letters, however, initials or no initials.

It was wiser to keep some things to yourself.

A phrase jumped out at him as he sorted: ". . . and we notice discrepancies in quarterly Town Tax Return 11 for the tax-year 1989 . . ."

He put it aside quickly.

Another: ". . . and in examining a sampling of Workmen's Compensation forms during the last quarter of 1987, we have serious questions concerning . . ."

Into the file.

Yet another: ". . . believe that your request for an examination deferral seems premature at this time . . ."

They blurred past him in a sickening swoop, making him feel as if he were on an out-of-control carnival ride.

". . . questions about these tree-farm funds are . . ."

". . . we find no record that the Town has filed . . ."

". . . dispersal of the State's share of funding has not been adequately documented . . ."

". . . missing expense-account receipts must be . . ."

". . . cash slips are not sufficient for . . ."

". . . may request complete documentation of expenses . . ."

And now this last, which had come yesterday. Which had in turn driven him to Lewiston, where he had vowed to never again go during harness-racing season, last night.

Keeton stared at it bleakly. His head pounded and throbbed; a large drop of sweat rolled slowly down the center of his back. There were dark, exhausted circles under his eyes. A cold sore clung to one corner of his mouth.

BUREAU OF TAXATION
State House
Augusta, Maine 04330

The letterhead, below the State Seal, screamed at him, and the salutation, which was cold and formal, threatened:

To the Selectmen of Castle Rock.

Just that. No more "Dear Dan" or "Dear Mr. Keeton." No more good wishes for his family at the closing. The letter was as cold and hateful as the stab of an icepick.

They wanted to audit the town books.

All the town books.

Town tax records, State and Federal revenue-sharing records, town expense records, road-maintenance records, municipal law-enforcement budgets, Parks Department budgets, even financial records pertaining to the State-funded experimental tree farm.

They wanted to see everything, and They wanted to see it on the 17th of October. That was only five days from now.

They.

The letter was signed by the State Treasurer, the State Auditor, and, even more ominous, by the Attorney General—Maine's top cop. And these were personal signatures, not reproductions.

"*They,*" Keeton whispered at the letter. He shook it in his fist and it rattled softly. He bared his teeth at it. "*Theyyyyyyy!*"

He slammed the letter down on top of the others. He closed the file. Typed neatly on the tab was CORRESPONDENCE, MAINE BUREAU OF TAXATION. Keeton stared at the closed file for a moment. Then he snatched a pen from its holder (the set had been a gift from the Castle County Jaycees) and slashed the words MAINE BUREAU OF KAKA! across the file in large, trembling letters. He stared at it a moment and then wrote MAINE BUREAU OF ASSHOLES! below it. He held the pen in his closed fist, wielding it like a knife. Then he threw it across the room. It landed in the corner with a small clatter.

Keeton closed the other file, the one which contained copies of letters he had written himself (and to which he always added his secretary's lower-case initials), letters he had concocted on long, sleepless nights, letters which had ultimately proved fruitless. A vein pulsed steadily in the center of his forehead.

He got up, took the two files over to the cabinet, put them in the bottom drawer, slammed it shut, checked to make sure it was locked. Then he went to the window and stood looking out over the sleeping town, taking deep breaths and trying to calm himself.

They had it in for him. The Persecutors. He found himself wondering for the thousandth time who had sicced Them on him in the first place. If he could find that person, that dirty Chief Persecutor, Keeton would take the gun from where it lay in its box under the motheaten sweaters and put an end to him. He would not do it quickly, however. Oh no. He would shoot off a piece at a time and make the dirty bastard sing the National Anthem while he did it.

His mind turned to the skinny deputy, Ridgewick. Could it have been him? He didn't seem bright enough . . . but looks could be deceiving. Pangborn said Ridgewick had ticketed the Cadillac on his orders, but that didn't make it true. And in the men's room, when Ridgewick had called him Buster, there had been a look of knowing, jeering contempt in his eyes. Had Ridgewick been around when the first letters from the Bureau of

Taxation began to come in? Keeton was quite sure he had been. Later today he would look up the man's employment record, just to be sure.

What about Pangborn himself? *He* was certainly bright enough, he most certainly hated Danforth Keeton (didn't They all? didn't They all hate him?), and Pangborn knew lots of people in Augusta. He knew Them well. Hell, he was on the phone to Them every fucking *day*, it seemed. The phone bills, even with the WATS line, were horrible.

Could it be both of them? Pangborn *and* Ridgewick?

In on it together?

"The Lone Ranger and his faithful Indian companion, Tonto," Keeton said in a low voice, and smiled balefully. "If it was you, Pangborn, you'll be sorry. And if it was both of you, you'll *both* be sorry," His hands slowly rolled themselves into fists. "I won't stand this persecution forever, you know."

His carefully manicured nails cut into the flesh of his palms. He did not notice the blood when it began to flow. Maybe Ridgewick. Maybe Pangborn, maybe Melissa Clutterbuck, the frigid bitch who was the Town Treasurer, maybe Bill Fullerton, the Second Selectman (he knew for a fact that Fullerton wanted his job and wouldn't rest until he had it) . . .

Maybe *all* of them.

All of them together.

Keeton let out his breath in a long, tortured sigh, making a fog-flower on the wire-reinforced glass of his office window. The question was, what was he going to do about it? Between now and the 17th of the month, what was he going to *do?*

The answer was simple: he didn't know.

2

Danforth Keeton's life as a young man had been a thing of clear blacks and whites, and he had liked that just fine. He had gone to Castle Rock High School and began working part-time at the family car dealership when he was fourteen, washing the demonstrators and waxing the showroom models. Keeton Chevrolet was one of the oldest Chevrolet franchises in New England and keystone of the Keeton financial structure. That had been a solid structure indeed, at least until fairly recently.

During his four years at Castle Rock High, he had been Buster to just about everyone. He took the commercial courses, maintained a solid B average, ran the student council almost single-handed, and went on to Traynor Business College in Boston. He made straight A's at Traynor and graduated three semesters early. When he came back to The Rock, he quickly made it clear that his Buster days were over.

It had been a fine life until the trip he and Steve Frazier had made to Lewiston nine or ten years ago. That was when the trouble had started; that was when his neat black-and-white life began to fill with deepening shades of gray.

He had never gambled—not as Buster at C.R.H.S., not as Dan at Traynor Business, not as Mr. Keeton of Keeton Chevrolet and the Board of Selectmen. As far as Keeton knew, no one in his whole family had gambled; he could not remember even such innocent pastimes as nickel skat or pitching pennies. There was no taboo against these things, no *thou shalt not,* but no one did them. Keeton had not laid down a bet on anything until that first trip to Lewiston Raceway with Steve Frazier. He had never placed a bet anywhere else, nor did he need to. Lewiston Raceway was all the ruin Danforth Keeton ever needed.

He had been Third Selectman then. Steve Frazier, now at least five years in his grave, had been Castle Rock's Head Selectman. Keeton and Frazier had gone "up the city" (trips to Lewiston were always referred to in this way) along with Butch Nedeau, The Rock's overseer of County Social Services, and Harry Samuels, who had been a Selectman for most of his adult life and would probably die as one. The occasion had been a statewide conference of county officials;

the subject had been the new revenue-sharing laws . . . and it was revenue-sharing, of course, that had caused most of his trouble. Without it, Keeton would have been forced to dig his grave with a pick and shovel. With it, he had been able to use a financial bucket-loader.

It was a two-day conference. On the evening between, Steve had suggested they go out and have a little fun in the big city. Butch and Harry had declined. Keeton had no interest in spending the evening with Steve Frazier, either—he was a fat old blowhard with lard for brains. He had gone, though. He supposed he would have gone if Steve had suggested they spend the evening touring the deepest shitpits of hell. Steve was, after all, the Head Selectman. Harry Samuels would be content to drone along as Second, Third, or Fourth Selectman for the rest of his life, Butch Nedeau had already indicated that he meant to step down after his current term . . . but Danforth Keeton had ambitions, and Frazier, fat old blowhard or not, was the key to them.

So they had gone out, stopping first at The Holly, BE JOLLY AT THE HOLLY! read the motto over the door, and Frazier had gotten very jolly indeed, drinking Scotch-and-waters as if the Scotch had been left out of them, and whistling at the strippers, who were mostly fat and mostly old and always slow. Keeton thought most of them looked stoned. He remembered thinking it was going to be a long evening.

Then they had gone to the Lewiston Raceway and everything changed.

They got there in time for the fifth pace, and Frazier had hustled a protesting Keeton over to the betting windows like a sheepdog nipping a wayward lamb back to the herd.

"Steve, I don't know anything about this—"

"*That* doesn't matter," Frazier replied happily, breathing Scotch fumes into Keeton's face. "We're gonna be lucky tonight, Buster. I can feel it."

He hadn't any idea of how to bet, and Frazier's constant

chatter made it hard to listen to what the other bettors in line were saying when they got to the two-dollar window.

When he got there, he pushed a five-dollar bill across to the teller and said, "Number four."

"Win, place, or show?" the teller asked, but for a moment Keeton had not been able to reply. Behind the teller he saw an amazing thing. Three clerks were counting and banding huge piles of currency, more cash than Keeton had ever seen in one place.

"Win, place, or show?" the teller repeated impatiently. "Hurry up, buddy. This is not the Public Library."

"Win," Keeton had said. He hadn't the slightest idea what "place" and "show" meant, but "win" he understood very well.

The teller thrust him a ticket and three dollars' change—a one and a two. Keeton looked at the two with curious interest as Frazier placed his bet. He had known there *were* such things as two-dollar bills, of course, but he didn't think he'd ever *seen* one before. Thomas Jefferson was on it. Interesting. In fact, the whole thing was interesting—the smells of horses, popcorn, peanuts; the hurrying crowds; the atmosphere of urgency. The place was *awake* in a way he recognized and responded to at once. He had felt this sort of wakefulness in himself before, yes, many times, but it was the first time he had ever sensed it in the wider world. Danforth "Buster" Keeton, who rarely felt a part of anything, not really, felt he was a part of this. Very much a part.

"This beats hell out of The Holly," he said as Frazier rejoined him.

"Yeah, harness racing's okay," Frazier said. "It won't ever re-place the World Series, but you know. Come on, let's get over to the rail. Which horse did you bet on?"

Keeton didn't remember. He'd had to check his ticket. "Number four," he said.

"Place or show?"

"Uh . . . win."

Frazier shook his head in good-natured contempt and clapped him on the shoulder. "Win's a sucker bet, Buster, It's a sucker bet even when the tote-board says it isn't. But you'll learn."

And, of course, he had.

Somewhere a bell went off with a loud *Brrrrrrannggg!* that made Keeton jump. A voice bellowed, *"And theyyy'rrre OFF!"* through the Raceway's speakers. A thunderous roar went up from the crowd, and Keeton had felt a sudden spurt of electricity course through his body. Hooves tattooed the dirt track. Frazier grabbed Keeton's elbow with one hand and used the other to make a path through the crowd to the rail. They came out less than twenty yards from the finish line.

Now the announcer was calling the race. Number seven, My Lass, leading at the first turn, with number eight, Broken Field, second, and number one, How Do?, third. Number four was named Absolutely—the dumbest name for a horse Keeton had ever heard in his life—and it was running sixth. He hardly cared. He was transfixed by the pelting horses, their coats gleaming under the floodlights, by the blur of wheels as the sulkies swept around the turn, the bright colors of the silks worn by the drivers.

As the horses entered the backstretch, Broken Field began to press My Lass for the lead. My Lass broke stride and Broken Field flew by her. At the same time, Absolutely began to move up on the outside—Keeton saw it before the disembodied voice of the announcer sent the news blaring across the track, and he barely felt Frazier elbowing him, barely heard him screaming, "That's your horse, Buster! That's your horse *and she's got a chance!"*

As the horses thundered down the final straightaway toward the place where Keeton and Frazier were standing, the entire crowd began to bellow. Keeton had felt the electricity whip through him again, not a spark this time but a storm. He began to bellow with them; the next day he would be so hoarse he could barely speak above a whisper.

"Absolutely!" he screamed. *"Come on Absolutely, come on you bitch and RUN!"*

"Trot," Frazier said, laughing so hard tears ran down his cheeks. "Come on you bitch and *trot.* That's what you mean, Buster."

Keeton paid no attention. He was in another world. He was sending brain-waves out to Absolutely, sending her telepathic strength through the air.

"Now it's Broken Field and How Do?, How Do? and Broken Field," the godlike voice of the announcer chanted, "and Absolutely is gaining fast as they come to the last eighth of a mile—"

The horses approached, raising a cloud of dust. Absolutely trotted with her neck arched and her head thrust forward, legs rising and falling like pistons; she passed How Do? and Broken Field, who was flagging badly, right where Keeton and Frazier were standing. She was still widening her lead when she crossed the finish line.

When the numbers went up on the tote-board, Keeton had to ask Frazier what they meant. Frazier had looked at his ticket, then at the board. He whistled soundlessly.

"Did I make my money back?" Keeton asked anxiously.

"Buster, you did a little better than that. Absolutely was a thirty-to-one shot."

Before he left the track that night, Keeton had made just over three hundred dollars. That was how his obsession was born.

3

He took his overcoat from the tree in the corner of his office, drew it on, started to leave, then stopped, holding the door-knob in his hand. He looked back across the room. There was a mirror on the wall opposite the window. Keeton looked at it for a long, speculative moment, then walked across to it. He had heard about how They used mirrors—he hadn't been born yesterday.

He put his face against it, ignoring the reflection of his pallid skin and bloodshot eyes. He cupped a hand to either cheek, cutting off the glare, narrowing his eyes, looking for a camera on the other side. Looking for Them.

He saw nothing.

After a long moment he stepped away, swabbed indifferently at the smeared glass with the sleeve of his overcoat, and left the office. Nothing *yet,* anyway. That didn't mean They wouldn't come in tonight, pull out his mirror, and replace it with one-way glass. Spying was just another tool of the trade for the Persecutors. He would have to check the mirror every day now.

"But I can," he said to the empty upstairs hallway. "I can do that. Believe me."

Eddie Warburton was mopping the lobby floor and didn't look up as Keeton stepped out onto the street.

His car was parked around back, but he didn't feel like driving. He felt too confused to drive; he would probably put the Caddy through someone's store window if he tried. Nor was he aware, in the depths of his confused mind, that he was walking away from his house rather than toward it. It was seven-fifteen on Saturday morning, and he was the only person out in Castle Rock's small business district.

His mind went briefly back to that first night at Lewiston Raceway. He couldn't do anything wrong, it seemed. Steve Frazier had lost thirty dollars and said he was leaving after the ninth race. Keeton said he thought he would stay awhile longer. He barely looked at Frazier, and barely noticed when Frazier was gone. He did remember thinking it was nice not to have someone at his elbow saying Buster This and Buster That all the time. He hated the nickname, and of course Steve knew it—that was why he used it.

The next week he had come back again, alone this time,

and had lost sixty dollars' worth of previous winnings. He hardly cared. Although he thought often of those huge stacks of banded currency, it wasn't the money, not really; the money was just the symbol you took away with you, something that said you had been there, that you had been, however briefly, part of the big show. What he really cared about was the tremendous, walloping excitement that went through the crowd when the starter's bell rang, the gates opened with their heavy, crunching thud, and the announcer yelled, *"Theyyy'rrre OFF!"* What he cared about was the roar of the crowd as the pack rounded the third turn and went hell-for-election down the backstretch, the hysterical camp-meeting exhortations from the stands as they rounded the fourth turn and poured on the coal down the homestretch. It was alive, oh, it was so alive. It was so alive that—

—that it was dangerous.

Keeton decided he'd better stay away. He had the course of his life neatly planned. He intended to become Castle Rock's Head Selectman when Steve Frazier finally pulled the pin, and after six or seven years of that, he intended to stand for the State House of Representatives. After that, who knew? National office was not out of reach for a man who was ambitious, capable . . . and sane.

That was the *real* trouble with the track. He hadn't recognized it at first, but he had recognized it soon enough. The track was a place where people paid their money, took a ticket . . . and gave up their sanity for a little while. Keeton had seen too much insanity in his own family to feel comfortable with the attraction Lewiston Raceway held for him. It was a pit with greasy sides, a snare with hidden teeth, a loaded gun with the safety removed. When he went, he was unable to leave until the last race of the evening had been run. He knew. He had tried. Once he had made it almost all the way to the exit turnstiles before something in the back of his brain, something powerful, enigmatic, and reptilian, had arisen, taken control, and turned his feet around. Keeton was terrified of fully waking that reptile. Better to let it sleep.

For three years he had done just that. Then, in 1984, Steve Frazier had retired, and Keeton had been elected Head Selectman. That was when his real troubles began.

He had gone to the track to celebrate his victory, and since he was celebrating, he decided to go whole hog. He bypassed the two- and five-dollar windows, and went straight to the ten-dollar window. He had lost a hundred and sixty dollars that night, more than he felt comfortable losing (he told his wife the next day that it had been forty), but not more than he could *afford* to lose. Absolutely not.

He returned a week later, meaning to win back what he had lost so he could quit evens. And he had almost made it. *Almost*—that was the key word. The way he had almost made it to the exit turnstiles. The week after, he had lost two hundred and ten dollars. That left a hole in the checking account Myrtle would notice, and so he had borrowed a little bit from the town's petty-cash fund to cover the worst of the shortfall. A hundred dollars. Peanuts, really.

Past that point, it all began to blur together. The pit had greased sides, all right, and once you started sliding you were doomed. You could expend your energy clawing at the sides and succeed in slowing your fall . . . but that, of course, only drew out the agony.

If there had been a point of no return, it had been the summer of 1989. The pacers ran nightly during the summer, and Keeton was in attendance constantly through the second half of July and all of August. Myrtle had thought for a while that he was using the racetrack as an excuse, that he was actually seeing another woman, and that was a laugh—it really was. Keeton couldn't have got a hard-on if Diana herself had driven down from the moon in her chariot with her toga open and a FUCK ME DANFORTH sign hung around her neck. The thought of how deep he'd dipped into the town treasury had caused his poor dick to shrivel to the size of a pencil eraser.

When Myrtle finally became convinced of the truth, that it was only horse racing after all, she had been relieved. It kept him out of the house, where he tended to be something of a tyrant, and he couldn't be losing too badly, she had reasoned, because the checkbook balance didn't fluctuate that much. It was just that Danforth had found a hobby to keep him amused in his middle age.

Only horse racing after all, Keeton thought as he walked down Main Street with his hands plunged deep into his overcoat pockets. He uttered a strange, wild laugh that would have turned heads if there had been anyone on the street. Myrtle kept her eye on the checking account. The thought that Danforth might have plundered the T-bills which were their life savings never occurred to her. Likewise, the knowledge that Keeton Chevrolet was tottering on the edge of extinction belonged to him alone.

She balanced the checkbook and the house accounts.

He was a CPA.

When it comes to embezzlement, a CPA can do a better job than most . . . but in the end the package always comes undone. The string and tape and wrapping paper on Keeton's package had begun to fall apart in the autumn of 1990. He had held things together as well as he could, hoping to recoup at the track. By then he had found a bookie, which enabled him to make bigger bets than the track would handle.

It hadn't changed his luck, however.

And then, this summer, the persecution had begun in earnest. Before, They had only been toying with him. Now They were moving in for the kill, and the Day of Armageddon was less than a week away.

I'll get Them, Keeton thought. *I'm not done yet. I've still got a trick or two up my sleeve.*

He didn't know what those tricks were, though; that was the trouble.

Never mind. There's a way. I know there's a w—

Here his thoughts ceased. He was standing in front of the new store, Needful Things, and what he saw in the window drove everything else slap out of his mind for a moment or two.

It was a rectangular cardboard box, brightly colored, with a picture on the front. A board game, he supposed. But it was a board game about horse racing, and he could have sworn that the painting, which showed two pacers sweeping down on the finish line neck-and-neck, was of the Lewiston Raceway. If that wasn't the main grandstand in the background, he was a monkey.

The name of the game was WINNING TICKET.

Keeton stood looking at it for almost five minutes, as hypnotized as a kid looking at a display of electric trains. Then, slowly, he walked under the dark-green canopy to see if the place kept Saturday hours. There was a sign hanging inside the door, all right, but it bore only one word, and the word, naturally, was

OPEN.

Keeton looked at it for a moment, thinking—as Brian Rusk had before him—that it must have been left there by mistake. Main Street shops didn't open at seven in Castle Rock, especially not on Saturday morning. All the same, he tried the knob. It turned easily in his hand.

As he opened the door, a small silver bell tinkled overhead.

4

"It's not really a game," Leland Gaunt was saying five minutes later, "you're wrong about that."

Keeton was seated in the plush high-backed chair where Nettie Cobb, Cyndi Rose Martin, Eddie Warburton, Everett Frankel, Myra Evans, and a good many other townsfolk had sat before him that week. He was drinking a cup of good Jamaican coffee. Gaunt, who seemed like one hell of a nice fellow for a flatlander, had insisted that he have one. Now Gaunt was leaning into his show window and carefully removing the box. He was dressed in a wine-colored smoking jacket, just as natty as you please, and not a hair out of place. He had told Keeton that he often opened at odd hours, because he was afflicted with insomnia.

"Ever since I was a young man," he had said with a rueful chuckle, "and that was many years ago." He looked fresh as a daisy to Keeton, however, except for his eyes—they were so bloodshot they looked as if red were actually their natural color.

Now he brought the box over and set it on a small table next to Keeton.

"The box was what caught my eye," Keeton said. "It looks quite a bit like the Lewiston Raceway. I go there once in awhile."

"You like a flutter, do you?" Gaunt asked with a smile.

Keeton was about to say he never bet, and changed his mind. The smile was not just friendly; it was a smile of commiseration, and he suddenly understood that he was in the presence of a fellow sufferer. Which just went to show how flaky he was getting around the edges, because when he had shaken Gaunt's hand, he'd felt a wave of revulsion so sudden and deep it had been like a muscle spasm. For that one moment he had been convinced that he had found his Chief Persecutor. He would have to watch that sort of thing; there was no sense going overboard.

"I have been known to wager," he said.

"Sadly, so have I," Gaunt said. His reddish eyes fixed upon Keeton's, and they shared a moment of perfect understanding . . . or so Keeton felt. "I've bet most of the tracks from the

Atlantic to the Pacific, and I'm quite sure the one on the box is Longacre Park, in San Diego. Gone, of course; there's a housing development there now."

"Oh," Keeton said.

"But let me show you this. I think you'll find it interesting."

He took the cover off the box, and carefully lifted out a tin raceway on a platform about three feet long and a foot and a half wide. It looked like toys Keeton had had as a child, the cheap ones made in Japan after the war. The track was a replica of a two-mile course. Eight narrow slots were set into it, and eight narrow tin horses stood behind the starting line. Each was mounted on a small tin post that poked out of its slot and was soldered to the horse's belly.

"Wow," Keeton said, and grinned. It was the first time he'd grinned in weeks, and the expression felt strange and out of place.

"You ain't seen nuthin yet, as the man said," Gaunt replied, grinning back. "This baby goes back to 1930 or '35, Mr. Keeton—it's a real antique. But it wasn't just a toy to the racing touts of the day."

"No?"

"No. Do you know what a Ouija board is?"

"Sure. You ask it questions and it's supposed to spell out answers from the spirit world."

"Exactly. Well, back in the Depression, there were a lot of racing touts who believed that Winning Ticket was the horse-player's Ouija board."

His eyes met Keeton's again, friendly, smiling, and Keeton was as unable to draw his own eyes away as he had been to leave the track before the last race was run on the one occasion when he had tried.

"Silly, isn't it?"

"Yes," Keeton said. But it didn't seem silly at all. It seemed perfectly . . . perfectly . . .

Perfectly reasonable.

Gaunt felt around in the box and brought out a little, tin key. "A different horse wins each time. There's some sort of random mechanism inside, I suppose—crude but effective enough. Now watch."

He inserted the key in a hole on the side of the tin platform on which, the tin horses stood, and turned it. There were small clicks and clacks and ratchets—winding-up sounds. Gaunt removed the key when it wouldn't turn anymore.

"What's your pick?" he asked.

"The five," Keeton said. He leaned forward, his heart picking up speed. It was foolish—and the ultimate proof of his compulsion, he supposed—but he could feel all the old excitement sweeping through him.

"Very well, I pick the six-horse. Shall we have a little wager, just to make it interesting?"

"Sure! How much?"

"Not money," Gaunt said. "My days of betting for money ended long ago, Mr. Keeton. They are the least interesting wagers of all. Let's say this: if your horse wins, I'll do you a little favor. Your choice. If mine wins, you have to do *me* a favor."

"And if another one wins, all bets are off?"

"Right. Are you ready?"

"Ayup," Keeton said tightly, and leaned close to the tin racecourse. His hands were clamped together between his large thighs.

There was a small metal lever sticking out of a slot by the starting line. "And they're off," Gaunt said softly, and pushed it.

The cogs and gears below the race-course began to grind. The horses moved away from the starting line, sliding along their appointed courses. They went slowly at first, wavering back and forth in the slots and progressing in little jerks as some mainspring—or a whole series of them—expanded inside the board, but as they approached the first turn they began to pick up speed.

The two-horse took the lead, followed by the seven; the others were back in the pack.

"Come on, five!" Keeton cried softly. "Come on five, pull, you bitch!"

As if hearing him, the small tin steed began to draw away from the pack. At the half, it had caught up with the seven. The six-horse—Gaunt's pick—had also begun to show some speed.

Winning Ticket rattled and vibrated on the small table. Keeton's face hung over it like a large, flawed moon. A drop of sweat fell on the tiny tin jockey piloting the three-horse; if he had been a real man, both he and his mount would have been drenched.

At the third turn the seven-horse put on a burst of speed and caught the two, but Keeton's five-horse was hanging on for dear life, and Gaunt's six was at its heels. These four rounded the turn in a bunch well ahead of the others, vibrating wildly in their slots.

"*Go you stupid bitch!*" Keeton yelled. He had forgotten that they were merely pieces of tin fashioned into the crude like-nesses of horses. He had forgotten he was in the shop of a man he had never met before. The old excitement had him. It shook him the way a terrier shakes a rat. "*Go on and go for it! Pull, you bitch, PULL! Pour it ON!*"

Now the five pulled even for the lead . . . and drew ahead. Gaunt's horse was moving up on its flank when Keeton's horse crossed the finish line, a winner.

The mechanism was running down, but most of the horses made it back around to the starting line before the clockwork ceased entirely. Gaunt used his finger to push the laggards up even with the others for another start.

"Whew!" Keeton said, and mopped his brow. He felt com-pletely wrung out . . . but he also felt better than he had in a long, long time. "That was pretty fine!"

"Fine as paint," Gaunt agreed.

"They knew how to make things in the old days, didn't they?"

"They did," Gaunt agreed, smiling. "And it looks as though I owe you a favor, Mr. Keeton."

"Aw, forget it—that was fun."

"No, indeed. A gentleman always pays his bets. Just let me know a day or two before you intend to call in your marker, as they say."

Before you call in your marker.

That brought it all crashing back on him. Markers! *They* held his! *They!* On Thursday They would call those markers home . . . and what then? What then?

Visions of damning newspaper headlines danced in his head.

"Would you like to know how the serious bettors of the thirties used this toy?" Gaunt asked softly.

"Sure," Keeton said, but he didn't care, not really . . . not until he looked up. Then Gaunt's eyes met his again, captured them again, and the idea of using a child's game to pick winners seemed to make perfect sense again.

"Well," Gaunt said, "they'd take that day's newspaper or *Racing Form* and run the races, one by one. On this board, you know. They would give each horse in each race a name from the paper—they'd do it by touching one of the tin horses and saying the name at the same time—and then wind the thing up and let it go. They'd ran the whole slate that way—eight, ten, a dozen races. Then they'd go to the track and bet on the horses that won at home."

"Did it work?" Keeton asked. His voice seemed to be coming to him from some other place. A far place. He seemed to be floating in Leland Gaunt's eyes. Floating on red foam. The sensation was queer but really quite pleasant.

"It seemed to," Gaunt said. "Probably just silly superstition, but . . . would you like to buy this toy and try it for yourself?"

"Yes," Keeton said.

"You're a man who needs a Winning Ticket quite badly, aren't you, Danforth?"

"I need more than one. I need a whole slew of them. How much?"

Leland Gaunt laughed. "Oh no—you don't get me *that* way! Not when I am already in your debt! I'll tell you what—open your wallet and give me the first bill you find in there. I'm sure it will be the right one."

So Keeton opened his wallet and drew out a bill without looking away from Gaunt's face, and of course it was the one with Thomas Jefferson's face on it—the kind of bill which had gotten him into all this trouble in the first place.

5

Gaunt made it disappear as neatly as a magician doing a trick and said: "There *is* one more thing."

"What?"

Gaunt leaned forward. He looked at Keeton earnestly, and touched him on the knee. "Mr. Keeton, do you know about . . . Them?"

Keeton's breath caught, the way the breath of a sleeper will sometimes catch when he finds himself in the throes of a bad dream. "Yes," he whispered. "God, yes."

"This town is full of Them," Gaunt went on in the same low, confidential tone. "Absolutely *infested*. I've been open less than a week, and I know it already. I think They may be after me. In fact, I'm quite sure of it. I may need your help."

"Yes," Keeton said. He spoke more strongly now. "By God, you'll have all the help you need!"

"Now, you just met me and you don't owe me a damned thing—"

Keeton, who felt already that Gaunt was the closest friend

he had made in the last ten years, opened his mouth to protest. Gaunt held up his hand, and the protests ceased at once.

"—and you don't have the slightest idea if I've sold you something which will really work or just another bag of dreams . . . the kind that turn into nightmares when you give them a poke and a whistle. I'm sure you believe all this now; I have a great gift of persuasion, if I do say so myself. But I believe in satisfied customers, Mr. Keeton, and *only* satisfied customers. I have been in business for many years, and I have built my reputation on satisfied customers. So take the toy. If it works for you, fine. If it doesn't, give it to the Salvation Army or throw it in the town dump. What are you out? Couple of bucks?"

"Couple of bucks," Keeton agreed dreamily.

"But if it *does* work, and if you can clear your mind of these ephemeral financial worries, come back and see me. We'll sit down and have coffee, just as we have this morning . . . and talk about Them."

"It's gone too far to just put the money back," Keeton said in the clear but disconnected tones of one who talks in his sleep. "There are more tracks than I can brush away in five days."

"A lot can change in five days," Mr. Gaunt said thoughtfully. He rose to his feet, moving with sinuous grace. "You've got a big day ahead of you . . . and so do I."

"But Them," Keeton protested. "What about Them?"

Gaunt placed one of his long, chilly hands on Keeton's arm, and even in his dazed state, Keeton felt his stomach curl up on itself at that touch. "We'll deal with Them later," he said. "Don't you worry about a thing."

6

"John!" Alan called as John LaPointe slipped into the Sheriff's Office by the alley door. "Good to see you!"

It was ten-thirty on Saturday morning and the Castle Rock Sheriff's Office was as deserted as it ever got. Norris was out fishing somewhere, and Seaton Thomas was down in Sanford, visiting his two old maid sisters. Sheila Brigham was at the Our Lady of Serene Waters rectory, helping her brother draft another letter to the paper explaining the essentially harmless nature of Casino Nite. Father Brigham also wanted the letter to express his belief that William Rose was as crazy as a cootiebug in a shitheap. One could not come right out and *say* such a thing, of course—not in a family newspaper—but Father John and Sister Sheila were doing the best they could to get the point across. Andy Clutterbuck was on duty somewhere, or so Alan assumed; he hadn't called in since Alan arrived at the office an hour ago. Until John showed up, the only other person in the Municipal Building seemed to be Eddie Warburton, who was fussing with the water-cooler in the corner.

"What's up, doc?" John asked, sitting on the corner of Alan's desk.

"On Saturday morning? Not much. But watch this." Alan unbuttoned the right cuff of his khaki shirt and pushed the sleeve up. "Please notice that my hand never leaves my wrist."

"Uh-huh," John said. He pulled a stick of Juicy Fruit out of his pants pocket, peeled off the wrapper, and stuck it in his mouth.

Alan showed his open right palm, flipped his hand to display the back, then closed the hand into a fist. He reached into it with his left index finger and pulled out a tiny ear of silk. He waggled his eyebrows at John. "Not bad, huh?"

"If that's Sheila's scarf, she's gonna be unhappy to find it all wrinkled up and smelling of your sweat," John said. He seemed less than poleaxed with wonder.

"Not my fault she left it on her desk," Alan replied. "Besides, magicians don't sweat. Now say-hey and abracadabra!" He pulled Sheila's scarf from his fist and puffed it dramatically into the air. It billowed out, then settled onto Norris's type-writer like a brightly colored butterfly. Alan looked at John, then sighed. "Not that great, huh?"

"It's a neat trick," John said, "but I've seen it a few times before. Like maybe thirty or forty?"

"What do you think, Eddie?" Alan called. "Not bad for a backwoods Deputy Dawg, huh?"

Eddie barely looked up from the cooler, which he was now filling from a supply of plastic jugs labelled SPRING WATER. "Didn't see, Shurf. Sorry."

"Hopeless, both of you," Alan said. "But I'm working on a variation, John. It's going to wow you, I promise."

"Uh-huh. Alan, do you still want me to check the bath-rooms at that new restaurant out on the River Road?"

"I still do," Alan said.

"Why do *I* always get the shit detail? Why can't Norris—"

"Norris checked the Happy Trails Campground johns in July *and* August," Alan said. "In June I did it. Quit bitching, Johnny. It's just your turn. I want you to take water samples, too. Use a couple of the special pouches they sent from Au-gusta. There's still a bunch in that cabinet in the hallway. I think I saw 'em behind Norris's box of Hi-Ho crackers."

"Okay," John said, "you got it. But at the risk of sounding like I'm bitching again, checking the water for wigglebugs is supposed to be the restaurant-owner's responsibility. I looked it up."

"Of course it is," Alan said, "but we're talking Timmy Gag-non here, Johnny—what does that tell you?"

"It tells me I wouldn't buy a hamburger at the new River-side B-B-Q Delish if I was dying of starvation."

"Correct!" Alan exclaimed. He rose to his feet and clapped John on the shoulder. "I'm hoping we can put the sloppy little son of a bitch out of business before the stray dog and cat population of Castle Rock starts to decline."

"That's pretty sick, Alan."

"Nope—that's Timmy Gagnon. Get the water samples this morning and I'll ship them off to State Health in Augusta before I leave tonight."

"What are you up to this morning?"

Alan rolled down his sleeve and buttoned the cuff. "Right now I'm going upstreet to Needful Things," he said. "I want to meet Mr. Leland Gaunt. He made quite an impression on Polly, and from what I hear around town, she's not the only one who's taken with him. Have you met him?"

"Not yet," John said. The started toward the door. "Been by the place a couple of times, though. Interesting mix of stuff in the window."

They walked past Eddie, who was now polishing the water-cooler's big glass bottle with a rag he had produced from his back pocket. He did not look at Alan and John as they went by; he seemed lost in his own private universe. But as soon as the rear door had clicked shut behind them, Eddie Warburton hurried into the dispatcher's office and picked up the telephone.

7

"All right . . . yes . . . yes, I understand."

Leland Gaunt stood beside his cash register, holding a Cobra cordless phone to his ear. A smile as thin as a new crescent moon curved his lips.

"Thank you, Eddie. Thank you very much."

Gaunt strolled toward the curtain which closed off the shop from the area behind it. He poked his upper body through the curtain and bent over. When he pulled back through the curtain, he was holding a sign.

"You can go home now . . . yes . . . you may be sure I won't forget. I never forget a face or a service, Eddie, and that is one of the reasons why I strongly dislike being reminded of either. Goodbye."

He pushed the END button without waiting for a response, collapsed the antenna, and dropped the telephone into the pocket of his smoking jacket. The shade was drawn over his door again. Mr. Gaunt reached between shade and glass to remove the sign which read

OPEN.

He replaced it with the one he had taken from behind the curtain, then went to the show window to watch Alan Pangborn approach. Pangborn looked into the window Gaunt was looking out of for some time before approaching the door; he even cupped his hands and pressed his nose against the glass for a few seconds. Although Gaunt was standing right in front of him with his arms folded, the Sheriff did not see him.

Mr. Gaunt found himself disliking Pangborn's face on sight. Nor did this much surprise him. He was even better at reading faces than he was at remembering them, and the words on this one were large and somehow dangerous.

Pangborn's face changed suddenly; the eyes widened a little, the good-humored mouth narrowed down to a tight slit. Gaunt felt a brief and totally uncharacteristic burst of fear. *He sees me!* he thought, although that, of course, was impossible. The Sheriff took half a step backward . . . and then laughed. Gaunt understood at once what had happened, but this did not moderate his instant deep dislike of Pangborn in the slightest.

"Get out of here, Sheriff," he whispered. "Get out and leave me alone."

8

Alan stood looking into the display window for a long time. He found himself wondering what, exactly, all the shouting was about. He had spoken to Rosalie Drake before going over to Polly's house yesterday evening, and Rosalie had made Needful

Things sound like northern New England's answer to Tiffany's, but the set of china in the window didn't look like anything to get up in the night and write home to mother about—it was rummage-sale quality at best. Several of the plates were chipped, and a hairline crack ran right through the center of one.

Oh well, Alan thought, different strokes for different folks. That china's probably a hundred years old, worth a fortune, and I'm just too dumb to know it.

He cupped his hands to the glass in order to see beyond the display, but there was nothing to look at—the lights were off and the place was deserted. Then he thought he caught sight of someone—a strange, transparent someone looking out at him with ghostly and malevolent interest. He took half a step backward before realizing it was the reflection of his own face he was seeing. He laughed a little, embarrassed by his mistake.

He strolled to the door. The shade was drawn; a hand-lettered sign hung from a clear plastic suction cup.

GONE TO PORTLAND TO RECEIVE
A CONSIGNMENT OF GOODS

SORRY TO HAVE MISSED YOU
PLEASE COME AGAIN

Alan pulled his wallet from his back pocket, removed one of his business cards, and scribbled a brief message on the back.

Dear Mr. Gaunt,
    I dropped by Saturday morning to say hello
and welcome you to town. Sorry to have missed
you. Hope you're enjoying Castle Rock! I'll drop
by again on Monday. Maybe we could have a cup
of coffee. If there's anything I can do for you, my
numbers—home and office—are on the other side.
                                    Alan Pangborn

He stooped, slid the card under the door, and stood up again. He looked into the display window a moment longer, wondering who would want that set of nondescript dishes. As he looked, a queerly pervasive feeling stole over him—a sense of being watched. Alan turned around and saw no one but Lester Pratt. Lester was putting one of those damned posters up on a telephone pole and not looking in his direction at all. Alan shrugged and headed back down the street toward the Municipal Building. Monday would be time enough to meet Leland Gaunt; Monday would be just fine.

9

Mr. Gaunt watched him out of sight, then went to the door and picked up the card Alan had slid beneath. He read both sides carefully, and then began to smile. The Sheriff meant to drop by again on Monday, did he? Well, that was just fine, because Mr. Gaunt had an idea that by the time Monday rolled around, Castle County's Sheriff was going to have other fish to fry. A whole mess of other fish. And that was just as well, because he had met men like Pangborn before, and they were good men to steer clear of, at least while one was still building up one's business and feeling out one's clientele. Men like Pangborn saw too much.

"Something happened to you, Sheriff," Gaunt said. "Something that's made you even more dangerous than you should be. *That's* on your face, too. What was it, I wonder? Was it something you did, something you saw, or both?"

He stood looking out onto the street, and his lips slowly pulled back from his large, uneven teeth. He spoke in the low, comfortable tones of one who has been his own best listener for a very long time.

"I'm given to understand you're something of a parlor prestidigitator, my uniformed friend. You like tricks. I'm going to show you a few new ones before I leave town. I'm confident they will amaze you."

He rolled his hand into a fist around Alan's business card, first bending and then crumpling it. When it was completely hidden, a lick of blue fire squirted out from between his second and third fingers. He opened his hand again, and although little tendrils of smoke drifted up from the palm, there was no sign of the card—not even a smear of ash.

"Say-hey and abracadabra," Gaunt said softly.

10

Myrtle Keeton went to the door of her husband's study for the third time that day and listened. When she got out of bed around nine o'clock that morning, Danforth had already been in there with the door locked. Now, at one in the afternoon, he was *still* in there with the door locked. When she asked him if he wanted some lunch, he told her in a muffled voice to go away, he was busy.

She raised her hand to knock again . . . and paused. She cocked her head slightly. A noise was coming from beyond the door—a grinding, rattling sound. It reminded her of the sounds her mother's cuckoo clock had made during the week before it broke down completely.

She knocked lightly. "Danforth?"

"Go away!" His voice was agitated, but she could not tell if the reason was excitement or fear.

"Danforth, are you all right?"

"Yes, dammit! Go away! I'll be out soon!"

Rattle and grind. Grind and rattle. It sounded like dirt in a dough-mixer. It made her a little afraid. She hoped Danforth wasn't having a nervous breakdown in there. He had been acting so *strange* lately.

"Danforth, would you like me to go down to the bakery and get some doughnuts?"

"Yes!" he shouted. "Yes! Yes! Doughnuts! Toilet paper! A nose job! Go anywhere! Get anything! *Just leave me alone!*"

She stood a moment longer, troubled. She thought about knocking again and decided not to. She was no longer sure she wanted to know what Danforth was doing in his study. She was no longer sure she even wanted him to open the door.

She put on her shoes and her heavy fall coat—it was sunny but chilly—and went out to the car. She drove down to The Country Oven at the end of Main Street and got half a dozen doughnuts—honey-glazed for her, chocolate coconut for Danforth. She hoped they would cheer him up—a little chocolate always cheered *her* up.

On her way back, she happened to glance in the show window of Needful Things. What she saw caused her to jam both feet down on the brake-pedal, hard. If anyone had been following her, she would have been rammed for sure.

There was the most *gorgeous* doll in the window.

The shade was up again, of course. And the sign hanging from the clear plastic suction cup again read

OPEN.

Of course.

11

Polly Chalmers spent that Saturday afternoon in what was, for her, a most unusual fashion: by doing nothing at all. She sat by the window in her bentwood Boston rocker with her hands folded neatly in her lap, watching the occasional traffic on the street outside. Alan had called her before going out on patrol, had told her of having missed Leland Gaunt, had asked her if she was all right and if there was anything she needed. She had told him that she was fine and that she didn't need a single thing, thanks. Both of these statements were lies; she was not fine at all and there were several things she needed. A cure for arthritis headed the list.

No, Polly—what you really need is some courage. Just enough to walk up to the man you love and say, "Alan, I bent the truth in places about the years when I was away from Castle Rock, and I outright lied to you about what happened to my son. Now I'd like to ask your forgiveness and tell you the truth."

It sounded easy when you stated it baldly like that. It only got hard when you looked the man you loved in the eyes, or when you tried to find the key that would unlock your heart without tearing it into bleeding, painful pieces.

Pain and lies; lies and pain. The two subjects her life seemed to revolve around just lately.

How are you today, Pol?

Fine, Alan. I'm fine.

In fact, she was terrified. It wasn't that her hands were so awfully painful at this very second; she almost wished they did hurt, because the pain, bad as it was when it finally came, was still better than the waiting.

Shortly after noon today, she had become aware of a warm tingling—almost a vibration—in her hands. It formed rings of heat around her knuckles and at the base of her thumb; she could feel it lurking at the bottom of each fingernail in small, steely arcs like humorless smiles. She had felt this twice before, and knew what it meant. She was going to have what her Aunt Betty, who'd been afflicted with the same sort of arthritis, called a real bad spell. "When my hands start to tingle like electric shocks, I always know it's time to batten down the hatches," Betty had said, and now Polly was trying to batten down her own hatches, with a notable lack of success.

Outside, two boys walked down the middle of the street, tossing a football back and forth between them. The one on the right—the youngest of the Lawes boys—went up for a high pass. The ball ticked off his fingers and bounced onto Polly's lawn. He saw her looking out the window as he went after it and waved to her. Polly raised her own hand in return . . . and felt the pain flare sullenly, like a thick bed of coals in an errant gust of wind. Then it was gone again and there was only that eerie tingling. It felt to her the way the air sometimes felt before a violent electrical storm.

The pain would come in its own time; she could do nothing about it. The lies she had told Alan about Kelton, though . . . that was quite another thing. And, she thought, it's not as though the truth is so awful, so glaring, so shocking . . . and it's not as though he doesn't already suspect or even know that you've lied. He does. I've seen it in his face. So why is this so hard, Polly? Why?

Partially because of the arthritis, she supposed, and partially because of the pain medication she had come to rely on more and more heavily—the two things together had a way of blurring rational thought, of making the clearest and cleanest of right angles look queerly skewed. Then there was the fact of Alan's own pain . . . and the honesty with which he had disclosed it. He had laid it out for her inspection without a single hesitation.

His feelings in the wake of the peculiar accident which had taken Annie's and Todd's lives were confused and ugly, surrounded by an unpleasant (and frightening) swirl of negative emotions, but he had laid them out for her just the same. He had done it because he wanted to find out if she knew things about Annie's state of mind that he did not . . . but he had also done it because playing fair and keeping such things in the open were just part of his nature. She was afraid of what he might think when he found out that playing fair wasn't always a part of hers; that her heart as well as her hands had been touched with early frost.

She stirred uneasily in the chair.

I *have* to tell him—sooner or later I *have* to. And none of that explains why it's so hard; none of that even explains why I told him the lies in the first place. I mean, it isn't as if I killed my son . . .

She sighed—a sound that was almost a sob—and shifted in her chair. She looked for the boys with the football, but they were gone. Polly settled back in her chair and closed her eyes.

12

She wasn't the first girl to ever turn up pregnant as the result of a date-night wrestling match, or the first to ever argue bitterly with her parents and other relations as a result. They had wanted her to marry Paul "Duke" Sheehan, the boy who had gotten her pregnant. She had replied that she wouldn't marry Duke if he was the last boy on earth. This was true, but what her pride would not let her tell them was that Duke didn't want to marry *her*—his closest friend had told her he was already making panicky preparations to join the Navy when he turned eighteen . . . which he would do in less than six weeks.

"Let me get this straight," Newton Chalmers said, and had then torn away the last tenuous bridge between his daughter and himself. "He was good enough to screw, but he's not good enough to marry—is that about right?"

She had tried to run out of the house then, but her mother had caught her. If she wouldn't marry the boy, Lorraine Chalmers said, speaking in the calm and sweetly reasonable voice that had driven Polly almost to madness as a teenager, then they would have to send her away to Aunt Sarah in Minnesota. She could stay in Saint Cloud until the baby came, then put it up for adoption.

"I know why you want me to leave," Polly said. "It's Great-aunt Evelyn, isn't it? You're afraid if she finds out I've got a bun in my oven, she'll cut you out of her will. It's all about money,

isn't it? You don't care about me at all. You don't give a *shit*
about m—"

Lorraine Chalmers's sweetly reasonable voice had always
masked a jackrabbit temper. She had torn away the last tenuous bridge between her daughter and herself by slapping Polly
hard across the face.

So Polly had run away. That had been a long, long time
ago—in July of 1970.

She stopped running for a while when she got to Denver,
and worked there until the baby was born in a charity ward
which the patients called Needle Park. She had fully intended
to put the child up for adoption, but something—maybe just
the feel of him when the maternity nurse had put him in her
arms after the delivery—had changed her mind.

She named the boy Kelton, after her paternal grandfather.
The decision to keep the baby had frightened her a little, because she liked to see herself as a practical, sensible girl, and
nothing which had happened to her over the last year or so fit
that image. First the practical, sensible girl had gotten pregnant out of wedlock in a time when practical, sensible girls
simply did not do such things. Then the practical, sensible
girl had run away from home and delivered her child in a city
where she had never been before and knew nothing about. And
to top it all off, the practical, sensible girl had decided to keep
the baby and take it with her into a future she could not see,
could not even sense.

At least she had not kept the baby out of spite or defiance;
no one could hang that on her. She found herself surprised
by love, that simplest, strongest, and most unforgiving of all
emotions.

She had moved on. No—*they* had moved on. She had worked
a number of menial jobs, and they had ended up in San Francisco, where she had probably intended to go all along. In that
early summer of 1971 it had been a kind of hippie Xanadu, a
hilly headshop full of freaks and folkies and yippies and bands

with names like Moby Grape and the Thirteenth Floor Elevators.

According to the Scott McKenzie song about San Francisco which had been popular during one of those years, summertime was supposed to be a love-in there. Polly Chalmers, who had been no one's idea of a hippie even back then, had somehow missed the love-in. The building where she and Kelton lived was full of jimmied mailboxes and junkies who wore the peace-sign around their necks and, more often than not, kept switchblades in their scuffed and dirty motorcycle boots. The most common visitors in this neighborhood were process servers, repo men, and cops. A lot of cops, and you didn't call them pigs to their faces; the cops had also missed the love-in, and were pissed about it.

Polly applied for welfare and found she had not lived in California long enough to qualify—she supposed things might be different now, but in 1971, it had been as hard for a young unwed mother to get along in San Francisco as it was anywhere else. She applied for Aid to Dependent Children, and waited—hoped—for something to come of it. Kelton never missed a meal, but she herself lived hand to mouth, a scrawny young woman who was often hungry and always afraid, a young woman very few of the people who knew her now would have recognized. Her memories of those first three years on the West Coast, memories stored at the back of her mind like old clothes, in an attic, were skewed and grotesque, images from a nightmare.

And wasn't that a large part of her reluctance to tell Alan about those years? Didn't she simply want to keep them dark? She hadn't been the only one who had suffered the nightmare consequences of her pride, her stubborn refusal to ask for help, and the vicious hypocrisy of the times, which proclaimed the triumph of free love while simultaneously branding unmarried women with babies as creatures beyond the pale of normal society; Kelton had been there as well. Kelton had been her hostage to fortune as she slogged angrily along the track of her sordid fool's crusade.

The horrible thing was that her situation had been slowly improving. In the spring of 1972 she had finally qualified for state help, her first ADC check had been promised for the following month, and she had been making plans to move into a slightly better place when the fire happened.

The call had come to her at the diner where she worked, and in her dreams, Norville, the short-order cook who had always been trying to get into her pants in those days, turned to her again, and again holding out the telephone. He said the same thing over and over: *Polly, it's the police. They want to talk to you. Polly, it's the police. They want to talk to you.*

They had indeed wanted to talk to her, because they had hauled the bodies of a young woman and a small child from the smoky third floor of the apartment building. They had both been burned beyond recognition. They knew who the child was; if Polly wasn't at work, they would know who the woman was, too.

For three months after Kelton's death she had gone on working. Her loneliness had been so intense that she was half-mad with it, so deep and complete that she hadn't even been aware of how badly she was suffering. At last she had written home, telling her mother and father only that she was in San Francisco, that she had given birth to a boy, and that the boy was no longer with her. She would not have given further details if she had been threatened with red-hot pokers. Going home had not been a part of her plans then—not her *conscious* plans, at least—but it began to seem to her that if she did not re-establish some of her old ties, a valuable inside part of her would begin dying by inches, the way a vigorous tree dies from the branches inward when it is deprived of water too long.

Her mother had replied at once to the box number Polly gave as a return address, pleading with her to come back to Castle Rock . . . to come home. She enclosed a money order for seven hundred dollars. It was very warm in the tenement flat where Polly had been living since Kelton's death, and she stopped halfway through the task of packing her bags for a cold glass of water. While she was drinking it, Polly realized that she was making ready to go home simply because her mother had asked—almost begged—her to do so. She hadn't really thought about it at all, which was almost certainly a mistake. It was that sort of leap-before-you-look behavior, not Duke Sheehan's puny little dingus, which had gotten her in trouble to begin with.

So she sat down on her narrow single-woman's bed and thought about it. She thought long and hard. At last she voided the money order and wrote a letter to her mother. It was less than a page long, but it had taken her nearly four hours to get it right.

I want to come back, or at least try it on for size, but I don't want us to drag out all the old bones and start chewing on them again if I do, she had written. *I don't know if what I really want—to start a new life in an old place—is possible for anyone, but I want to try. So I have an idea: let's be pen-pals for a while. You and me, and me and Dad. I have noticed that it's harder to be angry and resentful on paper, so let's talk that way for a while before we talk in person.*

They had talked that way for almost six months, and then one day in January of 1973, Mr. and Mrs. Chalmers had shown up at her door, bags in hand. They were registered at the Mark Hopkins Hotel, they said, and they were not going back to Castle Rock without her.

Polly had thought this over, feeling a whole geography of emotions: anger that they could be so high-handed, rueful amusement at the sweet and rather naive quality of that high-handedness, panic that the questions she had so neatly avoided answering in her letters would now be pressed home.

She had promised to go to dinner with them, no more than that—other decisions would have to wait. Her father told her he had only booked the room at the Mark Hopkins for a single night. You had better extend the reservation, then, Polly said.

She had wanted to talk with them as much as she could be- fore coming to any final decision—a more intimate form of the testing which had gone on in their letters. But that first night had been the only night they had had. It was the last night she had ever seen her father well and strong, and she had spent most of it in a red rage at him.

The old arguments, so easy to avoid in correspondence, had begun again even before pre-dinner glasses of wine were drunk. They were brash fires at first, but as her father contin- ued to drink, they developed into an uncontrollable wall of fire. He had struck the spark, saying they both felt Polly had learned her lesson and it was time to bury the hatchet. Mrs. Chalmers had fanned the flames, dropping into her old cool, sweetly reasonable voice. Where is the baby, dear? You might at least tell us *that* much. You turned him over to the Sisters, I suppose.

Polly knew these voices, and what they meant, from times long past. Her father's indicated his need to reestablish con- trol; at all costs there *must* be control. Her mother's indicated that she was showing love and concern in the only way she knew, by demanding information. Both voices, so familiar, so loved and despised, had ignited the old, wild anger in her.

They left the restaurant halfway through the main course, and the next day Mr. and Mrs. Chalmers had flown back to Maine alone.

After a three-month hiatus, the correspondence had begun again, hesitantly. Polly's mother wrote first, apologizing for the disastrous evening. The pleas to come home had been dropped. This surprised Polly . . . and filled some deep and barely acknowledged part of her with anxiety. She felt that her mother was finally denying her. This was, under the cir- cumstances, both foolish and self-indulgent, but that did not change those elemental feelings in the slightest.

I suppose you know your own mind best, she wrote to Polly. *That's hard for your father and me to accept, because we still see you as our little girl. I think it frightened him to see you looking so beautiful and so much older. And you mustn't blame him too much for the way he acted. He hasn't been feeling well; his stomach has been kicking up on him again. The doctor says it's only his gall bladder, and once he agrees to have it taken out all will be well, but I worry about him.*

Polly had replied in the same conciliatory tone. She found it easier to do so now that she had started taking business-school classes and shelved her plans to return to Maine indefinitely. And then, near the end of 1975, the telegram had come. It was short and brutal: YOUR DAD HAS CANCER. HE IS DYING. PLEASE COME HOME. LOVE, MOM.

He was still alive when Polly got to the hospital in Bridgton, her head spinning with jet-lag and the old memories seeing all the old places had prodded forth. The same wondering thought arose in her mind at each new turn of the road which led from the Portland Jetport into the high hills and low mountains of western Maine. *The last time I saw that, I was a child!*

Newton Chalmers lay in a private room, dozing in and out of consciousness, with tubes in his nose and machines gathered around him in a hungry semicircle. He died three days later. She had intended to go back to California right away—she almost thought of it as her home now—but four days after her father was buried, her mother suffered a crippling heart attack.

Polly had moved into the house. She nursed her mother for the next three and a half months, and at some point every night she would dream of Norville, the short-order cook at Yor Best Diner. Norville turned to her again and again in these dreams, holding the telephone out in his right hand, the one with the eagle and the words DEATH BEFORE DISHONOR tattooed on the back. *Polly, it's the police,* Norville said. *They want to talk to you. Polly, it's the police. They want to talk to you.*

Her mother was out of bed, on her feet again and talking about selling the house and moving to California with Polly (something she would never do, but Polly did not disabuse her of her dreams—she was older by then, and a little kinder) when the second heart attack struck. So it was that on a raw afternoon in March of 1976, Polly had found herself in Homeland Cemetery, standing next to her Great-aunt Evelyn, and looking at a coffin which stood on bands next to her father's fresh grave.

His body had lain in the Homeland crypt all winter, waiting for the earth to unlimber enough so it could be interred. In one of those grotesque coincidences which no decent novelist would dare invent, the interral of the husband had taken place just one day before the wife died. The sods on top of Newton Chalmers's final apartment had not yet been replaced; the earth was still raw and the grave looked obscenely naked. Polly's eyes kept straying from the coffin of her mother to the grave of her father. *It was as if she was just waiting for him to be decently buried,* she thought.

When the short service was over, Aunt Evvie had called her aside. Polly's last surviving relative stood by the Hay & Peabody funeral hack, a thin stick of a woman dressed in a man's black overcoat and strangely jolly red galoshes, a Herbert Tareyton tucked into the corner of her mouth. She flicked a wooden match alight with one thumbnail as Polly approached, and set fire to the tip of her cigarette. She inhaled deeply and then hacked the smoke back out into the cold spring air. Her cane (a simple ash stick; it would be three years yet before she would be awarded the Boston *Post* Cane as the town's oldest citizen) was planted between her feet.

Now, sitting in a Boston rocker that the old lady undoubtedly would have approved of, Polly calculated that Aunt Evvie must have been eighty-eight that spring—eighty-eight years old and still smoking like a chimney—although she had not looked much different to Polly than she had when Polly was a little girl, hoping for a penny sweet from the apparently endless supply Aunt Evvie kept in the pocket of her apron. Many things in Castle Rock had changed in the years she had been gone, but Aunt Evvie was not one of them.

"Well, *that's* over," Aunt Evvie had said in her cigarette-raspy voice. "They're in the ground, Polly. Mother and father both."

Polly had burst into tears then, a miserable flood of them. She thought at first that Aunt Evvie would try to comfort her, and her flesh was already shrinking from the old woman's touch—she didn't *want* to be comforted.

And need not have worried. Evelyn Chalmers had never been a woman who believed in comforting the grief-stricken; might in fact have believed, Polly sometimes thought later, that the very idea of comfort was an illusion. In any case, she only stood there with her cane planted between her red galoshes, smoking and waiting for Polly's tears to give way to sniffles as she brought herself under control.

When this had been accomplished, Aunt Evvie asked: "Your chap—the one they spent so much time fussing over—is dead, isn't he?"

Though she had guarded this secret jealously from everyone, Polly found herself nodding. "His name was Kelton."

"A goodish name," Aunt Evvie said. She drew on her cigarette and then exhaled slowly from her mouth so she could draw the smoke back up her nose—what Lorraine Chalmers had called a "double-pump," wrinkling her nose in distaste as she said it. "I knew it the first time you come over to see me after you got home. Saw it in your eyes."

"There was a fire," Polly said, looking up at her. She had a tissue but it was too soggy to do any more business; she put it in her coat pocket and used her fists instead, screwing them into her eyes like a little girl who has fallen off her scooter and banged her knee. "The young woman I hired to babysit him probably started it."

"Ayuh," Aunt Evvie said. "But do you want to know a secret, Trisha?"

Polly nodded her head, smiling a little. Her real name was Patricia, but she had been Polly to everyone since her baby-hood. Everyone except Aunt Evvie.

"Baby Kelton's dead . . . but *you're* not." Aunt Evvie tossed her cigarette away and used one bony forefinger to tap against Polly's chest for emphasis. "*You're* not. So what are you going to do about it?"

Polly thought it over. "I'm going back to California," she said finally. "That's all I know."

"Yes, and that's all right for a start. But it's not enough." And then Aunt Evvie said something very close to what Polly herself would say, some years later, when she went to dinner at The Birches with Alan Pangborn: "You're not the culprit here, Trisha. Have you got that sorted out?"

"I . . . I don't know."

"Then you don't. Until you realize that, it won't matter where you go, or what you do. There won't be any chance."

"What chance?" she had asked, bewildered.

"*Your* chance. Your chance to live your own life. Right how you have the look of a woman who is seeing ghosts. Not everybody believes in ghosts, but I do. Do you know what they are, Trisha?"

She had shaken her head slowly.

"Men and women who can't get over the past," Aunt Evvie said. "*That's* what ghosts are. Not *them.*" She flapped her arm toward the coffin which stood on its bands beside the coinciden-tally fresh grave. "The dead are dead. We bury them, and buried they stay."

"I feel . . ."

"Yes," Aunt Evvie said. "I know you do. But *they* don't. Your mother and my nephew don't. Your chap, the one who died while you been Away, *he* don't. Do you understand me?"

She had. A little, anyway.

"You're right not to want to stay here, Polly—at least,

you're right for now. Go back where you were. Or go someplace new—Salt Lake, Honolulu, Baghdad, wherever you want. It don't matter, because sooner or later you *will* come back here. I know that; this place belongs to you and you belong to it. That's written in every line of your face, in the way you walk, the way you talk, even the way you have of narrowin your eyes when you look at someone you ain't met before. Castle Rock was made for you and you for it. So there is no hurry. 'Go where ye list,' as the Good Book says. But go there *alive,* Trisha. Don't be no ghost. If you turn into one of those, it might be better if you stayed away."

The old woman looked around broodingly, her head rotating above her cane.

"Goddam town's got enough ghosts already," she said.

"I'll try, Aunt Evvie."

"Yes—I know you will. Trying—that's built into you, too." Aunt Evvie looked her over closely. "You were a fair child, and a likely child, although you weren't ever a lucky child. Well, luck is for fools. It's all they have to hope for, poor devils. It strikes me that you are still likely and fair, and that's the important thing. I think you'll make out." Then, briskly, almost arrogantly: "I love you, Trisha Chalmers. I always have."

"I love you, too, Aunt Evvie."

Then, in that careful way which the old and young have of showing affection, they embraced. Polly had smelled the old aroma of Aunt Evvie's sachet—a tremor of violets—and that made her weep again.

When she stood back, Aunt Evvie was reaching into her coat pocket. Polly watched for her to bring out a tissue, thinking in an amazed way that at last, after all the long years, she would see the old woman cry. But she hadn't. Instead of a tissue, Aunt Evvie brought out a single wrapped hard candy, just as she had in those days when Polly Chalmers had been a little girl with braids hanging over the front of her middy blouse.

"Would you like a sweet, honey?" she had asked cheerfully.

13

Twilight had begun to steal across the day.

Polly straightened up in the rocker, aware that she had almost fallen asleep. She bumped one of her hands, and a hard bolt of pain raced up her arm before being replaced once more by that hot anticipatory tingle. It was going to be bad, all right. Later tonight or tomorrow, it was going to be very bad indeed.

Never mind what you can't change, Polly—there's at least one thing you can *change,* must *change. You have to tell Alan the truth about Kelton. You have to stop harboring that ghost in your heart.*

But another voice rose up in response—an angry, frightened, clamorous voice. The voice of pride, she supposed, just that, but she was shocked by its strength and ardor as it demanded that those old days, that old life, not be exhumed . . . not for Alan, not for anybody. That, above all, her baby's short life and miserable death should not be given over to the sharp, wagging tongues of the town gossips.

What foolishness is that, Trisha? Aunt Evvie asked in her mind—Aunt Evvie, who had died so full of years, double-pumping her beloved Herbert Tareytons to the last. *What does it matter if Alan finds out how Kelton really died? What does it matter if every old gossip in town, from Lenny Partridge to Myrtle Keeton, knows? Do you think anyone cares a fig about your bun anymore, you silly goose? Don't flatter yourself—it's old news. Hardly worth a second cup of coffee in Nan's.*

Maybe so . . . but he had been *hers,* God damn it, *hers.* In his life and in his death, he had been hers. And *she* had been hers, too—not her mother's, her father's, Duke Sheehan's. *She had belonged to herself.* That frightened, lonely girl who had washed her panties out every night in the rusty kitchen sink because she had only three pairs, that frightened girl who always had a cold-sore waiting to happen at the corner of her lip or on the rim of one nostril, that girl who sometimes sat at the window overlooking the airshaft and laid her hot forehead on her arms and cried—that girl was *hers.* Her memories of herself and her son together in the dark of night, Kelton feeding at one small breast while she read a John D. MacDonald paperback and the disconnected sirens rose and raved through the cramped, hilly streets of the city, those memories were *hers.* The tears she had cried, the silences she had endured, the long, foggy afternoons in the diner trying to avoid Norville Bates's Roman hands and Russian fingers, the shame with which she had finally made an uneasy peace, the independence and the dignity she had fought so hard and so inconclusively to keep . . . those things were *hers,* and must not belong to the town.

Polly, this is not a question of what belongs to the town, and you know it. It's a question of what belongs to Alan.

She shook her head back and forth as she sat in the rocker, completely unaware she was making this gesture of negation. She supposed she had spent too many sleepless three o'clocks on too many endless dark mornings to give away her inner landscape without a fight. In time she would tell Alan everything—she had not meant to keep the complete truth a secret even this long—but the time wasn't yet. Surely not . . . especially when her hands were telling her that in the next few days she would not be able to think about much of anything at all except them.

The phone began to ring. That would be Alan, back from patrol and checking in with her. Polly got up and crossed the room to it. She picked it up carefully, using both hands, ready to tell him the things she believed he wanted to hear. Aunt Evvie's voice tried to intrude, tried to tell her this was bad behavior, childishly self-indulgent behavior, perhaps even dangerous behavior. Polly pushed that voice aside quickly and roughly.

"Hello?" she said brightly. "Oh, hi, Alan! How are you? Good."

She listened briefly, then smiled. If she had looked at her reflection in the hallway mirror, she would have seen a woman who appeared to be screaming . . . but she did not look.

"Fine, Alan," she said. "I'm just fine."

14

It was almost time to leave for the Raceway.

Almost.

"Come on," Danforth Keeton whispered. Sweat ran down his face like oil. "Come on, come on, *come on.*"

He was sitting hunched over Winning Ticket—he had swept everything off his desk to make room for it, and he had spent most of the day playing with it. He had started with his copy of *Bluegrass History: Forty Years of Kentucky Derby.* He had run at least two dozen Derbys, giving the tin Winning Ticket horses the names of the entrants in exactly the manner Mr. Gaunt had described. And the tin horses which got the names of the winning Derby horses from the book kept coming in first. It happened time after time. It was amazing—so amazing that it was four o'clock before he realized that he had spent the day running long-ago races when there were ten brand-new ones to be run at Lewiston Raceway that very evening.

Money was waiting to be made.

For the last hour, today's Lewiston *Daily Sun,* folded to the racing card, had lain to the left of the Winning Ticket board. To the right was a sheet of paper he had torn from his pocket notebook. Listed on the sheet in Keeton's large, hasty scrawl was this:

> 1st Race: BAZOOKA JOAN
> 2nd Race: FILLY DELFIA
> 3rd Race: TAMMY'S WONDER
> 4th Race: I'M AMAZED

5th Race: BY GEORGE
6th Race: PUCKY BOY
7th Race: CASCO THUNDER
8th Race: DELIGHTFUL SON
9th Race: TIKO-TIKO

It was only five in the afternoon, but Danforth Keeton was already running the last race of the night. The horses rattled and swayed around the track. One of them led by six lengths, and crossed the finish line far ahead of the others.

Keeton snatched up the newspaper and studied the evening's Raceway card again. His face shone so brightly that he looked sanctified. "Malabar!" he whispered, and shook his fists in the air. The pencil caught in one of them darted and plunged like a runaway sewing needle. "It's Malabar! Thirty-to-one! Thirty-to-one *at least!* Malabar, by God!"

He scribbled on the sheet of paper, panting raggedly as he did so. Five minutes later the Winning Ticket game was locked in his study closet and Danforth Keeton was on his way to Lewiston in his Cadillac.

CHAPTER NINE

1

At quarter to ten on Sunday morning, Nettie Cobb drew on her coat and buttoned it swiftly. An expression of grim determination was stamped on her face. She was standing in her kitchen. Raider was sitting on the floor, looking up at her as if to ask if she really meant to go through with it this time.

"Yes, I really mean it," she told him.

Raider thumped his tail against the floor, as if to say he knew she could do it.

"I've made a nice lasagna for Polly, and I'm going to take it to her. My lampshade is locked up in the armoire, and I *know* it's locked, I don't need to keep coming back to check because I know it in my *head.* That crazy Polish woman isn't going to keep me prisoner in my own house. If I see her on the street, I'll give her what-for! I warned her!"

She *had* to go out. She *had* to, and she knew it. She hadn't left the house in two days, and she had come to realize that the longer she put it off, the harder it would become. The longer she sat in the living room with the shades pulled down, the harder it would get to ever raise them again. She could feel the old confused terror creeping into her thoughts.

So she had gotten up early this morning—at five o'clock!— and had made a nice lasagna for Polly, just the way she liked it, with plenty of spinach and mushrooms. The mushrooms were canned, because she hadn't dared go out to the market last night, but she thought it had turned out very well despite that. It was now sitting on the counter, the top of the pan covered with aluminum foil.

She picked it up and marched through the living room to the door. "You be a good boy, Raider. I'll be back in an hour. Unless Polly gives me coffee, and then it might be a little longer. But I'll be fine. I don't have a thing to worry about. I didn't do anything to that crazy Polish woman's sheets, and if she bothers me, I'll give her the very dickens."

Raider uttered a stern bark to show he understood and believed.

She opened the door, peeked out, saw nothing. Ford Street was as deserted as only a small-town street can be early on Sunday morning. In the distance, one church-bell was calling Rev. Rose's Baptists to worship and another was summoning Father Brigham's Catholics.

Gathering all her courage, Nettie stepped out into the Sunday sunshine, set the pan of lasagna down on the step, pulled the door closed, and locked it. Then she took her housekey and scratched it up her forearm, leaving a thin red mark. As she stooped to pick up the pan again she thought, *Now when you get halfway down the block—maybe even sooner—you'll start thinking that you really didn't lock the door after all. But you did. You set the lasagna down to do it. And if you still can't believe it, just look at your arm and remember that you made that scratch with your very own housekey . . . after you used it to lock the house. Remember that, Nettie, and you'll be just fine when the doubts start to creep in.*

 This was a wonderful thought, and using the key to scratch her arm had been a wonderful idea. The red mark was something *concrete,* and for the first time in the last two days (and mostly sleepless nights), Nettie really *did* feel better. She marched down to the sidewalk, her head high, her lips pressed together so tightly that they almost disappeared. When she reached the sidewalk, she looked both ways for the crazy Polish woman's little yellow car. If she saw it, she intended to walk right up to it and tell the crazy Polish woman to leave her alone.

There wasn't a sign of it, though. The only vehicle in sight was an old orange truck parked up the street, and it was empty.

Good.

Nettie set sail for Polly Chalmers's house, and when the doubts assailed her, she remembered that the carnival glass lampshade was locked up, Raider was on guard, and the front door was locked. Especially that last. The front door was locked, and she only had to look at the fading red mark on her arm to prove it to herself.

So Nettie marched on with her head high, and when she reached the corner, she turned it without looking back.

2

When the nutty woman was out of sight, Hugh Priest sat up behind the wheel of the orange town truck he had drawn from the deserted motor pool at seven that morning (he had lain down on the seat as soon as he saw Crazy Nettie come out the door). He put the gearshift in neutral, and let the truck roll slowly and soundlessly down the slight grade to Nettie Cobb's house.

3

The doorbell woke Polly from a soupy state that wasn't really sleep but a kind of dream-haunted drug-daze. She sat up in bed and realized she was wearing her housecoat. When had she put it on? For a moment she couldn't remember, and that frightened her. Then it came. The pain she'd been expecting had arrived right on schedule, easily the worst arthritic pain of her entire life. It had awakened her at five. She had gone into the bathroom to urinate, then had discovered she couldn't even get a swatch of toilet paper off the roll to blot herself with. So she had taken a pill, put on her housecoat, and sat in the chair by the bedroom window to wait until it worked. At some point she must have gotten sleepy and gone back to bed.

Her hands felt like crude ceramic figures baked until they were on the verge of cracking. The pain was both hot and cold, set deep in her flesh like complex networks of poisoned wires. She held her hands up despairingly, scarecrow hands, awful, deformed hands, and downstairs the doorbell chimed again. She uttered a distracted little cry.

She went out onto the landing with her hands held out in front of her like the paws of a dog sitting up to beg a sweet. "Who is it?" she called down. Her voice was hoarse, gummy with sleep. Her tongue tasted like something which had been used to line a cat-box.

"It's Nettie!" The voice drifted back up. "Are you okay, Polly?"

Nettie. Good God, what was Nettie doing here before the crack of dawn on Sunday morning?

"I'm fine!" she called back. "I have to put something on! Use your key, dear!"

When she heard Nettie's key begin to rattle in the lock, Polly hurried back into her bedroom. She glanced at the clock on the table beside her bed and saw that dawn had cracked several hours before. Nor had she come back to put something on; her housecoat would do for Nettie just fine. But she needed a pill. She had never, never in her life, needed a pill as badly as she did now.

She didn't know how bad her condition really was until she tried to take one. The pills—actually caplets—were in a small glass dish on the mantel of the room's ornamental fireplace. She was able to get her hand into the dish all right, but found herself completely unable to grasp one of the caplets once it was there. Her fingers were like the pincers of some machine which had frozen solid for lack of oil.

She tried harder, concentrating all of her will on making

her fingers close upon one of the gelatine capsules. She was rewarded with slight movement and a great burst of agony. That was all. She made a little muttering sound of pain and frustration.

"Polly?" From the foot of the stairs now, Nettie's voice was concerned. People in Castle Rock might consider Nettie vague, Polly thought, but when it came to the vicissitudes of Polly's infirmity, Nettie was not vague at all. She had been around the house too long to be fooled . . . and had loved her too well. "Polly, are you really all right?"

"Be right down, dear!" she called back, trying to sound bright and lively. And as she took her hand out of the glass dish and bent her head over it, she thought, *Please, God. Don't let her come up now. Don't let her see me doing this.*

She lowered her face into the dish like a dog about to drink from its bowl and stuck out her tongue. Pain, shame, horror, and most of all a dark depression, all maroons and grays, enfolded her. She pressed her tongue against one of the caplets until it stuck. She drew it into her mouth, now not a dog but an anteater ingesting a tasty morsel, and swallowed.

As the pill traced its tiny hard trail down her throat, she thought again: *I would give anything to be free of this. Anything. Anything at all.*

4

Hugh Priest rarely dreamed anymore; these days he did not go to sleep so much as fall unconscious. But he'd had a dream last night, a real lulu. The dream had told him everything he had to know, and everything he was supposed to do.

In it he had been sitting at his kitchen table, drinking a beer and watching a game-show called *Sale of the Century.* All the things they were giving away were things he had seen in that shop, Needful Things. And all of the contestants were bleeding from their ears and the corners of their eyes. They were laughing, but they looked terrified.

All at once a muffled voice began to call, "Hugh! Hugh! Let me out, Hugh!"

It was coming from the closet. He went over and opened it, ready to coldcock whoever was hiding inside. But there was no one; only the usual tangle of boots, scarves, coats, fishing tackle, and his two shotguns.

"Hugh!"

He looked up, because the voice was coming from the shelf.

It was the fox-tail. The fox-tail was talking. And Hugh recognized the voice at once. It was the voice of Leland Gaunt. He had taken the brush down, revelling again in its plushy softness, a texture that was a little like silk, a little like wool, and really like nothing at all but its own secret self.

"Thanks, Hugh," the fox-tail said. "It's really stuffy in here. And you left an old pipe on the shelf. It really stinks. Whew!"

"Did you want to go to another place?" Hugh had asked. He felt a little stupid talking to a fox-tail, even in a dream.

"No—I'm getting used to it. But I have to talk to you. You have to do something, remember? You promised."

"Crazy Nettie," he agreed. "I have to play a trick on Crazy Nettie."

"That's right," said the fox-tail, "and you have to do it as soon as you wake up. So listen."

Hugh had listened.

The fox-tail had told him no one would be home at Nettie's but the dog, but now that Hugh was actually here, he decided it would be wise to knock. He did so. From inside he heard claws come clicking rapidly across a wooden floor, but nothing else. He knocked again, just to be safe. There was a single stern bark from the other side of the door.

"Raider?" Hugh asked. The fox-tail had told him that was the dog's name. Hugh thought it was a pretty good name, even if the lady who thought it up was nuttier than a fruitcake.

The single bark came again, not quite so stern this time.

Hugh took a key-ring from the breast pocket of the plaid hunting jacket he wore and examined it. He'd had this ring for a long time, and could no longer even remember what some of the keys had gone to. But four of them were skeleton keys, easily identified by their long barrels, and these were the ones he wanted.

Hugh glanced around once, saw the street was as deserted as it had been when he first arrived, and began to try the keys one by one.

5

When Nettie saw Polly's white, puffy face and haggard eyes, her own fears, which had gnawed at her like sharp weasel's teeth as she walked over, were forgotten. She didn't even have to look at Polly's hands, still held out at waist level (it hurt dreadfully to let them hang down when it was like this), to know how things were with her.

The lasagna was thrust unceremoniously on a table by the foot of the stairs. If it had gone tumbling to the floor, Nettie wouldn't have given it a second glance. The nervous woman Castle Rock had grown used to seeing on its streets, the woman who looked as if she were skulking away from some nasty piece of mischief even if she was only on her way to the post office, was not here. This was a different Nettie; Polly Chalmers's Nettie.

"Come on," she said briskly. "Into the living room. I'll get the thermal gloves."

"Nettie, I'm all right," Polly said weakly. "I just took a pill, and I'm sure that in a few minutes—"

But Nettie had an arm around her and was walking her into the living room. "What did you do? Did you sleep on them, do you think?"

"No—that would have woken me. It's just . . ." She laughed. It was a weak, bewildered sound. "It's just pain. I knew today was going to be bad, but I had no idea *how* bad. And the thermal gloves don't help."

"Sometimes they do. You know that sometimes they do. Now just sit there."

Nettie's tone brooked no refusal. She stood beside Polly until Polly sat in an overstuffed armchair. Then she went into the downstairs bathroom to get the thermal gloves. Polly had given up on them a year ago, but Nettie, it seemed, held for them a reverence that was almost superstitious. Nettie's version of chicken soup, Alan had once called them, and they had both laughed.

Polly sat with her hands resting on the arms of the chair like lumps of cast-off driftwood and looked longingly across the room at the couch where she and Alan had made love Friday night. Her hands hadn't hurt at all then, and that already seemed like a thousands years ago. It occurred to her that pleasure, no matter how deep, was a ghostly, ephemeral thing. Love might make the world go round, but she was convinced it was the cries of the badly wounded and deeply afflicted which spun the universe on the great glass pole of its axis.

Oh you stupid couch, she thought. *Oh you stupid empty couch, what good are you to me now?*

Nettie came back with the thermal gloves. They looked like quilted oven mitts connected by an insulated electric wire. A plug-in cord snaked out of the left glove's back. Polly had seen an ad for the gloves in *Good Housekeeping,* of all places. She had placed a call to The National Arthritis Foundation's 800 number and had ascertained that the gloves did indeed provide temporary relief in some cases. When she showed the ad to Dr. Van Allen, he added the coda which had been tiresomely familiar even two years ago: "Well, it can't hurt."

"Nettie, I'm sure that in a few minutes—"

"—you'll feel better," Nettie finished. "Yes, of course you will. And maybe these will help. Hold up your hands, Polly."

Polly gave in and held up her hands. Nettie held the gloves by their ends, squeezed them open, and slipped them on with the delicacy of a bomb-squad expert covering packets of C-4 with a blast-blanket. Her touch was gentle, expert, and compassionate. Polly didn't believe the thermal gloves would do a thing . . . but Nettie's obvious concern had already had its effect.

Nettie took the plug, got down on her knees, and slipped it into the baseboard socket near the chair. The gloves began to hum faintly, and the first tendrils of dry warmth caressed the skin of Polly's hands.

"You're too good to me," Polly said softly. "Do you know that?"

"I couldn't be," Nettie replied. "Not ever." Her voice was a trifle husky, and there was a bright, liquid shine in her eyes. "Polly, it's not my place to tell you your business, but I just can't keep quiet any longer. You have to do something about your poor hands. You *have* to. Things just can't go on this way."

"I know, dear. I know." Polly made a huge effort to climb over the wall of depression which had built itself up in her mind. "Why did you come over, Nettie? Surely it wasn't just to toast my hands."

Nettie brightened. "I made you a lasagna!"

"Did you? Oh, Nettie, you shouldn't have!"

"No? That's not what *I* think. *I* think you won't be up to cooking today, or tomorrow, either. I'll just put it in the refrigerator."

"Thank you. Thank you so much."

"I'm glad I did it. Doubly glad, now that I see you." She reached the hall doorway and looked back. A bar of sun fell across her face, and in that moment Polly might have seen how drawn and tired Nettie looked, if her own pain had not been so large. "Don't you move, now!"

Polly burst out laughing, surprising them both. "I can't! I'm trapped!"

In the kitchen, the refrigerator door opened and closed as Nettie put the lasagna away. Then she called, "Shall I put on the coffee? Would you like a cup? I could help you with it."

"Yes," Polly said, "that would be nice." The gloves were humming louder now; they were very warm. And either they were actually helping, or the pill was taking hold in a way the one at five o'clock hadn't. More probably it was a combination of the two, she thought. "But if you have to get back, Nettie—"

Nettie appeared in the doorway. She had taken her apron out of the pantry and put it on, and she held the old tin coffee pot in one hand. She wouldn't use the new digital Toshiba coffee-maker . . . and Polly had to admit that what came out of Nettie's tin pot was better.

"I've no place to go that's better than this," she said. "Besides, the house is all locked up and Raider's on guard."

"I'm sure," Polly said, smiling. She knew Raider very well. He weighed all of twenty pounds and rolled over to have his belly scratched when anyone—mailman, meter-reader, door-to-door salesman—came to the house.

"I think she'll leave me alone anyway," Nettie said. "I warned her. I haven't seen her around or heard from her, so I guess it finally sank in on her that I meant business."

"Warned who? About what?" Polly asked, but Nettie had already left the doorway, and Polly was indeed penned in her seat by the electric gloves. By the time Nettie reappeared with the coffee tray, the Percodan had begun to fog her in and she had forgotten all about Nettie's odd remark . . . which was not surprising in any case, since Nettie made odd remarks quite often.

Nettie put cream and sugar in Polly's coffee and held it up so she could sip from the cup. They chatted about one thing and another, and of course the conversation turned to the new shop before very long. Nettie told her about the purchase of the carnival glass lampshade again, but hardly in the breathless detail Polly would have expected, given the extraordinary nature of such an event in Nettie's life. But it kicked off something else in her mind: the note Mr. Gaunt had put in the cake container.

"I almost forgot—Mr. Gaunt asked me to stop by this afternoon. He said he might have an item I'd be interested in."

"You're not going, are you? With your hands like they are?"

"I might. They feel better—I think the gloves really did work this time, at least a little. And I have to do *something*." She looked at Nettie a trifle pleadingly.

"Well . . . I suppose." A sudden idea struck Nettie. "You know, I could walk by there on the way home, and ask him if he could come to *your* house!"

"Oh no, Nettie—that's out of your way!"

"Only a block or two." Nettie cast an endearingly sly sideglance Polly's way. "Besides, he might have another piece of carnival glass. I don't have enough money for another one, but *he* doesn't know that, and it doesn't cost anything to look, does it?"

"But to ask him to come here—"

"I'll explain how it is with you," Nettie said decisively, and began putting things back onto the tray. "Why, businessmen often have home demonstrations—if they have something worth selling, that is."

Polly looked at her with amusement and love. "You know, you're different when you're here, Nettie."

Nettie looked at her, surprised. "I am?"

"Yes."

"How?"

"In a good way. Never mind. Unless I have a relapse, I think I *will* want to go out this afternoon. But if you do happen to go by Needful Things—"

"I will." A look of ill-concealed eagerness shone in Nettie's eyes. Now that the idea had occurred to her, it took hold with all the force of a compulsion. Doing for Polly had been a tonic for her nerves, and no mistake.

"—and if he *does* happen to be in, give him my home number and ask him to give me a call if the item he wanted me to see came in. Could you do that?"

"You betcha!" Nettie said. She rose with the coffee-tray and took it into the kitchen. She replaced her apron on its hook in the pantry and came back into the living room to remove the thermal gloves. Her coat was already on. Polly thanked her again—and not just for the lasagna. Her hands still hurt badly, but the pain was manageable now. And she could move her fingers again.

"You're more than welcome," Nettie said. "And you know what? You *do* look better. Your color's coming back. It scared me to look at you when I first came in. Can I do anything else for you before I go?"

"No, I don't think so." She reached out and clumsily grasped one of Nettie's hands in her own, which were still flushed and very warm from the gloves. "I'm awfully glad you came over, dear."

On the rare occasions when Nettie smiled, she did it with her whole face; it was like watching the sun break through the clouds on an overcast morning. "I love you, Polly."

Touched, Polly replied: "Why, I love you, too, Nettie."

Nettie left. It was the last time Polly ever saw her alive.

6

The lock on Nettie Cobb's front door was about as complex as the lid of a candy-box; the first skeleton key Hugh tried worked after a little jiggling and joggling. He opened the door.

A small dog, yellow with a white bib, sat on the hall floor.

He uttered his single stern bark as morning sunlight fell around him and Hugh's large shadow fell on him.

"You must be Raider," Hugh said softly, reaching into his pocket.

The dog barked again and promptly rolled over on his back, all four paws splayed out limply.

"Say, that's cute!" Hugh said. Raider's stub of a tail thumped against the wooden floor, presumably in agreement. Hugh shut the door and squatted beside the dog. With one hand he scratched the right side of the dog's chest in that magic place that is somehow connected to the right rear paw, making it flail rapidly at the air. With his other he drew a Swiss Army knife out of his pocket.

"Aw, ain't you a good fella?" Hugh crooned. "Ain't you a one?"

He left off scratching and took a scrap of paper from his shirt pocket. Written on it in his labored schoolboy script was the message the fox-tail had given him—Hugh had sat down at his kitchen table and written it even before he got dressed, so he wouldn't forget a single word.

Nobody slings mud at my clean sheets. I told you I'd get you!

He pulled out the corkscrew hidden in one of the fat knife's slots and stuck the note on it. Then he turned the body of the knife sideways and closed his fist over it so the corkscrew protruded between the second and third fingers of his powerful right hand. He went back to scratching Raider, who had been lying on his back through all of this, eyeing Hugh cheerfully. He was cute as a bug, Hugh thought.

"Yes! Ain't you just the best old fella? Ain't you just the best old *one?*" Hugh asked, scratching. Now both rear legs were flailing. Raider looked like a dog pedaling an invisible bike.

"Yes you are! Yes you *are!* And do you know what I've got? I've got a fox-tail! Yes I do!"

Hugh held the corkscrew with the note pinned to it over the white bib on Raider's breast.

"And do you know what else? *I'm gonna keep it!*"

He brought his right hand down hard. The left, which had been scratching Raider, now pinned the dog as he gave the corkscrew three hard twists. Warm blood jetted up, dousing both of his hands. The dog rattled briefly on the floor and then lay still. He would utter his stern and harmless bark no more.

Hugh stood up, his heart thumping heavily. He suddenly felt very bad about what he had done—almost ill. Maybe she was crazy, maybe not, but she was alone in the world, and he had killed what was probably her only goddam friend.

He wiped his bloody hand across his shirt. The stain hardly showed at all on the dark wool. He couldn't take his eyes off the dog. He had done that. Yes, he had done it and he knew it, but he could hardly believe it. It was as if he had been in a trance, or something.

The inner voice, the one that sometimes talked to him about the A.A. meetings, spoke, up suddenly. *Yes—and I suppose you'll even be able to make yourself believe it, given time. But you weren't in any fucking trance; you knew just what you were doing.*

And why.

Panic began to race through him. He had to get out of here. He backed slowly down the hall, then uttered a hoarse cry as he ran into the closed front door. He fumbled behind him for the knob, and at last found it. He turned it, opened the door, and slid out of Crazy Nettie's house. He looked around wildly, somehow expecting to see half the town gathered here, watching him with solemn, judicial eyes. He saw no one but a kid pedaling up the street. There was a Playmate picnic cooler propped at an odd angle in the basket of the kid's bike. The kid spared Hugh Priest not so much as a glance as he went by, and when he was gone there were only the church-bells . . . this time they were calling the Methodists.

Hugh hurried down the walk. He told himself not to run, but he was trotting by the time he reached his truck, just the same. He fumbled the door open, slid in behind the wheel, and stabbed the ignition key at the slot. He did this three or four times, and the fucking key kept going astray. He had to steady his right hand with his left before he could finally get it to go where it belonged. His brow was dotted with fine beads of sweat. He had suffered through many hangovers, but he had never felt like this—this was like coming down with malaria, or something.

The truck started with a roar and a belch of blue smoke. Hugh's foot slipped off the clutch. The truck took two large, snapping jerks away from the curb and stalled. Breathing harshly through his mouth, Hugh got it started again and drove away fast.

By the time he got to the motor pool (it was still as deserted as the mountains of the moon) and exchanged the town truck for his old dented Buick, he had forgotten all about Raider and the horrible thing he had done with the corkscrew. He had something else, something much more important, to think about. During the drive back to the motor pool he had been gripped with a feverish certainty: someone had been in his house while he was gone, and that someone had stolen his fox-tail.

Hugh drove home at better than sixty, came to a stop four inches from his rickety porch in a squash of gravel and a cloud of dust, and ran up the steps two at a time. He burst in, ran to the closet, and yanked the door open. He stood on his toes and began to explore the high shelf with his panicky, fluttering hands.

At first they felt nothing but bare wood, and Hugh sobbed in fright and rage. Then his left hand sank deep into that rough plush that was neither silk nor wool, and a great sense of peace and fulfillment slipped over him. It was like food to the starving, rest to the weary . . . quinine to the malarial. The staccato drumroll in his chest finally began to ease. He drew the fox-tail down from its hiding place and sat at the kitchen table. He spread it across his fleshy thighs and began to stroke it with both hands.

Hugh sat like that for better than three hours.

7

The boy Hugh saw but failed to recognize, the one on the bike, was Brian Rusk. Brian had had his own dream last night, and had his own errand to run this morning in consequence.

In his dream, the seventh game of the World Series was about to start—some ancient Elvis-era World Series, featuring the old apocalyptic rivalry, that baseball avatar, the Dodgers versus the Yankees. Sandy Koufax was in the bullpen, warming up for Da Bums. He was also speaking to Brian Rusk, who stood beside him, between pitches. Sandy Koufax told Brian exactly what he was supposed to do. He was very clear about it; he dotted every *i* and crossed every *t*. No problem there.

The problem was this: Brian didn't want to do it.

He felt like a creep, arguing with a baseball legend like Sandy Koufax, but he had tried, just the same. "You don't understand, Mr. Koufax," he said. "I was supposed to play a trick on Wilma Jerzyck, and I did. I already *did*."

"So what?" Sandy Koufax said. "What's your point, bush?"

"Well, that was the deal. Eighty-five cents and one trick."

"You sure of that, bush? One trick? Are you sure? Did he say something like 'not more than one trick'? Something legal like that?"

Brian couldn't quite remember, but the feeling that he'd been had was growing steadily stronger inside him. No . . . not just *had*. *Trapped*. Like a mouse with a morsel of cheese.

"Let me tell you something, bush. The deal—"

He broke off and uttered a little *unhh!* as he threw a hard overhand fastball. It popped into the catcher's mitt with a rifleshot crack. Dust drifted up from the mitt, and Brian realized with dawning dismay that he knew the stormy blue eyes looking at them from behind the catcher's mask. Those eyes belonged to Mr. Gaunt.

Sandy Koufax caught Mr. Gaunt's return toss, then glanced at Brian with flat eyes like brown glass. "The deal is whatever I *say* the deal is, bush."

Sandy Koufax's eyes weren't brown at all, Brian had realized in his dream; they were also blue, which made perfect sense, since Sandy Koufax was *also* Mr. Gaunt.

"But—"

Koufax/Gaunt raised his gloved hand. "Let me tell you something, bush: I *hate* that word. Of all the words in the English language, it is easily the worst. I think it's the worst word in *any* language. You know what a butt is, bush? It's the place shit comes out of."

The man in the old-fashioned Brooklyn Dodgers uniform hid the baseball in his glove and turned to face Brian fully. It was Mr. Gaunt, all right, and Brian felt a freezing, dismal terror grip his heart. "I *did* say I wanted you to play a trick on Wilma, Brian, that's true, but I never said it was *the one and only* trick I wanted you to play on her. You just *assumed,* bush. Do you believe me, or would you like to hear the tape of our conversation?"

"I believe you," Brian said. He was perilously close to blubbering now. "I believe you, but—"

"What did I just tell you about that word, bush?"

Brian dropped his head and swallowed hard.

"You've got a lot to learn about dickering," Koufax/Gaunt said. "You and everyone else in Castle Rock. But that's one of the reasons I came—to conduct a seminar in the fine art of dickering. There was one fellow in town, a gent named Merrill, who knew a little something about it, but he's long gone and hard to find." He grinned, revealing Leland Gaunt's large, uneven teeth in Sandy Koufax's narrow, brooding face. "And the word 'bargain,' Brian—I have some tall teaching to do on that subject, as well."

"But—" The word was out of Brian's mouth before he could call it back.

"No buts about it," Koufax/Gaunt said. He leaned forward. His face stared solemnly at Brian from beneath the bill of his baseball cap. "Mr. Gaunt knows best. Can you say that, Brian?"

Brian's throat worked, but no sound came out. He felt hot, loose tears behind his eyes.

A large, cold hand descended upon Brian's shoulder. And gripped. "*Say* it!"

"Mr. Gaunt . . ." Brian had to swallow again to make room for the words. "Mr. Gaunt knows best."

"That's right, bush. That's exactly right. And what that means is you're going to do what I say . . . or else."

Brian summoned all his will and made one final effort.

"What if I say no, anyway? What if I say no because I didn't understand the whatdoyoucallems . . . the terms?"

Koufax/Gaunt picked the baseball out of his glove and closed his hand over it. Small drops of blood began to sweat out of the stitches.

"You really can't say no, Brian," he said softly. "Not anymore. Why, this is the seventh game of the World Series. All the chickens have come home to roost, and it's time to shit or git. Take a look around you. Go on and take a good look."

Brian looked around and was horrified to see that Ebbets Field was so full they were standing in the aisles . . . *and he knew them all.* He saw his Ma and Pa sitting with his little brother, Sean, in the Commissioner's Box behind home plate. His speech therapy class, flanked by Miss Ratcliffe on one end and her big dumb boyfriend, Lester Pratt, on the other, was ranged along the first-base line, drinking Royal Crown Cola and munching hotdogs. The entire Castle Rock Sheriff's Office was seated in the bleachers, drinking beer from paper cups with pictures of this year's Miss Rheingold contestants on them. He saw his Sunday School class, the town selectmen, Myra and Chuck Evans, his aunts, his uncles, his cousins. There, sitting behind third base, was Sonny Jackett, and when Koufax/Gaunt threw the bleeding ball and it made that rifleshot crack in the catcher's glove again, Brian saw that the face behind the mask now belonged to Hugh Priest.

"Run you down, little buddy," Hugh said as he threw the ball back. "Make you squeak."

"You see, bush, it's not just a question of the baseball card anymore," Koufax/Gaunt said from beside him. "You know that, don't you? When you slung that mud at Wilma Jerzyck's sheets, you started something. Like a guy who starts an avalanche just by shouting too loud on a warm winter day. Now your choice is simple. You can keep going . . . or you can stay where you are and get buried."

In his dream, Brian finally began to cry. He saw, all right. He saw just fine, now that it was too late to make any difference.

Gaunt squeezed the baseball. More blood poured out, and his fingertips sank deep into its white, fleshy surface. "If you don't want everybody in Castle Rock to know you were the one who started the avalanche, Brian, you had better do what I tell you."

Brian wept harder.

"When you deal with me," Gaunt said, winding up to throw, "you want to remember two things: Mr. Gaunt knows best . . . and the dealing isn't done until Mr. Gaunt *says* the dealing's done."

He threw with that sinuous all-of-a-sudden delivery which had made Sandy Koufax so hard to hit (that was, at least, the humble opinion of Brian's father), and when the ball hit

Hugh Priest's glove this time, it exploded. Blood and hair and stringy gobbets of flesh flew up in the bright autumn sun. And Brian had awakened, weeping into his pillow.

8

Now he was off to do what Mr. Gaunt had told him he must do. It had been simple enough to get away; he simply told his mother and father he didn't want to go to church that morning because he felt sick to his stomach (nor was this a lie). Once they were gone, he made his preparations.

It was hard to pedal his bike and even harder to keep it balanced, because of the Playmate picnic cooler in the bike basket. It was very heavy, and he was sweating and out of breath by the time he reached the Jerzyck house. There was no hesitation this time, no ringing the doorbell, no preplanned story. No one was here. Sandy Koufax/Leland Gaunt had told him in the dream that the Jerzycks would be staying late after the eleven o'clock Mass to discuss the upcoming Casino Nite festivities and would then be going to visit friends. Brian believed him. All he wanted now was to finish with this awful business just as fast as he could. And when it was done, he would go home, park his bike, and spend the rest of the day in bed.

He lifted the picnic cooler out of the bike basket, using both hands, and set it down on the grass. He was behind the hedge, where no one could see him. What he was about to do would be noisy, but Koufax/Gaunt had told him not to worry about that. He said most of the people on Willow Street were Catholics, and almost all of those not attending eleven o'clock Mass would have gone at eight and then left on their various Sunday day-trips. Brian didn't know if that was true or not. He only knew two things for sure: Mr. Gaunt knew best, and the deal wasn't done until Mr. Gaunt *said* the deal was done.

And this was the deal.

Brian opened the Playmate cooler. There were about a dozen good-sized rocks inside. Wrapped around each and held with a rubber band or two was a sheet of paper from Brian's school notebook. Printed on each sheet in large letters was this simple message:

I TOLD YOU TO LEAVE ME ALONE.
THIS IS YOUR LAST WARNING .

Brian took one of these and walked up the lawn until he was less than ten feet from the Jerzycks' big living-room window— what had been called a "picture window" back in the early sixties, when this house had been built. He wound up, hesitated for only a moment, and then let fly like Sandy Koufax facing the lead-off batter in the seventh game of the World Series. There was a huge and unmusical crash, followed by a thud as the rock hit the living-room carpet and rolled across the floor.

The sound had an odd effect on Brian. His fear left him, and his distaste for this further task—which could by no stretch of the imagination be dismissed as something so inconsequential as a prank—also evaporated. The sound of breaking glass excited him . . . made him feel, in fact, the way he felt when he had his daydreams about Miss Ratcliffe. Those had been foolish, and he knew that now, but there was nothing foolish about *this*. This was *real*.

Besides, he found that he now wanted the Sandy Koufax card more than ever. He had discovered another large fact about possessions and the peculiar psychological state they induce: the more one has to go through because of something one owns, the more one wants to keep that thing.

Brian took two more rocks and walked over to the broken picture window. He looked inside and saw the rock he had thrown. It was lying in the doorway between the living room and the kitchen. It looked very improbable there—like seeing a rubber boot on a church altar or a rose lying on the engine block of a tractor. One of the rubber bands holding the note to the rock had snapped, but the other was still okay. Brian's gaze shifted to the left and he found himself regarding the Jerzycks' Sony TV.

Brian wound up and threw. The rock hit the Sony dead-on. There was a hollow bang, a flash of light, and glass showered the carpet. The TV tottered on its stand but did not quite fall over. "Stee-rike *two!*" Brian muttered, then gave voice to a strange, strangled laugh.

He threw the other rock at a bunch of ceramic knick-knacks standing on a table by the sofa, but missed. It hit the wall with a thump and gouged out a chunk of plaster.

Brian laid hold of the Playmate's handle and lugged it around to the side of the house. He broke two bedroom windows. In back, he pegged a loaf-sized rock through the window in the top half of the kitchen door, then threw several more through the hole. One of these shattered the Cuisinart standing on the counter. Another blasted through the glass front of the RadarRange and landed right inside the microwave. "Stee-rike *three!* Siddown, bush!" Brian cried, and then laughed so hard he almost wet his pants.

When the throe had passed, he finished his circuit of the house. The Playmate was lighter now; he found he could carry it with one hand. He used his last three rocks to break the basement windows which showed among Wilma's fall flowers, then ripped up a few handfuls of the blooms for good measure. With that done, he closed the cooler, returned to his bicycle, put the Playmate into the basket, and mounted up for the ride home.

The Mislaburskis lived next door to the Jerzycks. As Brian pedaled out of the Jerzyck driveway, Mrs. Mislaburski opened her front door and came out on the stoop. She was dressed in a bright green wrapper. Her hair was bound up in a red doo-rag. She looked like an advertisement for Christmas in hell.

"What's going on over there, boy?" she asked sharply.

"I don't know, exactly. I think Mr. and Mrs. Jerzyck must be having an argument," Brian said, not stopping. "I just came over to ask if they needed anyone to shovel their driveway this winter, but I decided to come back another time."

Mrs. Mislaburski directed a brief, baleful glance at the Jerzyck house. Because of the hedges, only the second story was visible from where she stood. "If I were you, I wouldn't come back at all," she said. "That woman reminds me of those little fish they have down in South America. The ones that eat the cows whole."

"Piranha-fish," Brian said.

"That's right. Those."

Brian kept on pedaling. He was now drawing away from the woman in the green wrapper and red doo-rag. His heart was hustling right along, but it wasn't hammering or racing or anything like that. Part of him felt quite sure he was still dreaming. He didn't feel like himself at all—not like the Brian Rusk who got all A's and B's, the Brian Rusk who was a member of the Student Council and the Middle School Good Citizens' League, the Brian Rusk who got nothing but 1's in deportment.

"She'll kill somebody one of these days!" Mrs. Mislaburski called indignantly after Brian. "You just mark my words!"

Under his breath Brian whispered: "I wouldn't be a bit surprised."

He did indeed spend the rest of the day in bed. Under ordinary circumstances, this would have concerned Cora, perhaps enough to take Brian over to the Doc in the Box in Norway. Today, however, she hardly noticed that her son wasn't feeling well. This was because of the wonderful sunglasses Mr. Gaunt had sold her—she was absolutely entranced with them.

Brian got up around six o'clock, about fifteen minutes before his Pa came in from a day spent fishing on the lake with two friends. He got himself a Pepsi from the fridge and stood by the stove, drinking it. He felt quite a bit better.

He felt as if he might have finally fulfilled his part of the deal he had made with Mr. Gaunt.

He had also decided that Mr. Gaunt did indeed know best.

9

Nettie Cobb, without the slightest premonition of the unpleasant surprise awaiting her at home, was in high good spirits as she walked down Main Street toward Needful Things. She had a strong intuition that, Sunday morning or not, the shop would be open, and she was not disappointed.

"Mrs. Cobb!" Leland Gaunt said as she came in. "How very nice to see you!"

"It's nice to see you, too, Mr. Gaunt," she said . . . and it was.

Mr. Gaunt came over, his hand out, but Nettie shrank from his touch. It was dreadful behavior, so impolite, but she simply couldn't help herself. And Mr. Gaunt seemed to understand, God bless him. He smiled and changed course, closing the door behind her instead. He flipped the sign from OPEN to CLOSED with the speed of a professional gambler palming an ace.

"Sit down, Mrs. Cobb! Please! Sit down!"

"Well, all right . . . but I just came to tell you that Polly . . . Polly is . . ." She felt strange, somehow. Not bad, exactly, but strange. Swimmy in the head. She sat down rather gracelessly in one of the plush chairs. Then Mr. Gaunt was standing before her, his eyes fixed on hers, and the world seemed to center upon him and grow still again.

"Polly isn't feeling so well, is she?" Mr. Gaunt asked.

"That's it," Nettie agreed gratefully. "It's her hands, you know. She has . . ."

"Arthritis, yes, terrible, such a shame, shit happens, life's a bitch and then you die, tough titty said the kitty. I know, Nettie." Mr. Gaunt's eyes were growing again. "But there's no need for me to call her . . . or call *on* her, for that matter. Her hands are feeling better now."

"Are they?" Nettie asked distantly.

"You betcha! They still hurt, of course, which is good, but they don't hurt badly enough to keep her away, and that's better still—don't you agree, Nettie?"

"Yes," Nettie said faintly, but she had no idea of what she was agreeing to.

"You," Mr. Gaunt said in his softest, most cheerful voice, "have got a big day ahead of you, Nettie."

"I do?" It was news to her; she had been planning to spend the afternoon in her favorite living-room chair, knitting and watching TV with Raider at her feet.

"Yes. A *very* big day. So I want you to just sit there and rest for a moment while I go get something. Will you do that?"

"Yes . . ."

"Good. And close your eyes, why don't you? Have a really *good* rest, Nettie!"

Nettie obediently closed her eyes. An unknown length of time later, Mr. Gaunt told her to open them again. She did, and felt a pang of disappointment. When people told you to close your eyes, sometimes they wanted to give you something nice. A present. She had hoped that when she opened her eyes again, Mr. Gaunt might be holding another carnival glass lampshade, but all he had was a pad of paper. The sheets were small and pink. Each one was headed with the words

TRAFFIC VIOLATION WARNING.

"Oh," she said. "I thought it might be carnival glass."

"I don't think you'll be needing any more carnival glass, Nettie."

"No?" The pang of disappointment returned. It was stronger this time.

"No. Sad, but true. Still, I imagine you remember promising you'd do something for me." Mr. Gaunt sat down next to her. "You *do* remember that, don't you?"

"Yes," she said. "You want me to play a trick on Buster. You want me to put some papers in his house."

"That's right, Nettie—very good. Do you still have the key I gave you?"

Slowly, like a woman in an underwater ballet, Nettie brought the key from the right-hand pocket of her coat. She held it up so Mr. Gaunt could see it.

"That's very good!" he told her warmly. "Now put it back, Nettie. Put it back where it's safe."

She did.

"Now. Here are the papers." He put the pink pad in one of her hands. Into the other he placed a Scotch-tape dispenser. Alarm bells were going off somewhere inside her now, but they were far away, hardly audible.

"I hope this won't take long. I ought to go home soon. I have to feed Raider. He's my little dog."

"I know all about Raider," said Mr. Gaunt, and offered Nettie a wide smile. "But I have a feeling that he doesn't have much appetite today. I don't think you need to worry about him pooping on the kitchen floor, either."

"But—"

He touched her lips with one of his long fingers, and she felt suddenly sick to her stomach.

"Don't," she whined, pressing back into her chair. "Don't, it's awful."

"So they tell me," Mr. Gaunt agreed. "So if you don't want me to be awful to you, Nettie, you mustn't ever say that awful little word to me."

"What word?"

"*But.* I disapprove of that word. In fact, I think it's fair to say I *hate* that word. In the best of all possible worlds, there would be no need for such a puling little word. I want you to say something else for me, Nettie—I want you to say some words that I love. Words that I absolutely *adore*."

"What words?"

"Mr. Gaunt knows best. Say that."

"Mr. Gaunt knows best," she repeated, and as soon as the words were out of her mouth she understood how absolutely and completely true they were.

"Mr. Gaunt *always* knows best."

"Mr. Gaunt *always* knows best."

"Right! Just like Father," Mr. Gaunt said, and then laughed hideously. It was a sound like plates of rock moving deep in the earth, and the color of his eyes shifted rapidly from blue to green to brown to black when he did it. "Now, Nettie—listen carefully. You have this one little errand to do for me and then you can go home. Do you understand?"

Nettie understood.

And she listened very carefully.

CHAPTER TEN

1

South Paris is a small and squalid milltown eighteen miles northeast of Castle Rock. It is not the only jerkwater Maine town named after a European city or country; there is a Madrid (the natives pronounce it *Mad*-drid), a Sweden, an Etna, a Calais (pronounced so it rhymes with Dallas), a Cambridge, and a Frankfort. Someone may know how or why so many wide places in the road ended up with such an exotic variety of names, but I do not.

What I do know is that about twenty years ago a very good French chef decided to move out of New York and open his own restaurant in Maine's Lakes Region, and that he *further* decided there could be no better place for such a venture than a town named South Paris. Not even the stench of the tanning mills could dissuade him. The result was an eating establishment called Maurice. It is still there to this day, on Route 117 by the railroad tracks and just across the road from McDonald's. And it was to Maurice that Danforth "Buster" Keeton took his wife for lunch on Sunday, October 13th.

Myrtle spent a good deal of that Sunday in an ecstatic daze, and the fine food at Maurice was not the reason. For the last few months—almost a year, really—life with Danforth had been extremely unpleasant. He ignored her almost completely . . . except when he yelled at her. Her self-esteem, which had never been very high, plummeted to new depths. She knew as well as any woman ever has that abuse does not have to be administered with the fists to be effective. Men as well as women can wound with their tongues, and Danforth Keeton knew how to use his very well; he had inflicted a thousand invisible cuts on her with its sharp sides over the last year.

She did not know about the gambling—she really believed he went to the track mostly to watch. She didn't know about the embezzlement, either. She did know that several members of Danforth's family had been unstable, but she did not connect this behavior with Danforth himself. He didn't drink to excess, didn't forget to put on his clothes before going out in the morning, didn't talk to people who weren't there, and so she assumed he was all right. She assumed, in other words, that something was wrong with her. That at some point this something had simply caused Danforth to stop loving her.

She had spent the last six months or so trying to face the bleak prospect of the thirty or even forty loveless years which lay ahead of her as this man's mate, this man who had become by turns angry, coldly sarcastic, and unmindful of her. She had become just another piece of furniture as far as Danforth was concerned . . . unless, of course, she got in his way. If she did that—if his supper wasn't ready for him when he was ready for it, if the floor in his study looked dirty to him, even if the sections of the newspaper were in the wrong order when he came to the breakfast table—he called her dumb. He told her that if her ass fell off, she wouldn't know where to find it. He said that if brains were black powder, she wouldn't be able to blow her nose without a blasting cap. At first she had tried to defend herself from these tirades, but he cut her defenses apart as if they were the walls of a child's cardboard castle. If she grew angry in turn, he overtopped her into white rages that terrified her. So she had given anger up and had descended into dooms of bewilderment instead. These days she only smiled helplessly in the face of his anger, promised to do better, and went to their room, where she lay on the bed and wept and wondered whatever was to become of her and wished-wished-*wished* that she had a friend she could talk to.

She talked to her dolls instead. She'd started collecting them during the first few years of her marriage, and had always kept them in boxes in the attic. During the last year, though, she had brought them down to the sewing room, and sometimes, after her tears were shed, she crept into the sewing room and played with them. *They* never shouted. *They* never ignored. *They* never asked her how she got so stupid, did it come naturally or did she take lessons.

She had found the most wonderful doll of all yesterday, in the new shop.

And today everything had changed.

This morning, to be exact.

Her hand crept under the table and she pinched herself (not for the first time) just to make sure she wasn't dreaming. But after the pinch she was still here in Maurice, sitting in a bar of bright October sunshine, and Danforth was still there, across the table from her, eating with hearty good appetite, his face wreathed in a smile that looked almost alien to her, because she hadn't seen one there in such a long time.

She didn't know what had caused the change and was afraid to ask. She knew he had gone off to Lewiston Raceway last night, just as he almost always did during the evening (presumably because the people he met there were more interesting than the people he met every day in Castle Rock—his wife, for instance), and when she woke up this morning, she expected to find his half of the bed empty (or not slept in at all, which would mean that he had spent the rest of the night dozing in his study chair) and to hear him downstairs, muttering to himself in his bad-tempered way.

Instead, he had been in bed beside her, wearing the striped red pajamas she had given him for Christmas last year. This was the first time she had ever seen him wear them—the first time they'd been out of the box, as far as she knew. He was awake. He rolled over on his side to face her, already smiling. At first the smile frightened her. She thought it might mean he was getting ready to kill her.

Then he touched her breast and winked. "Want to, Myrt? Or is it too early in the day for you?"

So they had made love, for the first time in over five months they had made love, and he had been absolutely *magnificent,* and now here they were, lunching at Maurice on an early Sunday afternoon like a pair of young lovers. She didn't know what had happened to work this wondrous change in her husband, and didn't care. She only wanted to enjoy it, and to hope it would last.

"Everything okay, Myrt?" Keeton asked, looking up from his plate and scrubbing vigorously at his face with his napkin.

She reached shyly across the table and touched his hand. "Everything's fine. Everything is just . . . just wonderful."

She had to take her hand away so she could dab hastily at her eyes with her napkin.

2

Keeton went on chowing into his boof borgnine, or whatever it was the Froggies called it, with great appetite. The reason for his happiness was simple. Every horse he had picked yesterday afternoon with the help of Winning Ticket had come in for him last night. Even Malabar, the thirty-to-one shot in the tenth race. He had come back to Castle Rock not so much driving as floating on air, with better than eighteen thousand dollars stuffed into his overcoat pockets. His bookie was probably still wondering where the money went. Keeton knew; it was safely tucked away in the back of his study closet. It was in an envelope. The envelope was in the Winning Ticket box, along with the precious game itself.

He had slept well for the first time in months, and when he woke up, he had a glimmering of an idea about the audit. A glimmering wasn't much, of course, but it was better than the confused darkness that had been roaring through his head since that awful letter came. All he had needed to get his brain out of neutral, it seemed, was one winning night at the track.

He could not make total restitution before the axe fell, that much was clear. Lewiston Raceway was the only track which ran nightly during the fall season, for one thing, and it was pretty small potatoes. He could tour the local county fairs and make a few thousand at the races there, but that wouldn't be enough, either. Nor could he risk many nights like last night, even at the Raceway. His bookie would grow wary, then refuse to accept his bets at all.

But he believed he could make partial restitution and minimize the *size* of the fiddles at the same time. He could also spin a tale. A sure-fire development prospect that hadn't come off. A terrible mistake . . . but one for which he had taken complete responsibility and for which he was now making good. He could point out that a really unscrupulous man, if placed in such a position as this, might well have used the grace period to scoop even more money out of the town treasury—as much as he possibly could—and then to run for a place (some *sunny* place with lots of palm trees and lots of white beaches and lots of young girls in string bikinis) from which extradition was difficult or downright impossible.

He could wax Christlike and invite those among them without sin to cast the first stone. That should give them pause. If there was a man-jack among them who had not had his fingers in the state pie from time to time, Keeton would eat that man's shorts. Without salt.

They would have to give him time. Now that he was able to set his hysteria aside and think the situation over rationally, he was almost sure they would. After all, they were politicians, too. They would know that the press would have plenty of tar and feathers left over for them, the supposed guardians of the public trust, once they had finished with Dan Keeton. They would know the questions which would surface in the wake of a public investigation or even (God forbid) a trial for embezzlement. Questions like how long—in fiscal years, if you please, gentlemen—had Mr. Keeton's little operation been going on? Questions like how come the State Bureau of Taxation hadn't awakened and smelled the coffee some time ago? Questions ambitious men would find distressing.

He believed he could squeak through. No guarantees, but it looked possible.

All thanks to Mr. Leland Gaunt.

God, he loved Leland Gaunt.

"Danforth?" Myrt asked shyly.

He looked up. "Hmmm?"

"This is the nicest day I've had in years. I just wanted you to know that. How grateful I am to have such a nice day. With you."

"Oh!" he said. The oddest thing had just happened to him. For a moment he hadn't been able to remember the name of the woman sitting across from him. "Well, Myrt, it's been nice for me, too."

"Will you be going to the race-track tonight?"

"No," he said, "I think tonight I'll stay home."

"That's nice," she said. She found it so nice, in fact, that she had to dab at her eyes with her napkin again.

He smiled at her—it wasn't his old sweet smile, the one which had wooed and won her to begin with—but it was close. "Say, Myrt! Want dessert?"

She giggled and flapped her napkin at him. "Oh, *you!*"

3

The Keeton home was a split-level ranch in Castle View. It was a long walk uphill for Nettie Cobb, and by the time she got there her legs were tired and she was very cold. She met only three or four other pedestrians, and none of them looked at her; they were bundled deep into the collars of their coats, for the wind had begun to blow strongly and it had a keen edge. An ad supplement from someone's Sunday *Telegram* danced across the street, then took off into the hard blue sky like some strange bird as she turned into the Keetons' driveway. Mr. Gaunt had told her that Buster and Myrtle wouldn't be home, and Mr. Gaunt knew best. The garage door was up, and that showboat of a Cadillac Buster drove was gone.

Nettie went up the walk, stopped at the front door, and took the pad and the Scotch tape from her left-hand coat pocket. She very much wanted to be home with the Sunday Super Movie on TV and Raider at her feet. And that's where she would be as soon as she finished this chore. She might not even bother with her knitting. She might just sit there with her carnival glass lampshade in her lap. She tore off the first pink slip and taped it over the sign by the doorbell, the embossed one which said THE KEETONS and NO SALESMEN, PLEASE. She put the tape and the pad back in her left pocket, then took the key from her right and slipped it into the lock. Before turning it, she briefly examined the pink slip she had just taped up.

Cold and tired as she was, she just *had* to smile a little. It really was a pretty good joke, especially considering the way Buster drove. It was a wonder he hadn't killed anyone. She wouldn't like to be the man whose name was signed at the bottom of the warning-slip, though. Buster could be awfully grouchy. Even as a child he hadn't been one to take a joke.

She turned the key. The lock opened easily. Nettie went inside.

4

"More coffee?" Keeton asked.

"Not for me," Myrtle said. "I'm as full as a tick." She smiled.

"Then let's go home. I want to watch the Patriots on TV." He glanced at his watch. "If we hurry, I think I can make the kick-off."

Myrtle nodded, happier than ever. The TV was in the living room, and if Dan meant to watch the game, he wasn't going to spend the afternoon cooped up in his study. "Let's hurry, then," she said.

Keeton held up one commanding finger. "Waiter? Bring me the check, please."

5

Nettie had stopped wanting to hurry home; she liked being in Buster and Myrtle's house.

For one thing, it was warm. For another, being here gave Nettie an unexpected sense of power—it was like seeing behind the scenes of two actual human lives. She began by going upstairs and looking through all the rooms. There were a lot of them, too, considering there were no children, but, as her mother had always been fond of saying, them that has, gets.

She opened Myrtle's bureau drawers, investigating her underwear. Some of it was silk, quality stuff, but to Nettie most of the good things looked old. The same was true of the dresses hung on her side of the closet. Nettie went on to the bathroom, where she inventoried the pills in the medicine cabinet, and from there to the sewing room, where she admired the dolls. A nice house. A lovely house. Too bad the man who lived here was a piece of shit.

Nettie glanced at her watch and supposed she should start putting up the little pink slips. And she would, too.

Just as soon as she finished looking around downstairs.

6

"Danforth, isn't this a little *too* fast?" Myrtle asked breathlessly as they swung around a slow-moving pulp truck. An oncoming car blared its horn at them as Keeton swung back into his lane.

"I want to make the kick-off," he said, and turned left onto the Maple Sugar Road, passing a sign which read CASTLE ROCK 8 MILES.

7

Nettie snapped on the TV—the Keetons had a big color Mitsubishi—and watched some of the Sunday Super Movie. Ava Gardner was in it, and Gregory Peck. Gregory seemed to be in love with Ava, although it was hard to tell; it might be the other woman he was in love with. There had been a nuclear war. Gregory Peck drove a submarine. None of this interested Nettie very much, so she turned off the TV, taped a pink slip to the screen, and went into the kitchen. She looked at what was in the cupboards (the dishes were Corelle, very nice, but the pots and pans were nothing to write home about), then checked the refrigerator. She wrinkled her nose. Too many leftovers. Too many leftovers was a sure sign of slipshod housekeeping. Not that Buster would know; she'd bet her boots on *that*. Men like Buster Keeton wouldn't be able to find their way around the kitchen with a map and a guide-dog.

She checked her watch again and started. She had spent

an awfully long time wandering around the house. *Too* long. Quickly, she began to tear off slips of pink paper and tape them to things—the refrigerator, the stove, the telephone which hung on the kitchen wall by the garage doorway, the break-front in the dining room. And the more quickly she worked, the more nervous she became.

8

Nettie had just gotten down to business when Keeton's red Cadillac crossed the Tin Bridge and started up Watermill Lane toward Castle View.

"Danforth?" Myrtle asked suddenly. "Could you let me out at Amanda Williams's house? I know it's a little out of the way, but she's got my fondue pot. I thought—" The shy smile came and went on her face again. "I thought I might make you—*us*—a little treat. For the football game. You could just drop me off."

He opened his mouth to tell her the Williamses' was a *lot* out of his way, the game was about to start, and she could get her goddam fondue pot tomorrow. He didn't like cheese when it was hot and runny anyway. The goddamned stuff was probably full of bacteria.

Then he thought better of it. Aside from himself, the Board of Selectmen was made up of two dumb bastards and one dumb bitch. Mandy Williams was the bitch. Keeton had been at some pains to see Bill Fullerton, the town barber, and Harry Samuels, Castle Rock's only mortician, on Friday. He was also at pains to make these seem like casual calls, but they weren't. There was always the possibility that the Board of Taxation had begun sending *them* letters as well. He had satisfied himself that they were not—not yet, at least—but the Williams bitch had been out of town on Friday.

"All right," he said, then added: "You might ask her if any

town business has come to her attention. Anything I should get in touch with her about."

"Oh, honey, you know I can never keep that stuff straight—"

"I *do* know that, but you can *ask,* can't you? You're not too dumb to *ask,* are you?"

"No," she said hastily, in a small voice.

He patted her hand. "I'm sorry."

She looked at him with a wonderstruck expression. He had *apologized* to her. Myrtle thought he might have done this at some time or other in their years of marriage, but she could not remember when.

"Just ask her if the State boys have been bothering about anything lately," he said. "Land-use regulations, the damn sewage . . . taxes, maybe. I'd come in and ask myself, but I really want to catch the kick-off."

"All right, Dan."

The Williams house was halfway up Castle View. Keeton piloted the Cadillac into the driveway and parked behind the woman's car. It was foreign, of course. A Volvo. Keeton guessed she was a closet Communist, a lesbo, or both.

Myrtle opened her door and got out, flashing him the shy, slightly nervous smile again as she did so.

"I'll be home in half an hour."

"Fine. Don't forget to ask if she's aware of any new town business," he said. And if Myrt's description—garbled though it would surely be—of what Amanda Williams said raised even one single hackle on Keeton's neck, he would check in with the bitch personally . . . tomorrow. Not this afternoon. This afternoon was *his.* He was feeling much too good to even *look* at Amanda Williams, let alone make chit-chat with her.

He hardly waited for Myrtle to close her door before throwing the Cadillac in reverse and backing down to the street again.

9

Nettie had just taped the last of the pink sheets to the door of the closet in Keeton's study when she heard a car turn into the driveway. A muffled squeak escaped her throat. For a moment she was frozen in place, unable to move.

Caught! her mind screamed as she listened to the soft, well-padded burble of the Cadillac's big engine. *Caught! Oh Jesus Savior meek and mild I'm caught! He'll kill me!*

Mr. Gaunt's voice spoke in answer. It was not friendly now; it was cold and it was commanding and it came from a place deep in the center of her brain. *He probably WILL kill you if he catches you, Nettie. And if you panic, he'll catch you for sure. The answer is simple: don't panic. Leave the room. Do it now. Don't run, but walk fast. And as quietly as you can.*

She hurried across the second-hand Turkish rug on the study floor, her legs as stiff as sticks, muttering "Mr. Gaunt knows best" in a low litany, and entered the living room. Pink rectangles of paper glared at her from what seemed like every available surface. One even dangled from the central light-fixture on a long strand of tape.

Now the car's engine had taken on a hollow, echoey sound. Buster had driven into the garage.

Go, Nettie! Go right away! Now is your only chance!

She fled across the living room, tripped over a hassock, and went sprawling. She banged her head on the floor almost hard enough to knock herself out—*would* have knocked herself out, almost certainly, but for the thin cushion of a throw-rug. Bright globular lights skated across her field of vision. She scrambled up again, vaguely aware that her forehead was bleeding, and began fumbling at the knob of the front door as the car engine cut off in the garage. She cast a terrified glance back over her shoulder in the direction of the kitchen. She could see the door to the garage, the door he would come through. One of the pink slips of paper was taped to it.

The doorknob turned under her hand, but the door wouldn't open. It seemed stuck shut.

From the garage came a hefty *swoop-chunk* as Keeton slammed his car door. Then the rattle of the motorized garage door starting down on its tracks. She heard his footsteps gritting across the concrete. Buster was whistling.

Nettie's frantic gaze, partially obscured by blood from her cut forehead, fell upon the thumb-bolt. It had been turned. That was why the door wouldn't open for her. She must have turned it herself when she came in, although she couldn't remember doing it. She flicked it up, pulled the door open, and stepped through.

Less than a second later, the door between the garage and the kitchen opened. Danforth Keeton stepped inside, unbuttoning his overcoat. He stopped. The whistle died on his lips. He stood there with his hands frozen in the act of undoing one of the lower coat-buttons, his lips still pursed, and looked around the kitchen. His eyes began to widen.

If he had gone to the living-room window right then, he would have seen Nettie running wildly across his lawn, her unbuttoned coat billowing around her like the wings of a bat. He might not have recognized her, but he would surely have seen it was a woman, and this might have changed later events considerably. The sight of all those pink slips froze him in place, however, and in his first shock his mind was capable of producing two words and two words only. They flashed on and off inside his head like a giant neon sign with letters of screaming scarlet: THE PERSECUTORS! THE PERSECUTORS! THE PERSECUTORS!

10

Nettie reached the sidewalk and ran down Castle View as fast as she could. The heels of her loafers rattled a frightened tattoo, and her ears convinced her that she was hearing more feet than her own—Buster was behind her, Buster was chasing her, and when Buster caught her he might hurt her . . . but that didn't matter. It didn't matter because he could do worse than just hurt her. Buster was an important man in town, and if he wanted her sent back to Juniper Hill, she would be sent. So Nettie ran. Blood trickled down her forehead and into her eye, and for a moment she saw the world through a pale red lens, as if all the nice houses on the View had begun to ooze blood. She wiped it away with the sleeve of her coat and went on running.

The sidewalk was deserted, and most eyes inside the houses which were occupied this early Sunday afternoon were trained on the Patriots-Jets game. Nettie was seen by only one person.

Tansy Williams, fresh from two days in Portland where she and her mommy had gone to visit Grampa, was looking out the living-room window, sucking a lollypop and holding her teddy bear, Owen, under her left arm, when Nettie went by with wings on her heels.

"Mommy, a lady just ran by," Tansy reported.

Amanda Williams was sitting in the kitchen with Myrtle Keeton. They each had a cup of coffee. The fondue pot sat between them on the table. Myrtle had just asked if there was any town business going on that Dan should know about, and Amanda considered this a very odd question. If Buster wanted to know something, why hadn't he come in himself? For that matter, why such a question on a Sunday afternoon in the first place?

"Honey, Mommy's talking with Mrs. Keeton."

"She had blood on her," Tansy reported further.

Amanda smiled at Myrtle. "I *told* Buddy that if he was going to rent that *Fatal Attraction,* he should wait until Tansy was in bed to watch it."

Meantime, Nettie went on running. When she reached the intersection of Castle View and Laurel, she had to stop for a while. The Public Library was here, and there was a curved stone wall running around its lawn. She leaned against it, gasping and sobbing for breath as the wind tore past her, tugging at her coat. Her hands were pressed against her left side, where she had a deep stitch.

She looked back up the hill and saw that the street was empty. Buster had not been following her after all; that had just been her imagination. After a few moments she was able to hunt through her coat pockets for a Kleenex to wipe away some of the blood on her face. She found one, and she also discovered that the key to Buster's house was no longer there. It might have fallen out of her pocket as she ran down the hill, but she thought it more likely that she had left it in the lock of the front door. But what did that matter? She had gotten out before Buster saw her, that was the important thing. She thanked God that Mr. Gaunt's voice had spoken to her in the nick of time, forgetting that Mr. Gaunt was the reason she had been in Buster's home in the first place.

She looked at the smear of blood on the Kleenex and decided the cut probably wasn't as bad as it could have been. The flow seemed to be slowing down. The stitch in her side was going away, too. She pushed off the rock wall and began to plod toward home with her head down, so the cut wouldn't show.

Home, that was the thing to think about. Home and her beautiful carnival glass lampshade. Home and the Sunday Super Movie. Home and Raider. When she was at home with the door locked, the shades pulled, the TV on, and Raider sleeping at her feet, all of this would seem like a horrible dream—the sort of dream she'd had in Juniper Hill, after she had killed her husband.

Home, that was the place for her.

Nettie walked a little faster. She would be there soon.

11

Pete and Wilma Jerzyck had a light lunch with the Pulaskis after Mass, and following lunch, Pete and Jake Pulaski settled in front of the TV to watch the Patriots kick some New York ass. Wilma cared not a fig for football—baseball, basketball, or hockey, either, as far as that went. The only pro sport she liked was wrestling, and although Pete didn't know it, Wilma would have left him in the wink of an eye for Chief Jay Strongbow.

She helped Frieda with the dishes, then said she was going home to watch the rest of the Sunday Super Movie—it was *On the Beach,* with Gregory Peck. She told Pete she was taking the car.

"That's fine," he said, his eyes never leaving the TV. "I don't mind walking."

"Goddam good thing for you," she muttered under her breath as she went out.

Wilma was actually in a good mood, and the major reason had to do with Casino Nite. Father John wasn't backing down on it the way Wilma had expected him to do, and she had liked the way he'd looked that morning during the homily, which was called "Let Us Each Tend Our Own Garden." His tone had been as mild as ever, but there had been nothing mild about his blue eyes or his outthrust chin. Nor had all his fancy gardening metaphors fooled Wilma or anyone else about what he was saying: if the Baptists insisted on sticking their collective nose into the Catholic carrot-patch, they were going to get their collective ass kicked.

The thought of kicking ass (particularly on this scale) always put Wilma in a good mood.

Nor was the prospect of ass-kicking the only pleasure of Wilma's Sunday. She hadn't had to cook a heavy Sunday meal for once, and Pete was safely parked with Jake and Frieda. If she was lucky, he would spend the whole afternoon watching men try to rupture each other's spleens and she could watch the movie in peace. But first she thought she might call her old friend Nettie. She thought she had Crazy Nettie pretty well buffaloed, and that was all very well . . . for a start. But *only* for

a start. Nettie still had those muddy sheets to pay for, whether
she knew it or not. The time had come to put a few more moves
on Miss Mental Illness of 1991. This prospect filled Wilma
with anticipation, and she drove home as fast as she could.

12

Like a man in a dream, Danforth Keeton walked to his refrigerator and pulled off the pink slip which had been taped there.
The words

TRAFFIC VIOLATION WARNING

were printed across the top in black block letters. Below these
words was the following message:

> *Just a* WARNING—*but please read and heed!*
> *You have been observed breaking one or more traf-*
> *fic laws. The citing officer has elected to "let you off*
> *with a warning" this time, but he has recorded the*
> *make, model, and license number of your car, and*
> *next time you will be charged. Please remember that*
> *traffic laws are for* EVERYBODY.
> *Drive defensively!*
> *Arrive alive!*
> *Your Local Police Department thanks you!*

Below the sermon was a series of blanks labelled MAKE,
MODEL, and LIC. #. Printed on the slip in the first two blanks
were the words Cadillac and Seville. Neatly printed in the blank
for LIC. # was this:

BUSTER 1.

Most of the slip was taken up by a checklist of common
traffic violations such as failure to signal, failure to stop, and il-

legal parking. None of them was checked. Toward the bottom
were the words OTHER VIOLATION(S), followed by two blank
lines. OTHER VIOLATION(S) had been checked. The message on
the lines provided to describe the violation was also neatly
printed in small block capitals. It read:

> BEING THE BIGGEST COCKSUCKER
> IN CASTLE ROCK.

At the bottom was a line with the words CITING OFFICER
printed under it. The rubber-stamp signature on this line was
Norris Ridgewick.

Slowly, very slowly, Keeton clenched his fist on the pink
slip. It crackled and bent and crumpled. At last it disappeared
between Keeton's big knuckles. He stood in the middle of the
kitchen, looking around at all the other pink slips. A vein beat
time in the center of his forehead.

"I'll kill him," Keeton whispered. "I swear to God and all
the saints I'll kill that skinny little fuck."

13

When Nettie arrived home it was only twenty past one, but
it felt to her as if she had been gone for months, maybe even
years. As she walked up the cement path to her door, her terrors
slipped from her shoulders like invisible weights. Her head
still ached from the tumble she had taken, but she thought a
headache was a very small price to pay for being allowed to arrive back at her own little house safe and undetected.

She still had her own key; that was in the pocket of her dress.
She took it out and put it in the lock. "Raider?" she called as she
turned it. "Raider, I'm home!"

She opened the door.

"Where's Mummy's wittle boy, hmmm? Where *is* ums?
Izzum hungwy?" The hallway was dark, and at first she did not

see the small bundle lying on the floor. She took her key out of the lock and stepped; in. "Is Mummy's wittle boy *awful* hungwy? Izzum just *sooo* hung—"

Her foot struck something which was both stiff and yielding, and her voice halted in mid-simper. She looked down and saw Raider.

At first she tried to tell herself she wasn't seeing what her eyes *told* her she was seeing—wasn't, wasn't, wasn't. That wasn't Raider on the floor with something sticking out of his chest—how could it be?

She closed the door and beat frantically at the wall-switch with one hand. At last, the hall light jumped on and she saw. Raider was lying on the floor. He was lying on his back the way he did when he wanted to be scratched, and there was something red jutting out of him, something that looked like . . . looked like . . .

Nettie uttered a high, wailing scream—it was so high it sounded like the whine of some huge mosquito—and fell on her knees beside her dog.

"Raider! Oh Jesus Savior meek and mild! Oh my God, Raider, you ain't dead, are you? You ain't dead?"

Her hand—her cold, cold hand—beat at the red thing sticking out of Raider's chest the way it had beat at the light-switch a few seconds before. At last it caught hold and she tore it free, using a strength drawn from the deepest wells of her grief and horror. The corkscrew came out with a thick ripping sound, pulling chunks of flesh, small clots of blood, and tangles of hair with it. It left a ragged dark hole the size of a four-ten slug. Nettie shrieked. She dropped the gory corkscrew and gathered the small, stiff body in her arms.

"Raider!" she cried. *"Oh my little doggy! No! Oh no!"* She rocked him back and forth against her breast, trying to bring him back to life with her warmth, but it seemed she had no warmth to give. She was cold. Cold.

Some time later she put his body down on the hall floor

again and fumbled around with her hand until she found the Swiss Army knife with the murdering corkscrew jutting out of its handle. She picked it up dully, but some of that dullness left her when she saw that a note had been impaled upon the murder weapon. She pulled it off with numb fingers and held it up close in front of her. The paper was stiff with her poor little dog's blood, but she could still read the words scrawled on it:

Nobody slings mud at my clean sheets. I told you I'd get you!

The look of distracted grief and horror slowly left Nettie's eyes. It was replaced with a gruesome sort of intelligence that sparkled there like tarnished silver. Her cheeks, which had gone as pale as milk when she finally understood what had happened here, began to fill with dark red color. Her lips peeled slowly back from her teeth. She bared them at the note. Two harsh words slid out of her open mouth, hot and hoarse and rasping:

"You . . . bitch!"

She crumpled the paper in her fist and threw it against the wall. It bounced back and landed near Raider's body. Nettie pounced upon it, picked it up, and spat on it. Then she threw it away again. She got up and walked slowly down to the kitchen, her hands opening, snapping shut into fists, then springing open only to snap shut again.

14

Wilma Jerzyck drove her little yellow Yugo into her driveway, got out, and walked briskly toward the front door, digging in her purse for her housekey. She was humming "Love Makes the World Go Round" under her breath. She found the key,

put it in the lock . . . and then paused as some random movement caught the corner of her eye. She looked to her right, and
gaped at what she saw.

The living-room curtains were fluttering in the brisk afternoon wind. They were fluttering outside the house. And
the *reason* they were fluttering outside the house was that
the big picture window, which had cost the Clooneys four
hundred dollars to replace when their idiot son had broken
it with a baseball three years ago, was shattered. Long arrows
of glass pointed inward from the frame toward the central
hole.

"What the *fuck?*" Wilma cried, and turned the key in the
lock so hard she almost broke it off.

She rushed indoors, grabbing the door to slam it shut behind her, and then froze in place. For the first time in her adult
life, Wilma Wadlowski Jerzyck was shocked to complete im-
mobility.

The living room was a shambles. The TV—their beautiful
big-screen TV on which they still owed eleven payments—was
shattered. The innards were black and smoking. The picture-
tube lay in a thousand shiny fragments on the carpet. Across
the room, a huge hole had been knocked in one of the living-
room walls. A large package, shaped like a loaf, lay below this
hole. Another lay in the doorway to the kitchen.

She closed the door and approached the object in the doorway. One part of her mind, not quite coherent, told her to be
very careful—it might be a bomb. As she passed the TV, she
caught a hot, unpleasant aroma—a cross between singed insulation and burned bacon.

She squatted down by the package in the doorway and saw
it wasn't a package at all—at least, not in any ordinary, sense.
It was a rock with a piece of lined notebook paper wrapped
around it and held in place with a rubber band. She pulled the
paper out and read this message:

*I TOLD YOU TO LEAVE ME ALONE.
THIS IS YOUR LAST WARNING.*

When she had read it twice, she looked at the other rock. She went over to it and pulled off the sheet of paper rubberbanded to it. Identical paper, identical message. She stood up, holding one wrinkled sheet in each hand, looking from one to the other again and again, her eyes moving like those of a woman watching a hotly contested Ping-Pong match. Finally she spoke three words:

"Nettie. That cunt."

She walked into the kitchen and drew in breath over her teeth in a harsh, whistling gasp. She cut her hand on a sliver of glass taking the rock out of the microwave and picked the splinter absently out of her palm before removing the paper banded to the rock. It bore the same message.

Wilma walked quickly through the other rooms downstairs and observed more damage. She took all the notes. They were all the same. Then she walked back to the kitchen. She looked at the damage unbelievingly.

"Nettie," she said again.

At last the iceberg of shock around her was beginning to melt. The first emotion to replace it was not anger but incredulity. My, she thought, that woman really *must* be crazy. She really *must,* if she thought she could do something like this to me—to *me!*—and live to see the sun go down. Who did she think she was dealing with here, Rebecca of Fuckybrook Farm?

Wilma's hand closed on the notes in a spasm. She bent over and rubbed the crumpled carnation of paper sticking out of her fist briskly over her wide bottom.

"I wipe my fucking ass on your last warning!" she cried, and threw the papers away.

She looked around the kitchen again with the wondering

eyes of a child. A hole in the microwave. A big dent in the Amana refrigerator. Broken glass all over. In the other room the TV, which had cost them almost sixteen hundred dollars, smelled like a Fry-O-Lator full of hot dogshit. And who had done it all? Who?

Why, Nettie Cobb had done it, that was who. Miss Mental Illness of 1991.

Wilma began to smile.

A person who did not know Wilma might have mistaken it for a gentle smile, a kindly smile, a smile of love and good fellowship. Her eyes shone with some powerful emotion; the unwary might have mistaken it for exaltation. But if Peter Jerzyck, who knew her best, had seen her face at that moment, he would have run the other way as fast as his legs could carry him.

"No," Wilma said in a soft, almost caressing voice. "Oh, no, babe. You don't understand. You don't understand what it means to fuck with Wilma. You don't have the slightest *idea* what it means to fuck with Wilma Wadlowski Jerzyck."

Her smile widened.

"But you will."

Two magnetized steel strips had been mounted on the wall near the microwave. Most of the knives which had hung from these strips had been knocked loose by the rock Brian had pegged into the RadarRange; they lay on the counter in a pick-up-sticks jumble. Wilma picked out the longest, a Kingsford carving knife with a white bone handle, and slowly ran her wounded palm along the side of the blade, smearing the cutting edge with blood.

"I'm going to teach you everything you need to know."

Holding the knife in her fist, Wilma strode across the living room, crunching glass from the broken window and the TV picture-tube under the low heels of her black for-church shoes. She went out the door without closing it and cut across her lawn in the direction of Ford Street.

15

At the same time Wilma was selecting a knife from the clutter of them on the counter, Nettie Cobb was pulling a meat-cleaver from one of her kitchen drawers. She knew it was sharp, because Bill Fullerton down at the barber shop had put an edge on it for her less than a month ago.

Nettie turned and walked slowly down the hallway toward her front door. She stopped and knelt for a moment beside Raider, her poor little dog who had never done anything to anyone.

"I warned her," she said softly as she stroked Raider's fur. "I warned her, I gave that crazy Polish woman every chance. I gave her every chance in the world. My dear little doggy. You wait for me. You wait, because I'll be with you soon."

She got up and went out of her house, bothering with the door no more than Wilma had bothered with hers. Security had ceased to interest Nettie. She stood on the stoop for a moment, taking deep breaths, then cut across her lawn in the direction of Willow Street.

16

Danforth Keeton ran into his study and ripped open the closet door. He crawled all the way to the back. For a terrible moment he thought the game was gone, that the goddam intruding persecuting motherfucker Deputy Sheriff had taken it, and his future along with it. Then his hands fell upon the box and he tore back the lid. The tin racetrack was still there. And the envelope was still tucked beneath it. He bent it back and forth, listening to the bills crackle inside, and then replaced it.

He hurried to the window, looking out for Myrtle. She mustn't see the pink slips. He had to take them all down before

Myrtle got back, and how many were there? A hundred? He looked around his study and saw them stuck up everywhere. A thousand? Yes, maybe. Maybe a thousand. Even two thousand did not seem entirely out of the question. Well, if she got here before he was done cleaning up, she would just have to wait on the step, because he wasn't going to let her in until every one of these goddamned persecuting things was burning in the kitchen woodstove. Every . . . damned . . . one.

He snatched the slip dangling from the light-fixture. The tape stuck to his cheek and he pawed it away with a little squeal of anger. On this one, a single word glared up from the line reserved for OTHER VIOLATION(S):

EMBEZZLEMENT

He ran to the reading lamp by his easy chair. Snatched up the slip taped to the shade.

OTHER VIOLATION(S):

MISAPPROPRIATION OF TOWN FUNDS

The TV:

HORSE-FUCKING

The glass of his Lions Club Good Citizenship Award, mounted above the fireplace:

CORNHOLING YOUR MOTHER

The kitchen door:

COMPULSIVE MONEY-CHUCKING

AT LEWISTON RACEWAY

The door to the garage:

PSYCHOTIC GARBAGE-HEAD PARANOIA

He gathered them up as fast as he could, eyes wide and bulging from his fleshy face, his thinning hair standing up in wild disarray. He was soon panting and coughing, and an ugly reddish-purple color began to overspread his cheeks. He looked like a fat child with a grown-up's face on some strange, desperately important treasure hunt.

He pulled one from the front of the china closet:

STEALING FROM THE TOWN PENSION FUND
TO PLAY THE PONIES

Keeton hurried into his study with a pile of slips clutched in his right hand, strands of tape flying back from his fist, and began to pluck up more of the slips. The ones in here all stuck to a single subject, and with horrible accuracy:

EMBEZZLEMENT.

THEFT.

STEALING.

EMBEZZLEMENT.

FRAUD.

MISAPPROPRIATION.

BAD STEWARDSHIP.

EMBEZZLEMENT.

That word most of all, glaring, shouting, accusing:

OTHER VIOLATION(S): EMBEZZLEMENT.

He thought he heard something outside and ran to the window again. Maybe it was Myrtle. Maybe it was Norris Ridgewick, come by to gloat and laugh. If so, Keeton would get his gun and shoot him. But not in the head. No. In the head would be too good, too quick, for scum like Ridgewick. Keeton would guthole him, and leave him to scream himself to death on the lawn.

But it was only the Garsons' Scout, trundling down the View toward town. Scott Garson was the town's most important banker. Keeton and his wife sometimes took dinner with the Garsons—they were nice people, and Garson himself was politically important. What would *he* think if he saw these slips? What would he think of that word, EMBEZZLEMENT, screaming off the pink violation slips again and again, screaming like a woman being raped in the middle of the night?

He ran back into the dining room, panting. Had he missed any? He didn't think so. He'd gotten them all, at least down he—

No! There was one! Right on the newel post of the stairway! What if he had missed that one? My God!

He ran to it, snatched it up.

MAKE: SHITMOBILE
MODEL: OLD AND WEARY
LIC. #: OLDFUCK I
OTHER VIOLATION(S): FINANCIAL FAGGOTRY

More? Were there more? Keeton coursed through the down-stairs rooms at a dead run. His shirttail had come out of his pants and his hairy belly was bobbling wildly over his belt-buckle. He saw no more . . . at least not down here.

After another quick, frantic look out the window to make sure Myrt wasn't yet in sight, he pelted upstairs with his heart thundering in his chest.

17

Wilma and Nettie met on the corner of Willow and Ford. There they halted, staring at each other like gunslingers in a spaghetti Western. The wind flapped their coats briskly to and fro. The sun shuttered in and out of the clouds; their shadows came and went like fitful visitors.

No traffic moved on either of these two streets, or on the sidewalks. They owned this little corner of the autumn after-noon.

"You killed my dog, you bitch!"

"You broke my TV! You broke my windows! You broke my *microwave,* you crazy cunt!"

"I warned you!"

"Stick your warning up your old dirt road!"

"I'm going to kill you!"

"Take one step and *someone's* going to die here, all right, but it won't be me!"

Wilma spoke these words with alarm and dawning surprise; Nettie's face made her realize for the first time that the two of them might be about to engage in something a little more serious than pulling hair or ripping clothes. What was Nettie doing here in the first place? What had happened to the element of surprise? How had things come so quickly to the sticking point?

But there was a deep streak of Polish Cossack in Wilma's nature, a part that found such questions irrelevant. There was a battle to be fought here; that was the important thing.

Nettie ran at her, lifting the cleaver as she came. Her lips peeled back from her teeth and a long howl tore out of her throat.

Wilma crouched, holding her knife out like a giant switchblade. As Nettie closed with her, Wilma drove it forward. It thrust deep into Nettie's bowels and then rose, slitting her stomach open and letting out a spurt of stinking gruel. Wilma felt a moment's horror at what she had done—could it really be Wilma Jerzyck on the other end of the steel buried in Nettie?—and her arm muscles relaxed. The knife's upward momentum died before the blade could reach Nettie's frantically pumping heart.

"OOOOH YOU BIIIITCH!" Nettie screamed, and brought the cleaver down. It buried itself to the hilt in Wilma's shoulder, splitting the collarbone with a dull crunch.

The pain, a huge wooden plank of it, drove any objective thought from Wilma's mind. Only the raving Cossack was left. She yanked her knife free.

Nettie yanked her cleaver free. It took both hands to do it, and when she finally succeeded in wrenching it off the bone, a loose slew of guts slipped from the bloody hole in her dress and hung before her in a glistening knot.

The two women circled slowly, their feet printing tracks in their own blood. The sidewalk began to look like some weird Arthur Murray dance diagram. Nettie felt the world beginning to pulse in and out in great, slow cycles—the color would drain from things, leaving her in a blur of whiteness, and then it would slowly come back. She heard her heart in her ears, great slow snaffling thuds. She knew she was wounded but felt no pain. She thought Wilma might have cut her a little in the side, or something.

Wilma knew how badly she was hurt; was aware that she could no longer lift her right arm and that the back of her dress was drenched with blood. She had no intention of even trying to run away, however. She had never run in her life, and she wasn't going to start now.

"*Hi!*" someone screamed thinly at them from across the street. "*Hi! What are you two ladies doing there? You stop it, whatever it is! You stop it right now or I'll call the police!*"

Wilma turned her head in that direction. The moment her attention was diverted, Nettie stepped in and swung the cleaver in a flat, sweeping arc. It chopped into the swell of Wilma's hip and clanged off her pelvic bone, cracking it. Blood flew in a fan. Wilma screamed and flailed backward, sweeping the air in front of her with her knife. Her feet tangled together and she fell to the sidewalk with a thump.

"*Hi! Hi!*" It was an old woman, standing on her stoop and clutching a mouse-colored shawl to her throat. Her eyes were magnified into watery wheels of terror by her spectacles. Now she trumpeted in her clear and piercing old-lady voice: "*Help! Police! Murder! MURRRDURRRRR!*"

The women on the corner of Willow and Ford took no notice. Wilma had fallen in a bloody heap by the stop-sign, and as Nettie staggered toward her, she pushed herself into a sitting position against its post and held the knife in her lap, pointing upward.

"Come on, you bitch," she snarled. "Come for me, if you're coming."

Nettie came, her mouth working. The ball of her intestines swung back and forth against her dress like a misborn fetus. Her right foot struck Wilma's outstretched left foot and she fell forward. The carving knife impaled her just below the breastbone. She grunted through a mouthful of blood, raised the cleaver, and brought it down. It buried itself in the top of Wilma Jerzyck's head with a single dull sound—*chonk!* Wilma began to convulse, her body bucking and sunfishing under Nettie's. Each buck and thrash drove the carving knife in deeper.

"Killed . . . my . . . *doggy,*" Nettie gasped, spitting a fine mist of blood into Wilma's upturned face with every word. Then she shuddered all over and went limp. Her head bonked the post of the stop-sign as it fell forward.

Wilma's jittering foot slid into the gutter. Her good black for-church shoe flew off and landed in a pile of leaves with its low heel pointing up at the bustling clouds. Her toes flexed once . . . once more . . . and then relaxed.

The two women lay draped over each other like lovers, their blood painting the cinnamon-colored leaves in the gutter.

"*MURRRRRDURRRRRR!*" the old woman across the street trumpeted again, and then she rocked backward and fell full-length on her own hall floor in a faint.

Others in the neighborhood were coming to windows and opening doors now, asking each other what had happened, stepping out on stoops and lawns, first approaching the scene cautiously, then backing away in a hurry, hands over mouths, when they saw not only what had happened, but the gory extent of it.

Eventually, someone called the Sheriff's Office.

18

Polly Chalmers was walking slowly up Main Street toward Needful Things with her aching hands bundled into her warmest pair of mittens when she heard the first police siren. She stopped and watched as one of the county's three brown Plymouth cruisers belted through the intersection of Main and Laurel, lights flashing and twirling. It was doing fifty already and still accelerating. It was closely followed by a second cruiser.

She watched them out of sight, frowning. Sirens and racing police cruisers were a rarity in The Rock. She wondered what had happened—something a little more serious than a cat up a tree, she supposed. Alan would tell her when he called that evening.

Polly looked up the street again and saw Leland Gaunt standing in the doorway of his shop, also watching after the cruisers with an expression of mild curiosity on his face. Well, that answered one question: he *was* in. Nettie had never called her back to let her know one way or another. This hadn't surprised Polly much; the surface of Nettie's mind was slippery, and things had a way of sliding right off.

She walked on up the street. Mr. Gaunt looked around and saw her. His face lit up in a smile.

"Ms. Chalmers! How nice that you could drop by!"

She smiled wanly. The pain, which had abated for a while that morning, was now creeping back, thrusting its network of thin, cruel wires through the flesh of her hands. "I thought we'd agreed on Polly."

"Polly, then. Come inside—it's awfully good to see you. What's all the excitement?"

"I don't know," she said. He held the door for her and she went past him into the shop. "I suppose someone's been hurt and needs to go to the hospital. Medical Assistance in Norway is awfully slow on the weekends. Although why the dispatcher would send *two* cruisers . . ."

Mr. Gaunt closed the door behind them. The bell tinkled. The shade on the door was down, and with the sun now going the other way, the interior of Needful Things was gloomy . . . but, Polly thought, if gloom could ever be pleasant, this gloom was. A small reading lamp shed a golden circle on the counter by Mr. Gaunt's old-fashioned cash register. A book lay open there. It was *Treasure Island,* by Robert Louis Stevenson.

Mr. Gaunt was looking at her closely, and Polly had to smile again at the expression of concern in his eyes.

"My hands have been kicking up the very dickens these last few days," she said. "I guess I don't exactly look like Demi Moore."

"You look like a woman who is very tired and in quite a lot of discomfort," he said.

The smile on her face wavered. There was understanding and deep compassion in his voice, and for a moment Polly was afraid she might burst into tears. The thought which kept the tears at bay was an odd one: *His hands. If I cry, he'll try to comfort me. He'll put his hands on me.*

She buttressed the smile.

"I'll survive; I always have. Tell me—did Nettie Cobb happen to drop by?"

"Today?" He frowned. "No; not today. If she had, I would have shown her a new piece of carnival glass that came in yesterday. It's not as nice as the one I sold her last week, but I thought she might be interested. Why do you ask?"

"Oh . . . no reason," Polly said. "She said she might, but Nettie . . . Nettie often forgets things."

"She strikes me as a woman who has had a hard life," Mr. Gaunt said gravely.

"Yes. Yes, she has." Polly spoke these words slowly and mechanically. She could not seem to take her eyes from his. Then one of her hands brushed against the edge of a glass display case, and that caused her to break eye-contact. A little gasp of pain escaped her.

"Are you all right?"

"Yes, fine," Polly said, but it was a lie—she wasn't even within shouting distance of fine.

Mr. Gaunt clearly understood this. "You're not well," he said decisively. "Therefore I'm going to dispense with the small-talk. The item which I wrote you about did come in. I'm going to give it to you and send you home."

"*Give* it to me?"

"Oh, I'm not offering you a present," he said as he went behind the cash register. "We hardly know each other well enough for that, do we?"

She smiled. He was clearly a kind man, a man who, naturally enough, wanted to do something nice for the first person in Castle Rock who had done something nice for him. But she was having a hard time responding—was having a hard time even following the conversation. The pain in her hands was monstrous. She now wished she hadn't come, and, kindness or no kindness, all she wanted to do was get out and go home and take a pain-pill.

"This is the sort of item a vendor *has* to offer on trial—if he's an ethical man, that is." He produced a ring of keys, selected one, and unlocked the drawer under the cash register. "If you try it for a couple of days and discover it is worthless to you— and I have to tell you that will probably be the case—you return it to me. If, on the other hand, you find it provides you with some relief, we can talk price." He smiled at her. "And for you, the price would be rock-bottom, I can assure you."

She looked at him, puzzled. Relief? What was he talking about?

He brought out a small white box and set it on the counter. He took off the lid with his odd, long-fingered hands, and removed a small silver object on a fine chain from the cotton batting inside. It seemed to be a necklace of some sort, but the thing which hung down when Mr. Gaunt tented his fingers over the chain looked like a tea-ball, or an oversized thimble.

"This is Egyptian, Polly. Very old. Not as old as the Pyramids—gosh, no!—but still very old. There's something inside it. Some sort of herb, I think, although I'm not sure." He wiggled his fingers up and down. The silver tea-ball (if that was what it was) jounced at the bottom of the chain. Something shifted inside, something which made a dusty, slithery sound. Polly found it vaguely unpleasant.

"It's called an *azka,* or perhaps an *azakah,*" Mr. Gaunt said. "Either way, it's an amulet which is supposed to ward off pain."

Polly tried a smile. She wanted to be polite, but *really* . . . she had come all the way down here for *this?* The thing didn't even have any aesthetic value. It was ugly, not to put too fine a point on it.

"I really don't think . . ."

"I don't, either," he said, "but desperate situations often call for desperate measures. I assure you it is quite genuine . . . at least in the sense that it wasn't made in Taiwan. It is an authentic Egyptian artifact—not quite a relic, but an artifact most certainly—from the period of the Later Decline. It comes with a certificate of provenance which identifies it as a tool of *benka-litis,* or white magic. I want you to take it and wear it. I suppose it sounds silly. Probably it is. But there are stranger things in heaven and earth than some of us dream of, even in our wilder moments of philosophy."

"Do you really believe that?" Polly asked.

"Yes. I've seen things in my time that make a healing medallion or amulet look perfectly ordinary." A fugitive gleam flickered momentarily in his hazel eyes. "*Many* such things. The world's odd corners are filled with fabulous junk, Polly. But never mind that; *you* are the issue here.

"Even the other day, when I suspect the pain was not nearly as bad as it is right now, I got a good idea of just how unpleasant your situation had become. I thought this little . . .

item . . . might be worth a try. After all, what have you to lose? Nothing else you've tried has worked, has it?"

"I appreciate the thought, Mr. Gaunt, really I do, but—"

"Leland. Please."

"Yes, all right. I appreciate the thought, *Leland,* but I'm afraid I'm not superstitious."

She looked up and saw his bright hazel eyes were fixed upon her.

"It doesn't matter if *you* are or not, Polly . . . because this is." He wiggled his fingers. The *azka* bobbed gently at the end of its chain.

She opened her mouth again, but this time no words came out. She found herself remembering a day last spring. Nettie had forgotten her copy of *Inside View* when she went home. Leafing through it idly, glancing at stories about werewolf babies in Cleveland and a geological formation on the moon that looked like the face of JFK, Polly had come upon an ad for something called The Prayer Dial of the Ancients. It was supposed to cure headaches, stomach aches, and arthritis.

The ad was dominated by a black-and-white drawing. It showed a fellow with a long beard and a wizard's hat (either Nostradamus or Gandalf, Polly assumed) holding something that looked like a child's pinwheel over the body of a man in a wheelchair. The pinwheel gadget was casting a cone of radiance over the invalid, and although the ad did not come right out and say so, the implication seemed to be that the guy would be dancing up a storm at the Copa in a night or two. It was ridiculous, of course, superstitious pap for people whose minds had wavered or perhaps even broken under a steady onslaught of pain and disability, but still . . .

She had sat looking at that ad for a long time, and, ridiculous as it was, she had almost called the 800 number for phone orders given at the bottom of the page. Because sooner or later—

"Sooner or later a person in pain should explore even the

more questionable paths, if it's possible those paths might lead to relief," Mr. Gaunt said. "Isn't that so?"

"I . . . I don't . . ."

"Cold therapy . . . thermal gloves . . . even the radiation treatments . . . none of them have worked for you, have they?"

"How do you know about all that?"

"A good tradesman makes it his business to know the needs of his customers," Mr. Gaunt said in his soft, hypnotic voice. He moved toward her, holding the silver chain out in a wide ring with the *azka* hanging at the bottom. She shrank from the long hands with their leathery nails.

"Fear not, dear lady. I'll not touch the least hair upon your head. Not if you're calm . . . and remain quite still . . ."

And Polly did become calm. She did become still. She stood with her hands (still encased in the woolly mittens) crossed demurely in front of her, and allowed Mr. Gaunt to drop the silver chain over her head. He did it with the gentleness of a father turning down his daughter's bridal veil. She felt far away from Mr. Gaunt, from Needful Things, from Castle Rock, even from herself. She felt like a woman standing high on some dusty plain and under an endless sky, hundreds of miles from any other human being.

The *azka* dropped against the zipper of her leather car-coat with a small clink.

"Put it inside your jacket. And when you get home, put it inside your blouse, as well. It must be worn next to the skin for maximum effect."

"I can't put it in my jacket," Polly said in slow, dreaming tones. "The zipper . . . I can't pull down the zipper."

"No? Try."

So Polly stripped off one of the mittens and tried. To her great surprise, she found she was able to flex the thumb and first finger of her right hand just enough to grasp the zipper's tab and pull it down.

"There, you see?"

The little silver ball fell against the front of her blouse. It seemed very heavy to her, and the feel of it was not precisely comfortable. She wondered vaguely what was inside it, what had made that dusty slithery sound. Some sort of herb, he had said, but it hadn't sounded like leaves or even powder to Polly. It had seemed to her that something in there had shifted on its own.

Mr. Gaunt seemed to understand her discomfort. "You'll get used to it, and much sooner than you might think. Believe me, you will."

Outside, thousands of miles away, she heard more sirens. They sounded like troubled spirits.

Mr. Gaunt turned away, and as his eyes left her face, Polly felt her concentration begin to return. She felt a little bewildered, but she also felt good. She felt as if she had just had a short but satisfying nap. Her sense of mixed discomfort and disquiet was gone.

"My hands still hurt," she said, and this was true . . . but did they hurt as badly? It seemed to her there had been some relief, but that could be nothing more than suggestion—she had a feeling that Gaunt had imposed a kind of hypnosis on her in his determination to make her accept the *azka*. Or it might only be the warmth of the shop after the cold outside.

"I doubt very much if the promised effect is instantaneous," Mr. Gaunt said dryly. "Give it a chance, though—will you do that, Polly?"

She shrugged. "All right."

After all, what *did* she have to lose? The ball was small enough so it would barely make a bulge under a blouse and a sweater. She wouldn't have to answer any questions about it if no one knew it was there, and that would be just fine with her— Rosalie Drake would be curious, and Alan, who was about as superstitious as a tree-stump, would probably find it funny. As for Nettie . . . well, Nettie would probably be awed to silence if she knew Polly was wearing an honest-to-goodness magic charm, just like the ones they sold in her beloved *Inside View.*

"You shouldn't take it off, not even in the shower," Mr. Gaunt said. "There's no need to. The ball is real silver, and won't rust."

"But if I do?"

He coughed gently into his hand, as if embarrassed. "Well, the beneficial effect of the *azka* is cumulative. The wearer is a little better today, a little better still tomorrow, and so on. That's what I was told, at least."

Told by whom? she wondered.

"If the *azka* is removed, however, the wearer reverts to his or her former painful state not slowly but at once, and then has to wait for days or perhaps weeks in order to regain the lost ground once the *azka* is put back on."

Polly laughed a little. She couldn't help it, and was relieved when Leland Gaunt joined her.

"I know how it sounds," he said, "but I only want to help if I can. Do you believe that?"

"I do," she said, "and I thank you."

But as she allowed him to usher her from the shop, she found herself wondering about other things, too. There was the near trance-state she'd been in when he slipped the chain over her head, for instance. Then there was her strong dislike of being touched by him. Those things were very much at odds with the feelings of friendship, regard, and compassion which he projected like an almost visible aura.

But *had* he mesmerized her somehow? That was a foolish idea . . . wasn't it? She tried to remember exactly what she had felt like when they were discussing the *azka,* and couldn't do it. If he had done such a thing, it had no doubt been by accident, and with her help. More likely she had just entered the dazed state which too many Percodans sometimes induced. It was the thing she disliked most about the pills. No, she guessed that was the thing she disliked second to the most. What she really hated about them was that they didn't always work the way they were supposed to anymore.

"I'd drive you home, if I drove," Mr. Gaunt said, "but I'm afraid I never learned."

"Perfectly all right." Polly said. "I appreciate your kindness a great deal."

"Thank me if it works," he replied. "Have a lovely afternoon, Polly."

More sirens rose in the air. They were on the east side of town, over toward Elm, Willow, Pond, and Ford streets. Polly turned in that direction. There was something about the sound of sirens, especially on such a quiet afternoon, which conjured up vaguely threatening thoughts—not quite images—of impending doom. The sound began to die out, unwinding like an invisible clockspring in the bright autumn air.

She turned back to say something about this to Mr. Gaunt, but the door was shut. The sign reading

CLOSED

hung between the drawn shade and the glass, swinging gently back and forth on its string. He had gone back inside while her back was turned, so quietly she hadn't even heard him.

Polly began to walk slowly home. Before she got to the end of Main Street another police car, this one a State Police cruiser, blasted past her.

19

"Danforth?"

Myrtle Keeton stepped through the front door and into the living room. She balanced the fondue pot under her left arm as she struggled to remove the key Danforth had left in the lock.

"Danforth, I'm home!"

There was no answer, and the TV wasn't on. That was strange;

he had been so determined to get home in time for the kick-off. She wondered briefly if he might have gone somewhere else, up to the Garsons', perhaps, to watch it, but the garage door was down, which meant he had put the car away. And Danforth didn't walk anywhere if he could possibly avoid it. Especially not up the View, which was steep.

"Danforth? Are you here?"

Still no answer. There was an overturned chair in the dining room. Frowning, she set the fondue pot on the table and righted the chair. The first threads of worry, fine as cobweb, drifted through her mind. She walked toward the study door, which was closed. When she reached it, she tipped her head against the wood and listened. She was quite sure she could hear the soft squeak of his desk chair.

"Danforth? Are you in there?"

No answer . . . but she thought she heard a low cough. Worry became alarm. Danforth had been under a great deal of strain lately—he was the only one of the town's selectmen who worked really hard—and he weighed more than was good for him. What if he'd had a heart attack? What if he was in there lying on the floor? What if the sound she had heard was not a cough but the sound of Danforth trying to breathe?

The lovely morning and early afternoon they had spent together made such a thought seem horridly plausible: first the sweet build-up, then the crashing let-down. She reached for the knob of the study door . . . then drew her hand back and used it to pluck nervously at the loose skin under her throat instead. It had taken only a few blistering occasions to teach her that one did not disturb Danforth in his study without knocking . . . and that one never, never, *never* entered his *sanctum sanctorum* uninvited.

Yes, but if he's had a heart attack . . . or . . . or . . .

She thought of the overturned chair and fresh alarm coursed through her.

Suppose he came home and surprised a burglar? What if the bur-

glar conked Danforth over the head, knocked him out, and dragged him into his study?

She rapped a flurry of knuckles on the door. "Danforth? Are you all right?"

No answer. No sound in the house but the solemn tick-tock of the grandfather clock in the living room, and . . . yes, she was quite sure of it: the creak of the chair in Danforth's study.

Her hand began to creep toward the knob again.

"Danforth, are you . . ."

The tips of her fingers were actually touching the knob when his voice roared out at her, making her leap back from the door with a thin scream.

"Leave me alone! Can't you leave me alone, you stupid bitch?"

She moaned. Her heart was jackhammering wildly in her throat. It was not just surprise; it was the rage and unbridled hate in his voice. After the calm and pleasant morning they had spent, he could not have hurt her more if he had caressed her cheek with a handful of razor-blades.

"Danforth . . . I thought you were hurt . . ." Her voice was a tiny gasp she could hardly hear herself.

"Leave me alone!" Now he was right on the other side of the door, by the sound.

Oh my God, he sounds as if he's gone crazy. Can that be? How *can that be? What's happened since he dropped me off at Amanda's?*

But there were no answers to these questions. There was only ache. And so she crept away upstairs, got her beautiful new doll from the closet in the sewing room, then went into the bedroom. She eased off her shoes and then lay down on her side of their bed with the doll in her arms.

Somewhere, far off, she heard conflicting sirens. She paid them no attention.

Their bedroom was lovely at this time of day, full of bright October sunshine. Myrtle did not see it. She saw only darkness. She felt only misery, a deep, sick misery that not even the gorgeous doll could alleviate. The misery seemed to fill her throat and block her breathing.

Oh she had been so happy today—so very happy. *He* had been happy, too. She was sure of it. And now things were worse than they had been before. Much worse.

What had happened?

Oh God, what had happened and who was responsible?

Myrtle hugged the doll and looked up at the ceiling and after a while she began to weep in large, flat sobs that made her whole body quake.

CHAPTER ELEVEN

1

At fifteen minutes to midnight on that long, long Sunday in October, a door in the basement of Kennebec Valley Hospital's State Wing opened and Sheriff Alan Pangborn stepped through. He walked slowly, with his head down. His feet, clad in elasticized hospital slippers, shuffled on the linoleum. The sign on the door behind him could be read as it swung shut:

MORGUE

UNAUTHORIZED ENTRY PROHIBITED

At the far end of the corridor, a janitor in gray fatigues was using a buffer to polish the floor in slow, lazy sweeps. Alan walked toward him, stripping the hospital cap off his head as he went. He lifted the green-gown he was wearing and stuffed the cap in a back pocket of the blue-jeans he wore beneath. The soft drone of the buffer made him feel sleepy. A hospital in Augusta was the last place on earth he wanted to be tonight.

The janitor looked up as he approached, and switched off his machine.

"You don't look so well, my friend," he greeted Alan.

"I'm not surprised. Do you have a cigarette?"

The janitor took a pack of Luckies from his breast pocket and shook one out for Alan. "You can't smoke it in here, though," he said. He nodded his head toward the morgue door. "Doc Ryan throws a fit."

Alan nodded. "Where?"

The janitor took him to an intersecting corridor and pointed to a door about halfway down. "That goes to the alley beside the building. Prop it open with something, though, or you'll have to go all the way around to the front to get back in. You got matches?"

Alan started down the corridor. "I carry a lighter. Thanks for the smoke."

"I heard it was a double feature in there tonight," the janitor called after him.

"That's right," Alan said without turning around.

"Autopsies are bastards, ain't they?"

"Yes," Alan said.

Behind him, the soft drone of the floor-buffer recommenced. They were bastards, all right. The autopsies of Nettie Cobb and Wilma Jerzyck had been the twenty-third and twenty-fourth of his career, and they had all been bastards, but these two had been the worst by far.

The door the janitor had pointed out was the sort equipped with a panic-bar. Alan looked around for something he could use to prop it open and saw nothing. He pulled the green-gown off, wadded it up, and opened the door. Night air washed in, chilly but incredibly refreshing after the stale alcohol smell of the morgue and adjoining autopsy room. Alan placed the wadded-up gown against the door-jamb and stepped out. He carefully let the door swing back, saw that the gown would keep the latch from engaging, and forgot about it. He leaned against the cinderblock wall next to the pencil-line of light escaping through the slightly ajar door and lit his cigarette.

The first puff made his head feel swimmy. He had been try-ing to quit for almost two years and kept almost making it. Then something would come up. That was both the curse and the blessing of police work; something always came up.

He looked up at the stars, which he usually found calming, and couldn't see many—the high-intensity lights which ringed the hospital dulled them out. He could make out the Big Dipper, Orion, and a faint reddish point that was probably Mars, but that was all.

Mars, he thought. *That's it. That's undoubtedly it. The warlords of Mars landed in Castle Rock around noon, and the first people they met were Nettie and the Jerzyck bitch. The warlords bit them and turned them rabid. It's the only thing that fits.*

He thought about going in and telling Henry Ryan, the State of Maine's Chief Medical Examiner, *It was a case of alien intervention, Doc. Case closed.* He doubted if Ryan would be amused. It had been a long night for him, too.

Alan dragged deeply on the cigarette. It tasted absolutely grand, swimmy head or no swimmy head, and he felt he could understand perfectly why smoking was now off-limits in the public areas of every hospital in America. John Calvin had been dead right: nothing that made you feel this way could possibly be good for you. In the meantime, though, hit me wid dat nicotine, boss—it feel so fine.

He thought idly of how nice it would be to buy an entire carton of these selfsame Luckies, rip off both ends, and then light up the whole goddam thing with a blowtorch. He thought how nice it would be to get drunk. This would be a very bad time to get drunk, he supposed. Another inflexible rule of life—*When you really need to get drunk, you can never afford to do it.* Alan wondered vaguely if maybe the alcoholics of the world weren't the only ones who really had their priorities straight.

The pencil-line of light by his feet fattened to a bar. Alan looked around and saw Norris Ridgewick. Norris stepped out and leaned against the wall next to Alan. He was still wearing his green cap, but it was askew and the tie-ribbons hung down over the back of his gown. His complexion matched his gown.

"Jesus, Alan."

"They were your first ones, weren't they?"

"No, I saw an autopsy once when I was in North Wyndham. Smoke-inhalation case. But these . . . Jesus, Alan."

"Yeah," he said, and exhaled smoke. "Jesus."

"You got another cigarette?"

"No—sorry. I bummed this one from the janitor." He looked at the Deputy with mild curiosity. "I didn't know you smoked, Norris."

"I don't. I thought I might start."

Alan laughed softly.

"Man, I can't wait to get out fishing tomorrow. Or are off-days on hold while we sort this mess out?"

Alan thought about it, then shook his head. It hadn't really been the warlords of Mars; this business actually looked quite simple. In a way, that was what made it so horrible. He saw no reason to cancel Norris's off-days.

"That's great," Norris said, and then added, "But I'll come in if you want, Alan. No problem."

"Shouldn't need you to, Norris," he said. "John and Clut have both been in touch with me—Clut went with the CID guys to talk with Pete Jerzyck, and John went with the team investigating Nettie's end. They've both been in touch. It's pretty clear. Nasty, but clear."

And it was . . . yet he was troubled about it, just the same. On some deep level, he was very troubled indeed.

"Well, what happened? I mean, the Jerzyck bitch has been asking for it for years, but when somebody finally called her bluff, I thought she'd end up with a black eye or a broken arm . . . nothing like *this*. Was it just a case of picking on the wrong person?"

"I think that pretty well covers it," Alan said. "Wilma couldn't have picked a worse person in Castle Rock to start a feud with."

"Feud?"

"Polly gave Nettie a puppy last spring. It barked a little at first. Wilma did a lot of bitching about it."

"Really? I don't remember a complaint sheet."

"She only made one official complaint. I caught it. Polly asked me if I would. She felt partly responsible, since she gave

Nettie the dog in the first place. Nettie said she'd keep him inside as much as she could, and that finished it for me.

"The dog stopped the barking, but Wilma apparently went on bitching to Nettie. Polly says that Nettie'd cross the street when she saw Wilma coming, even if Wilma was two blocks away. Nettie did everything but fork the sign of the evil eye at her. Then, last week, she crossed the line. She went over to the Jerzycks' while Pete and Wilma were at work, saw the sheets hanging on the line, and covered them with mud from the garden."

Norris whistled. "Did we catch *that* complaint, Alan?"

Alan shook his head. "From then until this afternoon, it was all between the ladies."

"What about Pete Jerzyck?"

"Do you *know* Pete?"

"Well . . ." Norris stopped. Thought about Pete. Thought about Wilma. Thought about the two of them together. Slowly nodded his head. "He was afraid Wilma would chew him up one side and down the other if he tried playing referee . . . so he stood aside. Is that it?"

"Sort of. He actually may have headed things off, at least for a while. Clut says Pete told the CID guys that Wilma wanted to go over to Nettie's as soon as she got a look at her sheets. She was ready to rock and roll. She apparently called Nettie on the phone and told her she was going to rip off her head and shit down her neck."

Norris nodded. Between the autopsy on Wilma and the autopsy on Nettie, he had called dispatch in Castle Rock and asked for a list of complaints involving each of the two women. Nettie's list was short—one item. She had snapped and killed her husband. End of story. No flare-ups before and none since, including the last few years she'd spent back in town. Wilma was a different kettle of tripe entirely. She had never killed anyone, but the list of complaints—those made by her and those made about her—was a long one, and went back to what had then been Castle Rock Junior High, where she had punched a substitute teacher in the eye for giving her detention. On two occasions, worried women who'd had the ill luck or judgment to get into Wilma's bad books had requested police protection. Wilma had also been the subject of three assault complaints over the years. Ultimately all charges had been dropped, but it didn't take much study to figure out that no one in his or her right mind would have chosen Wilma Jerzyck to fuck with.

"They were bad medicine for each other," Norris murmured.

"The worst."

"Her husband talked Wilma out of going over there the first time she wanted to go?"

"He knew better than to even try. He told Clut he dropped two Xanax into a cup of tea and that lowered her thermostat. In fact, Jerzyck says he thought it was all over."

"Do you believe him, Alan?"

"Yeah—as much as I can believe anyone without actually talking to them face-to-face, that is."

"What's the stuff he dropped into her tea? Dope?"

"A tranquilizer. Jerzyck told CID he'd used it a couple of times before when she got hot, and it cooled her out pretty well. He said he thought it did this time, too."

"But it didn't."

"I think it did at first. Wilma didn't just go over and start chewing Nettie's ass, at least. But I'm pretty sure she went on harassing Nettie; it's the pattern she established when it was just the dog they were fighting over. Making phone-calls. Doing drive-bys. That sort of thing. Nettie's skin was pretty thin. Stuff like that would have really gotten to her. John LaPointe and the CID team I stuck him with went to see Polly around seven o'clock. Polly said she was pretty sure that Nettie was worried about something. She was over to see Polly this morning, and let something slip then. Polly didn't understand it at the time." Alan sighed. "I guess now she wishes she'd listened a little more closely."

"How's Polly taking it, Alan?"

"Pretty well, I think." He had spoken to her twice, once from a house near the crime scene, and a second time from here at K.V.H., just after he and Norris had arrived. On both occasions her voice had been calm and controlled, but he had sensed the tears and confusion just under the carefully maintained surface. He wasn't entirely surprised during the first call to find she already knew most of what had happened; news, particularly bad news, travels fast in small towns.

"What set off the big bang?"

Alan looked at Norris, surprised, and then realized he didn't know yet. Alan had gotten a more or less complete report from John LaPointe between the autopsies, while Norris had been on another phone, talking to Sheila Brigham and compiling lists of complaints involving the two women.

"One of them decided to escalate," he said. "My guess is Wilma, but the details of the picture are still hazy. Apparently Wilma went over to Nettie's while Nettie was visiting Polly this morning. Nettie must have left without locking her door, or even latching it securely, and the wind blew it open—you know how windy it was today."

"Yeah."

"So maybe it started out to be just another drive-by to keep Nettie's water hot. Then Wilma saw the door standing open and the drive-by turned into something else. Maybe it wasn't *quite* that way, but it feels right to me."

The words weren't even out of his mouth before he recognized them as a lie. It *didn't* feel right, that was the trouble. It *should* have felt right, he *wanted* it to feel right, and it didn't. What was driving him crazy was that there was no *reason* for that sense of wrongness, at least none he could put his finger on. The closest he could come was to wonder if Nettie would have been careless not only about locking her door but about shutting it tightly if she was as paranoid about Wilma Jerzyck as she had seemed . . . and that wasn't enough to hang a suspicion on. It wasn't enough because not all of Nettie's gear was stowed tightly, and you couldn't make any assumptions about what such a person would and wouldn't do. Still . . .

"What did Wilma do?" Norris asked. "Trash the place?"

"Killed Nettie's dog."

"What?"

"You heard me."

"Jesus! What a *bitch!*"

"Well, but we knew that about her, didn't we?"

"Yeah, but still . . ."

There it was again. Even from Norris Ridgewick, who could be depended on, even after all these years, to fill out at least twenty per cent of his paperwork bassackwards: *Yeah, but still.*

"She did it with a Swiss Army knife. Used the corkscrew attachment and stuck a note on it, saying it was payback for Nettie slinging mud at her sheets. So Nettie went over to Wilma's with a bunch of rocks. She wrapped notes of her own around them with rubber bands. The notes said the rocks were Wilma's last warning. She threw them through all of the Jerzycks' downstairs windows."

"Mother-a-God," Norris said, not without some admiration.

"The Jerzycks left for eleven o'clock Mass at ten-thirty or so. After Mass they had lunch with the Pulaskis. Pete Jerzyck stayed to watch the Patriots with Jake Pulaski, so there was no way he could even *try* to cool Wilma out this time."

"Did they meet on that corner by accident?" Norris asked.

"I doubt it. I think Wilma got home, saw the damage, and called Nettie out."

"You mean like in a duel?"

"That's what I mean."

Norris whistled, then stood quietly for a few moments, hands clasped behind his back, looking out into the darkness. "Alan, why are we supposed to attend these goddam autopsies, anyway?" he asked at last.

"Protocol, I guess," Alan said, but it was more than that . . .

at least for him. If you were troubled about the look of a case, or the feel of it (as he was troubled by the look and feel of this one), you might see something that would knock your brain out of neutral and into one of the forward gears. You might see a hook to hang your hat on.

"Well, then, I think it's time the county hired a protocol officer," Norris grumbled, and Alan laughed.

He wasn't laughing inside, though, and not just because this was going to hit Polly so hard over the next few days. Something about the case wasn't right. Everything looked all right on top, but down in the place where instinct lived (and sometimes hid), the Martian warlords still seemed to make more sense. At least to Alan.

Hey, come on! Didn't you just lay it out for Norris, A to Z, in the length of time it takes to smoke a cigarette?

Yes, he had. That was part of the trouble. Did two women, even when one was half-nuts and the other was poison-mean, meet on a street-corner and cut each other to ribbons like a couple of hopped-up crack addicts for such simple reasons?

Alan didn't know. And *because* he didn't know, he flipped the cigarette away and began to go over the whole thing again.

2

For Alan, it began with a call from Andy Clutterbuck. Alan had just turned off the Patriots-Jets game (the Patriots were already down by a touchdown and a field goal, and the second quarter was less than three minutes old) and was putting on his coat when the phone rang. Alan had been intending to go down to Needful Things and see if Mr. Gaunt was there. It was even possible, Alan supposed, that he might meet Polly there, after all. The call from Clut had changed all that.

Eddie Warburton, Clut said, had been hanging up the phone just as he, Clut, came back from lunch. There was some sort of ruckus going on over in the "tree-street" section of town. Women fighting or something. It might be a good idea, Eddie said, if Clut were to call the Sheriff and tell him about the trouble.

"What in the blue hell is Eddie Warburton doing answering the Sheriff's Office telephone?" Alan asked irritably.

"Well, I guess with the dispatch office empty, he thought—"

"He knows the procedure as well as anyone—when dispatch is empty, let The Bastard route the incoming calls."

"I don't know why he answered the phone," Clut said with barely concealed impatience, "but I don't think that's the important thing. Second call on the incident came in four minutes ago, while I was talking with Eddie. An old lady. I didn't get a name—either she was too upset to give me one or she just didn't want to. Anyhow, she says there's been some sort of serious fight on the corner of Ford and Willow. Two women involved. Caller says they were using knives. She says they're still there."

"Still fighting?"

"No—down, both of them. The fight's over."

"Right." Alan's mind began clicking along faster, like an express train picking up speed. "You logged the call, Clut?"

"You bet I did."

"Good. Seaton's on this afternoon, isn't he? Get him out there right away."

"Already sent him."

"God bless you. Now call the State Police."

"Do you want CIU?"

"Not yet. For the time being, just alert them to the situation. I'll meet you there, Clut."

When he got to the crime scene and saw the extent of the damage, Alan radioed the Oxford Barracks of the State Police and told them to send a Crime Investigation Unit right away . . . two, if they could spare them. By then Clut and Seaton Thomas were standing in front of the downed women with their arms spread, telling people to go back into their homes. Norris arrived, took a look, then got a roll of yellow tape marked CRIME SCENE DO NOT CROSS out of the trunk of his cruiser. There was a thick coating of dust on the tape, and Norris told Alan later that he hadn't been sure it would stick, it was so old.

It had, though. Norris strung it around the trunks of oak trees, forming a large triangle around the two women who appeared to be embracing at the foot of the stop-sign. The spectators had not returned to their houses, but did retreat to their own lawns. There were about fifty of them, and the number was growing as calls were made and neighbors hurried over to view the wreckage. Andy Clutterbuck and Seaton Thomas looked almost jumpy enough to pull their pieces and start firing warning shots. Alan sympathized with the way they felt.

In Maine, the Criminal Investigation Department of the State Police handles murder investigations, and for small-fry fuzz (which is almost all of them), the scariest time comes between the discovery of the crime and the arrival of CID. Local cops and county mounties both know perfectly well that it is the time when the so-called chain of evidence is most often broken. Most also know that what they do during that time will be closely scrutinized by Monday-morning quarterbacks—most of them from the judiciary and the Attorney General's Office—who believe that small-fry fuzz, even the County boys, are a bunch of Deputy Dawgs with ham hands and fumble fingers.

Also, those silent bunches of people standing on the lawns across the street were goddam spooky. They reminded Alan of the mall-zombies in *Dawn of the Dead*.

He got the battery-powered bullhorn out of the back seat of his cruiser and told them he wanted them to go inside, right away. They began to do it. He then reviewed the protocol in his head one more time, and radioed dispatch. Sandra

McMillan had come in to handle the chores there. She wasn't as steady as Sheila Brigham, but beggars could not be choosers . . . and Alan guessed Sheila would hear what had happened and come in before much longer. If her sense of duty didn't bring her, curiosity would.

Alan told Sandy to track down Ray Van Allen. Ray was Castle County's On-Call Medical Examiner—also the county coroner—and Alan wanted him here when CID arrived, if that was possible.

"Roger, Sheriff," Sandy said self-importantly. "Base is clear."

Alan went back to his officers on the scene. "Which one of you verified that the women are dead?"

Clut and Seat Thomas looked at each other in uneasy surprise, and Alan felt his heart sink. One point for the Monday-morning quarterbacks—or maybe not. The first Crime Investigation Unit wasn't here yet, although he could hear more sirens approaching. Alan ducked under the tape and approached the stop-sign, walking on tiptoe like a kid trying to sneak out of the house after curfew.

The spilled blood was mostly pooled between the victims and in the leaf-choked gutter beside them, but a fine spray of droplets—what the forensics boys called back-splatter—dotted the area around them in a rough circle. Alan dropped on one knee just outside this circle, stretched out a hand, and found he could reach the corpses—he had no doubt that was what they were—by leaning forward to the very edge of balance with one arm stretched out.

He looked back at Seat, Norris, and Clut. They were clustered together in a knot, staring at him with big eyes.

"Photograph me," he said.

Clut and Seaton only looked at him as if he had given an order in Tagalog, but Norris ran to Alan's cruiser and rooted around in back until he found the old Polaroid there, one of two they used for taking crime-scene photographs. When the appropriations committee met, Alan was planning to ask for at least one new camera, but this afternoon the appropriations committee meeting seemed very unimportant.

Norris hurried back with the camera, aimed, and triggered it. The drive whined.

"Better take another one just to be safe," Alan said. "Get the bodies, too. I'm not going to have those guys saying we broke the chain of evidence. Be damned if I will." He was aware that his voice sounded a shade querulous, but there was nothing he could do about it.

Norris took another Polaroid, documenting Alan's position outside the circle of evidence and the way the bodies were lying at the foot of the stop-sign. Then Alan leaned cautiously forward again and placed his fingers against the bloodstained neck of the woman lying on top. There was no pulse, of course, but after a second the pressure of his fingers caused her head to fall away from the sign-post and turn sideways. Alan recognized Nettie at once, and it was Polly he thought of.

Oh Jesus, he thought dolefully. Then he went through the motions of feeling for Wilma's pulse, even though there was a meat-cleaver buried in her skull. Her cheeks and forehead were printed with small dots of blood. They looked like heathen tattoos.

Alan got up and returned to where his men were standing on the other side of the tapes. He couldn't seem to stop thinking of Polly, and he knew that was wrong. He had to get her off his mind or he was going to bitch this up for sure. He wondered if any of the gawkers had ID'd Nettie already. If so, Polly would surely hear before he could call her. He hoped desperately that she wouldn't come down to see for herself.

You can't worry about that now, he admonished himself. *You've got a double murder on your hands, from the look.*

"Get out your book," he told Norris. "You're club secretary."

"Jesus, Alan, you know how lousy my spelling is."

"Just write."

Norris gave the Polaroid to Clut and got his notebook out

of his back pocket. A pad of Traffic Warnings with his name rubber-stamped at the bottom of each sheet fell out with it. Norris bent, picked the pad up off the sidewalk, and stuffed it absently into his pocket again.

"I want you to note that the head of the woman on top, designated Victim 1, was resting against the post of the stop-sign. I inadvertently pushed it off, checking for pulse."

How easy it is to slip into Police Speak, Alan thought, *where cars become "vehicles" and crooks become "perpetrators" and dead townspeople become "designated victims." Police Speak, the wonderful sliding glass barrier.*

He turned to Clut and told him to photograph this second configuration of the bodies, feeling extremely grateful that he'd had Norris document the original position before he touched the women.

Clut took the picture.

Alan turned back to Norris. "I want you to further note that when the head of Victim 1 moved, I was able to identify her as Netitia Cobb."

Seaton whistled. "You mean it's *Nettie?*"

"Yes. That's what I mean."

Norris wrote the information down on his pad. Then he asked, "What do we do now, Alan?"

"Wait for CID's Investigation Unit and try to look alive when they get here," Alan said.

The CIU arrived less than three minutes later in two cars, followed by Ray Van Allen in his cranky old Subaru Brat. Five minutes later a State Police ID team arrived in a blue station wagon. All the members of the State Police team then lit cigars. Alan had known they would do this. The bodies were fresh and they were outdoors, but the ritual of the cigars was immutable.

The unpleasant work known in Police Speak as "securing the scene" began. It went on until after dark. Alan had worked with Henry Payton, head of the Oxford Barracks (and thus in nominal charge of this case and the CIU guys working it), on several other occasions. He had never seen the slightest hint of imagination in Henry. The man was a plodder, but a thorough, conscientious plodder. It was because Henry had been assigned that Alan had felt safe to creep off for a bit and call Polly.

When he returned, the hands of the victims were being secured in gallon-sized Ziploc Baggies. Wilma Jerzyck had lost one of her shoes, and her stockinged foot was accorded the same treatment. The ID team moved in and took close to three hundred photos. More State Police had arrived by then. Some held back the crowd, which was trying to draw closer again, and others shunted the arriving TV people down to the Municipal Building. A police artist did a quick sketch on a Crime-Scene Grid.

At last the bodies themselves were taken care of—except, that was, for one final matter. Payton gave Alan a pair of disposable surgical gloves and a Ziploc Baggie. "The cleaver or the knife?"

"I'll take the cleaver," Alan said. It would be the messier of the two implements, still clotted with Wilma Jerzyck's brains, but he didn't want to touch Nettie. He had liked her.

With the murder weapons removed, tagged, bagged, and on their way to Augusta, the two CIU teams moved in and began to search the area around the bodies, which still lay in their terminal embrace with the blood pooled between them now hardening to a substance like enamel. When Ray Van Allen was finally allowed to load them into the Medical Assistance van, the scene was lit with police cruiser high beams and the orderlies first had to peel Wilma and Nettie apart.

During most of this, Castle Rock's Finest stood around feeling like bumps on a log.

Henry Payton joined Alan on the sidelines during the conclusion of the oddly delicate ballet known as On-Scene Investigation. "Lousy damned way to spend a Sunday afternoon," he said.

Alan nodded.

"I'm sorry the head moved on you. That was bad luck."

Alan nodded again.

"I don't think anyone's going to bother you about it, though. You've got at least one good pic of the original position." He looked toward Norris, who was talking with Clut and the newly arrived John LaPointe. "You're just lucky that old boy there didn't put his finger over the lens."

"Aw, Norris is all right."

"So's K-Y Jelly . . . in its place. Anyway, the whole thing looks pretty simple."

Alan agreed. That was the trouble; he had known that long before he and Norris finished their Sunday tour of duty in an alley behind Kennebec Valley Hospital. The whole thing was *too* pretty simple, maybe.

"You planning to attend the cutting party?" Henry asked.

"Yes. Is Ryan going to do it?"

"That's what I understand."

"I thought I might take Norris with me. The bodies will go to Oxford first, won't they?"

"Uh-huh. That's where we log them in."

"If Norris and I left now, we could be in Augusta before they get there."

Henry Payton nodded. "Why not? I think it's buttoned up here."

"I'd like to send one of my men with each of your CIU teams. As observers. Do you have a problem with that?"

Payton thought it over. "Nope—but who's going to keep the peace? Ole Seat Thomas?"

Alan felt a sudden flash of something which was a little too hot to be dismissed as mere annoyance. It had been a long day, he'd listened to Henry rag on his deputies about as much as he wanted to . . . yet he needed to stay on Henry's good side in order to hitch a ride on what was technically a State Police case, and so he held his tongue.

"Come on, Henry. It's Sunday night. Even The Mellow Tiger's closed."

"Why are you so hot to stick with this, Alan? Is there something hinky about it? I understand there was bad feeling between the two women, and that the one on top already offed someone. Her husband, no less."

Alan thought about it. "No—nothing hinky. Nothing that I know about, anyway. It's just that . . ."

"It doesn't quite jell in your head yet?"

"Something like that."

"Okay. Just as long as your men understand they're there to listen and no more."

Alan smiled a little. He thought of telling Payton that if he instructed Clut and John LaPointe to ask questions, they would probably run the other way, and decided not to. "They'll keep their lips zipped," he said. "You can count on it."

3

And so here they were, he and Norris Ridgewick, after the longest Sunday in living memory. But the day had one thing in common with the lives of Nettie and Wilma: it was over.

"Were you thinking about checking into a motel room for the night?" Norris asked hesitantly. Alan didn't have to be a mindreader to know what *he* was thinking about: the fishing he would miss tomorrow.

"Hell, no." Alan bent and picked up the gown he had used to prop the door open. "Let's beat feet."

"Great idea," Norris said, sounding happy for the first time since Alan had met him at the crime scene. Five minutes later they were headed toward Castle Rock along Route 43, the headlights of the County cruiser boring holes in the windy darkness. By the time they arrived, it had been Monday morning for almost three hours.

4

Alan pulled in behind the Municipal Building and got out of the cruiser. His station wagon was parked next to Norris's dilapidated VW Beetle on the far side of the lot.

"You headed right home?" he asked Norris.

Norris offered a small, embarrassed grin and dropped his eyes. "Soon's I change into my civvies."

"Norris, how many times have I told you about using the men's room as a changing booth?"

"Come on, Alan—I don't do it all the time." They both knew, however, that Norris did just that.

Alan sighed. "Never mind—it's been a hell of a long day for you. I'm sorry."

Norris shrugged. "It was murder. They don't happen around here very often. When they do, I guess everybody pulls together."

"Get Sandy or Sheila to write you up an overtime chit if either of them is still here."

"And give Buster something else to bitch about?" Norris laughed with some bitterness. "I think I'll pass. This one's on me, Alan."

"Has he been giving you shit?" Alan had forgotten all about the town's Head Selectman these last couple of days.

"No—but he gives me a real hairy eyeball when we pass on the street. If looks could kill, I'd be as dead as Nettie and Wilma."

"I'll write up the chit myself tomorrow morning."

"If your name's on it, that's okay," Norris said, starting for the door marked TOWN EMPLOYEES ONLY. "Goodnight, Alan."

"Good luck with the fishing."

Norris brightened at once. "Thanks—you should see the rod I got down at the new store, Alan—it's a dandy."

Alan grinned. "I bet it is. I keep meaning to go see that

fellow—he seems to have something for everyone else in town, so why not something for me?"

"Why not?" Norris agreed. "He's got all kinds of stuff, all right. You'd be surprised."

"Goodnight, Norris. And thanks again."

"Don't mention it." But Norris was clearly pleased.

Alan got into his car, backed out of the lot, and turned down Main Street. He checked the buildings on both sides automatically, not even registering his own examination . . . but storing the information just the same. One of the things he noticed was the fact that there was a light on in the living area above Needful Things. It was mighty late for small-town folks to be up. He wondered if Mr. Leland Gaunt was an insomniac, and reminded himself again that he had that call to make— but it would keep, he reckoned, until he had the sad business of Nettie and Wilma sorted out to his satisfaction.

He reached the corner of Main and Laurel, signalled a left turn, then halted in the middle of the intersection and turned right instead. To hell with going home. That was a cold and empty place with his remaining son living it up with his friend on Cape Cod. There were too many closed doors with too many memories lurking behind them in that house. On the other side of town there was a live woman who might need someone quite badly just now. Almost as badly, perhaps, as this live man needed her.

Five minutes later Alan killed the headlights and rolled quietly up Polly's driveway. The door would be locked, but he knew which corner of the porch steps to look under.

5

"What are you still doing here, Sandy?" Norris asked as he walked in, loosening his tie.

Sandra McMillan, a fading blonde who had been the county's part-time dispatcher for almost twenty years, was slipping into her coat. She looked very tired.

"Sheila had tickets to see Bill Cosby in Portland," she told Norris. "She said she'd stay here, but I made her go— practically pushed her out the door. I mean, how often does Bill Cosby come to Maine?"

How often do two women decide to cut each other to pieces over a dog that probably came from the Castle County Animal Shelter in the first place? Norris thought . . . but did not say. "Not that often, I guess."

"Hardly *ever.*" Sandy sighed deeply. "Tell you a secret, though—now that it's all over, I almost wish I'd said yes when Sheila offered to stay. It's been so *crazy* tonight—I think every TV station in the state called at least nine times, and until eleven o'clock or so, this place looked like a department store Christmas Eve sale."

"Well, go on home. You have my permission. Did you power up The Bastard?"

The Bastard was the machine which switched calls to Alan's home when no dispatcher was on duty at the station. If no one picked up at Alan's after four rings, The Bastard cut in and told callers to dial the State Police in Oxford. It was a jury-rig system that wouldn't have worked in a big city, but in Castle County, which had the smallest population of all Maine's six-teen counties, it worked fine.

"It's on."

"Good. I have a feeling that Alan might not have been going straight home."

Sandy raised her eyebrows knowingly.

"Hear anything from Lieutenant Payton?" Norris asked.

"Not a thing." She paused. "Was it awful, Norris? I mean . . . those two women?"

"It was pretty awful, all right," he agreed. His civvies were hung neatly on a hanger he had hooked over a filing-cabinet handle. He removed it and started for the men's room. It had been his habit to change in and out of his uniforms at work for the last three years or so, although the changes rarely came at such an outrageous hour as this. "Go home, Sandy—I'll lock up when I'm done."

He pushed through the bathroom door and hooked the hanger over the top of the door to the toilet stall. He was unbuttoning his uniform shirt when there was a light knock on the door.

"Norris?" Sandy called.

"I think I'm the only one here," he called back.

"I almost forgot—someone left a present for you. It's on your desk."

Norris paused in the act of unbuckling his pants. "A present? Who from?"

"I don't know—the place really was a madhouse. But it's got a card on it. Also a bow. It must be your secret lover."

"My lover's so secret even *I* don't know about her," Norris said with real regret. He stepped out of his pants and laid them over the stall door while he put on his jeans.

Outside, Sandy McMillan smiled with a touch of malice. "Mr. Keeton was by tonight," she said. "Maybe *he* left it. Maybe it's a kiss-and-make-up present."

Norris laughed. "That'll be the day."

"Well, make sure you tell me tomorrow—I'm dying to know. It's a pretty package. Goodnight, Norris."

"Night."

Who could have left me a present? he wondered, zipping up his fly.

6

Sandy left, pulling the collar of her coat up as she went out—the night was very cold, reminding her that winter was on its way. Cyndi Rose Martin, the lawyer's wife, was one of the many people she had seen that night—Cyndi Rose had turned up early in the evening. Sandy never thought of mentioning her to Norris, however; he did not move in the Martins' more rarefied social and professional circles. Cyndi Rose said she was looking for her husband, which made a certain amount of sense to Sandy (although the evening had been so harum-scarum that Sandy probably wouldn't have thought it odd if the woman had said she was looking for Mikhail Baryshnikov), because Albert Martin did some of the town's legal work.

Sandy said she hadn't seen Mr. Martin that evening, although Cyndi Rose was welcome to check upstairs and see if he was in with Mr. Keeton, if she wanted. Cyndi Rose said she thought she would do that, as long as she was here. By then the switchboard was lit up like a Christmas tree again, and Sandy did not see Cyndi Rose take the rectangular package with the bright foil paper and the blue velvet bow from her large handbag and put it on Norris Ridgewick's desk. Her pretty face had been lit with a smile as she did it, but the smile itself was not pretty at all. It was, in fact, rather cruel.

7

Norris heard the outer door shut and, dimly, the sound of Sandy starting her car. He tucked his shirt into his jeans, stepped into his loafers, and arranged his uniform carefully on its hanger. He sniffed the shirt at the armpits and decided it didn't have to go to the cleaners right away. That was good; a penny saved was a penny earned.

When he left the men's room, he put the hanger back on the same file-cabinet handle, where he could not help seeing it on his way out. That was *also* good, because Alan got pissed like a bear when Norris forgot and left his duds hanging around the police station. He said it made the place look like a laundrymat.

He went over to his desk. Someone really had left him a present—it was a box done up in light-blue foil wrapping paper and blue velvet ribbon exploding into a fluffy bow on top. There was a square white envelope tucked under the ribbon. Very curious now, Norris removed the envelope and tore it open. There was a card inside. Typed on it in capital letters was a short, enigmatic message:

!!!!!JUST A REMINDER!!!!!

He frowned. The only two persons he could think of who were always reminding him of things were Alan and his mother . . . and his mother had died five years ago. He picked up the package, broke the ribbon, and set the bow carefully aside. Then he took off the paper, revealing a plain white cardboard box. It was about a foot long, four inches wide, and four inches deep. The lid was taped shut.

Norris broke the tape and opened the box. There was a layer of white tissue paper over the object inside, thin enough to indicate a flat surface with a number of raised ridges running across it, but not thin enough to allow him to see what his present was.

He reached in to pull the tissue paper out, and his forefinger struck something hard—a protruding tongue of metal. A heavy steel jaw closed on the tissue paper and also on Norris Ridgewick's first three fingers. Pain ripped up his arm. He screamed and stumbled backward, grabbing his right wrist with his left hand. The white box tumbled to the floor. Tissue-paper crinkled.

Oh, son of a bitch, it *hurt!* He grabbed at the tissue, which hung down in a wrinkled ribbon, and tore it free. What he revealed was a large Victory rat-trap. Someone had armed it, stuck it in a box, put tissue-paper over it to hide it, and then wrapped it in pretty blue paper. Now it was clamped on the first three fingers of his right hand. It had torn the nail of his index finger right off, he saw; all that remained was a bleeding crescent of raw flesh.

"Whoremaster!" Norris cried. In his pain and shock, he at first beat the trap against the side of John LaPointe's desk instead of just prying back the steel bar. All he managed to do was bang his hurt fingers against the desk's metal corner and send a fresh snarl of pain up his arm. He screamed again, then grabbed the trap's bar and pulled it back. He released his fingers and dropped the trap. The steel bar snapped down again on the trap's wooden base as it fell to the floor.

Norris stood trembling for a moment, then bolted back into the men's room, turned on the cold water with his left hand, and thrust his right hand under the tap. It throbbed like an impacted wisdom tooth. He stood with his lips drawn back in a grimace, watching thin threads of blood swirl down the drain, and thought of what Sandy had said: *Mr. Keeton was by . . . maybe it's a kiss-and-make-up present.*

And the card: JUST A REMINDER.

Oh, it had been Buster, all right. He didn't doubt it a bit. It was just Buster's style.

"You son of a bitch," Norris groaned.

The cold water was numbing his fingers, damping down that sick throbbing, but he knew it would be back by the time he arrived home. Aspirin might dull it a little, but he still thought he could forget getting any real sleep tonight. Or any fishing tomorrow, for that matter.

Oh yes I will—I'll go fishing even if my fucking hand falls fucking off. I had it planned, I've been looking forward to it, and Danforth Fucking Buster Keeton isn't going to stop me.

He turned off the water and used a paper towel to blot his hand gently dry. None of the fingers which had been caught in the trap were broken—at least he didn't think so—but they were already beginning to swell, cold water or no cold water. The arm of the trap had left a dark red-purple weal which ran across the fingers between the first and second knuckles. The exposed flesh beneath what had been the nail of his index finger was sweating small beads of blood, and that sick throbbing was already beginning again.

He went back into the deserted bullpen and looked at the sprung trap, lying on its side by John's desk. He picked it up and went over to his own desk. He put the trap inside the gift-box and put it in the top drawer of his desk. He took his aspirin out of the lower drawer and shook three of them into his mouth. Then he got the tissue-paper, the wrapping paper, the ribbon, and the bow. These he stuffed into the trash basket, covering them with balls of discarded paper.

He had no intention of telling Alan or anyone else about the nasty trick Buster had played on him. They wouldn't laugh, but Norris knew what they would think . . . or thought he did: *Only Norris Ridgewick would fall for something like that—stuck his hand right into a loaded rat-trap, can you believe it?*

It must be your secret lover . . . Mr. Keeton was by tonight . . . maybe it's a kiss-and-make-up present.

"I'll take care of this myself," Norris said in a low, grim voice. He was holding his wounded hand against his chest. "In my own way, and in my own time."

Suddenly a new and urgent thought came to him: what if Buster hadn't been content with the rat-trap, which, after all, might not have worked? What if he had gone up to Norris's house? The Bazun fishing rod was there, and it wasn't even locked up; he had just leaned it in the corner of the shed, next to his creel.

What if Buster knew about it and had decided to break it in two?

"If he did that, I'd break *him* in two," Norris said. He spoke in a low, angry growl Henry Payton—nor many of his other law-enforcement colleagues, for that matter—would not have recognized. He forgot all about locking up when he left the office. He had even temporarily forgotten the pain in his hand. The only thing that mattered was getting home. Getting home and making sure the Bazun rod was still all right.

8

The shape under the blankets didn't move when Alan eased into the room, and he thought Polly was asleep—probably with the help of a Percodan at bedtime. He undressed quietly and slid into bed beside her. As his head settled on the pillow, he saw that her eyes were open, watching him. It gave him a momentary start and he jerked.

"What stranger comes to this maiden's bed?" she asked softly.

"Only I," he replied, smiling a little. "I apologize for waking you, maiden."

"I was awake," she said, and put her arms around his neck. He slipped his own about her waist. The deep bed-warmth of her pleased him—she was like a sleepy furnace. He felt something hard against his chest for a moment, and it almost registered that she was wearing something under her cotton nightgown. Then it shifted, tumbling down between her left breast and her armpit on its fine silver chain.

"Are you okay?" he asked her.

She pressed the side of her face against his cheek, still holding him. He could feel her hands locked together at the nape of his neck. "No," she said. The word came out in a trembling sigh, and then she began to sob.

He held her while she cried, stroking her hair.

"Why didn't she tell me what that woman was doing, Alan?" Polly asked at last. She drew away from him a little. Now his eyes had adjusted to the dark, and he could see her face—dark eyes, dark hair, white skin.

"I don't know," he said.

"If she'd told me, I would have taken care of it! I would have gone to see Wilma Jerzyck myself, and . . . and . . ."

It was not the moment to tell her that Nettie had apparently played the game with almost as much vigor and malice as Wilma herself. Nor was it the moment to tell her that there came a time when the Nettie Cobbs of the world—and the Wilma Jerzycks, too, he supposed—could no longer be fixed. There came a time when they went beyond anyone's ability to repair.

"It's three-thirty in the morning," he said. "That's a bad time to talk about should-haves and would-haves." He hesitated for a moment before speaking again. "According to John LaPointe, Nettie said something to you about Wilma this morning—yesterday morning, now. What was it?"

Polly thought it over. "Well, I didn't know it was about Wilma—not then, anyway. Nettie brought over a lasagna. And my hands . . . my hands were really bad. She saw it right away. Nettie is—was—may have been—*I* don't know—vague about some things, but I couldn't hide a thing from her."

"She loved you very much," Alan said gravely, and this brought on a fresh spate of sobbing. He had known it would, just as he knew that some tears have to be cried no matter what the hour—until they are, they simply rave and burn inside.

After a while, Polly was able to go on. Her hands crept back around Alan's neck as she spoke.

"She got those stupid thermal gloves out, only this time they really helped—the current crisis seems to have passed, anyway—and then she made coffee. I asked her if she didn't have things to do at home and she said she didn't. She said Raider was on guard and then she said something like, 'I think she'll leave me alone, anyway. I haven't seen her or heard from her, so I guess she finally got the message.' That isn't exact, Alan, but it's pretty close."

"What time did she come by?"

"Around quarter past ten. It might have been a little earlier or a little later, but not much. Why, Alan? Does it mean anything?"

When Alan slid between the sheets, he felt that he would be asleep ten seconds after his head hit the pillow. Now he was wide awake again, and thinking hard.

"No," he said after a moment. "I don't think it means anything, except that Nettie had Wilma on her mind."

"I just can't believe it. She seemed so much better—she
really did. Remember me telling you about how she got up
the courage to go into Needful Things all on her own last
Thursday?"

"Yes."

She released him and rolled fretfully onto her back. Alan
heard a small metallic *chink!* as she did so, and again thought
nothing of it. His mind was still examining what Polly had
just told him, turning it this way and that, like a jeweller examining a suspect stone.

"I'll have to make the funeral arrangements," she said. "Nettie has got people in Yarmouth—a few, anyway—but they
didn't want to have anything to do with her when she was
alive, and they'll want to have even less to do with her now
that she's dead. But I'll have to call them in the morning. Will
I be able to go into Nettie's house, Alan? I think she had an
address book."

"I'll bring you. You won't be able to take anything away, at
least not until Dr. Ryan has published his autopsy findings,
but I can't see any harm in letting you copy down a few telephone numbers."

"Thank you."

A sudden thought occurred to him. "Polly, what time did
Nettie leave here?"

"Quarter of eleven, I guess. It might have been as late as
eleven o'clock. She didn't stay a whole hour, I don't think.
Why?"

"Nothing," he said. He'd had a momentary flash: if Nettie had stayed long enough at Polly's, she might not have had
time to go back home, find her dog dead, collect the rocks,
write the notes, attach them to the rocks, go over to Wilma's,
and break the windows. But if Nettie had left Polly's at quarter
to eleven, that gave her better than two hours. Plenty of time.

Hey, Alan! the voice—the falsely cheery one that usually restricted its input to the subject of Annie and Todd—spoke up. *How come you're trying to bitch this up for yourself, good buddy?*

And Alan didn't know. There was something else he didn't know, either—how had Nettie gotten that load of rocks over to the Jerzyck house in the first place? She had no driver's license and didn't have a clue about operating a car.

Cut the crap, good buddy, the voice advised. *She wrote the notes at her house—probably right down the hall from her dog's dead body—and got the rubber bands from her own kitchen drawer. She didn't have to carry the rocks; there were plenty of those in Wilma's back-yard garden. Right?*

Right. Yet he could not get rid of the idea that the rocks had been brought with the notes already attached. He had no concrete reason to think so, but it just seemed right . . . the kind of thing you'd expect from a kid or someone who *thought* like a kid.

Someone like Nettie Cobb.

Quit it . . . let it go!

He couldn't, though.

Polly touched his cheek. "I'm awfully glad you came, Alan. It must have been a horrible day for you, too."

"I've had better, but it's over now. You should let it go, too. Get some sleep. You have a lot of arrangements to make tomorrow. Do you want me to get you a pill?"

"No, my hands are a little better, at least. Alan—" She broke off, but stirred restlessly under the covers.

"What?"

"Nothing," she said. "It wasn't important. I think I *can* sleep, now that you're here. Goodnight."

"Goodnight, honey."

She rolled away from him, pulled the covers up, and was still. For a moment he thought of how she had hugged him—the feel of her hands locked about his neck. If she was able to flex her fingers enough to do that, then she really *was* better.

That was a good thing, maybe the best thing that had happened to him since Clut had phoned during the football game. If only things would *stay* better.

Polly had a slightly deviated septum and now she began to snore lightly, a sound Alan actually found rather pleasant. It was good to be sharing a bed with another person, a real person who made real sounds . . . and sometimes filched the covers. He grinned in the dark.

Then his mind turned back to the murders and the grin faded.

I think she'll leave me alone, anyway. I haven't seen her or heard from her, so I guess she finally got the message.

I haven't seen her or heard from her.

I guess she finally got the message.

A case like this one didn't need to be solved; even Seat Thomas could have told you exactly what had happened after a single look at the crime-scene through his trifocals. It had been kitchen implements instead of duelling pistols at dawn, but the result was the same: two bodies in the morgue at K.V.H. with autopsy Y-cuts in them. The only question was why it had happened. He had had a few questions, a few vague disquiets, but they would no doubt have blown away before Wilma and Nettie had been seen into the ground.

Now the disquiets were more urgent, and some of them

(*I guess she finally got the message*)

had names.

To Alan, a criminal case was like a garden surrounded by a high wall. You had to get in, so you looked for the gate. Sometimes there were several, but in his experience there was always at least one; of course there was. If not, how had the gardener entered to sow the seeds in the first place? It might be large, with an arrow pointing to it and a flashing neon sign reading ENTER HERE, or it might be small and covered with so much ivy that you had to hunt for quite a while before you found it, but it was always there, and if you hunted long enough and weren't afraid of raising a few blisters on your hands from tearing away the overgrowth, you always found it.

Sometimes the gate was a piece of evidence found at a crime-scene. Sometimes it was a witness. Sometimes it was an assumption firmly based on events and logic. The assumptions he'd made in this case were: one, that Wilma had been follow-ing a long-established pattern of harassment and fuckery; two, that this time she had chosen the wrong person with whom to play mind-games; three, that Nettie had snapped again as she had when she'd killed her husband. But . . .

I haven't seen her or heard from her.

If Nettie had really said that, how much did it change? How many assumptions did that single sentence knock into cocked hats? Alan didn't know.

He stared into the darkness of Polly's bedroom and won-dered if he'd found the gate after all.

Maybe Polly hadn't heard what Nettie had said correctly.

It was technically possible, but Alan didn't believe it. Net-tie's actions, at least up to a certain point, supported what Polly claimed to have heard. Nettie hadn't come to work at Polly's on Friday—she'd said she was ill. Maybe she was, or maybe she was just scared of Wilma. That made sense; they knew from Pete Jerzyck that Wilma, after discovering that her sheets had been vandalized, had made at least one threatening call to Nettie. She might have made others the next day that Pete didn't know about. But Nettie had come to see Polly with a gift of food on Sunday morning. Would she have done that if Wilma was still stoking the fires? Alan didn't think so.

Then there was the matter of the rocks which had been thrown through Wilma's windows. Each of the attached notes said the same thing: I TOLD YOU TO LEAVE ME ALONE. THIS IS YOUR LAST WARNING. A warning usually means that the person being warned has more time to change his or her ways, but time had been up for Wilma and Nettie. They had met on that street-corner only two hours after the rocks had been thrown.

He supposed he could get around that one if he had to. When Nettie found her dog, she would have been furious. Ditto Wilma when she got home and saw the damage to her house. All it would have taken to strike the final spark was a single telephone call. One of the two women had made that call . . . and the balloon had gone up.

Alan turned over on his side, wishing that these were the old days, when you could still obtain records of local calls. If he could have documented the fact that Wilma and Nettie had spoken before their final meeting, he would have felt a lot better. Still—take the final phone-call as a given. That still left the notes themselves.

This is how it must have happened, he thought. *Nettie comes home from Polly's and finds her dog dead on the hall floor. She reads the note on the corkscrew. Then she writes the same message on fourteen or sixteen sheets of paper and puts them in the pocket of her coat. She also gets a bunch of rubber bands. When she gets to Wilma's she goes into the backyard. She piles up fourteen or sixteen rocks and uses the elastic bands to attach the notes. She must have done all that prior to throwing* any *rocks—it would have taken too long if she had to stop in the middle of the festivities to pick out more rocks and attach more notes. And when she's done, she goes home and broods over her dead pet some more.*

It felt all wrong to him.

It felt really lousy.

It presupposed a chain of thought and action that just didn't fit what he knew of Nettie Cobb. The murder of her husband had been the outcome of long cycles of abuse, but the murder itself had been an impulse crime committed by a woman whose sanity had broken. If the records in George Bannerman's old files were correct, Nettie sure hadn't written Albion Cobb any warning notes beforehand.

What felt right to him was much simpler: Nettie comes home from Polly's. She finds her dog dead in the hallway. She gets a cleaver from the kitchen drawer and heads up the street to cut herself a wide slice of Polish butt.

But if that was the case, who had broken Wilma Jerzyck's windows?

"Plus the times are all so *weird,*" he muttered, and rolled restlessly over onto his other side.

John LaPointe had been with the CIU team which had spent Sunday afternoon and evening tracing Nettie's movements—what movements there had been. She had gone to Polly's with the lasagna. She told Polly that she would probably go by the new shop, Needful Things, on her way home and speak to the owner, Leland Gaunt, if he was in—Polly said Mr. Gaunt had invited her to look at an item that afternoon and Nettie was going to tell Mr. Gaunt that Polly would probably show up, even though her hands were paining her quite badly.

If Nettie *had* gone into Needful Things, if Nettie *had* spent some time there—browsing, talking to the new shopkeeper that everyone in town thought was so fascinating and whom Alan kept not meeting—that might have bitched up her window of opportunity and re-opened the possibility of a mystery rock-thrower. But she hadn't. The shop had been closed. Gaunt had told both Polly, who had indeed dropped by later on, and the CID boys that he had seen neither hide nor hair of Nettie since the day she came in and bought her carnival glass lampshade. In any case, he had spent the morning in the back room, listening to classical music and cataloguing items. If someone had knocked, he probably wouldn't have heard anyway. So Nettie must have gone directly home, and that left her the time to do all those things which Alan found so unlikely.

Wilma Jerzyck's window of opportunity was even narrower. Her husband had some woodworking equipment in the basement; he had been down there Sunday morning from eight until just past ten. He saw it was getting late, he said, so he'd shut down the machinery and gone upstairs to dress for eleven o'clock Mass. Wilma, he told the officers, had been in the shower when he entered the bedroom, and Alan had no reason to doubt the new widower's testimony.

It must have gone like this: Wilma leaves her house on a drive-by mission at nine-thirty-five or nine-forty. Pete's in the basement, making birdhouses or whatever, and doesn't even know she's gone. Wilma gets to Nettie's at about quarter to ten—just minutes after Nettie must have left for Polly's—and sees the door standing open. To Wilma, this is as good as a gilt-edged invitation. She parks, goes inside, kills the dog and writes the note on impulse, and leaves again. None of the neighbors re-membered seeing Wilma's bright yellow Yugo—inconvenient, but hardly proof it hadn't been there. Most of the neighbors had been gone, anyway, either to church or visiting out of town.

Wilma drives back to her house, goes upstairs while Pete is shutting down his planer or jigsaw or whatever, and gets undressed. When Pete enters the master bathroom to wash the sawdust off his hands before putting on a coat and tie, Wilma has just stepped into the shower; in fact, she's probably still dry on one side.

Pete Jerzyck's finding his wife in the shower was the only thing in the whole mess that made perfect sense to Alan. The corkscrew which had been used on the dog was a lethal enough weapon, but a short one. She'd have wanted to wash off any bloodstains on her hands and arms.

Wilma just misses Nettie on one end and just misses her husband on the other. Was it possible? Yes. Only by a squeak and a gasp, but it *was* possible.

So let it go, Alan. Let it go and go to sleep.

But he still couldn't, because it still sucked. It sucked *hard*.

Alan rolled onto his back once more. Downstairs he heard the clock in the living room softly chiming four. This was getting him nowhere at all, but he couldn't seem to turn his mind off.

He tried to imagine Nettie sitting patiently at her kitchen table, writing THIS IS YOUR LAST WARNING over and over again while, less than twenty feet away, her beloved little dog lay dead. He couldn't do it no matter how he tried. What had seemed like a gate into this particular garden now seemed more and more like a clever painting of a gate on the high, unbroken wall. A *trompe l'oeil.*

Had Nettie walked over to Wilma's house on Willow Street and broken the windows? He didn't know, but he *did* know that Nettie Cobb was still a figure of interest in Castle Rock . . . the crazy lady who had killed her husband and then spent all those years in Juniper Hill. On the rare occasions when she deviated from the path of her usual routine, she was noticed. If she had gone stalking over to Willow Street on Sunday morning—perhaps muttering to herself as she went and almost certainly crying—she would have been noticed. Tomorrow Alan would start knocking on the doors between the two houses and asking questions.

He began to slip off to sleep at last. The image that followed him down was a pile of rocks with a sheet of note-paper banded around each one. And he thought again: *If Nettie didn't throw them, then who did?*

9

As the small hours of Monday morning crept toward dawn and the beginning of a new and interesting week, a young man named Ricky Bissonette emerged from the hedge surrounding the Baptist parsonage. Inside this neat-as-a-pin building, the Reverend William Rose slept the sleep of the just and the righteous.

Ricky, nineteen and not overburdened with brains, worked down at Sonny's Sunoco. He had closed up hours ago but had hung around in the office, waiting until it was late enough (or early enough) to play a little prank on Rev. Rose. On Friday afternoon, Ricky had stopped by the new shop, and had fallen into conversation with the proprietor, who was one interesting old fellow. One thing led to another, and at some point Ricky had realized he was telling Mr. Gaunt his deepest, most secret wish. He mentioned the name of a young actress-model—a *very* young actress-model—and told Mr. Gaunt he would give just about anything for some pictures of this young woman with her clothes off.

"You know, I have something that might interest you," Mr. Gaunt had said. He glanced around the store as if to verify that it was empty except for the two of them, then went to the door and turned the OPEN sign over to CLOSED. He returned to his spot by the cash register, rummaged under the counter, and came up with an unmarked manila envelope. "Have a look at these, Mr. Bissonette," Mr. Gaunt said, and then dropped a rather lecherous man-of-the-world wink. "I think you'll be startled. Perhaps even amazed."

Stunned was more like it. It was the actress-model for whom Ricky lusted—it *had* to be!—and she was a lot more than just nude. In some of the pictures she was with a well-known actor. In others, she was with *two* well-known actors, one of whom was old enough to be her grandfather. And in still others—

But before he could see any of the others (and it appeared there were fifty or more, all brilliant eight-by-ten glossy color shots), Mr. Gaunt had snatched them away.

"That's ——!" Ricky gulped, mentioning a name which was well known to readers of the glossy tabloids and watchers of the glossy talk-shows.

"Oh, no," Mr. Gaunt said, while his jade-colored eyes said Oh, yes. "I'm sure it can't be . . . but the resemblance *is* remarkable, isn't it? The sale of pictures such as these is illegal, of course—sexual content aside, the girl can't be a minute over seventeen, *whoever* she is—but I might be persuaded to deal for these just the same, Mr. Bissonette. The fever in my blood is not malaria but commerce. So! Shall we dicker?"

They dickered. Ricky Bissonette ended up purchasing seventy-two pornographic photographs for thirty-six dollars . . . and this little prank.

He ran across the parsonage lawn bent over at the waist, settled into the shadow of the porch for a moment to make sure he was unwatched, then climbed the steps. He produced a plain white card from his back pocket, opened the mail-slot, and dropped the card through. He eased the brass slot closed with the tips of his fingers, not wanting it to clack shut. Then he vaulted the porch railing and ran fleetly back across the lawn. He had big plans for the two or three hours of darkness which still remained to this Monday morning; they involved seventy-two photographs and a large bottle of Jergens hand lotion.

The card looked like a white moth as it fluttered from the mail-slot to the faded rug-runner in the front hall of the parsonage. It landed message-side up:

How you doing you Stupid Babtist Rat-Fuck.

We are writting you to say you better Quit talking out aginst our Casino Nite. We are just going to have a little fun we are not hurting You. Anyway a bunch of us Loyal Catholics are tired of your Babtist Bullshit. We know all You Babtists are a bunch of Cunt Lickers anyway. Now to THIS You better Pay Atention, Reverund Steam-Boat Willy. If you dont keept your Dick-Face out of Our business, we are going to stink You and your Ass-Face Buddies up so bad you will *Stink Forever!*

Leave us alone you Stupid Babtist Rat-Fuck or YOU WILL BE A SORRY SON OF A BITCH. "Just a Warning" from

> THE CONCERNED
> CATHOLIC MEN OF
> CASTLE ROCK

Rev. Rose discovered the note when he came downstairs in his bathrobe to collect the morning paper. His reaction is perhaps better imagined than described.

10

Leland Gaunt stood at the window of the front room above Needful Things with his hands clasped behind his back, looking out across the town of Castle Rock.

The four-room apartment behind him would have raised eyebrows in town, for there was nothing in it—nothing at all. Not a bed, not an appliance, not a single chair. The closets stood open and empty. A few dust-bunnies tumbled lazily across floors innocent of rugs in a slight draft that blew through the place at ankle level. The only furnishings were, quite literally, window-dressing: homey checked curtains. They were the only furnishings which mattered, because they were the only ones which could be seen from the street.

The town was sleeping now. The shops were dark, the houses were dark, and the only movement on Main Street was the blinker at the intersection of Main and Watermill, flashing on and off in sleepy yellow beats. He looked over the town with a tender loving eye. It wasn't his town just yet, but it soon would be. He had a lien on it already. They didn't know that . . . but they would. They would.

The grand opening had gone very, very well.

Mr. Gaunt thought of himself as an electrician of the human soul. In a small town like Castle Rock, all the fuse-boxes were lined up neatly side by side. What you had to do was open the boxes . . . and then start cross-wiring. You hot-wired a Wilma Jerzyck to a Nettie Cobb by using wires from two other fuse-boxes—those of a young fellow like Brian Rusk and a drunk fellow like Hugh Priest, let us say. You hot-wired other people in the same way, a Buster Keeton to a Norris Ridgewick, a Frank Jewett to a George Nelson, a Sally Ratcliffe to a Lester Pratt.

At some point you tested one of your fabulous wiring jobs just to make sure everything was working correctly—as he had done today—and then you laid low and sent a charge through the circuits every once in a while to keep things interesting. To keep things hot. But mostly you just laid low until everything was done . . . and then you turned on the juice.

All the juice.

All at once.

All it took was an understanding of human nature, and—

"Of course it's *really* a question of supply and demand," Leland Gaunt mused as he looked out over the sleeping town.

And why? Well . . . just because, actually. Just because.

People always thought in terms of souls, and of course he would take as many of those as he could when he closed up shop; they were to Leland Gaunt what trophies were to the hunter, what stuffed fish were to the fisherman. They were worth little to him these days in any practical sense, but he still bagged his limit if he possibly could, no matter what he might say to the contrary; to do any less would not be playing the game.

Yet it was mostly amusement, not souls, that kept him going. Simple amusement. It was the only reason that mattered after a while, because when the years were long, you took diversion where you could find it.

Mr. Gaunt took his hands from behind his back—those hands which revolted anyone unlucky enough to feel their crepitant touch—and locked them together tightly, the knuckles of his right hand pressing into the palm of his left, the knuckles of his left pressing into the palm of his right. His fingernails were long and thick and yellow. They were also very sharp, and after a moment or two they cut into the skin of his fingers, bringing a blackish-red flow of thick blood.

Brian Rusk cried out in his sleep.

Myra Evans thrust her hands into the fork of her crotch and began to masturbate furiously—in her dream, The King was making love to her.

Danforth Keeton dreamed he was lying in the middle of the

homestretch at Lewiston Raceway, and he covered his face with his hands as the horses bore down on him.

Sally Ratcliffe dreamed she opened the door of Lester Pratt's Mustang only to see it was full of snakes.

Hugh Priest screamed himself awake from a dream in which Henry Beaufort, the bartender at The Mellow Tiger, poured lighter fluid all over his fox-tail and set it on fire.

Everett Frankel, Ray Van Allen's Physician's Assistant, dreamed he slipped his new pipe into his mouth only to discover the stem had turned into a razor-blade and he had cut off his own tongue.

Polly Chalmers began to moan softly, and inside the small silver charm she wore something stirred and moved with a rustling like the whir of small dusty wings. And it sent up a faint, dusty aroma . . . like a tremor of violets.

Leland Gaunt relaxed his grip slowly. His big, crooked teeth were exposed in a grin which was both cheerful and surpassingly ugly. All over Castle Rock, dreams blew away and uneasy sleepers rested easy once more.

For now.

Soon the sun would be up. Not long after that a new day would begin, with all its surprises and wonders. He believed the time had come to hire an assistant . . . not that the assistant would be immune to the process which he had now set in motion. Heavens, no.

That would spoil all the fun.

Leland Gaunt stood at the window and looked at the town below, spread out, defenseless, in all that lovely darkness.

PART TWO

THE SALE OF THE CENTURY

CHAPTER TWELVE

1

Monday the 14th of October, Columbus Day, dawned fair and hot in Castle Rock. The residents grumbled about the heat, and when they met in groups—on the Town Common, at Nan's, on the benches in front of the Municipal Building— they told each other it was unnatural. Probably had something to do with the goddam oil-fires in Kuwait, they said, or maybe that hole in the ozone layer they were always blabbing about on TV. Several of the oldtimers declared it was never seventy degrees at seven o'clock in the morning during the second week of October when *they* were young.

This wasn't true, of course, and most (if not all) of them knew it; every two or three years you could count on Indian summer to get a little out of hand and there would be four or five days that felt like the middle of July. Then one morning you'd wake up with what felt like a summer cold only to see the front lawn stiff with frost and a snow-flurry or two breezing around in the chilly air. They knew all this, but as a topic of conversation, the weather was simply too good to ruin by acknowledging it. No one wanted to argue; arguments when the weather turned unseasonably hot were not a good idea. People were apt to get ugly, and if Castle Rock residents wanted a sobering example of what could happen when people got ugly, they only had to look as far as the intersection of Willow and Ford streets.

"Those two wimmin had it comin," Lenny Partridge, the

town's oldest resident and premier gossip, opined as he stood on the steps of the bandbox county courthouse which took up the west wing of the Municipal Building. "Both of em crazier'n a pair of rats in a backed-up shit-house. That Cobb woman stuck a meat-fork in her husband, you know." Lenny hitched at the truss beneath his baggy trousers. "Stuck him just like a pig, she did. Hot damn! Ain't some wimmin crazy?" He looked up at the sky and added: "Hot like this, there's apt to be more contention. I seen it before. First thing Sheriff Pangborn ort to do is order Henry Beaufort to keep the Tiger closed until the weather gets normal again."

"That's jake with me, oldtimer," Charlie Fortin said. "I c'n get my beer at Hemphill's for a day or two and do my drinkin at home."

This earned him laughter from the loose knot of men around Lenny and a fierce scowl from Mr. Partridge himself. The group broke up. Most of these men had to work, holiday or no holiday. Already some of the rickety pulp-trucks parked in front of Nan's were pulling out, headed for logging operations in Sweden and Nodd's Ridge and out by Castle Lake.

2

Danforth "Buster" Keeton sat in his study, wearing only his underpants. The underpants were soggy. He hadn't left the room since Sunday evening, when he had made a brief trip down to the Municipal Building. He'd gotten the Bureau of Taxation file and brought it home. Castle Rock's Head Selectman was oiling his Colt revolver for the third time. At some point this morning he meant to load it. Then he meant to kill his wife. Then he meant to go down to the Municipal Building, find that son of a bitch Ridgewick (he had no idea that it was Norris's day off) and kill *him*. Last of all, he intended to lock himself in his office and kill himself. He had decided that the only way he could escape the Persecutors forever was by taking these steps. He had been a fool to think otherwise. Not even a board game which magically picked winners at the race-track could stop Them. Oh no. He had learned that lesson yesterday when he had come home to find those terrible pink slips taped up all over the house.

The telephone on the desk rang. Startled, Keeton squeezed the Colt's trigger. There was a dry snap. If the gun had been loaded, he would have put a bullet spang through the study door.

He scooped the phone up. "Can't you people leave me alone for even a little while?" he shouted angrily.

The quiet voice which replied silenced him at once. It was the voice of Mr. Gaunt, and it poured over Keeton's blistered soul like soothing balm.

"What luck did you have with the toy I sold you, Mr. Keeton?"

"It worked!" Keeton said. His voice was jubilant. He forgot, at least for the moment, that he was planning a strenuous morning of murder and suicide. "I collected on every race, by God!"

"Well, that's fine," Mr. Gaunt said warmly.

Keeton's face clouded again. His voice dropped to what was almost a whisper. "Then . . . yesterday . . . when I got home . . ." He found he could not go on. A moment later he discovered— to his great amazement and even greater delight—that he didn't have to.

"You discovered They had been in your house?" Mr. Gaunt asked.

"Yes! *Yes!* How did you kn—"

"They are everywhere in this town," Mr. Gaunt said. "I told you that when last we met, did I not?"

"Yes! And—" Keeton broke off suddenly. His face twisted in alarm. "They could have this line tapped, do you realize that, Mr. Gaunt? *They could be listening in on our conversation right now!*"

Mr. Gaunt remained calm. "They could, but They're not. Please don't think I am naive, Mr. Keeton. I have encountered Them before. Many times."

"I'm sure you have," Keeton said. He was discovering that the wild joy he had taken in Winning Ticket was little or nothing compared to this; to finding, after what felt like centuries of struggle and darkness, a kindred soul.

"I have a small electronic device attached to my line," Mr. Gaunt went on in his calm and mellow voice. "If the line is tapped, a small light goes on. I am looking at that light now, Mr. Keeton, and it is dark. As dark as some of the hearts in this town."

"You *do* know, don't you?" Danforth Keeton said in a fervent, trembling voice. He felt as if he might weep.

"Yes. And I called to tell you that you mustn't do anything rash, Mr. Keeton." The voice was soft, lulling. As he listened to it, Keeton felt his mind begin to drift away like a child's helium-filled balloon. "That would make things far too easy for Them. Why, do you realize what would happen if you were to die?"

"No," Keeton murmured. He was looking out the window. His eyes were blank and dreamy.

"They would have a party!" Mr. Gaunt cried softly. "They would get liquored up in Sheriff Pangborn's office! They would go out to Homeland Cemetery and urinate on your grave!"

"Sheriff Pangborn?" Keeton said uncertainly.

"You don't really believe a drone like Deputy Ridgewick is allowed to operate in a case like this without orders from his higher-ups, do you?"

"No, of course not." He was beginning to see more clearly now. They; it had always been They, a tormenting dark cloud around him, and when you snatched at that cloud, you came away with nothing. Now he at last began to understand that They had faces and names. They might even be vulnerable. Knowing this was a tremendous relief.

"Pangborn, Fullerton, Samuels, the Williams woman, your own wife. They are all part of it, Mr. Keeton, but I suspect—yes, and rather strongly—that Sheriff Pangborn is the ringleader. If so, he would love it if you killed one or two of his underlings and then put yourself out of the way. Why, I suspect that is exactly what he has been aiming for all along. But you're going to fool him, Mr. Keeton, aren't you?"

"*Yessss!*" Keeton whispered fiercely. "What should I do?"

"Nothing today. Go about your business as usual. Go to the races tonight, if you like, and enjoy your new purchase. If you appear the same as always to Them, it will throw Them off balance. It will sow confusion and uncertainty amidst the enemy."

"Confusion and uncertainty." Keeton spoke the words slowly, tasting them.

"Yes. I'm laying my own plans, and when the time comes, I'll let you know."

"Do you promise?"

"Oh yes indeed, Mr. Keeton. You are quite important to me. In fact, I would go so far as to say I could not do without you."

Mr. Gaunt rang off. Keeton put his pistol and the gun-cleaning kit away. Then he went upstairs, dumped his soiled clothes in the laundry hamper, showered, and dressed. When he came down, Myrtle shrank away from him at first, but Keeton spoke kindly to her and kissed her cheek. Myrtle began to relax. Whatever the crisis had been, it seemed to have passed.

3

Everett Frankel was a big red-haired man who looked as Irish as County Cork . . . which was not surprising, since it was from Cork that his mother's ancestors had sprang. He had been Ray Van Allen's P.A. for four years, ever since he'd gotten out of the Navy. He arrived at Castle Rock Family Practice at quarter to eight that Monday morning, and Nancy Ramage, the head nurse, asked him if he could go right out to the Burgmeyer farm. Helen Burgmeyer had suffered what might have been an epileptic seizure in the night, she said. If Everett's diagnosis confirmed this, he was to bring her back to town in his car so the doctor—who would be in shortly—could examine her and decide if she needed to go to the hospital for tests.

Ordinarily, Everett would have been unhappy to be sent on a house-call first thing, especially one so far out in the country, but on an unseasonably hot morning like this, a ride out of town seemed like just the thing.

Besides, there was the pipe.

Once he was in his Plymouth, he unlocked the glove compartment and took it out. It was a meerschaum, with a bowl both deep and wide. It had been carved by a master craftsman, that pipe; birds and flowers and vines circled the bowl in a pattern that actually seemed to change when one looked at it from different angles. He had left the pipe in the glove compartment not just because smoking was forbidden in the doctor's office but because he didn't like the idea of other people (especially a snoop like Nancy Ramage) seeing it. First they would want to know where he had gotten it. Then they would want to know how much he had paid for it.

Also, some of them might covet it.

He put the stem between his teeth, marvelling again at how perfectly right it felt there, how perfectly *in its place.* He tilted down the rearview mirror for a moment so he could see himself, and approved completely of what he saw. He thought the pipe made him look older, wiser, handsomer. And when he had the pipe clenched between his teeth, the bowl pointed up a bit at just the right debonair angle, he *felt* older, wiser, handsomer.

He drove down Main Street, meaning to cross the Tin Bridge between the town and the country, and then slowed as he approached Needful Things. The green awning tugged at him like a fishhook. It suddenly seemed very important—imperative, in fact—that he stop.

He pulled in, started to get out of the car, then remembered that the pipe was still clenched between his teeth. He took it out (feeling a small pang of regret as he did so) and locked it in the glove compartment again. This time he actually reached the sidewalk before returning to the Plymouth to lock all four doors. With a nice pipe like that, it didn't do to take chances. Anybody might be tempted to steal a nice pipe like that. Anybody at all.

He approached the shop and then stopped, feeling disappointed. A sign hung in the window.

CLOSED COLUMBUS DAY

it read.

Everett was about to turn away when the door opened. Mr. Gaunt stood there, looking resplendent and quite debonair himself in a fawn-colored jacket with elbow patches and charcoal-gray pants.

"Come in, Mr. Frankel," he said. "I'm glad to see you."

"Well, I'm on my way out of town—business—and I thought I'd just stop and tell you again how much I like my pipe. I've always wanted one just like that."

Beaming, Mr. Gaunt said, "I know."

"But I see you're closed, so I won't bother y—"

"I am never closed to my favorite customers, Mr. Frankel, and I put you among that number. *High* among that number. Step in." And he held out his hand.

Everett shrank away from it. Leland Gaunt laughed cheerfully at this and stepped aside so the young Physician's Assistant could enter.

"I really can't stay—" Everett began, but he felt his feet carry him forward into the gloom of the shop as if they knew better.

"Of course not," Mr. Gaunt said. "The healer must be about

his appointed rounds, releasing the chains of illness which bind the body and . . ." His grin, a thing of raised eyebrows and clenched, jostling teeth, sprang forth. ". . . and driving out those devils which bind the spirit. Am I right?"

"I guess so," Everett said. He felt a pang of unease as Mr. Gaunt closed the door. He hoped his pipe would be all right. Sometimes people broke into cars. Sometimes they did that even in broad daylight.

"Your pipe will be fine," Mr. Gaunt soothed. From his pocket he drew a plain envelope with one word written across the front. The word was *Lovey.* "Do you remember promising to play a little prank for me, Dr. Frankel?"

"I'm not a doc—"

Mr. Gaunt's eyebrows drew together in a way that made Everett cease and desist at once. He took half a step backward.

"*Do* you remember or *don't* you?" Mr. Gaunt asked sharply. "You'd better answer me quickly, young man—I'm not as sure of that pipe as I was a moment ago."

"I remember!" Everett said. His voice was hasty and alarmed. "Sally Ratcliffe! The speech teacher!"

The bunched center of Mr. Gaunt's more or less single eyebrow relaxed. Everett Frankel relaxed with it. "That's right. And the time has come to play that little prank, Doctor. Here."

He held out the envelope. Everett took it, being careful that his fingers should not touch Mr. Gaunt's as he did so.

"Today is a school holiday, but the young Miss Ratcliffe is in her office, updating her files," Mr. Gaunt said. "I know that's not on your way to the Burgmeyer farm—"

"How do you know so *much?*" Everett asked in a dazed voice.

Mr. Gaunt waved this away impatiently. "—but you might make time to go by on your way back, yes?"

"I suppose—"

"And since outsiders at a school, even when the students aren't there, are regarded with some suspicion, you might explain your presence by dropping in at the school nurse's office, yes?"

"If she's there, I guess I could do that," Everett said. "In fact, I really should, because—"

"—you still haven't picked up the vaccination records," Mr. Gaunt finished for him. "That's fine. As a matter of fact she *won't* be there, but *you* don't know that, do you? Just poke your head into her office, then leave. But on your way in or your way out, I want you to put that envelope in the car Miss Ratcliffe has borrowed from her young man. I want you to put it under the driver's seat . . . but not *entirely* under. I want you to leave it with just a corner sticking out."

Everett knew perfectly well who "Miss Ratcliffe's young man" was: the high school Physical Education instructor. Given a choice, Everett would have preferred playing the trick on Lester Pratt rather than on his fiancée. Pratt was a beefy young Baptist who usually wore blue tee-shirts and blue sweat-pants with a white stripe running down the outside of each leg. He was the sort of fellow who exuded sweat and Jesus from his pores in apparently equal (and copious) amounts. Everett didn't care much for him. He wondered vaguely if Lester had slept with Sally yet—she was quite the dish. He thought the answer was probably no. He further thought that when Lester got het up after a little too much necking on the porch swing, Sally probably had him do sit-ups in the back yard or run a few dozen wind-sprints around the house.

"Sally has got the Prattmobile again?"

"Indeed," Mr. Gaunt said, a trifle testily. "Are you done being witty, Dr. Frankel?"

"Sure," he said. In truth, he felt a surprisingly deep sense of relief. He had been a little worried about the "prank" Mr. Gaunt wanted him to play. Now he saw that his worry had been foolish. It wasn't as if Mr. Gaunt wanted him to stick a firecracker in the lady's shoe or put Ex-Lax in her chocolate milk or anything like that. What harm could an envelope do?

Mr. Gaunt's smile, sunny and resplendent, burst forth once again. "Very good," he said. He came toward Everett, who observed with horror that Mr. Gaunt apparently meant to put an arm around him.

Everett moved hastily backward. In this way, Mr. Gaunt maneuvered him back to the front door and opened it.

"Enjoy that pipe," he said. "Did I tell you that it once belonged to Sir Arthur Conan Doyle, creator of the great Sherlock Holmes?"

"No!" Everett Frankel exclaimed.

"Of course I didn't," Mr. Gaunt said, grinning. "That would have been a lie . . . and I never lie in matters of business, Dr. Frankel. Don't forget your little errand."

"I won't."

"Then I'll wish you a good day."

"Same to y—"

But Everett was talking to no one. The door with its drawn shade had already been closed behind him.

He looked at it for a moment, then walked slowly back to his Plymouth. If he had been asked for an exact account of what he had said to Mr. Gaunt and what Mr. Gaunt had said to him, he would have made a poor job of it, because he couldn't exactly remember. He felt like a man who has been given a whiff of light anaesthetic.

Once he was sitting behind the wheel again, the first thing Everett did was unlock the glove compartment, put the envelope with *Lovey* written on the front in, and take the pipe out. One thing he *did* remember was Mr. Gaunt's teasing him, saying that A. Conan Doyle had once owned the pipe. And he had almost believed him. How silly! You only had to put it in your mouth and clamp your teeth on the stem to know better. The original owner of this pipe had been Hermann Göring.

Everett Frankel started his car and drove slowly out of town. And on his way to the Burgmeyer farm, he had to pull over to the side of the road only twice to admire how much that pipe improved his looks.

4

Albert Gendron kept his dental offices in the Castle Building, a graceless brick structure which stood across the street from the town's Municipal Building and the squat cement pillbox that housed the Castle County Water District. The Castle Building had thrown its shadow over Castle Stream and the Tin Bridge since 1924, and housed three of the county's five lawyers, an optometrist, an audiologist, several independent realtors, a credit consultant, a one-woman answering service, and a framing shop. The half dozen other offices in the building were currently vacant.

Albert, who had been one of Our Lady of Serene Waters' stalwarts since the days of old Father O'Neal, was getting on now, his once-black hair turning salt-and-pepper, his broad shoulders sloping in a way they never had in his young days, but he was still a man of imposing size—at six feet, seven inches tall and two hundred and eighty pounds, he was the biggest man in town, if not the entire county.

He climbed the narrow staircase to the fourth and top floor slowly, stopping on the landings to catch his breath before going on up, mindful of the heart-murmur Dr. Van Allen said he now had. Halfway up the final flight, he saw a sheet of paper taped to the frosted glass panel of his office door, obscuring the lettering which read ALBERT GENDRON D.D.S.

He was able to read the salutation on this note while he was still five steps from the top, and his heart began to pound harder, murmur or no murmur. Only it wasn't exertion causing it to kick up its heels; it was rage.

LISTEN UP YOU MACKEREL-SNAPPER! was printed at the top of the sheet in bright red Magic Marker.

Albert pulled the note from the door and read it quickly.

He breathed through his nose as be did so—harsh, snorting exhalations that made him sound like a bull about to charge.

LISTEN UP YOU MACKEREL-SNAPPER!

We have tried to reason with you—"Let him hear who hath understanding"—but it has been no use. YOU ARE SET ON YOUR COURSE OF DAMNATION AND BY THEIR WORKS SHALT YOU KNOW THEM. We have put up with your Popish idolatry and even with your licentious worship of the Babylon Whore. But now you have gone too far. THERE WILL BE NO DICING WITH THE DEVIL IN CASTLE ROCK!

Decent Christians can smell HELLFIRE and BRIMSTONE in Castle Rock this fall. If you cannot it is because your nose has been stuffed shut by your own sin and degradation. HEAR OUR WARNING AND HEED IT: GIVE UP YOUR PLAN TO TURN THIS TOWN INTO A DEN OF THIEVES AND GAMBLERS OR YOU *WILL* SMELL THE HELLFIRE! YOU *WILL* SMELL THE BRIMSTONE!

"The wicked shall be turned into hell, and all the nations that forget God." Psalm 9:17.

HEAR AND HEED, OR YOUR CRIES OF LAMENTATION WILL BE LOUD INDEED.

THE CONCERNED BAPTIST MEN
OF CASTLE ROCK

"Shit on toast," Albert said at last, and crumpled the note into one ham-sized fist. "That idiotic little Baptist shoe-salesman has finally gone out of his mind."

His first order of business after opening his office was to call Father John and tell him the game might be getting a little rougher between now and Casino Nite.

"Don't worry, Albert," Father Brigham said calmly. "If the idiot bumps us, he's going to find out how hard we mackerel-snappers can bump back . . . am I right?"

"Right you are, Father," Albert said. He was still holding the crumpled note in one hand. Now he looked down at it and an unpleasant little smile surfaced below his walrus moustache. "Right you are."

5

By quarter past ten that morning, the digital read-out in front of the bank announced the temperature in Castle Rock as seventy-seven degrees. On the far side of the Tin Bridge, the unseasonably hot sun produced a bright twinkle, a daystar at the place where Route 117 came over the horizon and headed toward town. Alan Pangborn was in his office, going over reports on the Cobb-Jerzyck murders, and did not see that reflection of sun on metal and glass. It wouldn't have interested him much if he had—it was, after all, only an approaching car. Nevertheless, the savagely bright twinkle of chrome and glass, heading toward the bridge at better than seventy miles an hour, heralded the arrival of a significant part of Alan Pangborn's destiny . . . and that of the whole town.

In the show window of Needful Things, the sign reading

CLOSED COLUMBUS DAY

was taken down by a long-fingered hand which emerged from the sleeve of a fawn sport-jacket. A new sign went up in its place. This one read

HELP WANTED.

6

The car was still doing fifty in a zone posted for twenty-five when it crossed the bridge. It was a unit the high school kids would have regarded with awe and envy: a lime-green Dodge Challenger that had been jacked in the back so the nose pointed toward the road. Through the smoked-glass windows, one could dimly make out the roll-bar which arched across the roof between the front and back seats. The rear end was covered with stickers: HEARST, FUELLY, FRAM, QUAKER STATE, GOODYEAR WIDE OVALS, RAM CHARGER. The straight-pipes burbled contentedly, fat on the ninety-six-octane fuel which could be purchased only at Oxford Plains Speedway once you got north of Portland.

It slowed a little at the intersection of Main and Laurel, then pulled into one of the slant-parking spaces in front of The Clip Joint with a low squeal of tires. There was no one in the shop getting a haircut just then; both Bill Fullerton and Henry Gendron, his number-two barber, were seated in the customers' chairs under the old Brylcreem and Wildroot Creme Oil signs. They had shared the morning paper out between them. As the driver gunned his engine briefly, causing exhaust to crackle and bang through the pipes, both looked up.

"A death-machine if I ever saw one," Henry said.

Bill nodded and plucked at his lower lip with the thumb and index finger of his right hand. "Ayuh."

They both watched expectantly as the engine died and the driver's door opened. A foot encased in a scuffed black engineer boot emerged from the Challenger's dark innards. It was attached to a leg clad in tight, faded denim. A moment later the driver got out and stood in the unseasonably hot daylight, removing his sunglasses and tucking them into the V of his shirt as he looked around in leisurely, contemptuous fashion.

"Uh-oh," Henry said. "Looks like a bad penny just turned up."

Bill Fullerton stared at the apparition with the sports section of the newspaper in his lap and his jaw hanging slightly agape. "Ace Merrill," he said. "As I live and breathe."

"What in the hell is he doing here?" Henry asked indignantly. "I thought he was over in Mechanic Falls, fuckin up *their* way of life."

"Dunno," Bill said, and pulled at his lower lip again. "Lookit im! Gray as a rat and probably twice as mean! How old is he, Henry?"

Henry shrugged. "More'n forty and less'n fifty is all I know. Who cares how old he is, anyway? He still looks like trouble to me."

As if he had overheard him, Ace turned toward the plate-glass window and raised his hand in a slow, sarcastic wave. The two men jerked and rustled indignantly, like a pair of old maids who have just realized that the insolent wolf-whistle coming from the doorway of the pool-hall is for them.

Ace shoved his hands into the pockets of his Low Riders and strolled away—portrait of a man with all the time in the world and all the cool moves in the known universe.

"You think you oughtta call Sheriff Pangborn?" Henry asked.

Bill Fullerton pulled at his lower lip some more. At last he shook his head. "He'll know Ace is back in town soon enough," he said. "Won't need me to tell him. Or you either."

They sat in silence and watched Ace stroll up Main Street until he had passed from their view.

7

No one would have guessed, watching Ace Merrill strut indolently up Main Street, that he was a man with a desperate problem. It was a problem Buster Keeton could have identified with to some extent; Ace owed some fellows a large chunk of money. Well over eighty thousand dollars, to be specific. But the worst Buster's creditors could do was put him in jail. If Ace didn't have the money soon, say by the first of November, *his* creditors were apt to put him in the ground.

The boys Ace Merrill had once terrorized—boys like Teddy Duchamp, Chris Chambers, and Vern Tessio—would have recognized him at once in spite of his graying hair. During the years when Ace had worked at the local textile mill (it had been closed for the last five years), that might not have been the case. In those days his vices had been beer and petty theft. He had put on a great deal of weight as a result of the former and had attracted a fair amount of attention from the late Sheriff George Bannerman as a result of the latter. Then Ace discovered cocaine.

He quit his job at the mill, lost fifty pounds running in high—*very* high—gear, and graduated to first-degree burglary as a result of this marvellous substance. His financial situation began to yo-yo in the grandiose way only high-margin traders on the stock market and cocaine dealers experience. He might start a month flat broke and end it with fifty or sixty thousand dollars tucked under the roots of the dead apple tree behind his place on Cranberry Bog Road. One day it was a seven-course French dinner at Maurice; the next it might be Kraft macaroni and cheese in the kitchen of his trailer. It all depended on the market and on the supply, because Ace, like most cocaine dealers, was his own best customer.

A year or so after the new Ace—long, lean, graying, and hooked through the bag—emerged from the suit of blubber he had been growing ever since he and public education parted company, he met some fellows from Connecticut. These fellows traded in firearms as well as blow. Ace saw eye to eye with them at once; like him, the Corson brothers were their own best customers. They offered Ace what amounted to a high-caliber franchise for the central Maine area, and Ace accepted gladly. This was a pure business decision no more than the decision to start dealing coke had been a pure business decision. If there was anything in the world Ace loved more than cars and coke, it was guns.

On one of the occasions when he found himself embarrassed for funds, he had gone to see his uncle, who had loaned money to half the people in town and was reputed to be rolling in dough. Ace saw no reason why he should not qualify for such a loan; he was young (well . . . forty-eight . . . *relatively* young), he had prospects, and he was blood.

His uncle, however, held a radically different view of things.

"Nope," Reginald Marion "Pop" Merrill told him. "I know where your money comes from—when you *have* money, that is. It comes from that white shit."

"Aw, Uncle Reginald—"

"Don't you Uncle Reginald *me*," Pop had replied. "You got a spot of it on y'nose right now. Careless. Folks who use that white shit and deal it *always* get careless. Careless people end up in the Shank. That's if they're lucky. If they ain't, they wind up fertilizing a patch of swamp about six feet long and three feet deep. I can't collect money if the people who owe it to me are dead or doing time. I wouldn't give you the sweat out of my dirty asshole, is what I mean to say."

That particular embarrassment had come shortly after Alan Pangborn had assumed his duties as Sheriff of Castle County. And Alan's first major bust had come when he surprised Ace and two of his friends trying to crack the safe in Henry Beaufort's office at The Mellow Tiger. It was a very good bust, a textbook bust, and Ace had found himself in Shawshank less than four months after his uncle had warned him of the place. The charges of attempted robbery were dropped in a plea-bargain, but Ace still got a pretty good dose of hard time on a nighttime breaking and entering charge.

He got out in the spring of 1989 and moved to Mechanic Falls. He had a job to go to; Oxford Plains Speedway participated in the state's pre-release program, and John "Ace" Merrill obtained a position as maintenance man and part-time pit mechanic.

A good many of his old friends were still around—not to mention his old customers—and soon Ace was doing business and having nosebleeds again.

He kept the job at the Speedway until his sentence was officially up, and quit the day it was. He'd gotten a phone call from the Flying Corson Brothers in Danbury, Connecticut, and soon he was dealing shooting irons again as well as the Bolivian marching powder.

The ante had gone up while he was in stir, it seemed; instead of pistols, rifles, and repeating shotguns, he now found himself doing a lively business in automatic and semi-automatic weapons. The climax had come in June of this year, when he sold a ground-fired Thunderbolt missile to a seafaring man with a South American accent. The seafaring man stowed the Thunderbolt below, then paid Ace seventeen thousand dollars in fresh hundreds with non-sequential serial numbers.

"What do you use a thing like that for?" Ace had asked with some fascination.

"Anytheeng you want to, *señor,*" the seafaring man had replied unsmilingly.

Then, in July, everything had crashed. Ace still didn't really understand how it could have happened, except that it probably would have been better if he had stuck with the Flying Corson Brothers for coke as well as guns. He had taken delivery of two pounds of Colombian flake from a guy in Portland, financing the deal with the help of Mike and Dave Corson. They had kicked in about eighty-five thousand. That particular pile of blow had seemed worth twice the asking price—it had tested high blue. Ace knew that eighty-five big ones was a lot more boost than he was used to handling, but he felt confident and ready to move up. In those days, "No problem!" had been Ace Merrill's main guidepost to living. Things had changed since then. Things had changed a lot.

These changes began when Dave Corson called from Danbury, Connecticut, to ask Ace what he thought he was doing, trying to pass off baking soda as cocaine. The guy in Portland had apparently managed to stiff Ace, high blue or no high blue, and when Dave Corson began to realize this, he stopped sounding so friendly. In fact, he began to sound positively *un-friendly*.

Ace could have done a fade. Instead, he gathered all his courage—which was not inconsiderable, even in his middle age—and went to see the Flying Corson Brothers. He gave them his view of what had happened. He did his explaining in the back of a Dodge van with wall-to-wall carpet, a heated mud-bed, and a mirror on the ceiling. He was very convincing. He *had* to be very convincing, because the van had been parked at the end of a rutted dirt road some miles west of Danbury, a black fellow named Too-Tall Timmy was behind the wheel, and the Flying Corson Brothers, Mike and Dave, were sitting on either side of Ace with H & K recoilless rifles.

As he talked, Ace found himself remembering what his uncle had said before the bust at The Mellow Tiger. *Careless people end up in the Shank. That's if they're lucky. If they ain't, they wind up fertilizing a patch of swamp about six feet long and three feet deep.* Well, Pop had been right about the first half; Ace intended to exercise all his persuasiveness to avoid the second half. There were no pre-release programs from the swamp.

He was very persuasive. And at some point he said two magic words: Ducky Morin.

"You bought that crap from *Ducky?*" Mike Corson said, his bloodshot eyes opening wide. "You sure that's who it was?"

"Sure I'm sure," Ace had replied. "Why?"

The Flying Corson Brothers looked at each other and began to laugh. Ace didn't know what they were laughing about, but he was glad they were doing it, just the same. It seemed like a good sign.

"What did he look like?" Dave Corson asked.

"He's a tall guy—not as tall as him"—Ace cocked a thumb at the driver, who was wearing a pair of Walkman earphones and rocking back and forth to a beat only he could hear—"but tall. He's a Canuck. Talks like dis, him. Got a little gold earring."

"That's ole Daffy Duck," Mike Corson agreed.

"Tell you the truth, I'm amazed nobody's whacked the guy yet," Dave Corson said. He looked at his brother, Mike, and they shook their heads at each other in perfectly shared wonder.

"I thought he was okay," Ace said. "Ducky always *used* to be okay."

"But you took some time off, dintcha?" Mike Corson asked.

"Little vacation at the Crossbar Hotel," Dave Corson said.

"You must have been inside when the Duckman discovered free-base," Mike said. "That was when his act started goin downhill fast."

"Ducky has a little trick he likes to pull these days," Dave said. "Do you know what bait-and-switch is, Ace?"

Ace thought about it. Then he shook his head.

"Yes, you do," Dave said. "Because that's the reason your ass is in a crack. Ducky showed you a lot of Baggies filled with white powder. One was full of good coke. The rest were full of shit. Like you, Ace."

"We tested!" Ace said. "I picked a bag at random, and we tested it!"

Mike and Dave looked at each other with dark drollery.

"They tested," Dave Corson said.

"He picked a bag at random," Mike Corson added.

They rolled their eyes upward and looked at each other in the mirror on the ceiling.

"Well?" Ace said, looking from one to the other. He was glad they knew who Ducky was, he was *also* glad they believed he hadn't meant to cheat them, but he was distressed just the same. They were treating him like a chump, and Ace Merrill was nobody's chump.

"Well *what?*" Mike Corson asked. "If you didn't think you picked the test bag yourself, the deal wouldn't go down, would it? Ducky is like a magician doing the same raggedy-ass card trick over and over again. 'Pick a card, any card.' You ever hear that one, Ace-Hole?"

Guns or no guns, Ace bridled. "Don't you call me that."

"We'll call you anything we want," Dave said. "You owe us eighty-five large, Ace, and what we've got for collateral on that money so far is a shitload of Arm & Hammer baking soda worth about a buck-fifty. We'll call you Hubert J. Mother-fucker if we want to."

He and his brother looked at each other. Wordless commu-nication passed between them. Dave got up and tapped Too-Tall Timmy on the shoulder. He gave Too-Tall his gun. Then Dave and Mike left the van and stood close together by a drift of sumac at the edge of some farmer's field, talking earnestly. Ace didn't know what words they were saying, but he knew perfectly well what was going on. They were deciding what to do with him.

He sat on the edge of the mud-bed, sweating like a pig, waiting for them to come back in. Too-Tall Timmy sprawled in the upholstered captain's chair Mike Corson had vacated, holding the H & K on Ace and nodding his head back and forth. Very faintly, Ace could hear the voices of Marvin Gaye and Tammi Terrell coming from the earphones. Marvin and Tammi, who were both the late great these days, were singing "My Mistake."

Mike and Dave came back in.

"We're going to give you three months to make good." Mike said. Ace felt himself go limp with relief. "Right now we want our money more than we want to rip your skin off. There's something else, too."

"We want to whack Ducky Morin," Dave said. "His shit has gone on long enough."

"Guy's giving us all a bad name," Mike said.

"We think you can find him," Dave said. "We think he'll figure once an Ace-Hole, always an Ace-Hole."

"You got any comment on that, Ace-Hole?" Mike asked him.

Ace had no comment on that. He was happy just knowing that he would be seeing another weekend.

"November first is the deadline," Dave said. "You bring us
our money by November first and then we all go after Ducky.
If you don't, we're going to see how many pieces of you we can
cut off before you finally give up and die."

8

When the balloon went up, Ace had been holding about a
dozen assorted heavy-caliber weapons of both the automatic
and semi-automatic varieties. He spent most of his grace period trying to turn these weapons into cash. Once he did that,
he could turn cash back into coke. You couldn't have a better
asset than cocaine when you needed to turn some big bucks in
a hurry.

But the market for guns was temporarily in the horse lati-
tudes. He sold half his stock—none of the big guns—and that
was it. During the second week in September he had met a
promising prospect at the Piece of Work Pub in Lewiston. The
prospect had hinted in every way it was possible to hint that he
would like to buy at least six and perhaps as many as ten automatic weapons, if the name of a reliable ammunition dealer
went with the shooting irons. Ace could do that; the Flying
Corson Brothers were the most reliable ammo dealers he knew.

Ace went into the grimy bathroom to do a couple of lines
before hammering the deal home. He was suffused with
the happy, relieved glow which has bedevilled a number of
American Presidents; he believed he saw light at the end of
the tunnel.

He laid the small mirror he carried in his shirt pocket on
the toilet tank and was spooning coke onto it when a voice
spoke from the urinal nearest the stall Ace was in. Ace never
found out who the voice belonged to; he only knew that its
owner might well have saved him fifteen years in a Federal
penitentiary.

"Man you be talking to wearin a wire," the voice from the
urinal said, and when Ace left the bathroom he went out the
back door.

9

Following that near miss (it never occurred to him that his un-
seen informant might just have been amusing himself), an odd
kind of paralysis settled over Ace. He became afraid to do anything but buy a little coke now and then for his own personal
use. He had never experienced such a sensation of dead stop
before. He hated it, but didn't know what to do about it. The
first thing he did every day was look at the calendar. November
seemed to be rushing toward him.

Then, this morning, he had awakened before dawn with a
thought blazing in his mind like strange blue light: he had to
go home. He had to go back to Castle Rock. That was where
the answer was. Going home felt right . . . but even if it turned
out to be wrong, the change of scenery might break the strange
vapor-lock in his head.

In Mechanic Falls he was just John Merrill, an ex-con who
lived in a shack with plastic on the windows and cardboard on
the door. In Castle Rock he had always been Ace Merrill, the
ogre who strode through the nightmares of a whole generation
of little kids. In Mechanic Falls he was poor-white back-road
trash, a guy who had a custom Dodge but no garage to put it
in. In Castle Rock he had been, at least for a little while, something like a king.

So he had come back, and here he was, and what now?

Ace didn't know. The town looked smaller, grimier, and
emptier than he remembered. He supposed Pangborn was
around someplace, and pretty soon old Bill Fullerton would get
him on the honker and tell him who was back in town. Then
Pangborn would find him and ask him what he thought he was

doing here. He would ask if Ace had a job. He didn't, and he couldn't even claim he had come back to visit his unc, because Pop had been in his junkshop when the place burned down. Okay then, Ace, Pangborn would say, why don't you just jump back into your street machine and cruise on out of here?

And what was he going to say to that?

Ace didn't know—he only knew that the flash of dark-blue light with which he had awakened was still glimmering somewhere inside him.

The lot where the Emporium Galorium had stood was still vacant, he saw. Nothing there but weeds, a few charred board-ends, and some road-litter. Broken glass twinkled back the sun in eye-watering shards of hot light. There was nothing there to look at, but Ace wanted to look, anyway. He started across the street. He had almost reached the far side when the green awning two storefronts up caught his eye.

NEEDFUL THINGS,

the side of the awning read. Now what kind of name for a store was that? Ace walked up the street to see. He could look at the vacant lot where his uncle's tourist-trap had stood later on; he didn't think anyone was going to move it.

The first thing to catch his eye was the

HELP WANTED

sign. He paid it little attention. He didn't know what he had come back to Castle Rock for, but a stockboy job wasn't it.

There were a number of rather classy-looking items in the window—the sort of stuff he would have taken away if he were doing a little nightwork in some rich guy's house. A chess set with carved jungle animals for pieces. A necklace of black pearls—it looked valuable to Ace, but he supposed the pearls were probably artificial. Surely no one in this dipshit burg could afford a string of genuine black pearls. Good job, though; they looked real enough to him. And—

Ace looked at the book behind the pearls with narrowed eyes. It had been set up on its spine so someone looking in the window could easily see the cover, which depicted the silhouettes of two men standing on a ridge at night. One had a pick, the other a shovel. They appeared to be digging a hole. The title of the book was *Lost and Buried Treasures of New England.* The author's name was printed below the picture in small white letters.

It was Reginald Merrill.

Ace went to the door and tried the knob. It turned easily. The bell overhead jingled. Ace Merrill entered Needful Things.

10

"No," Ace said, looking at the book Mr. Gaunt had taken from the window display and put into his hands. "This isn't the one I want. You must have gotten the wrong one."

"It's the only book in the show window, I assure you," Mr. Gaunt said in a mildly puzzled voice. "You can look for yourself if you don't believe me."

For a moment Ace did almost that, and then he let out an exasperated little sigh. "No, that's okay," he said.

The book the shopkeeper had handed him was *Treasure Island,* by Robert Louis Stevenson. What had happened was clear enough—he'd had Pop on his mind, and he'd made a mistake. The real mistake, though, had been coming back to Castle Rock in the first place. Why in the fuck had he done it?

"Listen, this is a very interesting place you've got here, but I ought to get a move on. I'll see you another time, Mr.—"

"Gaunt," the shopkeeper said, putting out his hand. "Leland Gaunt."

Ace put his own hand out and it was swallowed up. A great, galvanizing power seemed to rush through him at the moment of contact. His mind was filled with that dark-blue light again: a huge, sheeting flare of it this time.

He took his hand back, dazed and weak-kneed.

"What was *that?*" he whispered.

"I believe they call it 'an attention-getter,'" Mr. Gaunt said. He spoke with quiet composure. "You'll *want* to pay attention to me, Mr. Merrill."

"How did you know my name? I didn't tell you my name."

"Oh, I know who *you* are," Mr. Gaunt said with a little laugh. "I've been expecting you."

"How could you be expecting me? I didn't even know I was coming until I got in the damn car."

"Excuse me for a moment, please."

Gaunt stepped back toward the window, bent, and picked up a sign which was leaning against the wall. Then he leaned into the window, removed

HELP WANTED

and put up

CLOSED COLUMBUS DAY

in its place.

"Why'd you do that?" Ace felt like a man who has stumbled into a wire fence with a moderate electric charge running through it.

"It's customary for shopkeepers to remove help-wanted signs when they have filled the vacant position," Mr. Gaunt said, a little severely. "My business in Castle Rock has grown at a very satisfying rate, and I now find I need a strong back and an extra pair of hands. I tire so easily these days."

"Hey, I don't—"

"I also need a driver," Mr. Gaunt said. "Driving is, I believe, your main skill. Your first job, Ace, will be to drive to Boston. I have an automobile parked in a garage there. It will amuse you—it's a Tucker."

"A Tucker?" For a moment Ace forgot that he hadn't come

to town to take a stockboy's job . . . or a chauffeur's either, for that matter. "You mean like in that movie?"

"Not exactly," Mr. Gaunt said. He walked behind the counter where his old-fashioned cash register stood, produced a key, and unlocked the drawer beneath. He took out two small envelopes. One of them he laid on the counter. The other he held out to Ace. "It's been modified in some ways. Here. The keys."

"Hey, now, wait a minute! I told you—"

Mr. Gaunt's eyes were some strange color Ace could not quite pick up, but when they first darkened and then blazed out at him, Ace felt his knees grow watery again.

"You're in a jam, Ace, but if you don't stop behaving like an ostrich with its head stuck in the sand, I believe I am going to lose interest in helping you. Shop assistants are a dime a dozen. I know, believe me. I've hired hundreds of them over the years. Perhaps thousands. So stop fucking around *and take the keys.*"

Ace took the little envelope. As the tips of his fingers touched the tips of Mr. Gaunt's, that dark, sheeting fire filled his head once more. He moaned.

"You'll drive your car to the address I give you," Mr. Gaunt said, "and park it in the space where mine is now stored. I'll expect you back by midnight at the latest. I think it will actually be a good deal earlier than that.

"My car is much faster than it looks."

He grinned, revealing all those teeth.

Ace tried again. "Listen, Mr.—"

"Gaunt."

Ace nodded, his head bobbing up and down like the head of a marionette controlled by a novice puppet-master. "Under other circumstances, I'd take you up on it. You're . . . interesting." It wasn't the word he wanted, but it was the best one he could wrap his tongue around for the time being. "But you were right—I *am* in a jackpot, and if I don't find a large chunk of cash in the next two weeks—"

"Well, what about the book?" Mr. Gaunt asked. His tone was both amused and reproving. "Isn't that why you came in?"

"It isn't what I—"

He discovered he was still holding it in his hand, and looked down at it again. The picture was the same, but the title had changed back to what he had seen in the show window: *Lost and Buried Treasures of New England,* by Reginald Merrill.

"What *is* this?" he asked thickly. But suddenly he knew. He wasn't in Castle Rock at all; he was at home in Mechanic Falls, lying in his own dirty bed, dreaming all this.

"It looks like a book to me," Mr. Gaunt said. "And wasn't your late uncle's name Reginald Merrill? What a coincidence."

"My uncle never wrote anything but receipts and IOUs in his whole life," Ace said in that same thick, sleepy voice. He looked up at Gaunt again, and found he could not pull his eyes away. Gaunt's eyes kept changing color. Blue . . . gray . . . hazel . . . brown . . . black.

"Well," Mr. Gaunt admitted, "perhaps the name on the book is a pseudonym. Perhaps I wrote that particular tome myself."

"You?"

Mr. Gaunt steepled his fingers under his chin. "Perhaps it isn't even a book at all. Perhaps all the really special things I sell aren't what they appear to be. Perhaps they are actually gray things with only one remarkable property—the ability to take the shapes of those things which haunt the dreams of men and women." He paused, then added thoughtfully: "Perhaps they are dreams themselves."

"I don't get any of this."

Mr. Gaunt smiled. "I know. It doesn't matter. If your uncle *had* written a book, Ace, mightn't it have been about buried treasure? Wouldn't you say that treasure—whether buried in the ground or in the pockets of his fellow men—was a subject which greatly interested him?"

"He liked money, all right," Ace said grimly.

"Well, what happened to it?" Mr. Gaunt cried. "Did he leave any of it to you? Surely he did; are you not his only surviving relative?"

"He didn't leave me a red fucking cent!" Ace yelled back furiously. "Everyone in town said that old bastard had the first dime he ever made, but there was less than four thousand dollars in his bank accounts when he died. That went to bury him and clean up that mess he left downstreet. And when they opened his safe deposit box, do you know what they found?"

"Yes," Mr. Gaunt said, and although his mouth was serious— even sympathetic—his eyes were laughing. "Trading stamps. Six books of Plaid Stamps and fourteen of Gold Bond Stamps."

"That's right!" Ace said. He looked balefully down at *Lost and Buried Treasures of New England.* His disquiet and his sense of dreamy disorientation had been swallowed, at least for the time being, by his rage. "And you know what? You can't even redeem Gold Bond Stamps anymore. The company went out of business. Everyone in Castle Rock was afraid of him—even I was a little afraid of him—and everyone thought he was as rich as Scrooge McFucking Duck, but he died broke."

"Maybe he didn't trust banks," Mr. Gaunt said. "Maybe he buried his treasure. Do you think that's possible, Ace?"

Ace opened his mouth. Closed it again. Opened it. Closed it.

"Stop that," said Mr. Gaunt. "You look like a fish in an aquarium."

Ace looked at the book in his hand. He put it on the counter and riffled through the pages, which were crammed tight with small print. And something breezed out. It was a large and ragged chunk of brown paper, unevenly folded, and he recognized it at once—it had been torn from a Hemphill's Market shopping bag. How often, as a little boy, had he watched his uncle tear off a piece of brown paper just like this one from one of the bags he kept under his ancient Tokeheim cash register? How many times had he watched him add up figures on such a scrap . . . or write an IOU on it?

He unfolded it with shaking hands.

It was a map, that much was clear, but at first he could make nothing of it—it was just a bunch of lines and crosses and squiggly circles.

"What the fuck?"

"You need something to focus your concentration, that's all," Mr. Gaunt said. "This might help."

Ace looked up. Mr. Gaunt had put a small mirror in an ornate silver frame on the glass case beside his own cash register. Now he opened the other envelope he had taken from the locked drawer, and spilled a generous quantity of cocaine onto the mirror's surface. To Ace's not inexperienced eye, it looked to be of fabulously high quality; the spotlight over the display case kicked thousands of little sparkles from the clean flakes.

"Jesus, mister!" Ace's nose began to tingle in anticipation. "Is that Colombian?"

"No, this is a special hybrid," Mr. Gaunt said. "It comes from the Plains of Leng." He took a gold letter opener from the inside pocket of his fawn jacket and began to organize the pile of blow into long, chubby lines.

"Where's that?"

"Over the hills and far away," Mr. Gaunt replied without looking up. "Don't ask questions, Ace. Men who owe money do well to simply enjoy the good things which come their way."

He put the letter opener back and drew a short glass straw from the same pocket. He handed it to Ace. "Be my guest."

The straw was amazingly heavy—not glass after all but some sort of rock crystal, Ace guessed. He bent over the mirror, then hesitated. What if the old guy had AIDS or something like that?

Don't ask questions, Ace. Men who owe money do well to simply enjoy the good things which come their way.

"Amen," Ace said aloud, and tooted up. His head filled with that vague banana-lemon taste that really good cocaine always seemed to have. It was mellow, but it was also powerful. He felt his heart begin to pound. At the same time, his thoughts grew sharply focused and took on a polished chromium edge. He remembered something a guy had told him not long after he fell in love with this stuff: *Things have more names when you're coked up. A lot more names.*

He hadn't understood then, but he thought he did now.

He offered the straw to Gaunt, but Gaunt shook his head. "Never before five," he said, "but you enjoy, Ace."

"Thanks," Ace said.

He looked at the map again and found that he could now read it perfectly. The two parallel lines with the X between them was clearly the Tin Bridge, and once you realized that, everything else fell neatly into place. The squiggle which ran between the lines, through the X, and up to the top of the paper was Route 117. The small circle with the larger circle behind it must represent the Gavineaux dairy farm: the big circle would be the cowbarn. It all made sense. It was as clear and clean and sparkly as the crisp heap of dope this incredibly hip dude had poured out of the little envelope.

Ace bent over the mirror again. "Fire when ready," he murmured, and took another two lines. Bang! Zap! "Christ, that's powerful stuff," he said in a gasping voice.

"Sho nuff," Mr. Gaunt agreed gravely.

Ace looked up, suddenly sure the man was laughing at him, but Mr. Gaunt's face was calm and clear. Ace bent over the map again.

Now it was the crosses which caught his eye. There were seven of them—no, actually there were eight. One appeared to be on the dead, swampy ground owned by old man Treblehorn . . . except old man Treblehorn was dead, had been for years, and hadn't there been talk at one time that his uncle Reginald had gotten most of that land as repayment of a loan?

Here was another, on the edge of the Nature Conservancy on the other side of Castle View, if he had his geography right. There were two out on Town Road #3, near a circle that was probably the old Joe Camber place, Seven Oaks Farm. Two more on the land supposedly owned by Diamond Match on the west side of Castle Lake.

Ace stared up at Gaunt with wild, bloodshot eyes. "Did he bury his money? Is that what the crosses mean? *Are they the places he buried his money?*"

Mr. Gaunt shrugged elegantly. "I'm sure I don't know. It seems logical, but logic often has little to do with the way people behave."

"But it *could* be," Ace said. He was becoming frantic with excitement and cocaine overload; what felt like stiff bundles of copper wire were exploding in the big muscles of his arms and belly. His sallow face, pocked with the scars of adolescent acne, had taken on a dark flush. "It *could* be! All the places those crosses are . . . *all that could be Pop's property!* Do you see? He might have put all that land in a blind trust or whatever the fuck they call it . . . so nobody could buy it . . . so nobody could find what he put there . . ."

He snorted the rest of the coke on the mirror and then leaned over the counter. His bulging, bloodshot eyes jittered in his face.

"I could be more than just out of the shithole," he said in a low, trembling whisper. "I could be fucking *rich.*"

"Yes," Mr. Gaunt said, "I'd say that's a good possibility. But remember that, Ace." He cocked his thumb toward the wall, and the sign there which read

I DO NOT ISSUE REFUNDS OR MAKE EXCHANGES
CAVEAT EMPTOR!

Ace looked at the sign. "What's it mean?"

"It means that you're not the first person who ever thought he had found the key to great riches in an old book," Mr. Gaunt said. "It also means that I still need a stockboy and a driver."

Ace looked at him, almost shocked. Then he laughed. "You kidding?" He pointed at the map. "I've got a lot of digging to do."

Mr. Gaunt sighed regretfully, folded the sheet of brown paper, put it back into the book, and placed the book in the drawer under the cash register. He did all this with incredible swiftness.

"Hey!" Ace yelled. "What are you doing?"

"I just remembered that book is already promised to another customer, Mr. Merrill. I'm sorry. And I really am closed—it's Columbus Day, you know."

"Wait a minute!"

"Of course, if you had seen fit to take the job, I'm sure something could have been worked out. But I can see that you're very busy; you undoubtedly want to make sure your affairs are in order before the Corson Brothers turn you into coldcuts."

Ace's mouth had begun to open and close again. He was trying to remember where the little crosses had been and was discovering that he couldn't do it. All of them seemed to blend together into one big cross in his jazzed-up, flying mind . . . the sort of cross you saw in cemeteries.

"All right!" he cried. "All right, I'll take the fucking job!"

"In that case, I believe this book is for sale after all," Mr. Gaunt said. He drew it out of the drawer and checked the flyleaf. "It goes for a dollar and a half." His jostling teeth appeared in a wide, sharky smile. "That's a dollar thirty-five, with the employee discount."

Ace drew his wallet from his back pocket, dropped it, and almost clouted his head on the edge of the glass case bending over to pick it up.

"But I've got to have some time off," he told Mr. Gaunt.

"Indeed."

"Because I really do have some digging to do."

"Of course."

"Time is short."

"How wise of you to know it."

"How about when I get back from Boston?"

"Won't you be tired?"

"Mr. Gaunt, I can't afford to be tired."

"I might be able to help you there," Mr. Gaunt said. His smile widened and his teeth bulged from it like the teeth of a skull. "I might have a little pick-me-up for you, is what I mean to say."

"What?" Ace asked, his eyes widening. "What did you say?"

"I beg your pardon?"

"Nothing," Ace said. "Never mind."

"All right—do you still have the keys I gave you?"

Ace was surprised to discover that he had stuffed the envelope containing the keys into his back pocket.

"Good." Mr. Gaunt rang up $1.35 on the old register, took the five-dollar bill Ace had laid on the counter, and rendered three dollars and sixty-five cents change. Ace took it like a man in a dream.

"Now," Mr. Gaunt said. "Let me give you a few directions, Ace. And remember what I said: I want you back by midnight. If you're not back by midnight, I will be unhappy. When I'm unhappy, I sometimes lose my temper. You wouldn't want to be around when that happens."

"Do you Hulk out?" Ace asked jestingly.

Mr. Gaunt looked up with a grinning ferocity that caused Ace to retreat a step. "Yes," he said. "That's just what I do, Ace. I Hulk out. Indeed I do. Now pay attention."

Ace paid attention.

11

It was quarter of eleven and Alan was just getting ready to go down to Nan's and catch a quick cup of coffee when Sheila

Brigham buzzed him. It was Sonny Jackett on line one, she said. He insisted on talking to Alan and nobody else.

Alan picked up the phone. "Hello, Sonny—what can I do for you?"

"Well," Sonny said in his drawling downeast accent, "I hate to put more trouble on your plate after the double helpin you got yesterday, Sheriff, but I think an old friend of yours is back in town."

"Who's that?"

"Ace Merrill. I seen his car parked upstreet from here."

Oh shit, what next? Alan thought. "Did you see him?"

"Nope, but you can't miss the car. Puke-green Dodge Challenger—what the kids call a ramrod. I seen it up to the Plains."

"Well, thanks, Sonny."

"Don't mention it—what do you suppose that booger's doin back in Castle Rock, Alan?"

"I don't know," Alan said, and thought as he hung up: *But I guess I better find out.*

12

There was a space empty next to the green Challenger. Alan swung Unit 1 in next to it and got out. He saw Bill Fullerton and Henry Gendron looking out the barber-shop window at him with bright-eyed interest and raised a hand to them. Henry pointed across the street. Alan nodded and crossed. Wilma Jerzyck and Nettie Cobb kill each other on a street-corner one day and Ace Merrill turns up the next, he thought. This town's turning into Barnum & Bailey's Circus.

As he reached the sidewalk on the far side, he saw Ace come sauntering out of the shadow cast by the green awning of Needful Things. He had something in one hand. At first Alan couldn't tell what it was, but as Ace drew closer, he decided he *had* been able to tell; he just hadn't been able to believe it. Ace Merrill wasn't the sort of guy you expected to see with a book in his hand.

They drew together in front of the vacant lot where the Emporium Galorium had once stood.

"Hello, Ace," Alan said.

Ace didn't seem in the least surprised to see him. He took his sunglasses from the V of his shirt, shook them out one-handed, and slipped them on. "Well, well, well—how they hangin, boss?"

"What are you doing in Castle Rock, Ace?" Alan asked evenly.

Ace looked up at the sky with exaggerated interest. Little glints of light twinkled on the lenses of his Ray-Bans. "Nice day for a ride," he said. "Summery."

"Very nice," Alan agreed. "Have you got a valid license, Ace?"

Ace looked at him reproachfully. "Would I be out driving if I didn't? That wouldn't be legal, would it?"

"I don't think that's an answer."

"I took the re-exam as soon as they gave me my pink sheet," Ace said. "I'm street-legal. How's that, boss? Is that an answer?"

"Maybe I could check for myself." Alan held out his hand.

"Why, I don't think you trust me!" Ace said. He spoke in the same jocular, teasing voice, but Alan heard the anger beneath it.

"Let's just say I'm from Missouri."

Ace shifted the book to his left hand so he could dig the wallet out of his hip pocket with his right, and Alan got a better look at the cover. The book was *Treasure Island,* by Robert Louis Stevenson.

He looked at the license. It was signed and valid.

"The car registration is in the glove compartment, if you want to cross the street and look at that, too," Ace said. Alan could hear the anger in his voice more clearly now. And the old arrogance as well.

"I think I'll trust you on that one, Ace. Why don't you tell me what you're really doing back here in town?"

"I came to look at *that*," Ace said, and pointed to the vacant lot. "I don't know why, but I did. I doubt if you believe me, but it happens to be the truth."

Oddly enough, Alan did believe him.

"I see you bought a book, too."

"I can read," Ace said. "I doubt if you believe that, either."

"Well, well." Alan hooked his thumbs into his belt. "You had a look and you bought a book."

"He's a poet and he don't know it."

"Why, I guess I am. It's good of you to point it out, Ace. Now I guess you'll be sliding on out of town, won't you?"

"What if I don't? You'd find something to bust me for, I guess. Is the word 'rehabilitation' in your vocabulary, Sheriff Pangborn?"

"Yes," Alan said, "but the definition isn't Ace Merrill."

"You don't want to push me, man."

"I'm not. If I start, you'll know it."

Ace took off his sunglasses. "You guys never quit, do you? You never . . . fucking . . . quit."

Alan said nothing.

After a moment Ace seemed to regain his composure.

He put his Ray-Bans back on. "You know," he said, "I think I *will* leave. I've got places to go and things to do."

"That's good. Busy hands are happy hands."

"But if I want to come back, I will. Do you hear me?"

"I hear you, Ace, and I want to tell you that I don't think that would be wise at all. Do you hear *me?*"

"You don't scare me."

"If I don't," Alan said, "you're even dumber than I thought."

Ace looked at Alan for a moment through his dark glasses, then laughed. Alan didn't care for the sound of it—it was a creepy sort of laugh, strange and off-center. He stood and watched as Ace crossed the street in his outdated hood's strut, opened the door of his car, and got in. A moment later the engine roared into life. Exhaust blatted through the straight-pipes; people stopped on the street to look.

That's an illegal muffler, Alan thought. A glasspack. I could cite him for that.

But what would be the point? He had bigger fish to fry than Ace Merrill, who was leaving town anyway. For good this time, he hoped.

He watched the green Challenger make an illegal U-turn on Main Street and head back toward Castle Stream and the edge of town. Then he turned and looked thoughtfully up the street at the green awning. Ace had come back to his old home town and bought a book—*Treasure Island,* to be exact. He had bought it in Needful Things.

I thought that place was closed today, Alan thought. Wasn't that what the sign said?

He walked up the street to Needful Things. He had not been wrong about the sign; it read

CLOSED COLUMBUS DAY.

If he'll see Ace, maybe he'll see me, Alan thought, and raised his fist to knock. Before he could bring it down, the pager clipped to his belt went off. Alan pushed the button that turned the hateful gadget off and stood indecisively in front of the shop door a moment longer . . . but there was really no question about what he had to do now. If you were a lawyer or a business executive, maybe you could afford to ignore your pages for a while, but when you were a County Sheriff—and one who was elected rather than appointed—there wasn't much question about priorities.

Alan crossed the sidewalk, then paused and spun around quickly. He felt a little like the player who is "it" in a game of Red Light, the one whose job it is to catch the other players in motion so he can send them all the way back to the beginning. The feeling that he was being watched had returned, and it was very strong. He was positive he would see the surprised twitch of the drawn shade on Mr. Gaunt's side of the door.

But there was nothing. The shop just went on dozing in the unnaturally hot October sunlight, and if he hadn't seen Ace coming out with his own eyes, Alan would have sworn the place was empty, watched feeling or no watched feeling.

He crossed to his cruiser, leaned in to grab the mike, and radioed in.

"Henry Payton called," Sheila told him. "He's already got preliminary reports on Nettie Cobb and Wilma Jerzyck from Henry Ryan—by?"

"I copy. By."

"Henry said if you want him to give you the high spots, he'll be in from right now until about noon. By."

"Okay. I'm just up Main Street. I'll be right in. By."

"Uh, Alan?"

"Yeah?"

"Henry also asked if we're going to get a fax machine before the turn of the century, so he can just send copies of this stuff instead of calling all the time and reading it to you. By."

"Tell him to write a letter to the Head Selectman," Alan said grumpily. "I'm not the one who writes the budget and he knows it."

"Well, I'm just telling you what he *said*. No need to get all huffy about it. By."

Alan thought Sheila sounded rather huffy herself, however. "Over and out," he said.

He got into Unit 1 and racked the mike. He glanced at the bank in time to see the big digital read-out over the door announce the time as ten-fifty and the temperature as eighty-two degrees. Jesus, we don't need this, he thought. Everyone in town's got a goddam case of prickly heat.

Alan drove slowly back to the Municipal Building, lost in thought. He couldn't shake the feeling that there was something going on in Castle Rock, something which was on the verge of slipping out of control. It was crazy, of course, crazy as hell, but he just couldn't shake it.

CHAPTER THIRTEEN

1

The town's schools were closed for the holiday, but Brian Rusk wouldn't have gone even if they had been open.

Brian was sick.

It wasn't any kind of physical illness, not measles or chicken pox or even the Hershey Squirts, the most humiliating and debilitating of them all. Nor was it a mental disease, exactly—his mind was involved, all right, but it felt almost as if that involvement were a side-effect. The part of him which had taken sick was deeper inside him than his mind; some essential part of his make-up which was available to no doctor's needle or microscope had gone gray and ill. He had always been a sunshiny sort of boy, but that sun was gone now, buried behind heavy banks of cloud which were still building.

The clouds had begun to gather on the afternoon he had thrown the mud at Wilma Jerzyck's sheets, they had thickened when Mr. Gaunt had come to him in a dream, dressed in a Dodger uniform, and told him he wasn't done paying for his Sandy Koufax card yet . . . but the overcast had not become total until he had come down to breakfast this morning.

His father, dressed in the gray fatigues he wore to work at the Dick Perry Siding and Door Company in South Paris, was seated at the kitchen table with the Portland *Press-Herald* open in front of him.

"Goddam Patriots," he said from behind his newspaper barricade. "When the hell are they gonna get a quarterback that can throw the goddam ball?"

"Don't swear in front of the boys," Cora said from the stove, but she didn't speak with her usual exasperated forcefulness— she sounded distant and preoccupied.

Brian slipped into his chair and poured milk on his corn flakes.

"Hey Bri!" Sean said cheerfully. "You wanna go downtown today? Play some video games?"

"Maybe," Brian said. "I guess—" Then he saw the headline on the front page of the paper and stopped talking.

MURDEROUS SPAT LEAVES TWO WOMEN DEAD

IN CASTLE ROCK

"It was a duel," State Police Source Claims

There were photographs of two women, side by side. Brian recognized both of them. One was Nettie Cobb, who lived around the corner on Ford Street. His mom said she was a nut, but she had always seemed okay to Brian. He had stopped a couple of times to pet her dog when she was walking him, and she seemed pretty much like anyone else.

The other woman was Wilma Jerzyck.

He poked at his cereal but didn't actually eat any of it. After his father left for work, Brian dumped the soggy corn flakes into the garbage pail and then crept upstairs to his room. He expected his mother to come cawing after him, asking how come he was throwing away good food while children were starving in Africa (she seemed to believe the thought of starving kids could improve your appetite), but she didn't; she seemed lost in a world of her own this morning.

Sean was right there, however, bugging him just like always.

"So what do you say, Bri? You want to go downtown? Do you?" He was almost dancing from one foot to the other in his excitement. "We could play some video games, maybe check out that new store with all the neat stuff in the window—"

"You stay out of there!" Brian shouted, and his little brother recoiled, a look of shock and dismay spreading over his face.

"Hey," Brian said, "I'm sorry. But you don't want to go in there, Sean-O. That place sucks."

Sean's lower lip was trembling. "Kevin Pelkey says—"

"Who are you going to believe? That wet end or your own brother? It's no good, Sean. It's . . ." He wet his lips and then said what he understood as the bottom of the truth: "It's bad."

"What's the matter with you?" Sean asked. His voice was fierce and teary. "You've been acting like a dope all weekend! Mom, too!"

"I don't feel so good, that's all."

"Well . . ." Sean considered. Then he brightened. "Maybe some video games would make you feel better. We can play Air Raid, Bri! They got Air Raid! The one where you sit right inside, and it tilts back and forth! It's awesome!"

Brian considered it briefly. No. He couldn't imagine going down to the video arcade, not today, maybe not ever again. All the other kids would be there—today you'd have to wait in line to get at the good games like Air Raid—but he was different from them now, and he might always be different.

After all, *he* had a 1956 Sandy Koufax card.

Still, he wanted to do something nice for Sean, for *anyone*—something that would make up a little for the monstrous thing he had done to Wilma Jerzyck. So he told Sean he might want to play some video games that afternoon, but to take some quarters in the meantime. Brian shook them out of his big plastic Coke bottle bank.

"Jeepers!" Sean said, his eyes round. "There's eight . . . nine . . . ten quarters here! You really *must* be sick!"

"Yeah, I guess I must be. Have fun, Sean-O. And don't tell Mom, or she'll make you put them back."

"She's in her room, moonin around in those dark glasses,"

Sean said. "She doesn't even know we're alive." He paused for a moment and then added: "I hate those dark glasses. They're totally creepy." He looked more closely at his big brother. "You really don't look so great, Bri."

"I don't feel so great," Brian said truthfully. "I think I'll lie down."

"Well . . . I'll wait for you awhile. See if you feel any better. I'll be watchin cartoons on channel fifty-six. Come on down if you feel better." Sean shook the quarters in his cupped hands.

"I will," Brian said, and closed his door softly as his little brother walked away.

But he hadn't felt any better. As the day drew on, he just went on feeling

(*cloudier*)

worse and worse. He thought of Mr. Gaunt. He thought of Sandy Koufax. He thought of that glaring newspaper headline—MURDEROUS SPAT LEAVES TWO WOMEN DEAD IN CASTLE ROCK. He thought of those pictures, familiar faces swimming up from clumps of black dots.

Once he almost fell asleep, and then the little record player started up in his mother and father's bedroom. Mom was playing her scratchy Elvis 45s again. She had been doing it almost all weekend.

Thoughts went whirling and rocking through Brian's head like bits of clutter caught up in a cyclone.

MURDEROUS SPAT.

"*You know they said you was high-class . . . but that was just a lie . . .*"

It was a duel.

MURDEROUS: *Nettie Cobb, the lady with the dog.* "*You ain't never caught a rabbit . . .*" *When you deal with me, you want to remember two things.*

SPAT: *Wilma Jerzyck, the lady with the sheets.*

Mr. Gaunt knows best . . .

"*. . . and you ain't no friend of mine.*"

. . . and the duelling isn't done until Mr. Gaunt says it's done.

Around and around these thoughts went, a jumble of terror, guilt, and misery set to the beat of Elvis Presley's golden hits. By noon, Brian's stomach had begun to roil and knot. He hurried down to the bathroom at the end of the hall in his stocking feet, closed the door, and vomited into the toilet bowl as quietly as he could. His mother didn't hear. She was still in her room, where Elvis was now telling her he wanted to be her teddy bear.

As Brian walked slowly back to his room, feeling more miserable than ever, a horrible, haunting certainty came to him: his Sandy Koufax card was gone. Someone had stolen it last night while he slept. He had participated in a murder because of that card, and now it was gone.

He broke into a run, almost slipped on the rug in the middle of his bedroom floor, and snatched his baseball-card book from the top of the dresser. He turned through the pages with such terrified speed that he tore several loose from the ring-binders. But the card—*the* card—was still there: that narrow face looking out at him from beneath its plastic covering on the last page. Still there, and Brian felt a great, miserable relief sweep through him.

He slipped the card from its pocket, went over to the bed, and lay down with it in his hands. He didn't see how he could ever let go of it again. It was all he had gotten out of this nightmare. The only thing. He didn't like it anymore, but it was his. If he could have brought Nettie Cobb and Wilma Jerzyck back to life by burning it up, he would have been hunting for matches at once (or so he really believed), but he *couldn't* bring them back, and since he couldn't, the thought of losing the card and having nothing at all was insupportable.

So he held it in his hands and looked at the ceiling and listened to the dim sound of Elvis, who had moved on to "Wooden Heart." It was not surprising that Sean had told him he looked bad; his face was white, his eyes huge and dark and listless. And his own heart felt pretty wooden, now that he thought about it.

Suddenly a new thought, a really horrible thought, cut across the darkness inside his head with the affrighted, speeding brilliance of a comet: *He had been seen!*

He sat bolt upright on his bed. staring at himself in the mirror on his closet door with horror. Bright green wrapper! Bright red kerchief over a bunch of hair-rollers! Mrs. Mislaburski!

What's going on over there, boy?

I don't know, exactly. I think Mr. and Mrs. Jerzyck must be having an argument.

Brian got off his bed and went over to the window, half-expecting to see Sheriff Pangborn turning into the driveway in his police cruiser right this minute. He wasn't, but he would be coming soon. Because when two women killed each other in a murderous spat, there was an investigation. Mrs. Mislaburski would be questioned. And she would say that she had seen a boy at the Jerzycks' house. That boy, she would tell the Sheriff, had been Brian Rusk.

Downstairs, the telephone began to ring. His mother didn't pick it up, even though there was an extension in the bedroom. She just went on singing along with the music. At last he heard Sean answer. "Who is it please?"

Brian thought calmly: *He'll get it out of me. I can't lie, not to a policeman. I couldn't even lie to Mrs. Leroux about who broke the vase on her desk when she had to go down to the office that time. He'll get it out of me and I'll go to jail for murder.*

That was when Brian Rusk first began to think of suicide. These thoughts were not lurid, not romantic; they were very calm, very rational. His father kept a shotgun in the garage, and at that moment the shotgun seemed to make perfect sense. The shotgun seemed to be the answer to everything.

"Bri-unnn! Telephone!"

"I don't want to talk to Stan!" he yelled. "Tell him to call back tomorrow!"

"It's not Stan," Sean called back. "It's a guy. A grown-up."

Large icy hands seized Brian's heart and squeezed it. This was it—Sheriff Pangborn was on the phone.

Brian? I have some questions to ask you. They're very serious questions. I'm afraid if you don't come right down to answer them, I'll have to come and get you. I'll have to come in my police car. Pretty soon your name is going to be in the paper, Brian, and your picture is going to be on TV, and all your friends will see it. Your mother and father will see it, too, and your little brother. And when they show the picture, the man on the news will say, "This is Brian Rusk, the boy who helped murder Wilma Jerzyck and Nettie Cobb."

"Huh-huh-who is it?" he called downstairs in a shrieky little voice.

"I dunno!" Sean had been torn away from *The Transformers* and sounded irritated. "I think he said his name was Crowfix. Something like that."

Crowfix?

Brian stood in the doorway, his heart thumping in his chest. Two big clown-spots of color now burned in his pallid face.

Not Crowfix.

Koufax.

Sandy Koufax had called him on the phone. Except Brian had a pretty good idea of who it *really* was.

He went down the stairs on leaden feet. The telephone handset seemed to weigh at least five hundred pounds.

"Hello, Brian," Mr. Gaunt said softly.

"Huh-Huh-Hello," Brian replied in the same shrieky little voice.

"You don't have a thing to worry about," Mr. Gaunt said. "If Mrs. Mislaburski had *seen* you throw those rocks, she wouldn't have asked you what was going on over there, now would she?"

"How do you know about that?" Brian again felt like throwing up.

"That doesn't matter. What matters is that you did the right thing, Brian. Exactly the right thing. You said you thought

Mr. and Mrs. Jerzyck were having an argument. If the police *do* find you, they'll just think you heard the person who was throwing the rocks. They'll think you didn't see him because he was behind the house."

Brian looked through the archway into the TV room to make sure Sean wasn't snooping. He wasn't; he was sitting cross-legged in front of the TV with a bag of microwave popcorn in his lap.

"I can't lie!" he whispered into the telephone. "I always get caught out when I lie!"

"Not this time, Brian," Mr. Gaunt said. "This time you're going to do it like a champ."

And the most horrible thing of all was that Brian thought Mr. Gaunt knew best about this, too.

2

While her older son was thinking of suicide and then dicker-ing in a desperate, quiet whisper with Mr. Gaunt, Cora Rusk was dancing quietly around her bedroom in her housecoat.

Except it wasn't her bedroom.

When she put on the sunglasses Mr. Gaunt had sold her, she was in Graceland.

She danced through fabulous rooms which smelled of Pine-Sol and fried food, rooms where the only sounds were the quiet hum of air conditioners (only a few of the windows at Graceland actually opened; many were nailed shut and all were shaded), the whisper of her feet on deep-pile rugs, and the sound of Elvis singing "My Wish Came True" in his haunt-ing, pleading voice. She danced beneath the huge chandelier of French crystal in the dining room and past the trademark stained-glass peacocks. She trailed her hands across the rich blue velvet drapes. The furniture was French Provincial. The walls were blood red.

The scene changed like a slow dissolve in a movie and Cora found herself in the basement den. There were racks of animal horns on one wall and columns of framed gold records on another. Blank TV screens bulged from a third wall. Behind the long, curved bar were shelves stocked with Gatorade: orange, lime, lemon flavors.

The record-changer on her old portable phonograph with the picture of The King on its vinyl cover clicked. Another forty-five dropped down. Elvis began to sing "Blue Hawaii," and Cora hula-hulaed into the Jungle Room with its frowning Tiki gods, the couch with the gargoyle armrests, the mirror with its lacy frame of feathers plucked from the breasts of living pheasants.

She danced. With the sunglasses she had purchased in Needful Things masking her eyes, she danced. She danced at Graceland while her son crept back upstairs and lay down on his bed again and looked at the narrow face of Sandy Koufax and thought about alibis and shotguns.

3

Castle Rock Middle School was a frowning pile of red brick standing between the Post Office and the Library, a hold-over from the time when the town elders didn't feel entirely comfortable with a school unless it looked like a reformatory. This one had been built in 1926 and filled that particular bill admirably. Each year the town got a little closer to deciding to build a new one, one with actual windows instead of loopholes and a playground that didn't look like a penitentiary exercise yard and classrooms that actually stayed warm in the winter.

Sally Ratcliffe's speech therapy room was an afterthought in the basement, tucked away between the furnace room and the supply closet with its stacks of paper towels, chalk, Ginn and Company textbooks, and barrels of fragrant red sawdust. With her teacher's desk and six smaller pupil desks in the room there was barely enough space to turn around, but Sally had tried to make the place as cheery as possible, just the same. She knew that most kids who were tapped for speech therapy—the stutterers, the lispers, the dyslexics, the nasal blocks—found the experience a frightening, unhappy one. They were teased by their peers and closely questioned by their parents. There was no need for the environment to be unnecessarily grim on top of all that.

So there were two mobiles hanging from the dusty ceiling pipes, pictures of TV and rock stars on the walls, and a big Garfield poster on the door. The words in the balloon coming out of Garfield's mouth said, "If a cool cat like me can talk that trash, so can you!"

Her files were woefully behind even though school had been in session for only five weeks. She had meant to spend the whole day updating them, but at quarter past one Sally gathered them all up, stuck them back into the file-drawer they had come from, slammed it shut, and locked it. She told herself she was quitting early because the day was too nice to spend cooped up in this basement room, even with the furnace mercifully silent for a change. This wasn't entirely the truth, however. She had very definite plans for this afternoon.

She wanted to go home, she wanted to sit in her chair by the window with the sun flooding into her lap, and she wanted to meditate upon the fabulous splinter of wood she had bought in Needful Things.

She had become more and more sure that the splinter was an authentic miracle, one of the small, divine treasures God had scattered around the earth for His faithful to find. Holding it was like being refreshed by a dipper of well-water on a hot day. Holding it was like being fed when you were hungry. Holding it was . . .

Well, holding it was ecstasy.

And something had been nagging at her, as well. She had

put the splinter in the bottom drawer of her bedroom dresser, beneath her underwear, and she had been careful to lock her house when she went out, but she had a terrible, nagging feeling that someone might break in and steal the

(*relic holy relic*)

splinter. She knew it didn't make much sense—what robber would want to steal an old gray piece of wood, even if he found it? But if the robber happened to *touch* it . . . if those sounds and images filled *his* head as they filled hers every time she closed the splinter in her small fist . . . well . . .

So she'd go home. She'd change into shorts and a halter and spend an hour or so in quiet

(*exaltation*)

meditation, feeling the floor beneath her turn into a deck which heaved slowly up and down, listening to the animals moo and low and baa, feeling the light of a different sun, waiting for the magic moment—she was sure it would come if she held the splinter long enough, if she remained very, very quiet and very, very prayerful—when the bow of the huge, lumbering boat should come to rest on the mountain top with a low grinding sound. She did not know why God had seen fit to bless her, of all the world's faithful, with this bright and shining miracle, but since He had, Sally meant to experience it as fully and as completely as she could.

She went out the side door and crossed the playground to the faculty parking lot, a tall, pretty young woman with darkish blonde hair and long legs. There was a good deal of talk about those legs in the barber shop when Sally Ratcliffe went strolling by in her sensible low heels, usually with her purse in one hand and her Bible—stuffed with tracts—in the other.

"Christ, that woman's got legs right up to her chin," Bobby Dugas said once.

"Don't let em worry you," Charlie Fortin replied. "You ain't never gonna feel em wrapped around *your* ass. She belongs to Jesus and Lester Pratt. In that order."

The barber shop had exploded into hearty male laughter on the day when Charlie had gotten that one—a genuine Knee-Slapper—off. And outside, Sally Ratcliffe had walked along on her way to Rev. Rose's Thursday Evening Bible Study for Young Adults, unknowing, uncaring, wrapped securely in her own cheerful innocence and virtue.

No jokes were made about Sally's legs or Sally's *anything* if Lester Pratt happened to be in The Clip Joint (and he went there at least once every three weeks to have the bristles of his crewcut sharpened). It was clear to most of those in town who cared about such things that he believed Sally farted perfume and shit petunias, and you didn't argue about such things with a man who was put together like Lester. He was an amiable enough guy, but on the subjects of God and Sally Ratcliffe he was always dead serious. And a man like Lester could pull off your arms and legs before putting them back on in new and interesting ways, if he wanted to.

He and Sally had had some pretty hot sessions, but they had never gone All the Way. Lester usually returned home after these sessions in a state of total discomposure, his brain bursting with joy and his balls bursting with frustrated jizz, dreaming of the night, not too far away now, when he wouldn't have to stop. He sometimes wondered if he might not drown her the first time they actually Did It.

Sally was also looking forward to marriage and an end to sexual frustration . . . although these last few days, Lester's embraces had seemed a little less important to her. She had debated telling him about the splinter of wood from the Holy Land she had purchased at Needful Things, the splinter with the miracle inside it, and in the end she hadn't. She *would,* of course; miracles should be shared. It was undoubtedly a sin *not* to share them. But she had been surprised (and a little dismayed) by the feeling of jealous possessiveness which rose up in her each time she thought of showing Lester the splinter and inviting him to hold it.

No! an angry, childish voice had cried out the first time she had considered this. *No, it's mine! It wouldn't mean as much to him as it does to me! It* couldn't!

The day would come when she *would* share it with him, just as the day would come when she would share her body with him—but it was not time for either of those things to happen yet.

This hot October day belonged strictly to *her.*

There were only a few cars in the faculty lot, and Lester's Mustang was the newest and nicest of them. She'd been having lots of problems with her own car—something in the drive-train kept breaking down—but that was no real problem. When she had called Les this morning and asked if she could have his car yet again (she'd only returned it after a six-day loan at noon the day before), he agreed to drive it over right away. He could jog back, he said, and later he and a bunch of The Guys were going to play touch football. She guessed he would have insisted that she take the car even if he *had* needed it, and that seemed perfectly all right to her. She was aware—in a vague, unfocused way that was the result of intuition rather than experience—that Les would jump through hoops of fire if she asked him to, and this established a chain of adoration which she accepted with naive complacency. Les worshipped her; they both worshipped God; everything was as it should be; world without end, amen.

She slipped into the Mustang, and as she turned to put her purse on the console, her eye happened on something white sticking out from beneath the passenger seat. It looked like an envelope.

She bent over and plucked it up, thinking how odd it was to find such a thing in the Mustang; Les usually kept his car as scrupulously neat as his person. There was one word on the front of the envelope, but it gave Sally Ratcliffe a nasty little jolt. The word was *Lovey,* written in lightly flowing script.

Feminine script.

She turned it over. Nothing written on the back, and the envelope was sealed.

"Lovey?" Sally asked doubtfully, and suddenly realized she was sitting in Lester's car with all the windows still rolled up, sweating like mad. She started the engine, rolled down the driver's window, then leaned across the console to roll down the passenger window.

She seemed to catch a faint whiff of perfume as she did it. If so, it wasn't hers; she didn't wear perfume, or make-up either. Her religion taught her that such things were the tools of harlots. (And besides, she didn't need them.)

It wasn't perfume, anyway. Just the last of the honeysuckle growing along the playground fence—that's all you smelled.

"Lovey?" she said again, looking at the envelope.

The envelope said nothing. It just lay there smugly in her hands.

She fluttered her fingers over it, then bent it back and forth. There was a piece of paper in there, she thought—at least one—and something else, too. The something else felt like it might be a photograph.

She held the envelope up to the windshield, but that was no good; the sun was going the other way now. After a moment's debate she got out of the car and held the envelope up in front of the sun. She could only make out a light rectangle—the letter, she thought—and a darker square shape that was probably an enclosed photo from

(*Lovey*)

whoever had sent Les the letter.

Except, of course, it hadn't been *sent*—not through the mails, anyway. There was no stamp, no address. Just that one troubling word. It hadn't been opened, either, which meant . . . what? That someone had slipped it into Lester's Mustang while Sally had been working on her files?

That might be. It might also mean that someone had slipped it into the car last night—even yesterday—and Lester hadn't seen it. After all, only a corner had been sticking out; it might have slid forward a little from its place under the seat while she had been driving to school this morning.

"Hi, Miss Ratcliffe!" someone called. Sally jerked the envelope down and hid it in the folds of her skirt. Her heart bumped guiltily.

It was little Billy Marchant, cutting across the playground with his skateboard under his arm. Sally waved to him and then got quickly back into the car. Her face felt hot. She was blushing. It was silly—no, *crazy*—but she was behaving almost as if Billy had caught her doing something she shouldn't.

Well, weren't you? Weren't you trying to peek at a letter that isn't yours?

She felt the first twinges of jealousy then. Maybe it *was* hers; a lot of people in Castle Rock knew she had been driving Lester's car as much as she had been driving her own these past few weeks. And even if it *wasn't* hers, Lester Pratt *was.* Hadn't she just been thinking, with the solid, pleasant complacency which only Christian women who are young and pretty feel so exquisitely, that he would jump through hoops of fire for her?

Lovey.

No one had left that envelope for *her,* she was sure of that much. *She* didn't have any women friends who called her Sweetheart or Darling or Lovey. It had been left for *Lester.* And—

The solution suddenly struck her, and she collapsed against the powder-blue bucket seat with a little sigh of relief. Lester taught Phys Ed at Castle Rock High. He only had the boys, of course, but lots of girls—young girls, impressionable girls— saw him every day. And Les was a good-looking young man.

Some little high school girl with a crush slipped a note into his car. That's all it is. She didn't even dare leave it on the dashboard where he would see it right away.

"He wouldn't mind if I opened it," Sally said aloud, and tore off the end of the envelope in a neat strip which she put in the ashtray where no cigarette had ever been parked. "We'll have a good laugh about it tonight."

She tilted the envelope, and a Kodak print fell out into her hand. She saw it, and her heart stuttered to a stop for a moment. Then she gasped. Bright red suffused her cheeks, and her hand covered her mouth, which had pursed itself into a small, shocked O of dismay.

Sally had never been in The Mellow Tiger and so she didn't know that was the background, but she wasn't a *total* innocent; she had watched enough TV and been to enough movies to know a bar when she saw one. The photo showed a man and a woman sitting at a table in what appeared to be one corner (a *cozy* corner, her mind insisted on calling it) of a large room. There was a pitcher of beer and two Pilsner glasses on the table. Other people were sitting at other tables behind and around them. In the background was a dance-floor.

The man and the woman were kissing.

She was wearing a sparkly sweater top which left her midriff exposed and a skirt of what appeared to be white linen. A very *short* skirt. One of the man's hands pressed familiarly against the skin of her waist. The other was actually *under her skirt,* pushing it up even further. Sally could see the blur of the woman's panties.

That little chippie, Sally thought with angry dismay.

The man's back was to the photographer; Sally could make out only his chin and one ear. But she could see that he was very muscular, and that his black hair was mown into a rigorously short crewcut. He was wearing a blue tee-shirt—what the schoolkids called a muscle-shirt—and blue sweatpants with a white stripe on the side.

Lester.

Lester exploring the landscape under that chippie's skirt.

No! her mind proclaimed in panicky denial. It *can't* be him! Lester doesn't go out to bars! He doesn't even drink! And he'd never kiss another woman, because he loves me! I know he does, because . . .

"Because he says so." Her voice, dull and listless, was shocking to her own ears. She wanted to crumple the picture up and throw it out of the car, but she couldn't do that—someone might find it if she did, and what would that someone think?

She bent over the photograph again, studying it with jealous, intent eyes.

The man's face blocked most of the woman's, but Sally could see the line of her brow, the corner of one eye, her left cheek, and the line of her jaw. More important, she could see how the woman's dark hair was cut—in a shag, with bangs feathered across the forehead.

Judy Libby had dark hair. And Judy Libby had it cut in a shag, with bangs feathered across the forehead.

You're wrong. No, worse than that—you're crazy. Les broke up with Judy when she left the church. And then she went away. To Portland or Boston or someplace like that. This is someone's twisted, mean idea of a joke. You know Les would never—

But *did* she know? Did she really?

All of her former complacency now rose up to mock her, and a voice which she had never heard before today suddenly spoke up from some deep chamber of her heart: *The trust of the innocent is the liar's most useful tool.*

It didn't *have* to be Judy, though; it didn't *have* to be Lester, either. After all, you couldn't really tell *who* people were when they were kissing, could you? You couldn't even tell for sure at the movies if you came in late, not even if they were two famous stars. You had to wait until they stopped and looked at the camera again.

This was no movie, the new voice assured her. *This was real life. And if it isn't them, what was that envelope doing in this car?*

Now her eyes fixed upon the woman's right hand, which was pressed lightly against

(Lester's)

her boyfriend's neck. She had long, shaped nails, painted with some dark polish. Judy Libby had had nails like that. Sally remembered that she hadn't been at all surprised when Judy stopped coming to church. A girl with fingernails like that, she remembered thinking, has got a lot more than the Lord of Hosts on her mind.

All right, so it's probably Judy Libby. That doesn't mean it's Lester with her. This could just be her nasty way of getting back at both of us because Lester dropped her when he finally realized she was about as Christian as Judas Iscariot. After all, lots of men have crewcuts, and any man can put on a blue tee-shirt and a pair of pants with white coach-stripes running up the sides.

Then her eye happened upon something else, and her heart suddenly seemed to fill up with lead shot. The man was wearing a wristwatch—the digital kind. She recognized it even though it wasn't in perfect focus. She ought to have recognized it; hadn't she given it to Lester herself, for his birthday last month?

It could be a coincidence, her mind insisted feebly. It was only a Seiko, that was all I could afford. Anyone could have a watch like that. But the new voice laughed raucously, despairingly. The new voice wanted to know who she thought she was kidding. And there was more. She couldn't see the hand under the girl's skirt (thank God for small favors!), but she could see the arm to which it was attached. There were two large moles on that arm, just below the elbow. They almost touched, making a shape like a figure-eight.

How often had she run her finger lovingly over those very same moles as she and Lester sat on the porch swing? How often had she kissed them lovingly as he caressed her breasts (armored in a heavy J. C. Penney bra carefully selected for just such conflicts of love on the back porch) and panted terms of endearment and promises of unflagging loyalty in her ear?

It was Lester, all right. A watch could be put on and taken

off, but moles couldn't be . . . A snatch of an old disco song occurred to her: *"Bad girls . . . toot-toot . . . beep-beep . . ."*

"Chippie, chippie, *chippie!*" she hissed at the picture in a sudden vicious undertone. How could he have gone back to her? *How?*

Maybe, the voice said, *because she lets him do what you won't.*

Her breast rose sharply; a hissy little gasp of dismay tore over her teeth and down her throat.

But they're in a bar! Lester doesn't—

Then she realized that was very much a secondary consideration. If Lester was seeing Judy, if he was lying about *that,* a lie about whether or not he drank beer wasn't very important, was it?

Sally put the photograph aside with a shaking hand and pawed out of the envelope the folded note which accompanied it. It was on a single sheet of peach-colored stationery with a deckle edge. Some light smell, dusty and sweet, came from it when she took it out. Sally held it to her nose and inhaled deeply.

"Chippie!" she cried in a hoarse, agonized undertone.

If Judy Libby had appeared in front of her at that moment, Sally would have attacked her with her own nails, sensibly short though they were. She wished Judy were. She wished Lester were, too. It would be awhile before he played any more touch football after *she* got through with him. *Quite* awhile.

She unfolded the note. It was short, the words written in the rolling Palmer Method hand of a schoolgirl.

Darling Les,

    Felicia took this when we were at the Tiger
the other night. She said she ought to use it to
blackmail us! But she was only teasing. She gave
it to me, and I am giving it to you as a souvenier
of our BIG NIGHT. It was TERRIBLY NAUGHTY of
you to put your hand under my skirt like that
"right out in public," but it got me SO HOT.

Besides, you are SO STRONG. The more I looked
at it the more "hot" it started to make me. If
you look close, you can see my underwear! It's a
good thing Felicia wasn't around later, when I
wasn't wearing any!!! I will see you soon. In the
meantime, keep this picture "in remembrance
of me." I will be thinking of you and your BIG
THING. I better stop now before I get any hotter
or I'll have to do something naughty. And please
stop worrying about YOU KNOW WHO. She is
two busy going steady with Jesus to worry
about us.

Your

Judy

Sally sat behind the wheel of Lester's Mustang for almost
half an hour, reading this note again and again, her mind and
her emotions in a stew of anger, jealousy, and hurt. There was
also an undertone of sexual excitement in her thoughts and
feelings—but this was something she would never have admitted to anyone, least of all herself.

The stupid slut doesn't even know how to spell "too," she thought.

Her eyes kept finding new phrases to fix upon. Most of them
were the ones which had been capitalized.

Our BIG NIGHT.

TERRIBLY NAUGHTY.

SO HOT.

SO STRONG.

Your BIG THING.

But the phrase she kept returning to, the one which fed her
rage most successfully, was that blasphemous perversion of the
Communion ritual:

. . . keep this picture "in remembrance of me."

Obscene images rose in Sally's mind, unbidden. Lester's mouth closing on one of Judy Libby's nipples while she crooned: "Take, drink ye all of this, in remembrance of me." Lester on his knees between Judy Libby's spread legs while she told him to take, eat this in remembrance of me.

She crumpled the peach-colored sheet of paper into a ball and threw it onto the floor of the car. She sat bolt upright behind the wheel, breathing hard, her hair fuzzed out in sweaty tangles (she had been running her free hand distractedly through it as she studied the note). Then she bent, picked it up, smoothed it out, and stuffed both it and the photograph back into the envelope. Her hands were shaking so badly she had to try three times to get it in, and when she finally did, she tore the envelope halfway down the side.

"Chippie!" she cried again, and burst into tears. The tears were hot; they burned like acid. *"Bitch!* And *you! You!* Lying *bastard!"*

She jammed the key into the ignition. The Mustang awoke with a roar that sounded as angry as she felt. She dropped the gearshift into drive and tore out of the faculty parking lot in a cloud of blue smoke and a wailing shriek of burned rubber.

Billy Marchant, who was practicing nosies on his skateboard across the playground, looked up in surprise.

4

She was in her bedroom fifteen minutes later, digging through her underwear, looking for the splinter and not finding it. Her anger at Judy and her lying bastard of a boyfriend had been eclipsed by an overmastering terror—what if it was gone? What if it had been stolen after all?

Sally had brought the torn envelope in with her, and became aware that it was still clutched in her left hand. It was impeding her search. She threw it aside and tore her sensible cotton underwear out of her drawer in big double handfuls, throwing it everywhere. Just as she felt she must scream with a combination of panic, rage, and frustration, she saw the splinter. She had pulled the drawer open so hard that it had slid all the way into the left rear corner of the drawer.

She snatched it up, and at once felt peace and serenity flood through her. She grabbed the envelope with her other hand and then held both hands in front of her, good and evil, sacred and profane, alpha and omega. Then she put the torn envelope in the drawer and tossed her underwear on top of it in helter-skelter piles.

She sat down, crossed her legs, and bowed her head over the splinter. She shut her eyes, expecting to feel the floor begin to sway gently beneath her, expecting the peace which came to her when she heard the voices of the animals, the poor dumb animals, saved in a time of wickedness by the grace of God.

Instead, she heard the voice of the man who had sold her the splinter. *You really ought to take care of this, you know,* Mr. Gaunt said from deep within the relic. *You really ought to take care of this . . . this nasty business.*

"Yes," Sally Ratcliffe said. "Yes, I know."

She sat there all afternoon in her hot maiden's bedroom, thinking and dreaming in the dark circle which the splinter spread around her, a darkness which was like the hood of a cobra.

5

"Lookit my king, all dressed in green . . . iko-iko one day . . . he's not a man, he's a lovin' machine . . ."

While Sally Ratcliffe was meditating in her new darkness, Polly Chalmers was sitting in a bar of brilliant sunlight by a window she had opened to let in a little of the unseasonably warm October afternoon. She was running her Singer Dress-O-Matic and singing "Iko Iko" in her clear, pleasant alto voice.

Rosalie Drake came over and said, "I know someone who's feeling better today. A *lot* better, by the sound."

Polly looked up and offered Rosalie a smile which was strangely complex. "I do and don't," she said.

"What you mean is that you do and can't help it."

Polly considered this for a few moments and then nodded her head. It wasn't exactly right, but it would do. The two women who had died together yesterday were together again today, at the Samuels Funeral Home. They would be buried out of different churches tomorrow morning, but by tomorrow afternoon Nettie and Wilma would be neighbors again . . . in Homeland Cemetery, this time. Polly counted herself partially responsible for their deaths—after all, Nettie would never have come back to Castle Rock if not for her. She had written the necessary letters, attended the necessary hearings, had even found Netitia Cobb a place to live. And why? The hell of it was, Polly couldn't really remember now, except it had seemed an act of Christian charity and the last responsibility of an old family friendship.

She would not duck this culpability, nor let anyone try to talk her out of it (Alan had wisely not even tried), but she was not sure she would have changed what she had done. The core of Nettie's madness had been beyond Polly's power to control or alter, apparently, but she had nevertheless spent three happy, productive years in Castle Rock. Perhaps three such years were better than the long gray time she would have spent in the institution, before old age or simple boredom cashed her in. And if Polly had, by her actions, signed her name to Wilma Jerzyck's death-warrant, hadn't Wilma written the particulars of that document herself? After all, it had been Wilma, not Polly, who had stabbed Nettie Cobb's cheery and inoffensive little dog to death with a corkscrew.

There was another part of her, a simpler part, which simply grieved for the passing of her friend, and puzzled over the fact that Nettie could have done such a thing when it really had seemed to Polly that she was getting better.

She had spent a good part of the morning making funeral arrangements and calling Nettie's few relatives (all of them had indicated that they wouldn't be at the funeral, which was only what Polly had expected), and this job, the clerical processes of death, had helped to focus her own grief . . . as the rituals of burying the dead are undoubtedly supposed to do.

There were some things, however, which would not yet leave her mind.

The lasagna, for instance—it was still sitting in the refrigerator with the foil over the top to keep it from drying out. She supposed she and Alan would eat it for dinner tonight—if he could come over, that was. She wouldn't eat it by herself. She couldn't stand that.

She kept remembering how quickly Nettie had seen she was in pain, how exactly she had gauged that pain, and how she had brought her the thermal gloves, insisting that this time they really might help. And, of course, the last thing Nettie had said to her: "I love you, Polly."

"Earth to Polly, Earth to Polly, come in, Pol, do you read?" Rosalie chanted. She and Polly had remembered Nettie together that morning, trading these and other reminiscences, and had cried together in the back room, holding each other amid the bolts of cloth. Now Rosalie also seemed happy— perhaps just because she had heard Polly singing.

Or because she wasn't entirely real to either of us, Polly mused. There was a shadow over her—not one that was completely black, mind you; it was just thick enough to make her hard to see. That's what makes our grief so fragile.

"I hear you," Polly said. "I *do* feel better, I *can't* help it, and I'm very grateful *for* it. Does that about cover the waterfront?"

"Just about," Rosalie agreed. "I don't know what surprised me more when I came back in—hearing you singing, or hearing you running a sewing machine again. Hold up your hands."

Polly did. They would never be mistaken for the hands of a beauty queen, with their crooked fingers and the Heberden's nodes, which grotesquely enlarged the knuckles, but Rosalie could see that the swelling had gone down dramatically since last Friday, when the constant pain had caused Polly to leave early.

"Wow!" Rosalie said. "Do they hurt at all?"

"Sure—but they're still better than they've been in a month. Look."

She slowly rolled her fingers into loose fists. Then she opened them again, using the same care. "It's been at least a month since I've been able to do that." The truth, Polly knew, was a little more extreme; she hadn't been able to make fists without suffering serious pain since April or May.

"*Wow!*"

"So I feel better," Polly said. "Now if Nettie were here to share it, that would make things just about perfect."

The door at the front of the shop opened.

"Will you see who that is?" Polly asked. "I want to finish sewing this sleeve."

"You bet." Rosalie started off, then stopped for a moment and looked back. "Nettie wouldn't mind you feeling good, you know."

Polly nodded. "I do know," she said gravely.

Rosalie went out front to wait on the customer. When she was gone, Polly's left hand went to her chest and touched the small bulge, not much bigger than an acorn, that rested under her pink sweater and between her breasts.

Azka—what a wonderful word, she thought, and began to run the sewing machine again, turning the fabric of the dress— her first original since last summer—back and forth under the jittery silver blur of the needle.

She wondered idly how much Mr. Gaunt would want for the amulet. Whatever he wants, she told herself, it won't be enough. I won't—I *can't*—think that way when it comes time to dicker, but it's the simple truth. Whatever he wants for it will be a bargain.

CHAPTER FOURTEEN

1

The Castle Rock selectmen (and selectwoman) shared a single full-time secretary, a young woman with the exotic name of Ariadne St. Claire. She was a happy young woman, not over-burdened with intelligence but tireless and pleasing to look at. She had large breasts which rose in soft, steep hills beneath an apparently endless supply of angora sweaters, and lovely skin. She also had very bad eyes. They swam, brown and enlarged, behind the thick lenses of her horn-rimmed spectacles. Buster liked her. He considered her too dumb to be one of Them.

Ariadne poked her head into his office at quarter to four. "Deke Bradford came by, Mr. Keeton. He needs a signature on a fund-release form. Can you do it?"

"Well, let's see what it is," Buster said, slipping that day's sports section of the Lewiston *Daily Sun,* folded to the racing card, deftly into his desk drawer.

He felt better today; purposeful and alert. Those wretched pink slips had been burned in the kitchen stove, Myrtle had stopped sidling away like a singed cat when he approached (he no longer cared much for Myrtle, but it was still annoying to live with a woman who thought you were the Boston Strangler), and he expected to clear another large bundle of cash at the Raceway that night. Because of the holiday, the crowds (not to mention the payoffs) would be bigger.

He had, in fact, started to think in terms of quinellas and trifectas.

As for Deputy Dickface and Sheriff Shithead and all the rest of their merry crew . . . well, he and Mr. Gaunt knew about Them, and Buster believed the two of them were going to make one hell of a team.

For all these reasons he was able to welcome Ariadne into his office with equanimity—he was even able to take some of his old pleasure in observing the gentle way her bosom swayed within its no doubt formidable harness.

She put a fund-release form on his desk. Buster picked it up and leaned back in his swivel chair to look it over. The amount requested was noted in a box at the top—nine hundred and forty dollars. The payee was to be Case Construction and Supply in Lewiston. In the space reserved for *Goods and/ or Services to Be Supplied,* Deke had printed 16 CASES OF DY-NAMITE. Below, in the *Comments/Explanations* section, he had written:

> *We've finally come up against that granite ridge at the gravel pit out on Town Road #5, the one the state geologist warned us about back in '87 (see my report for details). Anyway, there is plenty more gravel beyond it, but we'll have to blow out the rock to get at it. This should be done before it gets cold and the winter snowfall starts. If we have to buy a winter's worth of gravel over in Norway, the taxpayers are going to howl blue murder. Two or three bangs should take care of it, and Case has a big supply of Taggart Hi-Impact on hand—I checked. We can have it by noon tomorrow, if we want, and start blasting on Wednesday. I have the spots marked if anyone from the Selectmen's Office wants to come out and take a look.*

Below this, Deke had scrawled his signature.

Buster read Deke's note twice, tapping his front teeth thoughtfully as Ariadne stood waiting. At last he rocked forward in his chair, made a change, added a sentence, initialed both the change and the addition, then signed his own name below Deke's with a flourish. When he handed the pink sheet of paper back to Ariadne, he was smiling.

"There!" he said. "And everyone thinks I'm such a skin-flint!"

Ariadne looked at the form. Buster had changed the amount from nine hundred and forty dollars to fourteen hundred dollars. Below Deke's explanation of what he wanted the dynamite for, Buster had added this: *Better get at least twenty cases while the supply is good.*

"Will you want to go out and look at the gravel pit, Mr. Keeton?"

"Nope, nope, won't be necessary." Buster leaned back in his chair again and locked his hands together behind his neck. "But ask Deke to give me a call when the stuff arrives. That's a lot of bang. We wouldn't want it to fall into the wrong hands, would we?"

"No indeed," Ariadne said, and went out. She was glad to go. There was something in Mr. Keeton's smile which she found . . . well, a little creepy.

Buster, meanwhile, had swivelled his chair around so he could look out at Main Street, which was a good deal busier than it had been when he had looked out over the town with such despair on Saturday morning. A lot had happened since then, and he suspected that a lot more *would* happen in the next couple of days. Why, with twenty cases of Taggart Hi-Impact Dynamite stored in the town's Public Works shed—a shed to which he, of course, had a key—almost anything could happen.

Anything at all.

2

Ace Merrill crossed the Tobin Bridge and entered Boston at four o'clock that afternoon, but it was well past five before he finally reached what he hoped was his destination. It was in a strange, mostly deserted slum section of Cambridge, near the center of a meandering snarl of streets. Half of them seemed to be posted one-way; the other half were dead ends. The ruined buildings of this decayed area were throwing long shadows over the streets when Ace stopped in front of a stark one-story cinderblock building on Whipple Street. It stood in the center of a weedy vacant lot.

There was a chainlink fence around the property, but it presented no problem; the gate had been stolen. Only the hinges remained. Ace could see what were probably bolt-cutter scars on them. He eased the Challenger through the gap where the gate had been and drove slowly toward the cinderblock building.

Its walls were blank and windowless. The rutted track he was on led to a closed garage door in the side of the building which faced the River Charles. There were no windows in the garage door, either. The Challenger rocked on its springs and bounced unhappily through holes in what might once have been an asphalt surface. He passed an abandoned baby carriage sitting in a strew of broken glass. A decayed doll with half a face reclined inside, staring at him with one moldy blue eye as he passed. He parked in front of the closed garage door. What the hell was he supposed to do now? The cinderblock building had the look of a place which had been deserted since 1945 or so.

Ace got out of the car. He took a scrap of paper from his breast pocket. Written on it was the address of the place where Gaunt's car was supposed to be stored. He looked doubtfully at it again. The last few numbers he had passed suggested that this was *probably* 85 Whipple Street, but who the fuck could tell for sure? Places like this never had street numbers, and there didn't seem to be anyone around he could ask. In fact, this whole section of town had a deserted, creepy feel Ace didn't much like. Vacant lots. Stripped cars which had been looted of every useful part and every centimeter of copper wire. Empty tenements waiting for the politicians to get their kickbacks straight before they fell under the wrecking ball. Twisty side-streets that dead-ended in dirty courtyards and trashy cul-de-sacs. It had taken him an hour to find Whipple Street, and now that he had, he almost wished it had stayed lost. This was the part of town where the cops sometimes found the bodies of infants stuffed into rusty garbage cans and discarded refrigerators.

He walked over to the garage door and looked for a pushbell. There was none. He leaned the side of his head against the rusty metal and listened for the sounds of someone inside. It could be a chop-shop, he supposed; a dude with a supply of high-tension coke like the stuff Gaunt had laid on him might very well know the sort of people who sold Porsches and Lamborghinis for cash after the sun went down.

He heard nothing but silence.

Probably not even the right place, he thought, but he had been up and down the goddam street and it was the only place on it big enough—and strong enough—to store a classic car in. Unless he had fucked up royally and come to the wrong part of town. The idea made him nervous. *I want you back by midnight,* Mr. Gaunt had said. *If you're not back by midnight, I will be unhappy. When I'm unhappy, I sometimes lose my temper.*

Mellow out, Ace told himself uneasily. He's just some old dude with a bad set of false teeth. Probably a fag.

But he *couldn't* mellow out, and he didn't really think Mr. Leland Gaunt was just some old dude with a bad set of false teeth. He also thought he didn't want to find out for sure one way or the other.

But the current thing was this: it was going to be dark before long, and Ace didn't want to be in this part of town after dark. There was something wrong with it. Something that went beyond the spooky tenements with their blank, staring windows and the cars standing on naked wheelrims in the gutter. He hadn't seen a single person on the sidewalk or sitting on a stoop or looking out a window since he started getting close to Whipple Street . . . but he had had the sensation that he was being watched, just the same. Still had it, in fact: a busy crawling in the short hairs on the back of his neck.

It was almost as though he were not in Boston at all anymore. This place was more like the motherfucking Twilight Zone.

If you're not back by midnight, I will be unhappy.

Ace made a fist and hammered on the rusty, featureless face of the garage door. "Hey! Anybody in there want to look at some Tupperware?"

No answer.

There was a handle at the bottom of the door. He tried it. No joy. The door wouldn't even rattle in its frame, let alone roll up on its tracks.

Ace hissed air out between his teeth and looked around nervously. His Challenger was standing nearby, and he had never in his life wanted so much to just get in and *go*. But he didn't dare.

He walked around the building and there was nothing. Nothing at all. Just expanses of cinderblock, painted an unpleasant snot-green. An odd piece of graffiti had been spray-painted on the back of the garage, and Ace looked at it for some moments, not understanding why it made his skin crawl.

YOG-SOTHOTH RULES,

it read in faded red letters.

He arrived back at the garage door and thought, *Now what?*

Because he could think of nothing else, he got back into the Challenger and just sat there, looking at the garage door. At last, he laid both hands on the horn and honked a long, frustrated blast.

At once the garage door began to roll silently up on its tracks.

Ace sat watching it, gape-mouthed, and his first urge was to simply start the Challenger up and drive away as fast as he could and as far as he could. Mexico City might do for a start. Then he thought of Mr. Gaunt again and got slowly out of his car. He walked over to the garage as the door came to rest below the ceiling inside.

The interior was brightly lit by half a dozen two-hundred-watt bulbs hanging at the ends of thick electrical cords. Each bulb had been shaded with a piece of tin shaped into a cone, so that the lights cast circular pools of brightness on the floor. On the far side of the cement floor was a car covered with a dropcloth. There was a table littered with tools standing against one wall. Three crates were stacked against another wall. On top of them was an old-fashioned reel-to-reel tape recorder.

The garage was otherwise empty.

"Who opened the door?" Ace asked in a dry little voice. "Who opened the fucking *door?*"

But to this there was no answer.

3

He drove the Challenger inside and parked it against the rear wall—there was plenty of room. Then he walked back to the doorway. There was a control box mounted on the wall next to it. Ace pushed the DOWN button. The waste ground on which this enigmatic blockhouse of a building stood was filling up with shadows, and they made him nervous. He kept thinking he saw things moving out there.

The door rolled down without a single squeak or rattle. While he waited for it to close all the way, Ace looked around for the sonic sensor which had responded to the sound of his horn. He couldn't see it. It had to be here someplace, though—garage doors did not open all by themselves.

Although, he thought, if shit like that happens anywhere in this town, Whipple Street's probably the place.

Ace walked over to the stack of crates with the tape recorder on top. His feet made a hollow gritting sound on the cement. *Yog-Sothoth rules,* he thought randomly, and then shivered. He didn't know who the fuck Yog-Sothoth was, probably some Rastafarian reggae singer with ninety pounds of dreadlocks growing out of his dirty scalp, but Ace still didn't like the sound that name made in his head. Thinking about that name in this place seemed like a bad idea. It seemed like a dangerous idea.

A scrap of paper had been taped to one of the recorder's reels. Two words were written on it in large capital letters:

PLAY ME.

Ace pulled off the note and pushed the PLAY button. The reels began to turn, and when he heard that voice, he jumped a little. Still, whose voice had he expected? Richard Nixon's?

"Hello, Ace," Mr. Gaunt's recorded voice said. "Welcome to Boston. Please remove the tarp from my car and load the crates. They contain rather special merchandise which I expect to need quite soon now. I'm afraid you'll have to put at least one crate in the back seat; the Tucker's trunk leaves something to be desired. Your own car will be quite safe here, and your ride back will be uneventful. And please remember this—the sooner you get back, the sooner you can begin investigating the locations on your map. Have a pleasant trip."

The message was followed by the empty hiss of tape and the low whine of the capstan drive.

Ace left the reels turning for almost a minute, nevertheless. This whole situation was weird . . . and getting weirder all the time. Mr. Gaunt had been here during the afternoon—*had* to have been, because he had mentioned the map, and Ace hadn't laid eyes on either the map or Mr. Leland Gaunt until this morning. The old buzzard must have taken a plane down while he, Ace, was driving. But why? What the fuck did it all mean?

He *hasn't* been here, he thought. I don't care if it's impossible or not—he *hasn't* been here. Look at that goddam tape recorder, for instance. *Nobody* uses tape recorders like that anymore. And look at the dust on the reels. The note was dusty, too. This set-up has been waiting for you a long time. Maybe it's been sitting here and catching dust ever since Pangborn sent you to Shawshank.

Oh, but that was crazy.

That was just bullshit.

Nevertheless, there was a deep core-part of him that believed it was true. Mr. Gaunt hadn't been anywhere near Boston this afternoon. Mr. Gaunt had spent the afternoon in Castle Rock—Ace knew it—standing by his window, watching the passersby, perhaps even removing the

CLOSED COLUMBUS DAY

sign every now and then and putting up

OPEN

in its place. If he saw the right person approaching, that was— the sort of person with whom a fellow like Mr. Gaunt might want to do a spot of business.

Just what *was* his business?

Ace wasn't sure he wanted to know. But he wanted to know what was in those crates. If he was going to transport them from here all the way back to Castle Rock, he had a goddam *right* to know.

He pushed the STOP button on the tape recorder and lifted it aside. He took a hammer from the tools on top of the worktable and the crowbar which leaned against the wall next to it. He returned to the crates and slid the crowbar's flat end under the wooden lid of the one on top. He levered it up. The nails let go with a thin shriek. The contents of the crate were covered with a heavy oilcloth square. He lifted it aside and simply gaped at what he saw beneath.

Blasting caps.

Dozens of blasting caps.

Maybe *hundreds* of blasting caps, each resting in its own cozy little nest of excelsior.

Jesus Christ, what's he planning to do? Start World War III?

Heart thumping heavily in his chest, Ace hammered the nails back down and lifted the crate of blasting caps aside. He opened the second crate, expecting to see neat rows of fat red sticks that looked like road-flares.

But it wasn't dynamite. It was guns.

There were maybe two dozen in all—high-powered automatic pistols. The smell of the deep grease in which they had been packed drifted up to him. He didn't know what kind they were—German, maybe—but he knew what they meant: twenty-to-life if he was caught with them in Massachusetts. The Commonwealth took an extremely dim view of guns, especially automatic weapons.

This case he set aside without putting the lid back on. He opened the third crate. It was full of ammo clips for the pistols.

Ace stepped back, rubbing his mouth nervously with the palm of his left hand.

Blasting caps.

Automatic handguns.

Ammunition.

This was merchandise?

"Not me," Ace said in a low voice, shaking his head. "Not this kid. Uh-uh, no way."

Mexico City was looking better and better. Maybe even Rio. Ace didn't know if Gaunt was building a better mousetrap or a better electric chair, but he did know he wanted no part of it, whatever it was. He was leaving, and he was leaving right now.

His eyes fixed on the crate of automatic pistols.

And I'm taking one of those babies with me, he thought. A little something for my trouble. Call it a souvenir.

He started toward the crate, and at that instant the reels of the tape recorder began to turn again, although none of the buttons had been depressed.

"Don't even think about it, Ace," the voice of Mr. Gaunt advised coldly, and Ace screamed. "You don't want to fuck with me. What I do to you if you even try will make what the Corson Brothers were planning look like a day in the country. You're my boy now. Stick with me and we'll have fun. Stick with me and you'll get back at everyone in Castle Rock who ever did the nasty to you . . . and you'll leave a rich man. Go against me and you'll never stop screaming."

The tape recorder stopped.

Ace's bulging eyes followed its power cord to the plug. It lay on the floor, covered with a fine spill of dust.

Besides, there wasn't an outlet in sight.

4

Ace suddenly began to feel a little calmer, and this was not quite so odd as it might have seemed. There were two reasons for the steadying of his emotional barometer.

The first was that Ace was a kind of throwback. He would have been perfectly at home living in a cave and dragging his woman around by the hair when he wasn't busy throwing rocks at his enemies. He was the sort of man whose response is only completely predictable when he is confronted with superior strength and authority. Confrontations of this kind didn't happen often, but when they did, he bowed to the superior force almost at once. Although he did not know it, it was this characteristic which had kept him from simply running away from the Flying Corson Brothers in the first place. In men like Ace Merrill, the only urge stronger than the urge to dominate is the deep need to roll over and humbly expose the undefended neck when the real leader of the pack puts in an appearance.

The second reason was even simpler: he chose to believe he

was dreaming. There was some part of him which knew this wasn't true, but the idea was still easier to believe than the evidence of his senses; he didn't even want to *consider* a world which might admit the presence of a Mr. Gaunt. It would be easier—safer—to just close down his thinking processes for a while and march along to the conclusion of this business. If he did that, he might eventually wake up to the world he had always known. God knew that world had its dangers, but at least he understood it.

He hammered the tops back onto the crate of pistols and the crate of ammo. Then he went over to the stored automobile and grasped the canvas tarpaulin, which was also covered with a mantle of dust. He pulled it off . . . and for a moment he forgot everything else in wonder and delight.

It was a Tucker, all right, and it was beautiful.

The paint was canary yellow. The streamlined body gleamed with chrome along the sides and beneath the notched front bumper. A third headlight stared from the center of the hood, below a silver ornament that looked like the engine of a futuristic express train.

Ace walked slowly around it, trying to eat it up with his eyes.

There was a pair of chromed grilles on either side of the back deck; he had no idea what they were for. The fat Goodyear whitewalls were so clean they almost glowed under the hanging lights. Written in flowing chrome script across the back deck were the words "Tucker Talisman." Ace had never heard of such a model. He had thought the Torpedo was the only car Preston Tucker had ever turned out.

You have another problem, old buddy—there are no license plates on this thing. Are you going to try getting all the way back to Maine in a car that sticks out like a sore thumb, a car with no plates, a car loaded with guns and explosive devices?

Yes. He was. It was a bad idea, of course, a really bad idea . . . but the alternative—which would involve trying to fuck over

Mr. Leland Gaunt—seemed *so* much worse. Besides, this was a *dream*.

He shook the keys out of the envelope, went around to the trunk, and hunted in vain for a keyhole. After a few moments he remembered the movie with Jeff Bridges and understood. Like the German VW Beetle and the Chevy Corvair, the Tucker's *engine* was back here. The trunk was up front.

Sure enough, he found the keyhole directly under that weird third headlight. He opened the trunk. It was indeed very cozy, and empty except for a single object. It was a small bottle of white dust with a spoon attached to the cap by a chain. A small piece of paper had been taped to the chain. Ace pulled it free and read the message which had been written there in teeny capital letters:

Ace followed orders.

5

Feeling much better with a little of Mr. Gaunt's incomparable blow lighting up his brain like the front of Henry Beaufort's Rock-Ola, Ace loaded the guns and the clips of ammo into the trunk. He put the crate of blasting caps into the back seat, pausing for just a moment to inhale deeply. The sedan had that incomparable new-car smell, nothing like it in the world (except maybe for pussy), and when he got behind the wheel, he saw that it *was* brand new: the odometer of Mr. Gaunt's Tucker Talisman was set at 00000.0.

Ace pushed the ignition key into the slot and turned it.

The Talisman started up with a low, throaty, delightful rumble. How many horses under the hood? He didn't know, but it felt like a whole herd of them. There had been lots of automotive books in prison, and Ace had read most of them. The Tucker Torpedo had been a flathead six, about three hundred and fifty cubic inches, a lot like the cars Mr. Ford had built between 1948 and 1952. It had had something like a hundred and fifty horses under the hood.

This one felt bigger. A *lot* bigger.

Ace felt an urge to get out, go around back, and see if he could worry the hood open . . . but it was like thinking too much about that crazy name—Yog-whatever. Somehow it seemed like a bad idea. What seemed like a *good* idea was to get this thing back to Castle Rock just as fast as he could.

He started to get out of the car to use the door control, then honked the horn instead, just to see if anything would happen. Something did. The door trundled silently up on its rails.

There's a sound sensor around someplace for sure, he told himself, but he no longer believed it. He no longer even cared. He shifted into first and the Talisman throbbed out of the garage. He honked again as he started down the rutty path to the hole in the fence, and in the rearview mirror he saw the garage lights go out and the door start to descend. He also caught a glimpse of his Challenger, standing with its nose to the wall and the crumpled tarp on the floor beside it. He had an odd feeling that he was never going to see it again. Ace found he didn't care about that, either.

6

The Talisman not only ran like a dream, it seemed to know its own way back to Storrow Drive and the turnpike north. Every now and then the turnblinkers went on by themselves. When this happened, Ace simply made the next turn. In no time at all the creepy little Cambridge slum where he had found the Tucker was behind him, and the shape of the Tobin Bridge, more familiarly known as the Mystic River Bridge, was looming in front of him, a black gantry against the darkening sky.

Ace pulled the light-switch, and a sharply defined fan of radiance at once sprang out before him. When he turned the wheel, the fan of light turned with it. That center headlight was a hell of a rig. No wonder they drove the poor bastard who thought this car up out of business, Ace thought.

He was about thirty miles north of Boston when he noticed the needle of the fuel gauge was sitting on the peg beyond E. He pulled off at the nearest exit and cruised Mr. Gaunt's ride to a stop at the pumps of a Mobil station which stood at the ramp's foot. The pump jockey pushed his cap back on his head with one greasy thumb and walked around the car admiringly. "Nice car!" he said. "Where'd you get it?"

Without thinking, Ace said, "The Plains of Leng. Yog-Sothoth Vintage Motors."

"Huh?"

"Just fill it up, son—this isn't Twenty Questions."

"Oh!" the pump jockey said, taking a second look at Ace and becoming obsequious at once. "Sure! You bet!"

And he tried, but the pump clicked off after running just fourteen cents into the tank. The pump jockey tried to squeeze more in by running the pump manually, but the gas only slopped out, running down the Talisman's gleaming yellow flank and dripping onto the tarmac.

"I guess it doesn't need gas," the jockey said timidly.

"Guess not."

"Maybe your fuel gauge is bust—"

"Wipe that gas off the side of my car. You want the paint to blister? What's the matter with you?"

The kid sprang to do it, and Ace went into the bathroom to help his nose a little. When he came out, the pump jockey was standing at a respectful distance from the Talisman, twisting his rag nervously in both hands.

He's scared, Ace thought. Scared of what? Me?

No; the kid in the Mobil coverall barely glanced in Ace's direction. It was the Tucker that kept drawing his gaze.

He tried to touch it, Ace thought.

The revelation—and that was what it was, exactly what it was—brought a grim little smile to the corners of his mouth.

He tried to touch it and something happened. What it was don't really matter. It taught him that he can look but he better not touch, and that's all that *does* matter.

"Won't be no charge," the pump jockey said.

"You got *that* right." Ace slid behind the wheel and got rolling in a hurry. He had a brand-new idea about the Talisman. In a way it was a scary idea, but in another way it was a really *great* idea. He thought that maybe the gas gauge always read empty . . . and that the tank was always full.

7

The toll-gates for passenger cars in New Hampshire are the automated kind; you throw a buck's worth of change (No Pennies Please) into the basket, the red light turns green, and you go. Except when Ace rolled the Tucker Talisman up to the basket jutting out from the post, the light turned green on its own and the little sign shone out:

TOLL PAID, THANK U.

"Betcha *fur*," Ace muttered, and drove on toward Maine.

By the time he left Portland behind, he had the Talisman cruising along at just over eighty miles an hour, and there was plenty left under the hood. Just past the Falmouth exit, he topped a rise and saw a State Police cruiser lurking beside the highway. The distinctive torpedo-shape of a radar gun jutted from the driver's window. *Uh-oh,* Ace thought. *He got me. Dead-bang. Jesus Christ, why was I speeding anyway, with all the shit I'm carrying?*

But he knew why, and it wasn't the coke he had snorted. Maybe on another occasion, but not this time. It was the Talisman. It *wanted* to go fast. He would look at the speedometer, ease his foot off the go-pedal a little . . . and five minutes later he would realize he had it three quarters of the way to the floor again.

He waited for the cruiser to come alive in a blaze of pulsing blue lights and rip out after him, but it didn't happen. Ace blipped past at eighty, and the State Bear never made a move.

Hell, he must have been cooping.

But Ace knew better. When you saw a radar gun poking out of the window, you knew the guy inside was wide awake and hot to trot. No, what had happened was this: the State cop hadn't been able to see the Talisman. It sounded crazy, but it felt exactly right. The big yellow car with its three headlights screaming out of the front was invisible to both high-tech hardware and the cops that used it.

Grinning, Ace walked Mr. Gaunt's Tucker Talisman up to a hundred and ten. He arrived back in The Rock at quarter past eight, with almost four hours to spare.

8

Mr. Gaunt emerged from his shop and stood beneath the canopy to watch Ace baby the Talisman into one of the three slant parking spaces in front of Needful Things.

"You made good time, Ace."

"Yeah. This is some car."

"Bet your fur," Mr. Gaunt said. He ran a hand along the Tucker's smoothly sloping front deck. "One of a kind. You have brought my merchandise, I take it?"

"Yeah. Mr. Gaunt, I got some idea of just how special this car of yours is on the way back, but I think you still might consider getting some license plates for it, and maybe an inspection stick—"

"They are not necessary," Mr. Gaunt said indifferently. "Park it in the alley behind the shop, Ace, if you please. I'll take care of it later."

"How? Where?" Ace found himself suddenly reluctant to turn the car over to Mr. Gaunt. It was not just that he'd left his own car in Boston and needed wheels for his night's work; the Talisman made every other car he had ever driven, including the Challenger, seem like street-trash.

"That," said Mr. Gaunt, "is my business." He looked at Ace imperturbably. "You'll find that things go more smoothly for you, Ace, if you look at working for me the way you would look at serving in the Army. There are three ways of doing things for you now—the right way, the wrong way, and Mr. Gaunt's way. If you always opt for the third choice, trouble will never find you. Do you understand me?"

"Yeah. Yeah, I do."

"That's fine. Now drive around to the back door."

Ace piloted the yellow car around the corner and drove slowly up the narrow alley which ran behind the business buildings on the west side of Main Street. The rear door of Needful Things was open. Mr. Gaunt stood in a slanted ob-long of yellow light, waiting. He made no effort to help as Ace carried the crates into the shop's back room, puffing with the effort. He did not know it, but a good many customers would have been surprised if they had seen that room. They had heard Mr. Gaunt back there behind the hanging velvet drape which divided the shop from the storage area, shifting goods, moving boxes around . . . but there was nothing at all in the room until Ace stacked the crates in one corner at Mr. Gaunt's direction.

Yes—there was one thing. On the far side of the room, a brown Norway rat was lying beneath the sprung arm of a large Victory rat-trap. Its neck was broken, its front teeth exposed in a dead snarl.

"Good job," Mr. Gaunt said, rubbing his long-fingered hands together and smiling. "This has been a good evening's work, all told. You have performed to the top of my expectations, Ace—the very top."

"Thanks, sir." Ace was astounded. He had never in his life called any man sir until this moment.

"Here's a little something for your trouble." Mr. Gaunt handed Ace a brown envelope. Ace pressed at it with the tips of his fingers and felt the loose grit of powder inside. "I believe you will want to do some investigating tonight, won't you? This might give you a little extra go-power, as the old Esso ads used to say."

Ace started. "Oh, shit! *Shit!* I left that book—the book with the map in it—in my car! It's back in Boston! God *damn* it!" He made a fist and slammed it against his thigh.

Mr. Gaunt was smiling. "I don't think so," he said. "I think it's in the Tucker."

"No, I—"

"Why not check for yourself?"

So Ace did, and of course the book was there, sitting on the dashboard with its spine pressing against the Tucker's patented pop-out windshield. *Lost and Buried Treasures of New England.* He took it and thumbed it. The map was still inside. He looked at Mr. Gaunt with dumb gratitude.

"I won't require your services again until tomorrow evening, around this same time," Mr. Gaunt said. "I suggest you spend the daylight hours at your place in Mechanic Falls. That should suit you well enough; I believe you'll want to sleep late. You still have a busy night ahead of you, if I am not mistaken."

Ace thought of the little crosses on the map and nodded.

"And," Mr. Gaunt added, "it might be prudent for you to avoid the notice of Sheriff Pangborn for the next day or two. After that, I don't think it will matter." His lips pulled back; his teeth sprang forward in large, predatory clumps. "By the end of the week, I think a lot of things which heretofore mattered a great deal to the citizens of this town are going to cease to matter at all. Don't you think so, Ace?"

"If you say so," Ace replied. He was falling into that strange, dazed state again, and he didn't mind at all. "I don't know how I'm going to get around, though."

"All taken care of," Mr. Gaunt said. "You'll find a car parked out front with the keys in the ignition. A company car, so to speak. I'm afraid it's only a Chevrolet—a perfectly *ordinary* Chevrolet—but it will provide you with reliable, unobtrusive transportation, just the same. You'll enjoy the TV newsvan more, of course, but—"

"Newsvan? What newsvan?"

Mr. Gaunt elected not to answer. "But the Chevrolet will meet all your current transportation needs, I assure you. Just don't try to run any State Police speed-traps in it. I'm afraid that wouldn't do. Not with this vehicle. Not at all."

Ace heard himself say: "I sure would like to have a car like your Tucker, Mr. Gaunt, sir. It's great."

"Well, perhaps we can do a deal. You see, Ace, I have a very simple business policy. Would you like to know what it is?"

"Sure." And Ace was sincere.

"Everything is for sale. That's my philosophy. Everything is for sale."

"Everything's for sale," Ace said dreamily. "Wow! Heavy!"

"Right! Heavy! Now, Ace, I believe I'll have a bite to eat. I've just been too busy to do it, holiday or no holiday. I'd ask you to join me, but—"

"Gee, I really can't."

"No, of course not. You have places to go and holes to dig, don't you? I'll expect you tomorrow night, between eight and nine."

"Between eight and nine."

"Yes. After dark."

"When nobody knows and nobody sees," Ace said dreamily.

"Got it in one! Goodnight, Ace."

Mr. Gaunt held out his hand. Ace began to reach for it . . . and then saw there was already something in it. It was the brown rat from the trap in the storeroom. Ace pulled back with a little grunt of disgust. He hadn't the slightest idea when Mr. Gaunt had picked up the dead rat. Or perhaps it was a different one?

Ace decided he didn't care, one way or another. All he knew was that he had no plans to shake hands with a dead rat, no matter how cool a dude Mr. Gaunt was.

Smiling, Mr. Gaunt said: "Excuse me. Every year I grow a little more forgetful. I believe I just tried to give you my dinner, Ace!"

"Dinner," Ace said in a faint little voice.

"Yes indeed." A thick yellow thumbnail plunged into the white fur which covered the rat's belly; a moment later, its intestines were oozing into Mr. Gaunt's unmarked palm. Before Ace could see more, Mr. Gaunt had turned away and was pulling the alley door closed. "Now, where did I put that cheese—?"

There was a heavy metallic *snick!* as the lock engaged.

Ace leaned over, sure he was going to vomit between his shoes. His stomach clenched, his gorge rose . . . and then sank back again.

Because he hadn't seen what he thought he'd seen. "It was a joke," he muttered. "He had a rubber rat in his coat pocket, or something. It was just a joke."

Was it? What about the intestines, then? And the cold, jelly-like mung which had surrounded them? What about that?

You're just tired, he thought. You imagined it, that's all. It was a rubber rat. As for the rest . . . poof.

But for a moment everything—the deserted garage, the self-directed Tucker, even that ominous piece of graffiti, YOG-SOTHOTH RULES—tried to cram in on him, and a powerful voice yelled: Get out of here! Get out while there's still time!

But that was the *really* crazy thought. There was money waiting for him out there in the night. Maybe a lot of it. Maybe a son-of-a-bitching *fortune*.

Ace stood in the darkness for a few minutes like a robot with a flat power-pack. Little by little some sense of reality—some sense of *himself*—returned, and he decided the rat didn't matter. Neither did the Tucker Talisman. The blow mattered, and the map mattered, and he had an idea that Mr. Gaunt's very simple business policy mattered, but nothing else. He couldn't *let* anything else matter.

He walked down the alley and around the corner to the front of Needful Things. The shop was closed and dark, like all the shops on Lower Main Street. A Chevy Celebrity was parked in one of the slant spaces in front of Mr. Gaunt's shop, just as promised. Ace tried to remember if it had been there when he arrived with the Talisman, and really couldn't do it. Every time he tried to cast his mind back to any memories before the last few minutes, it ran into a roadblock; he saw himself moving to accept Mr. Gaunt's offered hand, most natural thing in the world, and suddenly realizing that Mr. Gaunt was holding a large dead rat.

I believe I'll have a bite to eat. I'd ask you to join me, but—

Well, it was just something else that didn't matter. The Chevy was here now, and that was all that did. Ace opened the door, put the book with the precious map inside it on the seat, then pulled the keys out of the ignition. He went around to the back of the car and opened the trunk. He had a good idea of what he would find, and he wasn't disappointed. A pick and a short-handled spade were neatly crossed over each other in an X. Ace looked more closely and saw Mr. Gaunt had even put in a pair of heavy work gloves.

"Mr. Gaunt, you think of everything," he said, and slammed the trunk. As he did, he saw there was a sticker on the Celebrity's rear bumper, and he bent closer to read it:

I ♥ ANTIQUES

Ace began to laugh. He was still laughing as he drove across the Tin Bridge and headed toward the old Treblehorn place, which he intended to make the site of his first dig. As he drove up Panderly's Hill on the other side of the bridge, he passed a convertible headed in the other direction, toward town. The convertible was filled with young men. They were singing "What a Friend We Have in Jesus" at the top of their voices, and in perfect one-part Baptist harmony.

9

One of those young men was Lester Ivanhoe Pratt. Following the touch-football game, he and a bunch of the guys had driven up to Lake Auburn, about twenty-five miles away. There was a week-long tent revival going on up there, and Vic Tremayne had said there would be a special five o'clock Columbus Day prayer-meeting and hymn-sing. Since Sally had Lester's car and they'd made no plans for the evening—no movie, no dinner out at McDonald's in South Paris—he'd gone along with Vic and the other guys, good Christian fellows every one.

He knew, of course, why the other guys were so eager to make the trip, and the reason wasn't religion—not *entirely* religion, anyway. There were always lots of pretty girls at the tent revivals which crisscrossed northern New England between May and the last state fair ox-pull at the end of October, and a good hymn-sing (not to mention a mess of hot preaching and a dose of that oldtime Jesus spirit) always put them in a merry, eager mood.

Lester, who had a girl, looked upon the plans and schemes of his friends with the indulgence an old married man might show for the antics of a bunch of young bucks. He went along mostly to be friendly, and because he always liked to listen to some good preaching and do some singing after an exhilarating afternoon of head-knocking and body-blocking. It was the best way of cooling down he knew.

It had been a good meeting, but an awful lot of people had

wanted to be saved at the end of it. As a result, it had gone on a little longer than Lester would have wished. He had been planning to call Sally and ask her if she wanted to go out to Weeksie's for an ice-cream soda or something. Girls liked to do things like that on the spur of the moment sometimes, he had noticed.

They crossed the Tin Bridge, and Vic let him out on the corner of Main and Watermill.

"Great game, Les!" Bill MacFarland called from the back seat.

"Sure was!" Lester called back cheerily. "Let's do it again Saturday—maybe I can break your arm instead of just spraining it!"

The four young men in Vic's car roared heartily at this piece of wit and then Vic drove away. The sound of "Jesus Is a Friend Forever" drifted back on air which was still strangely summery. You expected a chill to creep into it even during the warmest spells of Indian summer weather after the sun went down. Not tonight, though.

Lester walked slowly up the hill toward home, feeling tired and sore and utterly contented. Every day was a fine day when you'd given your heart to Jesus, but some days were finer than others. This had been one of the finest kind, and all he wanted right now was to shower up, call Sally, and then jump into bed.

He was looking up at the stars, trying to make out the constellation Orion, when he turned into his driveway. As a result he ran balls-first, and at a brisk walking pace, into the rear end of his Mustang.

"*Oooof!*" Lester Pratt cried. He backed up, bent over, and clasped his wounded testicles. After a few moments, he managed to raise his head and look at his car through eyes which were watering with pain. What the heck was his car doing here, anyway? Sally's Honda wasn't supposed to be out of the shop until at least Wednesday—probably Thursday or Friday, with the holiday and all.

Then, in a burst of bright pink-orange light, it came to

him. Sally was inside! She had come over while he was out, and now she was waiting for him! Maybe she had decided that tonight was *the* night! Premarital sex was wrong, of course, but sometimes you had to break a few eggs in order to make an omelette. And he was certainly up to the task of atoning for that particular sin if she was.

"Rooty-toot-toot!" cried Lester Pratt enthusiastically. "Sweet little Sally in her birthday suit!"

He ran for the porch in a crabby little strut, still clutching his throbbing balls. Now, however, they were throbbing with anticipation as well as pain. He took the key from beneath the doormat and let himself in.

"Sally?" he called. "Sal, are you here? Sorry I'm late—I went over to the Lake Auburn revival meeting with some of the guys, and . . ."

He trailed off. There was no response, and that meant she wasn't here, after all. Unless . . . !

He hurried upstairs as fast as he could, suddenly sure he would find her asleep in his bed. She would open her eyes and sit up, the sheet falling away from her lovely breasts (which he had felt—well, sort of—but never actually seen); she would hold her arms out to him, those lovely, sleepy, cornflower-blue eyes opening wide, and by the time the clock struck ten, they would be virgins no longer. Rooty-toot!

But the bedroom was as empty as the kitchen and living room had been. The sheets and blankets were on the floor, as they almost always were; Lester was one of those fellows so full of energy and the holy spirit that he could not simply sit up and get out of bed in the morning; he *bounded* up, eager not just to meet the day but to blitz it, knock it to the greensward, and force it to cough up the ball.

Now, however, he walked downstairs with a frown creasing his wide, ingenuous face. The car was here, but Sally wasn't. What did that mean? He didn't know, but he didn't much like it.

He flipped on the porch light and went out to look in the car; maybe she had left him a note. He got as far as the head of the porch steps, then froze. There was a note, all right. It had been written across the Mustang's windshield in hot-pink spray-paint, probably from his own garage. The big capital letters glared at him:

GO TO HELL YOU CHEATING BASTARD

Lester stood on the top porch step for a long time, reading this message from his fiancée over and over and over again. The prayer-meeting? Was that it? Did she think he'd gone over to the prayer-meeting in Lake Auburn to meet some floozy? In his distress, it was the only idea that made any sense to him at all.

He went inside and called Sally's house. He let the phone ring two dozen times, but no one answered.

10

Sally knew he would call, and so she had asked Irene Lutjens if she could spend the night at Irene's place. Irene, all but bursting with curiosity, said yes, sure, of course. Sally was so distressed about *something* that she hardly looked pretty at all. Irene could hardly believe it, but it was true.

For her own part, Sally had no intention of telling Irene or anyone else what had happened. It was too awful, too shameful. She would carry it with her to the grave. So she refused to answer Irene's questions for over half an hour. Then the whole story came pouring out of her in a hot flood of tears. Irene held her and listened, her eyes growing big and round.

"That's all right," Irene crooned, rocking Sally in her arms. "That's all right, Sally—Jesus loves you, even if that son of a bitch doesn't. So do I. So does Reverend Rose. And you certainly gave the musclebound creep something to remember you by, didn't you?"

Sally nodded, sniffling, and the other girl stroked her hair and made soothing sounds. Irene could hardly wait until tomorrow, when she could start calling her other girlfriends. They wouldn't *believe* it! Irene felt sorry for Sally, she really did, but she was also sort of glad this had happened. Sally was so *pretty,* and Sally was so darned *holy.* It was sort of nice to see her crash and burn, just this once.

And Lester's the best-looking guy in church. If he and Sally really *do* break up, I wonder if he might not ask me out? He looks at me sometimes like he's wondering what kind of underwear I've got on, so I guess it's not impossible . . .

"I feel so horrible!" Sally wept. "So *d-d-dirty!*"

"Of *course* you do," Irene said, continuing to rock her and stroke her hair. "You don't still have the letter and that picture, do you?"

"I b-b-burned them!" Sally cried loudly against Irene's damp bosom, and then a fresh storm of grief and loss carried her away.

"Of course you did," Irene murmured. "It's just what you *should* have done." Still, she thought, you could have waited until I had at least one look, you wimpy thing.

Sally spent the night in Irene's guest-room, but she hardly slept at all. Her weeping passed eventually, and she spent most of that night staring dry-eyed into the dark, gripped by those dark and bitterly satisfying fantasies of revenge which only a jilted and previously complacent lover can fully entertain.

CHAPTER FIFTEEN

1

Mr. Gaunt's first "by appointment only" customer arrived promptly at eight o'clock on Tuesday morning. This was Lucille Dunham, one of the waitresses at Nan's Luncheonette. Lucille had been struck by a deep, hopeless aching at the sight of the black pearls in one of the display cases of Needful Things. She knew she could never hope to buy such an expensive item, never in a million years. Not on the salary that skinflint Nan Roberts paid her. All the same, when Mr. Gaunt suggested that they talk about it without half the town leaning over their shoulders (so to speak), Lucille had leaped at the offer the way a hungry fish might leap at a sparkling lure.

She left Needful Things at eight-twenty, an expression of dazed, dreaming happiness on her face. She had purchased the black pearls for the unbelievable price of thirty-eight dollars and fifty cents. She had also promised to play a little prank, perfectly harmless, on that stuffed-shirt Baptist minister William Rose. That wouldn't be work, as far as Lucille was concerned; it would be pure pleasure. The Bible-quoting stinker had never once left her a tip, not even so much as one thin dime. Lucille (a good Methodist who didn't in the slightest mind shaking her tail to a hot boogie beat on Saturday night) had heard of storing up your reward in heaven; she wondered if Rev. Rose had heard that it was more blessed to give than to receive.

Well, she would pay him back a little . . . and it was really quite harmless. Mr. Gaunt had told her so.

That gentleman watched her go with a pleasant smile on his face. He had an extremely busy day planned, *extremely* busy, with appointments every half hour or so and lots of telephone calls to make. The carnival was well established: one major attraction had been tested successfully; the time to start up all the rides at once was now near at hand. As always when he reached this point, whether in Lebanon, Ankara, the western provinces of Canada, or right here in Hicksville, U.S.A., he felt there were just not enough hours in the day. Yet one bent every effort toward one's goal, for busy hands were happy hands, and to strive was in itself noble, and . . .

. . . and if his old eyes did not deceive him, the day's second customer, Yvette Gendron, was hurrying up the sidewalk toward the canopy right now.

"Busy, busy, busy day," Mr. Gaunt murmured, and fixed a large, welcoming smile on his face.

2

Alan Pangborn arrived at his own office at eight-thirty, and there was already a message slip taped to the side of his phone. Henry Payton of the State Police had called at seven-forty-five. He wanted Alan to return the call ASAP. Alan settled into his chair, placed the telephone between his ear and his shoulder, and hit the button which auto-dialed the Oxford Barracks. From the top drawer of his desk he took four silver dollars.

"Hello, Alan," Henry said. "I'm afraid I've got some bad news about your double murder."

"Oh, so all at once it's *my* double murder," Alan said. He closed his fist around the four cartwheels, squeezed, and opened his hand again. Now there were three. He leaned back in his chair and cocked his feet up on his desk. "It really must be bad news."

"You don't sound surprised."

"Nope." He squeezed his fist shut again and used his pinky finger to "force" the lowest silver dollar in the stack. This was an operation of some delicacy . . . but Alan was more than equal to the challenge. The silver dollar slipped from his fist and tumbled down his sleeve. There was a quiet *chink!* sound as it struck the first one, a sound that would be covered by the magician's patter in an actual performance. Alan opened his hand again, and now there were only two cartwheels.

"Maybe you wouldn't mind telling me why not," Henry said. He sounded slightly testy.

"Well, I've spent most of the last two days thinking about it," Alan said. Even this was an understatement. From the moment on Sunday afternoon when he had first seen that Nettie Cobb was one of the two women lying dead at the foot of the stop-sign, he had thought of little else. He even dreamed about it, and the feeling that all the numbers added up short had become a nagging certainty. This made Henry's call not an annoyance but a relief, and saved Alan the trouble of calling him.

He squeezed the two silver dollars in his hand.

Chink.

Opened his hand. Now there was one.

"What bothers you?" Henry asked.

"Everything," Alan said flatly. "Starting with the fact that it happened at all. I suppose the thing that itches the worst is the way the time-table of the crime works . . . or *doesn't* work. I keep trying to see Nettie Cobb finding her dog dead and then sitting down to write all those notes. And do you know what? I keep not being able to do it. And every time I can't do it, I wonder how much of this stupid goddam business I'm not seeing."

Alan squeezed his fist viciously shut, opened it, and then there were none.

"Uh-huh. So maybe my bad news is your good news. Someone else was involved, Alan. We don't know who killed the

Cobb woman's dog, but we can be almost positive that it wasn't Wilma Jerzyck."

Alan's feet came off the desk in a hurry. The cartwheels slid out of his sleeve and hit the top of his desk in a little silver runnel. One of them came down on edge and rolled for the side of the desk. Alan's hand flicked out, spooky-quick, and snatched it back before it could get away. "I think you better tell me what you got, Henry."

"Uh-huh. Let's start with the dog. The body was turned over to John Palin, a D.V.M. in South Portland. He is to animals what Henry Ryan is to people. He says that because the corkscrew penetrated the dog's heart and it died almost instantly, he can give us a fairly restricted time of death."

"*That's* a nice change," Alan said. He was thinking of the Agatha Christie novels which Annie had read by the dozen. In those, it seemed there was always some doddering village doctor who was more than willing to set the time of death as between 4:30 p.m. and quarter past five. After almost twenty years as a law-enforcement officer, Alan knew a more realistic response to the time-of-death question was "Sometime last week. Maybe."

"It is, isn't it? Anyway, this Dr. Palin says the dog died between ten o'clock and noon. Peter Jerzyck says that when he came into the master bedroom to get ready for church—*at a little past ten*—his wife was in the shower."

"Yes, we knew it was tight," Alan said. He was a little disappointed. "But this guy Palin must allow for a margin of error, unless he's God. Fifteen minutes is all it takes to make Wilma look good for it."

"Yeah? How good does she look to you, Alan?"

He considered the question, then said heavily: "To tell you the truth, old buddy, she doesn't look that good. She never did." Alan forced himself to add: "Just the same, we'd look pretty silly keeping this case open on the basis of some dog-doctor's report and a gap of—what?—fifteen minutes?"

"Okay, let's talk about the note on the corkscrew. You re-member the note?"

" 'Nobody slings mud at my clean sheets. I told you I'd get you.' "

"The very one. The handwriting expert in Augusta is still mooning over it, but Peter Jerzyck provided us with a sample of his wife's handwriting, and I've got Xerox copies of both the note and the sample on the desk in front of me. They don't match. No *way* do they match."

"The hell you say!"

"The hell I don't. I thought you were the guy who wasn't surprised."

"I knew something was wrong, but it's been those rocks with the notes on them that I haven't been able to get out of my mind. The time sequence is screwy, and that's made me un-comfortable, yeah, but on the whole I guess I was willing to sit still for it. Mostly because it seems like such a Wilma Jerzyck thing to do. You're sure she didn't disguise her handwriting?" He didn't believe it—the idea of travelling incognito had never been Wilma Jerzyck's style—but it was a possibility that had to be covered.

"Me? I'm positive. But I'm not the expert, and what I think won't stand up in court. That's why the note's in graphanalysis."

"When will the handwriting guy file his report?"

"Who knows? Meantime, take my word for it, Alan—they're apples and oranges. Nothing alike."

"Well, if Wilma didn't do it, someone sure wanted Nettie to *believe* she did. Who? And why? *Why,* for God's sake?"

"I dunno, scout—it's your town. In the meantime, I have two more things for you."

"Shoot." Alan put the silver dollars back into his drawer, then made a tall, skinny man in a top-hat walk across the wall. On the return trip, the top-hat became a cane.

"Whoever killed the dog left a set of bloody finger-prints on the inner knob of Nettie's front door—that's big number one."

"Hot damn!"

"Warm damn at the best, I'm afraid. They're blurry. The perp probably left them grasping the doorknob to go out."

"No good at all?"

"We've got some fragments that *might* be useful, although there isn't much chance that they'd stand up in court. I've sent them to FBI Print-Magic in Virginia. They're doing some pretty amazing reconstructive work on partials these days. They're slower than cold molasses—it'll probably be a week or even ten days before I hear back—but in the meantime, I compared the partials with the Jerzyck woman's prints, which were delivered to me by the ever-thoughtful Medical Examiner's office last evening."

"No match?"

"Well, it's like the handwriting, Alan—it's comparing partials to totals, and if I testified in court on something like that, the defense would chew me a new asshole. But since we're sitting at the bullshit table, so to speak, no—they're nothing alike. There's the question of size, for one thing. Wilma Jerzyck had small hands. The partials came from someone with big hands. Even when you allow for the blurring, they are damned big hands."

"A man's prints?"

"I'm sure of it. But again, it'd never stand up in court."

"Who gives a fuck?" On the wall, a shadow lighthouse suddenly appeared, then turned into a pyramid. The pyramid opened like a flower and became a goose flying through the sunshine. Alan tried to see the face of the man—not Wilma Jerzyck but some *man*—who had gone into Nettie's house after Nettie had left on Sunday morning. The man who had killed Nettie's Raider with a corkscrew and then framed Wilma for it. He looked for a face and saw nothing but shadows. "Henry, who would even *want* to do something like this, if it wasn't Wilma?"

"I don't know. But I think we might have a witness to the rock-throwing incident."

"*What?* Who?"

"I said *might,* remember."

"I know what you said. Don't tease me. Who is it?"

"A kid. The woman who lives next door to the Jerzycks heard noises and came out to try and see what was going on. She said she thought maybe 'that bitch'—her words—had finally gotten mad enough at her husband to throw him out a window. She saw the kid pedaling away from the house, looking scared. She asked him what was going on. He said he thought maybe Mr. and Mrs. Jerzyck were having a fight. Well, that was what *she* thought, too, and since the noises had stopped by then, she didn't think any more about it."

"That must have been Jillian Mislaburski," Alan said. "The house on the other side of the Jerzyck place is empty—up for sale."

"Yeah. Jillian Misla-whatski. That's what I've got here."

"Who was the kid?"

"Dunno. She recognized him but couldn't come up with the name. She says he's from the neighborhood, though—probably from right there on the block. We'll find him."

"How old?"

"She said between eleven and fourteen."

"Henry? Be a pal and let *me* find him. Would you do that?"

"Yep," Henry said at once, and Alan relaxed. "I don't understand why we have to roll these investigations when the crime happens right in the county seat, anyway. They let them fry their own fish in Portland and Bangor, so why not Castle Rock? Christ, I wasn't even sure how to pronounce that woman's *name* until you said it out loud!"

"There are a lot of Poles in The Rock," Alan said absently. He tore a pink Traffic Warning form from the pad on his desk and jotted *Jill Mislaburski* and *Boy, 11–14* on the back.

"If my guys find this kid, he's gonna see three big State Troops and be so scared everything goes out of his head," Henry said. "He probably knows you—don't you go around and talk at the schools?"

"Yes, about the D.A.R.E. program and on Law and Safety Day," Alan said. He was trying to think of families with kids on the block where the Jerzycks and the Mislaburskis lived. If Jill Mislaburski recognized him but didn't know his name, that probably meant the kid lived around the corner, or maybe on Pond Street. Alan wrote three names quickly on the sheet of scrap paper: *DeLois, Rusk, Bellingham.* There were probably other families with boys in the right age-group that he couldn't remember right off the bat, but those three would do for a start. A quick canvass would almost certainly turn the kid up.

"Did Jill know what time she heard the ruckus and saw the boy?" Alan asked.

"She's not sure, but she thinks it was after eleven."

"So it wasn't the Jerzycks fighting, because the Jerzycks were at Mass."

"Right."

"Then it was the rock-thrower."

"Right again."

"This one's *real* weird, Henry."

"That's three in a row. One more and you win the toaster oven."

"I wonder if the kid saw who it was?"

"Ordinarily I'd say 'too good to be true,' but the Mislaburski woman said he looked scared, so maybe he did. If he *did* see the perp, I'll bet you a shot and a beer it wasn't Nettie Cobb. I think somebody played them off against each other, scout, and maybe just for the kick of the thing. Just for that."

But Alan, who knew the town better than Henry ever would, found this fantastical. "Maybe the kid did it himself," he said. "Maybe *that's* why he looked scared. Maybe what we've got here is a simple case of vandalism."

"In a world where there's a Michael Jackson and an asshole like Axl Rose, anything's possible, I suppose," Henry said, "but I'd like the possibility of vandalism a lot better if the kid was sixteen or seventeen, you know?"

"Yes," Alan said.

"And why speculate at all, if you can find the kid? You can, can't you?"

"I'm pretty sure, yeah. But I'd like to wait until school lets out, if that's okay with you. It's like you said—scaring him won't do any good."

"Fine by me; the two ladies aren't going anywhere but into the ground. The reporters are around here, but they're only a nuisance—I swat em like flies."

Alan looked out the window in time to see a newsvan from WMTW-TV go cruising slowly past, probably bound for the main courthouse entrance around the corner.

"Yeah, they're here, too," he said.

"Can you call me by five?"

"By four," Alan said. "Thanks, Henry."

"Don't mention it," Henry Payton said, and hung up.

Alan's first impulse was to go get Norris Ridgewick and tell him all about this—Norris made a hell of a good sounding-board, if nothing else. Then he remembered that Norris was probably parked in the middle of Castle Lake with his new fishing rod in his hand.

He made a few more shadow-animals on the wall, then got up. He felt restless, oddly uneasy. It wouldn't hurt to cruise around the block where the murders had taken place. He might remember a few more families with kids in the right age-brackets if he actually looked at the houses . . . and who knew? Maybe what Henry had said about kids also held true for middle-aged Polish ladies who bought their clothes at Lane Bryant. Jill Mislaburski's memory might improve if the questions were coming from someone with a familiar face.

He started to grab his uniform hat off the top of the coat tree by the door and then left it where it was. It might be better today, he decided, if I only look semi-official. As far as that goes, it wouldn't kill me to take the station wagon.

He left the office and stood in the bullpen for a moment, bemused. John LaPointe had turned his desk and the space around it into something that looked in need of Red Cross flood-relief. Papers were stacked up everywhere. The drawers were nested inside each other, making a Tower of Babel on John's desk-blotter. It looked ready to fall over at any second. And John, ordinarily the most cheerful of police officers, was red-faced and cursing.

"I'm going to wash your mouth out with soap, Johnny," Alan said, grinning.

John jumped, then turned around. He answered Alan with a grin of his own, one which was both shamefaced and distracted. "Sorry, Alan. I—"

Then Alan was moving. He crossed the room with the same liquid, silent speed that had so struck Polly Chalmers on Friday evening. John LaPointe's mouth fell open. Then, from the corner of his eye, he saw what Alan was up to—the two drawers on top of the stack he had made were starting to tumble.

Alan was fast enough to avert an utter disaster, but not fast enough to catch the first drawer. It landed on his feet, scattering papers, paper-clips, and loose bunches of staples everywhere. He pinned the other two against the side of John's desk with his palms.

"Holy Jesus! That was lickety-split, Alan!" John exclaimed.

"Thank you, John," Alan said with a pained smile. The drawers were starting to slip. Pushing harder did no good; it only made the desk start to move. Also, his toes hurt. "Toss all the compliments you want, by all means. But in between, maybe you could take the goddam drawer off my feet."

"Oh! Shit! Right! Right!" John hurried to do it. In his eagerness to remove the drawer, he bumped Alan. Alan lost his tenuous pressure-hold on the two drawers he had caught in time. They also landed on his feet.

"Ouch!" Alan yelled. He started to grab his right foot and then decided the left one hurt worse. *"Bastard!"*

"Holy Jesus, Alan, I'm sorry!"

"What have you got in there?" Alan asked, hopping away with his left foot in his hand. "Half of Castle Land Quarry?"

"I guess it *has* been awhile since I cleaned em out." John smiled guiltily and began stuffing papers and office supplies helter-skelter back into the drawers. His conventionally handsome face was flaming scarlet. He was on his knees, and when he pivoted to get the paper-clips and staples which had gone under Clut's desk, he kicked over a tall stack of forms and reports that he had stacked on the floor. Now the bullpen area of the Sheriff's Office was beginning to resemble a tornado zone.

"Whoops!" John said.

"Whoops," Alan said, sitting on Norris Ridgewick's desk and trying to massage his toes through his heavy black police-issue shoes. "Whoops is good, John. A very accurate description of the situation. This is a whoops if I ever saw one."

"Sorry," John said again, and actually wormed under his desk on his stomach, sweeping errant clips and staples toward him with the sides of his hands. Alan was not sure if he should laugh or cry. John's feet were wagging back and forth as he moved his hands, spreading the papers on the floor widely and evenly.

"John, get out of there!" Alan yelled. He was trying hard not to laugh, but he could tell already it was going to be a lost cause.

LaPointe jerked. His head bonked briskly against the underside of his desk. And another stack of papers, one which had been deposited on the very edge of gravity to make room for the drawers, fell over the side. Most floomped straight to the floor, but dozens went seesawing lazily back and forth through the air.

He's gonna be filing those all day, Alan thought resignedly. Maybe all week.

Then he could hold on no longer. He threw back his head and bellowed laughter. Andy Clutterbuck, who had been in the dispatcher's office, came out to see what was going on.

"Sheriff?" he asked. "Everything okay?"

"Yeah," Alan said. Then he looked at the reports and forms, scattered hell to breakfast, and began to laugh again. "John's doing a little creative paperwork here, that's all."

John crawled out from under his desk and stood up. He looked like a man who wishes mightily that someone would ask him to stand at attention, or maybe hit the deck and do forty pushups. The front of his previously immaculate uniform was covered with dust, and in spite of his amusement, Alan made a mental note—it had been a long time since Eddie Warburton had taken care of the floor under these bullpen desks. Then he began laughing again. There was simply no help for it. Clut looked from John to Alan and then back to John again, puzzled.

"Okay," Alan said, getting himself under control at last. "What were you looking for, John? The Holy Grail? The Lost Chord? What?"

"My wallet," John said, brushing ineffectually at the front of his uniform. "I can't find my goddam wallet."

"Did you check your car?"

"Both of them," John said. He passed a disgusted glance over the asteroid belt of junk around his desk. "The cruiser I was driving last night and my Pontiac. But sometimes when I'm here I stick it in a desk drawer because it makes a lump against my butt when I sit down. So I was checking—"

"It wouldn't bust your ass like that if you didn't keep your whole goddam life in there, John," Andy Clutterbuck said reasonably.

"Clut," Alan said, "go play in the traffic, would you?"

"Huh?"

Alan rolled his eyes. "Go find something to do. I think John and I can handle this; we're trained investigators. If it turns out we can't, we'll let you know."

"Oh, sure. Just trying to help, you know. I've seen his wallet. It looks like he's got the whole Library of Congress in there. In fact—"

"Thanks for your input, Clut. We'll see you."

"Okay," Clut said. "Always glad to help. Later, dudes."

Alan rolled his eyes. He felt like laughing again, but controlled himself. It was clear from John's unhappy expression that it was no joke to him. He was embarrassed, but that was only part of it. Alan had lost a wallet or two in his time, and he knew what a shitty feeling it was. Losing the money in it and the hassle of reporting credit cards gone west was only part of it, and not necessarily the worst part, either. You kept remembering stuff you had tucked away in there, stuff that might seem like junk to someone else but was irreplaceable to you.

John was hunkered down on his hams, picking up papers, sorting them, stacking them, and looking disconsolate. Alan helped.

"Did you really hurt your toes, Alan?"

"Nah. You know these shoes—it's like wearing Brinks trucks on your feet. How much was in the wallet, John?"

"Aw, no more'n twenty bucks, I guess. But I got my hunting license last week, and that was in there. Also my MasterCard. I'll have to call the bank and tell them to cancel the number if I can't find the damned wallet. But what I really want are the pictures. Mom and Dad, my sisters . . . you know. Stuff like that."

But it wasn't the picture of his mother and father or the ones of his sisters that John really cared about; the really important one was the picture of him and Sally Ratcliffe. Clut had taken it at the Fryeburg State Fair about three months before Sally had broken up with John in favor of that stonebrain Lester Pratt.

"Well," Alan said, "it'll turn up. The money and the plastic may be gone, but the wallet and pictures will probably come home, John. They usually do. You know that."

"Yeah," John said with a sigh. "It's just that . . . damn, I keep trying to remember if I had it this morning when I came in to work. I just can't."

"Well, I hope you find it. Stick a LOST notice up on the bulletin board, why don't you?"

"I will. And I'll get the rest of this mess cleaned up."

"I know you will, John. Take it easy."

Alan went out to the parking lot, shaking his head.

3

The small silver bell over the door of Needful Things tinkled and Babs Miller, member in good standing of the Ash Street Bridge Club, came in a little timidly.

"Mrs. Miller!" Leland Gaunt welcomed her, consulting the sheet of paper which lay beside his cash register. He made a small tick-mark on it. "How good that you could come! And right on time! It was the music box you were interested in, wasn't it? A lovely piece of work."

"I wanted to speak to you about it, yes," Babs said. "I suppose it's sold." It was difficult for her to imagine that such a lovely thing could *not* have been sold. She felt her heart break a little just at the thought. The tune it played, the one Mr. Gaunt claimed he could not remember . . . she thought she knew just which one it must be. She had once danced to that tune on the Pavillion at Old Orchard Beach with the captain of the football team, and later that same evening she had willingly given up her virginity to him under a gorgeous May moon. He had given her the first and last orgasm of her life, and all the while it had been roaring through her veins, that tune had been twisting through her head like a burning wire.

"No, it's right here," Mr. Gaunt said. He took it from the glass case where it had been hiding behind the Polaroid camera and set it on top. Babs Miller's face lit up at the sight of it.

"I'm sure it's more than I could afford," Babs said, "all at once, that is, but I *really* like it, Mr. Gaunt, and if there was any chance that I could pay for it in installments . . . any chance at *all* . . ."

Mr. Gaunt smiled. It was an exquisite, comforting smile. "I think you're needlessly worried," said he. "You're going to be surprised at how reasonable the price of this lovely music box is, Mrs. Miller. Very surprised. Sit down. Let's talk about it."

She sat down.

He came toward her.

His eyes captured hers.

That tune started up in her head again.

And she was lost.

4

"I remember now," Jillian Mislaburski told Alan. "It was the Rusk boy. Billy, I think his name is. Or maybe it's Bruce."

They were standing in her living room, which was dominated by the Sony TV and a gigantic plaster crucified Jesus which hung on the wall behind it. Oprah was on the tube. Judging from the way Jesus had His eyes rolled up under His crown of thorns, Alan thought He would maybe have preferred Geraldo. Or *Divorce Court.* Mrs. Mislaburski had offered Alan a cup of coffee, which he had refused.

"Brian," he said.

"That's right!" she said. "Brian!"

She was wearing her bright green wrapper but had dispensed with the red doo-rag this morning. Curls the size of the cardboard cylinders one finds at the centers of toilet-paper rolls stood out around her head in a bizarre corona.

"Are you sure, Mrs. Mislaburski?"

"Yes. I remembered who he was this morning when I got up. His father put the aluminum siding on our house two years ago. The boy came over and helped out for awhile. He seemed like a nice boy to me."

"Do you have any idea what he might have been doing there?"

"He said he wanted to ask if they'd hired anyone to shovel their driveway this winter. I think that was it. He said he'd come back later, when they weren't fighting. The poor kid looked scared to death, and I don't blame him." She shook her head. The large curls bounced softly. "I'm sorry she died the way she did . . ." Jill Mislaburski lowered her voice confidentially. "But I'm happy for *Pete*. No one knows what he had to put up with, married to that woman. No one." She looked meaningfully at Jesus on the wall, then back at Alan again.

"Uh-huh," Alan said. "Did you notice anything else, Mrs. Mislaburski? Anything about the house, or the sounds, or the boy?"

She put a finger against her nose and cocked her head. "Well, not really. The boy—Brian Rusk—had a cooler in his bike basket. I remember that, but I don't suppose that's the kind of thing—"

"Whoa," Alan said, raising his hand. A bright light had gone on for a moment at the front of his mind. "A cooler?"

"You know, the kind you take on picnics or to tailgate parties? I only remember it because it was really too big for his bike basket. It was in there crooked. It looked like it might fall out."

"Thank you, Mrs. Mislaburski," Alan said slowly. "Thank you very much."

"Does it mean something? Is it a clue?"

"Oh, I doubt it." But he wondered.

I'd like the possibility of vandalism a lot better if the kid was sixteen or seventeen, Henry Payton had said. Alan had felt the same way . . . but he had come across twelve-year-old vandals before, and he guessed you could tote a pretty fair number of rocks in one of those picnic coolers.

Suddenly he began to feel a good deal more interested in the talk he would be having with young Brian Rusk this afternoon.

5

The silver bell tinkled. Sonny Jackett came into Needful Things slowly, warily, kneading his grease-stained Sunoco cap in his hands. His manner was that of a man who sincerely believes he will soon break many expensive things no matter how much he doesn't want to; breaking things, his face proclaimed, was not his desire but his karma.

"Mr. Jackett!" Leland Gaunt cried his customary welcome with his customary vigor, and then made another tiny checkmark on the sheet beside the cash register. "So glad you could stop by!"

Sonny advanced three steps farther into the room and then stopped, glancing warily from the glass cases to Mr. Gaunt.

"Well," he said, "I didn't come in to buy nuthin. Got to put you straight on that. Ole Harry Samuels said you ast if I'd stop by this mornin if I had a chance. Said you had a socket-wrench set that was some nice. I been lookin for one, but this ain't no store for the likes of me. I'm just makin my manners to you, sir."

"Well, I appreciate your honesty," Mr. Gaunt said, "but you don't want to speak too soon, Mr. Jackett. This is one nice set of sockets—double-measure adjustable."

"Oh, ayuh?" Sonny raised his eyebrows. He knew there *were* such things, which made it possible to work on both foreign and domestic cars with the same socket-wrenches, but he had never actually seen such a rig. "That so?"

"Yes. I put them in the back room, Mr. Jackett, as soon as I heard you were looking. Otherwise they would have gone almost at once, and I wanted you to at least see them before I sold the set to someone else."

Sonny Jackett reacted to this with instant Yankee suspicion. "Now, why would you want to do that?"

"Because I have a classic car, and classic cars need frequent repairs. I've been told you're the best mechanic this side of Derry."

"Oh." Sonny relaxed. "Mayhap I am. What've you got for wheels?"

"A Tucker."

Sonny's eyebrows shot up and he looked at Mr. Gaunt with a new respect. "A Torpedo! Fancy that!"

"No. I have a Talisman."

"Ayuh? Never heard of a Tucker Talisman."

"There were only two built—the prototype and mine. In 1953, that was. Mr. Tucker moved to Brazil not long after, where he died." Mr. Gaunt smiled mistily. "Preston was a sweet fellow, and a wizard when it came to auto design . . . but he was no businessman."

"That so?"

"Yes." The mist in Mr. Gaunt's eyes cleared. "But that's yesterday, and this is today! Turn the page, eh, Mr. Jackett? Turn the page, I always say—face front, march cheerily into the future, and never look back!"

Sonny regarded Mr. Gaunt from the corners of his eyes with some unease and said nothing.

"Let me show you the socket-wrenches."

Sonny didn't agree at once. Instead, he looked doubtfully at the contents of the glass cases again. "Can't afford nothing too nice. Got bills a mile high. Sometimes I think I ought to get right the hell out of bi'ness and go on the County."

"I know what you mean," Mr. Gaunt said. "It's the damned Republicans, that's what *I* think."

Sonny's knotted, distrustful face relaxed all at once. "You're goddamned right about *that,* chummy!" he exclaimed. "George Bush has damn near *ruint* this country . . . him and his goddam war! But do you think the Democrats have anyone to put up against 'im next year who can win?"

"Doubtful," Mr. Gaunt said.

"Jesse Jackson, for instance—a nigger."

He looked truculently at Mr. Gaunt, who inclined his head slightly, as if to say *Yes, my friend—speak your mind. We are both men of the world who are not afraid to call a spade a spade.* Sonny Jackett relaxed a little more, less self-conscious about the grease on his hands now, more at home.

"I got nothing against niggers, you understand, but the idear of a jig in the White House—the *White* House!—gives me the shivers."

"Of course it does," Mr. Gaunt agreed.

"And that wop from New York—Mar-i-o Koo-whoa-mo! Do you think a guy with a name like that can beat that four-eyed dink in the White House?"

"No," Mr. Gaunt said. He held up his right hand, the long first finger placed about a quarter of an inch from his spatulate, ugly thumb. "Besides, I mistrust men with tiny heads."

Sonny gaped for a moment, then slapped his knee and gasped wheezy laughter. "Mistrust men with tiny— Say! That's pretty good, mister! That's pretty goddam good!"

Mr. Gaunt was grinning.

They grinned at each other.

Mr. Gaunt got the set of socket-wrenches, which came in a leather case lined with black velvet—the most beautiful set of chrome-steel alloy socket-wrenches Sonny Jackett had ever seen.

They grinned over the socket-wrenches, baring their teeth like monkeys that will soon fight.

And, of course, Sonny bought the set. The price was amazingly low—a hundred and seventy dollars, plus a couple of really amusing tricks to be played on Don Hemphill and the Rev. Rose. Sonny told Mr. Gaunt it would be a pleasure—he would enjoy stinking up those psalm-singing Republican son-ofawhores' lives.

They grinned over the tricks to be played on Steamboat Willie and Don Hemphill.

Sonny Jackett and Leland Gaunt—just a couple of grinning men of the world.

And over the door, the little silver bell jingled.

6

Henry Beaufort, owner and operator of The Mellow Tiger, lived in a house about a quarter of a mile from his place of business. Myra Evans parked in the Tiger's parking-lot—empty now in the hot, unseasonable morning sunshine—and walked to the house. Considering the nature of her errand, this seemed a reasonable precaution. She needn't have worried. The Tiger didn't close until one in the a.m., and Henry rarely rose much before that same hour in the p.m. All the shades, both upstairs and down, were drawn. His car, a perfectly maintained 1960 Thunderbird that was his pride and joy, stood in the driveway.

Myra was wearing a pair of jeans and one of her husband's blue work-shirts. The tail of the shirt was out and hung almost to her knees. It concealed the belt she wore beneath, and the scabbard hanging from the belt. Chuck Evans was a collector of World War II memorabilia (and, although she did not know it, he had already made a purchase of his own in this area at the town's new shop), and there was a Japanese bayonet in the scabbard. Myra had taken it half an hour ago from the wall of Chuck's basement den. It bumped solidly against her right thigh at every step.

She was very anxious to get this job done, so she could get back to the picture of Elvis. Holding the picture, she had discovered, produced a kind of story. It wasn't a real story, but in most ways—*all* ways, actually—she considered it *better* than a real story. Act I was The Concert, where The King pulled her up on stage to dance with him. Act II was The Green Room After The Show, and Act III was In the Limo. One of Elvis's Memphis guys was driving the limo, and The King didn't even bother to put up the black glass between the driver and them before doing the most outrageous and delicious things to her in the back seat as they drove to the airport.

Act IV was titled On the Plane. In this act they were in the *Lisa Marie,* Elvis's Convair jet . . . in the big double bed behind the partition at the back of the cabin, to be exact. That was the act Myra had been enjoying yesterday and this morning: cruising at thirty-two thousand feet in the *Lisa Marie,* cruising in bed with The King. She wouldn't have minded staying there with him forever, but she knew that she wouldn't. They were bound for Act V: Graceland. Once they were there, things could only get better.

But she had this little piece of business to take care of first.

She had been lying in bed this morning after her husband left, naked except for her garter-belt (The King had been very clear in his desire for Myra to leave that on), the picture clasped tightly in her hands, moaning and writhing slowly on the sheets. And then, suddenly, the double bed was gone. The whisper-drone of the *Lisa Marie*'s engines was gone. The smell of The King's English Leather was gone.

In the place of these wonderful things was Mr. Gaunt's face . . . only he no longer looked as he did in his shop. The skin on his face looked blistered, seared with some fabulous secret heat. It pulsed and writhed, as if there were things beneath, struggling to get out. And when he smiled, his big square teeth had become a double row of fangs.

"It's time, Myra," Mr. Gaunt had said.

"I want to be with Elvis," she whined. "I'll do it, but not right now—please, not right now."

"Yes, right now. You promised, and you're going to make good on your promise. You'll be very sorry if you don't, Myra."

She had heard a brittle cracking. She looked down and saw with horror that a jagged crack now split the glass over The King's face.

"*No!*" she cried. "*No, don't do that!*"

"*I'm* not doing it," Mr. Gaunt had responded with a laugh. "*You're* doing it. You're doing it by being a silly, lazy little cunt. This is America, Myra, where only whores do business in bed. In America respectable people have to get out of bed and *earn* the things they need, or lose them forever. I think you forgot that. Of course, I can always find somebody else to play that little trick on Mr. Beaufort, but as for your beautiful *affaire de coeur* with The King—"

Another crack raced like a silver lightning-bolt across the glass covering the picture. And the face beneath it, she observed with mounting horror, was growing old and wrinkled and raddled as the corrupting air seeped in and went to work on it.

"*No! I'll do it! I'll do it right now! I'm getting up right now, see? Only make it stop! MAKE IT STOP!*"

Myra had leaped to the floor with the speed of a woman who has discovered she is sharing her bed with a nest of scorpions.

"When you keep your promise, Myra," Mr. Gaunt said. Now he was speaking from some deep sunken hollow in her mind. "You know what to do, don't you?"

"Yes, I know!" Myra looked despairingly at the picture— the image of an old, ill man, his face puffy from years of excess and indulgence. The hand which held the microphone was a vulture's talon.

"When you come back with your mission accomplished," Mr. Gaunt said, "the picture will be fine. Only don't let anyone see you, Myra. If anyone sees you, you'll never see *him* again."

"I won't!" she babbled. "I swear I won't!"

And now, as she reached Henry Beaufort's house, she remembered that admonition. She looked around to make sure no one was coming along the road. It was deserted in both directions.

A crow cawed somnolently in someone's October-barren field. There was no other sound. The day seemed to throb like a living thing, and the land lay stunned within the slow beat of its unseasonable heart.

Myra walked up the driveway, pulling up the tail of the blue shirt, feeling to make sure of the scabbard and the bayonet inside it. Sweat ran, trickling and itching, down the center of her back and under her bra. Although she didn't know it and wouldn't have believed it if told, she had achieved a momentary beauty in the rural stillness. Her vague, unthoughtful face had filled, at least during these moments, with a deep purpose and determination which had never been there before. Her cheekbones were clearly defined for the first time since high school, when she had decided her mission in life was to eat every Yodel and Ding-Dong and Hoodsie Rocket in the world. During the last four days or so, she had been much too busy having progressively weirder and weirder sex with The King to think much about eating. Her hair, which usually hung around her face in a lank, floppy rug, was tied back in a tight little horsetail, exposing her brow. Perhaps shocked by the sudden overdose of hormones and the equally sudden cutback in sugar consumption after years of daily overdoses, most of the pimples that had flared on her face like uneasy volcanoes ever since she was twelve had gone into remission. Even more remarkable were her eyes—wide, blue, almost feral. They were not the eyes of Myra Evans, but of some jungle beast that might turn vicious at any moment.

She reached Henry's car. *Now* something was coming along 117—an old, rattling farm-truck headed for town. Myra slipped around to the front of the T-Bird and crouched behind its grille until the truck was gone. Then she stood up again. From the breast pocket of her shirt she took a folded sheet of paper. She opened it, smoothed it carefully, and then stuck it under one of the Bird's windshield wipers so the brief message written there showed clearly.

DON'T YOU EVER CUT ME OFF AND
THEN KEEP MY CAR-KEYS YOU DAMN
FROG!

it read.

It was time for the bayonet.

She took another quick glance around, but the only thing moving in the whole hot daylight world was a single crow, perhaps the one which had called before. It flapped down to the top of a telephone pole directly across from the driveway and seemed to watch her.

Myra took the bayonet out, gripped it tightly in both hands, stooped, and rammed it up to the hilt in the whitewall on the driver's-side front. Her face was pulled back in a wincing snarl, anticipating a loud bang, but there was only a sudden breathless *booooosh!*—the sound a big man might make after a sucker-punch to the gut. The T-Bird settled appreciably to the left. Myra yanked the bayonet, tearing the hole wider, grateful Chuck liked to keep his toys sharp.

When she had cut a ragged rubber smile in the rapidly deflating tire, she went around to the one on the passenger-side front and did it again. She was still anxious to get back to her picture, but she found she was glad she had come, just the same. This was sort of exciting. The thought of Henry's face when he saw what had happened to his precious Thunderbird was actually making her horny. God knew why, but she thought that when she finally got back on board the *Lisa Marie,* she might have a new trick or two to show The King.

She moved on to the rear tires. The bayonet did not cut quite so easily now, but she made up for it with her own enthusiasm, sawing energetically through the side-walls of the tires.

When the job was done, when all four tires were not just punctured but gutted, Myra stepped back to survey her work. She was breathing rapidly, and she armed sweat off her forehead in a quick, mannish gesture. Henry Beaufort's Thunderbird now sat a good six inches lower on the driveway than it had when she arrived. It rested on its wheel-rims with the expensive radials spread out around them in wrinkled rubber puddles. And then, although she had not been asked to do so, Myra decided to add the extra touch that means so much. She raked the tip of the bayonet down the side of the car, splitting the deeply polished surface with a long, jagged scratch.

The bayonet made a small, wailing screech against the metal and Myra looked at the house, suddenly sure that Henry Beaufort must have heard, that the shade in the bedroom window was suddenly going to flap up and he would be looking out at her.

It didn't happen, but she knew it was time to leave. She had overstayed her welcome here, and besides—back in her own bedroom, The King awaited. Myra hurried down the driveway, reseating the bayonet in its scabbard and then dropping the tail of Chuck's shirt over it again. One car passed her before she got back to The Mellow Tiger, but it was going the other way—assuming the driver wasn't ogling her in his rearview mirror, he would have seen only her back.

She slid into her own car, yanked the rubber band out of her hair, allowing her locks to fall around her face in their usual limp fashion, and drove back to town. She did this one-handed. Her other hand had business to take care of below her waist. She let herself into her house and bounded up the stairs by twos. The picture was on the bed, where she had left it. Myra kicked off her shoes, pushed her jeans down, grabbed the picture, and jumped into bed with it. The cracks in the glass were gone; The King had been restored to youth and beauty.

The same could be said for Myra Evans . . . at least temporarily.

7

Over the door, the silver bell sang its jingly little tune.

"Hello, Mrs. Potter!" Leland Gaunt said cheerily. He made a tick-mark on the sheet by the cash register. "I'd about decided you weren't going to come by."

"I almost didn't," Lenore Potter said. She looked upset, distracted. Her silver hair, usually coiffed to perfection, had been tacked up in an indifferent bun. An inch of her slip was showing beneath the hem of her expensive gray twill skirt, and there were dark circles beneath her eyes. The eyes themselves were restless, shooting from place to place with baleful, angry suspicion.

"It was the Howdy Doody puppet you wanted to look at, wasn't it? I believe you told me you have quite a collection of children's memorab—"

"I really don't believe I can look at such gentle things today, you know," Lenore said. She was the wife of the richest lawyer in Castle Rock, and she spoke in clipped, lawyerly tones. "I'm in an extremely poor frame of mind. I'm having a magenta day. Not just red, but *magenta!*"

Mr. Gaunt stepped around the main display case and came toward her, his face instantly filled with concern and sympathy. "My dear lady, what's happened? You look dreadful!"

"Of *course* I look dreadful!" she snapped. "The normal flow of my psychic aura has been disrupted—*badly* disrupted! Instead of blue, the color of calm and serenity, my entire *calava* has gone bright magenta! And it's all the fault of that bitch across the street! That high-box *bitch!*"

Mr. Gaunt made peculiar soothing gestures which never quite touched any part of Lenore Potter's body. "What bitch is that, Mrs. Potter?" he asked, knowing perfectly well.

"Bonsaint, of course! Bonsaint! That nasty lying Stephanie Bonsaint! My aura has *never* been magenta before, Mr. Gaunt! Deep pink a few times, yes, and once, after I was almost run down in the street by a drunk in Oxford, I think it might have turned red for a few minutes, but it has *never* been *magenta!* I simply cannot *live* like this!"

"Of course not," Mr. Gaunt soothed. "No one could *expect* you to, my dear."

His eyes finally captured hers. This was not easy with Mrs. Potter's gaze darting around in such a distracted manner, but he did finally manage. And when he did, Lenore calmed almost at once. Looking into Mr. Gaunt's eyes, she discovered, was almost like looking into her own aura when she had been doing all her exercises, eating the right foods (bean-sprouts and tofu, mostly), and maintaining the surfaces of her *calava* with at least an hour of meditation when she arose in the morning and again before she went to bed at night. His eyes were the faded, serene blue of desert skies.

"Come," he said. "Over here." He led her to the short row of three high-backed plush velvet chairs where so many citizens of Castle Rock had sat over the last week. And when she was seated, Mr. Gaunt invited: "Tell me all about it."

"She's always hated me," Lenore said. "She's always thought that her husband hasn't risen in the Firm as fast as she wanted because *my* husband kept him back. And that *I* put him up to it. She is a woman with a small mind and a big bosom and a dirty-gray aura. You know the type."

"Indeed," Mr. Gaunt said.

"But I never knew how *much* she hated me until this morning!" Lenore Potter was growing agitated again in spite of Mr. Gaunt's settling influence. "I got up and my flowerbeds were absolutely ruined! *Ruined!* Everything that was lovely yesterday is dying today! Everything which was soothing to the aura and nourishing to the *calava* has been *murdered!* By that bitch! By that *fucking Bonsaint BITCH!*"

Lenore's hands closed into fists, hiding the elegantly manicured nails. The fists drummed on the carved arms of the chair.

"Chrysanthemums, cimicifuga, asters, marigolds . . . that

bitch came over in the night and tore them all out of the ground! Threw them everywhere! Do you know where my ornamental cabbages are this morning, Mr. Gaunt?"

"No—where?" he asked her tenderly, still making those stroking motions just above her body.

He actually had a good idea of where they were, and he knew beyond a shadow of a doubt who was responsible for the *calava*-destroying mess: Melissa Clutterbuck. Lenore Potter did not suspect Deputy Clutterbuck's wife because she didn't *know* Deputy Clutterbuck's wife—nor did Melissa Clutterbuck know Lenore, except to say hello to on the street. There had been no malice on Melissa's part (except, of course, Mr. Gaunt thought, for the normal malicious pleasure *anyone* feels when tearing hell out of someone else's much-beloved possessions). She had torn up Lenore Potter's flowerbeds in partial payment for a set of Limoges china. When you got right down to the bottom of the thing, it was strictly business. Enjoyable, yes, Mr. Gaunt thought, but whoever said that business always had to be a drag?

"My flowers are in the street!" Lenore shouted. "In the middle of Castle View! She didn't miss a trick! Even the African daisies are gone! All gone! *All . . . gone!*"

"Did you see her?"

"I didn't *need* to see her! She's the only one who hates me enough to do something like that. And the flowerbeds are full of the marks of her high heels. I swear that little trollop wears her heels even to *bed.*"

"Oh Mr. Gaunt," she wailed, "every time I close my eyes everything goes all *purple!* What am I going to *do?*"

Mr. Gaunt said nothing for a moment. He only looked at her, fixing her with his eyes until she grew calm and distant.

"Is that better?" he asked finally.

"Yes!" she replied in a faint, relieved voice. "I believe I can see the blue again . . ."

"But you're too upset to even *think* about shopping."

"Yes . . ."

"Considering what that bitch did to you."

"Yes . . ."

"She ought to pay."

"Yes."

"If she ever tries anything like that again, she *will* pay."

"*Yes!*"

"I may have just the thing. Sit right there, Mrs. Potter. I'll be back in a jiffy. In the meantime, think blue thoughts."

"Blue," she agreed dreamily.

When Mr. Gaunt returned, he put one of the automatic pistols Ace had brought back from Cambridge into Lenore Potter's hands. It was fully loaded and gleamed a greasy blue-black under the display lights.

Lenore raised the gun to eye level. She looked at it with deep pleasure and even deeper relief.

"Now, I would never urge anyone to shoot anyone else," Mr. Gaunt said. "Not without a very good *reason,* at least. But you sound like a woman who might *have* a very good reason, Mrs. Potter. Not the flowers—we both know they are not the important thing. Flowers are replaceable. But your karma . . . your *calava* . . . well, what else do we—any of us—really have?" And he laughed deprecatingly.

"Nothing," she agreed, and pointed the automatic at the wall. "Pow. Pow, pow, pow. That's for you, you envying little roundheels trollop. I hope your husband ends up town garbage collector. It's what he deserves. It's what you *both* deserve."

"You see that little lever there, Mrs. Potter?" He pointed it out to her.

"Yes, I see it."

"That's the safety catch. If the bitch should come over again, trying to do more damage, you'd want to push that first. Do you understand?"

"Oh yes," Lenore said in her sleeper's voice. "I understand perfectly. Ka-*pow.*"

"No one would blame you. After all, a woman has to protect

her property. A woman has to protect her karma. The Bonsaint creature probably won't come again, but if she does . . ."

He looked at her meaningfully.

"If she does, it will be for the last time." Lenore raised the short barrel of the automatic to her lips and kissed it softly.

"Now put that in your purse," Mr. Gaunt said, "and get on home. Why, for all you know, she could be in your yard right now. In fact, she could be in your house."

Lenore looked alarmed at this. Thin threads of sinister purple began to twist and twine through her blue aura. She got up, stuffing the automatic into her purse. Mr. Gaunt looked away from her and she blinked her eyes rapidly several times as soon as he did.

"I'm sorry, but I'll have to look at Howdy Doody another time, Mr. Gaunt. I think I'd better go home. For all I know, that Bonsaint woman could be in my yard right now, while I'm here. She might even be in my *house!*"

"What a terrible idea," Mr. Gaunt said.

"Yes, but property is a responsibility—it must be protected. We have to face these things, Mr. Gaunt. How much do I owe you for the . . . the . . ." But she could not remember exactly what it was he had sold her, although she was sure she would very soon now. She gestured vaguely at her purse instead.

"No charge to you. Those are on special today. Think of it as . . ." His smile widened. ". . . as a free get-acquainted gift."

"Thank you," Lenore said. "I feel ever so much better."

"As always," said Mr. Gaunt with a little bow, "I am glad to have been of service."

8

Norris Ridgewick was not fishing.

Norris Ridgewick was looking in Hugh Priest's bedroom window.

Hugh lay on his bed in a loose heap, snoring at the ceiling. He wore only a pair of pee-stained boxer shorts. Clutched in his big, knuckly hands was a matted piece of fur. Norris couldn't be sure—Hugh's hands were very big and the window was very dirty—but he thought it was an old moth-eaten foxtail. It didn't matter what it was, anyway; what mattered was that Hugh was asleep.

Norris walked back down the lawn to where his personal car stood parked behind Hugh's Buick in the driveway. He opened the passenger door and leaned in. His fishing creel was sitting on the floor. The Bazun rod was in the back seat—he found he felt better, *safer,* if he kept it with him.

It was still unused. The truth was just this simple: he was *afraid* to use it. He had taken it out on Castle Lake yesterday, all fitted up and ready to go . . . and then had hesitated just before making his first cast, with the rod cocked back over his shoulder.

What if, he thought, *a really big fish takes the lure? Smokey, for instance?*

Smokey was an old brown trout, the stuff of legend among the fisherpeople of Castle Rock. He was reputed to be over two feet long, wily as a weasel, strong as a stoat, tough as nails. According to the oldtimers, Smokey's jaw bristled with the steel of anglers who had hooked him . . . but had been unable to hold him.

What if he snaps the rod?

It seemed crazy to believe that a lake-trout, even a big one like Smokey (if Smokey actually existed), could snap a Bazun rod, but Norris supposed it was possible . . . and the way his luck had been running just lately, it might really happen. He could hear the brittle snap in his head, could feel the agony of seeing the rod in two pieces, one of them in the bottom of the boat and the other floating alongside. And once a rod was broken, it was Katy bar the door—there wasn't a thing you could do with it except throw it away.

So he had ended up using the old Zebco after all. There had been no fish for dinner last night . . . but he *had* dreamed of Mr. Gaunt. In the dream Mr. Gaunt had been wearing hipwaders and an old fedora with feathered lures dancing jauntily around the brim. He was sitting in a rowboat about thirty feet out on Castle Lake while Norris stood on the west shore with his dad's old cabin, which had burned down ten years before, behind him. He stood and listened while Mr. Gaunt talked. Mr. Gaunt had reminded Norris of his promise, and Norris had awakened with a sense of utter certainty: he had done the right thing yesterday, putting the Bazun aside in favor of the old Zebco. The Bazun rod was too nice, far too nice. It would be criminal to risk it by actually *using* it.

Now Norris opened his creel. He took out a long fishgutting knife and walked over to Hugh's Buick.

Nobody deserves it more than this drunken slob, he told himself, but something inside didn't agree. Something inside told him he was making a black and woeful mistake from which he might never recover. He was a policeman; part of his job was to arrest people who did the sort of thing he was about to do. It was vandalism, that was exactly what it came down to, and vandals were bad guys.

You decide, Norris. The voice of Mr. Gaunt spoke up suddenly in his mind. *It's your fishing rod. And it's your God-given right of free will, too. You have a choice. You always have a choice. But—*

The voice in Norris Ridgewick's head didn't finish. It didn't need to. Norris knew what the consequences of turning away now would be. When he went back to his car, he would find the Bazun broken in two. Because every choice had consequences. Because in America, you could have anything you wanted, just as long as you could pay for it. If you couldn't pay, or *refused* to pay, you would remain needful forever.

Besides, he'd do it to me, Norris thought petulantly. And not for a nice fishing rod like my Bazun, either. Hugh Priest would cut his own mother's throat for a bottle of Old Duke and a pack of Luckies.

Thus he refuted guilt. When the something inside tried to protest again, tried to tell him to please think before he did this, *think,* he smothered it. Then he bent down and began to carve up the tires of Hugh's Buick. His enthusiasm, like Myra Evans's, grew as he worked. As an extra added attraction, he smashed the Buick's headlights and the taillights, too. He finished by putting a note which read

> JUST A WARNING
>
> YOU KNOW WHAT I'LL COME AFTER NEXT TIME HUBERT. YOU HAVE KICKED MY ROCKOLA FOR THE LAST TIME. STAY OUT OF MY BAR!

under the windshield wiper on the driver's side.

With the job done he crept back up to the bedroom window, his heart hammering heavily in his narrow chest. Hugh Priest was still deeply asleep, clutching that ratty runner of fur.

Who in God's name would want a dirty old thing like that? Norris wondered. He's holding onto it like it was his fucking teddy bear.

He went back to his car. He got in, shifted into neutral, and let his old Beetle roll soundlessly down the driveway. He didn't start the engine until the car was on the road. Then he drove away as fast as he could. He had a headache. His stomach was rolling around nastily in his guts. And he kept telling himself it didn't matter; he felt good, he felt good, goddammit, he felt *really good.*

It didn't work very well until he reached back between the seats and grasped the limber, narrow fishing rod in his left fist. Then he began to feel calm again.

Norris held it like that all the way home.

9

The silver bell jingled.

Slopey Dodd walked into Needful Things.

"Hullo, Slopey," Mr. Gaunt said.

"Huh-Huh-Hello, Mr. G-G-Guh—"

"You don't need to stutter around me, Slopey," Mr. Gaunt said. He raised one of his hands with the first two fingers extended in a fork. He drew them down through the air in front of Slopey's homely face, and Slopey felt something—a tangled, knotted snarl in his mind—magically dissolve. His mouth fell open.

"What did you do to me?" he gasped. The words ran perfectly out of his mouth, like beads on a string.

"A trick Miss Ratcliffe would undoubtedly love to learn," Mr. Gaunt said. He smiled and made a mark beside Slopey's name on his sheet. He glanced at the grandfather clock ticking contentedly away in the corner. It was quarter to one. "Tell me how you got out of school early. Will anyone be suspicious?"

"No." Slopey's face was still amazed, and he appeared to be trying to look down at his own mouth, as if he could actually see the words tumbling from it in such unprecedented good order. "I told Mrs. DeWeese I felt sick to my stomach. She sent me to the school nurse. I told the nurse I felt better, but still sick. She asked me if I thought I could walk home. I said yes, so she let me go." Slopey paused. "I came because I fell asleep in study hall. I dreamed you were calling me."

"I was." Mr. Gaunt tented his oddly even fingers beneath his chin and smiled at the boy. "Tell me—did your mother like the pewter teapot you got her?"

A blush mounted into Slopey's cheeks, turning them the color of old brick. He started to say something, then gave up and inspected his feet instead.

In his softest, kindest voice, Mr. Gaunt said: "You kept it yourself, didn't you?"

Slopey nodded, still looking at his feet. He felt ashamed and confused. Worst of all, he felt a terrible sense of loss and grief: somehow Mr. Gaunt had dissolved that tiresome, infuriating knot in his head . . . and what good did it do? He was too embarrassed to talk.

"Now what, pray tell, does a twelve-year-old boy want with a pewter teapot?"

Slopey's cowlick, which had bobbed up and down a few seconds ago, now waved from side to side as he shook his head. He didn't *know* what a twelve-year-old boy wanted with a pewter teapot. He only knew that he wanted to keep it. He liked it. He really . . . really . . . liked it.

". . . feels," he muttered at last.

"Pardon me?" Mr. Gaunt asked, raising his single wavy eyebrow.

"I like the way it *feels,* I said!"

"Slopey, Slopey," Mr. Gaunt said, coming around the counter, "you don't have to explain to *me.* I know all about that peculiar thing people call 'pride of possession.' I have made it the cornerstone of my career."

Slopey Dodd shrank away from Mr. Gaunt in alarm. "Don't you touch me! *Please* don't!"

"Slopey, I have no more intention of touching you than I do of telling you to give your mother the teapot. It's *yours.* You can do anything you want with it. In fact, I *applaud* your decision to keep it."

"You . . . you do?"

"I do! *Indeed* I do! Selfish people are happy people. I believe that with all my heart. But Slopey . . ."

Slopey raised his head a little and looked fearfully through the hanging fringe of his red hair at Leland Gaunt.

"The time has come for you to finish paying for it."

"Oh!" An expression of vast relief filled Slopey's face. "Is *that* all you wanted me for? I thought maybe . . ." But he either couldn't or didn't dare finish. He hadn't been sure *what* Mr. Gaunt had wanted.

"Yes. Do you remember who you promised to play a trick on?"

"Sure. Coach Pratt."

"Right. There are two parts to this prank—you have to put something somewhere, plus you have to tell Coach Pratt something. And if you follow directions exactly, the teapot will be yours forever."

"Can I talk like this, too?" Slopey asked eagerly. "Can I talk without stuttering forever, too?"

Mr. Gaunt sighed regretfully. "I'm afraid you'll go back to the way you were as soon as you leave my shop, Slopey. I believe I *do* have an anti-stuttering device somewhere in stock, but—"

"Please! Please, Mr. Gaunt! I'll do anything! I'll do *anything* to *anyone!* I *hate* to stutter!"

"I know you would, but that's just the problem, don't you see? I am rapidly running out of pranks which need to be played; my dance-card, you might say, is nearly full. So you couldn't pay me."

Slopey hesitated a long time before speaking again. When he did, his voice was low and diffident. "Couldn't you . . . I mean, do you ever just . . . *give* things away, Mr. Gaunt?"

Leland Gaunt's face grew deeply sorrowful. "Oh, Slopey! How often I've thought of it, and with such *longing!* There is a deep, untapped well of charity in my heart. But . . ."

"But?"

"It just wouldn't be business," Mr. Gaunt finished. He favored Slopey with a compassionate smile . . . but his eyes sparkled so wolfishly that Slopey took a step backward. "You understand, don't you?"

"Uh . . . yeah! Sure!"

"Besides," Mr. Gaunt went on, "the next few hours are

crucial to me. Once things really get rolling, they can rarely be stopped . . . but for the time being, I must make prudence my watchword. If you suddenly stopped stuttering, it might raise questions. That would be bad. The Sheriff is already asking questions he has no business asking." His face darkened momentarily, and then his ugly, charming, jostling smile burst forth again. "But I intend to take care of him, Slopey. Ah, yes."

"Sheriff Pangborn, you mean?"

"Yes—Sheriff Pangborn, that's what I mean to say." Mr. Gaunt raised his first two fingers and once again drew them down in front of Slopey Dodd's face, from forehead to chin. "But we never talked about him, did we?"

"Talked about *who?*" Slopey asked, bewildered.

"Exactly."

Leland Gaunt was wearing a jacket of dark-gray suede today, and from one of its pockets he produced a black leather wallet. He held it out to Slopey, who took it gingerly, being careful not to touch Mr. Gaunt's fingers.

"You know Coach Pratt's car, don't you?"

"The Mustang? Sure."

"Put this in it. Under the passenger seat, with just a corner sticking out. Go to the high school right now—it wants to be there before the last bell. Do you understand?"

"Yes."

"Then you're to wait until he comes out. And when he does . . ."

Mr. Gaunt went on speaking in a low murmur, and Slopey looked up at him, jaw slack, eyes dazed, nodding every once in a while.

Slopey Dodd left a few minutes later with John LaPointe's wallet tucked into his shirt.

CHAPTER SIXTEEN

1

Nettie lay in a plain gray casket which Polly Chalmers had paid for. Alan had asked her to let him help share the expense, and she'd refused in that simple but final way he had come to know, respect, and accept. The coffin stood on steel runners above a plot in Homeland Cemetery near the area where Polly's people were buried. The mound of earth next to it was covered with a carpet of bright green artificial grass which sparkled feverishly in the hot sunlight. That fake grass never failed to make Alan shudder. There was something obscene about it, something hideous. He liked it even less than the morticians' practice of first rouging the dead and then dolling them up in their finest clothes they looked as if they were bound for a big business meeting in Boston instead of a long season of decay amid the roots and the worms.

Reverend Tom Killingworth, the Methodist minister who conducted twice-weekly services at Juniper Hill and who had known Nettie well, performed the service at Polly's request. The homily was brief but warm, full of reference to the Nettie Cobb this man had known, a woman who had been slowly and bravely coming out of the shadows of insanity, a woman who had taken the courageous decision to try to treat once more with the world which had hurt her so badly.

"When I was growing up," Tom Killingworth said, "my mother kept a plaque with a lovely Irish saying on it in her sewing room. It said 'May you be in heaven half an hour before the devil knows you're dead.' Nettie Cobb had a hard life, in many ways a sad life, but in spite of that I do not believe she and the devil ever had much to do with each other. In spite of her terrible, untimely death, my heart believes that it is to heaven she has gone, and that the devil still hasn't gotten the news." Killingworth raised his arms in the traditional gesture of benediction. "Let us pray."

From the far side of the hill, where Wilma Jerzyck was being buried at the same time, came the sound of many voices rising and falling in response to Father John Brigham. Over there, cars were lined up from the burial site all the way to the cemetery's east gate; they had come for Peter Jerzyck, the living, if not for his dead wife. Over here there were only five mourners: Polly, Alan, Rosalie Drake, old Lenny Partridge (who went to all funerals on general principles, so long as it wasn't one of the Pope's army getting buried), and Norris Ridgewick. Norris looked pale and distracted. Fish must not have been biting, Alan thought.

"May the Lord bless you and keep your memories of Nettie Cobb fresh and green in your hearts," Killingworth said, and beside Alan, Polly began to cry again. He put an arm around her and she moved against him gratefully, her hand finding his and twining in it tightly. "May the Lord lift up His face upon you; may He shower His grace upon you; may He cheer your souls and give you peace. Amen."

The day was even hotter than Columbus Day had been, and when Alan raised his head, darts of bright sunlight bounced off the casket-rails and into his eyes. He wiped his free hand across his forehead, where a solid summer sweat had broken. Polly fumbled in her purse for a fresh Kleenex and wiped her streaming eyes with it.

"Honey, are you all right?" Alan asked.

"Yes . . . but I have to cry for her, Alan. Poor Nettie. Poor, poor Nettie. Why did this happen? *Why?*" And she began to sob again.

Alan, who wondered exactly the same thing, gathered her into his arms. Over her shoulder he saw Norris wandering away toward where the cars belonging to Nettie's mourners were huddled, looking like a man who either doesn't know where he is going or who isn't quite awake. Alan frowned. Then Rosalie Drake approached Norris, said something to him, and Norris gave her a hug.

Alan thought, *He knew her, too—he's just sad, that's all. You're jumping at an almighty lot of shadows these days— maybe the real question here is what's the matter with you?*

Then Killingworth was there and Polly was turning to thank him, getting herself under control. Killingworth held out his hands. With guarded amazement Alan watched the fearless way Polly allowed her own hand to be swallowed up in the minister's larger ones. He could not remember ever seeing Polly offer one of her hands so freely and unthoughtfully.

She's not just a little better; she's a lot better. What in the hell happened?

On the other side of the hill, Father John Brigham's nasal, rather irritating voice proclaimed: "Peace be with you."

"And with you," the mourners replied *en masse.*

Alan looked at the plain gray casket beside that hideous swath of fake green grass and thought, *Peace be with you, Nettie. Now and at last, peace be with you.*

2

As the twin funerals at Homeland were winding up, Eddie Warburton was parking in front of Polly's house. He slipped from his car—not a nice new car like the one that honky bastard down at the Sunoco had wrecked, just transportation—and looked cautiously both ways. Everything seemed fine; the street was dozing through what might have been an afternoon in early August.

Eddie hurried up Polly's walk, fumbling an official-looking

envelope out of his shirt as he went. Mr. Gaunt had called him only ten minutes ago, telling him it was time to finish paying for his medallion, and here he was . . . of course. Mr. Gaunt was the sort of guy who, when he said frog, you jumped.

Eddie climbed the three steps to Polly's porch. A hot little gust of breeze stirred the windchimes above the door, making them jingle softly together. It was the most civilized sound imaginable, but Eddie jumped slightly anyway. He took another look around, saw no one, then looked down at the envelope again. Addressed to "Ms. Patricia Chalmers"—pretty hoity-toity! Eddie hadn't the slightest idea that Polly's real first name was Patricia, nor did he care. His job was to do this little trick and then get the hell out of here.

He dropped the letter into the mail-slot. It fluttered down and landed on top of the other mail: two catalogues and a cable-TV brochure. Just a business-length envelope with Polly's name and address centered below the metered mail stamp in the upper right corner and the return address in the upper left:

San Francisco Department of Child Welfare
666 Geary Street
San Francisco, California 94112

3

"What is it?" Alan asked as he and Polly walked slowly down the hill toward Alan's station wagon. He had hoped to pass at least a word with Norris, but Norris had already gotten into his VW and taken off. Back to the lake for a little more fishing before the sun went down, probably.

Polly looked up at him, still red-eyed and too pale, but smiling tentatively. "What is what?"

"Your hands. What's made them all better? It's like magic."

"Yes," she said, and held them out before her, splay-fingered, so they could both look at them. "It is, isn't it?" Her smile was a little more natural now.

Her fingers were still twisted, still crooked, and the joints were still bunched, but the acute swelling which had been there Friday night was almost completely gone.

"Come on, lady. Give."

"I'm not sure I want to tell you," she said. "I'm a little embarrassed, actually."

They stopped and waved at Rosalie as she drove by in her old blue Toyota.

"Come on," Alan said. " 'Fess up."

"Well," she said, "I guess it was just a matter of finally meeting the right doctor." Slow color was rising in her cheeks.

"Who's that?"

"Dr. Gaunt," she said with a nervous little laugh. "Dr. Leland Gaunt."

"Gaunt!" He looked at her in surprise. "What does he have to do with your hands?"

"Drive me down to his shop and I'll tell you on the way."

4

Five minutes later (one of the nicest things about living in Castle Rock, Alan sometimes thought, was that almost everything was only five minutes away), he swung into one of the slant spaces in front of Needful Things. There was a sign in the window, one Alan had seen before:

TUESDAYS AND THURSDAYS
BY APPOINTMENT ONLY.

It suddenly occurred to Alan—who hadn't thought about this aspect of the new store at all until now—that closed except "by appointment" was one fuck of a strange way to run a small-town business.

"Alan?" Polly asked hesitantly. "You look mad."

"I'm not mad," he said. "What in the world do I have to be mad about? The truth is, I don't know *how* I feel. I guess—" He uttered a short laugh, shook his head, and started again. "I guess I'm what Todd used to call 'gabberflasted.' Quack remedies? It just doesn't seem like you, Pol."

Her lips tightened at once, and there was a warning in her eyes when she turned to look at him. " 'Quack' isn't the word I'd have used. Quack is for ducks and . . . and prayer-wheels from the ads in the back of *Inside View.* 'Quack' is the wrong word to use if a thing works, Alan. Do you think I'm wrong?"

He opened his mouth—to say what, he wasn't sure—but she went on before he could say anything.

"Look at this." She held her hands out in the sunshine flooding through the windshield, then opened them and closed them effortlessly several times.

"All right. Poor choice of words. What I—"

"Yes, I'd say so. A very poor choice."

"I'm sorry."

She turned all the way around to face him then, sitting where Annie had so often sat, sitting in what had once been the Pangborn family car. Why haven't I traded this thing yet? Alan wondered. What am I—crazy?

Polly placed her hands gently over Alan's. "Oh, this is starting to feel really uncomfortable—we *never* argue, and I'm not going to start now. I buried a good companion today. I'm not going to have a fight with my boyfriend, as well."

A slow grin lit his face. "That what I am? Your boyfriend?"

"Well . . . you're my *friend.* Can I at least say that?"

He hugged her, a little astonished at how close they had come to having harsh words. And not because she felt worse; because she felt *better.* "Honey, you can say anything you want. I love you a bunch."

"And we're not going to fight, no matter what."

He nodded solemnly. "No matter what."

"Because I love you, too, Alan."

He kissed her cheek, then let her go. "Let me see this ashcan thing he gave you."

"It's not an ashcan, it's an *azka*. And he didn't *give* it to me, he loaned it to me on a trial basis. That's why I'm here—to buy it. I told you that. I just hope he doesn't want the moon and stars for it."

Alan looked at the sign in the display window, and at the shade pulled down over the door. He thought, I'm afraid that's just what he *is* going to want, darlin.

He didn't like any of this. He had found it hard to take his eyes away from Polly's hands during the funeral service—he had watched her manipulate the catch on her purse effortlessly, dip into her bag for a Kleenex, then close the catch with the tips of her fingers instead of shuffling the bag awkwardly around so she could do it with her thumbs, which were usually a good deal less painful. He knew her hands were better, but this story about a magic charm—and that was what it came down to when you scraped the frosting off the cake—made him extremely nervous. It reeked of confidence game.

TUESDAYS AND THURSDAYS
BY APPOINTMENT ONLY.

No—except for a few fancy restaurants like Maurice, he hadn't seen a business that kept appointment-only hours since he'd come to Maine. And you could walk right off the street and get a table at Maurice nine times out of ten . . . except in the summer, of course, when the tourists were spawning.

BY APPOINTMENT ONLY.

Nevertheless, he had seen (out of the corner of his eye, as it were) people going in and out all week long. Not in *droves,* maybe, but it was clear that Mr. Gaunt's way of doing business hadn't hurt him any, odd or not. Sometimes his customers came in little groups, but far more often they seemed to be on their own . . . or so it seemed to Alan now, casting his mind back over the previous week. And wasn't that how con-men worked? They split you off from the herd, got you on your own, made you comfortable, and then showed you how you could own the Lincoln Tunnel for this one-time-only low price.

"Alan?" Her fist knocked lightly on his forehead. "Alan, are you in there?"

He looked back at her with a smile. "I'm here, Polly."

She had worn a dark-blue jumper with a matching blue stock tie to Nettie's funeral. While Alan was thinking, she had taken off the tie and dextrously unbuttoned the top two buttons of the white blouse underneath.

"More!" he said with a leer. "Cleavage! We want cleavage!"

"Stop," she said primly but with a smile. "We're sitting in the middle of Main Street and it's two-thirty in the afternoon. Besides, we've just come from a funeral, in case you forgot."

He started. "Is it really that late?"

"If two-thirty's late, it's late." She tapped his wrist. "Do you ever look at the thing you've got strapped on there?"

He looked at it now and saw it was closer to two-forty than two-thirty. Middle School broke at three o'clock. If he was going to be there when Brian Rusk got out, he had to get moving right away.

"Let me see your trinket," he said.

She grasped the fine silver chain around her neck and pulled out the small silver object on the end of it. She cupped it in her palm . . . then closed her hand over it when he moved to touch it.

"Uh . . . I don't know if you're supposed to." She was smiling, but the move he'd made had clearly left her uncomfortable. "It might screw up the vibrations, or something."

"Oh, come on, Pol," he said, annoyed.

"Look," she said, "let's get something straight, okay? Want to?" The anger was back in her voice. She was trying to control it, but it was there. "It's easy for you to make light of this.

You're not the one with the oversized buttons on the tele-phone, or the oversized Percodan prescription."

"Hey, Polly! That's—"

"No, never mind hey Polly." Bright spots of color had mounted in her cheeks. Part of her anger, she would think later, sprang from a very simple source: on Sunday, she had felt exactly as Alan felt now. Something had happened since then to change her mind, and dealing with that change was not easy. "This thing *works.* I know it's crazy, but it *does work.* On Sunday morning, when Nettie came over, I was in agony. I'd started thinking about how the real solution to all my problems might be a double amputation. The pain was so bad, Alan, that I turned that thought over with a feeling that was almost sur-prise. Like 'Oh yeah—amputation! Why haven't I thought of *that* before? It's so obvious!' Now, just two days later, all I've got is what Dr. Van Allen calls 'fugitive pain,' and even that seems to be going away. I remember about a year ago I spent a week on a brown-rice diet because *that* was supposed to help. Is this so different?"

The anger had gone out of her voice as she spoke, and now she was looking at him almost pleadingly.

"I don't know, Polly. I really don't."

She had opened her hand again, and she now held the *azka* between her thumb and forefinger. Alan bent close to look at it, but made no move to touch it this time. It was a small silver object, not quite round. Tiny holes, not much bigger than the black dots which make up newsprint photographs, studded its lower half. It gleamed mellowly in the sunlight.

And as Alan looked at it, a powerful, irrational feeling swept him: he didn't like it. He didn't like it at all. He resisted a brief, powerful urge to simply rip it off Polly's neck and throw it out the open window.

Yes! Good idea, sport! You do that and you'll be picking your teeth out of your lap!

"Sometimes it almost feels like something is moving around

inside of it," Polly said, smiling. "Like a Mexican jumping bean, or something. Isn't that silly?"

"I don't know."

He watched her drop it back inside her blouse with a strong sense of misgiving . . . but once it was out of sight and her fingers—her undeniably limber fingers—had gone to work re-buttoning the top of her blouse, the feeling began to fade. What didn't was his growing suspicion that Mr. Leland Gaunt was conning the woman he loved . . . and if he was, she would not be the only one.

"Have you thought it could be something else?" Now he was moving with the delicacy of a man using slick stepping-stones to cross a swift-running stream. "You've had remissions before, you know."

"Of *course* I know," Polly said with edgy patience. "They're *my* hands."

"Polly, I'm just trying—"

"I knew you'd probably react just the way you *are* reacting, Alan. The fact is simple enough: I know what arthritic remission feels like, and brother, this isn't it. I've had times over the last five or six years when I felt pretty good, but I never felt *this* good even during the best of them. This is different. This is like . . ." She paused, thought, then made a small frustrated gesture that was mostly hands and shoulders. "This is like being *well* again. I don't expect you to understand exactly what I mean, but I can't put it any better than that."

He nodded, frowning. He *did* understand what she was saying, and he also understood that she meant it. Perhaps the *azka* had unlocked some dormant healing power in her own mind. Was that possible, even though the disease in question wasn't psychosomatic in origin? The Rosicrucians thought stuff like that happened all the time. So did the millions of people who had bought L. Ron Hubbard's book on Dianetics, for that matter. He himself didn't know; the only thing he could say for sure was that he had never seen a blind person think himself back to sight or a wounded person stop his bleeding by an effort of concentration.

What he *did* know was this: something about the situation smelled wrong. Something about it smelled as high as dead fish that have spent three days in the hot sun.

"Let's cut to the chase," Polly said. "Trying not to be mad at you is wearing me out. Come inside with me. Talk to Mr. Gaunt yourself. It's time you met him anyway. Maybe he can explain better what the charm does . . . and what it doesn't do."

He looked at his watch again. Fourteen minutes of three now. For a brief moment he thought of doing as she suggested, and leaving Brian Rusk for later. But catching the boy as he came out of school—catching him while he was away from home—felt right. He would get better answers if he talked to him away from his mother, who would hang around them like a lioness protecting her cub, interrupting, perhaps even telling her son not to answer. Yes, that was the bottom line: if it turned out her son had something to hide, or if Mrs. Rusk even *thought* he did, Alan might find it difficult or impossible to get the information he needed.

Here he had a potential con artist; in Brian Rusk he might have the key that would unlock a double murder.

"I can't, honey," he said. "Maybe a little later today. I have to go over to the Middle School and talk to someone, and I ought to do it right away."

"Is it about Nettie?"

"It's about Wilma Jerzyck . . . but if my hunch is right, Nettie comes into it, yes. If I find anything out, I'll tell you later. In the meantime, will you do something for me?"

"Alan, I'm buying it! They're not your hands!"

"No, I expect you to buy it. I want you to pay him by check, that's all. There's no reason why he shouldn't take one—if he's a reputable businessman, that is. You live in town and you bank right across the street. But if something shakes out funny, you've got a few days to put a stop on payment."

"I see," Polly said. Her voice was calm, but Alan realized with a sinking feeling that he had finally missed his footing on one of those slippery stepping-stones and fallen headlong into the stream. "You think he's a crook, don't you, Alan? You think he's going to take the gullible little lady's money, fold his tent, and steal off into the night."

"I don't know," Alan said evenly. "What I *do* know is that he's only been doing business here in town for a week. So a check seems like a reasonable precaution to take."

Yes, he was being reasonable. Polly recognized that. It was that very reasonableness, that stubborn rationality in the face of what seemed to her to be an authentic miracle cure, that was now driving her anger. She fought an urge to begin snapping her fingers in his face, shouting *Do you* SEE *that, Alan? Are you* BLIND? as she did so. The fact that Alan was right, that Mr. Gaunt should have no problem at all with her check if he was on the up-and-up, only made her angrier.

Be careful, a voice whispered. Be careful, don't be hasty, turn on brain before throwing mouth in gear. Remember that you love this man.

But another voice answered, a colder voice, one she barely recognized as her own: Do I? Do I really?

"All right," she said, tight-lipped, and slid across the seat and away from him. "Thank you for looking after my best interests, Alan. Sometimes I forget how badly I need someone to do that, you see. I'll be sure to write him a check."

"Polly—"

"No, Alan. No more talk now. I can't not be mad at you any longer today." She opened the door and got out in one lithe gesture. The jumper rode up, revealing a momentary heart-stopping length of thigh.

He started to get out on his own side, wanting to catch her, talk to her, smooth it over, make her see that he had only voiced his doubts because he cared about her. Then he looked at his watch again. It was nine minutes of three. Even if he pushed it, he might miss Brian Rusk.

"I'll talk to you tonight," he called out the window.

"Fine," she said. "You do that, Alan." She went directly to the door beneath the canopy without turning around. Before he put the station wagon in reverse and backed out into the street, Alan heard the tinkle of a small silver bell.

5

"Ms. Chalmers!" Mr. Gaunt cried cheerfully, and made a small check-mark on the sheet beside the cash register. He was nearing the bottom of it now: Polly's was the last name but one.

"Please . . . Polly," she said.

"Excuse me." His smile widened. *"Polly."*

She smiled back at him, but the smile was forced. Now that she was in here, she felt a keen sorrow at the angry way she and Alan had parted. Suddenly she found herself struggling just to keep from bursting into tears.

"Ms. Chalmers? Polly? Are you feeling unwell?" Mr. Gaunt came around the counter. "You look a trifle pale." His face was furrowed with genuine concern. This is the man Alan thinks is a crook, Polly thought. If he could only see him now—

"It's the sun, I think," she said in a voice that was not quite even. "It's so warm outside."

"But cool in here," he said soothingly. "Come, Polly. Come and sit down."

He led her, his hand near but not quite touching the small of her back, to one of the red velvet chairs. She sat upon it, knees together.

"I happened to be looking out the window," he said, sitting in the chair next to hers and folding his long hands into his lap. "It looked to me as if you and the Sheriff might be argu-ing."

"It's nothing," she said, but then a single large tear over-spilled the corner of her left eye and rolled down her cheek.

"On the contrary," he said. "It means a great deal."

She looked up at him, surprised . . . and Mr. Gaunt's hazel eyes captured hers. Had they been hazel before? She couldn't remember, not for certain. All she knew was that as she looked into them, she felt all the day's misery—poor Nettie's funeral, then the stupid fight she'd had with Alan—begin to dissolve.

"It . . . it does?"

"Polly," he said softly, "I think everything is going to turn out just fine. If you trust me. Do you? Do you trust me?"

"Yes," Polly said, although something inside, something far and faint, cried out a desperate warning. "I do—no matter what Alan says, I trust you with all my heart."

"Well, that's fine," Mr. Gaunt said. He reached out and took one of Polly's hands. Her face wrinkled in disgust for a mo-ment, and then relaxed into its former blank and dreaming ex-pression. "That's just fine. And your friend the Sheriff needn't have worried, you know; your personal check is just as good as gold with me."

6

Alan saw he was going to be late unless he turned on the flasher-bubble and stuck it on the roof. He didn't want to do that. He didn't want Brian Rusk to see a police car; he wanted him to see a slightly down-at-the-heels station wagon, just like the kind his own dad probably drove.

It was too late to make it to the school before it let out for the day. Alan parked at the intersection of Main and School streets instead. This was the most logical way for Brian to come; he would just have to hope that logic would work somewhere along the line today.

Alan got out, leaned against the station wagon's bumper, and felt in his pocket for a stick of chewing gum. He was unwrapping it when he heard the three o'clock bell at the Middle School, dreamy and distant in the warm air.

He decided to talk to Mr. Leland Gaunt of Akron, Ohio, as soon as he finished with Brian Rusk, appointment or no appointment . . . and just as abruptly changed his mind. He'd call the Attorney General's Office in Augusta first, have them check Gaunt's name against the con file. If there was nothing there, they could send the name on to the LAWS R & I computer in Washington—LAWS, in Alan's opinion, was one of the few good things the Nixon administration had ever done.

The first kids were coming down the street now, yelling, skipping, laughing. A sudden idea struck Alan, and he opened the driver's door of the station wagon. He reached across the seat, opened the glove compartment, and pawed through the stuff inside. Todd's joke can of nuts fell out onto the floor as he did so.

Alan was about to give up when he found what he wanted. He took it, slammed the glove compartment shut, and backed out of the car. He was holding a small cardboard envelope with a sticker on it that said:

> *The Folding Flower Trick*
> *Blackstone Magic Co.*
> *19 Greer St.*
> *Paterson, N.J.*

From this packet Alan slipped an even smaller square—a thick block of multicolored tissue-paper. He slipped it beneath his watchband. All magicians have a number of "palming wells" on their persons and about their clothes, and each has his own favorite well. Under the watchband was Alan's.

With the famous Folding Flowers taken care of, Alan went

back to watching for Brian Rusk. He saw a boy on a bike, cutting jazzily in and out through the clots of pint-sized pedestrians, and was alert at once. Then he saw it was one of the Hanlon twins, and allowed himself to relax again.

"Slow down or I'll give you a ticket," Alan growled as the boy shot past. Jay Hanlon looked at him, startled, and almost ran into a tree. He pedaled on at a much more sedate speed.

Alan watched him for a moment, amused, then turned back in the direction of the school and resumed his watch for Brian Rusk.

7

Sally Ratcliffe climbed the stairs from her little speech therapy room to the first floor of the Middle School five minutes after the three o'clock bell and walked down the main hall toward the office. The hall was clearing rapidly, as it always did on days when the weather was fair and warm. Outside, droves of kids were shouting their way across the lawn to where the #2 and #3 buses idled sleepily at the curb. Sally's low heels clicked and clacked. She was holding a manila envelope in one hand. The name on this envelope, Frank Jewett, was turned in against her gently rounded breast.

She paused at Room 6, one door down from the office, and looked in through the wire-reinforced glass. Inside, Mr. Jewett was talking to the half-dozen teachers who were involved in coaching fall and winter sports. Frank Jewett was a pudgy little man who always reminded Sally of Mr. Weatherbee, the principal in the Archie comics. Like Mr. Weatherbee's, his glasses were always sliding down on his nose.

Sitting to his right was Alice Tanner, the school secretary. She appeared to be taking notes.

Mr. Jewett glanced to his left, saw Sally looking in the window, and gave her one of his prissy little smiles. She raised one hand in a wave and made herself smile back. She could remember the days when smiling had come naturally to her; next to praying, smiling had been the most natural thing in the world.

Some of the other teachers looked over to see who their fearless leader was looking at. So did Alice Tanner. Alice waggled her fingers coyly at Sally, smiling with saccharine sweetness.

They know, Sally thought. Every one of them knows that Lester and I are history. Irene was so sweet last night . . . so sympathetic . . . and so anxious to spill her guts. That little bitch.

Sally waggled her fingers right back, feeling her own coy—and totally bogus—smile stretch her lips. I hope you get hit by a dump-truck on your way home, you whory-looking thing, she thought, and then walked on, her sensible low heels clicking and clacking.

When Mr. Gaunt had called her during her free period and told her it was time to finish paying for the wonderful splinter, Sally had reacted with enthusiasm and a sour kind of pleasure. She sensed that the "little joke" she had promised to play on Mr. Jewett was a mean one, and that was all right with her. She felt mean today.

She put her hand on the office door . . . then paused.

What's the matter with you? she wondered suddenly. You have the splinter . . . the wonderful, holy splinter with the wonderful, holy vision caught inside it. Aren't things like that supposed to make a person feel better? Calmer? More in touch with God the Father Almighty? *You* don't feel calmer and more in touch with anyone. You feel like someone filled your head up with barbed wire.

"Yes, but that's not my fault, or the splinter's fault," Sally muttered. "That's Lester's fault. Mr. Lester Big-Prick Pratt."

A short girl wearing glasses and heavy braces turned from the Pep Club poster she'd been studying and glanced curiously at Sally.

"What are *you* looking at, Irvina?" Sally asked.

Irvina blinked. "Nuffink, Miz Rat-Cliff."

"Then go look at it someplace else," Sally snapped. "School is out, you know."

Irvina hurried down the hall, throwing an occasional distrustful glance back over her shoulder.

Sally opened the door to the office and went in. The envelope she carried had been right where Mr. Gaunt had told her it would be, behind the garbage cans outside the cafeteria doors. She had written Mr. Jewett's name on it herself.

She took one more quick glance over her shoulder to make sure that little whore Alice Tanner wasn't coming in. Then she opened the door to the inner office, hurried across the room, and laid the manila envelope on Frank Jewett's desk. Now there was the other thing.

She opened the top desk drawer and removed a pair of heavy scissors. She bent and yanked on the lower left-hand drawer. It was locked. Mr. Gaunt had told her that would probably be the case. Sally glanced into the outer office, saw it was still empty, the door to the hallway still shut. Good. Great. She jammed the tips of the scissors into the crack at the top of the locked drawer and levered them up, hard. Wood splintered, and Sally felt her nipples grow strangely, pleasantly hard. This was sort of fun. Scary, but fun.

She re-seated the scissors—the points went in farther this time—and levered them up again. The lock snapped and the drawer rolled open on its casters, revealing what was inside. Sally's mouth dropped open in shocked surprise. Then she began to giggle—breathy, stifled sounds that were really closer to screams than to laughter.

"Oh Mr. Jewett! What a naughty boy you are!"

There was a stack of digest-sized magazines inside the drawer, and *Naughty Boy* was, in fact, the name of the one on top. The blurry picture on the cover showed a boy of about nine. He was wearing a '50's-style motorcycle cap and nothing else.

Sally reached into the drawer and pulled out the magazines—there were a dozen of them, maybe more. *Happy Kids. Nude Cuties. Blowing in the Wind. Bobby's Farm World.* She looked into one and could barely believe what she was seeing. Where did things like this come from? They surely didn't sell them down at the drugstore, not even on the top rack Rev. Rose sometimes preached about in church, the one with the sign that said ONLY EYES 18 YRS AND OLDER PLEASE.

A voice she knew very well suddenly spoke up in her head. *Hurry, Sally. The meeting's almost over, and you don't want to be caught in here, do you?*

And then there was another voice as well, a woman's voice, one Sally could almost put a name to. Hearing this second voice was like being on the telephone with someone while someone else spoke in the background on the other end of the line.

More than fair, this second voice said. *It seems* divine.

Sally tuned the voice out and did what Mr. Gaunt had told her to do: she scattered the dirty magazines all over Mr. Jewett's office. Then she replaced the scissors and left the room quickly, pulling the door shut behind her. She opened the door of the outer office and peeked out. No one there . . . but the voices from Room 6 were louder now, and people were laughing. They *were* getting ready to break up; it had been an unusually short meeting.

Thank God for Mr. Gaunt! she thought, and slipped out into the hall. She had almost reached the front doors when she heard them coming out of Room 6 behind her. Sally didn't look around. It occurred to her that she hadn't thought of Mr. Lester Big-Prick Pratt for the last five minutes, and that was really fine. She thought she might go home and draw herself a nice bubble-bath and get into it with her wonderful splinter and spend the next two *hours* not thinking about Mr. Lester Big-Prick Pratt, and what a lovely change *that* would be! Yes, indeed! Yes, ind—

What did you do in there? What was in that envelope? Who put it there, outside the cafeteria? When? And, most important of all, Sally, what are you starting?

She stood still for a moment, feeling little beads of sweat form on her forehead and in the hollows of her temples. Her eyes went wide and startled, like the eyes of a frightened doe. Then they narrowed and she began to walk again. She was wearing slacks, and they chafed at her in a strangely pleasant way that made her think of her frequent necking sessions with Lester.

I don't *care* what I did, she thought. In fact, I hope it's something really mean. He *deserves* a mean trick, looking like Mr. Weatherbee but having all those disgusting magazines. I hope he *chokes* when he walks into his office.

"Yes, I hope he fucking *chokes*," she whispered. It was the first time in her life she had actually said the f-word out loud, and her nipples tightened and began to tingle again. Sally began to walk faster, thinking in some vague way that there might be something *else* she could do in the bathtub. It suddenly seemed to her that she had a need or two of her own. She wasn't sure exactly how to satisfy them . . . but she had an idea she could find out.

The Lord, after all, helped those who helped themselves.

8

"Does that seem like a fair price?" Mr. Gaunt asked Polly.

Polly started to reply, then paused. Mr. Gaunt's attention suddenly seemed to be diverted; he was gazing off into space and his lips were moving soundlessly, as if in prayer.

"Mr. Gaunt?"

He started slightly. Then his eyes returned to her and he smiled. "Pardon me, Polly. My mind wanders sometimes."

"The price seems more than fair," Polly told him. "It seems *divine*." She took her checkbook from her purse and began to write. Every now and then she would wonder vaguely just what she was up to here, and then she would feel Mr. Gaunt's eyes call hers. When she looked up and met them, the questions and doubts subsided again.

The check she handed to him was drawn in the amount of forty-six dollars. Mr. Gaunt folded it neatly and tucked it into the lapel pocket of his sport-jacket.

"Be sure to fill out the counterfoil," Mr. Gaunt said. "Your snoopy friend will undoubtedly want to see it."

"He's coming to see you," Polly said, doing exactly as Mr. Gaunt had suggested. "He thinks you're a confidence man."

"He's got lots of thoughts and lots of plans," Mr. Gaunt said, "but his plans are going to change and his thoughts are going to blow away like fog on a windy morning. Take my word for it."

"You . . . you're not going to hurt him, are you?"

"Me? You do me a very great wrong, Patricia Chalmers. I am a pacifist—one of the world's *great* pacifists. I wouldn't raise a hand against our Sheriff. I just meant that he's got business on the other side of the bridge this afternoon. He doesn't know it yet, but he does."

"Oh."

"Now, Polly?"

"Yes?"

"Your check does not constitute complete payment for the *azka.*"

"It doesn't?"

"No." He was holding a plain white envelope in his hands. Polly didn't have the slightest idea where it had come from, but that seemed perfectly all right. "In order to finish paying for your amulet, Polly, you have to help me play a little trick on someone."

"Alan?" Suddenly she was as alarmed as a woods-rabbit which gets a dry whiff of fire on a hot summer afternoon. "Do you mean *Alan?*"

"I most certainly do *not*," he said. "Asking you to play a trick on someone you *know,* let alone someone you think you *love,* would be unethical, my dear."

"It would?"

"Yes . . . although I believe you really ought to think carefully about your relationship with the Sheriff, Polly. You may find that it all comes down to a fairly simple choice: a little pain now to save a great deal of pain later. Put another way, those who marry in haste often live to repent in leisure."

"I don't understand you."

"I know you don't. You'll understand me better, Polly, after you check your mail. You see, I'm not the only one who has attracted his snooping, sniffy nose. For now, let us discuss the small prank I want you to play. The butt of this joke is a fellow whom I have just recently employed. His name is Merrill."

"*Ace* Merrill?"

His smile faded. "Don't interrupt me, Polly. Don't ever interrupt me when I am speaking. Not unless you want your hands to swell up like innertubes filled with poison gas."

She shrank away from him, her dreamy, dreaming eyes wide. "I . . . I'm sorry."

"All right. Your apology is accepted . . . this time. Now listen to me. Listen very carefully."

9

Frank Jewett and Brion McGinley, the Middle School's geography teacher and basketball coach, walked from Room 6 into the outer office just behind Alice Tanner. Frank was grinning and telling Brion a joke he'd heard earlier that day from a textbook salesman. It had to do with a doctor who was finding it difficult to diagnose a woman's illness. He had narrowed it down to two possibles—AIDS or Alzheimer's—but that was as far as he could go.

"So the gal's husband takes the doctor aside," Frank went on as they walked into the outer office. Alice was bending over her desk, thumbing through a little pile of messages there, and Frank lowered his voice. Alice could be quite the stick when it came to jokes which were even slightly off-color.

"Yeah?" Now Brion was also beginning to grin.

"Yeah. He's real upset. He says, 'Jeez, Doc—is that the best you can do? Isn't there some way we can figure out which one she has?'"

Alice selected two of the pink message forms and started into the inner office with them. She got as far as the doorway and then stopped short, as if she'd walked into an invisible stone wall. Neither of the grinning middle-aged small-town white guys noticed.

"'Sure, it's easy,' the doc says. 'Take her about twenty-five miles into the woods and leave her there. If she finds her way back, don't fuck her.'"

Brion McGinley gaped foolishly at his boss for a moment, then exploded into hearty guffaws of laughter. Principal Jewett joined him. They were laughing so hard that neither of them heard Alice the first time she called Frank's name. There was no problem the second time. The second time she nearly shrieked it.

Frank hurried over to her. "Alice? What—" Then he *saw* what, and a terrible, glassy fright filled him. His words dried up. He felt the flesh of his testicles crawling madly; his balls seemed to be trying to pull themselves back to where they had come from.

It was the magazines.

The secret magazines from the bottom drawer.

They had been spread all over the office like nightmare confetti: boys in uniforms, boys in haylofts, boys in straw hats, boys riding hobby-horses.

"What in God's name?" The voice, hoarse with horror and fascination, came from Frank's left. He turned his head in that direction (the tendons in his neck creaking like rusty screen-door springs) and saw Brion McGinley staring at the wild strew of magazines. His eyes were all but falling out of his face.

A prank, he tried to say. *A stupid prank, that's all, those magazines are not mine. You only have to look at me to know that magazines like that would hold no . . . hold no interest for a man . . . a man of my . . . my . . .*

His what?

He didn't know, and it didn't really matter, anyway, because he had lost his ability to speak. Entirely lost it.

The three adults stood in shocked silence, staring into the office of Middle School Principal Frank Jewett. A magazine which had been precariously balanced on the edge of the visitor's chair riffled its pages in response to a puff of hot air through the half-open window and then fell to the floor. *Saucy Young Guys,* the cover promised.

A prank, yes, I'll say it was a prank, but will they believe me? Suppose the desk drawer was forced? Will they believe me if it was?

"Mrs. Tanner?" a girl's voice asked from behind them.

All three of them—Jewett, Tanner, McGinley—whirled around guiltily. Two girls in red-and-white cheerleading outfits, eighth-graders, stood there. Alice Tanner and Brion McGinley moved almost simultaneously to block the view into Frank's office (Frank Jewett himself seemed rooted to the spot, turned to stone), but they moved just a little too late. The cheerleaders' eyes widened. One of them—Darlene Vickery—clapped her hands to her small rosebud mouth and stared at Frank Jewett unbelievingly.

Frank thought: Oh good. By noon tomorrow, every student in this school will know. By supper tomorrow night, everyone in town will know.

"You girls leave," Mrs. Tanner said. "Someone has played a nasty joke on Mr. Jewett—a *very* nasty joke—and you are not to say one word. Do you understand?"

"Yes, Mrs. Tanner," Erin McAvoy said; three minutes later

she would be telling her best friend, Donna Beaulieu, that Mr. Jewett's office had been decorated with pictures of boys wearing heavy metal bracelets and little else.

"Yes, Mrs. Tanner," Darlene Vickery said; five minutes later she would be telling *her* best friend, Natalie Priest.

"Go on," Brion McGinley said. He was trying to sound brisk, but his voice was still thick with shock. "Off you go."

The two girls fled, cheerleader skirts flipping about their sturdy knees.

Brion turned slowly to Frank. "I think—" he began, but Frank paid no notice. He walked into his office, moving slowly, like a man in a dream. He closed the door with the word PRIN-CIPAL lettered on it in neat black strokes, and slowly began picking up the magazines.

Why don't you just give them a written confession? part of his mind screamed.

He ignored the voice. A deeper part of him, the primitive voice of survival, was also speaking, and this part told him that right now he was at his most vulnerable. If he talked to Alice or Brion now, if he tried to explain this, he would hang himself as high as Haman.

Alice was knocking on the door. Frank ignored her and continued his dream-walk around the office, picking up the magazines he had accumulated over the last nine years, writing away for them one by one and picking them up at the post office in Gates Falls, sure each time that the State Police or a team of Postal Inspectors would fall on him like a ton of bricks. None ever had. But now . . . this.

They won't believe they belong to you, the primitive voice said. They won't *allow* themselves to believe it—to do that would upset too many of their comfy small-town conceptions of life. Once you get yourself under control, you should be able to put it over. But . . . who would have done something like this? Who *could* have done something like this? (It never occurred to Frank to ask himself what mad compulsion had caused him to bring the magazines here—*here,* of all places—in the first place.)

There was only one person Frank Jewett could think of—the one person from The Rock with whom he'd shared his secret life. George T. Nelson, the high school wood shop teacher. George T. Nelson, who, under his bluff, macho exterior, was just as gay as old dad's hatband. George T. Nelson, with whom Frank Jewett had once attended a sort of party in Boston, the sort of party where there were a great many middle-aged men and a small group of undressed boys. The sort of party that could land you in jail for the rest of your life. The sort of party—

There was a manila envelope sitting on his desk blotter. His name was written on the center of it. Frank Jewett felt a horrible sinking sensation in the pit of his belly. It felt like an elevator out of control. He looked up and saw Alice and Brion peering in at him, almost cheek to cheek. Their eyes were wide, their mouths open, and Frank thought: Now I know what it feels like to be a fish in an aquarium.

He waved at them—*go away!* They didn't go, and this somehow did not surprise him. This was a nightmare, and in nightmares, things never went the way you wanted them to. That was why they were nightmares. He felt a terrible sense of loss and disorientation . . . but somewhere beneath it, like a living spark beneath a heap of wet kindling, was a little blue flame of anger.

He sat behind his desk and put the stack of magazines on the floor. He saw that the drawer they'd been in had been forced, just as he had feared. He ripped open the envelope and spilled out the contents. Most of them were glossy photographs. Photographs of him and George T. Nelson at that party in Boston. They were cavorting with a number of nice young fellows (the oldest of the nice young fellows might have been twelve), and in each picture George T. Nelson's face was obscured but Frank Jewett's was crystal clear.

This didn't much surprise Frank, either.

There was a note in the envelope. He took it out and read it.

Frank old Buddy,

    Sorry to do this, but I have to leave town and
have no time to fuck around. I want $2,000.
Bring it to my house tonight at 7:00 p.m. So
far you can wiggle out of this thing, it will be
tough but no real problem for a slippery bastard
like you, but ask yourself how you're going to
like seeing copies of these pix nailed up on every
phone pole in town, right under those Casino
Nite posters. They will run you out of town on a
rail, old Buddy. Remember, $2,000 at my house
by 7:15 at the latest or you will wish you were
born without a dick.

                                Your friend,
                                George

Your friend.

Your *friend!*

His eyes kept returning to that closing line with a kind of
incredulous, wondering horror.

Your motherfucking backstabbing Judas-kissing *FRIEND!*

Brion McGinley was still hammering on the door, but
when Frank Jewett finally looked up from whatever it was on
his desk which had taken his attention, Brion's fist paused in
mid-stroke. The principal's face was waxy white except for two
bright clown-spots of flush on his cheeks. His lips were drawn
back from his teeth in a narrow smile.

He didn't look in the least like Mr. Weatherbee.

My *friend,* Frank thought. He crumpled the note with one
hand as he shoved the glossy photographs back into the envelope with the other. Now the blue spark of anger had turned or-

ange. The wet kindling was catching fire. *I'll be there, all right.*
I'll be there to discuss this matter with my friend George T. Nelson.

"Yes indeed," Frank Jewett said. "Yes *indeed.*" He began to
smile.

10

It was going on quarter past three and Alan had decided Brian
Rusk must have taken a different route; the flood of home-
going students had almost dried up. Then, just as he was reaching into his pocket for his car-keys, he saw a lone figure biking
down School Street toward him. The boy was riding slowly,
seeming almost to trudge over the handlebars, and his head
was bent so low Alan couldn't see his face.

But he could see what was in the carrier basket of the boy's
bike: a Playmate cooler.

11

"Do you understand?" Gaunt asked Polly, who was now holding the envelope.

"Yes, I . . . I understand. I do." But her dreaming face was
troubled.

"You don't look happy."

"Well . . . I . . . ."

"Things like the *azka* don't always work very well for people
who aren't happy," Mr. Gaunt said. He pointed at the tiny
bulge where the silver ball lay against her skin, and again she
seemed to feel something shift strangely inside. At the same
moment, horrible cramps of pain invaded her hands, spreading
like a network of cruel steel hooks. Polly moaned loudly.

Mr. Gaunt crooked the finger he had pointed in a come-along gesture. She felt that shift in the silver ball again, more clearly this time, and the pain was gone.

"You don't want to go back to the way things were, do you, Polly?" Mr. Gaunt asked in a silky voice.

"No!" she cried. Her breast was moving rapidly up and down. Her hands began to make frantic washing gestures, one against the other, and her wide eyes never left his. "Please, no!"

"Because things could go from bad to worse, couldn't they?"

"Yes! Yes, they could!"

"And nobody understands, do they? Not even the Sheriff. *He* doesn't know what it's like to wake up at two in the morning with hell in his hands, does he?"

She shook her head and began to weep.

"Do as I say and you'll never have to wake up that way again, Polly. And here is something else—do as I say and if anyone in Castle Rock finds out that your child burned to death in a San Francisco tenement, they won't find it out from *me.*"

Polly uttered a hoarse, lost cry—the cry of a woman hopelessly ensnarled in a grinding nightmare.

Mr. Gaunt smiled.

"There are more kinds of hell than one, aren't there, Polly?"

"How do you know about him?" she whispered. "No one knows. Not even Alan. I told Alan—"

"I know because knowing is my business. And suspicion is his, Polly—Alan never believed what you told him."

"He said—"

"I'm sure he said all kinds of things, but he never believed you. The woman you hired to baby sit was a drug addict, wasn't she? That wasn't *your* fault, but of course the things which led to that situation were all a matter of personal choice, Polly, weren't they? *Your* choice. The young woman you hired to watch Kelton passed out and dropped a cigarette—or maybe it was a joint—into a waste-basket. Hers was the finger that pulled the trigger, you might say, but the gun was loaded because of your pride, your inability to bend your neck before your parents and the other good people of Castle Rock."

Polly was sobbing harder now.

"Yet is a young woman not entitled to her pride?" Mr. Gaunt asked gently. "When everything else is gone, is she not at least entitled to this, the coin without which her purse is entirely empty?"

Polly raised her streaming, defiant face. "I thought it was my business," she said. "I still do. If that's pride, so what?"

"Yes," he said soothingly. "Spoken like a champion . . . but they *would* have taken you back, wouldn't they? Your mother and father? It might not have been pleasant—not with the child always there to remind them, not with the way tongues wag in pleasant little backwaters like this one—but it would have been possible."

"Yes, and I would have spent every day trying to stay out from under my mother's thumb!" she burst out in a furious, ugly voice which bore almost no resemblance to her normal tone.

"Yes," Mr. Gaunt said in that same soothing voice. "So you stayed where you were. You had Kelton, and you had your pride. And when Kelton was dead, you still had your pride . . . didn't you?"

Polly screamed in grief and agony and buried her wet face in her hands.

"It hurts worse than your hands, doesn't it?" Mr. Gaunt asked. Polly nodded her head without taking her face out of her hands. Mr. Gaunt put his own ugly, long-fingered hands behind his head and spoke in the tone of one who gives a eulogy: "Humanity! So noble! So willing to sacrifice the other fellow!"

"Stop!" she moaned. "Can't you stop?"

"It's a secret thing, isn't it, Patricia?"

"Yes."

He touched her forehead. Polly uttered a gagging moan but did not draw away.

"That's one door into hell you'd like to keep locked, isn't it?" She nodded inside her hands.

"Then do as I say, Polly," he whispered. He took one of her hands away from her face and began caressing it. "Do as I say, and keep your mouth shut." He looked closely at her wet cheeks and her streaming, reddened eyes. A little *moue* of disgust puckered his lips for a moment.

"I don't know which makes me sicker—a crying woman or a laughing man. Wipe your goddamned face, Polly."

Slowly, dreamily, she took a lace-edged handkerchief from her purse and began to do it.

"That's good," he said, and rose. "I'll let you go home now, Polly; you have things to do. But I want you to know it has been a great pleasure doing business with you. I have always *so* enjoyed ladies who take pride in themselves."

12

"Hey, Brian—want to see a trick?"

The boy on the bicycle looked up fast, the hair flying off his forehead, and Alan saw an unmistakable expression on his face: naked, unadulterated fear.

"Trick?" the boy said in a trembling voice. "What trick?"

Alan didn't know what the boy was afraid of, but he understood one thing—his magic, which he had relied upon often as an ice breaker with children, had for some reason been exactly the wrong thing this time. Best to get it out of the way as soon as possible and start over again.

He held up his left arm—the one watch on it—and smiled into Brian Rusk's pale, watchful, frightened face. "You'll notice that there's nothing up my sleeve and that my arm goes all the way up to my shoulder. But now . . . *presto!*"

Alan passed his open right hand slowly down his left arm, snapping the little packet effortlessly out from beneath his watch with his right thumb as he did so. As he closed his fist, he slipped the almost microscopic loop that held the packet closed. He clasped his left hand over his right, and when he spread them apart, a large tissue-paper bouquet of unlikely flowers bloomed where there had been nothing but thin air a moment before.

Alan had done this trick hundreds of times and never better than on this hot October afternoon, but the expected reaction—a moment of stunned surprise followed by a grin that was one part amazement and two parts admiration—didn't dawn on Brian's face. He gave the bouquet a cursory glance (there seemed to be relief in that brief look, as if he had expected the trick to be of a far less pleasant nature) and then returned his gaze to Alan's face.

"Pretty neat, huh?" Alan asked. He stretched his lips in a big smile that felt every bit as genuine as his grandfather's dentures.

"Yeah," Brian said.

"Uh-huh. I can see you're blown away." Alan brought his hands together, deftly collapsing the bouquet again. It was easy—too easy, really. It was time to buy a new copy of the Folding Flower Trick; they only lasted so long. The tiny spring in this one was getting loose and the brightly colored paper would soon begin to rip.

He opened his hands again, smiling rather more hopefully now. The bouquet was gone; was once more just a small packet of paper under his watchband. Brian Rusk did not return his smile; his face wore no real expression at all. The remnants of his summer tan could not cover the pallor beneath, nor the fact that his complexion was in an unusual state of pre-pubescent revolt: a scatter of pimples on the forehead, a bigger one by the corner of his mouth, blackheads nesting on either side of his nose. There were purplish shadows under his eyes, as if his last good night's sleep had been a long time ago.

This kid is a long way from right, Alan thought. There's

something badly sprained, maybe even broken here. There seemed to be two likely possibilities: either Brian Rusk had seen whoever had vandalized the Jerzyck house, or he had done it himself. It was paydirt either way, but if it was the second choice, Alan could barely imagine the size and weight of the guilt which must now be harrowing this boy.

"That's a great trick, Sheriff Pangborn," Brian said in a colorless, emotionless voice. "Really."

"Thanks—glad you liked it. Do you know what I want to talk to you about, Brian?"

"I . . . guess I do," Brian said, and Alan was suddenly sure the boy was going to confess to breaking the windows. Right here on this street-corner he was going to confess, and Alan was going to take a giant step toward unravelling what had happened between Nettie and Wilma.

But Brian said nothing more. He only looked up at Alan with his tired, slightly bloodshot eyes.

"What happened, son?" Alan asked in the same quiet voice. "What happened while you were at the Jerzycks' house?"

"Don't know," Brian said. His voice was listless. "But I dreamed about it last night. Sunday night, too. I dream about going to that house, only in my dream I see what's really making all the noise."

"And what's that, Brian?"

"A monster," Brian said. His voice did not change, but a large tear had appeared in each of his eyes, growing on the lower arcs of the lids. "In my dream I knock on the door instead of riding away like I did and the door opens and it's a monster and it eats . . . me . . . up." The tears brimmed, then rolled slowly down the disturbed skin of Brian Rusk's cheeks.

And yes, Alan thought, it could be that, too—simple fright. The sort of fright a little kid might feel when he opens the bedroom door at the wrong time and sees his mother and father screwing. Only because he's too young to know the look of screwing, he thinks they're fighting. Maybe he even thinks, if they're making a lot of noise, that they're trying to kill each other.

But—

But it didn't feel right. It was just that simple. It felt as if this kid were lying his head off, in spite of the haggard look in his eyes, the look that said *I want to tell you everything.* What did that mean? Alan didn't know for sure, but experience taught him that the likeliest solution was that Brian knew whoever had thrown the rocks. Maybe it was someone Brian felt obliged to protect. Or maybe the rock-thrower knew Brian had seen him, and Brian knew *that.* Maybe the kid was afraid of reprisals.

"A person threw a bunch of rocks into the Jerzycks' house," Alan said in a low and (he hoped) soothing voice.

"Yes, sir," Brian said—almost sighed. "I guess so. I guess it could have been that, I thought they were fighting, but it could have been someone throwing rocks. Crash, boom, bang."

The whole rhythm section was the Purple Gang, Alan thought but did not say. "You thought they were fighting?"

"Yes, sir."

"Is that what you really thought?"

"Yes, sir."

Alan sighed. "Well, you know what it was now. And you know it was a bad thing to do. Throwing rocks through somebody's windows is a pretty serious business, even if nothing else comes of it."

"Yes, sir."

"But this time, something else *did* come of it. You know that, don't you, Brian?"

"Yes, sir."

Those eyes, looking up at him from that calm, pallid face. Alan began to understand two things: this boy *did* want to tell him what had happened, but he was almost certainly not going to do so.

"You look very unhappy, Brian."

"Yes, sir?"

" 'Yes, sir' . . . does that mean you *are* unhappy?"

Brian nodded, and two more tears spilled from his eyes and rolled down his cheeks. Alan felt two strong, conflicting emotions: deep pity and wild exasperation.

"What are you unhappy about, Brian? Tell me."

"I used to have this really nice dream," Brian said in a voice which was almost too low to hear. "It was stupid, but it was nice, just the same. It was about Miss Ratcliffe, my speech teacher. Now I know it's stupid. I didn't used to know, and that was better. But guess what? I know more than that now."

Those dark, terribly unhappy eyes rose to meet Alan's again.

"The dream I have . . . the one about the monster who throws the rocks . . . it scares me, Sheriff Pangborn . . . but what makes me unhappy are the things I know now. It's like knowing how the magician does his tricks."

He nodded his head a little, and Alan could have sworn Brian was looking at the band of his watch.

"Sometimes it's better to be dumb. I know that now."

Alan put a hand on the boy's shoulder. "Brian, let's cut through the bullshit, all right? Tell me what happened. Tell me what you saw and what you did."

"I came to see if they wanted their driveway shovelled this winter," the boy said in a mechanical rote voice that frightened Alan badly. The kid looked like almost any American child of eleven or twelve—Converse sneakers, jeans, a tee-shirt with Bart Simpson on it—but he sounded like a robot which has been badly programmed and is now in danger of overloading. For the first time, Alan wondered if Brian Rusk had maybe seen one of his own parents throwing rocks at the Jerzyck house.

"I heard noises," the boy was continuing. He spoke in simple declarative sentences, talking as police detectives are trained to talk in court. "They were scary noises. Bangs and crashes and things breaking. So I rode away as fast as I could. The lady from next door was out on her stoop. She asked me what was going on. I think she was scared, too."

"Yes," Alan said. "Jillian Mislaburski. I talked to her." He touched the Playmate cooler sitting crookedly in the basket of Brian's bike. He was not unaware of the way Brian's lips tightened when he did this. "Did you have this cooler with you on Sunday morning, Brian?"

"Yes, sir," Brian said. He wiped his cheeks with the backs of his hands and watched Alan's face warily.

"What was in it?"

Brian said nothing, but Alan thought his lips were trembling.

"What was in it, Brian?"

Brian said a little more nothing.

"Was it full of rocks?"

Slowly and deliberately, Brian shook his head—no.

For the third time, Alan asked: "What was in it?"

"Same thing that's in it now," Brian whispered.

"May I open it and see?"

"Yes, sir," Brian said in his listless voice. "I guess so."

Alan rotated the cover to one side and looked into the cooler.

It was full of baseball cards: Topps, Fleer, Donruss.

"These are my traders. I carry them with me almost everywhere," Brian said.

"You . . . carry them with you."

"Yes, sir."

"Why, Brian? Why do you cart a cooler filled with baseball cards around with you?"

"I *told* you—they're traders. You never know when you'll get a chance to make a boss trade with someone. I'm still looking for a Joe Foy—he was on the Impossible Dream team in '67—and a Mike Greenwell rookie card. The Gator's my favorite player." And now Alan thought he saw a faint, fugitive gleam of amusement in the boy's eyes; could almost hear a telepathic voice chanting *Fooled ya! Fooled ya!* But surely that was only him; only his own frustration mocking the boy's voice.

Wasn't it?

Well, what did you *expect* to find inside that cooler, anyway? A pile of rocks with notes tied around them? Did you actually think he was on his way to do the same thing to someone *else's* house?

Yes, he admitted. Part of him had thought exactly that. Brian Rusk, The Pint-Sized Terror of Castle Rock. The Mad Rocker. And the worst part was this: he was pretty sure Brian Rusk knew what was going through his head.

Fooled ya! Fooled ya, Sheriff!

"Brian, please tell me what's going on around here. If you know, please tell me."

Brian closed the lid of the Playmate cooler and said nothing. It made a soft little *snick!* in the drowsy autumn afternoon.

"Can't say?"

Brian nodded slowly—meaning, Alan thought, that he was right: he couldn't say.

"Tell me this, at least: are you scared? Are you scared, Brian?"

Brian nodded again, just as slowly.

"Tell me what you're scared of, son. Maybe I can make it go away." He tapped one finger lightly against the badge he wore on the left side of his uniform shirt. "I think that's why they pay me to lug this star around. Because sometimes I can make the scary stuff go away."

"I—" Brian began, and then the police radio Alan had installed beneath the dash of the Town and Country wagon three or four years ago squawked to life.

"Unit One, Unit One, this is base. Do you copy? Over?"

Brian's eyes broke away from Alan's. They turned toward the station wagon and the sound of Sheila Brigham's voice—the voice of authority, the voice of the police. Alan saw that, if the boy had been on the verge of telling him something (and it might only be wishful thinking to believe he had been), he wasn't anymore. His face had closed up like a clamshell.

"You go on home now, Brian. We're going to talk about this . . . this dream of yours . . . more later on. Okay?"

"Yes, sir," Brian said. "I guess so."

"In the meantime, think about what I said: most of what being Sheriff's about is making the scary stuff go away."

"I have to go home now, Sheriff. If I don't get home pretty soon, my mom's gonna be mad at me."

Alan nodded. "Well, we don't want that. Go on, Brian."

He watched the boy go. Brian's head was down, and once again he did not seem to be riding the bike so much as trudging along with it between his legs. Something was wrong there, so wrong that Alan's finding out what had happened to Wilma and Nettie seemed secondary to finding out what had put the tired, haunted expression on that kid's face.

The women, after all, were dead and buried. Brian Rusk was still alive.

He went to the tired old station wagon he should have traded a year ago, leaned in, grabbed the Radio Shack mike, and depressed the transmit button. "Yeah, Sheila, this is Unit One. I copy—come on back."

"Henry Payton called for you, Alan," Sheila said. "He told me to tell you it's urgent. He wants me to patch you through to him. Ten-four?"

"Go for it," Alan said. He felt his pulse pick up.

"It may take a couple of minutes, ten-four?"

"That's fine. I'll be right here. Unit One clear."

He leaned against the side of the car in the dappled shade, mike in hand, waiting to see what was urgent in Henry Payton's life.

13

By the time Polly reached home, it was twenty minutes past three, and she felt torn in two completely different directions. On one hand, she felt a deep, drumming need to be about the errand Mr. Gaunt had given her (she didn't like to think of it in his terms, as a prank—Polly Chalmers was not much of a prankster), to get it done so that the *azka* would finally belong to her. The concept that the dealing wasn't done until Mr. Gaunt *said* the dealing was done had not so much as crossed her mind.

On the other hand, she felt a deep, drumming need to get in touch with Alan, to tell him exactly what had happened . . . or as much of it as she could remember. One thing she *could* remember—it filled her with shame and a low sort of horror, but she could remember it, all right—was this: Mr. Leland Gaunt hated the man Polly loved, and Mr. Gaunt was doing something—*something*—that was very wrong. Alan should know. Even if the *azka* stopped working, he should know.

You don't mean that.

But yes—part of her meant *exactly* that. The part that was terrified of Leland Gaunt even though she couldn't remember what, exactly, he had done to induce that feeling of terror.

Do you want to go back to the way things were, Polly? Do you want to go back to owning a pair of hands that feel full of shrapnel?

No . . . but neither did she want Alan hurt. Neither did she want Mr. Gaunt to do whatever he was planning to do, if it was something (she suspected it was) that would hurt the town. Nor did she want to be a part of that something, by going out to the old deserted Camber place at the end of Town Road #3 and playing some sort of trick she didn't even understand.

So these conflicting wants, each championed by its own hectoring voice, pulled at her as she walked slowly home. If

Mr. Gaunt had hypnotized her in some way (she had been positive of this when she left the store, but she became less and less sure as time passed), the effects had worn off now. (Polly really believed this.) And she had never in her life found herself so incapable of deciding what to do next. It was as if her whole supply of some vital decision-making chemical had been stolen from her brain.

In the end she went home to do what Mr. Gaunt had advised (although she no longer precisely remembered the advice). She would check her mail, and then she would call Alan and tell him what Mr. Gaunt wanted her to do.

If you do that, the interior voice said grimly, the *azka* really *will* stop working. And you know it.

Yes—but there was still the question of right and wrong. There was still that. She would call Alan, and apologize for being so short with him, and then tell him what Mr. Gaunt wanted of her. Perhaps she would even give him the envelope Mr. Gaunt had given her, the one she was supposed to put in the tin can.

Perhaps.

Feeling a little better, Polly put her key in the front door of her house—again rejoicing at the ease of this operation, almost without being aware of it—and turned it. The mail was in its usual place on the carpet—not very much today. Usually there was more junk mail after the Post Office had taken a day off. She bent and picked it up. A cable-TV brochure with Tom Cruise's smiling, impossibly handsome face on the front; one catalogue from the Horchow Collection and another from The Sharper Image. Also—

Polly saw the one letter and a ball of dread began to grow deep in her stomach. To Patricia Chalmers of Castle Rock, from the San Francisco Department of Child Welfare . . . from 666 Geary. She remembered 666 Geary so very well from her trips down there. Three trips in all. Three interviews with three Aid to Dependent Children bureaucrats, two of whom had been men—men who had looked at her the way you looked at a candy-wrapper that's gotten stuck on one of your best shoes. The third bureaucrat had been an extremely large black woman, a woman who had known how to listen and how to laugh, and it was from this woman that Polly had finally gotten an approval. But she remembered 666 Geary, second floor, so very, very well. She remembered the way the light from the big window at the end of the hall had laid a long, milky stain on the linoleum; she remembered the echoey sound of typewriters from offices where the doors always stood open; she remembered the cluster of men smoking cigarettes by the sand-filled urn at the far end of the hall, and how they had looked at her. Most of all she remembered how it had felt to be dressed in her one good outfit—a dark polyester pants suit, a white silk blouse, L'Eggs Nearly Nude pantyhose, her low heels—and how terrified and lonely she had felt, for the dim second-floor corridor of 666 Geary seemed to be a place with neither heart nor soul. Her ADC application had finally been approved there, but it was the turndowns she remembered, of course—the eyes of the men, how they had crawled across her breasts (they were better dressed than Norville down at the diner, but otherwise, she thought, not really much different); the mouths of the men, how they had pursed in decorous disapproval as they considered the problem of Kelton Chalmers, the bastard offspring of this little trollop, this Janey-come-lately who didn't look like a hippie *now,* oh *no,* but who would undoubtedly take off her silk blouse and nice pants suit as soon as she got out of here, not to mention her brassiere, and put on a pair of tight bellbottom jeans and a tie-dyed blouse that would showcase her nipples. Their eyes said all that and more, and although the response of the Department had come in the mail, Polly had known immediately that she would be turned down. She had wept as she left the building on each of those first two occasions, and it seemed to her now that she could remember the acid-trickle of each tear as it slid down her cheek.

That, and the way the people on the street had looked at her. No caring in their eyes; just a certain dull curiosity.

She had never wanted to think about those times or that dim second-floor hallway again, but now it was back with her—so clearly she could smell the floor polish, could see the milky reflected light from the big window, could hear the echoey, dreamy sound of old manual typewriters chewing through another day in the bowels of the bureaucracy.

What did they want? Dear God, what could the people at 666 Geary want with her at this late date?

Tear it up! a voice inside nearly screamed, and the command was so imperative that she came very close to doing just that. She ripped the envelope open instead. There was a single sheet of paper inside. It was a Xerox. And although the envelope had been addressed to her, she saw with astonishment that the letter was not; it was addressed to Sheriff Alan Pangborn.

Her eyes dropped to the foot of the letter. The name typed below the scrawled signature was John L. Perlmutter, and this name rang a very faint bell for her. Her eyes dropped a little further and she saw, at the very foot of the letter, the notation "cc: Patricia Chalmers." Well, this was a Xerox, not a carbon, but it still cleared up the puzzling matter of this being Alan's letter (and settled her first confused idea that it had been delivered to her by mistake). But what, in God's name . . .

Polly sat on the Shaker bench in the hallway and began to read the letter. As she did so, a remarkable series of emotions lensed across her face, like cloud formations on an unsettled, windy day: puzzlement, understanding, shame, horror, anger, and finally fury. She screamed aloud once—*"No!"*—and then went back and forced herself to read the letter again, slowly, all the way to the end.

San Francisco Department of Child Welfare

666 Geary Street

San Francisco, California 94112

September 23, 1991

Sheriff Alan J. Pangborn
Castle County Sheriff's Office
2 The Municipal Building
Castle Rock, Maine 04055

Dear Sheriff Pangborn:

I am in receipt of your letter of September 1, and am writing to tell you I can offer you no help whatever in this matter. It is the policy of this Department to give out information on applicants for Aid to Dependent Children (ADC) only when we are compelled to do so by a valid court order. I have shown your letter to Martin D. Chung, our chief legal counsel, who instructs me to tell you that a copy of your letter has been forwarded to the California Attorney General's Office. Mr. Chung has asked for an opinion as to whether your request may be illegal in and of itself. Whatever the result of that inquiry, I must tell you that I find your curiosity about this woman's life in San Francisco to be both inappropriate and offensive.

I suggest, Sheriff Pangborn, that you lay this matter to rest before you incur legal difficulties.

Sincerely,

John L. Perlmutter
Deputy Director

cc: Patricia Chalmers

After her fourth reading of this terrible letter, Polly rose from the bench and walked into the kitchen. She walked slowly and gracefully, more like one who swims than one who walks. At first her eyes were dazed and confused, but by the time she had taken the handset from the wall mounted phone and tapped out the number of the Sheriff's Office on the oversized pads, they had cleared. The look which lit them was simple and unmistakable: an anger so strong it was nearly hate.

Her lover had been sniffing around in her past—she found the idea simultaneously unbelievable and strangely, hideously plausible. She had done a lot of comparing herself to Alan Pangborn in the last four or five months, and that meant she had done a lot of coming off second best. His tears; her deceptive calm, which hid so much shame and hurt and secret defiant pride. His honesty; her little stack of lies. How saintlike he had seemed! How dauntingly perfect! How hypocritical her own insistence that he put the past away!

And all the time he had been sniffing around, trying to find out the real story on Kelton Chalmers.

"You bastard," she whispered, and as the telephone began to ring, the knuckles of the hand holding the telephone turned white with strain.

14

Lester Pratt usually left Castle Rock High in the company of several friends; they would all go down to Hemphill's Market for sodas, then head off to someone's house or apartment for a couple of hours to sing hymns or play games or just shoot the bull. Today, however, Lester left school alone with his knapsack on his back (he disdained the traditional teacher's briefcase) and his head down. If Alan had been there to watch Lester walk slowly across the school lawn toward the faculty parking lot, he would have been struck by the man's resemblance to Brian Rusk.

Three times that day Lester had tried to get in touch with Sally, to find out what in the land of Goshen had made her so mad. The last time had been during his period five lunchbreak. He knew she was at the Middle School, but the closest he got to her was a call-back from Mona Lawless who taught sixth- and seventh-grade math and chummed with Sally.

"She can't come to the phone," Mona told him, displaying all the warmth of a deep-freeze stuffed with Popsicles.

"Why not?" he had asked—almost whined. "Come on, Mona—give!"

"I don't know." Mona's tone had progressed from Popsicles in the deep-freeze to the verbal equivalent of liquid nitrogen. "All I know is that she's been staying with Irene Lutjens, she looks like she spent all last night crying, and she says she doesn't want to talk to you." *And this is all your fault,* Mona's frozen tone said. *I know that because you're a man and all men are dogshit—this is just another specific example illustrating the general case.*

"Well I don't have the slightest idea what it's all about!" Lester shouted. "Will you tell her that, at least? Tell her I don't know, why she's mad at me! Tell her whatever it is, it must be a misunderstanding, *because I don't get it!*"

There was a long pause. When Mona spoke again, her voice had warmed up a little. Not much, but it was a lot better than liquid nitrogen. "All right, Lester. I'll tell her."

Now he raised his head, half-hoping Sally might be sitting in the passenger seat of the Mustang, ready to kiss and make up, but the car was empty. The only person close to it was softheaded Slopey Dodd, goofing around on his skateboard.

Steve Edwards came up behind Lester and clapped him on the shoulder. "Les, boy! Want to come over to my place for a Coke? A bunch of the guys said they'd drop by. We have to talk about this outrageous Catholic harassment. The big meeting's at the church tonight, don't forget, and it would be good if we Y.A.'s could present a united front when it comes to deciding what to do. I mentioned the idea to Don Hemphill and he said yeah, great, go for it." He looked at Lester as if he expected a pat on the head.

"I can't this afternoon, Steve. Maybe another time."

"Hey, Les—don't you get it? There may not *be* another time! The Pope's boys aren't fooling around anymore!"

"I can't come over," Les said. And if you're wise, his face said, you'll stop pushing it.

"Well, but . . . why not?"

Because I have to find out what the heck I did to make my girl so angry, Lester thought. And I *am* going to find out, even if I have to shake it out of her.

Out loud he said, "I've got stuff to do, Steve. Important stuff. Take my word for it."

"If this is about Sally, Les—"

Lester's eyes flashed dangerously. "You just shut up about Sally."

Steve, an inoffensive young man who had been set aflame by the strife over Casino Nite, was not yet burning brightly enough to overstep the line Lester Pratt had so clearly drawn. But neither was he quite ready to give up. Without Lester Pratt, a Young Adults' Policy Meeting was a joke, no matter how many from the Y.A. group turned out. Pitching his voice more reasonably, he said: "You know the anonymous card Bill got?"

"Yes," Lester said. Rev. Rose had found it on the floor of the parsonage front hallway: the already-notorious "Babtist Rat-Fuck" card. The Reverend had passed it around at a hastily called Guys Only Y.A. meeting because, he said, it was impossible to credit unless you saw the vile thing for yourself. It was hard to fully understand, Rev. Rose had added, the depths to which the Catholics would sink-uh in order to stifle righteous opposition to their Satan-inspired night of gambling; perhaps actually seeing this vile spew of filth would help these "fine young men" comprehend what they were up against. "For do we not say that forewarned is-uh forearmed?" Rev. Rose had finished grandly. He then produced the card (it was inside a Baggie, as if those who handled it needed to be guarded from infection) and handed it around.

As Lester finished reading it, he had been more than ready to ring a few sets of Catholic chimes, but now the entire affair seemed distant and somehow childish. Who really cared if the Catholics gambled for play money and gave away a few new tires and kitchen appliances? When it came down to a choice between the Catholics and Sally Ratcliffe, Lester knew which one he had to worry about.

"—a meeting to try and work out the next step!" Steve was continuing. He was starting to get hot again. "We have to seize the initiative here, Les . . . we *have* to! Reverend Bill says he's worried that these so called Concerned Catholic Men are through talking. Their next step may be—"

"Look, Steve, do whatever you want, *but leave me out of it!*"

Steve stopped and stared at him, clearly shocked and just as clearly expecting Lester, normally the most eventempered of fellows, to come to his senses and apologize. When he realized no apology was forthcoming, he started to walk back toward the school, putting distance between himself and Lester. "Boy, you're in a rotten mood," he said.

"That's right!" Lester called back truculently. He rolled his big hands into fists and planted them on his hips.

But Lester was more than just angry; he hurt, damn it, he hurt all over, and what hurt the worst was his *mind,* and he wanted to strike out at someone. Not poor old Steve Edwards; it was just that allowing himself to get pissed at Steve seemed to have turned on a switch inside him. That switch had sent electricity flowing to a lot of mental appliances which were usually dark and silent. For the first time since he'd fallen in love with Sally, Lester—normally the most placid of men—felt angry at her, too. What right had she to tell him to go to hell? What right did she have to call him a bastard?

She was mad about something, was she? All right, she was mad. Maybe he had even give a her something to be mad about. He hadn't the slightest idea what that something might be, but say (just for the sake of argument) that he had. Did that give her the right to fly off the handle at him without even doing him the courtesy of asking for an explanation first? Did it give her the right to stay with Irene Lutjens so he couldn't crash his way into wherever she was, or to refuse all his telephone calls, or to employ Mona Lawless as a go-between?

I'm going to find her, Lester thought, and I'm going to find out what's eating her. Then, once it's out, we can make up. And after we do, I'm going to give her the same lecture I give my freshmen when basketball practice starts—about how trust is the key to teamwork.

He stripped off his pack, chucked it into the back seat, and climbed into his car. As he did, he saw something sticking out from under the passenger seat. Something black. It looked like a wallet.

Lester seized it eagerly, thinking at first that it must be Sally's. If she had left it in his car at some point during the long holiday weekend, she must have missed it by now. She'd be anxious. And if he could relieve her anxiety about her lost wallet, the rest of their conversation might become a little easier.

But it wasn't Sally's; he saw that as soon as he got a close look at the item which had been under the passenger seat. It was black leather. Sally's was scuffed blue suede, and much smaller.

Curiously, he opened it. The first thing he saw struck him like a hard blow to the solar plexus. It was John LaPointe's Sheriff's Department ID.

What in the name of God had John LaPointe been doing in *his* car?

Sally had it all weekend, his mind whispered. So just what the hell do you *think* he was doing in your car?

"No," he said. "Uh-uh, no *way*—she wouldn't. She wouldn't see *him*. No way in hell."

But she *had* seen him. She and Deputy John LaPointe had gone out together for over a year, in spite of the developing bad feelings between Castle Rock's Catholics and Baptists. They had broken up before the current hooraw over Casino Nite, but—

Lester got out of the car again and flipped through the wallet's see-through pockets. His sense of incredulity grew. Here was LaPointe's driver's license—in the picture on it, he was wearing the little moustache he'd cultivated when he'd been going out with Sally. Lester knew what some fellows called moustaches like that: pussy-ticklers. Here was John LaPointe's fishing license. Here was a picture of John LaPointe's mother and father. Here was his hunting license. And here . . . *here* . . .

Lester stared fixedly at the snapshot he'd come upon. It was a snapshot of John and Sally. A snap of a fellow and his best girl. They were standing in front of what looked like a carnival shooting-gallery. They were looking at each other and laughing. Sally was holding a big stuffed teddy bear. LaPointe had probably just won it for her.

Lester stared, at the picture. A vein had risen in the center of his forehead, quite a prominent one, and it pulsed steadily.

What had she called him? A cheating bastard?

"Well, look who's talking," Lester Pratt whispered.

Rage began to build up in him. It happened very quickly. And when someone touched him on the shoulder he swung around, dropping the wallet and doubling up his fists. He came very close to punching inoffensive, stuttering Slopey Dodd into the middle of next week.

"Cuh-Coach P-Pratt?" Slopey asked. His eyes were big and round, but he didn't look frightened. Interested, but not frightened. "Are yuh-yuh-you o-k-k-kay?"

"I'm fine," Lester said thickly, "Go home, Slopey. You don't have any business with that skateboard in the faculty parking lot."

He bent down to pick up the dropped wallet, but Slopey was two feet closer to the ground and beat him to it. He looked curiously at LaPointe's driver's-license photo before handing the wallet back to Coach Pratt. "Yep," Slopey said. "That's the same guh-guh-guy, all r-right."

He hopped onto his board and prepared to ride away. Lester grabbed him by the shirt before he could do so. The board squirted out from under Slopey's foot, rolled away on its own, hit a pothole and turned over. Slopey's AC/DC shirt—FOR THOSE ABOUT TO ROCK, WE SALUTE YOU, it said—tore at the neck, but Slopey didn't seem to mind; didn't even seem to be much surprised by Lester's actions, let alone frightened. Lester didn't notice. Lester was beyond noticing nuances. He was one of those large and normally placid men who own a short, nasty temper beneath that placidity, a damaging emotional tornado-in-waiting. Some men go through their entire lives without ever discovering that ugly storm-center. Lester however, had discovered his (or rather it had discovered him) and he was now completely in its grip.

Holding a swatch of Slopey's tee-shirt in a fist which was nearly the size of a Daisy canned ham, he bent his sweating face down to Slopey's. The vein in the center of his forehead was pulsing faster than ever.

"What do you mean, 'that's the same guy, all right'?"

"He's the same g-g-guy who muh-met M-Miss Ruh-Ruh-Ratcliffe after school last Fuh-Friday."

"He met her *after school?*" Lester asked hoarsely. He gave Slopey a shake brisk enough to rattle the boy's teeth in his head. "Are you sure of that?"

"Yeah," Slopey said. "They w-went off in your cuh-cuh-har. Coach P-Pratt. The guh-guy was d-d-driving."

"Driving? He was driving my car? *John LaPointe was driving my car with Sally in it?*"

"Well, that g-g-guy," Slopey said, pointing at the driver's-license photograph again. "B-But before they g-g-got ih-in, he g-gave her a kuh-kuh-kiss."

"*Did* he," Lester said. His face had become very still. "*Did* he, now."

"Oh, shuh-shuh-*shore*," Slopey said. A wide (and rather sala-cious) grin lit his face.

In a soft, silky tone utterly unlike his usual rough hey-guys-let's-go-get-em voice, Lester asked: "And did she kiss him back? What do you think, Slopey?"

Slopey rolled his eyes happily. "*I'll* suh-say she d-d-did! They were r-really suh-suh-huckin face, C-Coach Puh-Pratt!"

"Sucking face," Lester mused in his new soft and silky voice. "Yep."

"*Really* sucking face," Lester marvelled in his new soft and silky voice.

"You b-b-bet."

Lester let go of the Slopester (as his few friends called him) and straightened up. The vein in the center of his forehead was pulsing and pumping away. He had begun to grin. It was an unpleasant grin, exposing what seemed like a great many more white, square teeth than a normal man should have. His blue eyes had become small, squinty triangles. His crewcut screamed off his head in all directions.

"Cuh-Cuh-Coach Pratt?" Slopey asked. "Is something ruh-ruh-hong?"

"Nope," Lester Pratt said in his new soft and silky voice. His grin never wavered. "Nothing I can't put right." In his mind, his hands were already locked around the neck of that lying, Pope-loving, teddy-bear-winning, girl-stealing, shit-eating French frog of a John LaPointe. The asshole that walked like a man. The asshole who had apparently taught the girl Lester loved, the girl who would do no more than part her lips the tiniest bit when Lester kissed her, how to really suck face.

First he would take care of John LaPointe. No problem there. Once that was done, he'd have to talk to Sally.

Or something.

"Not a thing in the world I can't put right," he repeated in his new soft and silky voice, and slid back behind the Mustang's wheel. The car leaned appreciably to the left as Lester's two hundred and twenty pounds of solid hock and loin settled into the bucket seat. He started the engine, gunned it in a series of hungry tiger-cage roars, then drove away in a screech of rubber. The Slopester, coughing and theatrically waving dust away from his face, walked over to where his skateboard lay.

The neck of his old tee-shirt had been torn completely away from the shirt's body, leaving what looked like a round black necklace lying over Slopey's prominent collarbones. He was grinning. He had done just what Mr. Gaunt had asked him to do, and it had gone like gang-busters. Coach Pratt had looked madder than a wet hen.

Now he could go home and look at his teapot.

"I j-j-just wish I didn't have to stuh-stuh-hutter," he remarked to no one in particular.

Slopey mounted his skateboard and rode away.

15

Sheila had a hard time connecting Alan with Henry Payton— once she was positive she'd lost Henry, who sounded really excited, and would have to call him back—and she had no more than accomplished this technological feat when Alan's personal line lit up. Sheila put aside the cigarette she'd been about to light and answered it. "Castle County Sheriff's Office, Sheriff Pangborn's line."

"Hello, Sheila. I want to talk to Alan."

"Polly?" Sheila frowned. She was sure that was who it was, but she had never heard Polly Chalmers sound exactly as she did now—cold and clipped, like an executive secretary in a big company. "Is that you?"

"Yes," Polly said. "I want to talk to Alan."

"Gee, Polly, you can't. He's talking with Henry Payton right n—"

"Put me on hold," Polly interrupted. "I'll wait."

Sheila began to feel flustered. "Well . . . uh . . . I would, but it's a little more complicated than that. You see, Alan's . . . you know, in the field. I had to patch Henry through."

"If you can patch Henry Payton through, you can patch me through," Polly said coldly. "Right?"

"Well, yes, but I don't know how long they'll be—"

"I don't care if they talk until hell freezes over," Polly said. "Put me on hold, and when they're done, patch me through to Alan. I wouldn't ask you to do it if it weren't important—you know that, Sheila, don't you?"

Yes—Sheila knew it. And she knew something else, too: Polly was beginning to scare her. "Polly, are you okay?"

There was a long pause. Then Polly answered with a question of her own. "Sheila, did you type any correspondence for Sheriff Pangborn that was addressed to the Department of Child Welfare in San Francisco? Or see any envelopes addressed that way go out?"

Red lights—a whole series of them—suddenly went on in Sheila's mind. She nearly idolized Alan Pangborn, and Polly Chalmers was accusing him of something. She wasn't sure what, but she knew the tone of accusation when she heard it. She knew it very well.

"That isn't the sort of information I could give out to anyone," she said, and her own tone had dropped twenty degrees. "I suppose you'd better ask the Sheriff, Polly."

"Yes—I guess I'd better. Put me on hold and connect me when you can, please."

"Polly, what's wrong? Are you angry at Alan? Because you must know he'd never do anything that was—"

"I don't know anything anymore," Polly said. "If I asked you something that was out of line, I'm sorry. Now will you put me on hold and connect me as soon as you can, or do I have to go out and find him for myself?"

"No, I'll connect you," Sheila said. Her heart felt strangely troubled, as if something terrible had happened. She, like many of the women in Castle Rock, had believed Alan and Polly were deeply in love, and, like many of the other women in town, Sheila tended to see them as characters in a dark-tinged fairytale where everything would come right in the end . . . somehow love would find a way. But now Polly sounded more than angry; she sounded full of pain, and something else as well. To Sheila, the something else sounded almost like hate. "You're going on hold now, Polly—it may be awhile."

"That's fine. Thanks, Sheila."

"Welcome." She pushed the hold button and then found her cigarette. She lit it and dragged deeply, looking at the small flickering light with a frown.

16

"Alan?" Henry Payton called. "Alan, you there?" He sounded like an announcer broadcasting from inside a large empty Saltines box.

"Right here, Henry."

"I got a call from the FBI just half an hour ago," Henry said from inside his cracker-box. "We caught an incredibly lucky break on those prints."

Alan's heartbeat kicked into a higher gear. "The ones on the doorknob of Nettie's house? The partials?"

"Right. We have a tentative match with a fellow right there in town. One prior—petty larceny in 1977. We've also got his service prints."

"Don't keep me hanging—who is it?"

"The name of the individual is Hugh Albert Priest."

"Hugh Priest!" Alan exclaimed. He could not have been more surprised if Payton had named J. Danforth Quayle. To the best of Alan's knowledge, the two men had known Nettie Cobb equally well. "Why would Hugh Priest kill Nettie's dog? Or break Wilma Jerzyck's windows, for that matter?"

"I don't know the gentleman, so I can't say," Henry replied. "Why don't you pick him up and ask him? In fact, why don't you do it right away, before he gets nervous and decides to visit relatives in Dry Hump, South Dakota?"

"Good idea," Alan said. "I'll talk to you later, Henry. Thanks."

"Just keep me updated, scout—this *is* supposed to be my case, you know."

"Yeah. I'll talk to you."

There was a sharp metallic sound—*bink!*—as the connection broke, and then Alan's radio was transmitting the open hum of a telephone line. Alan wondered briefly what Nynex and AT&T would think of the games they were playing, then bent to rack the mike. As he did so, the telephone line hum was broken by Sheila Brigham's voice—her uncharacteristically hesitant voice.

"Sheriff, I have Polly Chalmers on hold. She's asked to be patched through to you as soon as you're available. Ten-four?"

Alan blinked. "Polly?" He was suddenly afraid, the way you're afraid when the telephone rings at three in the morning. Polly had never requested such a service before, and if asked, Alan would have said she never would—it would have gone against her idea of correct behavior, and to Polly, correct behavior was very important. "What is it, Sheila—did she say? Ten-four."

"No, Sheriff. Ten-four."

No. Of course she hadn't. He had known that, too. Polly didn't spread her business around. The fact that he'd even asked showed how surprised he was.

"Sheriff?"

"Patch her through, Sheila. Ten-four."

"Ten-forty, Sheriff."

Bink!

He stood there in the sunshine, his heart beating too hard and too fast. He didn't like this.

The *bink!* sound came again, followed by Sheila's voice—

distant, almost lost. "Go ahead, Polly—you should be connected."

"Alan?" The voice was so loud he recoiled. It was the voice of a giant . . . an angry giant. He knew that much already; one word was enough.

"I'm here, Polly—what is it?"

For a moment there was only silence. Somewhere, deep within it, was the faint mutter of other voices on other calls. He had time to wonder if he had lost the connection . . . time to almost hope he had.

"Alan, I know this line is open," she said, "but you'll know what I'm talking about. How could you? How *could* you?"

Something was familiar about this conversation. Something.

"Polly, I'm not understanding you—"

"Oh, I think you are," she replied. Her voice was growing thicker, harder to understand, and Alan realized that if she wasn't crying, she soon would be. "It's hard to find out you don't know a person the way you thought you did. It's hard to find out the face you thought you loved is only a mask."

Something familiar, right, and now he knew what it was. This was like the nightmares he'd had following the deaths of Annie and Todd, the nightmares in which he stood on the side of the road and watched them go past in the Scout. They were on their way to die. He knew it, but he was helpless to change it. He tried to wave his arms but they were too heavy. He tried to shout and couldn't remember how to open his mouth. They drove by him as if he were invisible, and this was like that, too—as if he had become invisible to Polly in some weird way.

"Annie—" He realized with horror whose name he had said, and backtracked. "*Polly.* I don't know what you're talking about, Polly, but—"

"*You do!*" she screamed at him suddenly. "Don't say you don't when *you do!* Why couldn't you wait for me to tell you, Alan? And if you couldn't wait, why couldn't you *ask?* Why did you have to go behind my back? *How could you go behind my back?"*

He shut his eyes tight in an effort to catch hold of his racing, confused thoughts, but it did no good. A hideous picture came instead: Mike Horton from the Norway *Journal-Register,* bent over the newspaper's Bearcat scanner, furiously taking notes in his pidgin shorthand.

"I don't know what it is you think I've done, but you've got it wrong. Let's get together, talk—"

"No. I don't think I can see you now, Alan."

"Yes. You can. And you're going to. I'll be—"

Then Henry Payton's voice cut in. *Why don't you do it right away, before he gets nervous and decides to visit relatives in Dry Hump, South Dakota?*

"You'll be what?" she was asking. "You'll be what?"

"I just remembered something," Alan said slowly.

"Oh, did you? Was it a letter you wrote at the beginning of September, Alan? A letter to San Francisco?"

"I don't know what you're talking about, Polly. I can't come now because there's been a break in . . . in the other thing. But later—"

She spoke to him through a series of gasping sobs that should have made her hard to understand but didn't. "Don't you get it, Alan? There *is* no later, not anymore. You—"

"Polly, *please*—"

"*No!* Just leave me alone! Leave me alone, you snooping, prying son of a bitch!"

Bink!

And suddenly Alan was listening to that open telephone line hum again. He looked around the intersection of Main and School like a man who doesn't know where he is and has no clear understanding of how he got there. His eyes had the faraway, puzzled expression often seen in the eyes of fighters in the last few seconds before their knees come unhinged and they go sprawling to the canvas for a long winter's nap.

How had this happened? And how had it happened so *quickly?*

He hadn't the slightest idea. The whole town seemed to have gone slightly nuts in the last week or so . . . and now Polly was infected, too.

Bink!

"Um . . . Sheriff?" It was Sheila, and Alan knew from her hushed, tentative tone that she'd had her ears on during at least part of his conversation with Polly. "Alan, are you there? Come back?"

He felt a sudden urge, amazingly strong, to rip the mike out of its socket and throw it into the bushes beyond the sidewalk. Then drive away. Anywhere. Just stop thinking about everything and drive down the sun.

Instead he gathered all of his forces and made himself think of Hugh Priest. That's what he had to do, because it now looked as if maybe Hugh had brought about the deaths of two women. Hugh was his business right now, not Polly . . . and he discovered a great sense of relief hiding in that.

He pushed the TRANSMIT button. "Here, Sheila. Ten-four."

"Alan, I think I lost the connection with Polly. I . . . um . . . I didn't mean to listen, but—"

"That's okay, Sheila; we were done." (There was something horrible about that, but he refused to think of it now.) "Who's there with you right now? Ten-four?"

"John's catching," Sheila said, obviously relieved at the turn in the conversation. "Clut's out on patrol. Near Castle View, according to his last ten-twenty."

"Okay." Polly's face, suffused with alien anger, tried to swim to the surface of his mind. He forced it back and concentrated on Hugh Priest again. But for one terrible second he could see no faces at all; only an awful blankness.

"Alan? You there? Ten-four?"

"Yes. You bet. Call Clut and tell him to get on over to Hugh Priest's house near the end of Castle Hill Road. He'll know where. I imagine Hugh's at work, but if he does happen to be taking the day off, I'll want Clut to pick him up and bring him in for questioning. Ten-four?"

"Ten-four, Alan."

"Tell him to proceed with extreme caution. Tell him Hugh is wanted for questioning in the deaths of Nettie Cobb and Wilma Jerzyck. He should be able to fill in the rest of the blanks for himself. Ten-four."

"Oh!" Sheila sounded both alarmed and excited. "Ten-four, Sheriff."

"I'm on my way to the town motor pool. I expect to find Hugh there. Ten-forty over and out."

As he racked the mike (it felt as if he had been holding it for at least four years) he thought: If you'd told Polly what you just put on the air to Sheila, this situation you've got on your hands might be a little less nasty.

Or it might not—how could he tell such a thing when he didn't know what the situation *was?* Polly had accused him of prying . . . of snooping. That covered a lot of territory, none of it mapped. Besides, there was something else. Telling the dispatcher to put out a pick-up and hold was part of what the job was all about. So was making sure your field officers knew that the man they were after might be dangerous. Giving out the same information to your girlfriend on an open radio/telephone patch was a different matter entirely. He had done the right thing and he knew it.

This did not quiet the ache in his heart, however, and he made another effort to focus his mind on the business ahead— finding Hugh Priest, bringing him in, getting him a goddam lawyer if he wanted one, and then asking him why he had stuck a corkscrew into Nettie's dog, Raider.

For a moment it worked, but as he started the station wagon's engine and pulled away from the curb, it was still Polly's face— not Hugh's—he saw in his mind.

CHAPTER SEVENTEEN

1

At about the same time Alan was heading across town to arrest Hugh Priest, Henry Beaufort was standing in his driveway and looking at his Thunderbird. The note he'd found under the windshield wiper was in one hand. The damage the chicken-shit bastard had done to the tires was bad, but the tires could be replaced. It was the scratch he had drawn along the car's right-hand side that really toasted Henry's ass.

He looked at the note again and read it aloud. "Don't you *ever* cut me off and then keep my car-keys you damn *frog!*"

Who had he cut off lately? Oh, all kinds of people. A night when he didn't have to cut *someone* off was a rare night, indeed. But cut off *and* car-keys kept on the board behind the bar? Only one of those just lately.

Only one.

"You motherfucker," The Mellow Tiger's owner and operator said in a soft, reflective voice. "You stupid crazy mother-fucking sonofabitch."

He thought about going back inside to get his deer rifle and then thought better of it. The Tiger was just up the road, and he kept a rather special box under the bar. Inside it was a double-barrelled Winchester shotgun sawed off at the knees. He'd kept it there ever since that numb fuck Ace Merrill had tried to rob him a few years back. It was a highly illegal weapon, and Henry had never used it.

He thought he might just use it today.

He touched the ugly scratch Hugh had laid into the side of his T-Bird, then crumpled up the note and tossed it aside. Billy Tupper would be up at the Tiger by now, sweeping the floor and swamping out the heads. Henry would get the sawed-off, then borrow Billy's Pontiac. It seemed he had a little asshole-hunting to do.

Henry kicked the balled-up note into the grass. "You been taking those stupid-pills again, Hugh, but you aren't going to be taking any more after today—I guarantee it." He touched the scratch a final time. He had never been so angry in his whole life. "I guaran-fuckin-tee it."

Henry set off up the road toward The Mellow Tiger, walking fast.

2

In the process of tearing apart George T. Nelson's bedroom, Frank Jewett found half an ounce of coke under the mattress of the double bed. He flushed it down the john, and as he watched it swirl away, he felt a sudden cramp in his belly. He started to unbuckle his pants, then walked back into the trashed bedroom again instead. Frank supposed he had gone utterly crazy, but he no longer cared much. Crazy people didn't have to think about the future. To crazy people, the future was a very low priority.

One of the few undisturbed things in George T. Nelson's bedroom was a picture on the wall. It was a picture of an old lady. It was in an expensive gold frame, and this suggested to Frank that it was a picture of George T. Nelson's sainted mother. The cramp struck again. Frank removed the picture from the wall and put it on the floor. Then he unbuckled his pants, squatted carefully above it, and did what came naturally.

It was the high point of what had been, up 'til then, a very bad day.

3

Lenny Partridge, Castle Rock's oldest resident and holder of the Boston *Post* Cane which Aunt Evvie Chalmers had once possessed, also drove one of Castle Rock's oldest cars. It was a 1966 Chevrolet Bel-Air which had once been white. It was now a generic smudged no-color—call it Dirt Road Gray. It wasn't in very good shape. The glass in the back window had been replaced by a flapping sheet of all-weather plastic some years ago, the rocker panels had rusted out so badly that Lenny could view the road through a complicated lacework of rust as he drove along, and the exhaust pipe hung down like the rotted arm of a man who had died in a dry climate. Also, the oil-seals were gone. When Lenny drove the Bel-Air, he spread great clouds of fragrant blue smoke out behind him, and the fields he passed on his daily trip into town looked as if a homicidal aviator had just dusted them with paraquat. The Chevy gobbled three (sometimes four) quarts of oil a day. This gaudy consumption did not bother Lenny in the least; he bought recycled Diamond motor oil from Sonny Jackett in the five-gallon economy size, and he always made sure that Sonny deducted ten per cent . . . his Golden Ager discount. And because he hadn't driven the Bel-Air at a speed greater than thirty-five miles an hour in the last ten years, it would probably hold together longer than Lenny himself.

While Henry Beaufort was starting up the road to The Mellow Tiger on the other side of the Tin Bridge, almost five miles away, Lenny was guiding his rusty Bel-Air over the top of Castle Hill.

There was a man standing in the middle of the road with his arms held up in an imperial stop gesture. The man was bare chested and barefooted. He wore only a pair of khaki pants with the fly unzipped, and, around his neck, a moth-eaten runner of fur.

Lenny's heart took a large wheezy leap in his scrawny chest and he slammed both of his feet, clad in a pair of slowly disintegrating high-tops, down on the brake pedal. It sank almost to the floor with an unearthly moan and the Bel-Air finally stopped less than three feet from the man in the road, whom Lenny now recognized as Hugh Priest. Hugh had not so much as flinched. When the car stopped, he strode rapidly around to where Lenny was sitting, hands pressed against the front of his thermal undershirt, trying to catch his breath and wondering if this was the final cardiac arrest.

"Hugh!" he gasped. "Why, what in the tarnal hell are you doin? I almost run you down! I—"

Hugh opened the driver's door and leaned in. The fur stole he was wearing around his neck swung forward and Lenny flinched back from it. It looked like a half-rotten fox-tail with great hunks of fur missing from the hide. It smelled bad.

Hugh seized him by the straps of his overalls and hauled him out of the car. Lenny uttered a squawk of terror and outrage.

"Sorry, oldtimer," Hugh said in the absent voice of a man who has much greater problems than this one on his mind. "I need your car. Mine's a little under the weather."

"You can't—"

But Hugh most definitely could. He tossed Lenny across the road as if the old fellow were no more than a bag of rags. When Lenny came down, there was a clear snapping sound and his squawks turned to mournful, hooting cries of pain. He had broken one collarbone and two ribs.

Ignoring him, Hugh got behind the wheel of the Chevy, pulled the door shut, and floored the accelerator. The engine let out a scream of surprise and a blue fog of oilsmoke rolled out of the sagging tailpipe. He was rolling down the hill at better than fifty miles an hour before Lenny Partridge could even manage to thrash his way over onto his back.

4

Andy Clutterbuck swung onto Castle Hill Road at approximately 3:35 p.m. He passed Lenny Partridge's old oil-guzzler going the other way and didn't give it a thought; Clut's mind was totally occupied with Hugh Priest, and the rusty old Bel-Air was just another part of the scenery.

Clut didn't have the slightest idea of why or how Hugh might have been involved in the deaths of Wilma and Nettie, but that was all right; he was a footsoldier and that was all. The whys and hows were someone else's job, and this was one of those days when he was damned glad of it. He *did* know that Hugh was a nasty drunk whom the years had not sweetened. A man like that might do anything . . . especially when he was deep in his cups.

He's probably at work, anyway, Clut thought, but as he approached the ramshackle house which Hugh called home, he unsnapped the strap on his service revolver just the same. A moment later he saw the sun twinkling off glass and chrome in Hugh's driveway and his nerves cranked up until they were humming like telephone wires in a gale. Hugh's *car* was here, and when a man's car was at home, the man usually was, too. It was just a fact of country life.

When Hugh had left his driveway on foot, he had turned right, away from town and toward the top of Castle Hill. If Clut had looked in that direction, he would have seen Lenny Partridge lying on the soft shoulder of the road and flopping around like a chicken taking a dustbath, but he didn't look that way. All of Clut's attention was focused on Hugh's house. Lenny's thin, birdlike cries went in one of Clut's ears, directly across his brain without raising the slightest alarm, and out the other.

Clut drew his gun before getting out of the cruiser.

5

William Tupper was only nineteen and he was never going to be a Rhodes Scholar, but he was smart enough to be terrified by Henry's behavior when Henry came into the Tiger at twenty minutes to four on the last real day of Castle Rock's existence. He was also smart enough to know trying to refuse Henry the keys to his Pontiac would do no good; in his present mood, Henry (who was, under ordinary circumstances, the best boss Billy had ever had) would just knock him down and take them.

So for the first—and perhaps the only—time in his life, Billy tried guile. "Henry," he said timidly, "you look like you could use a drink. I know *I* could. Why don't you let me pour us both a short one before you go?"

Henry had disappeared behind the bar. Billy could hear him back there, rummaging around and cursing under his breath. Finally he stood up again, holding a rectangular wooden box with a small padlock on it. He put the box on the bar and then began to pick through the ring of keys he wore at his belt.

He considered what Billy had said, began to shake his head, then reconsidered. A drink really wasn't such a bad idea; it would settle both his hands and his nerves. He found the right key, popped the lock on the box, and laid the lock aside on the bar. "Okay," he said. "But if we're gonna do it, let's do it right. Chivas. Single for you, double for me." He pointed his finger at Billy. Billy flinched—he was suddenly sure Henry was going to add: *But you're coming with me.* "And don't you tell your mother I let you have hard liquor in here, do you understand me?"

"Yessir," Billy said, relieved. He went quickly to get the bottle before Henry could change his mind. "I understand you perfect."

6

Deke Bradford, the man who ran Castle Rock's biggest and most expensive operation—Public Works—was utterly disgusted.

"Nope, he's not here," he told Alan. "Hasn't been in all day. But if you see him before I do, do me a favor and tell him he's fired."

"Why have you held onto him as long as you have, Deke?"

They were standing in the hot afternoon sunlight outside Town Garage #1. Off to the left, a Case Construction and Supply truck was backed up to a shed. Three men were offloading small but heavy wooden cases. A red diamond shape—the symbol for high explosives—was stencilled on each of these. From inside the shed, Alan could hear the whisper of air conditioning. It seemed very odd to hear an air conditioner running this late in the year, but in Castle Rock, this had been an extremely odd week.

"I kep' him on longer than I should," Deke admitted, and ran his hands through his short, graying hair. "I did it because I thought there was a good man hidin somewhere inside of him." Deke was one of those short, stocky men—fireplugs with legs—who always looked ready to take a large chomp out of someone's ass. He was, however, one of the sweetest, kindest men Alan had ever met. "When he wasn't drunk or too hung over, wasn't nobody in this town'd work harder for you than Hugh would. And there was somethin in his face made me think he might not be one of those men who just has to go on drinkin until the devil knocks em down. I thought maybe with a steady job, he'd straighten up and fly right. But this last week."

"What about this last week?"

"Man's been going to hell in a handbasket. Looked like he was all the time on something, and I don't necessarily mean booze. It seemed like his eyes sank way back in his head, and he was always lookin over your shoulder when you talked to him, never right at you. Also, he started talking to himself."

"About what?"

"I dunno. I doubt if the other guys do, either. I hate to fire a man, but I'd made up my mind on Hugh even before you pulled in here this afternoon. I'm done with him."

"Excuse me, Deke." Alan went back to the car, called Sheila, and told her Hugh hadn't been at work all day.

"See if you can reach Clut, Sheila, and tell him to really watch his ass. And send John out there as backup," He hesitated over the next part, knowing the caution had resulted in more than a few needless shootings, and then went ahead. He had to; he owed it to his officers in the field. "Clut and John are to consider Hugh armed and dangerous. Got it?"

"Armed and dangerous, ten-four."

"Okay. Ten-forty, Unit One out."

He racked the microphone and walked back to Deke.

"Do you think he might have left town, Deke?"

"*Him?*" Deke cocked his head to one side and spat tobacco juice. "Guys like him *never* leave town until they've picked up their last paycheck. Most of em never leave at all. When it comes to remembering what roads lead out of town, guys like Hugh seem to have some sort of forgetting disease."

Something caught Deke's eye and he turned toward the men offloading the wooden crates. "Watch what you're doing with those, you guys! You're s'posed to be unloadin em, not playin pepper with em!"

"That's a lot of bang you got there," Alan said.

"Ayuh—twenty cases. We're gonna blow a granite jar-top over at the gravel-pit out on #5. The way it looks to me, we'll have enough left over to blow Hugh all the way to Mars, if you want to."

"Why did you get so much?"

"It wasn't my idea; Buster added to my purchase order, God

knows why. I can tell you one thing, though—he's gonna shit when he sees the electrical bill for this month . . . unless a cold front moves in. That air conditioner sucks up the juice somethin wicked, but you got to keep that stuff cool or it sweats. They all tell you this new bang don't do it, but I believe in better safe than sorry."

"Buster topped your order," Alan mused.

"Yeah—by four or six cases, I can't remember which. Wonders'll never cease, huh?"

"I guess not. Deke, can I use your office phone?"

"Be my guest."

Alan sat behind Deke's desk for a full minute, sweating dark patches beneath the arms of his uniform shirt and listening to the telephone at Polly's house ring again and again and again. At last he dropped the handset back into the cradle.

He left the office in a slow walk, head down. Deke was padlocking the door of the dynamite shack, and when he turned to Alan, his face was long and unhappy. "There was a good man somewhere inside of Hugh Priest, Alan. I swear to God there was. A lot of times that man comes out. I seen it happen before. More often than most people'd believe. With Hugh . . ." He shrugged. "Huh-uh. No soap."

Alan nodded.

"Are you okay, Alan? You look like you come over funny."

"I'm fine," Alan said, smiling a little. But it was the truth; he *had* come over funny. Polly too. And Hugh. And Brian Rusk. It seemed as if everyone had come over funny today.

"Want a glass of water or cold tea? I got some."

"Thanks, but I better get going."

"All right. Let me know how it turns out."

That was something Alan couldn't promise to do, but he had a sickening little feeling in the pit of his stomach that Deke would be able to read all about it for himself in a day or two. Or watch it on TV.

7

Lenny Partridge's old Chevy Bel-Air pulled into one of the slant parking spaces in front of Needful Things shortly before four, and the man of the hour got out. Hugh's fly was still unzipped, and he was still wearing the fox-tail around his neck. He crossed the sidewalk, his bare feet slapping on the hot concrete, and opened the door. The small silver bell overhead jingled.

The only person who saw him go in was Charlie Fortin. He was standing in the doorway of Western Auto and smoking one of his stinky home-rolled cigarettes. "Old Hugh finally flipped," Charlie said to no one in particular.

Inside, Mr. Gaunt looked at old Hugh with a pleasant, expectant little smile . . . as if barefooted, bare-chested men wearing moth-eaten fox-tails around their necks showed up in his shop every day. He made a small checkmark on the sheet beside the cash register. The last checkmark.

"I'm in trouble," Hugh said, advancing on Mr. Gaunt. His eyes rolled from side to side in their sockets like pinballs. "I'm in a real mess this time."

"I know," Mr. Gaunt said in his most soothing voice.

"This seemed like the right place to come. I dunno—I keep dreaming about you. I . . . I didn't know where else to turn."

"This *is* the right place, Hugh."

"He cut my tires," Hugh whispered. "Beaufort, the bastard who owns The Mellow Tiger. He left a note. 'You know what I'll come after next time Hubert,' it said. I know what *that* means. You bet I do." One of Hugh's grubby, large-fingered hands caressed the mangy fur, and an expression of adoration spread across his face, it would have been sappy if it had not been so clearly genuine. "My beautiful, beautiful fox-tail."

"Perhaps you ought to take care of him," Mr. Gaunt suggested thoughtfully, "before he can take care of you. I know that sounds a little . . . well . . . *extreme* . . . but when you consider—"

"Yes! Yes! That's just what I want to do!"

"I think I have just the thing," Mr. Gaunt said. He bent down, and when he straightened up he had an automatic pistol in his left hand. He pushed it across the glass top of the case. "Fully loaded."

Hugh picked it up. His confusion seemed to blow away like smoke as the gun's solid weight filled his hand. He could smell gun-grease, low and fragrant.

"I . . . I left my wallet at home," he said.

"Oh, you don't need to worry about *that,*" Mr. Gaunt told him. "At Needful Things, Hugh, we insure the things we sell." Suddenly his face hardened. His lips peeled back from his teeth and his eyes blazed. "Go get him!" he cried in a low, harsh voice. "Go get the bastard that wants to destroy what is yours! Go get him, Hugh! Protect yourself! Protect your *property!*"

Hugh grinned suddenly. "Thanks, Mr. Gaunt. Thanks a lot."

"Don't mention it," Mr. Gaunt said, dropping immediately back into his normal tone of voice, but the small silver bell was already jangling as Hugh went back out, stuffing the automatic into the sagging waistband of his trousers as he walked.

Mr. Gaunt went to the window and watched Hugh get behind the wheel of the tired Chevy and back it into the street. A Budweiser truck rolling slowly down Main Street blared its horn and swerved to avoid him.

"Go get him, Hugh," Mr. Gaunt said in a low voice. Small wisps of smoke began to rise from his ears and his hair; thicker threads emerged from his nostrils and from between the square white tombstones of his teeth. "Get all of them you can. Party down, big fella."

Mr. Gaunt threw back his head and began to laugh.

8

John LaPointe hurried toward the side door of the Sheriff's Office, the one that gave on the Municipal Building parking lot. He was excited. Armed and dangerous. It wasn't often that you got to assist in arresting an armed and dangerous suspect. Not in a sleepy little town like Castle Rock, anyway. He had forgotten all about his missing wallet (at least for the time being), and Sally Ratcliffe was even further from his mind.

He reached for the door just as someone opened it from the other side. All at once John was facing two hundred and twenty pounds of angry Phys Ed coach.

"Just the man I wanted to see," Lester Pratt said in his new soft and silky voice. He held up a black leather wallet. "Lose something, you ugly two-timing gambling godless son of a bitch?"

John didn't have the slightest idea what Lester Pratt was doing here, or how he could have found his lost wallet. He only knew that he was Clut's designated backup and he had to get going right away.

"Whatever it is, I'll talk to you about it later, Lester," John said, and reached for his wallet. When Lester first pulled it back out of his reach and then brought it down hard, smacking him in the center of the face with it, John was more astounded than angry.

"Oh, I don't want to *talk*," Lester said in his new soft and silky voice. "I wouldn't waste my time." He dropped the wallet, grabbed John by the shoulders, picked him up, and threw him back into the Sheriff's Office. Deputy LaPointe flew six feet through the air and landed on top of Norris Ridgewick's desk. His butt skated across it, plowing a path through the heaped paperwork and knocking Norris's IN/OUT basket onto the floor. John followed, landing on his back with a painful thump.

Sheila Brigham was staring through the dispatcher's window, her mouth wide open.

John began to pick himself up. He was shaken and dazed, without the slightest clue as to what was going on here.

Lester was walking toward him in a fighting strut. His fists were held up in an old fashioned John L. Sullivan pose that should have been comic but wasn't. "I'm going to learn you a lesson," Lester said in his new soft and silky voice. "I'm going to teach you what happens to Catholic fellows who steal Baptist fellows' girls. I'm going to teach you all about it, and when I'm done, you'll have it so right you'll never forget it."

Lester Pratt closed in to teaching distance.

9

Billy Tupper might not have been an intellectual, but he was a sympathetic ear, and a sympathetic ear was the best medicine for Henry Beaufort's rage that afternoon. Henry drank his drink and told Billy what had happened . . . and as he talked, he felt himself calming down. It occurred to him that if he had gotten the shotgun and just kept rolling, he might have ended this day not behind his bar but behind those of the holding cell in the Sheriff's Office. He loved his T-Bird a lot, but he began to realize he didn't love it enough to go to prison for it. He could replace the tires, and the scratch down the side would eventually buff out. As for Hugh Priest, let the law take care of him.

He finished the drink and stood up.

"You still goin after him, Mr. Beaufort?" Billy asked apprehensively.

"I wouldn't waste my time," Henry said, and Billy breathed a sigh of relief. "I'm going to let Alan Pangborn take care of him. Isn't that what I pay my taxes for, Billy?"

"I guess so." Billy looked out the window and brightened a little more. A rusty old car, a car which had once been white but was now a faded no-color—call it Dirt Road Gray—was coming up the hill toward The Mellow Tiger, spreading a thick blue fog of exhaust behind it. "Look! It's old Lenny! I ain't seen him in a coon's age!"

"Well, we still don't open until five," Henry said. He went behind the bar to use the telephone. The box containing the sawed off shotgun was still on the bar. I think I was planning to use that, he mused. I think I really was. What the hell gets into people—some kind of poison?

Billy walked toward the door as Lenny's old car pulled into the parking lot.

10

"Lester—" John LaPointe began, and that was when a fist almost as large as a Daisy canned ham—but much harder—collided with the center of his face. There was a dirty crunching sound as his nose broke in a burst of horrible pain. John's eyes squeezed shut and brightly colored sparks of light fountained up in the darkness. He went reeling and flailing across the room, waving his arms, fighting a losing battle to stay on his feet. Blood was pouring out of his nose and over his mouth. He struck the bulletin board and knocked it off the wall.

Lester began to walk toward him again, his brow wrinkled into a beetling frown of concentration below his screaming haircut.

In the dispatcher's office, Sheila got on the radio and began yelling for Alan.

11

Frank Jewett was on the verge of leaving the home of his good old "friend" George T. Nelson when he had a sudden cautionary thought. This thought was that, when George T. Nelson arrived home to find his bedroom trashed, his coke flushed, and the likeness of his mother beshitted, he might come looking for his old party-buddy. Frank decided it would be nuts to leave without finishing what he had started . . . and if finishing what he had started meant blowing the blackmailing bastard's oysters off, so be it. There was a gun cabinet downstairs, and the idea of doing the job with one of George T. Nelson's own guns felt like poetic justice to Frank. If he was unable to unlock the gun cabinet, or force the door, he would help himself to one of his old party-buddy's steak-knives and do the job with *that*. He would stand behind the front door, and when George T. Nelson came in, Frank would either blow his motherfucking oysters off or grab him by the hair and cut his motherfucking throat. The gun would probably be the safer of the two options, but the more Frank thought of the hot blood jetting from George T. Nelson's slit neck and splashing all over his hands, the more fitting it seemed. *Et tu,* Georgie. *Et tu,* you blackmailing fuck.

Frank's reflections were disturbed at this point by George T. Nelson's parakeet, Tammy Faye, who had picked the most inauspicious moment of its small avian life to burst into song. As Frank listened, a peculiar and terribly unpleasant smile began to surface on his face. How did I miss that goddam bird the first time? he asked himself as he strode into the kitchen.

He found the drawer with the sharp knives in it after a little exploration and spent the next fifteen minutes poking it through the bars of Tammy Faye's cage, forcing the small bird into a fluttery, feather-shedding panic before growing bored with the game and skewering it. Then he went downstairs to see what he could do with the gun cabinet. The lock turned out to be easy, and as Frank climbed the stairs to the first floor again, he burst into an unseasonal but nonetheless cheery song:

Ohh . . . you better not fight, you better not cry,
You better not pout, I'm telling you why,
Santa Claus is coming to town!
He sees you when you're sleeping!
He knows when you're awake!
He knows if you've been bad or good,
So you better be good for goodness' sake!

Frank, who had never failed to watch Lawrence Welk every Saturday night with his own beloved mother, sang the last line in a low Larry Hooper basso. Gosh, he felt good! How could he have ever believed, only an hour or so earlier, that his life was at an end? This wasn't the end; it was the beginning! Out with the old—especially dear old "friends" like George T. Nelson—and in with the new!

Frank settled in behind the door. He was pretty well loaded for bear; there was a Winchester shotgun leaning against the wall, a Llama .32 automatic stuffed into his belt, and a Sheffington steak-knife in his hand. From where he stood he could see the heap of yellow feathers that had been Tammy Faye. A small grin twitched Frank's Mr. Weatherbee mouth and his eyes—utterly mad eyes now—rolled ceaselessly back and forth behind his round rimless Mr. Weatherbee spectacles.

"You better be good for goodness' sake!" he admonished under his breath. He sang this line several times as he stood there, and several more times after he had made himself more comfortable, sitting behind the door with his legs crossed, his back propped against the wall, and his weapons in his lap.

He began to feel alarmed at how sleepy he was becoming. It seemed nuts to be on the verge of dozing off when he was waiting to cut a man's throat, but that didn't change the fact. He thought he had read someplace (perhaps in one of his classes at the University of Maine at Farmington, a cow college from which he had graduated with absolutely no honors at all) that

a severe shock to the nervous system sometimes had that very
effect . . . and he'd suffered a severe shock, all right. It was a
wonder his heart hadn't blown like an old tire when he saw
those magazines scattered all over his office.

Frank decided it would be unwise to take chances. He
moved George T. Nelson's long, oatmeal-colored sofa away
from the wall a little bit, crawled behind it, and lay down on
his back with the shotgun by his left hand. His right hand, still
curled around the handle of the steak-knife, lay on his chest.
There. Much better. George T. Nelson's deep-pile carpeting
was actually quite comfortable.

"You better be good for goodness' sake," Frank sang under
his breath. He was still singing in a low, snory voice ten minutes later, when he finally dozed off.

12

"Unit One!" Sheila screamed from the radio slung under the
dash as Alan crossed the Tin Bridge on his way back into town.
"Come in, Unit One! Come in *right now!*"

Alan felt a sickening lift-drop in his stomach. Clut had run
into a hornet's nest up at Hugh Priest's house on Castle Hill
Road—he was sure of it. Why in Christ's name hadn't he told
Clut to rendezvous with John before bracing Hugh?

You know why—because not all your attention was on your
job when you were giving orders. If something's happened to
Clut because of that, you'll have to face it and own the part of
it that's yours. But that comes later. Your job right now is to
do your job. So do it, Alan—forget about Polly and do your
damned job.

He snatched the microphone off its prongs. "Unit One, come
back?"

"Someone's beating John up!" she screamed. "Come quick,
Alan, he's hurting him *bad!*"

This information was so completely at odds with what Alan had expected that he was utterly flummoxed for a moment.

"What? Who? *There?*"

"*Hurry up, he's killing him!*"

All at once it clicked home. It was Hugh Priest, of course. For some reason Hugh had come to the Sheriff's Office, had arrived before John could get rolling for Castle Hill, and had started swinging. It was John LaPointe, not Andy Clutter-buck, who was in danger.

Alan grabbed the dash-flash, turned it on, and stuck it on the roof. When he reached the town side of the bridge he of-fered the old station wagon a silent apology and floored the accelerator.

13

Clut began to suspect Hugh wasn't home when he saw that all the tires on the man's car were not just flat but cut to pieces. He was about to approach the house anyway when he finally heard thin cries for help.

He stood where he was for a moment, undecided, then hur-ried back down the driveway. This time he saw Lenny lying on the side of the road and ran, holster flapping, to where the old man lay.

"Help me!" Lenny wheezed as Clut knelt by him. "Hugh Priest's gone crazy, tarnal fool's busted me right to Christ up!"

"Where you hurt, Lenny?" Clut asked. He touched the old man's shoulder. Lenny let out a shriek. It was as good an an-swer as any. Clut stood up, unsure of exactly what to do next. Too many things had gotten crammed up in his mind. All he knew for sure was that he desperately did not want to fuck this up.

"Don't move," he said at last. "I'm going to go call Medical Assistance."

"I ain't got no plans to get up and do the tango, y'goddam fool," Lenny said. He was crying and snarling with pain. He looked like an old bloodhound with a broken leg.

"Right," Clut said. He started to run back to his cruiser, then returned to Lenny again. "He took your car, right?"

"No!" Lenny gasped, holding his hands against his broken ribs. "He busted me up and then flew off on a magic fuckin carpet. Sure, he took my car! Why do you think I'm layin here? Get a fuckin tan?"

"Right," Clut repeated, and sprinted back down the road. Dimes and quarters bounced out of his pockets and spun across the macadam in bright little arcs.

He leaned in the window of his car so fast he almost knocked himself out on the door-ledge. He snagged the mike. He had to get Sheila to send help for the old man, but that wasn't the most important thing. Both Alan and the State Police had to know that Hugh Priest was now driving Lenny Partridge's old Chevrolet Bel-Air. Clut wasn't sure what year it was, but no-body could miss that dust-colored oil-burner.

But he could not raise Sheila in dispatch. He tried three times and there was no answer. No answer at all.

Now he could hear Lenny starting to scream again, and Clut went into Hugh's house to call Rescue Services in Norway on the telephone.

One hell of a fine time for Sheila to have to be on the john, he thought.

14

Henry Beaufort was also trying to reach the Sheriff's Office. He stood at the bar with the telephone pressed against his ear. It rang again and again and again. "Come on," he said, "answer the fucking phone. What are you guys doing over there? Play-ing gin rummy?"

Billy Tupper had gone outside. Henry heard him yell something and looked up impatiently. The yell was followed by a sudden loud bang. Henry's first thought was that one of Lenny's old tires had blown . . . and then there were two more bangs.

Billy walked back into the Tiger. He was walking very slowly. He was holding one hand against his throat, and blood was pouring through his fingers.

"*'Enry!*" Billy cried in a weird, strangled Cockney voice. "*'Enry! 'En—*"

He reached the Rock-Ola, stood there swaying for a moment, and then everything in his body seemed to let go at once and he collapsed in a loose tumble.

A shadow fell over his feet, which were almost out the door, and then the shadow's owner appeared. He was wearing a foxtail around his neck and holding a pistol in one hand. Smoke drifted from its barrel. Tiny jewels of perspiration nestled in the sparse mat of hair between his nipples. The skin under his eyes was puffy and brown. He stepped over Billy Tupper and into the dimness of The Mellow Tiger.

"Hello, Henry," said Hugh Priest.

15

John LaPointe didn't know why this was happening, but he knew Lester was going to kill him if he kept it up—and Lester showed no sign of even slowing down, let alone stopping. He tried to slide down the wall and out of Lester's reach, but Lester grabbed his shirt and yanked him back up. Lester was still breathing easily. His own shirt had not even come untucked from the elastic waistband of his sweatpants.

"Here you go, Johnny-boy," Lester said, and smashed another fist into John's upper lip. John felt it split apart on his teeth. " Grow your goddam pussy-tickler over *that.*"

Blindly, John stuck out one leg behind Lester and pushed as hard as he could. Lester uttered a surprised yell and went over, but he shot both hands out as he toppled, snagged them in John's blood-spattered shirt, and pulled the Deputy over on top of him. They began to roll across the floor, butting and punching.

Both were far too busy to see Sheila Brigham dart out of the dispatcher's cubicle and into Alan's office. She snatched the shotgun off the wall, cocked it, and ran back into the bullpen area, which was now a shambles. Lester was sitting on top of John, industriously banging his head against the floor.

Sheila knew how to use the gun she held; she had been target-shooting since she was eight years old. Now she socked the butt-plate against her shoulder and screamed: *"Get away from him, John! Give me a clear field!"*

Lester turned at the sound of her voice, his eyes glaring. He bared his teeth at Sheila like an angry bull gorilla, then went back to banging John's head on the floor.

16

As Alan approached the Municipal Building, he saw the first unqualifiedly good thing of the day: Norris Ridgewick's VW approaching from the other direction. Norris was in plain clothes, but Alan cared not at all about that. He could use him this afternoon. Oh boy, how he could use him.

Then that went to hell, too.

A large red car—a Cadillac, license plate KEETON 1— suddenly shot out of the narrow alley which gave access to the Municipal Building's parking lot. Alan watched, gape-mouthed, as Buster drove his Cadillac into the side of Norris's Beetle. The Caddy wasn't going fast, but it was roughly four times the size of Norris's car. There was a crunch of crimping metal and the VW toppled over onto the passenger side with a hollow bang and a tinkle of glass.

Alan slammed on the brakes and got out of his cruiser.

Buster was getting out of his Cadillac.

Norris was struggling out through the window of his Volkswagen with a dazed expression on his face.

Buster began to stalk toward Norris, his hands closing into fists. A frozen grin was rising on his fat round face.

Alan took one look at that grin and began to run.

17

The first shot Hugh fired shattered a bottle of Wild Turkey on the backbar. The second shattered the glass over a framed document which hung on the wall just above Henry's head and left a round black hole in the liquor license beneath. The third tore off Henry Beaufort's right cheek in a pink cloud of blood and vaporized flesh.

Henry shrieked, grabbed the box with the sawed-off shotgun inside, and dropped behind the bar. He knew Hugh had shot him, but he didn't know if it was bad or not. He was only aware that the right side of his face was suddenly as hot as a furnace, and that blood, warm, wet, and sticky, was pouring down the side of his neck.

"Let's talk about cars, Henry," Hugh was saying as he approached the bar. "Even better than that, let's talk about my fox-tail—what do you say?"

Henry opened the box. It was lined with red velvet. He stuck his jittery, unstable hands in and pulled out the sawed-off Winchester. He started to break it, then realized there was no time. He would just have to hope it was loaded.

He gathered his legs under him, getting ready to spring up and give Hugh what he sincerely hoped would be a big surprise.

18

Sheila realized John wasn't going to get out from under the crazy man, who she now believed was Lester Platt or Pratt . . . the gym teacher at the high school, anyway. She didn't think John *could* get out from under. Lester had stopped banging John's head against the floor and had closed his big hands around John's throat instead.

Sheila reversed the gun, locked her hands on the barrel, and cocked it back over her shoulder like Ted Williams. Then she brought it around in a hard, smooth swing.

Lester turned his head at the last moment, just in time to catch the gun's steel-edged walnut stock between his eyes. There was a nasty crunch as the gunstock smashed a hole into Lester's skull and turned his forebrain to jelly. It sounded as if someone had stepped very hard on a full box of popcorn. Lester Pratt was dead before he hit the floor.

Sheila Brigham looked at him and began to scream.

19

"Did you think I wouldn't know who it was?" Buster Keeton was grunting as he dragged Norris—who was dazed but unhurt—the rest of the way out of the VW's driver's-side window. "Did you think I wouldn't know, with your name right at the bottom of every goddam sheet of paper you taped up? Did you? Did you?"

He cocked one fist back to strike Norris, and Alan Pangborn slipped a handcuff around it just as neatly as you please.

"Huh!" Buster exclaimed, and wheeled ponderously around.

Inside the Municipal Building, someone started to scream.

Alan glanced in that direction, then used the cuff on the other end of the chain to pull Buster over to the open door of his own Cadillac. Buster flailed at him as he did so. Alan took several punches harmlessly on his shoulder, and snapped the free cuff around the door handle of the car.

He turned around and Norris was there. He had time to register the fact that Norris looked just terrible, and to dismiss it as a consequence of being rammed amidships by the Head Selectman.

"Come on," he said to Norris. "We've got trouble."

But Norris ignored him, at least for the moment. He brushed past Alan and punched Buster Keeton squarely in the eye. Buster let out a startled squawk and fell back against the door of his car. It was still open and his weight drove it shut, catching the tail of his sweat-soaked white shirt in the latch.

"That's for the rattrap, you fat shit!" Norris cried.

"I'll get you!" Buster screamed back. "Don't think I won't! I'll get *All of You People!*"

"Get *this*," Norris growled. He was moving in again with his fists cocked at the sides of his puffed-up pigeon chest when Alan grabbed him and hauled him back.

"Quit it!" he shouted into Norris's face. "We've got trouble inside! Bad trouble!"

The scream lifted in the air again. People were gathering on the sidewalks of Lower Main Street now. Norris looked toward them, then back at Alan. His eyes had cleared, Alan saw with relief, and he looked like himself again. More or less.

"What is it, Alan? Something to do with *him?*" He jerked his chin toward the Cadillac. Buster was standing there, looking sullenly at them and plucking at the handcuff on his wrist with his free hand. He seemed not to have heard the screams at all.

"No," Alan said. "Have you got your gun?"

Norris shook his head.

Alan unsnapped the safety-strap on his holster, drew his service .38, and handed it to Norris.

"What about you, Alan?" Norris asked.

"I want my hands free. Come on, let's go. Hugh Priest is in the office, and he's gone crazy."

20

Hugh Priest had gone crazy, all right—not much doubt about that—but he was a good three miles from the Castle Rock Municipal Building.

"Let's talk about—" he began, and that was when Henry Beaufort leaped up from behind the bar like a jack-in-the-box, blood soaking the right side of his shirt, the shotgun levelled.

Henry and Hugh fired at the same time. The crack of the automatic pistol was lost in the shotgun's blurred, primal roar. Smoke and fire leaped from the truncated barrel. Hugh was lifted off his feet and driven across the room, bare heels dragging, his chest a disintegrating swamp of red muck. The gun flew out of his hand. The ends of the fox-tail were burning.

Henry was thrown against the back bar as Hugh's bullet punctured his right lung. Bottles tumbled and crashed all around him. A large numbness swarmed through his chest. He dropped the shotgun and staggered toward the telephone. The air was full of crazy perfume: spilled booze and burning fox-hair. Henry tried to draw in breath, and although his chest heaved, he seemed to get no air. There was a thin, shrill sound as the hole in his chest sucked wind.

The telephone seemed to weigh a thousand pounds, but he finally got it up to his ear and pressed the button which automatically dialed the Sheriff's Office.

Ring . . . ring . . . ring . . .

"What the fuck's the *matter* with you people?" Henry gasped raggedly. "I'm *dying* up here! Answer the goddam telephone!"

But the telephone just went on ringing.

21

Norris caught up with Alan halfway down the alley and they walked side by side into the Municipal Building's small parking lot. Norris was holding Alan's service revolver with his finger curled around the trigger guard and the stubby barrel pointed up into the hot October sky. Sheila Brigham's Saab was in the lot along with Unit 4, John LaPointe's cruiser, but that was all. Alan wondered briefly where Hugh's car was, and then the side door to the Sheriff's Office burst open. Someone carrying the shotgun from Alan's office in a pair of bloody hands bolted out. Norris levelled the short-barrelled .38 and slid his finger inside the trigger-guard.

Alan registered two things at once. The first was that Norris was going to shoot. The second was that the screaming person with the gun was not Hugh Priest but Sheila Brigham.

Alan Pangborn's almost heavenly reflexes saved Sheila's life that afternoon, but it was a very close thing. He didn't bother trying to shout or even using his hand to deflect the pistol barrel. Neither would have stood much chance of success. He stuck out his elbow instead, then jerked it up like a man doing an enthusiastic buck-and-wing at a country dance. It struck Norris's gun-hand an instant before Norris fired, driving the barrel upward. The pistol-shot was an amplified whip-crack in the enclosed courtyard. A window in the Town Services Office on the second floor shattered. Then Sheila dropped the shotgun she had used to brain Lester Pratt and was running toward them, screaming and weeping.

"Jesus," Norris said in a small, shocked voice. His face was as pale as paper as he thrust the pistol, butt first, toward Alan. "I almost shot *Sheila*—oh dear Jesus Christ."

"*Alan!*" Sheila was crying. "Thank God!"

She ran into him without slowing, almost knocking him

over. He holstered his revolver and then put his arms around her. She was trembling like an electric wire with too much current running through it. Alan suspected he was trembling pretty badly himself, and he had come close to wetting his pants. She was hysterical blind with panic, and that was probably a blessing: he didn't think she had the slightest idea how close she had come to taking a round.

"What's going on in there, Sheila?" he asked. "Tell me quick." His ears were ringing so badly from the gunshot and the succeeding echo that he could almost swear he heard a telephone somewhere.

22

Henry Beaufort felt like a snowman melting in the sun. His legs were giving way beneath him. He crumpled slowly into a kneeling position with the ringing, unanswered phone still tolling in his ear. His head swam with the mingled stench of booze and burning fur. Another hot smell was mingling with these now. He suspected it was Hugh Priest.

He was vaguely aware that this wasn't working and he ought to dial another number for help, but he didn't think he could. He was beyond wringing another number out of the telephone—this was it. So he knelt behind the bar in a growing pool of his own blood, listening to the chimney-hoot of air from the hole in his chest, clinging desperately to consciousness. The Tiger didn't open for an hour yet, Billy was dead, and if no one answered this telephone soon, he would also be dead when the first customers came trickling in for their various happy-hour potations.

"Please," Henry whispered in a screamy, breathless voice. "Please answer the phone, someone please answer this fucking phone."

23

Sheila Brigham began to regain some control, and Alan got the most important thing out of her right away: she had decommissioned Hugh with the butt of the shotgun. No one was going to try to shoot them when they went through the door.

He hoped.

"Come on," he said to Norris, "let's go."

"Alan . . . When she came out . . . I thought . . ."

"I know what you thought, but no harm was done. Forget it, Norris. John's inside. Come on."

They went to the door and stood on either side of it. Alan looked at Norris. "Go in low," he said.

Norris nodded his head.

Alan grabbed the doorknob, jerked the door open, and lunged inside. Norris went in under him in a crouch.

John had managed to find his feet and stagger most of the way to the door. Alan and Norris hit him like the front line of the old Pittsburgh Steelers and John suffered a final painful indignity: he was knocked flat by his colleagues and sent skidding across the tiled floor like one of the weights in a barroom bowling game. He struck the far wall with a thud and let out a scream of pain which was both surprised and somehow weary.

"Jesus, that's *John!*" Norris cried. "What a French fire-drill!"

"Help me with him," Alan said.

They hurried across the room to John, who was slowly sitting up on his own. His face was a mask of blood. His nose was canted severely to the left. His upper lip was swelling like an overinflated innertube. As Alan and Norris reached him, he cupped one hand under his mouth and spat a tooth into it.

"He'th craythee," John said in a mushy, dazed voice. "Theela hit him with the thotgun. I think thee killed him."

"John, are you all right?" Norris asked.

"I'm a fuckin *meth*," John said. He leaned forward and vomited extravagantly between his own spread legs to prove it.

Alan looked around. He was vaguely aware that it wasn't just his ears; a telephone really *was* ringing. But the phone wasn't the important thing now. He saw Hugh lying face-down by the rear wall and went over. He dropped his ear against the back of Hugh's shirt, listening for a heartbeat. All he could hear at first was the ringing in his ears. The goddam telephones were ringing on every desk, it sounded like.

"Answer that fucking thing or take it off the hook!" Alan snapped at Norris.

Norris went to the closest phone—it happened to be on his own desk—punched the button that was flashing, and picked it up. "Don't bother us now," he said. "We have an emergency situation here. You'll have to call back later." He dropped it back into its cradle without waiting for a response.

24

Henry Beaufort took the telephone—the heavy, heavy telephone—away from his ear and looked at it with dimming, unbelieving eyes.

"*What* did you say?" he whispered.

Suddenly he could no longer hold the telephone receiver; it was just too damned heavy. He dropped it on the floor, slowly collapsed onto his side, and lay there panting.

25

As far as Alan could tell, Hugh was all finished. He grabbed him by the shoulders, rolled him over . . . and it wasn't Hugh at all. The face was too completely covered with blood, brains, and bits of bone for him to be able to tell who it *was,* but it surely wasn't Hugh Priest.

"What in the fuck is going on here?" he said in a low, amazed voice.

26

Danforth "Buster" Keeton stood in the middle of the street, handcuffed to his own Cadillac, and watched Them watching him. Now that the Chief Persecutor and his Deputy Persecutor were gone, They had nothing else to watch.

He looked at Them and knew Them for what They were— each and every one of Them.

Bill Fullerton and Henry Gendron were standing in front of the barber shop. Bobby Dugas was standing between them with a barber's apron still snapped around his neck and hanging down in front of him like an oversized dinner napkin. Charlie Fortin was standing in front of the Western Auto. Scott Garson and his puke lawyer friends Albert Martin and Howard Potter were standing in front of the bank, where they had probably been talking about him when the ruckus broke out.

Eyes.

Fucking *eyes.*

There were eyes everywhere.

All looking at *him.*

"I see you!" Buster cried suddenly. "I see You all! All You People! And I know what to do! Yes! You bet!"

He opened the door of his Cadillac and tried to get in. He couldn't do it. He was cuffed to the outside doorhandle. The chain between the cuffs was long, but not *that* long.

Someone laughed.

Buster heard that laugh quite clearly.

He looked around.

Many residents of Castle Rock stood in front of the businesses along Main Street, looking back at him with the black buckshot eyes of intelligent rats.

Everyone was there but Mr. Gaunt.

Yet Mr. Gaunt *was* there; Mr. Gaunt was inside Buster's head, telling him exactly what to do.

Buster listened . . . and began to smile.

27

The Budweiser truck Hugh had almost sideswiped in town stopped at a couple of the little mom-n-pops on the other side of the bridge and finally pulled into the parking lot of The Mellow Tiger at 4:01 p.m. The driver got out, grabbed his clipboard, hitched up his green khaki pants, and marched toward the building. He stopped five feet away from the door, eyes widening. He could see a pair of feet in the bar's doorway.

"Holy Joe!" the driver exclaimed. "You okay, buddy?"

A faint wheezing cry drifted to his ears:

". . . . . . help . . . . . ."

The driver ran inside and discovered Henry Beaufort, barely alive, crumpled behind the bar.

28

"Ith Lethter Pratt," John LaPointe croaked. Supported by Norris on one side and Sheila on the other, he had hobbled over to where Alan knelt by the body.

"*Who?*" Alan asked. He felt as if he had accidentally stumbled into some mad comedy. Ricky and Lucy Go to Hell. Hey Lester, you got some 'splainin to do.

"Lethter Pratt," John said again with painful patience. "He'th the Phidthical Educaythun teather at the high thcool."

"What's *he* doing here?" Alan asked.

John LaPointe shook his head wearily. "Dunno, Alan. He jutht came in and went craythee."

"Somebody give me a break," Alan said. "Where's Hugh Priest? Where's Clut? What in God's name is going on here?"

29

George T. Nelson stood in the doorway of his bedroom, looking around unbelievingly. The place looked as if some punk band—the Sex Pistols, maybe the Cramps—had had a party in it, along with all their fans.

"What—" he began, and could say no more. Nor did he need to. He *knew* what. It was the coke. Had to be. He'd been dealing among the faculty at Castle Rock High for the last six years (not all the teachers were appreciators of what Ace Merrill sometimes called Bolivian Bingo Dust, but the ones who were qualified as *big* appreciators), and he'd left half an ounce of almost pure coke under the mattress. It was the blow, sure it was. Someone had talked and someone else had gotten greedy. George supposed he'd known that as soon as he'd pulled into the driveway and saw the broken kitchen window.

He crossed the room and yanked up the mattress with hands that felt dead and numb. Nothing underneath. The coke was gone. Nearly two thousand dollars' worth of almost pure coke, gone. He sleepwalked toward the bathroom to see if his own small stash was still in the Anacin bottle on the top shelf of the medicine cabinet. He'd never needed a hit as badly as he did just now.

He reached the doorway and stopped, eyes wide. It wasn't the mess that riveted his attention, although this room had also been turned upside down with great zeal; it was the toilet. The ring was down, and it was thinly dusted with white stuff.

George had an idea that white stuff was not Johnson's Baby Powder.

He walked across to the toilet, wetted his finger, and touched it to the dust. He put his finger in his mouth. The tip of his tongue went numb almost at once. Lying on the floor between the john and the tub was an empty plastic Baggie. The picture was clear. Crazy, but clear. Someone had come in, found the coke . . . and then *flushed it down the crapper.* Why? *Why?* He didn't know, but he decided when he found the person who had done this, he would ask. Just before he tore his head right off his shoulders. It couldn't hurt.

His own three-gram stash was intact. He carried it out of the bathroom and then stopped again as a fresh shock struck his eyes. He hadn't seen this particular abomination as he crossed the bedroom from the hall, but from this angle it was impossible to miss.

He stood where he was for a long moment, eyes wide with amazed horror, his throat working convulsively. The nests of veins at his temples beat rapidly, like the wings of small birds. He finally managed to produce one small, strangled word:

". . . . . . mom . . . . . . !"

Downstairs, behind George T. Nelson's oatmeal-colored sofa, Frank Jewett slept on.

30

The bystanders on Lower Main, who had been called out to the sidewalk by the yelling and the gunshot, were now being entertained by a new novelty: the slow-motion escape of their Head Selectman.

Buster leaned as far into his Cadillac as he could and turned the ignition switch to the ON position. He then pushed the button that lowered the power window on the driver's side.

He closed the door again and carefully began to wriggle in through the window.

He was still sticking out from the knees down, his left arm pulled back behind him at a severe angle by the handcuff around the doorhandle, the chain lying across his large left thigh, when Scott Garson came up.

"Uh, Danforth," the banker said hesitantly, "I don't think you're supposed to do that. I believe you're arrested."

Buster looked under his right armpit, smelling his own aroma—quite spicy by now, quite spicy indeed—and saw Garson upside down. He was standing directly behind Buster. He looked as if he might be planning to try to haul Buster back out of his own car.

Buster pulled his legs up as much as he could and then shot them out, hard, like a pony kicking up dickens in the pasture. The heels of his shoes struck Garson's face with a smack which Buster found entirely satisfying. Garson's gold-rimmed spectacles shattered. He howled, reeled backward with his bleeding face in his hands, and fell on his back in Main Street.

"Hah!" Buster grunted. "Didn't expect that, did you? Didn't expect that at *all,* you persecuting son of a bitch, did you?"

He wriggled the rest of the way into his car. There was just enough chain. His shoulder-joint creaked alarmingly and then rotated enough in its socket to allow him to wriggle under his own arm and scoot his ass back along the seat. Now he was sitting behind the wheel with his cuffed arm out the window. He started the car.

Scott Garson sat up in time to see the Cadillac bearing down on him. Its grille seemed to leer at him, a vast chrome mountain which was going to crush him.

He rolled frantically to the left, avoiding death by less than a second. One of the Cadillac's large front tires rolled over his right hand, squashing it pretty efficiently. Then the rear tire rolled over it, finishing the job. Garson lay on his back, looking at his grotesquely mashed fingers, which were now roughly the size of putty-knives, and began to scream up into the hot blue sky.

31

"TAMMMEEEEE FAYYYYE!"

This shriek hauled Frank Jewett out of his deepening doze. He had absolutely no idea where he was in those first confused seconds—only that it was some tight, close place. An *unpleasant* place. There was something in his hand, too . . . what was it?

He raised his right hand and almost poked out his own eye with the steak-knife.

"Ooooooohhhh, nooooooooh! TAMMEEEEEEE FAYYYYE!"

It came back to him all at once. He was behind the couch of his good old "friend," George T. Nelson, and that was George T. Nelson himself, in the flesh, noisily mourning his dead parakeet. Along with this realization, everything else returned to Frank: the magazines scattered all over the office, the blackmail note, the possible (no, probable—the more he thought about it, the more probable it seemed) ruin of his career and his life.

Now, incredibly, he could hear George T. Nelson sobbing. Sobbing over a goddam flying shithouse. Well, Frank thought, I'm going to put you out of your misery, George. Who knows—maybe you'll even wind up in bird heaven.

The sobs were approaching the sofa. Better and better. He would jump up—surprise, George!—and the bastard would be dead before he had any idea of what was up. Frank was on the verge of making his spring when George T. Nelson, still sobbing as if his heart would break, seat-dropped onto his sofa. He was a heavy man, and his weight drove the sofa back smartly toward the wall. He did not hear the surprised, breathless "Oooof!" from behind him; his own sobs covered it. He fumbled for the telephone, dialed through a shimmer of tears and got (almost miraculously) Fred Rubin on the first ring.

"Fred!" he cried. "Fred, something terrible has happened! Maybe it's still happening! Oh Jesus, Fred! Oh Jesus!"

Below and behind him, Frank Jewett was struggling for breath. Edgar Allan Poe stories he'd read as a kid, stories about being buried alive, raced through his head. His face was slowly turning the color of old brick. The heavy wooden leg which had been forced against his chest when George T. Nelson collapsed onto the sofa felt like a bar of lead. The back of the sofa lay against his shoulder and the side of his face.

Above him, George T. Nelson was spilling a garbled description of what he'd found when he finally got home into Fred Rubin's ear. At last he paused for a moment and then cried out, "I don't *care* if I shouldn't be talking about it on the phone—*HOW CAN I CARE WHEN HE KILLED TAMMY FAYE? THE BASTARD KILLED TAMMY FAYE!* Who could have done it, Fred? *Who?* You have to help me!"

Another pause as George T. Nelson listened, and Frank realized with growing panic that he was soon going to pass out. He suddenly understood what he had to do—use the Llama automatic to shoot up through the sofa. He might not kill George T. Nelson, he might not even *hit* George T. Nelson, but he could sure as hell get George T. Nelson's *attention,* and once he did that he thought the odds were good that George T. Nelson would get his fat ass off this sofa before Frank died down here with his nose squashed against the baseboard heating unit.

Frank opened the hand holding the steak-knife and tried to reach for the pistol tucked into the waistband of his pants. Dreamlike horror washed through him as he realized he couldn't get it—his fingers were opening and closing two full inches above the gun's ivory-inlaid handle. He tried with all his remaining strength to get the hand down lower, but his pinned shoulder would not move at all; the big sofa—and George T. Nelson's considerable weight—held it firmly against the wall. It might have been nailed there.

Black roses—harbingers of approaching asphyxiation—began to bloom before Frank's bulging eyes.

As from some impossible distance, he heard his old "friend" screaming at Fred Rubin, who undoubtedly had been George T. Nelson's partner in the cocaine deal. "What are you *talking* about? I call to tell you I've been violated and you tell me to go see the new guy downstreet? I don't need knick-knacks, Fred, I need—"

He broke off, got up, and paced across the room. With what was literally the last of his strength, Frank managed to push the sofa a few inches away from the wall. It wasn't much, but he was able to take small sips of incredibly wonderful air.

"He sells *what?*" George T. Nelson shouted. "Well, Jesus! Jesus H. Christ! Why didn't you say so in the first place?"

Silence again. Frank lay behind the sofa like a beached whale, sipping air and hoping his monstrously pounding head would not explode. In a moment he would arise and blow his old "friend" George T. Nelson's oysters off. In a moment. When he got his breath back. And when the big black flowers currently filling his sight shrank back into nothing. In a moment. Two at the most.

"Okay," George T. Nelson said. "I'll go see him. I doubt if he's the miracle-worker you think he is, but any goddam port in a storm, right? I have to tell you something, though—I don't give much of a shit if he's dealing or not. I'm going to find the son of a bitch who did this—that's the first goddam order of business—and I'm going to nail him to the nearest wall. Have you got that?"

I got it, Frank thought, but just who nails who to that fabled wall still remains to be seen, my dear old party-buddy.

"Yes, I *did* get the name!" George T. Nelson screamed into the phone. "Gaunt, Gaunt, fucking *Gaunt!*"

He slammed the phone down, then must have thrown it across the room—Frank heard the shatter of breaking glass. Seconds later, George T. Nelson uttered a final oath and stormed out of the house. The engine of his Iroc-Z raved to life. Frank heard him backing down the driveway as he himself slowly pushed the sofa away from the wall. Rubber screamed against pavement outside and then Frank's old "friend" George T. Nelson was gone.

Two minutes later, a pair of hands rose into view and clutched the back of the oatmeal-colored sofa. A moment after that, the face of Frank M. Jewett—pale and crazed, the rimless Mr. Weatherbee glasses sitting askew on his small pug nose and one lens cracked—appeared between the hands. The sofa-back had left a red, stippled pattern on his right cheek. A few dust-bunnies danced in his thinning hair.

Slowly, like a bloated corpse rising from the bed of a river until it floats just below the surface, the grin reappeared on Frank's face. He had missed his old "friend" George T. Nelson this time, but George T. Nelson had no plans to leave town. His phone conversation had made that quite clear. Frank would find him before the day was over. In a town the size of Castle Rock, how could he miss?

32

Sean Rusk stood in the kitchen doorway of his house, looking anxiously out at the garage. Five minutes before, his older brother had gone out there—Sean had been looking out of his bedroom window and had just happened to see him. Brian had been holding something in one hand. The distance had been too great for Sean to see what it was, but he didn't *need* to see. He knew. It was the new baseball card, the one Brian kept creeping upstairs to look at. Brian didn't know Sean knew about that card, but Sean did. He even knew who was on it, because he'd gotten home much earlier from school today than Brian, and he had sneaked into Brian's room to look at it. He didn't have the slightest idea why Brian cared about it so much; it was old, dirty, dog-eared, and faded. Also, the player was somebody Sean had never heard of—a pitcher for the Los Angeles Dodgers named Sammy Koberg, lifetime record one win, three losses. The guy had never even spent a whole year in the majors. Why would Brian care about a worthless card like that?

Sean didn't know. He only knew two things for sure: Brian *did* care, and the way Brian had been acting for the last week or so was scary. It was like those TV ads you saw about kids on drugs. But Brian wouldn't use drugs . . . would he?

Something about Brian's face when he went out to the garage had scared Sean so badly he had gone to tell his mother. He wasn't sure exactly what to say, and it turned out not to matter because he didn't get a chance to say anything. She was mooning around in the bedroom, wearing her bathrobe and those stupid sunglasses from the new store downtown.

"Mom, Brian's—" he began, and that was as far as he got.

"Go away, Sean. Mommy's busy right now."

"But Mom—"

"Go *away,* I said!"

And before he had a chance to go on his own, he'd found himself hustled unceremoniously out of the bedroom. Her bathrobe fell open as she pushed him, and before he could look away, he saw that she was wearing nothing beneath it, not even a nightgown.

She had slammed the door behind him. And locked it.

Now he stood in the kitchen doorway, waiting anxiously for Brian to come back out of the garage . . . but Brian didn't.

His unease had grown in some stealthy way until it was barely controlled terror. Sean went out the kitchen door, trotted through the breezeway, and entered the garage.

It was dark and oily-smelling and explosively hot inside.

For a moment he didn't see his brother in the shadows and thought he must have gone out through the back door into the yard. Then his eyes adjusted, and he uttered a small, whimpery gasp.

Brian was sitting against the rear wall, next to the Lawnboy. He had gotten Daddy's rifle. The butt was propped on the floor. The muzzle was pointed at his own face. Brian was supporting the barrel with one hand while the other clutched the dirty old baseball card which had somehow gained such a hold over his life this last week.

"Brian!" Sean cried. "What are you doing?"

"Don't come any closer, Sean, you'll get the mess on you."

"Brian, don't!" Sean cried, beginning to weep. "Don't be such a wussy! You're . . . you're scaring me!"

"I want you to promise me something," Brian said. He had taken off his socks and sneakers, and now he wriggled one of his big toes inside the Remington's trigger-guard.

Sean felt his crotch grow wet and warm. He had never been so scared in his life. "Brian, please! *Pleeease!*"

"I want you to promise me you'll never go to the new store," Brian said. "Do you hear me?"

Sean took a step toward his brother. Brian's toe tightened on the trigger of the rifle.

"*No!*" Sean screamed, drawing back at once. "I mean yes! *Yes!*"

Brian let the barrel drop a little when he saw his brother retreat. His toe relaxed a bit. "Promise me."

"*Yes!* Anything you want! Only don't do that! Don't . . . don't tease me anymore, Bri! Let's go in and watch *The Transformers!* No . . . *you* pick! Anything you want! Even Wapner! We can watch Wapner if you want to! All week! All *month!* I'll watch with you! Only stop scaring me, Brian, *please stop scaring me!*"

Brian Rusk might not have heard. His eyes seemed to float in his distant, serene face.

"Never go there," he said. "Needful Things is a poison place, and Mr. Gaunt is a poison man. Only he's really not a man, Sean. He's not a man at all. Swear to me you'll never buy any of the poison things Mr. Gaunt sells."

"I swear! I swear!" Sean babbled. "I swear on Mommy's name!"

"No," Brian said, "you can't do that, because he got her, too. Swear on your *own* name, Sean. Swear it on your very own name."

"I do!" Sean cried out in the hot, dim garage. He held his hands out imploringly to his brother. "I really do, I swear on my very own name! Now please put the gun down, Bri—"

"I love you, baby brother." He looked down at the baseball card for a moment. "Sandy Koufax sucks," Brian Rusk remarked, and pulled the trigger with his toe.

Sean's drilling shriek of horror rose over the blast, which was flat and loud in the hot dark garage.

33

Leland Gaunt stood at his shop window, looking out on Main Street and smiling gently. The sound of the shot from up on Ford Street was faint, but his ears were sharp and he heard it.

His smile broadened a little.

He took down the sign in the window, the one which said he was open by appointment only, and put up a new one. This one read

CLOSED UNTIL FURTHER NOTICE.

"We're having fun now," Leland Gaunt said to no one at all. "Yessirree."

CHAPTER EIGHTEEN

1

Polly Chalmers knew nothing of these things.

While Castle Rock was bearing the first real fruits of Mr. Gaunt's labors, she was out at the end of Town Road #3, at the old Camber place. She had gone there as soon as she had finished her conversation with Alan.

Finished it? she thought. Oh my dear, that's much too civilized. After you hung up on him—isn't that what you mean?

All right, she agreed. After I hung up on him. But he went behind my back. And when I called him on it, he got all flustered and then lied about it. He *lied* about it. I happen to think that behavior like that *deserves* an uncivilized response.

Something stirred uneasily in her at this, something which might have spoken if she had given it time and room, but she gave it neither. She wanted no dissenting voices; did not, in fact, want to think about her last conversation with Alan Pangborn at all. She just wanted to take care of her business out here at the end of Town Road #3 and then go back home. Once she was there, she intended to take a cool bath and then go to bed for twelve or sixteen hours.

That deep voice managed just five words: But, Polly . . . have you thought—

No. She hadn't. She supposed she would have to think in time, but now was too soon. When the thinking began, the hurting would begin, too. For now she only wanted to take care of business . . . and not think at all.

The Camber place was spooky . . . reputed by some to be haunted. Not so many years ago, two people—a small boy and Sheriff George Bannerman—had died in the dooryard of this house. Two others, Gary Pervier and Joe Camber himself, had died just down the hill. Polly parked her car over the place where a woman named Donna Trenton had once made the fatal mistake of parking her Ford Pinto, and got out. The *azka* swung back and forth between her breasts as she did.

She looked around uneasily for a moment at the sagging porch, the paintless walls overrun by climbing ivy, the windows which were mostly broken and stared blindly back at her. Crickets sang their stupid songs in the grass, and the hot sun beat down as it had on those terrible days when Donna Trenton had fought for her life here, and for the life of her son.

What am I doing here? Polly thought. *What in God's name am I doing here?*

But she knew, and it had nothing to do with Alan Pangborn or Kelton or the San Francisco Department of Child Welfare. This little field-trip had nothing to do with love. It had to do with pain. That was all . . . but that was enough.

There was something inside the small silver charm. Something that was alive. If she did not live up to her side of the bargain she had made with Leland Gaunt, it would die. She didn't know if she could stand to be tumbled back down into the horrible, grinding pain to which she had awakened on Sunday morning. If she had to face a lifetime of such pain, she thought she would kill herself.

"And it's not Alan," she whispered as she walked toward the barn with its gaping doorway and its ominous swaybacked roof. "He said he wouldn't raise a hand against him."

Why do you even care? that worrisome voice whispered.

She cared because she didn't want to hurt Alan. She was angry at him, yes—*furious,* in fact—but that didn't mean she had to stoop to his level, that she had to treat *him* as shabbily as he had treated her.

But, Polly . . . have you thought—

No. *No!*

She was going to play a trick on Ace Merrill, and she didn't care about Ace at all—had never even met him, only knew him by reputation. The trick was on Ace, but . . .

But Alan, who had sent Ace Merrill away to Shawshank, came into it someplace. Her heart told her so.

And could she back out of this? Could she, even if she wanted to? Now it was Kelton, as well. Mr. Gaunt hadn't exactly told her that the news of what had happened to her son would end up all over town unless she did what he told her to do . . . but he had hinted as much. She couldn't bear for that to happen.

Is a woman not entitled to her pride? When everything else is gone, is she not at least entitled to this, the coin without which her purse is entirely empty?

Yes. And yes. And yes.

Mr. Gaunt had told her she'd find the only tool she would need in the barn; now Polly began to walk slowly in that direction.

Go where ye list, but go there alive, *Trisha,* Aunt Evvie had told her. *Don't be no ghost.*

But now, stepping into the Camber barn through doors which hung gaping and frozen on their rusty tracks, she *felt* like a ghost. She had never felt more like a ghost in her life. The *azka* moved between her breasts . . . on its own now. Something inside. Something alive. She didn't like it, but she liked the idea of what would happen if that thing died even less.

She would do what Mr. Gaunt had told her to do, at least this once, cut all her ties with Alan Pangborn (it had been a mistake to ever begin with him, she saw that now, saw it clearly), and keep her past her own. Why not?

After all, it was such a little thing.

2

The shovel was exactly where he had told her it would be, leaning against one wall in a dusty shaft of sunlight. She took hold of its smooth, worn handle.

Suddenly she seemed to hear a low, purring growl from the deep shadows of the barn, as if the rabid Saint Bernard which had killed Big George Bannerman and caused the death of Tad Trenton were still here, back from the dead and meaner than ever. Gooseflesh danced up her arms and Polly left the barn in a hurry. The dooryard was not exactly cheery—not with that empty house glaring sullenly at her—but it was better than the barn.

What am I doing here? her mind asked again, woefully, and it was Aunt Evvie's voice that came back: *Going ghost. That's what you're doing. You're going ghost.*

Polly squeezed her eyes shut. "Stop it!" she whispered fiercely. "Just *stop it!*"

That's right, Leland Gaunt said. *Besides, what's the big deal? It's only a harmless little joke. And if something serious were to come of it—it won't, of course, but just supposing, for the sake of argument, that it did—whose fault would that be?*

"Alan's," she whispered. Her eyes rolled nervously in their sockets and her hands clenched and unclenched nervously between her breasts. "If he were here to talk to . . . if he hadn't cut himself off from me by snooping around in things that are none of his business . . ."

The little voice tried to speak up again, but Leland Gaunt cut it off before it could say a word.

Right again, Gaunt said. *As to what you're doing here, Polly, the answer to that is simple enough: you're paying. That's what you're doing, and that's all you're doing. Ghosts have nothing to do with it. And remember this, because it is the simplest, most wonderful aspect of commerce: once an item is paid for, it belongs to you. You didn't expect such a wonderful thing to come cheap, did you? But when you finish paying, it's yours. You have clear title to the thing you have paid for. Now will you stand here listening to those old frightened voices all day, or will you do what you came to do?*

Polly opened her eyes again. The *azka* hung movelessly at the end of its chain. If it had moved—and she was no longer sure it had—it had stopped now. The house was just a house, empty too long and showing the inevitable signs of neglect. The windows were not eyes, but simply holes rendered glassless by adventuresome boys with rocks. If she had heard something in the barn—and she was no longer sure she had—it had only been the sound of a board expanding in the unseasonable October heat.

Her parents were dead. Her sweet little boy was dead. And the dog which had ruled this dooryard so terribly and completely for three summer days and nights eleven years ago was dead.

There were no ghosts.

"Not even me," she said, and began to walk around the barn.

3

When you go around to the back of the barn, Mr. Gaunt had said, *you'll see the remains of an old trailer.* She did; a silver-sided Air-Flow, almost obscured by goldenrod and high tangles of late sunflowers.

You'll see a large flat rock at the left end of the trailer.

She found it easily. It was as large as a garden paving stone.

Move the rock and dig. About two feet down you'll find a Crisco can.

She tossed the rock aside and dug. Less than five minutes after she started, the shovel's blade clunked on the can. She discarded the shovel and dug into the loose earth with her fingers, breaking the light webwork of roots with her fingers. A minute later she was holding the Crisco can. It was rusty but intact. The rotting label came loose and she saw a recipe for Pineapple Surprise Cake on the back (the list of ingredients was mostly obscured by a black blotch of mold), along with a Bisquick coupon that had expired in 1969. She got her fingers under the lid of the can and pried it loose. The whiff of air that escaped made her wince and draw her head back for a moment. That voice tried one last time to ask what she was doing here, but Polly shut it out.

She looked into the can and saw what Mr. Gaunt had told her she would see: a bundle of Gold Bond trading stamps and several fading photographs of a woman having sexual intercourse with a collie dog.

She took these things out, stuffed them into her hip pocket, and then wiped her fingers briskly on the leg of her jeans. She would wash her hands as soon as she could, she promised herself. Touching these things which had lain so long under the earth made her feel unclean.

From her other pocket she took a sealed business envelope. Typed on the front in capital letters was this:

A MESSAGE FOR THE INTREPID
TREASURE-HUNTER.

Polly put the envelope in the can, pressed the cover back down, and dropped it into the hole again. She used the shovel to fill in the hole, working quickly and carelessly. All she wanted right now was to get the hell out of here.

When she was done, she walked away fast. The shovel she slung into the high weeds. She had no intention of taking it back to the barn, no matter how mundane the explanation of the sound she had heard might be.

When she reached her car, she opened first the passenger door and then the glove compartment. She pawed through the litter of paper inside until she found an old book of matches. It took her four tries to produce one small flame. The pain had almost entirely left her hands, but they were shaking so badly that she struck the first three much too hard, bending the paper heads uselessly to the side.

When the fourth flared alight, she held it between two fingers of her right hand, the flame almost invisible in the hot afternoon sunlight, and took the matted pile of trading stamps and dirty pictures from her jeans pocket. She touched the flame to the bundle and held it there until she was sure it had caught. Then she cast the match aside and dipped the papers down to produce the maximum draft. The woman was mal-nourished and hollow-eyed. The dog looked mangy and just smart enough to be embarrassed. It was a relief to watch the surface of the one photograph she could see bubble and turn brown. When the pictures began to curl up, she dropped the flaming bundle into the dirt where a woman had once beaten another dog, this one a Saint Bernard, to death with a baseball bat.

The flames flared. The little pile of stamps and photos quickly crumpled to black ash. The flames guttered, went out . . . and at the moment they did, a sudden gust of wind blew through the stillness of the day, breaking the clot of ash up into flakes. They whirled upward in a funnel which Polly followed with eyes that had gone suddenly wide and fright-ened. Where, exactly, had that freak gust of wind come from?

Oh, please! Can't you stop being so damned—

At that moment the growling sound, low, like an idling outboard motor, rose from the hot, dark maw of the barn again. It wasn't her imagination and it wasn't a creaking board.

It was a *dog*.

Polly looked that way, frightened, and saw two sunken red circles of light peering out at her from the darkness.

She ran around the car, bumping her hip painfully against the right side of the hood in her hurry, got in, rolled up the windows, and locked the doors. She turned the ignition key. The engine cranked over . . . but did not start.

No one knows where I am, she realized. No one but Mr. Gaunt . . . and he wouldn't tell.

For a moment she imagined herself trapped out here, the way Donna Trenton and her son had been trapped. Then the engine burst into life and she backed out of the driveway so fast she almost ran her car into the ditch on the far side of the road. She dropped the transmission into drive and headed back to town as fast as she dared to go.

She had forgotten all about washing her hands.

4

Ace Merrill rolled out of bed around the same time that Brian Rusk was blowing his head off thirty miles away.

He went into the bathroom, shucking out of his dirty skivvies as he walked, and urinated for an hour or two. He raised one arm and sniffed his pit. He looked at the shower and decided against it. He had a big day ahead of him. The shower could wait.

He left the bathroom without bothering to flush—*if it's yellow, let it mellow* was an integral part of Ace's philosophy—and went directly to the bureau, where the last of Mr. Gaunt's blow was laid out on a shaving mirror. It was great stuff—easy on the nose, hot in the head. It was also almost gone. Ace had needed a lot of go-power last night, just as Mr. Gaunt had said, but he had a pretty good idea there was more where this had come from.

Ace used the edge of his driver's license to shape a couple of lines. He snorted them with a rolled-up five-dollar bill, and something that felt like a Shrike missile went off in his head.

"Boom!" cried Ace Merrill in his best Warner Wolf voice. "Let's go to the videotape!"

He pulled a pair of faded jeans up over his naked hips and then got into a Harley-Davidson tee-shirt. It's what all the well-dressed treasure-hunters are wearing this year, he thought, and laughed wildly. My, that coke was fine!

He was on his way out the door when his eye fell on last night's take and he remembered that he had meant to call Nat Copeland in Portsmouth. He went back into the bedroom, dug through the clothes which were balled helter-skelter in his top bureau drawer, and finally came up with a battered address book. He went back into the kitchen, sat down, and dialled the number he had. He doubted that he would actually catch Nat in, but it was worth a try. The coke buzzed and whipsawed in his head, but he could already feel the rush tapering off. A headshot of cocaine made a new man of you. The only trouble was, the first thing the new man wanted was another one, and Ace's supply was severely depleted.

"Yeah?" a wary voice said in his ear, and Ace realized he had beaten the odds again—his luck was in.

"Nat!" he cried.

"Who the fuck says so?"

"*I* do, old hoss! *I* do!"

"Ace? That you?"

"None other! How you doin, ole Natty?"

"I've been better." Nat sounded less than overjoyed to hear from his old machine-shop buddy at Shawshank. "What do you want, Ace?"

"Now, is that any way to talk to a pal?" Ace asked reproachfully. He cocked the phone between his ear and shoulder and pulled a pair of rusty tin cans toward him.

One of them had come out of the ground behind the old Treblehorn place, the other from the cellar-hole of the old Masters farm, which had burned flat when Ace was only ten years old. The first can had contained only four books of S & H Green Stamps and several banded packets of Raleigh cigarette coupons. The second had contained a few sheafs of mixed trading stamps and six rolls of pennies. Except they didn't look like regular pennies.

They were white.

"Maybe I just wanted to touch base," Ace teased. "You know, check on the state of your piles, see how your supply of K-Y's holdin out. Things like that."

"What do you want, Ace?" Nat Copeland repeated wearily.

Ace plucked one of the penny-rolls out of the old Crisco can. The paper had faded from its original purple to a dull wash pink. He shook two of the pennies out into his hand and looked at them curiously. If anyone would know about these things, Nat Copeland was the guy.

He had once owned a shop in Kittery called Copeland's Coins and Collectibles. He'd also had his own private coin collection—one of the ten best in New England, at least according to Nat himself. Then he too had discovered the wonders of cocaine. In the four or five years following this discovery, he had dismantled his coin collection item by item and put it up his nose. In 1985, police responding to a silent alarm at the Long John Silver coin-shop in Portland had found Nat Copeland in the back room, stuffing Lady Liberty silver dollars into a chamois bag. Ace met him not long after.

"Well, I *did* have a question, now that you mention it."

"A question? That's all?"

"That's absolutely all, good buddy."

"All right." Nat's voice relaxed the smallest bit. "Ask, then. I don't have all day."

"Right," Ace said. "Busy, busy, busy. Places to go and people to eat, am I right, Natty?" He laughed crazily. It wasn't just the blow; it was the *day.* He hadn't gotten in until first light, the coke he had ingested had kept him awake until almost ten this morning in spite of the drawn shades and his physical exertions, and he still felt ready to eat steel bars and spit out tenpenny nails. And why not? Why the fuck *not?* He was standing on the rim of a fortune. He knew it, he felt it in every fiber.

"Ace, is there really something on that thing you call your mind or did you phone just to rag me?"

"No, I didn't call to rag you. Give me the straight dope, Natty, and I might give *you* some straight dope. *Very* straight."

"Really?" Nat Copeland's voice lost its edge at once. It became hushed, almost awed. "Are you shitting me, Ace?"

"The best, primoest shit I ever had, Natty Bumppo, my lad."

"Can you cut me in?"

"I wouldn't doubt it a bit," Ace said, meaning to do no such thing. He had pried three or four more of the strange pennies out of their old, faded roll. Now he pushed them into a straight line with his finger. "But you've got to do me a favor."

"Name it."

"What do you know about white pennies?"

There was a pause on the other end of the line. Then Nat said cautiously, "White pennies? Do you mean *steel* pennies?"

"I don't know what I mean—you're the coin collector, not me."

"Look at the dates. See if they're from the years 1941 to 1945."

Ace turned over the pennies in front of him. One was a 1941; four were 1943s; the last was from 1944.

"Yeah. They are. What are they worth, Nat?" He tried to disguise the eagerness in his voice and was not entirely successful.

"Not a lot taken one by one," Nat said, "but a hell of a lot more than ordinary pennies. Maybe two bucks apiece. Three if they're U.C."

"What's that?"

"Uncirculated. In mint condition. Have you got a lot, Ace?"

"Quite a few," Ace said, "quite a few, Natty my man." But

he was disappointed. He had six rolls, three hundred pennies, and the ones he was looking at didn't look in particularly good shape to him. They weren't exactly beat to shit, but they were a long way from being shiny and new. Six hundred dollars, eight hundred tops. Not what you'd call a big strike.

"Well, bring them down and let me look," Nat said. "I can get you top dollar." He hesitated, then added: "And bring some of that marching powder with you."

"I'll think about it," Ace said.

"Hey, Ace! Don't hang up!"

"Fuck you very much, Natty," Ace replied, and did just that.

He sat where he was for a moment, brooding over the pennies and the two rusty cans. There was something very weird about all of this. Useless trading stamps and six hundred dollars' worth of steel pennies. What did that add up to?

That's the bitch of it, Ace thought. It doesn't add up to anything. Where's the real stuff? Where's the goddam LOOT?

He pushed back from the table, went into the bedroom, and snorted the rest of the blow Mr. Gaunt had laid on him. When he came out again, he had the book with the map in it and he was feeling considerably more cheerful. It *did* add up. It added up just fine. Now that he had helped his head a little bit, he could see that.

After all, there had been lots of crosses on that map. He had found two caches right where those crosses suggested they would be, each marked with a large, flat stone. Crosses + Flat Stones = Buried Treasure. It *did* seem that Pop had been a little softer in his old age than people from town had believed, that he'd had a bit of a problem telling the difference between diamonds and dust there at the end, but the big stuff—gold, currency, maybe negotiable securities—had to be out there *someplace,* under one or more of those flat rocks.

He had *proved* that. His uncle had buried things of *value,* not just bunches of moldy old trading stamps. At the old Masters farm he had found six rolls of steel pennies worth at least six hundred dollars. Not much . . . but an indication.

"It's out there," Ace said softly. His eyes sparkled madly. "It's all out there—in one of those other seven holes. Or two. Or three."

He *knew* it.

He took the brown-paper map out of the book and let his finger wander from one cross to the next, wondering if some were more likely than others. Ace's finger stopped on the old Joe Camber place. It was the only location where there were two crosses close together. His finger began to move slowly back and forth between them.

Joe Camber had died in a tragedy that had taken three other lives. His wife and boy had been away at the time. On vacation. People like the Cambers didn't ordinarily take vacations, but Charity Camber had won some money in the state lottery, Ace seemed to recall. He tried to remember more, but it was hazy in his mind. He'd had his own fish to fry back then— plenty of them.

What had Mrs. Camber done when she and her boy had returned from their little trip to find that Joe—a world-class shit, according to everything Ace had heard—was dead and gone? Moved out of state, hadn't they? And the property? Maybe she'd wanted to turn it over in a hurry. In Castle Rock, one name stood above all the rest when it came to turning things over in a hurry; that name was Reginald Marion "Pop" Merrill. Had she gone to see him? He would have offered her short commons—that was his way—but if she was anxious enough to move, short commons might have been okay with her. In other words, the Camber place might also have belonged to Pop at the time of his death.

This possibility solidified to a certainty in Ace's mind only moments after it occurred to him.

"The Camber place," he said. "I bet that's where it is! I *know* that's where it is!"

Thousands of dollars! Maybe *tens* of thousands! Hopping Jesus!

He snatched up the map and slammed it back into the book. Then he headed out to the Chevy Mr. Gaunt had loaned him, almost running.

One question still nagged: If Pop really *had* been able to tell the difference between diamonds and dust, why had he bothered to bury the trading stamps at all?

Ace pushed this question impatiently aside and got on the road to Castle Rock.

5

Danforth Keeton arrived back home in Castle View just as Ace was leaving for the town's more rural environs. Buster was still handcuffed to the doorhandle of his Cadillac, but his mood was one of savage euphoria. He had spent the last two years fighting shadows, and the shadows had been winning. It had gotten to the point where he had begun fearing that he might be going insane . . . which, of course, was just what They wanted him to believe.

He saw several "satellite dishes" on his drive from Main Street to his home on the View. He had noticed them before, and had wondered if they might not be a part of what was going on in this town. Now he felt sure. They weren't "satellite dishes" at all. They were mind-disrupters. They might not *all* be aimed at his house, but you could be sure any which weren't were aimed at the few other people like him who understood that a monstrous conspiracy was afoot.

Buster parked in his driveway and pushed the garage-door opener clipped to his sun visor. The door began to rise, but he felt a monstrous bolt of pain go through his head at the same instant. He understood *that* was a part of it, too—They had replaced his *real* Wizard garage-door opener with something else, something that shot bad rays into his head at the same time it was opening the door.

He pulled it off the visor and threw it out the window before driving into the garage.

He turned off the ignition, opened the door, and got out. The handcuff tethered him to the door as efficiently as a choke-chain. There were tools mounted neatly on wall-pegs, but they were well out of reach. Buster leaned back into the car and began to blow the horn.

6

Myrtle Keeton, who'd had her own errand to run that afternoon, was lying on her bed upstairs in a troubled semi-doze when the horn began to blow. She sat bolt upright, eyes bulging in terror. *"I did it!"* she gasped. "I did what you told me to do, now please leave me alone!"

She realized that she had been dreaming, that Mr. Gaunt was not here, and let out her breath in a long, trembling sigh.

WHONK! WHONK! WHOOOONNNNNNK!

It sounded like the Cadillac's horn. She picked up the doll which lay next to her on the bed, the beautiful doll she had gotten at Mr. Gaunt's shop, and hugged it to her for comfort. She had done something this afternoon, something which a dim, frightened part of her believed to be a bad thing, a *very* bad thing, and since then the doll had become inexpressibly dear to her. Price, Mr. Gaunt might have said, always enhances value . . . at least in the eyes of the purchaser.

WHOOONNNNNNNNNNNNNNNNNKK!

It *was* the Cadillac's horn. Why was Danforth sitting in the garage, blowing his horn? She supposed she had better go see.

"But he better not hurt my doll," she said in a low voice. She placed it carefully in the shadows under her side of the bed. "He just better not, because that's where I draw the line."

Myrtle was one of a great many people who had visited Needful Things that day, just another name with a checkmark beside it on Mr. Gaunt's list. She had come, like many others, because Mr. Gaunt had *told* her to come. She got the message in a way her husband would have understood completely: she heard it in her head.

Mr. Gaunt told her the time had come to finish paying for her doll . . . if she wanted to keep it, that was. She was to take a metal box and a sealed letter to the Daughters of Isabella Hall, next to Our Lady of Serene Waters. The box had grilles set in every side but the bottom. She could hear a faint ticking noise from inside. She had tried to look into one of the round grilles—they looked like the speakers in old-fashioned table radios—but she had been able to see only a vague cube-shaped object. And in truth, she hadn't looked very hard. It seemed better—safer—not to.

There had been one car in the parking lot of the little church complex when Myrtle, who was on foot, arrived. The parish hall itself had been empty, though. She peeked over the sign taped to the window set in the top half of the door to make sure, then read the sign.

DAUGHTERS OF ISABELLA

MEET TUESDAY AT 7 P.M.

HELP US PLAN "CASINO NITE"!

Myrtle slipped inside. To her left was a stack of brightly painted compartments standing against the wall—this was where the daycare children kept their lunches and where the Sunday School children kept their various drawings and work projects. Myrtle had been told to put her item into one of these compartments, and she did so. It just fit. At the front of the room was the Chairwoman's table, with an American flag on the left and a banner depicting the Infant of Prague on the right. The table was already set up for the evening meeting, with pens, pencils, Casino Nite sign-up sheets, and, in the middle, the Chairwoman's agenda. Myrtle had put the envelope Mr. Gaunt had given her under this sheet so Betsy Vigue, this year's Daughters of Isabella Activities Chairwoman, would see it as soon as she picked up her agenda.

READ THIS RIGHT AWAY YOU POPE WHORE

was typed across the front of the envelope in capital letters.

Heart bumping rapidly in her chest, her blood-pressure somewhere over the moon, Myrtle had tiptoed out of the Daughters of Isabella Hall. She paused for a moment outside, hand pressed above her ample bosom, trying to catch her breath.

And saw someone hurrying out of the Knights of Columbus Hall beyond the church.

It was June Gavineaux. She looked as scared and guilty as Myrtle felt. She raced down the wooden steps to the parking lot so fast she almost fell and then walked rapidly toward that single parked car, low heels tip-tapping briskly on the hot-top.

She looked up, saw Myrtle, and paled. Then she looked more closely at Myrtle's face . . . and understood.

"You too?" she asked in a low voice. A strange grin, both jolly and nauseated, rose on her face. It was the expression of a normally well-behaved child who has, for reasons she does not understand herself, put a mouse in her favorite teacher's desk drawer.

Myrtle felt an answering grin of exactly the same type rise on her own face. Yet she tried to dissemble. "Mercy's sake! I don't know what you're talking about!"

"Yes you do." June had looked around quickly, but the two women had this corner of that strange afternoon to themselves. "Mr. Gaunt."

Myrtle nodded and felt her cheeks heat in a fierce, unaccustomed blush.

"What did you get?" June asked.

"A doll. What did *you* get?"

"A vase. The most beautiful cloisonné vase you ever saw."

"What did you do?"

Smiling slyly, June countered: "What did *you* do?"

"Never mind." Myrtle looked back toward the Daughters of Isabella Hall and then sniffed. "It doesn't matter anyway. They're only Catholics."

"That's right," June (who was a lapsed Catholic herself) replied. Then she had gone to her car. Myrtle had not asked for a ride and June Gavineaux did not offer one. Myrtle had walked rapidly out of the parking lot. She had not looked up when June shot by her in her white Saturn. All Myrtle had wanted was to go home, take a nap while she cuddled her lovely doll, and forget what she had done.

That, she was now discovering, was not going to be as easy as she had hoped.

7

WHHHHHHOOOOOOOONNNNNNNNNNNNNNNNNKKKKK*!*

Buster planted his palm on the horn and held it down. The blare rang and blasted in his ears. Where in hell's name *was* that bitch?

At last the door between the garage and the kitchen opened. Myrtle poked her head through. Her eyes were large and frightened.

"Well, finally," Buster said, letting go of the horn. "I thought you'd died on the john."

"Danforth? What's wrong?"

"Nothing. Things are better than they've been for two years. I just need a little help, that's all."

Myrtle didn't move.

"Woman, get your fat ass over here!"

She didn't want to go—he scared her—but the habit was old and deep and hard to break. She came around to where he stood in the wedge of space behind the car's open door. She walked slowly, her slippers scuffing the concrete floor in a way that made Buster grind his teeth together.

She saw the handcuffs, and her eyes widened. "Danforth, what *happened?*"

"Nothing I can't handle. Pass me that hacksaw, Myrt. The one on the wall. No—on second thought, never mind the hacksaw right now. Give me the big screwdriver instead. And that hammer."

She started to draw away from him, her hands going up to her chest and joining there in an anxious knot. Quick as a snake, moving before she could back out of his reach, Buster shot his free hand through the open window and seized her by the hair.

"*Ow!*" she screamed, grabbing futilely at his fist. "*Danforth, ow! OWWW!*"

Buster dragged her toward him, his face clenched in a horrible grimace. Two large veins pulsed in his forehead. He felt her hand beating against his fist no more than he would have felt a bird's wing.

"*Get what I tell you!*" he cried, and pulled her head forward. He thumped it against the top of the open door once, twice, three times. "*Were you born foolish or did you just grow that way? Get it, get it, get it!*"

"*Danforth, you're hurting me!*"

"*Right!*" he screamed back, and thumped her head once more against the top of the Cadillac's open door, much harder this time. The skin of her forehead split and thin blood began to flow down the left side of her face. "*Are you going to mind me, woman?*"

"*Yes! Yes! Yes!*"

"Good." He relaxed his grip on her hair. "Now give me the big screwdriver and the hammer. And don't try any funny business, either."

She waved her right arm toward the wall. "I can't reach."

He leaned forward, extending his own reach a little and allowing her to take a step toward the wall where the tools hung. He kept his fingers wrapped firmly in her hair as she groped. Dime-sized drops of blood splattered on and between her slippers.

Her hand closed on one of the tools, and Danforth shook her head briskly, the way a terrier might shake a dead rat. "Not that, Dumbo," he said. "That's a drill. Did I ask for a drill? *Huh?*"

"But Danforth—*oww!*—I can't *see!*"

"I suppose you'd like me to let you go. Then you could run into the house and call Them, couldn't you?"

"I don't know what you're talking about!"

"Oh no. You're such an innocent little lamb. It was just an accident that you got me out of the way on Sunday so that fucking Deputy could put those lying stickers up all over the house—is that what you expect me to believe?"

She looked back at him through the tangles of her hair. Blood had formed fine beads in her eyelashes. "But . . . but Danforth . . . *you* asked *me* out on Sunday. You said—"

He jerked hard on her hair. Myrtle screamed.

"Just get what I asked for. We can discuss this later."

She felt along the wall again, head down, hair (except for Buster's fistful) hanging in her face. Her groping fingers touched the big screwdriver.

"That's one," he said. "Let's try for two, what do you say?"

She fumbled some more, and at last her fluttering fingers happened on the perforated rubber sleeve which covered the handle of the Craftsman hammer.

"Good. Now give them to me."

She pulled the hammer off its pegs, and Buster reeled her in. He let go of her hair, ready to snatch a fresh handful if she showed any sign of bolting. Myrtle didn't. She was cowed. She only wanted to be allowed back upstairs, where she would cuddle her beautiful doll to her and go to sleep. She felt like sleeping forever.

He took the tools from her unresisting hands. He placed the tip of the screwdriver against the doorhandle, then whacked the top of the screwdriver several times with the hammer. On the fourth blow, the doorhandle snapped off. Buster slipped the loop of the cuff out of it, then dropped both the handle and the screwdriver to the concrete floor. He went first to the button which closed the garage door. Then, as it rattled noisily down on its tracks, he advanced on Myrtle with the hammer in his hand.

"Did you sleep with him, Myrtle?" he asked softly.

"What?" She looked at him with dull, apathetic eyes.

Buster began to whack the hammerhead into the palm of his hand. It made a soft, fleshy sound—*thuck! thuck! thuck!*

"Did you sleep with him after the two of you put up those goddam pink slips all over the house?"

She looked at him dully, not understanding, and Buster himself had forgotten that she had been with him at Maurice when Ridgewick broke in and did his thing.

"Buster, what are you talking ab—"

He stopped, his eyes widening. *"What did you call me?"*

The apathy left her eyes. She began to retreat from him, hunching her shoulders protectively. Behind them, the garage door came to rest. Now the only sounds in the garage were their scuffling feet and the soft clink of the handcuff chain as it swung back and forth.

"I'm sorry," she whispered. "I'm sorry, Danforth." Then she turned and ran for the kitchen door.

He caught her three steps from it, once again using her hair to draw her to him. *"What* did you call me?" he screamed, and raised the hammer.

Her eyes turned up to follow its ascent. *"Danforth, no, please!"*
"What did you call me? What did you call me?"

He screamed it over and over again, and each time he asked the question he punctuated it with that soft, fleshy sound: *Thuck. Thuck. Thuck.*

8

Ace drove into the Camber dooryard at five o'clock. He stuffed the treasure map into his back pocket, then opened the trunk. He got the pick and shovel which Mr. Gaunt had thoughtfully provided and then walked over to the leaning, overgrown porch which ran along one side of the house. He took the map out of his back pocket and sat on the steps to examine it. The short-term effects of the coke had worn off, but his heart was still thudding briskly along in his chest. Treasure-hunting, he had discovered, was also a stimulant.

He looked around for a moment at the weedy yard, the sagging barn, the clusters of blindly staring sunflowers. It's not much, but I think this is it, just the same, he thought. The place where I put the Corson Brothers behind me forever and get rich in the bargain. It's here—some of it or all of it. Right here. I can feel it.

But it was more than feeling—he could *hear* it, singing softly to him. Singing from beneath the ground. Not just tens of thousands, but hundreds of thousands. Perhaps as much as a million.

"A million dollars," Ace whispered in a hushed, choked voice, and bent over the map.

Five minutes later he was hunting along the west side of the Camber house. Most of the way down toward the back, almost obscured in tall weeds, he found what he was looking for—a large, flat stone. He picked it up, threw it aside, and began to dig frantically. Less than two minutes later, there was a muffled clunk as the blade struck rusty metal. Ace fell on his knees, rooted in the dirt like a dog hunting a buried bone, and a minute later he had unearthed the Sherwin-Williams paint-can which had been buried here.

Most dedicated cocaine users are also dedicated nail-biters and Ace was no exception. He had no fingernails to pry with and he couldn't get the lid off. The paint around the rim had dried to an obstinate glue. With a grunt of frustration and rage, Ace pulled out his pocket-knife, got the blade under the can's rim, and levered the cover off. He peered in eagerly.

Bills!

Sheafs and sheafs of bills!

With a cry he seized them, pulled them out . . . and saw that his eagerness had deceived him. It was only more trading stamps. Red Ball Stamps this time, a kind which had been redeemable only south of the Mason-Dixon line . . . and there only until 1964, when the company had gone out of business.

"Shit fire and save matches!" Ace cried. He threw the stamps aside. They unfolded and began to tumble away in the light, hot breeze that had sprung up. Some of them caught and fluttered from the weeds like dusty banners. *"Cunt! Bastard! Sonofawhore!"*

He rooted in the can, even turned it over to see if there was anything taped to the bottom, and found nothing. He threw it away, stared at it for a moment, then rushed over and booted it like a soccer ball.

He felt in his pocket for the map again. There was one panicky second when he was afraid it wasn't there, that he had lost it somehow, but he had only pushed it all the way down to the bottom in his eagerness to get cracking. He yanked it out and looked at it. The other cross was out behind the barn . . . and suddenly a wonderful idea came into Ace's mind, lighting up the angry darkness in there like a Roman candle on the Fourth of July.

The can he had just dug up was a blind! Pop might have thought someone would tumble to the fact that he had marked his various stashes with flat rocks. Thus, he had practiced a little of the old bait-and-switch out here at the Camber place. Just to be safe. A hunter who found one useless treasure-trove would never guess that there was *another* stash, right here on this same property but in a more out-of-the-way place . . .

"Unless they had the map," Ace whispered. "Like *I* do."

He grabbed the pick and shovel and raced for the barn, eyes wide, sweaty, graying hair matted to the sides of his head.

9

He saw the old Air-Flow trailer and ran toward it. He was almost there when his foot struck something and he fell sprawling to the ground. He was up in a moment, looking around. He saw what he had stumbled over at once.

It was a shovel. One with fresh dirt on the blade.

A bad feeling began to creep over Ace; a very bad feeling indeed. It began in his belly, then spread upward to his chest and down to his balls. His lips peeled back from his teeth, very slowly, in an ugly snarl.

He got to his feet and saw the rock marker lying nearby, dirt side up. It had been thrown aside. Someone had been here first . . . and not long ago, from the look. Someone had beaten him to the treasure.

"No," he whispered. The word fell from his snarling mouth like a drop of tainted blood or infected saliva. *"No!"*

Not far from the shovel and the uprooted rock, Ace saw a pile of loose dirt which had been scraped indifferently back into a hole. Ignoring both his own tools and the shovel which the thief had left behind, Ace fell on his knees again and began pawing dirt out of the hole. In no time at all, he had found the Crisco can.

He brought it out and pried off the lid.

There was nothing inside but a white envelope.

Ace took it out and tore it open. Two things fluttered out: a sheet of folded paper and a smaller envelope. Ace ignored the second envelope for the time being and unfolded the paper. It was a typed note. His mouth dropped open as he read his own name at the top of the sheet.

Dear Ace,

I can't be sure you'll find this, but there's no law against hoping. Sending you to Shawshank was fun, but this has been better. I wish I could see your face when you finish reading this!

Not long after I sent you up, I went to see Pop. I saw him pretty often—once a month, in fact. We had an arrangement: he gave me a hundred a month and I let him go on making his illegal loans. All very civilized. Halfway through this particular meeting, he excused himself to use the toilet— "something he et," he said. Ha-ha! I took the opportunity to peek in his desk, which he had left unlocked. Such carelessness was not like him, but I think he was afraid he might load his pants if he didn't go "to visit his Uncle John" right away. Ha!

I only found one item of interest, but that one was a corker. It looked like a map. There were lots of crosses on it, but one of the crosses—the one marking this spot—was marked in red. I put the map back before Pop returned. He never knew I looked at it. I came out here right after he died and dug up this Crisco can. There was better than two hundred thousand dollars in it, Ace. Don't worry, though—I decided to "share and share alike" and am going to leave you exactly what you deserve.

Welcome back to town, Ace-Hole!

Yours sincerely,
Alan Pangborn
Castle County Sheriff

P.S.: A word to the wise, Ace: now that you know, "take your lumps" and forget the whole thing. You know the old saying—finders keepers.

If you ever try to brace me about your uncle's
money, I will tear you a new asshole and stuff
your head into it.

Trust me on this.

A.P.

Ace let the sheet of paper slide from his numb fingers and
opened the second envelope.

A single one-dollar bill fell out of it.

*I decided to "share and share alike" and am going to leave you
exactly what you deserve.*

"You crab-infested *bastard*," Ace whispered, and picked up
the dollar bill with shaking fingers.

Welcome back to town, Ace-Hole!

"*You SONOFAWHORE!*" Ace screamed so loudly that he felt
something in his throat strain and almost rupture. The echo
came back dimly: *... whore ... whore ... whore ...*

He began to tear the dollar up, then forced his fingers to
relax.

Huh-uh. No way, José.

He was going to save this. The son of a bitch had wanted
Pop's money, had he? He had stolen what rightfully belonged
to Pop's last living relative, had he? Well, all right. Good.
Fine. But he should have *all* of it. And Ace intended to see that
the Sheriff had just that. So, after he removed Pusbag's testicles
with his pocketknife, he intended to stuff this dollar bill into
the bloody hole where they had been.

"You want the money, Daddy-O?" Ace asked in a soft, mus-
ing voice. "Okay. That's okay. No problem. No ... fucking ...
problem."

He got to his feet and began walking back toward the car in
a stiff, staggering version of his usual hood strut.

By the time he got there, he was almost running.

PART THREE

———

EVERYTHING
MUST GO

CHAPTER NINETEEN

1

By quarter to six, a weird twilight had begun to creep over Castle Rock; thunderheads were stacking up on the southern horizon. Low, distant boomings muttered over the woods and fields from that direction. The clouds were moving toward town, growing as they came. The streetlights, governed by a master photoelectric cell, came on a full half hour earlier than they usually did at that time of year.

Lower Main Street was a crowded confusion. It had been overrun by State Police vehicles and TV newsvans. Radio calls crackled and entwined in the hot, still air. TV technicians paid out cable and yelled at the people—kids, mostly—who tripped over the loose lengths of it before they could anchor it temporarily to the pavement with duct tape. Photographers from four daily papers stood outside the barricades in front of the Municipal Building and took stills which would appear on front pages the following day. A few locals—surprisingly few, if anyone had bothered to notice such things—rubbernecked. A TV correspondent stood in the glare of a hi-intensity lamp and taped his report with the Municipal Building in the background. "A senseless wave of violence swished through Castle Rock this afternoon," he began, then stopped. *"Swished?"* he asked himself disgustedly. "Shit, let's take it again from the top." To his left, a TV-dude from another station was watching his crew prepare for what would be a live feed in less than twenty minutes. More of the onlookers had been drawn to the familiar faces of the TV correspondents than to the barricades, where there had been nothing to see since two orderlies from Medical Assistance had brought out the unfortunate Lester Pratt in a black plastic bag, loaded him into the back of their ambulance, and driven away.

Upper Main, away from the blue strobes of the State Police cruisers and the bright pools of the TV lights, was almost entirely deserted.

Almost.

Every now and then a car or a pick-up truck would park in one of the slant spaces in front of Needful Things. Every now and then a pedestrian would saunter up to the new shop, where the display lights were off and the shade was pulled down on the door under the canopy. Every now and then one of the rubberneckers on Lower Main would break away from the shifting knot of onlookers and walk up the street, past the vacant lot where the Emporium Galorium had once stood, past You Sew and Sew, closed and dark, to the new store.

No one noticed this trickle of visitors—not the police, not the camera crews, not the correspondents, not the majority of the bystanders. They were looking at THE SCENE OF THE CRIME, and their backs were turned to the place where, less than three hundred yards away, the crime was still going on.

If some disinterested observer *had* been keeping an eye on Needful Things, he or she would have quickly detected a pattern. The visitors approached. The visitors saw the sign in the window which read

CLOSED UNTIL FURTHER NOTICE.

The visitors stepped back, identical expressions of frustration and distress on their faces—they looked like hurting junkies who had discovered the pusherman wasn't where he'd promised to be. *What do I do now?* their faces said. Most stepped forward to read the sign again, as if a second, closer scrutiny would somehow change the message.

A few got into their cars and left or wandered down toward the Municipal Building to stare at the free show for a while, looking dazed and vaguely disappointed. On the faces of most, however, an expression of sudden comprehension dawned. They had the look of people suddenly understanding some basic concept, like how to diagram simple sentences or reduce a pair of fractions to their lowest common denominator.

These people walked around the corner to the service alley which ran behind the business buildings on Main Street—the alley where Ace had parked the Tucker Talisman the night before.

Forty feet down, an oblong of yellow light fell out of an open door and across the patched concrete. This light grew slowly brighter as day slipped into evening. A shadow lay in the center of the oblong, like a silhouette cut from mourner's crepe. The shadow belonged, of course, to Leland Gaunt.

He had placed a table in the doorway. On it was a Roi-Tan cigar box. He put the money which his customers tendered into this box and made change from it. These patrons approached hesitantly, even fearfully in some cases, but all of them had one thing in common: they were angry people with heavy grudges to tote. A few—not many—turned away before they reached Mr. Gaunt's makeshift counter. Some went running, with the wide eyes of men and women who have glimpsed a frightful fiend licking its chops in the shadows. Most, however, stayed to do business. And as Mr. Gaunt bantered with them, treating this odd back-door commerce as an amusing diversion at the end of a long day, they relaxed.

Mr. Gaunt had enjoyed his shop, but he never felt so comfortable behind plate-glass and under a roof as he did here, on the edge of the air, with the first breezes of the coming storm stirring his hair. The shop, with its clever display lights on ceiling-mounted tracks, was all right . . . but this was better. This was *always* better.

He had begun business many years ago—as a wandering

peddler on the blind face of a distant land, a peddler who carried his wares on his back, a peddler who usually came at the fall of darkness and was always gone the next morning, leaving bloodshed, horror, and unhappiness behind him. Years later, in Europe, as the Plague raged and the deadcarts rolled, he had gone from town to town and country to country in a wagon drawn by a slat-thin white horse with terrible burning eyes and a tongue as black as a killer's heart. He had sold his wares from the back of the wagon . . . and was gone before his customers, who paid with small, ragged coins or even in barter, could discover what they had *really* bought.

Times changed; methods changed; faces, too. But when the faces were needful they were always the same, the faces of sheep who have lost their shepherd, and it was with this sort of commerce that he felt most at home, most like that wandering peddler of old, standing not behind a fancy counter with a Sweda cash register nearby but behind a plain wooden table, making change out of a cigar-box and selling them the same item over and over and over again.

The goods which had so attracted the residents of Castle Rock—the black pearls, the holy relics, the carnival glass, the pipes, the old comic books, the baseball cards, the antique kaleidoscopes—were all gone. Mr. Gaunt had gotten down to his *real* business, and at the end of things, the real business was always the same. The ultimate item had changed with the years, just like everything else, but such changes were surface things, frosting of different flavors on the same dark and bitter cake.

At the end, Mr. Gaunt always sold them weapons . . . and they always bought.

"Why, thank you, Mr. Warburton!" Mr. Gaunt said, taking a five-dollar bill from the black janitor. He handed him back a single and one of the automatic pistols Ace had brought from Boston.

"Thank you, Miss Milliken!" He took ten and gave back eight.

He charged them what they could afford—not a penny more or a penny less. Each according to his means was Mr. Gaunt's motto, and never mind each according to his needs, because they were *all* needful things, and he had come here to fill their emptiness and end their aches.

"Good to see you, Mr. Emerson!"

Oh, it was always good, so very good, to be doing business in the old way again. And business had never been better.

2

Alan Pangborn wasn't in Castle Rock. While the reporters and the State Police gathered at one end of Main Street and Leland Gaunt conducted his going-out-of-business sale halfway up the hill, Alan was sitting at the nurses' station of the Blumer Wing in Northern Cumberland Hospital in Bridgton.

The Blumer Wing was small—only fourteen patient rooms—but what it lacked in size it made up for in color. The walls of the inpatient rooms were painted in bright primary shades. A mobile hung from the ceiling in the nurses' station, the birds depending from it swinging and dipping gracefully around a central spindle.

Alan was sitting in front of a huge mural which depicted a medley of Mother Goose rhymes. One section of the mural showed a man leaning across a table, holding something out to a small boy, obviously a hick, who looked both frightened and fascinated. Something about this particular image had struck Alan, and a snatch of childhood rhyme rose like a whisper in his mind:

Simple Simon met a pie-man
going to the fair.
"Simple Simon," said the pie-man,
"come and taste my wares!"

A ripple of gooseflesh had broken out on Alan's arms—tiny bumps like beads of cold sweat. He couldn't say why, and that seemed perfectly normal. Never in his entire life had he felt as shaken, as scared, as deeply confused as he did right now. Something totally beyond his ability to understand was happening in Castle Rock. It had become clearly apparent only late this afternoon, when everything had seemed to blow sky-high at once, but it had begun days, maybe even a week, ago. He didn't know what it was, but he knew that Nettie Cobb and Wilma Jerzyck had been only the first outward signs.

And he was terribly afraid that things were still progressing while he sat here with Simple Simon and the pie man.

A nurse, Miss Hendrie according to the small nameplate on her breast, walked up the corridor on faintly squeaking crepe soles weaving her way gracefully among the toys which littered the hall. When Alan came in, half a dozen kids, some with limbs in casts or slings, some with the partial baldness he associated with chemotherapy treatments, had been playing in the hall, trading blocks and trucks, shouting amiably to each other. Now it was the supper hour, and they had gone either down to the cafeteria or back to their rooms.

"How is he?" Alan asked Miss Hendrie.

"No change." She looked at Alan with a calm expression which contained an element of hostility. "Sleeping. He *should* be sleeping. He has had a great shock."

"What do you hear from his parents?"

"We called the father's place of employment in South Paris. He had an installation job over in New Hampshire this afternoon. He's left for home, I understand, and will be informed when he arrives. He should get here around nine, I would think, but of course it's impossible to tell."

"What about the mother?"

"I don't know," Miss Hendrie said. The hostility was more apparent now, but it was no longer aimed at Alan. "I didn't make that call. All I know is what I see—she's not here. This little boy saw his brother commit suicide with a rifle, and although it happened at home, the mother is not here yet. You'll have to excuse me now—I have to fill the med-cart."

"Of course," Alan muttered. He watched her as she started away, then rose from his chair. "Miss Hendrie?"

She turned to him. Her eyes were still calm, but her raised brows expressed annoyance.

"Miss Hendrie, I really do need to talk with Sean Rusk. I think I need to talk to him very badly."

"Oh?" Her voice was cool.

"Something—" Alan suddenly thought of Polly and his voice cracked. He cleared his throat and pushed on. "Something is going on in my town. The suicide of Brian Rusk is only part of it, I believe. And I also believe that Sean Rusk may have the key to the rest of it."

"Sheriff Pangborn, Sean Rusk is only seven years old. And if he *does* know something, why aren't there other policemen here?"

Other policemen, he thought, What she means are *qualified* policemen. Policemen who don't interview eleven-year-old boys on the street and then send them home to commit suicide in the garage.

"Because they've got their hands full," Alan said, "and because they don't know the town the way I do."

"I see." She turned to go again.

"Miss Hendrie."

"Sheriff, I'm short-handed this evening and very b—"

"Brian Rusk wasn't the only Castle Rock fatality today. There were at least three others. Another man, the owner of the local tavern, has been taken to the hospital in Norway with gunshot trauma. He may live, but it's going to be touch and go with him for the next thirty-six hours or so. And I have a hunch the killing isn't done."

He had finally succeeded in capturing all of her attention.

"You believe Sean Rusk knows something about this?"

"He may know why his brother killed himself. If he does, that may open up the rest of it. So if he wakes up, will you tell me?"

She hesitated, then said, "That depends on his mental state when he does, Sheriff. I'm not going to allow you to make a hysterical little boy's condition worse, no matter what is going on in your town."

"I understand."

"Do you? Good." She gave him a look which said, *Just sit there and don't make trouble for me, then,* and went back behind the high desk. She sat down, and he could hear her putting bottles and boxes on the med-cart.

Alan got up, went to the pay phone in the hall, and dialled Polly's number again. And once again it simply rang on and on. He dialled You Sew and Sew, got the answering machine and racked the phone. He went back to his chair, sat in it, and stared at the Mother Goose mural some more.

You forgot to ask me one question, Miss Hendrie, Alan thought. You forgot to ask me why I'm here if there's so much going on in the seat of the county I was elected to preserve and protect. You forgot to ask me why I'm not leading the investigation while some less essential officer—old Seat Thomas, for instance—sits here, waiting for Sean Rusk to wake up. You forgot to ask those things, Miss Hendrie, and I know a secret. I'm *glad* you forgot. That's the secret.

The reason was as simple as it was humiliating. Except in Portland and Bangor, murder belonged not to the Sheriff's Office but to the State Police. Henry Payton had winked at that in the wake of Nettie and Wilma's duel, but he was not winking anymore. He couldn't afford to. Representatives of every southern Maine newspaper and TV station were either in Castle Rock right now or on their way. They would be joined by their colleagues from all over the state before very much longer . . . and if this really was not over, as Alan suspected, they would shortly be joined by more media people from points south.

That was the simple reality of the situation, but it didn't change the way Alan felt. He felt like a pitcher who can't get the job done and is sent to the showers by the coach. It was an indescribably shitty way to feel. He sat in front of Simple Simon and once again began to add up the score.

Lester Pratt, dead. He had come to the Sheriff's Office in a jealous frenzy and had attacked John LaPointe. It was over his girl, apparently, although John had told Alan before the ambulance came that he had not dated Sally Ratcliffe in over a year. "I only thaw her to thpeek to wunth in awhile on the thtreet, and even then thee cut me dead motht of the time. Thee dethided I'm one of the hellbound." He had touched his broken nose and winced. "Right now I *feel* hellbound."

John was now hospitalized in Norway with a broken nose, a fractured jaw, and possible internal injuries.

Sheila Brigham was also in the hospital. Shock.

Hugh Priest and Billy Tupper were both dead. That news had come in just as Sheila was beginning to fall apart. The call came from a beer deliveryman, who'd had the sense to call Medical Assistance before calling the Sheriff. The man had been almost as hysterical as Sheila Brigham, and Alan hadn't blamed him. By then he had been feeling pretty hysterical himself.

Henry Beaufort, in critical condition as a result of multiple gunshot wounds.

Norris Ridgewick, missing . . . and that somehow hurt the most.

Alan had looked around for him after receiving the deliveryman's call, but Norris was just gone. Alan had assumed at the time that he must have gone outside to formally arrest Danforth and would return with the Head Selectman in tow, but events shortly proved that no one had arrested Keeton. Alan supposed the Staties would arrest him if they ran across him while they pursued other lines of investigation, but otherwise, no. They had more important things to do. In the meantime,

Norris was just gone. Wherever he was, he'd gotten there on foot; when Alan left town, Norris's VW had still been lying on its side in the middle of Lower Main Street.

The witnesses said Buster had crawled into his Cadillac through the window and simply driven away. The only person who had tried to stop him had paid a steep price. Scott Garson was hospitalized here at Northern Cumberland with a broken jaw, broken cheekbone, broken wrist, and three broken fingers. It could have been worse; the bystanders claimed Buster had actively tried to run the man down as he lay in the street.

Lenny Partridge, broken collarbone and God knew how many broken ribs, was also here someplace. Andy Clutterbuck had weighed in with news of this fresh disaster while Alan was still trying to comprehend the fact that the town's Head Selectman was now a fugitive from justice handcuffed to a big red Cadillac. Hugh Priest had apparently stopped Lenny, tossed him across the road, and driven away in the old man's car. Alan supposed they would find Lenny's car in the parking lot of The Mellow Tiger, since Hugh had bitten the dust there.

And, of course, there was Brian Rusk, who had eaten a bullet at the ripe old age of eleven. Clut had barely begun to tell his tale when the phone rang again. Sheila was gone by then, and Alan had picked up on the voice of a screaming, hysterical little boy—Sean Rusk, who had dialled the number on the bright orange sticker beside the kitchen telephone.

All in all, Medical Assistance ambulances and Rescue Services units from four different towns had made afternoon stops in Castle Rock.

Now, sitting with his back to Simple Simon and the pieman, watching the plastic birds as they swung and dipped around their spindle, Alan turned once more to Hugh and Lenny Partridge. Their confrontation was hardly the biggest to take place in Castle Rock today, but it was one of the oddest . . . and Alan sensed that a key to this business might be hidden in its very oddity.

"Why in God's name didn't Hugh take his own car, if he had a hard-on for Henry Beaufort?" Alan had asked Clut, running his hands through hair which was already wildly disarranged. "Why bother with Lenny's old piece of shit?"

"Because Hugh's Buick was standing on four flats. Looked like somebody ripped the shit out of them with a knife." Clut had shrugged, looking uneasily at the shambles the Sheriff's Office had become. "Maybe he thought Henry Beaufort did it."

Yes, Alan thought now. Maybe so. It was crazy, but was it any crazier than Wilma Jerzyck thinking Nettie Cobb had first splattered mud on her sheets and then thrown rocks through the windows of her house? Any crazier than Nettie thinking Wilma had killed her dog?

Before he had a chance to question Clut any further, Henry Payton had come in and told Alan, as kindly as he could, that he was taking the case. Alan nodded. "There's one thing you need to find out, Henry, as soon as you can."

"What's that, Alan?" Henry had asked, but Alan saw with a sinking feeling that Henry was listening to him with only half an ear. His old friend—the first real friend Alan had made in the wider law-enforcement community after winning the job as Sheriff, and a very valuable friend he had turned out to be—was already concentrating on other things. How he would deploy his forces, given the wide spread of the incidents, was probably chief among them.

"You need to find out if Henry Beaufort was as angry at Hugh Priest as Hugh apparently was at him. You can't ask him now, I understand he's unconscious, but when he wakes up—"

"Will do," Henry said, and clapped Alan on the shoulder. "Will do." Then, raising his voice: "Brooks! Morrison! Over here!"

Alan watched him move off and thought of going after him. Of grabbing him and *making* him listen. He didn't do it, because Henry and Hugh and Lester and John—even Wilma and

Nettie—were beginning to lose any feeling of real importance to him. The dead were dead; the wounded were being looked after; the crimes had been committed.

Except Alan had a terrible, sneaking suspicion that the real crime was still going on.

When Henry had walked away to brief his men, Alan had called Clut over once again. The Deputy came with his hands stuffed into his pockets and a morose look on his face. "We been replaced, Alan," he said. "Taken right out of the picture. God *damn!*"

"Not entirely," Alan said, hoping he sounded as if he really believed this. "You're going to be my liaison here, Clut."

"Where are you going?"

"To the Rusk house."

But when he got there, both Brian and Sean Rusk were gone. The ambulance which was taking care of the unfortunate Scott Garson had swung by to pick up Sean; they were on their way to Northern Cumberland Hospital. Harry Samuels's second hearse, an old converted Lincoln, had gotten Brian Rusk and would take him to Oxford, pending autopsy. Harry's better hearse—the one he referred to as "the company car"—had already left for the same place with Hugh and Billy Tupper.

Alan thought, The bodies will be stacked in that tiny morgue over there like cordwood.

It was when he got to the Rusk home that Alan realized—in his gut as well as in his head—how completely he had been taken out of the play. Two of Henry's C.I.D. men were there ahead of him, and they made it clear that Alan could hang around only as long as he didn't try to stick in an oar and help them row. He had stood in the kitchen doorway for a moment, watching them, feeling about as useful as a third wheel on a motor-scooter. Cora Rusk's responses were slow, almost doped. Alan thought it might be shock, or perhaps the ambulance attendants who were transporting her remaining son to the hospital had given her some prescription mercy before they left. She reminded him eerily of the way Norris had looked as he had crawled from the window of his overturned VW. Whether it was because of a tranquilizer or just shock, the detectives weren't getting much of value from her. She wasn't quite weeping, but she was clearly unable to concentrate on their questions enough to make helpful responses. She didn't know anything, she told them; she had been upstairs, taking a nap. Poor Brian, she kept saying. Poor, poor Brian. But she expressed this sentiment in a drone which Alan found creepy, and she kept toying with a pair of old sunglasses which lay beside her on the kitchen table. One of the bows had been mended with adhesive tape, and one of the lenses was cracked.

Alan had left in disgust and come here, to the hospital.

Now he got up and went to the pay telephone down the hall in the main lobby. He tried Polly again, got no answer, and then dialled the Sheriff's Office. The voice which answered growled, "State Police," and Alan felt a childish surge of jealousy. He identified himself and asked for Clut. After a wait of almost five minutes, Clut came on the line.

"Sorry, Alan. They just let the phone lay there on the desk. Lucky I came over to check, or you'd still be waiting. Darned old Staties don't care one bit about us."

"Don't worry about it, Clut. Has anyone collared Keeton yet?"

"Well . . . I don't know how to tell you this, Alan, but . . ."

Alan felt a sinking in the pit of his stomach and closed his eyes. He had been right; it wasn't over.

"Just tell me," he said. "Never mind the protocol."

"Buster—Danforth, I mean—drove home and used a screwdriver to knock the doorhandle off his Cadillac. You know, where he was cuffed."

"I know," Alan agreed. His eyes were still shut.

"Well . . . he killed his wife, Alan. With a hammer. It wasn't a State cop that found her, because the Staties weren't much interested in Buster up to twenty minutes ago. It was Seat

Thomas. He drove by Buster's house to double check. He reported in what he found, and got back here not five minutes ago. He's having chest pains, he says, and I'm not surprised. He told me that Buster took her face 'bout right off. Said there's guts and hair everyplace. There's a platoon or so of Payton's bluejackets up there on the View now. I put Seat in your office. Figured he better sit down before he fell down."

"Jesus Christ, Clut—take him over to Ray Van Allen, fast. He's sixty-two and been smoking Camels all his damn life."

"Ray went to Oxford, Alan. He's trying to help the doctors patch up Henry Beaufort."

"His P.A. then—what's his name? Frankel. Everett Frankel."

"Not around. I tried both the office and his house."

"Well, what does his wife say?"

"Ev's a bachelor, Alan."

"Oh. Christ." Someone had scrawled a bit of graffiti over the telephone. *Don't worry, be happy,* it said. Alan considered this sourly.

"I can take him to the hospital myself," Clut offered.

"I need you right where you are," Alan said. "Have the reporters and TV people shown up?"

"Yeah. The place is crawling with them."

"Well, check on Seat as soon as we're done here. If he doesn't feel any better, here's what you do: go out front, grab a reporter who looks halfway bright to you, deputize him, and have him drive Seat over here to Northern Cumberland."

"Okay." Clut hesitated, then burst out: "I wanted to go over to the Keeton place, but the State Police . . . they won't let me onto the crime-scene! How do you like that, Alan? Those bastards won't let a County Deputy Sheriff onto the crime-scene!"

"I know how you feel. I don't like it much myself. But they're doing their job. Can you see Seat from where you are, Clut?"

"Yuh."

"Well? Is he alive?"

"He's sitting behind your desk, smoking a cigarette and looking at this month's *Rural Law Enforcement.*"

"Right," Alan said. He felt like laughing or crying or doing both at the same time. "That figures. Has Polly Chalmers called, Clut?"

"N . . . wait a minute, here's the log. I thought it was gone. She did call, Alan. Just before three-thirty."

Alan grimaced. "I know about that one. Anything later?"

"Not that I see here, but that doesn't mean much. With Sheila gone and these darned old State Bears clumping around, who can tell for sure?"

"Thanks, Clut. Is there anything else I should know?"

"Yeah, a couple of things."

"Shoot."

"They've got the gun Hugh used to shoot Henry, but David Friedman from State Police Ballistics says he doesn't know what it is. An automatic pistol of some kind, but the guy said he's never seen one quite like it."

"Are you sure it was David Friedman?" Alan asked.

"Friedman, yeah—that was the guy's name."

"He *must* know. Dave Friedman's a walking *Shooter's Bible.*"

"He doesn't, though. I stood right there while he was talking to your pal Payton. He said it's a little like a German Mauser, but it lacked the normal markings and the slide was different. I think they sent it to Augusta with about a ton of other evidence."

"What else?"

"They found an anonymous note in Henry Beaufort's yard," Clut said. "It was crumpled into a ball beside his car—you know that classic T-Bird of his? It was vandalized, too. Just like Hugh's."

Alan felt as if a large soft hand had just whacked him across the face. "What did the note say, Clut?"

"Just a minute." He heard a faint *whick-whick* sound as Clut paged through his notebook. "Here it is. 'Don't you *ever* cut me off and then keep my car-keys you damn *frog.*'"

"*Frog?*"

"That's what it says." Clut giggled nervously. "The word 'ever' and the word 'frog' have got lines drawn under them."

"And you say the car was vandalized?"

"That's right. Tires slashed, just like Hugh's. And a big long scratch down the passenger side. Ouch!"

"Okay," Alan said, "here's something else for you to do. Go to the barber shop, and then to the billiard parlor if you need to. Find out who it was Henry cut off this week or last."

"But the State Police—"

"*Fuck* the State Police!" Alan said feelingly. "It's *our* town. We know who to ask and where to find them. Do you want to tell me you can't lay hands on someone who'll know this story in just about five minutes?"

"Of course not," Clut said. "I saw Charlie Fortin when I came back from Castle Hill, noodling with a bunch of guys in front of the Western Auto. If Henry was bumping heads with somebody, Charlie will know who. Hell, the Tiger's Charlie's home away from home."

"Yes. But were the State Police questioning him?"

"Well . . . no."

"No. So *you* question him. But I think we both already know the answer, don't we?"

"Hugh Priest," Clut said.

"It has the unmistakable clang of a ringer to me," Alan said. He thought, This is maybe not so different from Henry Payton's first guess after all.

"Okay, Alan. I'll get on it."

"And call me back the minute you know for sure. The *second.*" He gave Clut the number, then made him recite it back so he could be sure Clut had copied it down correctly.

"I will," Clut said, and then burst out furiously, "What's going on, Alan? Goddammit, *what's going on around here?*"

"I don't know." Alan felt very old, very tired . . . and angry. No longer angry at Payton for shunting him off the case, but angry at whoever was responsible for these gruesome fireworks. And he felt more and more sure that, when they got to the bottom of it, they would discover that a single agency had been at work all along. Wilma and Nettie. Henry and Hugh. Lester and John. Someone had wired them together like packets of high explosive. "I don't know, Clut, but we're going to find out."

He hung up and dialled Polly's number again. His urge to make things right with her to understand what had happened to make her so furious with him, was fading. The replacement feeling which had begun to creep over him was even less comforting: a deep, unfocused dread; a growing feeling that she was in danger.

Ring, ring, ring . . . but no answer.

Polly, I love you and we need to talk. Please pick up the phone. Polly, I love you and we need to talk. Please pick up the phone. Polly, I love you—

The litany ran around in his head like a wind-up toy. He wanted to call Clut back and ask him to check on her right away, before he did anything else, but couldn't. That would be very wrong when there might be other packets of explosive still waiting to explode in The Rock.

Yes, but Alan . . . suppose Polly's one of them?

That thought poked some buried association loose, but he was unable to grasp it before it floated away.

Alan slowly hung up the telephone, cutting it off in mid-ring as he settled it into its cradle.

3

Polly could stand it no longer. She rolled on her side, reached for the telephone . . . and it stilled in mid-ring.

Good, she thought. But was it?

She was lying on her bed, listening to the sound of approaching thunder. It was hot upstairs—as hot as the middle of July—but opening the windows was not an option, because she'd had Dave Phillips, one of the local handymen and caretakers, put on her storm windows and doors just the week before. So she had taken off the old jeans and shirt she had worn on her expedition to the country and folded them neatly over the chair by the door. Now she lay on the bed in her underwear, wanting a little nap before she got up and showered, but unable to go to sleep.

Some of it was the sirens, but more of it was Alan; what Alan had done. She could not comprehend this grotesque betrayal of all she had believed and all she had trusted, but neither could she escape it. Her mind would turn to something else (those sirens, for instance, and how they sounded like the end of the world) and then suddenly it would be there again, how he had gone behind her back, how he had *sneaked*. It was like being poked by the splintery end of a board in some tender, secret place.

Oh Alan, how could you? she asked him—and herself—again.

The voice which replied surprised her. It was Aunt Evvie's voice, and beneath the dry lack of sentiment that had always been her way, Polly felt a disquieting, powerful anger.

If you had told him the truth in the first place, girl, he never would have had to.

Polly sat up quickly. That was a disturbing voice, all right, and the most disturbing thing about it was the fact that it was her *own* voice. Aunt Evvie was many years dead. This was her own subconscious, using Aunt Evvie to express its anger the way a shy ventriloquist might use his dummy to ask a pretty girl for a date, and—

Stop it, girl—didn't I once tell you this town is full of ghosts? Maybe it is *me. Maybe it* is.

Polly uttered a whimpering, frightened cry and then pressed her hand against her mouth.

Or maybe it isn't. In the end, who it is don't matter much, does it? The question is this, Trisha: Who sinned first? Who lied first? Who covered up first? Who cast the first stone?

"That's not fair!" Polly shouted into the hot room, and then looked at her own frightened, wide-eyed reflection in the bedroom mirror. She waited for the voice of Aunt Evvie to come back, and when it didn't, she slowly lay back down again.

Perhaps she *had* sinned first, if omitting part of the truth and telling a few white lies was sinning. Perhaps she *had* covered up first. But did that give Alan the right to open an investigation on her, the way a law officer might open an investigation on a known felon? Did it give him the right to put her name on some interstate law-enforcement wire . . . or send out a tracer on her, if that was what they called it . . . or . . . or . . .

Never mind, Polly, a voice—one she knew—whispered. *Stop tearing yourself apart over what was very proper behavior on your part. I mean, after all! You heard the guilt in his* voice, *didn't you?*

"Yes!" she muttered fiercely into the pillow. "That's right, I *did!* What about *that,* Aunt Evvie?" There was no answer . . . only a queer, light tugging

(*the question is this Trisha*)

at her subconscious mind. As if she had forgotten something, left something out

(*would you like a sweet Trisha*)

of the equation.

Polly rolled restlessly onto her side, and the *azka* tumbled across the fullness of one breast. She heard something inside scratch delicately at the silver wall of its prison.

No, Polly thought, it's just something shifting. Something inert. This idea that there really *is* something alive in there . . . it's just your imagination.

Scratch-scritch-scratch.

The silver ball jiggled minutely between the white cotton cup of her bra and the coverlet of the bed.

Scratchy-scritch-scratch.

That thing is alive, Trisha, Aunt Evvie said. *That thing is alive, and you know it.*

Don't be silly, Polly told her, tossing over to the other side. How could there possibly be some creature in there? I suppose it might be able to breathe through all those tiny holes, but what in God's name would it eat?

Maybe, Aunt Evvie replied with soft implacability, *it's eating* YOU, *Trisha.*

"Polly," she murmured. "My name is *Polly.*"

This time the tug at her subconscious mind was stronger—somehow alarming—and for a moment she was almost able to grasp it. Then the telephone began to ring again. She gasped and sat up, her face wearing a look of tired dismay. Pride and longing were at war there.

Talk to him, Trisha—what can it hurt? Better still, listen to him. You didn't do much of that before, did you?

I don't want to talk to him. Not after what he did.

But you still love him.

Yes; that was true. The only thing was, now she hated him as well.

The voice of Aunt Evvie rose once more, gusting angrily in her mind. *Do you want to be a ghost all your life, Trisha? What's the matter with you, girl?*

Polly reached out for the telephone in a mockery of decisiveness. Her hand—her limber, pain-free hand—faltered just short of the handset. Because maybe it *wasn't* Alan. Maybe it was Mr. Gaunt. Maybe Mr. Gaunt wanted to tell her that he wasn't finished with her yet, that she hadn't finished paying yet.

She made another move toward the telephone—this time the tips of her fingers actually brushed the plastic casing—and then she drew back. Her hand clutched its partner and they folded into a nervous ball on her belly. She was afraid of Aunt

Evvie's dead voice, of what she had done this afternoon, of what Mr. Gaunt (or Alan!) might tell the town about her dead son, of what yonder confusion of sirens and racing cars might mean.

But more than all of these things, she had discovered, she was afraid of Leland Gaunt himself. She felt as if someone had tied her to the clapper of a great iron bell, a bell which would simultaneously deafen her, drive her mad, and crush her to a pulp if it began to ring.

The telephone fell quiet.

Outside, another siren began to scream, and as it began to fade toward the Tin Bridge, the thunder rolled again. Closer than ever now.

Take it off, the voice of Aunt Evvie whispered. *Take it off, honey. You can do it—his power is over need, not will. Take it off. Break his hold on you.*

But she was looking at the telephone and remembering the night—was it less than a week ago?—when she had reached for it and struck it with her fingers, knocking it to the floor. She remembered the pain which had clawed its way up her arm like a hungry rat with broken teeth. She couldn't go back to that. She just couldn't.

Could she?

Something nasty is going on in The Rock tonight, Aunt Evvie said. *Do you want to wake up tomorrow and have to figure out how much of it was YOUR nastiness? Is that really a score you want to add up, Trisha?*

"You don't understand," she moaned. "It wasn't on Alan, it was on Ace! Ace Merrill! And he deserves whatever he gets!"

The implacable voice of Aunt Evvie returned: *Then so do you, honey. So do you.*

4

At twenty minutes past six on that Tuesday evening, as the thunderheads neared and real dark began to overtake twilight, the State Police officer who had replaced Sheila Brigham in dispatch came out into the Sheriff's Office bullpen. He skirted the large area, roughly diamond-shaped, which was marked with CRIME-SCENE tape and hurried over to where Henry Payton stood.

Payton looked dishevelled and unhappy. He had spent the previous five minutes with the ladies and gentlemen of the press, and he felt as he always did after one of these confrontations: as if he had been coated with honey and then forced to roll in a large pile of ant-infested hyena-shit. His statement had not been as well prepared—or as unassailably vague—as he would have liked. The TV people had forced his hand. They wanted to do live updates during the six–to–six-thirty time-slot when the local news was broadcast—felt they *had* to do live updates—and if he didn't throw them some kind of bone, they were apt to crucify him at eleven. They had almost crucified him anyway. He had come as close as he ever had in his entire career to admitting he didn't have a fucking clue. He had not left this impromptu press conference; he had escaped it.

Payton found himself wishing he had listened more closely to Alan. When he arrived, it had seemed that the job was essentially damage control. Now he wondered, because there had been *another* murder since he took the case—a woman named Myrtle Keeton. Her husband was still out there someplace, probably headed over the hills and far away by now, but just possibly still galloping gaily around this weird little town. A man who had offed his wife with a hammer. A prime psycho, in other words.

The trouble was, he didn't *know* these people. Alan and his deputies did, but both Alan and Ridgewick were gone. LaPointe was in the hospital, probably hoping the doctors could get his nose on straight again. He looked around for Clutterbuck and was somehow not surprised to see that he had also melted away.

You want it, Henry? he heard Alan say inside his head. *Fine. Take it. And as far as suspects go, why not try the phone book?*

"Lieutenant Payton? Lieutenant Payton!" It was the officer from dispatch.

"What?" Henry growled.

"I've got Dr. Van Allen on the radio. He wants to talk to you."

"About what?"

"He wouldn't say. He only told me he *had* to speak to you."

Henry Payton walked into the dispatcher's office feeling more and more like a kid riding a bike with no brakes down a steep hill with a drop-off on one side, a rock wall on the other, and a pack of hungry wolves with reporters' faces behind him.

He picked up the mike. "This is Payton, come back."

"Lieutenant Payton, this is Dr. Van Allen. County Medical Examiner?" The voice was hollow and distant, broken up occasionally by heavy bursts of static. That would be the approaching storm, Henry knew. More fun with Dick and Jane.

"Yes, I know who you are," Henry said. "You took Mr. Beaufort to Oxford. How is he, come back?"

"He's—"

Crackle crackle buzz snacker.

"You're breaking up, Dr. Van Allen," Henry said, speaking as patiently as he could. "We've got what looks to be a really first-class electrical storm on the way here. Please say again. K."

"Dead!" Van Allen shouted through a break in the static. "He died in the ambulance, but we do not believe it was gunshot trauma which killed him. Do you understand? *We do not believe this patient died of gunshot trauma.* His brain first underwent atypical edema and then ruptured. The most likely diagnosis is that some toxic substance, some *extremely* toxic substance, was introduced into his blood when he was shot. This same substance appears to have literally burst his heart open. Please acknowledge."

Oh Jesus, Henry Payton thought. He pulled down his tie,

unbuttoned his collar, and then pressed the transmit button again.

"I acknowledge your message, Dr. Van Allen, but I'll be damned if I understand it. K."

"The toxin was very likely on the bullets in the gun that shot him. The infection appears to spread slowly at first, then to pick up speed. We have two clear, fan-shaped areas of introduction here—the cheek-wound and the chest-wound. It's very important to—"

Crackle snackle buzzzit.

"—has it? Ten-four?"

"Say again, Dr. Van Allen." Henry wished to Christ the man had simply picked up the telephone. "Please say again, come back."

"*Who has that gun?*" Van Allen shrieked. "*Ten-four!*"

"David Friedman. Ballistics. He's taken it to Augusta. K."

"Would he have unloaded it first—ten-four?"

"Yes. That's standard practice. Come back."

"Was it a revolver or an automatic, Lieutenant Payton? That's of prime importance right now. Ten-four."

"An automatic. K."

"Would he have unloaded the clip? Ten-four."

"He'd do that at Augusta." Payton sat down heavily in the dispatcher's chair. Suddenly he needed to take a heavy dump. "Ten-four."

"No! No, he mustn't! *He must not do that*—do you copy?"

"I copy," Henry said. "I'll leave a message for him at the Ballistics Lab, saying he's to leave the goddam bullets in the goddam clip until we get this latest goddam snafu sorted the goddam hell out." He felt a childish pleasure at the realization that this was going out on the air . . . and then he wondered how many of the reporters out front were monitoring him on their Bearcats. "Listen, Dr. Van Allen, we've got no business talking about this on the radio. Ten-four."

"Never mind the public-relations aspect," Van Allen came

back harshly. "We're talking about a man's *life* here, Lieutenant Payton—I tried to get you on the telephone and couldn't get through. Tell your man Friedman to examine his hands carefully for scratches, small nicks, even hangnails. If he has the smallest break in the skin of his hands, he's to go to the nearest hospital *immediately*. I have no way of knowing if the crap we're dealing with was on the casing of the ammunition clip as well as on the bullets themselves. And it isn't the kind of thing he wants to take the slightest chance with. This stuff is *deadly*. Ten-four?"

"I acknowledge," Henry heard himself say. He found himself wishing he were anywhere but here—but since he *was* here, he wished that Alan Pangborn were here beside him. Since arriving in Castle Rock, he had come more and more to feel like Brer Rabbit stuck in the Tar Baby. "What *is* it? K?"

"We don't know yet. Not curare, because there was no paralysis until the very end. Also, curare is relatively painless, and Mr. Beaufort suffered a great deal. All we know right now is that it started slowly and then moved like a freight-train. Ten-four."

"That's *all?* Ten-four."

"Jesus Christ," Ray Van Allen ejaculated. "Isn't it enough? Ten-four."

"Yes. I guess it is. K."

"Just be glad—"

Crackle crackle brrack!

"Say again, Dr. Van Allen. Say again. Ten-four."

Through the swelling ocean of static he heard Dr. Van Allen say, "Just be glad you've got the gun in custody. That you don't have to worry about it doing any more damage. Ten-four."

"You got *that* right, buddy. Ten-forty, out."

5

Cora Rusk turned onto Main Street and walked slowly toward Needful Things. She passed a bright yellow Ford Econoline van with WPTD CHANNEL 5 ACTION NEWS emblazoned on the side, but did not see Danforth "Buster" Keeton looking out of the driver's window at her with unblinking eyes. She probably wouldn't have recognized him in any case; Buster had become, in a manner of speaking, a new man. And even if she had seen and recognized him, it would have meant nothing to Cora. She had her own problems and sorrows. Most of all, she had her own anger. And none of this concerned her dead son.

In one hand, Cora Rusk held a pair of broken sunglasses.

It had seemed to her that the police were going to question her forever . . . or at least until she went mad. *Go away!* she wanted to scream at them. *Stop asking me all these stupid questions about Brian! Arrest him if he's in trouble, his father will fix it, fixing things is all he's good for, but leave me alone! I've got a date with The King, and I can't keep him waiting!*

At one point she had seen Sheriff Pangborn leaning in the doorway between the kitchen and the back stoop, his arms folded across his chest, and she had been on the very verge of blurting this out, thinking *he* would understand. He wasn't like these others—he was from town, he would know about Needful Things, he would have bought his own special item there, he would understand.

Except Mr. Gaunt had spoken up in her mind just then, as calm and as reasonable as ever. *No, Cora—don't talk to him. He wouldn't understand. He's not like you. He's not a smart shopper. Tell them you want to go to the hospital and see your other boy. That will get rid of them, at least for a while. After that it won't matter.*

So she had told them just that, and it worked like a charm. She had even managed to squeeze out a tear or two, thinking not about Brian but about how sad Elvis must feel, wandering around Graceland without her. Poor lost King!

They had left, all but the two or three who were out in the garage. Cora didn't know what they were doing or what they could possibly want out there, and she didn't care. She grabbed her magic sunglasses off the table and hurried upstairs. Once she was in her room she slipped out of her robe, lay down on her bed, and put them on.

At once she was in Graceland again. Relief, anticipation, and amazing horniness filled her.

She swept up the curving staircase, cool and nude, to the upstairs hall, hung with jungle tapestries and nearly as wide as a freeway. She walked down to the closed double doors at the far end, her bare feet whispering in the deep nap of the carpet. She saw her fingers reach out and close around the handles. She pushed the doors open, revealing The King's bedroom, a room which was all black and white—black walls, white shag rug, black drapes over the windows, white trim on the black bedspread—except for the ceiling, which was painted midnight blue with a thousand twinkly electric stars.

Then she looked at the bed and that was when the horror struck.

The King was on the bed, but The King was not alone.

Sitting on top of him, riding him like a pony, was Myra Evans. She had turned her head and stared at Cora when the doors opened. The King only kept looking up at Myra, blinking those sleepy, beautiful blue eyes of his.

"Myra!" Cora had exclaimed. "What are you doing here?"

"Well," Myra said smugly, "I'm sure not vacuuming the floor."

Cora gasped for breath, utterly stunned. "Well . . . well . . . *well I'll be butched!*" she cried, her voice rising as her wind returned.

"Then go *be* butched," Myra said, pumping her hips faster, "and take those silly sunglasses off while you're at it. They look stupid. Get out of here. Go back to Castle Rock. We're busy . . . aren't we, E?"

"That's raht, sweet thang," The King said. "Just as busy as two twiddlybugs in a carpet."

Horror turned to fury, and Cora's paralysis broke with a snap. She rushed at her so-called friend, meaning to rip her deceitful eyes from their sockets. But when she raised one clawed hand to do so, Myra reached out—never missing a stroke with her pumping hips as she did—and tore the sunglasses from Cora's face with her own hand.

Cora had squeezed her eyes shut in surprise . . . and when she opened them, she had been lying in her own bed again. The sunglasses were on the floor, both lenses shattered.

"No," Cora moaned, lurching out of bed. She wanted to shriek, but some inner voice—not her own—warned her that the police in the garage would hear if she did, and come running. "No, please no, please, *pleeeease*—"

She tried to fit chunks of the broken lenses back into the streamlined gold frames, but it had been impossible. They were broken. Broken by that evil whoring slut. Broken by her *friend,* Myra Evans. Her *friend* who had somehow found her own way to Graceland, her *friend* who was even now, as Cora tried to put together a priceless artifact that was irretrievably broken, making love to The King.

Cora looked up. Her eyes had become glittering black slits. "I'll butch *her,*" she had whispered hoarsely. "See if I don't."

6

She read the sign in the window of Needful Things, paused for a moment, thinking, and then walked around to the service alley. She brushed by Francine Pelletier, who was on her way out of the alley, putting something into her purse. Cora hardly even looked at her.

Halfway down the alley she saw Mr. Gaunt standing behind a wooden table which lay across the open back door of his shop like a barricade.

"Ah, Cora!" he exclaimed. "I was wondering when you'd drop by."

"That *bitch!*" Cora spat. "That double-crossing little slut-*bitch!*"

"Pardon me, Cora," Mr. Gaunt said with urbane politeness, "but you seem to have missed a button or two." He pointed one of his odd, long fingers at the front of her dress.

Cora had slipped the first thing she'd found in the closet on over her nakedness, and had managed to do only the top button. Below that one, the dress gaped open to the curls of her pubic hair. Her belly, swelled by a great many Ring-Dings, Yodels, and chocolate-covered cherries during *Santa Barbara* (and all her other shows), curved smoothly out.

"Who gives a shit?" Cora snapped.

"Not I," Mr. Gaunt agreed serenely. "How may I help you?"

"That bitch is fucking The King. She broke my sunglasses. I want to kill her."

"*Do* you," Mr. Gaunt said, raising his eyebrows. "Well, I can't say that I don't sympathize, Cora, because I do. It may be that a woman who would steal another woman's man deserves to live. I wouldn't care to say on that subject one way or the other—I've been a businessman all my life, and know very little about matters of the heart. But a woman who deliberately breaks another woman's most treasured possession . . . well, that is a much more serious thing. Do you agree?"

She began to smile. It was a hard smile. It was a merciless smile. It was a smile utterly devoid of sanity. "Too fucking right," said Cora Rusk.

Mr. Gaunt turned around for a moment. When he faced Cora again, he was holding an automatic pistol in one hand.

"Might you be looking for something like this?" he asked.

CHAPTER TWENTY

1

After Buster finished with Myrtle, he fell into a deep fugue state. All sense of purpose seemed to desert him. He thought of Them—the whole town was crawling with Them—but instead of the clear, righteous anger the idea had brought only minutes before, he now felt only weariness and depression. He had a pounding headache. His arm and back ached from wielding the hammer.

He looked down and saw that he was still holding it. He opened his hand and it fell to the kitchen linoleum, making a bloody splatter there. He stood looking at this splatter for almost a full minute with a kind of idiot attention. It looked to him like a sketch of his father's face drawn in blood.

He plodded through the living room and into his study, rubbing his shoulder and upper arm as he went. The handcuff chain jingled maddeningly. He opened the closet door, dropped to his knees, crawled beneath the clothes which hung at the front, and dug out the box with the pacers on the front. He backed clumsily out of the closet again (the handcuff caught in one of Myrtle's shoes and he threw it to the back of the closet with a sulky curse), took the box over to his desk, and sat down with it in front of him. Instead of excitement, he felt only sadness. Winning Ticket was wonderful, all right, but what good could it possibly do him now? It didn't matter if he put the money back or not. He had murdered his wife. She had undoubtedly deserved it, but *They* wouldn't see it that way. They would happily throw him in the deepest, darkest Shawshank Penitentiary cell they could find and throw away the key.

He saw that he had left large bloody smears on the box-top, and he looked down at himself. For the first time he noticed that he was covered with blood. His meaty forearms looked as though they belonged to a Chicago hog-butcher. Depression folded over him again in a soft, black wave. They had beaten him . . . okay. Yet he would escape Them. He would escape Them just the same.

He got up, weary to his very center, and plodded slowly upstairs. He undressed as he went, kicking off his shoes in the living room, dropping his pants at the foot of the stairs, then sitting down halfway up to peel off his socks. Even they were bloody. The shirt gave him the hardest time; pulling off a shirt while you were wearing a handcuff was the devil's own job.

Almost twenty minutes passed between the murder of Mrs. Keeton and Buster's trudge to and through the shower. He might have been taken into custody without a problem at almost any time during that period . . . but on Lower Main Street a transition of authority was going on, the Sheriff's Office was in almost total disarray, and the whereabouts of Danforth "Buster" Keeton simply did not seem very important.

Once he had towelled dry, he put on a clean pair of pants and a tee-shirt—he didn't have the energy to tussle again with long sleeves—and went back down to his study. Buster sat in his chair and looked at Winning Ticket again, hoping that his depression might prove to be just an ephemeral thing, that some of his earlier joy might return. But the picture on the box seemed to have faded, dulled. The brightest color in evidence was a smear of Myrtle's blood across the flanks of the two-horse.

He took the top off and looked inside. He was shocked to see that the little tin horses were leaning sadly every which-way. Their colors had also faded. A broken bit of spring poked through the hole where you inserted the key to wind the machinery.

Someone's been in here! his mind cried. Someone's been at it! One of Them! Ruining *me* wasn't enough! They had to ruin my game, too!

But a deeper voice, perhaps the fading voice of sanity, whispered that this was not true. *This is how it was from the very start,* the voice whispered. *You just didn't see it.*

He went back to the closet, meaning to take down the gun after all. It was time to use it. He was feeling around for it when the telephone rang. Buster picked it up very slowly, knowing who was on the other end.

Nor was he disappointed.

2

"Hello, Dan," said Mr. Gaunt. "How are you this fine evening?"

"Terrible," Buster said in a glum, draggy voice. "The world has turned to boogers. I'm going to kill myself."

"Oh?" Mr. Gaunt sounded a trifle disappointed, nothing more.

"Nothing's any good. Even the game you sold me is no good."

"Oh, I doubt that very much," Mr. Gaunt replied with a touch of asperity. "I check all my merchandise very carefully, Mr. Keeton. Very carefully indeed. Why don't you look again?"

Buster did, and what he saw astounded him. The horses stood up straight in their slots. Each coat looked freshly painted and glistening. Even their eyes seemed to spark fire. The tin race-course was all bright greens and dusty summer browns. *The track looks fast,* he thought dreamily, and his eyes shifted to the box-top.

Either his eyes, dulled by his deep depression, had tricked him or the colors there had deepened in some amazing way in the few seconds since the telephone had rung. Now it was Myrtle's blood he could barely see. It was drying to a drab maroon.

"My God!" he whispered.

"Well?" Mr. Gaunt asked. "Well, Dan? Am I wrong? Because if I am, you must defer your suicide at least long enough to return your purchase to me for a full refund. I stand behind my merchandise. I have to, you know. I have my reputation to protect, and that's a proposition I take very seriously in a world where there's billions of Them and only one of me."

"No . . . no!" Buster said. "It's . . . it's *beautiful!*"

"Then you were in error?" Mr. Gaunt persisted.

"I . . . I guess I must have been."

"You *admit* you were in error?"

"I . . . yes."

"Good," Mr. Gaunt said. His voice lost its edge. "Then by all means, go ahead and kill yourself. Although I must admit I am disappointed. I thought I had finally met a man who had guts enough to help me kick Their asses. I guess you're just a talker, like all the rest." Mr. Gaunt sighed. It was the sigh of a man who realizes he has not glimpsed light at the end of the tunnel after all.

A strange thing was happening to Buster Keeton. He felt his vitality and purpose surging back. His own interior colors seemed to be brightening, intensifying again.

"You mean it's not too late?"

"You must have skipped Poetry 101. 'Tis never too late to seek a newer world. Not if you're a man with some spine. Why, I had everything all set up for you, Mr. Keeton. I was counting on you, you see."

"I like plain old Dan a lot better," Buster said, almost shyly.

"All right. Dan. Are you really set on making such a cowardly exit from life?"

"No!" Buster cried. "It's just . . . I thought, what's the use? There's too many of Them."

"Three good men can do a lot of damage, Dan."

"Three? Did you say *three?*"

"Yes . . . there's another of us. Someone else who sees the danger, who understands what They are up to."

"Who?" Buster asked eagerly. "Who?"

"In time," Mr. Gaunt said, "but for now, time is in short supply. They'll be coming for you."

Buster looked out the study window with the narrowed eyes of a ferret which smells danger on the wind. The street was empty, but only for the time being. He could feel Them, sense Them massing against him.

"What should I do?"

"Then you're on my team?" Mr. Gaunt asked. "I *can* count on you after all?"

"Yes!"

"All the way?"

" 'Til hell freezes over or you say different!"

"Very good," Mr. Gaunt said. "Listen carefully, Dan." And as Mr. Gaunt talked and Buster listened, gradually sinking into that hypnotic state which Mr. Gaunt seemed to induce at will, the first rumbles of the approaching storm had begun to shake the air outside.

3

Five minutes later, Buster left his house. He had put a light jacket on over his tee-shirt and stuffed the hand with the cuff still on it deep into one of his pockets. Halfway down the block he found a van parked against the curb just where Mr. Gaunt had told him he would find it. It was bright yellow, a guarantee most passersby would look at the paint instead of the driver. It was almost windowless, and both sides were marked with the logo of a Portland TV station.

Buster took a quick but careful look in both directions, then got in. Mr. Gaunt had told him the keys would be under the seat. They were. Sitting on the passenger seat was a paper shopping bag. In it Buster found a blonde wig, a pair of yuppie wire-rimmed glasses, and a small glass bottle.

He put the wig on with some misgivings—long and shaggy, it looked like the scalp of a dead rock singer—but when he looked at himself in the van's rearview mirror, he was astounded by how well it fit. It made him look younger. *Much* younger. The lenses of the yuppie spectacles were clear glass, and they changed his appearance (at least in Buster's opinion) even more than the wig. They made him look smart, like Harrison Ford in *The Mosquito Coast.* He stared at himself in fascination. All at once he looked thirty something instead of fifty-two, like a man who might very well work for a TV station. Not as a news correspondent, nothing glamorous like that, but perhaps as a cameraman or even a producer.

He unscrewed the top of the bottle and grimaced—the stuff inside smelled like a melting tractor battery. Tendrils of smoke rose from the mouth of the bottle. *Got to be careful with this stuff,* Buster thought. *Got to be real careful.*

He put the empty cuff under his right thigh and pulled the chain taut. Then he poured some of the bottle's contents on the chain just below the cuff on his wrist, being careful not to drip any of the dark, viscous liquid on his skin. The steel immediately began to smoke and bubble. A few drops struck the rubber floormat and it also began to bubble. Smoke and a horrid frying smell rose from it. After a few moments Buster pulled the empty cuff out from under his thigh, hooked his fingers through it, and yanked briskly. The chain parted like paper and he threw it on the floor. He was still wearing a bracelet, but he could live with that; the chain and the swinging empty cuff had been the real pain in the keister. He slotted the key in the ignition, started the engine, and drove away.

Not three minutes later, a Castle County Sheriff's car driven by Seaton Thomas turned into the driveway of the Keeton home, and old Seat discovered Myrtle Keeton sprawled half in and half out of the doorway between the garage and the kitchen. Not long after, his car was joined by four State Police units. The cops tossed the house from top to bottom, looking for either Buster or some sign of where he might have gone. No one gave the game sitting on his study desk a second glance. It was old, dirty, and obviously broken. It looked like something that might have come out of a poor relation's attic.

4

Eddie Warburton, the janitor at the Municipal Building, had been pissed off at Sonny Jackett for more than two years. Over the last couple of days, this anger had built into a red rage.

When the transmission of Eddie's neat little Honda Civic had seized up during the summer of 1989, Eddie hadn't wanted to take it to the nearest Honda dealership. That would have involved a large towing fee. Bad enough that the tranny hadn't expired until three weeks after the drive-train warranty had done the same thing. So he had gone to Sonny Jackett first, had asked Sonny if he had any experience working on foreign cars.

Sonny told him he did. He spoke in that expansive, patronizing way most back-country Yankees had of talking to Eddie. *We're not prejudiced, boy,* that tone said. *This is the north, you know. We don't hold with all that southern crap. Of COURSE you're a nigger, anyone can see that, but it don't mean a thing to us. Black, yellow, white, or green, we rook em all like you've never seen. Bring it on in here.*

Sonny had fixed the Honda's transmission, but the bill had been a hundred dollars more than Sonny had said it would be, and they'd almost gotten into a fist-fight over it one night at the Tiger. Then Sonny's *lawyer* (Yankees or crackers, it was Eddie Warburton's experience that all white men had *lawyers*) called Eddie and told him Sonny was going to take him to small claims court. Eddie ended up fifty dollars out of pocket as a result of that little experience and the fire in the Honda's electrical system happened five months later. The car had been parked in the Municipal Building's lot. Someone had yelled to Eddie, but by the time he got outside with a fire extinguisher, the interior of his car was a dancing mass of yellow fire. It had been a total loss.

He'd wondered ever since if Sonny Jackett had set that fire. The insurance investigator said it was a *bona fide* accident which had been caused by a short-circuit . . . a one-in-a-million type of thing. But what did that fellow know? Probably nothing, and besides, it wasn't *his* money. Not that the insurance had been enough to cover Eddie's investment.

And now he knew. He knew for sure.

Earlier today he had gotten a little package in the mail. The items inside had been extremely enlightening: a number of blackened alligator clips, an old, lop-eared photograph, and a note.

The clips were of the sort a man could use to start an electrical fire. One simply stripped the insulation from the right pairs of wires in the right places, clipped the wires together, and *voilà*.

The snapshot showed Sonny and a number of his whitebread friends, the fellows who were always lounging on kitchen chairs in the gas station office when you went down there. The location was not Sonny's Sunoco, however; it was Robicheau's Junkyard out on Town Road #5. The hankies were standing in front of Eddie's burned-out Civic, drinking beer, laughing . . . and eating chunks of watermelon.

The note was short and to the point. *Dear Nigger: Fucking with me was a bad mistake.*

At first Eddie wondered why Sonny would send him such a note (although he did not relate it to the letter he himself had slipped through Polly Chalmers's mail-slot at Mr. Gaunt's behest). He decided it was because Sonny was even dumber and meaner than most honkies. Still—if the business was still rankling in Sonny's guts, why had he waited so long to reopen it? But the more he brooded over those old times

(*Dear Nigger:*)

the less the questions seemed to matter. The note and the blackened alligator clips and that old photograph got into his head, buzzing there like a cloud of hungry mosquitoes.

Earlier tonight he had bought a gun from Mr. Gaunt.

The fluorescents in the Sunoco station's office threw a white trapezoid on the macadam of the service tarmac as Eddie pulled in—driving the second-hand Olds which had replaced the Civic. He got out, one hand in his jacket pocket, holding the gun.

He paused outside the door for a minute, looking in. Sonny was sitting beside his cash register in a plastic chair which was rocked back on its rear legs. Eddie could just see the top of Sonny's cap over his open newspaper. Reading the paper. Of course. White men always had *lawyers,* and after a day of shafting black fellows like Eddie, they always sat in their offices, rocked back in their chairs and reading the paper.

Fucking white men, with their fucking *lawyers* and their fucking *newspapers.*

Eddie drew the automatic pistol and went inside. A part of him which had been asleep suddenly woke up and screamed in alarm that he shouldn't do this, it was a mistake. But the voice didn't matter. It didn't matter because suddenly Eddie didn't seem to be inside himself at all. He seemed to be a spirit hovering over his own shoulder, watching all this happen. An evil imp had taken over his controls.

"I got something for you, you cheating sumbitch," Eddie heard his mouth say, and watched his finger pull the trigger of the automatic twice. Two small black circles appeared in a headline which said MCKERNAN APPROVAL RATING SOARS. Sonny Jackett screamed and jerked. The rear legs of the tipped-back chair skidded and Sonny went tumbling to the floor with blood soaking into his coverall . . . except the name stitched on the coverall in gold thread was RICKY. It wasn't Sonny at all but Ricky Bissonette.

"Ah, shit!" Eddie screamed. "I shot the wrong fuckin honky!"

"Hello, Eddie," Sonny Jackett remarked from behind him. "Good thing for me I was in the shithouse, wasn't it?"

Eddie began to turn. Three bullets from the automatic pistol Sonny had bought from Mr. Gaunt late that afternoon entered his lower back, pulverizing his spine, before he could get even halfway around.

He watched, eyes wide and helpless, as Sonny bent down toward him. The muzzle of the gun Sonny held was as big as the mouth of a tunnel and as dark as forever. Above it, Sonny's face was pale and set. A streak of grease ran down one cheek.

"Planning to steal my new socket-wrench set wasn't your mistake," Sonny said as he pressed the barrel of the automatic against the center of Eddie Warburton's forehead. "Writing and *telling* me you were gonna do it . . . *that* was your mistake."

A great white light—the light of understanding—suddenly went on in Eddie's mind. *Now* he remembered the letter he had pushed through the Chalmers woman's mail-slot, and he found himself able to put that piece of mischief together with the note he had received and the one Sonny was talking about.

"Listen!" he whispered. "You have to listen to me, Jackett— we been played for suckers, both of us. We—"

"Goodbye, black boy," Sonny said, and pulled the trigger.

Sonny looked fixedly at what remained of Eddie Warburton for almost a full minute, wondering if he should have listened to what Eddie had to say. He decided the answer was no. What could a fellow dumb enough to send a note like that have to say that could possibly matter?

Sonny got up, walked into the office, and stepped over Ricky Bissonette's legs. He opened the safe and took out the adjustable socket-wrenches Mr. Gaunt had sold him. He was still looking at them, picking each one up, handling it lovingly, then putting it back in the custom case again, when the State Police arrived to take him into custody.

5

Park at the corner of Birch and Main, Mr. Gaunt had told Buster on the telephone, *and just wait. I will send someone to you.*

Buster had followed these instructions to the letter. He had seen a great many comings and goings at the mouth of the service alley from his vantage point one block up—almost all his friends and neighbors, it seemed to him, had a little business to do with Mr. Gaunt this evening. Ten minutes ago the Rusk woman had walked down there with her dress unbuttoned, looking like something out of a bad dream.

Then, not five minutes after she came back out of the alley, putting something into her dress pocket (the dress was still unbuttoned and you could see a lot, but who in his right mind, Buster wondered, would want to look), there had been several gunshots from farther up Main Street. Buster couldn't be sure, but he thought they came from the Sunoco station.

State Police cruisers came winding up Main from the Municipal Building, their blue lights flashing, scattering reporters like pigeons. Disguise or no disguise, Buster decided it would be prudent to climb into the back of the van for a little while.

The State Police cars roared by, and their whirling blue lights picked out something which leaned against the van's rear doors—a green canvas duffle bag. Curious, Buster undid the knot in the drawstring, pulled the mouth of the bag open, and looked inside.

There was a box on top of the bag's contents. Buster took it out and saw the rest of the duffle was full of timers. Hotpoint clock-timers. There were easily two dozen of them. Their smooth white faces stared up at him like pupilless Orphan Annie eyes. He opened the box he had removed and saw it was full of alligator clips—the kind electricians sometimes used to make quick connections.

Buster frowned . . . and then, suddenly, his mind's eye saw an office form—a Castle Rock fund-release form, to be exact. Typed neatly in the space provided for *Goods and/or Services to Be Supplied* were these words: 16 CASES OF DYNAMITE.

Sitting in the back of the van, Buster began to grin. Then he began to laugh. Outside, thunder boomed and rolled. A tongue of lightning licked out of the dragging belly of a cloud and jabbed down into Castle Stream.

Buster went on laughing. He laughed until the van shook with it.

"Them!" he cried, laughing. "Oh, boy, have we got something for Them! Have we *ever!*"

6

Henry Payton, who had come to Castle Rock to pull Sheriff Pangborn's smoking irons out of the fire, stood in the doorway of the Sunoco station's office with his mouth open. They had two more men down. One was white and one was black, but both were dead.

A third man, the station owner according to the name on his coverall, sat on the floor by the open safe with a dirty steel case cradled in his arms as if it were a baby. Beside him on the floor was an automatic pistol. Looking at it, Henry felt an elevator go down in his guts. It was the twin of the one Hugh Priest had used to shoot Henry Beaufort.

"Look," one of the officers behind Henry said in a quiet, awed voice. "There's another one."

Henry turned his head to look, and heard the tendons in his neck creak. Another gun—a third automatic pistol—lay near the outstretched hand of the black guy.

"Don't touch em," he said to the other officers. "Don't even get near em." He stepped over the pool of blood, seized Sonny Jackett by the lapels of his coverall, and pulled him to his feet. Sonny did not resist, but he clutched the steel case tighter against his breast.

"What went on here?" Henry yelled into his face. "What in God's name went on?"

Sonny gestured toward Eddie Warburton, using his elbow so he would not have to let go of the case. "He came in. He had a gun. He was crazy. You can see he was crazy; look what he did to Ricky. He thought Ricky was me. He wanted to steal my adjustables. Look."

Sonny smiled and tilted the steel case so Henry could look at the jumble of rusty ironmongery inside.

"I couldn't let him do that, could I? I mean . . . these are *mine*. I paid for them, and they're *mine*."

Henry opened his mouth to say something. He had no idea what it would have been, and it never got out. Before he could say the first word, there were more gunshots, this time from up on Castle View.

7

Lenore Potter stood over the body of Stephanie Bonsaint with a smoking automatic pistol in her hand. The body lay in the flowerbed behind the house, the only one the evil, vindictive bitch hadn't torn up on her previous two trips.

"You shouldn't have come back," Lenore said. She had never fired a gun in her life before and now she had killed a woman . . . but the only feeling she had was one of grim exultation. The woman had been on her property, tearing up her garden (Lenore had waited until the bitch actually got going—*her* mamma hadn't raised any fools), and she had been within her rights. *Perfectly* within her rights.

"Lenore?" her husband called. He was leaning out of the upstairs bathroom window with shaving cream on his face. His voice was alarmed. "Lenore, what's going on?"

"I've shot a trespasser," Lenore said calmly, without looking around. She placed her foot under the heavy weight of the body and lifted. Feeling her toe sink into the Bonsaint bitch's unresisting side gave her a sudden mean pleasure. "It's Stephanie Bon—"

The body rolled over. It was not Stephanie Bonsaint. It was that nice Deputy Sheriff's wife.

She had shot Melissa Clutterbuck.

Quite suddenly, Lenore Potter's *calava* went past blue, past purple, past magenta. It went all the way to midnight black.

8

Alan Pangborn sat looking down at his hands, looking past them into a darkness so black it could only be felt. It had occurred to him that he might have lost Polly this afternoon, not for just a little while—until this current misunderstanding was ironed out—but forever. And that was going to leave him with about thirty-five years to kill.

He heard a small scuffing sound and looked up quickly. It was Miss Hendrie. She looked nervous, but she also looked as if she had come to a decision.

"The Rusk boy is stirring," she said. "He's not awake—they gave him a tranquilizer and he won't be *really* awake for some time yet—but he *is* stirring."

"Is he?" Alan asked quietly, and waited.

Miss Hendrie bit at her lip and then pressed on. "Yes. I'd let you see him if I could, Sheriff Pangborn, but I really can't. You understand, don't you? I mean, I know you have problems in your home town, but this little boy is only seven."

"Yes."

"I'm going down to the caff for a cup of tea. Mrs. Evans is late—she always is—but she'll be here in a minute or two. If you went down to Sean Rusk's room—Room Nine—right after I leave, she probably wouldn't know you were here at all. Do you see?"

"Yes," Alan said gratefully.

"Rounds aren't until eight, so if you *were* in his room, she probably wouldn't notice you. Of course if she did, you would tell her that I followed hospital directives and refused you admission. That you snuck in while the desk was temporarily unattended. Wouldn't you?"

"Yes," Alan said. "You bet I would."

"You could leave by the stairs at the far end of the corridor. If you went into Sean Rusk's room, that is. Which, of course, I told you not to do."

Alan stood up and impulsively kissed her cheek.

Miss Hendrie blushed.

"Thanks," Alan said.

"For what? I haven't done a thing. I believe I'll go get my tea now. Please sit right where you are until I'm gone, Sheriff."

Alan obediently sat down again. He sat there, his head positioned between Simple Simon and the pie-man until the double doors had whooshed most of the way shut behind Miss Hendrie. Then he got up and walked quietly down the brightly painted corridor, with its litter of toys and jigsaw puzzles, to Room 9.

9

Sean Rusk looked totally awake to Alan.

This was the pediatric wing and the bed he was in was a small one, but he still seemed lost in it. His body created only a small hump beneath the counterpane, making him seem like a disembodied head resting on a crisp white pillow. His face was very pale. There were purple shadows, almost as dark as bruises, beneath his eyes, which looked at Alan with a calm lack of surprise. A curl of dark hair lay across the center of his forehead like a comma.

Alan took the chair by the window and pulled it to the side of the bed, where bars had been raised to keep Sean from falling out. Sean did not turn his head, but his eyes moved to follow him.

"Hello, Sean," Alan said quietly. "How are you feeling?"

"My throat is dry," Sean said in a husky whisper.

There was a pitcher of water and two glasses on the table by the bed. Alan poured a glass of water and bent with it over the hospital bars.

Sean tried to sit up and couldn't do it. He fell back against the pillow with a small sigh that hurt Alan's heart. His mind turned to his own son—poor, doomed Todd. As he slipped a hand beneath Sean Rusk's neck to help him sit up, he had a moment of hellish total recall. He saw Todd standing by the Scout that day, answering Alan's goodbye wave with one of his own, and in the eye of memory a kind of nacreous, failing light seemed to play around Todd's head, illuminating every loved line and feature.

His hand shook. A little water spilled down the front of the hospital johnny Sean wore.

"Sorry."

"S'okay," Sean replied in his husky whisper, and drank thirstily. He almost emptied the glass. Then he burped.

Alan lowered him carefully back down. Sean seemed a little more alert now, but there was still no luster in his eyes. Alan thought he had never seen a little boy who looked so dreadfully alone, and his mind tried once again to call up that final image of Todd.

He pushed it away. There was work to do here. It was distasteful work, and damned ticklish in the bargain, but he felt more and more that it was also desperately important work. Regardless of what might be going on in Castle Rock right now, he felt increasingly sure that at least some of the answers lay here, behind that pale forehead and those sad, lusterless eyes.

He looked around the room and forced a smile. "Boring room," he said.

"Yeah," Sean said in his low, husky voice. "Totally dopey."

"Maybe a few flowers would liven it up," Alan said, and passed his right hand in front of his left forearm, deftly plucking the folding bouquet from its palming well beneath his watchband.

He knew he was pressing his luck but had decided, on the spur of the moment, to go for it anyway. He was almost sorry. Two of the tissue-paper blooms tore as he slipped the loop and popped the bouquet open. He heard the spring give a tired twang. It was undoubtedly the final performance of this version of the Folding Flower Trick, but Alan *did* get away with it . . . just. And Sean, unlike his brother, was clearly amused and delighted in spite of his state of mind and the drugs perking through his system.

"*Awesome!* How'd you do that?"

"Just a little magic . . . Want them?" He moved to put the spray of tissue-paper flowers in the water pitcher.

"Naw. They're just paper. Also, they're ripped in a few places." Sean thought about this, apparently decided it sounded ungrateful, and added: "Neat trick, though. Can you make them disappear?"

I doubt it, son, Alan thought. Aloud he said, "I'll try."

He held the bouquet up so Sean could see it clearly, then curved his right hand slightly and drew it downward. He made this pass much more slowly than usual in deference to the sad state of the MacGuffin, and found himself surprised and impressed with the result. Instead of snapping out of sight as they usually did, the Folding Flowers seemed to disappear into his loosely curled fist like smoke. He felt the loosened, overstressed spring try to buckle and jam, but in the end it decided to cooperate one last time.

"That's really radical," Sean said respectfully, and Alan privately agreed. It was a wonderful variation on a trick he'd wowed schoolkids with for years, but he doubted that it could be done with a new version of the Folding Flower Trick. A brand-new spring would make that slow, dreamy pass impossible.

"Thanks," he said, and stowed the folding bouquet under his watchband for the last time. "If you don't want flowers, how about a quarter for the Coke machine?"

Alan leaned forward and casually plucked a quarter from Sean's nose. The boy grinned.

"Whoops, I forgot—it takes seventy-five cents these days, doesn't it? Inflation. Well, no problem." He pulled a coin from Sean's mouth and discovered a third one in his own ear. By then Sean's smile had faded a little and Alan knew that he had better get down to business quickly. He stacked the three quarters on the low dresser beside the bed. "For when you feel better," he said.

"Thanks, mister."

"You're welcome, Sean."

"Where's my daddy?" Sean asked. His voice was marginally stronger now.

The question struck Alan as odd. He would have expected Sean to ask first for his mother. The boy was, after all, only seven.

"He'll be here soon, Sean."

"I hope so. I want him."

"I know you do." Alan paused and said, "Your mommy will be here soon, too."

Sean thought about this, then shook his head slowly and deliberately. The pillowcase made little rustling noises as he did it. "No she won't. She's too busy."

"Too busy to come and see you?" Alan asked.

"Yes. She's very busy. Mommy's visiting with The King. That's why I can't go in her room anymore. She shuts the door and puts on her sunglasses and visits with The King."

Alan saw Mrs. Rusk responding to the State Police who were questioning her. Her voice slow and disconnected. A pair of sunglasses on the table beside her. She couldn't seem to leave them alone; one hand toyed with them almost constantly. She would draw it back, as if afraid someone would notice, and then, after only a few seconds, her hand would return to them again, seemingly on its own. At the time he had thought she was either suffering from shock or under the influence of a tranquilizer. Now he wondered. He also wondered if he should ask Sean about Brian or pursue this new avenue. Or were they both the same avenue?

"You're not really a magician," Sean said. "You're a policeman, aren't you?"

"Uh-huh."

"Are you a State Policeman with a blue car that goes really fast?"

"No—I'm County Sheriff. Usually I have a brown car with a star on the side, and it does go pretty fast, but tonight I'm driving my old station wagon that I keep forgetting to trade in." Alan grinned. "It goes really slow."

This sparked some interest. "Why aren't you driving your brown policeman car?"

So I wouldn't spook Jill Mislaburski or your brother, Alan thought. I don't know about Jill, but I guess it didn't work so well with Brian.

"I really don't remember," he said. "It's been a long day."

"Are you a Sheriff like in *Young Guns?*"

"Uh-huh. I guess so. Sort of like that."

"Me and Brian rented that movie and watched it. It was most totally awesome. We wanted to go see *Young Guns II* when it was at The Magic Lantern in Bridgton last summer but my mom wouldn't let us because it was an R-picture. We ain't allowed to see R-pictures, except sometimes our dad lets us watch them at home on the VCR. Me and Brian really liked *Young Guns.*" Sean paused, and his eyes darkened. "But that was before Brian got the card."

"What card?"

For the first time, a real emotion appeared in Sean's eyes. It was terror.

"The baseball card. The great special baseball card."

"Oh?" Alan thought of the Playmate cooler and the baseball cards—traders, Brian had called them—inside. "Brian liked baseball cards, didn't he, Sean?"

"Yes. That was how *he* got him. I think he must use different things to get different people."

Alan leaned forward. "Who, Sean? *Who* got him?"

"Brian killed himself. I saw him do it. It was in the garage."

"I know. I'm sorry."

"Gross stuff came out of the back of his head. Not just blood. *Stuff.* It was yellow."

Alan could think of nothing to say. His heart was pounding slowly and heavily in his chest, his mouth was as dry as a desert, and he felt sick to his stomach. His son's name clanged in his mind like a funeral bell rung by idiot hands in the middle of the night.

"I wished he didn't," Sean said. His voice was strangely matter-of-fact, but now a tear rose in each of his eyes, grew, and spilled down his smooth cheeks. "We won't get to see *Young Guns II* together when they put it out for VCRs. I'll have to watch it by myself, and it won't be any fun without Brian making all his stupid jokes. I know it won't."

"You loved your brother, didn't you?" Alan said hoarsely. He reached through the hospital bars. Sean Rusk's hand crept into his and then closed tightly upon it. It was hot. And small. Very small.

"Yeah. Brian wanted to pitch for the Red Sox when he grew up. He said he was gonna learn to throw a dead-fish curve, just like Mike Boddicker. Now he never will. He told me not to come any closer or I'd get the mess on me. I cried. I was scared. It wasn't like a movie. It was just our *garage.*"

"I know," Alan said. He remembered Annie's car. The shattered windows. The blood on the seats in big black puddles. That hadn't been like a movie, either. Alan began to cry. "I know, son."

"He asked me to promise, and I did, and I'm going to keep it. I'll keep that promise all my life."

"What did you promise, son?"

Alan swiped at his face with his free hand, but the tears would not stop. The boy lay before him, his skin almost as white as the pillowcase on which his head rested; the boy had seen his brother commit suicide, had seen the brains hit the garage wall like a fresh wad of snot, and where was his mother? Visiting with The King, he had said. *She shuts the door and puts on her sunglasses and visits with The King.*

"What did you promise, son?"

"I tried to swear it on Mommy's name, but Brian wouldn't let me. He said I had to swear on my own name. Because he got her, too. Brian said he gets everyone who swears on anyone else's name. So I swore on my own name like he wanted, but Brian made the gun go bang anyway." Sean was crying harder now, but he looked earnestly up at Alan through his tears. "It wasn't just blood, Mr. Sheriff. It was other stuff. *Yellow* stuff."

Alan squeezed his hand. "I know, Sean. What did your brother want you to promise?"

"Maybe Brian won't go to heaven if I tell."

"Yes he will. *I* promise. And I'm a Sheriff."

"Do Sheriffs ever break their promises?"

"They never break them when they're made to little kids in the hospital," Alan said. "Sheriffs *can't* break their promises to kids like that."

"Do they go to hell if they do?"

"Yes," Alan said. "That's right. They go to hell if they do."

"Do you swear Brian will go to heaven even if I tell? Do you swear on your very own name?"

"On my very own name," Alan said.

"Okay," Sean said. "He made me promise I would never go to the new store where he got the great special baseball card. He thought Sandy Koufax was on that card, but that wasn't who it was. It was some other player. It was old and dirty, but I don't think Brian knew that." Sean paused a moment, thinking, and then went on in his eerily calm voice. "He came home one day and later on I heard him in his room, crying."

The sheets, Alan thought. Wilma's sheets. It *was* Brian.

"Brian said Needful Things is a poison place and *he's* a poison man and I should never go there."

"Brian *said* that? He *said* Needful Things?"

"Yes."

"Sean—" He paused, thinking. Electric sparks were shooting through him everywhere, jigging and jagging in tiny blue splinters.

"What?"

"Did . . . did your mother get her sunglasses at Needful Things?"

"Yes."

"She told you that she did?"

"No. But I know she did. She wears the sunglasses and that's how she visits with The King."

"What King, Sean? Do you know?"

Sean looked at Alan as though he were crazy. "Elvis. *He's* The King."

"Elvis," Alan muttered. "Sure—who else?"

"I want my father."

"I know, honey. Just a couple more questions and I'll leave you alone. Then you'll go back to sleep and when you wake up, your father will be here." He hoped. "Sean, did Brian say who the poison man was?"

"Yes. Mr. Gaunt. The man who runs the store. *He's* the poison man."

Now his mind jumped to Polly—Polly after the funeral, saying *I guess it was just a matter of finally meeting the right doctor . . . Dr. Gaunt. Dr. Leland Gaunt.*

He saw her holding out the little silver ball she had bought in Needful Things so he could see it . . . but cupping her hand protectively over it when he put a hand out to touch it. There had been an expression on her face in that moment which was totally unlike Polly. A look of narrow suspicion and possessiveness. Then, later, speaking in a strident, shaky, tear-filled voice which was also totally unlike her: *It's hard to find out the face you thought you loved is only a mask . . . How could you go behind my back? . . . How could you?*

"What did you tell her?" he muttered. He was totally unaware that he had seized the counterpane of the hospital bed in one hand and was twisting it slowly into his clenched fist. "What did you tell her? And how the hell did you make her believe it?"

"Mr. Sheriff? Are you okay?"

Alan forced himself to open his fist. "Yes—fine. You're sure Brian said Mr. Gaunt, aren't you, Sean?"

"Yes."

"Thank you," Alan said. He bent over the bars, took Sean's hand, and kissed his cool, pale cheek. "Thank you for talking to me." He let go of the boy's hand and stood up.

During the last week, there had been one piece of business on his agenda which simply hadn't gotten done—a courtesy call on Castle Rock's newest businessman. No big deal; just a friendly hello, a welcome to town, and a quick rundown on what the procedure was in case of trouble. He had meant to do it, had once even dropped by, but it kept not getting done. And today, when Polly's behavior began to make him wonder if Mr. Gaunt was on the up-and-up, the shit had *really* hit the fan, and he had wound up here, more than twenty miles away.

Is he keeping me away? Has he been keeping me away all along?

The idea should have seemed ridiculous, but in this quiet, shadowy room, it did not seem ridiculous at all.

Suddenly he needed to get back. He needed to get back just as fast as he could.

"Mr. Sheriff?"

Alan looked down at him.

"Brian said something else, too," Sean said.

"Did he?" Alan asked. "What was that, Sean?"

"Brian said Mr. Gaunt wasn't really a man at all."

10

Alan walked down the hall toward the door with the EXIT sign over it as quietly as he could, expecting to be frozen in his tracks by a challenging shout from Miss Hendrie's replacement at any moment. But the only person who spoke to him was a little girl. She stood in the doorway of her room, her blonde hair tied in braids which lay on the front of her faded pink flannel nightie. She was holding a blanket. Her favorite, from its ragged well-used look. Her feet were bare, the ribbons at the ends of her braids were askew, and her eyes were enormous in her haggard face. It was a face which knew more about pain than any child's face should know.

"You've got a gun," she announced.

"Yes."

"My dad has a gun."

"Does he?"

"Yes. It's bigger than yours. It's bigger than the world. Are you the Boogeyman?"

"No, honey," he said, and thought: I think maybe the Boogeyman is in my home town tonight.

He pushed through the door at the end of the corridor, went downstairs, and pushed through another door into a late twilight as sultry as any midsummer evening. He hurried around to the parking lot, not quite running. Thunder bumbled and grumbled out of the west, from the direction of Castle Rock.

He unlocked the driver's door of the station wagon, got in, and pulled the Radio Shack microphone off its prongs. "Unit One to base. Come back."

His only response was a rush of brainless static.

The goddam storm.

Maybe the Boogeyman ordered it up special, a voice whispered from somewhere deep inside. Alan smiled with his lips pressed together.

He tried again, got the same response, then tried the State Police in Oxford. They came through loud and clear. Dispatch told him there was a big electrical storm in the vicinity of Castle Rock, and communications had become spotty. Even the telephones only seemed to be working when they wanted to.

"Well, you get through to Henry Payton and tell him to take a man named Leland Gaunt into custody. As a material witness will do to begin with. That's *Gaunt,* G as in George. Do you copy? Ten-four."

"I copy you five-by, Sheriff. Gaunt, G as in George. Ten-four."

"Tell him I believe Gaunt may be an accessory before the fact in the murders of Nettie Cobb and Wilma Jerzyck. Ten-four."

"Copy. Ten-four."

"Ten-forty, over and out."

He replaced the mike, keyed the engine, and headed back toward The Rock. On the outskirts of Bridgton, he swerved

into the parking lot of a Red Apple store and used the telephone to dial his office. He got two clicks and then a recorded
voice telling him the number was temporarily out of service.

He hung up and went back to his car. This time he *was* running. Before he pulled out of the parking lot and back onto
Route 117, he turned on the Porta-Bubble and stuck it on the
roof again. By the time he was half a mile down the road he
had the shuddering, protesting Ford wagon doing seventy-five.

11

Ace Merrill and full dark returned to Castle Rock together.

He drove the Chevy Celebrity across Castle Stream Bridge
while thunder rolled heavily back and forth in the sky overhead and lightning jabbed the unresisting earth. He drove
with the windows open; there was still no rain falling and the
air was as thick as syrup.

He was dirty and tired and furious. He had gone to three
more locations on the map in spite of the note, unable to believe what had happened, unable to believe it *could* have happened. To coin a phrase, he was unable to believe he had been
aced out. At each one of the spots he had found a flat stone and
a buried tin can. Two had contained more wads of dirty trading stamps. The last, in the marshy ground behind the Strout
farm, had contained nothing but an old ball-point pen. There
was a woman with a forties hairdo on the pen's barrel. She was
wearing a forties tank-style bathing suit as well. When you
held the pen up, the bathing suit disappeared.

Some treasure.

Ace had driven back to Castle Rock at top speed, his eyes
wild and his jeans splattered with swamp-goo up to the knees,
for one reason and one reason only: to kill Alan Pangborn.
Then he would simply haul ass for the West Coast—he should
have done it long before. He might get some of the money out

of Pangborn; he might get none of it. Either way, one thing was certain: that son of a bitch was going to die, and he was going to die *hard*.

Still three miles from the bridge, he realized that he didn't have a weapon. He had meant to take one of the autos from the crate in the Cambridge garage, but then that damned tape recorder had started up, scaring the life out of him. But he knew where they were.

Oh yes.

He crossed the bridge . . . and then stopped at the intersection of Main Street and Watermill Lane, although the right-of-way was his.

"What the *fuck?*" he muttered.

Lower Main was a tangled confusion of State Police cruisers, flashing blue lights, TV vans, and little knots of people. Most of the action was swirling around the Municipal Building. It looked almost as though the town fathers had decided to throw a street-carnival on the spur of the moment.

Ace didn't care what had happened; the whole town could dry up and blow away as far as he was concerned. But he wanted Pangborn, wanted to tear the fucking thief's scalp off and hang it on his belt, and how was he supposed to do that with what looked like every State cop in Maine hanging out at the Sheriff's Office?

The answer came at once. *Mr. Gaunt will know. Mr. Gaunt has the artillery, and he'll have the answers to go with it. Go see Mr. Gaunt.*

He glanced in his mirror and saw more blue lights top the nearest rise on the other side of the bridge. Even more cops on the way. What the fuck happened here this afternoon? he wondered again, but that was a question which could be answered another time . . . or not at all, if that was how things fell out. Meantime, he had his own business, and it began with getting out of the way before the arriving cops rear-ended him.

Ace turned left on Watermill Lane, then right onto Cedar

Street, skirting the downtown area before cutting back to Main Street. He paused at the stop-light for a moment, looking at the nest of flashing blue lights at the bottom of the hill. Then he parked in front of Needful Things.

He got out of the car, crossed the street, and read the sign in the window. He felt a moment of crashing disappointment—it was not just a gun he needed, but a little more of Mr. Gaunt's blow as well—and then he remembered the service entrance in the alley. He walked up the block and around the corner, not noticing the bright yellow van parked twenty or thirty yards farther up, or the man who sat inside it (Buster had moved to the passenger seat now), watching him.

As he entered the alley, he bumped into a man who was wearing a tweed cap pulled low over his forehead.

"Hey, watch where you're going, Daddy-O," Ace said.

The man in the tweed cap raised his head, bared his teeth at Ace, and snarled. At the same moment he pulled an automatic from his pocket and pointed it in Ace's general direction. "Don't fuck with me, my friend, unless you want some, too."

Ace raised his hands and stepped back. He was not afraid; he was utterly astonished. "Not me, Mr. Nelson," he said. "Leave me out of it."

"Right," the man in the tweed cap said. "Have you seen that cocksucker Jewett?"

"Uh . . . the one from the junior high?"

"The Middle School, right—are there any other Jewetts in town? Get real, for Christ's sake!"

"I just got here," Ace said cautiously. "I really haven't seen anyone, Mr. Nelson."

"Well, I'm going to find him, and he's going to be one sorry sack of shit when I do. He killed my parakeet and shit on my mother." George T. Nelson narrowed his eyes and added: "This is a good night to stay out of my way."

Ace didn't argue.

Mr. Nelson stuffed the gun back into his pocket and disappeared around the corner, walking with the purposeful strides of one who is indeed highly pissed off. Ace stood right where he was for a moment, hands still raised. Mr. Nelson taught wood shop and metal shop at the high school. Ace had always believed he was one of those guys who wouldn't have nerve enough to slap a deerfly if it lit on his eyeball, but he thought he might just have to change his opinion on that. Also, Ace had recognized the gun. He should have; he had brought a whole case of them back from Boston just the night before.

12

"Ace!" Mr. Gaunt said. "You're just in time."

"I need a gun," Ace said. "Also, some more of that high-class boogerjuice, if you've got any."

"Yes, yes . . . in time. All things in time. Help me with this table, Ace."

"I'm going to kill Pangborn," Ace said. "He stole my fucking treasure and I'm going to kill him."

Mr. Gaunt looked at Ace with the flat yellow stare of a cat stalking a mouse . . . and in that moment, Ace *felt* like a mouse. "Don't waste my time telling me things I already know," he said. "If you want my help, Ace, help *me*."

Ace grabbed one side of the table, and they carried it back into the storeroom. Mr. Gaunt bent down and picked up a sign which leaned against the wall.

THIS TIME I'M *REALLY* CLOSED,

it read. He put it on the door and then shut it. He was turning the thumb-lock before Ace realized there had been nothing on the sign to hold it in place—no tack, no tape, no nothing. But it had stayed up just the same.

Then his eye fell upon the crates which had contained the

automatic pistols and the clips of ammunition. There were only three guns and three clips left.

"Holy Jesus! Where'd they all go?"

"Business has been good this evening, Ace," Mr. Gaunt said, rubbing his long-fingered hands together. "Extremely good. And it's going to get even better. I have work for you to do."

"I *told* you," Ace said. "The Sheriff stole my—"

Leland Gaunt was upon him before Ace even saw him move. Those long, ugly hands seized him by the front of the shirt and lifted him into the air as if he were made of feathers. A startled cry fell out of his mouth. The hands which held him were like iron. Mr. Gaunt lifted him high, and Ace suddenly found himself looking down into that blazing, hellish face with only the haziest idea of how he had gotten there. Even in the extremity of his sudden terror, he noticed that smoke—or perhaps it was steam—was coming out of Mr. Gaunt's ears and nostrils. He looked like a human dragon.

"*You tell me NOTHING!*" Mr. Gaunt screamed up at him. His tongue licked out between those jostling tombstone teeth, and Ace saw it came to a double point, like the tongue of a snake. "*I tell you EVERYTHING! Shut up when you are in the company of your elders and betters, Ace! Shut up and listen! Shut up and listen! SHUT UP AND LISTEN!*"

He whirled Ace twice around his head like a carnival wrestler giving his opponent an airplane spin, and threw him against the far wall. Ace's head connected with the plaster. A large fireworks display went off in the center of his brain. When his vision cleared, he saw Leland Gaunt bearing down on him. His face was a horror of eyes and teeth and blowing steam.

"*No!*" Ace shrieked. "*No, Mr. Gaunt, please! NO!*"

The hands had become talons, the nails grown long and sharp in a moment's time . . . *or were they that way all along?* Ace's mind gibbered. *Maybe they were that way all along and you just didn't see it.*

They cut through the fabric of Ace's shirt like razors, and Ace was jerked back up into that fuming face.

"Are you ready to listen, Ace?" Mr. Gaunt asked. Hot blurts of steam stung Ace's cheeks and mouth with each word. "Are you ready, or should I just unzip your worthless guts and have done with it?"

"Yes!" he sobbed. "I mean *no!* I'll listen!"

"Are you going to be a good little errand boy and follow orders?"

"*Yes!*"

"Do you know what will happen if you don't?"

"*Yes! Yes! Yes!*"

"You're disgusting, Ace," Mr. Gaunt said. "I like that in a person." He slung Ace against the wall. Ace slid down it into a loose kneeling position, gasping and sobbing. He looked down at the floor. He was afraid to gaze directly into the monster's face.

"If you should even think of going against my wishes, Ace, I'll see that you get the grand tour of hell. You'll have the Sheriff, don't worry. For the moment, however, he is out of town. Now. Stand up."

Ace got slowly to his feet. His head throbbed; his tee-shirt hung in ribbons.

"Let me ask you something." Mr. Gaunt was urbane and smiling again, not a hair out of place. "Do you like this little town? Do you love it? Do you keep snapshots of it on the walls of your shitty little shack to remind yourself of its rustic charm on those days when the bee stings and the dog bites?"

"Hell, no," Ace said in an unsteady voice. His voice rose and fell with the pounding of his heart. He made it to his feet only with the greatest effort. His legs felt as if they were made of spaghetti. He stood with his back to the wall, watching Mr. Gaunt warily.

"Would it appall you if I said I wanted you to blow this shitty little burg right off the face of the map while you wait for the Sheriff to come back?"

"I . . . I don't know what that word means," Ace said nervously.

"I'm not surprised. But I think you understand what I *mean,* Ace. Don't you?"

Ace thought back. He thought back all the way to a time, many years ago, when four snotnosed kids had cheated him and his friends (Ace had *had* friends back in those days, or at least a reasonable approximation thereof) out of something Ace had wanted. They had caught one of the snotnoses—Gordie LaChance—later on and had beaten the living shit out of him, but it hadn't mattered. These days LaChance was a bigshot writer living in another part of the state, and he probably wiped his ass with ten-dollar bills. Somehow the snotnoses had won, and things had never been the same for Ace after that. That was when his luck had turned bad. Doors that had been open to him had begun to close, one by one. Little by little he had begun to realize that he was not a king and Castle Rock was not his kingdom. If that had ever been true, those days had begun to pass that Labor Day weekend when he was sixteen, when the snots had cheated him and his friends out of what was rightfully theirs. By the time Ace was old enough to drink legally in The Mellow Tiger, he had gone from being a king to being a soldier without a uniform, skulking through enemy territory.

"I *hate* this fucking toilet," he said to Leland Gaunt.

"Good," Mr. Gaunt said. "Very good. I have a friend—he's parked just up the street—who is going to help you do something about that, Ace. You'll have the Sheriff . . . and you'll have the whole town, too. Does that sound good?" He had captured Ace's eyes with his own. Ace stood before him in the tattered rags of his tee-shirt and began to grin. His head no longer ached.

"Yeah," he said. "It sounds absolutely t-fine."

Mr. Gaunt reached into his coat pocket and brought out a plastic sandwich bag filled with white powder. He held it out to Ace.

"There's work to do, Ace," he said.

Ace took the sandwich bag, but it was still Mr. Gaunt's eyes he looked at, and into.

"Good," he said. "I'm ready."

13

Buster watched as the last man he had seen enter the service alley came back out again. The guy's tee-shirt hung in ragged strips now, and he was carrying a crate. Tucked into the waistband of his bluejeans were the butts of two automatic pistols.

Buster drew back in sudden alarm as the man, whom he now recognized as John "Ace" Merrill, walked directly to the van and set the crate down.

Ace tapped on the glass. "Open up the back, Daddy-O," he said. "We got work to do."

Buster unrolled his window. "Get out of here," he said. "Get out, you ruffian! Or I'll call the police!"

"Good fucking luck," Ace grunted.

He drew one of the pistols from the waistband of his pants. Buster stiffened, and then Ace thrust it through the window at him, butt first. Buster blinked at it.

"Take it," Ace said impatiently, "and then open the back. If you don't know who sent me, you're even dumber than you look." He reached out with his other hand and felt the wig. "Love your hair," he said with a small smile. "Simply marvellous."

"Stop that," Buster said, but the anger and outrage had gone out of his voice. *Three good men can do a lot of damage,* Mr. Gaunt had said. *I will send someone to you.*

But Ace? Ace *Merrill?* He was a *criminal!*

"Look," Ace said, "if you want to discuss the arrangements with Mr. Gaunt, I think he might still be in there. But as you can see"—he fluttered his hands through the long strips of tee-shirt hanging over his chest and belly—"his mood is a little touchy."

"You're supposed to help me get rid of Them?" Buster asked.

"That's right," Ace said. "We're gonna turn this whole town into a Flame-Broiled Whopper." He picked up the crate. "Although I don't know how we're supposed to do any real damage with just a box of blasting caps. He said you'd know the answer to that one."

Buster had begun to grin. He got up, crawled into the back of the van, and slid the door open on its track. "I believe I do," he said. "Climb in, Mr. Merrill. We've got an errand to run."

"Where?"

"The town motor pool, to start with," Buster said. He was still grinning.

CHAPTER TWENTY-ONE

1

The Rev. William Rose, who had first stepped into the pulpit of The United Baptist Church of Castle Rock in May of 1983, was a bigot of the first water; no question about it. Unfortunately, he was also energetic, sometimes witty in an odd, cruel way, and extremely popular with his congregation. His first sermon as leader of the Baptist flock had been a sign of things to come. It was called "Why the Catholics are Hellbound." He had kept up in this vein, which was extremely popular with his congregation, ever since. The Catholics, he informed them, were blasphemous, misguided creatures who worshipped not Jesus but the woman who had been chosen to bear Him. Was it any wonder they were so prone to error on other subjects as well?

He explained to his flock that the Catholics had perfected the science of torture during the Inquisition; that the Inquisitors had burned the *true* faithful at what he called The Smoking-uh Stake right up until the end of the nineteenth century, when heroic Protestants (Baptists, mostly) had made them stop; that forty different Popes through history had known their own mothers and sisters, and even their illegitimate daughters, in-uh unholy sexual congress-uh; that the Vatican was built on the gold of Protestant martyrs and plundered nations.

This sort of ignorant twaddle was hardly news to the Catholic Church, which had had to put up with similar heresies for hundreds of years. Many priests would have taken it in stride, perhaps even making gentle fun of it. Father John Brigham, however, was not the sort to take things in his stride. Quite the contrary. A bad-tempered, bandy-legged Irishman, Brigham was one of those humorless men who cannot suffer fools, especially strutting fools of Rev. Rose's stripe.

He had borne Rose's strident Catholic-baiting in silence for almost a year before finally cutting loose from his own pulpit. His homily, which pulled no punches at all, was called "The Sins of Reverend Willie." In it he characterized the Baptist minister as "a psalm-singin jackass of a man who thinks Billy Graham walks on water and Billy Sunday sits at the right hand of God the Father Almighty."

Later that Sunday, Rev. Rose and four of his largest deacons had paid a visit on Father Brigham. They were shocked and angered, they said, by the slanderous things Father Brigham had said.

"You've got your nerve tellin *me* to tone down," Father Brigham said, "after a hard mornin of tellin the faithful that I serve the Whore of Babylon."

Color rose quickly in Rev. Rose's normally pale cheeks and overspread his mostly bald pate. He had *never* said anything about the Whore of Babylon, he told Father Brigham, although he *had* mentioned the Whore of Rome several times, and if the shoe fit, why, Father Brigham had just better slip his heel in and wear it.

Father Brigham had stepped out of the rectory's front door with his fists bunched. "If you want to discuss this on the front walk, my friend," he said, "just ask your little Gestapo unit there to stand aside and we'll discuss it all you want."

Rev. Rose, who was three inches taller than Father Brigham—but perhaps twenty pounds lighter—stepped back with a sneer. "I would not soil-uh my hands," he said.

One of the deacons was Don Hemphill. He was both taller *and* heavier than the combative priest. "*I'll* discuss it with you if you want," he said. "I'll wipe the walk with your Pope-loving, bog-trotting *ass.*"

Two of the other deacons, who knew Don was capable of just that, had restrained him in the nick of time . . . but after that, the rumble was on.

Until this October, it had been mostly *sub rosa*—ethnic jokes and malicious chatter in the ladies' and men's groups of the two churches, schoolyard taunting between children of the two factions, and, most of all, rhetorical grenades tossed from pulpit to pulpit on Sundays, that day of peace when, history teaches, most wars actually start. Every now and then there were ugly incidents—eggs were thrown at the Parish Hall during a Baptist Youth Fellowship dance, and once a rock was winged through the living-room window of the rectory—but it had been mostly a war of words.

Like all wars, it had had both its heated moments and its lulls, but a steadily deepening anger had run through it since the day the Daughters of Isabella announced their plans for Casino Nite. By the time Rev. Rose received the infamous "Babtist Rat-Fuck" card, it was probably too late to avoid a confrontation of some sort; the over-the-top crudity of the message only seemed to guarantee that when the confrontation came, it would be a wowser. The kindling had been laid; all that remained was for someone to strike a match and light the bonfire.

If anyone had fatally underestimated the volatility of the situation, it was Father Brigham. He had known his Baptist counterpart would not like the idea of Casino Nite, but he did not understand how deeply the concept of church-supported gaming enraged and offended the Baptist preacher. He did not know that Steamboat Willie's father had been a compulsive gambler who had abandoned the family on many occasions when the gambling fever took him, or that the man had finally shot himself in the back room of a dance-hall after a losing night at craps. And the unlovely truth about Father Brigham was this: it probably would not have made any difference to him even if he had known.

Rev. Rose mobilized his forces. The Baptists began with a No Casino Nite letter-writing campaign to the Castle Rock *Call* (Wanda Hemphill, Don's wife, wrote most of them herself), and followed up the letters with the DICE AND THE DEVIL posters. Betsy Vigue, Casino Nite Chairwoman and Grand Regeant of the local Daughters of Isabella chapter, organized the counterattack. For the previous three weeks, the *Call* had expanded to sixteen pages to handle the resulting debate (except it was more a shouting-match than a reasonable airing of different views). More posters went up; they were just as quickly torn down again. An editorial urging temperance on both sides was ignored. Some of the partisans were having fun; it was sort of neat to be caught up in such a teapot tempest. But as the end drew near, Steamboat Willie was not having fun, and neither was Father Brigham.

"I loathe that self-righteous little piece of shit!" Brigham burst out at a surprised Albert Gendron on the day Albert brought him the infamous "LISTEN UP YOU MACKEREL-SNAPPER" letter which Albert had found taped to the door of his dental office.

"Imagine that whore's son accusing good Baptists of such a thing!" Rev. Rose had spat at an equally surprised Norman Harper and Don Hemphill. That had been on Columbus Day, following a call from Father Brigham. Brigham had tried to read the mackerel-snapper letter to Rev. Rose; Rev. Rose had (quite properly, in the view of his deacons) refused to listen.

Norman Harper, a man who outweighed Albert Gendron by twenty pounds and stood nearly as tall, was made uneasy by the shrill, almost hysterical quality of Rose's voice, but he didn't say so. "I'll tell you what it is," he rumbled. "Old Father Bog-Trotter's gotten a little nervous about that card you got at the parsonage, Bill, that's all. He's realized that was going too far. He figures if he says one of his buddy-boys got a letter full of the same kind of filth, it'll spread the blame around."

"Well, it won't work!" Rose's voice was shriller than ever. "No one in my congregation would be a party to such filth! *No one!*" His voice splintered on the last word. His hands opened and closed convulsively. Norman and Don exchanged a quick, uneasy glance. They had discussed just this sort of behavior, which was becoming more and more common in Rev. Rose, on several occasions over the last few weeks. The Casino Nite business was tearing Bill apart. The two men were afraid he might actually have a nervous breakdown before the situation was finally resolved.

"Don't you fret," Don said soothingly. "We know the truth of the thing, Bill."

"Yes!" Rev. Rose cried, fixing the two men with a trembling, liquid gaze. "Yes, *you* know—you two. And I—*I* know! But what about the rest of this town-uh? Do *they* know?"

Neither Norman nor Don could answer this.

"I hope someone rides the lying idol-worshipper out on a rail!" William Rose cried, clenching his fists and shaking them impotently. "On a rail! I would pay to see that! I would pay handsomely!"

Later on Monday, Father Brigham had phoned around, asking those interested in "the current atmosphere of religious repression in Castle Rock" to drop by the rectory for a brief meeting that evening. So many people showed up that the meeting had to be moved to the Knights of Columbus Hall next door.

Brigham began by speaking of the letter Albert Gendron had found on his door—the letter purporting to be from The Concerned Baptist Men of Castle Rock—and then recounted his unrewarding telephone conversation with Rev. Rose. When he told the assembled group that Rose claimed to have received his own obscene note, a note which purported to be from The Concerned *Catholic* Men of Castle Rock, there was a rumble from the crowd . . . shocked at first, then angry.

"The man's a damned liar!" someone called from the back of the room.

Father Brigham seemed to nod and shake his head at the same time. "Perhaps, Sam, but that's not the real issue. He is quite mad—I think *that* is the issue."

Thoughtful, worried silence greeted this, but Father Brigham felt a sense of almost palpable relief, just the same. *Quite mad:* it was the first time he had spoken the words aloud, although they had been circling in his mind for at least three years.

"I don't want to be stopped by a religious nut," Father Brigham went on. "Our Casino Nite is harmless and whole-some, no matter what the Reverend Steamboat Willie may think about it. But I feel, since he has grown increasingly stri-dent and increasingly less stable, that we should take a vote. If you are in favor of cancelling Casino Nite—of bowing to this pressure in the name of safety—you should say so."

The vote to hold Casino Nite just as planned had been unanimous.

Father Brigham nodded, pleased. Then he looked at Betsy Vigue. "You're going to have a planning session tomorrow night, aren't you, Betsy?"

"Yes, Father."

"Then may I suggest," Father Brigham said, "that we men meet here, at the K of C Hall, at just the same time."

Albert Gendron, a ponderous man who was both slow to anger and slow to recover from anger, got up slowly and stood to his full height. Necks craned to follow his rise. "Are you suggesting those Baptist clunks might try to bother the ladies, Father?"

"No, no, not at all," Father Brigham soothed. "But I think it might be wise if we discussed some plans to ensure that Ca-sino Nite *itself* goes smoothly—"

"Guards?" someone else asked enthusiastically. "Guards, Father?"

"Well . . . eyes and ears," Father Brigham said, leaving no doubt at all that guards were what he meant. "And, if we meet Tuesday evening while the ladies are meeting, we'll be there just in case there *is* trouble."

So, while the Daughters of Isabella were gathering at the building on one side of the parking lot, the Catholic men were gathering at the building on the other. And, across town, Rev. William Rose had called a meeting at this same time to discuss the latest Catholic slander and to plan the making of signs and the organizing of Casino Nite picketers.

The various alarums and excursions in The Rock that early evening did not dent attendance at these meetings very much—most of the gawkers milling around the Municipal Building as the storm approached were people who were neutral in The Great Casino Nite Controversy. As far as the Catholics and Baptists actually embroiled in the brouhaha were concerned, a couple of murders could not hold a candle to the prospect of a really good holy grudge-match. Because, after all, other things had to take a back seat when it came to questions of religion.

2

Over seventy people showed up at the fourth meeting of what Rev. Rose had dubbed The Baptist Anti-Gambling Christian Soldiers of Castle Rock. This was a great turnout; attendance had fallen off sharply at the last meeting, but rumors of the obscene card dropped through the parsonage mail-slot had pumped it up again. The showing relieved Rev. Rose, but he was both disappointed and puzzled to realize that Don Hemphill wasn't in attendance. Don had promised he would be here, and Don was his strong right arm.

Rose glanced at his watch and saw it was already five after seven—no time to call the market and see if Don had forgotten. Everyone who was coming was here, and he wanted to catch them while their indignation and curiosity were at flood-tide. He gave Hemphill one more minute, then mounted the pulpit and raised his skinny arms in a gesture of welcome. His congregation—dressed tonight in their working clothes, for the most part—filed into the pews and sat down on the plain wooden benches.

"Let us begin this endeavor as all great-uh endeavors are begun," Rev. Rose said quietly. "Let us bow our heads-uh in prayer."

They dropped their heads, and that was when the vestibule door banged open behind them with gunshot force. A few of the women screamed and several men leaped to their feet.

It was Don. He was his own head butcher, and he still wore his bloodstained white apron. His face was as red as a beefsteak tomato. His wild eyes were streaming water. Runners of snot were drying on his nose, his upper lip, and the creases which bracketed his mouth.

Also, he stank.

Don smelled like a pack of skunks which had been first run through a vat of sulphur, then sprayed with fresh cowshit, and finally let loose to rant and racket their panicky way through a closed room. The smell preceded him; the smell followed him; but mostly the smell hung around him in a pestilential cloud. Women shrank away from the aisle and groped for their hand-kerchiefs as he stumbled past them with his apron flapping in front and his untucked white shirt flapping behind. The few children in attendance began to cry. Men roared out cries of mingled disgust and bewilderment.

"Don!" Rev. Rose cried in a prissy, surprised voice. His arms were still raised, but as Don Hemphill neared the pulpit, Rose lowered them and involuntarily clapped one hand over his nose and mouth. He thought he might vomit. It was the most incredible nose-buster of a stink he had ever encountered. "What . . . what has happened?"

"Happened?" Don Hemphill roared. "*Happened?* I'll tell you what happened! I'll tell you *all* what happened!"

He wheeled on the congregation, and in spite of the stink which both clung to him and spread out from him, they grew still as his furious, maddened eyes fell upon them.

"The sons of bitches stink-bombed my store, that's what happened! There weren't more than half a dozen people there because I put up a sign saying I was closing early, and thank God for that, but the stock is ruined! All of it! Forty thousand dollars' worth! Ruined! I don't know what the bastards used, but it's going to stink for *days!*"

"Who?" Rev. Rose asked in a timorous voice. "Who did it, Don?"

Don Hemphill reached into the pocket of his apron. He brought out a curved black band with a white notch in it and a stack of leaflets. The band was a Roman collar. He held it up for them all to see.

"*WHO THE HELL DO YOU THINK?*" he screamed. "*My store! My stock! All shot to hell, and who do you think?*"

He threw the leaflets at the stunned members of The Baptist Anti-Gambling Christian Soldiers. They separated in the air and fluttered down like confetti. Some of those present reached out and grabbed at them. Each one was the same; each showed a crowd of laughing men and women standing around a roulette table.

JUST FOR FUN!

it said over the picture. And, below it:

JOIN US FOR "CASINO NITE"
AT THE KNIGHTS OF COLUMBUS HALL
OCTOBER 31, 1991
TO BENEFIT THE
CATHOLIC BUILDERS' FUND

"Where did you find these pamphlets, Don?" Len Milliken asked in a rumbling, ominous voice. "And this collar?"

"Somebody put them inside the main doors," Don said, "just before everything went to he—"

The vestibule door boomed again, making them all jump, only this time it was not opening but closing.

"Hope you like the smell, you Baptist faggots!" someone shouted. This was followed by a burst of shrill, nasty laughter.

The congregation stared at Rev. William Rose with frightened eyes. He stared back at them with eyes which were equally frightened. And that was when the box hidden in the choir suddenly began to hiss. Like the box placed in the Daughters of Isabella Hall by the late Myrtle Keeton, this one (planted by Sonny Jackett, now also late) contained a timer which had ticked all afternoon.

Clouds of incredibly potent stink began to pour out of the grilles set into the sides of the box.

At The United Baptist Church of Castle Rock, the fun had just begun.

3

Babs Miller skulked along the side of the Daughters of Isabella Hall, freezing in place each time a blue-white flash of lightning smoked across the sky. She had a crowbar in one hand and one of Mr. Gaunt's automatic pistols in the other. The music box she had bought at Needful Things was tucked into one pocket of the man's overcoat she wore, and if anyone tried to steal it, that person was going to eat an ounce or so of lead.

Who would want to do such a low, nasty, mean thing? Who would want to steal the music box before Babs could even find out what tune it played?

Well, she thought, let's just put it this way—I hope Cyndi

Rose Martin doesn't show her face in front of mine tonight. If she does, she isn't ever going to show her face again *anywhere*— not on *this* side of hell, anyway. What does she think I am . . . stupid?

Meanwhile, she had a little trick to perform. A prank. At Mr. Gaunt's request, of course.

Do you know Betsy Vigue? Mr. Gaunt had asked. *You do, don't you?*

Of course she did. She had known Betsy ever since grade school, when they were often hall-monitors together and inseparable comrades.

Good. Watch through the window. She will sit down. She will pick up a piece of paper, and see something beneath it.

What? Babs had asked, curious.

Never mind what. If you ever expect to find the key that unlocks the music box, you had better just shut your mouth and open your ears— do you understand, dear?

She had understood. She understood something else, as well. Mr. Gaunt was a scary man sometimes. A *very* scary man.

She'll pick up the thing she's found. She'll examine it. She'll begin to open it. By then you should be by the door to the building. Wait until everyone looks around toward the left rear of the hall.

Babs had wanted to ask why they would all do that, but decided it would be safer not to ask.

When they turn to look, you will slip the crowbar's split end under the doorknob. Prop the other end against the ground. Wedge it firmly.

When do I shout? Babs had asked.

You'll know. They'll all look like somebody stuck Flit-guns full of red pepper up their butts. Do you remember what you're supposed to shout, Babs?

She had. It seemed like sort of a mean trick to pull on Betsy Vigue, with whom she had skipped hand-in-hand to school, but it also seemed harmless (well . . . *fairly* harmless), and they were not children anymore, she and the little girl she had for some reason always called Betty La-La; all of that had been a long time ago. And, as Mr. Gaunt had pointed out, no one would ever connect it with her. Why should they? Babs and her husband were, after all, Seventh-Day Adventists, and as far as *she* was concerned, the Catholics and the Baptists deserved just what they got—Betty La-La included.

Lightning flashed. Babs froze, then scurried a window closer to the door, peering in to make sure Betsy wasn't sitting down at the head table yet.

And the first hesitant drops of that mighty storm began to patter down around her.

4

The stench which began to fill the Baptist Church was like the stench which had clung to Don Hemphill . . . but a thousand times worse.

"Oh shit!" Don roared. He had completely forgotten where he was, and remembering probably wouldn't have changed his language much. *"They've set one up here, too! Out! Out! Everybody out!"*

"Move!" Nan Roberts bellowed in her lusty rush-hour-at-the-diner baritone. *"Move! Hoss your freight, folks!"*

They could all see where the stink was coming from—thick runners of whitish-yellow smog were pouring over the choir's waist-high railing and through the diamond-shaped cut-outs in the low panels. The side door was just beneath the choir balcony, but no one thought of going in that direction. A stench that strong would kill you . . . but first your eyeballs would pop and your hair would fall out and your asshole would seal itself shut in outraged horror.

The Baptist Anti-Gambling Christian Soldiers of Castle Rock became a routed army in less than five seconds. They stampeded toward the vestibule at the back of the church, screaming and gagging. One of the pews was overturned and hit the floor with a loud bang. Deborah Johnstone's foot was pinned beneath it, and Norman Harper struck her broadside while she was struggling to pull it free. Deborah fell over and there was a loud crack as her ankle broke. She shrieked with pain, her foot still caught under the pew, but her cries went unheeded among so many others.

Rev. Rose was closest to the choir, and the stink closed over his head like a large, smelly mask. This is the smell of Catholics burning in hell, he thought confusedly, and leaped from the pulpit. He landed squarely on Deborah Johnstone's midriff with both feet, and her shrieks became a long, choked wheeze that trailed away to nothing as she passed out. Rev. Rose, unaware that he had just knocked one of his most faithful parishioners unconscious, clawed his way toward the back of the church.

Those who reached the vestibule doors first discovered there was no escape to be had that way; the doors had been locked shut somehow. Before they could turn back, these leaders of the proposed exodus were smashed flat against the locked doors by those behind them.

Screams, roars of outrage, and furious curses blued the air. And as the rain started outside, the vomiting began inside.

5

Betsy Vigue took her place at the Chairwoman's table between the American flag and the Infant of Prague banner. She rapped her knuckles for order, and the ladies—about forty in all— began to take their seats. Outside, thunder banged across the sky. There were little screams and nervous laughter.

"I call this meeting of the Daughters of Isabella to order," Betsy said, and picked up her agenda. "We'll begin, as usual, by reading—"

She stopped. There was a white business envelope lying on

the table. It had been beneath her agenda. The words typed on it glared up at her.

READ THIS RIGHT AWAY YOU POPE WHORE

Them, she thought. Those Baptists. Those ugly, nasty, small-minded people.

"Betsy?" Naomi Jessup asked. "Is something wrong?"

"I don't know," she said, "I think so."

She tore the envelope open. A sheet of paper slid out. Typed on it was the following message:

THIS IS THE SMELL OF CATHOLIC CUNTS!

A hissing noise suddenly began to come from the left rear corner of the hall, a sound like an overburdened steam-pipe. Several of the women exclaimed and turned in that direction. Thunder whacked heartily overhead, and this time the screams were in earnest.

A whitish-yellow vapor was pouring from one of the cubbyholes at the side of the room. And suddenly the small one-room building was filled with the most awful smell any of them had ever experienced.

Betsy got to her feet, knocking over her chair. She had just opened her mouth—to say what, she had no idea—when a woman's voice outside cried, *"This is because of Casino Nite, you bitches! Repent! Repent!"*

She caught a glimpse of someone outside the rear door before the foul cloud coming from the cubbyhole obscured the window in the door completely . . . and then she no longer cared. The stink was unbearable.

Pandemonium broke loose. The Daughters of Isabella plunged back and forth in the cloudy, stinking room like maddened sheep. When Antonia Bissette was shoved backward and broke her neck against the steel edge of the Chairwoman's table, no one heard or noticed.

Outside, thunder roared and lightning flashed.

6

The Catholic men in the K of C Hall had formed a loose circle around Albert Gendron. Using the note he'd found taped to his office door as a take-off point ("Aw, this ain't nothing—you should have been there when . . ."), he was regaling them with horrible yet fascinating stories of Catholic-baiting and Catholic revenge in Lewiston back in the thirties.

"So when he seen how that bunch of ignorant Holy Rollers had covered the feet of the Blessed Virgin with cow-patty, he right away jumped in his car and drove—"

Albert broke off suddenly, listening.

"What's that?" he asked.

"Thunder," Jake Pulaski said. "It's gonna be one big storm."

"No—*that*," Albert said, and got up. "Sounds like screamin."

The thunder retreated temporarily to mere grumbles, and in the hiatus they all heard it: women. Women screaming.

They turned toward Father Brigham, who had risen from his chair. "Come on, men!" he said. "Let's see—"

Then the hissing began, and the stink began to billow from the back of the hall toward where the men stood in a knot. A window shattered and a rock bounced crazily across the floor, which had been polished to a mellow gloss over the years by dancing feet. Men yelled and skipped back from the carom. The rock rolled across to the far wall, bounced once more, and lay still.

"*Hellfire from the Baptists!*" someone yelled from outside. "*No gambling in Castle Rock! Spread the word, nun-fuckers!*"

The foyer door of the K of C Hall had also been propped shut with a crowbar. The men struck it and began to pile up.

"*No!*" Father Brigham yelled. He fought his way through the rising stench to a small side door. It was unlocked. "*This way! THIS WAY!*"

At first no one listened; in their panic they continued to pile

up against the Hall's immovable front door. Then Albert Gendron reached out with his big hands and knocked two heads
together.

"Do what the Father says!" he roared. *"They're killing the
women!"*

Albert bulled his way back through the crush by main force,
and the others began to follow him. They made their way in a
rough, stumbling line through the streaming murk, coughing
and cursing. Meade Rossignol could hold his churning gut no
longer. He opened his mouth and yarked supper all over the
wide back of Albert Gendron's shirt. Albert hardly noticed.

Father Brigham was already stumbling toward the steps
which led to the parking lot and the Daughters of Isabella Hall
on the far side. He paused every now and then to retch dryly.
The stink clung to him like flypaper. The men began to follow
him in ragged procession, barely noticing the rain, which had
now begun to fall harder.

When Father Brigham was halfway down the short flight
of steps, a flash of lightning showed him the crowbar propped
against the door of the Daughters of Isabella Hall. A moment
later one of the windows on the right side of the building shattered outward and women began to hurl themselves through
the hole, tumbling on the lawn like large rag dolls which had
learned how to vomit.

7

Rev. Rose never reached the vestibule; there were too many
people stacked up in front of him. He turned, holding his
nose, and staggered back into the church. He tried to yell to
the others, but when he opened his mouth, he sprayed a great
jet of puke instead. His feet tangled in each other and he fell,
knocking his head hard on the top of a pew. He tried to get
to his feet and could not do it. Then large hands thrust them-

selves into his armpits and pulled him up. "Out the window, Rev'rund!" Nan Roberts shouted. "Hoss y'freight!"

"The glass—"

"Never mind the glass! We're going to choke in here!"

She propelled him forward, and Rev. Rose just had time to throw a hand over his eyes before he shattered his way through a stained-glass window depicting Christ leading His sheep down a hill the exact color of lime Jell-O. He flew through the air, struck the lawn, and bounced. His upper plate shot from his mouth and he grunted.

He sat up, suddenly aware of the dark, the rain . . . and the blessed perfume of open air. He had no time to savor this; Nan Roberts grabbed him by the hair of his head and jerked him to his feet.

"Come on, Rev'rund!" she shouted. Her face, glimpsed in a blue-white flash of lightning, was the twisted face of a harpy. She was still wearing her white rayon uniform—she had always made it a habit to dress just as she had her waitresses dress—but the swell of her bosom was now wearing a bib of vomit.

Rev. Rose stumbled along beside her, head down. He wished she would let go of his hair, but each time he tried to say so, the thunder drowned him out.

A few others had followed them out the broken window, but most were still stacked up on the other side of the vestibule door. Nan saw why immediately; two crowbars had been propped under the handles. She kicked them aside as a bolt of lightning struck down on the Town Common, blowing the bandstand, where a tormented young man named Johnny Smith had once discovered the name of a killer, to flaming matchwood. Now the wind began to blow harder, whipping the trees against the dark, racing sky.

The moment the crowbars were gone, the doors flew open—one was torn entirely off its hinges and tumbled into the flowerbed on the left side of the steps. A flood of wild-eyed

Baptists poured out, stumbling and falling all over one another as they pelted down the church steps. They stank. They wept. They coughed. They vomited.

And they were all as mad as hell.

8

The Knights of Columbus, led by Father Brigham, and the Daughters of Isabella, led by Betsy Vigue, came together in the center of the parking lot as the skies opened and the rain began to drive down in buckets. Betsy groped for Father Brigham and held him, her red eyes streaming tears, her hair plastered against her skull in a wet, gleaming cap.

"There are others still inside!" she cried. "Naomi Jessup . . . 'Tonia Bissette . . . I don't know how many others!"

"Who was it?" Albert Gendron roared. "Who in the hell did it?"

"*Oh, it was the Baptists! Of course it was!*" Betsy screamed, and then she began to weep as lightning jumped across the sky like a white-hot tungsten filament. "*They called me a Pope whore! It was the Baptists! The Baptists! It was the God damned Baptists!*"

Father Brigham, meanwhile, had disengaged himself from Betsy and leaped to the door of the Daughters of Isabella Hall. He booted the crowbar aside—the door had splintered all around it in a circle—and yanked it open. Three dazed, retching women and a cloud of stinking smoke came out.

Through it he saw Antonia Bissette, pretty 'Tonia who was so quick and clever with her needle and always so eager to help out on any new church project. She lay on the floor near the Chairwoman's table, partly hidden by the overturned banner depicting the Infant of Prague. Naomi Jessup knelt beside her, wailing. 'Tonia's head was twisted at a weird, impossible angle. Her glazed eyes glared up at the ceiling. The stench had ceased to bother Antonia Bissette, who had not bought a single thing from Mr. Gaunt or participated in any of his little games.

Naomi saw Father Brigham standing in the doorway, got to her feet, and staggered toward him. In the depth of her shock, the smell of the stink-bomb no longer seemed to bother her, either. "Father," she cried. "Father, *why?* Why did they do this? It was only supposed to be a little fun . . . that was all it was supposed to be. *Why?*"

"Because that man is insane," Father Brigham said. He folded Naomi into his arms.

Beside him in a voice which was both low and deadly, Albert Gendron said: "Let's go get them."

9

The Baptist Anti-Gambling Christian Soldiers strode up Harrington Street from the Baptist Church in the pouring rain with Don Hemphill, Nan Roberts, Norman Harper, and William Rose in the forefront. Their eyes were reddened, furious orbs peering from puffy, irritated sockets. Most of the Christian Soldiers had vomit on their pants, their shirts, their shoes, or all three. The rotten-egg smell of the stink-bomb clung to them in spite of the sheeting rain, refusing to be washed away.

A State Police car stopped at the intersection of Harrington and Castle Avenue, which, half a mile farther up, became Castle View. A Trooper got out and gaped at them. "Hey!" he shouted. "Where do you folks think you're going?"

"We're gonna kick us some Pope-sucker butt, and if you know what's good for you, you'll stay the hell out of our way!" Nan Roberts shouted back at him.

Suddenly Don Hemphill opened his mouth and began to sing in a full, rich baritone voice.

"Onward, Christian soldiers, marching as to war—"

Others joined in. Soon the entire congregation had taken it

up and they began to move faster, not just walking now but marching to the beat. Their faces were pallid and angry and empty of all thought as they began not just to sing but to roar out the words. Rev. Rose sang along with them, although he lisped quite badly with his upper plate gone.

"Christ, the royal master, leads against the foe,
Forward into battle, see His banners go!"

Now they were almost running.

10

Trooper Morris stood beside the door of his car with his microphone in his hand, staring after them. Water ran from the waterproof over the brim of his Smokey Bear hat in little streamlets.

"Come back, Unit Sixteen," Henry Payton's voice crackled.

"You better get some men up here right away!" Morris cried. His voice was both scared and excited. He had been a State Trooper for less than a year. "Something's going down! Something bad! A crowd of about seventy people just walked past me! Ten-four!"

"Well, what were they doing?" Payton asked. "Ten-four."

"They were singing 'Onward Christian Soldiers'! Ten-four!"

"Is that you, Morris? Ten-four."

"Yessir! Ten-four!"

"Well, so far as I know, Trooper Morris, there is still no law against singing hymns, even in the pouring rain. I believe it to be a stupid activity but not an illegal one. Now I only want to say this once: I've got about four different messes on my hands, I don't know where the Sheriff or any of his goddam deputies are, *and I don't want to be bothered with trivialities! Do you copy this? Ten-four!*"

Trooper Morris swallowed hard. "Uh, yessir, I copy, I sure do, but someone in the crowd—it was a woman, I think—said they were going to, uh, 'kick us some Pope-sucker butt' is how I believe she put it. I know that doesn't make a whole lot of sense, but I didn't much like the sound of it." Then Morris added timidly: "Ten-four?"

The silence was so long Morris was about to try Payton again—the electricity in the air had made long-range radio communication impossible and even in-town chatter difficult—and then Payton said in a weary, frightened voice, "Aw. Aw, Jesus. Aw, Jesus Tiddlywinks *Christ.* What's going on here?"

"Well, the lady said they were going to—"

"I heard you the first time!" Payton yelled it so loudly that his voice distorted and broke up. "Get over to the Catholic Church! If something's happening, try to break it up but don't get hurt. I repeat, *don't get hurt.* I'll send backup as soon as I can—if I have any backup left. Do it now! Ten-four!"

"Uh, Lieutenant Payton? Where *is* the Catholic Church in this town?"

"How the fuck should I know?" Payton screamed. *"I don't worship there! Just follow the crowd! Ten-forty out!"*

Morris hung up the mike. He could no longer *see* the crowd, but he could still hear them between the thunderclaps. He put the cruiser in gear and followed the singing.

11

The path which led up to the kitchen door of Myra Evans's house was lined with rocks painted in various pastel colors.

Cora Rusk picked up a blue one and bounced it in the hand which was not holding her gun, testing its weight. She tried the door. It was locked, as she had expected. She tossed the rock through the glass and used the barrel of her pistol to clear away the shards and splinters still clinging to the frame. Then she reached through, unlocked the door, and stepped inside. Her hair clung to her cheeks in wet snaggles and commas. Her dress still gaped open, and droplets of rainwater ran down the pimple-studded swells of her breasts.

Chuck Evans wasn't home, but Garfield, Chuck and Myra's Angora cat, was. He came trotting into the kitchen, miaowing, hoping for food, and Cora let him have it. The cat flew backward in a cloud of blood and fur. "Eat *that,* Garfield," Cora remarked. She strode through the puff of gunsmoke and into the hall. She started up the stairs. She knew where she would find the slut. She would find her in bed. Cora knew that as well as she knew her own name.

"It's bedtime, all right," she said. "You just want to believe it, Myra my dear."

Cora was smiling.

12

Father Brigham and Albert Gendron led a platoon of pissed-off Catholics down Castle Avenue toward Harrington Street. Halfway there, they heard singing. The two men exchanged a glance.

"Do you think we might be able to teach em a different tune, Albert?" Father Brigham asked softly.

"I think so, Father," Albert replied.

"Shall we teach them to sing 'I Ran All the Way Home'?"

"A very good tune, Father. I think maybe even muck like them might be able to learn that one."

Lightning flew across the sky. It illuminated Castle Avenue with momentary brilliance, and showed the two men a small crowd advancing up the hill toward them. Their eyes gleamed white and empty, like the eyes of statues, in the lightning-flash.

"There they are!" someone shouted, and a woman cried: "Get the dirty Mickey Finn sons of bitches!"

"Let's bag some trash," Father John Brigham breathed happily, and charged the Baptists.

"Amen, Father," Albert said, running at his side.

They *all* began to run then.

As Trooper Morris rounded the corner, a fresh bolt of lightning jigged across the sky, felling one of the old elms by Castle Stream. In the glare, he saw two mobs of people running toward each other. One mob was running up the hill, the other mob was running down, and both mobs were screaming for blood. Trooper Morris suddenly found himself wishing he had called in sick that afternoon.

13

Cora opened the door of Chuck and Myra's bedroom and saw exactly what she had expected: the bitch lying naked in a rumpled double bed which looked as if it had seen a hard tour of duty lately. One of her hands was behind her, tucked under the pillows. The other held a framed picture. The picture was between Myra's meaty thighs. She appeared to be humping it. Her eyes were half-closed in ecstasy.

"Oooh, E!" she moaned. "Ooooh, E! *OOOHH, EEEE-EEEEEEE!*"

Horrified jealousy flared in Cora's heart and rose up her throat until she could taste its bitter juice in her mouth.

"Oh you shithouse mouse," she breathed, and brought up the automatic.

At that moment Myra looked at her, and Myra was smiling. She brought her free hand out from under her pillow. In it she held an automatic pistol of her own.

"Mr. Gaunt *said* you'd come, Cora," she said, and fired.

Cora felt the bullet beat the air beside her cheek; heard it thud into the plaster on the left side of the door. She fired her own gun. It struck the picture between Myra's legs, shattering the glass and burying itself in Myra's upper thigh.

It also left a bullet-hole in the center of Elvis Presley's forehead.

"Look what you did!" Myra shrieked. *"You shot The King, you stupid cunt!"*

She fired three shots at Cora. Two went wild but the third hit Cora in the throat, driving her backward against the wall in a pink spray of blood. As Cora collapsed to her knees, she fired again. The bullet punched a hole in Myra's kneecap and knocked her out of bed. Then Cora fell face-forward onto the floor, the gun slipping from her hand.

I'm coming to you, Elvis, she tried to say, but something was terribly, terribly wrong. There seemed to be only darkness, and no one in it but her.

14

Castle Rock's Baptists, led by the Rev. William Rose, and Castle Rock's Catholics, led by Father John Brigham, came together near the foot of Castle Hill with an almost audible crunch. There was no polite fist-fighting, no Marquis of Queensberry rules; they had come to gouge out eyes and tear off noses. Quite possibly to kill.

Albert Gendron, the huge dentist who was slow to anger but terrible once his wrath was roused, grabbed Norman Harper by the ears and jerked Norman's head forward. He brought his own head forward at the same time. Their skulls crashed together with a sound like crockery in an earthquake. Norman shuddered, then went limp. Albert threw him aside like a bag of laundry and grabbed for Bill Sayers, who sold tools at the Western Auto. Bill dodged, then threw a punch. Albert took it squarely on the mouth, spat a tooth, grabbed Bill in a bear-hug, and squeezed until he heard a rib snap. Bill began to shriek. Albert threw him most of the way across the street, where Trooper Morris stopped just in time to avoid running him down.

The area was now a tangle of struggling, punching, gouging, yelling figures. They tripped each other, they slipped in the rain, they got up again, they hit out and were hit in return. The gaudy splashes of lightning made it seem that some weird dance was going on, one where you threw your partner into the nearest tree instead of allemanding her, or dug your knee into his crotch instead of doing a do-si-do.

Nan Roberts grabbed Betsy Vigue by the back of the dress as Betsy tore tattoos into Lucille Dunham's cheeks with her nails. Nan yanked Betsy toward her, whirled her around, and poked two of her fingers up Betsy's nose all the way to the second knuckles. Betsy uttered a nasal foghorn screech as Nan began to shake her enthusiastically back and forth by her nose.

Frieda Pulaski belted Nan with her pocket-book. Nan was driven to her knees. Her fingers came out of Betsy Vigue's nose with an audible pop. When she tried to get up, Betsy kicked her in the face and knocked her sprawling in the middle of the street. "You bidch, you wregged by dodze!" Betsy shrieked. "You wregged by *DODZE!*" She tried to stamp her foot down into Nan's belly. Nan grabbed her foot, twisted her, and dumped the once-upon-a-time Betty La-La face-first into the street. Nan crawled to her; Betsy was waiting; a moment later they were both rolling over and over in the street, biting and scratching.

"STOP!!!"

Trooper Morris bellowed, but his voice was drowned out in a volley of thunder which shook the entire street.

He pulled his gun, raised it skyward . . . but before he could fire, someone—God only knows who—shot him in the crotch with one of Leland Gaunt's special sale items. Trooper Morris flew backward against the hood of his cruiser and rolled into

the street, clutching the ruins of his sexual equipment and trying to scream.

It was impossible to tell just how many of the combatants
had brought weapons purchased from Mr. Gaunt that day. Not
many, and some of those who *had* been armed had lost the au-
tomatics in the confusion of trying to escape the stink-bombs.
But at least four more shots were fired in rapid succession,
shots that were largely overlooked in the confusion of shouting
voices and booming thunder.

Len Milliken saw Jake Pulaski aiming one of the guns at
Nan, who had allowed Betsy to get away and was now trying to
choke Meade Rossignol. Len grabbed Jake's wrist and forced it
upward into the lightning-dazzled sky a second before the gun
went off. Then he brought Jake's wrist down and snapped it
over his knee like a stick of kindling wood. The gun clattered
onto the wet street. Jake began to howl. Len stepped back and
said, "That'll teach you to—" He got no further, for someone
chose that moment to sink the blade of a pocket-knife into the
nape of his neck, severing Len's spinal cord at the brain-stem.

Other police-cars were arriving now, their blue lights swinging crazily in the rain-swept dark. The combatants did not
heed the amplified yells to cease and desist. When the Troopers
attempted to break things up, they found themselves sucked
into the brawl instead.

Nan Roberts saw Father Brigham, his damned black shirt
split right up the back. He was holding Rev. Rose by the nape
of the neck with one hand. His other hand was rolled up into a
tight fist, and he was popping Rev. Rose repeatedly in the nose
with it. His fist would slam home, the hand holding the nape
of Rev. Rose's neck would rock backward a little, and then it
would haul Rev. Rose back into position for the next blow.

Bellowing at the top of her lungs, ignoring the confused
State Trooper who was telling her—almost begging her—to
stop and stop *right now,* Nan slung away Meade Rossignol and
launched herself at Father Brigham.

CHAPTER TWENTY-TWO

1

The onslaught of the storm slowed Alan down to a crawl in spite of his growing feeling that time had become vitally, bitterly important, and that if he didn't get back to Castle Rock soon, he might just as well stay away forever. Much of the information he had really needed, it seemed to him now, had been in his mind all along, locked up behind a stout door. The door had a legend printed neatly on it—but not OFFICE OF THE PRESIDENT or BOARD ROOM or even PRIVATE DO NOT ENTER. The legend printed on the door in Alan's mind had been THIS MAKES NO SENSE. All he'd needed to unlock it was the right key . . . the key which Sean Rusk had given him. And what was behind the door?

Why, Needful Things. And its proprietor, Mr. Leland Gaunt.

Brian Rusk had bought a baseball card in Needful Things, and Brian was dead. Nettie Cobb had bought a lampshade in Needful Things, and *she* was dead, too. How many others in Castle Rock had gone to the well and bought poisoned water from the poison man? Norris had—a fishing rod. Polly had—a magic charm. Brian Rusk's mother had—a pair of cheap sunglasses that had something to do with Elvis Presley. Even Ace Merrill had—an old book. Alan was willing to bet that Hugh Priest had also made a purchase . . . and Danforth Keeton . . .

How many others? How many?

He pulled up on the far side of the Tin Bridge just as a bolt of lightning stroked down from the sky and severed one of the old elms on the other side of Castle Stream. There was a huge electrical crackle and a wild streak of brilliance. Alan threw an arm across his eyes, but an afterimage was still printed on them in stark blue as the radio uttered a loud blurt of static and the elm toppled with ponderous grandeur into the stream.

He dropped his arm, then yelled as thunder bellowed directly overhead, sounding loud enough to crack the world. For a moment his dazzled eyes could make out nothing and he was afraid the tree might have fallen on the bridge, blocking his way into town. Then he saw it lying just upstream of the rusty old structure, buried in a loom of rapids. Alan put the cruiser in gear and made the crossing. As he did, he could hear the wind, which was now blowing a gale, hooting in the struts and girders of the bridge. It was a creepy, lonely sound.

Rain pelted against the old station wagon's windshield, turning everything beyond it into a wavering hallucination. As Alan came off the bridge and onto Lower Main Street at its intersection with Watermill Lane, the rain began to come so hard that the wipers, even on fast speed, were entirely useless. He unrolled his window, stuck his head out, and drove that way. He was instantly soaked.

The area around the Municipal Building was loaded with police cars and newsvans, but it also had a weird, deserted look, as if the people who belonged to all these vehicles had suddenly been teleported to the planet Neptune by evil aliens. Alan saw a few newspeople peering out from the shelter of their vans, and one State cop ran down the alley which led to the Municipal Building's parking lot, rainwater spatting up from his shoes, but that was all.

Three blocks up, toward Castle Hill, an S.P. cruiser shot across Upper Main at high speed, heading west along Laurel Street. A moment later, another cruiser shot across Main. This one was on Birch Street and headed in the opposite direction from the first. It happened so fast—zip, zip—that it was like something you'd see in a comedy movie about bumbling police. *Smokey and the Bandit,* perhaps. Alan, however, saw nothing funny in it. It gave him a sense of action without purpose, a kind of panicky, helter-skelter movement. He was suddenly sure that Henry Payton had lost control of whatever was happening in Castle Rock tonight . . . if he'd ever had anything more than an illusion of control in the first place, that was.

He thought he could hear faint cries coming from the direction of Castle Hill. With the rain, thunder, and driving wind it was hard to tell for sure, but he did not think those cries were just imagination. As if to prove this, a State Police car roared out of the alley next to the Municipal Building, flashing headlights and whirling domelights illuminating silvery streaks of rain, and headed in that direction. It nearly sideswiped an oversized WMTW newswagon in the process.

Alan remembered feeling, earlier this week, that there was something badly out of joint in his little town—that things he could not see were going wrong and Castle Rock was trembling on the edge of some unthinkable disorder. And now the disorder had come, and it had all been planned by the man

(Brian said Mr. Gaunt wasn't really a man at all)

Alan had never quite managed to see.

A scream rose in the night, high and drilling. It was followed by the sound of shattering glass . . . and then, from somewhere else, a gunshot and a burst of cracked, idiot laughter. Thunder banged in the sky like a pile of dropped boards.

But I have time now, Alan thought. Yes. Plenty of time. Mr. Gaunt, I think we ought to say hello to each other, and I think it's high time you found out what happens to people who fuck with my town.

Ignoring the faint sounds of chaos and violence he heard through his open window, ignoring the Municipal Building where Henry Payton was presumably coordinating the forces of law and order—or trying to—Alan drove up Main Street toward Needful Things.

As he did, a violent white-purple bolt of lightning flared across the sky like an electric firetree, and while the accompanying cannonade of thunder was still roaring overhead, all the lights in Castle Rock went out.

2

Deputy Norris Ridgewick, clad in the uniform he kept for parades and other dress occasions, was in the shed attached to the little house he had shared with his mother until she died of a stroke in the fall of 1986, the house where he had lived alone since then. He was standing on a stool. A heavy length of noosed rope hung down from one of the overhead beams. Norris ran his head into this noose and was pulling it tight against his right ear when lightning flashed and the two electric bulbs which lit the shed winked out.

Still, he could see the Bazun fishing rod leaning against the wall by the door which led into the kitchen. He had wanted that fishing rod so badly and had believed he had gotten it so cheaply, but in the end the price had been high. Too high for Norris to pay.

His house was on the upper arm of Watermill Lane, where the Lane hooks back toward Castle Hill and the View. The wind was right, and he could hear the sounds of the brawl which was still going on there—the screams, the yells, the occasional gunshot.

I'm responsible for that, he thought. Not completely—hell, no—but I'm a part of it. I participated. I'm the reason Henry Beaufort is hurt or dying, maybe even dead over in Oxford. I'm the reason Hugh Priest is on a cooling-board. Me. The fellow who always wanted to be a policeman and help folks, the fellow who wanted that ever since he was a kid. Stupid, funny, clumsy old Norris Ridgewick, who thought he needed a Bazun fishing rod and could get one cheap.

"I'm sorry for what I did," Norris said. "That doesn't fix it, but for whatever it's worth, I'm *real* sorry."

He prepared to jump off the stool, and suddenly a new voice spoke up inside his head. *Then why don't you try to put it right, you chickenshit coward?*

"I can't," Norris said. Lightning blazed; his shadow jumped crazily on the shed wall, as if he were already doing the airdance. "It's too late."

Then at least take a look at what you did it FOR, the angry voice insisted. *You can do that much, can't you? Take a look! Take a really GOOD look!*

The lightning flashed again. Norris stared at the Bazun rod . . . and let out a scream of agony and disbelief. He jerked, almost tumbling off the stool and hanging himself by accident.

The sleek Bazun, so limber and strong, was no longer there. It had been replaced by a dirty, splintery bamboo pole, really no more than a stick with a kid's Zebco reel attached to it by one rusty screw.

"Someone stole it!" Norris cried. All of his bitter jealousy and paranoid covetousness returned in a flash, and he felt that he must rush out into the streets and find the thief. He must kill them all, everyone in town, if that was necessary, to get the evil man or woman responsible. *"SOMEONE STOLE MY BAZUN!"* he wailed again, swaying on the stool.

No, the angry voice replied. *This is how it always was. All that's been stolen is your blinders—the ones you put on yourself, of your own free will.*

"No!" Monstrous hands seemed to be clapped against the sides of Norris's head; now they began to squeeze. "No, no, *no!*"

But the lightning flashed, again showing him the dirty bamboo rod where the Bazun had been only moments before. He had put it there so it would be the last thing he ever saw when he stepped off the stool. No one had been in here; no one had moved it; consequently the voice had to be right.

This is how it always was, the angry voice insisted. *The only question is this: are you going to do something about it, or are you going to run away into the darkness?*

He began to grope for the noose, and at that moment he sensed he was not alone in the shed. In that moment he seemed to smell tobacco and coffee and some faint cologne—Southern Gentleman, perhaps—the smells of Mr. Gaunt.

Either he lost his balance or angry, invisible hands pushed him from the stool. One foot clipped it as he swayed outward and knocked it over.

Norris's shout was choked off as the slip-knot pulled tight. One flailing hand found the overhead beam and caught it. He yanked himself partway up, providing himself with some slack. His other hand clawed at the noose. He could feel hemp pricking at his throat.

No is right! he heard Mr. Gaunt cry out angrily. *No is exactly right, you damned welsher!*

He wasn't here, not really; Norris knew he hadn't been pushed. Yet he felt a complete certainty that part of Mr. Gaunt *was* here just the same . . . and Mr. Gaunt was not pleased, because this was not the way it was supposed to go. The suckers were supposed to see *nothing.* Not, at least, until it was too late to matter.

He yanked and clawed at the noose, but it was as if the slip-knot had been dipped in concrete. The arm which was holding him up trembled wildly. His feet scissored back and forth three feet above the floor. He could not hold this half-chin-up much longer. It was amazing he had been able to keep any slack in the rope at all.

At last he managed to wiggle two of his fingers under the noose and pull it partway open. He shook his head out of it just as a horrible, numbing cramp struck the arm that was holding him up. He toppled to the floor in a sobbing heap, holding his cramped arm to his chest. Lightning flew and turned the spit on his bared teeth into tiny purple arcs of light. He grayed out then . . . for how long he didn't know, but the rain was still pelting and the lightning was still flashing when his mind swam back into itself.

He staggered to his feet and walked over to the fishing pole, still holding his arm. The cramp was beginning to loosen now, but Norris was still panting. He seized the pole and examined it closely and angrily.

Bamboo. Dirty, filthy bamboo. It wasn't worth everything; it was worth *nothing*.

Norris's thin chest hitched in breath, and he uttered a scream of shame and rage. At the same moment he raised his knee and snapped the fishing rod over it. He doubled the pieces and snapped them again. They felt nasty—almost germy—in his hands. They felt *fraudulent*. He cast them aside and they rattled to a stop by the overturned stool like so many meaningless pick-up sticks.

"There!" he cried. "There! *There! THERE!*"

Norris's thoughts turned to Mr. Gaunt. Mr. Gaunt with his silver hair and his tweed and his hungry, jostling smile.

"I'm going to get you," Norris Ridgewick whispered. "I don't know what happens after that, but I am going to get you *so* good."

He walked to the shed door, yanked it open, and stepped out into the pouring rain. Unit 2 was parked in the driveway. He bent his thin Barney Fife body into the wind and walked over to it.

"I dunno what you are," Norris said, "but I'm coming for your lying, conning ass."

He got into the cruiser and backed down the driveway. Humiliation, misery, and anger were equally at war on his face. At the foot of the driveway he turned left and began driving toward Needful Things as fast as he dared.

3

Polly Chalmers was dreaming.

In her dream she was walking into Needful Things, but the figure behind the counter was not Leland Gaunt; it was Aunt Evvie Chalmers. Aunt Evvie was wearing her best blue dress and her blue shawl, the one with the red edging. Gripped between her large and improbably even false teeth was a Herbert Tareyton.

Aunt Evvie! Polly cried in her dream. A vast delight and an even vaster relief—that relief we only know in happy dreams, and in the moment of waking from horrid ones—filled her like light. *Aunt Evvie, you're alive!*

But Aunt Evvie showed no sign of recognition. *Buy anything you want, Miss,* Aunt Evvie said. *By the way—was your name Polly or Patricia? I disremember, somehow.*

Aunt Evvie, you know my name—I'm Trisha. I've always been Trisha to you.

Aunt Evvie took no notice. *Whatever your name is, we're having a special today. Everything must go.*

Aunt Evvie, what are you doing here?

I BELONG here, Aunt Evvie said. *Everyone in town belongs here, Miss Two-Names. In fact, everyone in the WORLD belongs here, because everyone loves a bargain. Everyone loves something for nothing . . . even if it costs everything.*

The good feeling was suddenly gone. Dread replaced it. Polly looked into the glass cases and saw bottles of dark fluid marked DR. GAUNT'S ELECTRIC TONIC. There were badly made wind-up toys that would cough up their cogs and spit out their springs the second time they were wound. There were crude sex-toys. There were small bottles of what looked like cocaine; these were labelled DR. GAUNT'S KICKAPOO POTENCY POWDER. Cheap novelties abounded: plastic dog-puke, itching powder, cigarette loads, joy buzzers. There was a pair of those X-ray glasses that were supposed to allow you to look through closed doors and ladies' dresses but actually did nothing except put raccoon rings around your eyes. There were plastic flowers and marked playing cards and bottles of cheap perfume labelled DR. GAUNT'S LOVE POTION #9, TURNS LASSITUDE INTO LUST. The cases were a catalogue of the timeless, the tasteless, and the useless.

Anything you want, Miss Two-Names, Aunt Evvie said.

Why are you calling me that, Aunt Evvie? Please—don't you recognize me?

It's all guaranteed to work. The only thing not guaranteed to work after the sale is YOU. *So step right up and buy, buy, buy.*

Now she looked directly at Polly, and Polly was struck through with terror like a knife. She saw compassion in Aunt Evvie's eyes, but it was a terrible, merciless compassion.

What IS your name, child? Seems to me I once knew.

In her dream (and in her bed) Polly began to weep.

Has someone else forgotten your name? Aunt Evvie asked. *I wonder. Seems like they have.*

Aunt Evvie, you're scaring me!

You're scaring yourself, child, Aunt Evvie responded, looking directly at Polly for the first time. *Just remember that when you buy here, Miss Two-Names, you're also selling.*

But I need it! Polly cried. She began to weep harder. *My hands—!*

Yes, this does it, Miss Polly Frisco, Aunt Evvie said, and brought out one of the bottles marked DR. GAUNT'S ELECTRIC TONIC. She set it on the counter, a small, squat bottle filled with something that looked like loose mud. *It can't make your pain gone, of course—nothing can do that—but it can effect a transferral.*

What do you mean? Why are you scaring me?

It changes the location of your arthritis, Miss Two-Names— instead of your hands, the disease attacks your heart.

No!

Yes.

No! No! NO!

Yes. Oh yes. And your soul as well. But you'll have your pride. That'll be left to you, at least. And isn't a woman entitled to her pride? When everything else is gone—heart, soul, even the man you love—you'll have that, little Miss Polly Frisco, won't you? You'll have that one coin without which your purse would be empty. Let it be your dark and bitter comfort for the rest of your life. Let it serve. It MUST serve, because if you keep on the way you're going, there surely won't be no other.

Stop, please, can't you—

4

"Stop," she muttered in her sleep. "Please stop. *Please.*"

She rolled over on her side. The *azka* chinked softly against its chain. Lightning lit up the sky, striking the elm by Castle Stream, toppling it into the rushing water as Alan Pangborn sat behind the wheel of his station wagon, dazzled by the flash.

The follow-shot crack of thunder woke Polly up. Her eyes flew open. Her hand went to the *azka* at once and closed protectively around it. The hand was limber; the joints moved as easily as ball bearings packed in deep clean oil.

Miss Two-Names . . . little Miss Polly Frisco.

"What . . . ?" Her voice was thick, but her mind already felt clear and alert, as if she hadn't been asleep at all but in a daze of thought so deep it was nearly a trance. Something was looming in her mind, something the size of a whale. Outside, lightning flashed and flickered across the sky like bright purple sparklers.

Has someone else forgotten your name? . . . Seems like they have.

She reached for the night-table and switched on the lamp. Lying next to the Princess phone, the phone equipped with the oversized keypads which she no longer needed, was the envelope she had found lying in the hall with the rest of the mail when she returned home this afternoon. She had re-folded the terrible letter and slid it back inside.

Somewhere in the night, between the racketing bursts of thunder, she thought she could hear people shouting. Polly ignored them; she was thinking about the cuckoo bird, which lays its egg in a strange nest while the owner is away. When the mother-to-be returns, does she notice that something new has been added? Of course not; she simply accepts it as her own. The way Polly had accepted this goddamned letter simply because it happened to be lying on the hall floor with two catalogues and a come-on from Western Maine Cable TV.

She had just accepted it . . . but *anyone* could drop a letter through a mail-slot, wasn't that true?

"Miss Two-Names," she murmured in a dismayed voice. "Little Miss Polly Frisco." And that was the thing, wasn't it? The thing her subconscious had remembered and had manufactured Aunt Evvie to tell her. She *had* been Miss Polly Frisco.

Once upon a time, she had.

She reached for the envelope.

No! a voice told her, and that was a voice she knew very well. *Don't touch that, Polly—not if you know what's good for you!*

Pain as dark and strong as day-old coffee flared deep in her hands.

It can't make your pain gone . . . but it can effect a transferral.

That whale-sized thing was coming to the surface. Mr. Gaunt's voice couldn't stop it; nothing could stop it.

YOU can stop it, Polly, Mr. Gaunt said. *Believe me, you MUST.*

Her hand drew back before it touched the letter. It returned to the *azka* and became a protective fist around it. She could feel something inside it, something which had been warmed by her heat, scurrying frantically inside the hollow silver amulet, and revulsion filled her, making her stomach feel weak and loose, her bowels rotten.

She let go and reached for the letter again.

Last warning, Polly, the voice of Mr. Gaunt told her.

Yes, Aunt Evvie's voice replied. *I think he means it, Trisha. He has always so enjoyed ladies who take pride in themselves, but do you know what? I don't think he's got much use for those who decide it goeth before a fall. I think the time has come for you to decide, once and for all, what your name* REALLY *is.*

She took hold of the envelope, ignoring another warning twinge in her hands, and looked at the neatly typed address. This letter—*purported* letter, *purported* Xerox—had been sent to "Ms. Patricia Chalmers."

"No," she whispered. "Wrong. Wrong *name.*" Her hand closed slowly and steadily on the letter, crumpling it. A dull ache filled her fist, but Polly ignored it. Her eyes were bright, feverish. "I was always Polly in San Francisco—I was Polly to everyone, *even to Child Welfare!*"

That had been part of her attempt to break clean with every aspect of the old life which she fancied had hurt her so badly, never in her darkest nights allowing herself to dream that most of the wounds had been self-inflicted. In San Francisco there had been no Trisha or Patricia; only Polly. She had filled out all three of her ADC applications that way, and had signed her name that way—as Polly Chalmers, no middle initial.

If Alan really *had* written to the Child Welfare people in San Francisco, she supposed he might have given her name as Patricia, but wouldn't any resulting records search have come up blank? Yes, of course. Not even the addresses would correlate, because the one she'd printed in the space for ADDRESS OF LAST RESIDENCE all those years ago had been her parents' address, and that was on the other side of town.

Suppose Alan gave them both names? Polly and *Patricia?*

Suppose he had? She knew enough about the workings of government bureaucracies to believe it didn't matter what name or names *Alan* had given them; when writing to her, the letter would have come to the name and address they had on file. Polly had a friend in Oxford whose correspondence from the University of Maine still came addressed to her maiden name, although she had been married for twenty years.

But this envelope had come addressed to *Patricia* Chalmers, not Polly Chalmers. And who in Castle Rock had called her Patricia just today?

The same person who had known that Nettie Cobb was really Netitia Cobb. Her good friend Leland Gaunt.

All of that about the names is interestin, Aunt Evvie said suddenly, *but it ain't really the important thing. The important thing is the man—YOUR man. He IS your man, ain't he? Even now. You know he would never go behind your back like that letter said he done. Don't matter what name was on it or how convincing it might sound . . . you KNOW that, don't you?*

"Yes," she whispered. "I know *him.*"

Had she really believed *any* of it? Or had she put her doubts about that absurd, unbelievable letter aside because she was afraid—in terror, actually—that Alan would see the nasty truth of the *azka* and force her to make a choice between him and it?

"Oh no—that's too simple," she whispered. "You believed it, all right. Only for half a day, but you did *believe* it. Oh Jesus. Oh Jesus, what have I done?"

She tossed the crumpled letter onto the floor with the revolted expression of a woman who has just realized she's holding a dead rat.

I didn't tell him what I was angry about; didn't give him a chance to explain; just . . . just BELIEVED it. Why? In God's name, WHY?

She knew, of course. It had been the sudden, shameful fear that her lies about the cause of Kelton's death had been discovered, the misery of her years in San Francisco suspected, her culpability in the death of her baby being evaluated . . . and all this by the one man in the world whose good opinion she wanted and needed.

But that wasn't all of it. That wasn't even most of it. Mostly it had been pride—wounded, outraged, throbbing, swollen, malignant pride. Pride, the coin without which her purse would be entirely empty. She had believed because she had been in a panic of shame, a shame which had been born of pride.

I have always so *enjoyed ladies who take pride in themselves.*

A terrible wave of pain broke in her hands; Polly moaned and held them against her breasts.

Not too late, Polly, Mr. Gaunt said softly. *Not too late, even now.*

"Oh, fuck pride!" Polly shrieked suddenly into the dark of her closed, stuffy bedroom, and ripped the *azka* from her neck. She held it high overhead in her clenched fist, the fine silver chain whipping wildly, and she felt the surface of the charm crack like the shell of an egg inside her hand. *"FUCK PRIDE!"*

Pain instantly clawed its way into her hands like some small and hungry animal . . . but she knew even then that the pain was not as great as she had feared; nowhere near as great as she had feared. She knew it as surely as she knew that Alan had never written to Child Welfare in San Francisco, asking about her.

"FUCK PRIDE! FUCK IT! FUCK IT! FUCK IT!" she screamed, and threw the *azka* across the room.

It hit the wall, bounced to the floor, and split open. Lightning flashed, and she saw two hairy legs poke out through the crack. The crack widened, and what crawled out was a small spider. It scuttered toward the bathroom. Lightning flashed again, printing its elongated, ovate shadow on the floor like an electric tattoo.

Polly leaped from her bed and chased after it. She had to kill it, and quickly . . . because even as she watched, the spider was swelling. It had been feeding on the poison it had sucked out of her body, and now that it was free of its containment, there was no telling how big it might grow.

She slapped the bathroom light-switch, and the fluorescent over the sink flickered into life. She saw the spider scurrying toward the tub. When it went through the door, it had been no bigger than a beetle. Now it was the size of a mouse.

As she came in, it turned and scurried toward her—that horrid clittering sound of its legs beating against the tiles— and she had time to think, It was between my breasts, it was lying AGAINST me, it was lying against me ALL THE TIME—

Its body was a bristly blackish-brown. Tiny hairs stood out on its legs. Eyes as dull as fake rubies stared at her . . . and she saw that two fangs stuck out of its mouth like curved vampire teeth. They were dripping some clear liquid. Where the droplets struck the tiles, they left small, smoking craters.

Polly screamed and grabbed the bathroom plunger which stood beside the toilet. Her hands screamed back at her, but she closed them around the plunger's wooden handle just the same and struck the spider with it. It retreated, one of its legs now broken and hanging uselessly askew. Polly chased after it as it ran for the tub.

Hurt or not, it was still growing. Now it was the size of a rat. Its bulging belly had dragged against the tiles, but it went up the shower-curtain with weird agility. Its legs made a sound against the plastic like tiny spats of water. The rings jingled on the steel bar running overhead.

Polly swung the plunger like a baseball bat, the heavy rubber cup whooshing through the air, and struck the horrid thing again. The rubber cup covered a lot of area but was not, unfortunately, very effective when it connected. The shower-curtain billowed inward and the spider dropped off into the tub with a meaty plop.

In that instant the light went out.

Polly stood in the dark, the plunger in her hand, and listened to the spider scurrying. Then the lightning flashed again and she could see its humped, bristly back protruding over the lip of the tub. The thing which had come out of the thimble-sized *azka* was as big as a cat now—the thing which had been nourishing itself on her heart's blood even as it abstracted the pain from her hands.

The envelope I left out at the old Camber place—what was that?

With the *azka* no longer around her neck, with the pain awake and yelling in her hands, she could no longer tell herself it had nothing to do with Alan.

The spider's fangs clicked on the porcelain edge of the tub. It sounded like someone clicking a penny deliberately on a hard surface for attention. Its listless doll's eyes now regarded her over the lip of the tub.

It's too late, those eyes seemed to say. *Too late for Alan, too late for you. Too late for everyone.*

Polly launched herself at it.

"What did you make me do?" she screamed. *"What did you make me do? Oh you monster, WHAT DID YOU MAKE ME DO?"*

And the spider rose up on its rear legs, pawing obscenely at the shower-curtain for balance with its front ones, to meet her attack.

5

Ace Merrill began to respect the old dude a little when Keeton produced a key which opened the locked shed with the red diamond-shaped HIGH EXPLOSIVES signs on the door. He began to respect him a little more when he felt the chilly air, heard the steady low whoosh of the air conditioner, and saw the stacked crates. Commercial dynamite. Lots of commercial dynamite. It wasn't quite the same thing as having an arsenal filled with Stinger missiles, but it was close enough for rock and roll. My, yes.

There had been a powerful eight-cell flashlight in the carry-compartment between the van's front seats, along with a supply of other useful tools, and now—as Alan neared Castle Rock in his station wagon, as Norris Ridgewick sat in his kitchen, fashioning a hangman's noose with a length of stout hemp rope, as Polly Chalmers's dream of Aunt Evvie moved toward its conclusion—Ace ran the flashlight's bright spotlight from one crate to the next. Overhead, the rain drummed on the shed's roof. It was coming down so hard that Ace could almost believe he was back in the prison showers.

"Let's get on with it," Buster said in a low, hoarse voice.

"Just a minute, Dad," Ace said. "It's break-time." He handed Buster the flashlight and took out the plastic bag Mr. Gaunt had given him. He tipped a little pile of coke into the snuff-hollow on his left hand, and snorted it quickly.

"What's that?" Buster asked suspiciously.

"South American bingo-dust, and it's just as tasty as taters."

"Huh," Keeton snorted. "Cocaine. They sell cocaine."

Ace didn't have to ask who They were. The old dude had talked about nothing else on the ride up here, and Ace suspected he would talk about nothing else all night.

"Not true, Dad," Ace said. "They don't sell it; They're the ones who want it all to Themselves." He tipped a little more into the snuff-hollow at the base of his thumb and held his hand out. "Try it and tell me I'm wrong."

Keeton looked at him with a mixture of doubt, curiosity, and suspicion. "Why do you keep calling me Dad? I'm not *old* enough to be your dad."

"Well, I doubt if you ever read the underground comics, but there is this guy named R. Crumb," Ace said. The coke was at work in him now, sparking all his nerve-endings alight. "He does these comics about a guy named Zippy. And to me, you look just like Zippy's Dad."

"Is that good?" Buster asked suspiciously.

"Awesome," Ace assured him. "But I'll call you Mr. Keeton, if you want." He paused and then added deliberately, "Just like They do."

"No," Buster said at once, "that's all right. As long as it's not an insult."

"Absolutely not," Ace said. "Go on—try it. A little of *this* shit and you'll be singing 'Heigh ho, heigh ho, it's off to work we go' until the break of dawn."

Buster gave him another look of dark suspicion, then snorted the coke Ace had offered. He coughed, sneezed, then clapped a hand to his nose. His watering eyes stared balefully at Ace. "It *burns!*"

"Only the first time," Ace assured him happily.

"Anyway, I don't feel a thing. Let's stop fooling around and get this dynamite into the van."

"You bet, Dad."

It took them less than ten minutes to load the crates of dynamite. After they had put the last one in, Buster said: "Maybe that stuff of yours *does* do something, after all. Can I have a little more?"

"Sure, Dad." Ace grinned. "I'll join you."

They tooted up and headed back to town. Buster drove, and now he began to look not like Zippy's Dad but Mr. Toad in Walt Disney's *The Wind in the Willows*. A new, frantic light had come into the Head Selectman's eyes. It was amazing how fast the confusion had dropped out of his mind; he now felt he could understand everything They had been up to—every plan, every plot, every machination. He told Ace all about it as Ace sat in the back of the van with his legs crossed, hooking up Hotpoint timers to blasting caps. For the time being at least, Buster had forgotten all about Alan Pangborn, who was Their ringleader. He was entranced by the idea of blowing Castle Rock—or as much of it as possible—to kingdom come.

Ace's respect became solid admiration. The old fuck was crazy, and Ace *liked* crazy people—always had. He felt at home with them. And, like most people on their first cocaine high, old Dad's mind was touring the outer planets. He couldn't shut up. All Ace had to do was keep saying, "Uh-huh," and "That's right, Dad," and "Fuckin-A, Dad."

Several times he almost called Keeton Mr. Toad instead of Dad, but caught himself. Calling this guy Mr. Toad might be a very bad idea.

They crossed the Tin Bridge while Alan was still three miles from it and got out in the pouring rain. Ace found a blanket in one of the van's bench compartments and draped it over a bundle of dynamite and one of the cap equipped timers.

"Do you want help?" Buster asked nervously.

"You better let me handle it, Dad. You'd be apt to fall in the goddam stream, and I'd have to waste time fishing you out. Just keep your eyes open, okay?"

"I will Ace . . . why don't we sniff a little more of that cocaine first?"

"Not right now," Ace said indulgently, and patted one of Buster's meaty arms. "This shit is almost pure. You want to explode?"

"Not *me*," Buster said. "Everything else, but not *me*." He began to laugh wildly. Ace joined him.

"Havin some fun tonight, huh, Dad?"

Buster was amazed to find this was true. His depression following Myrtle's . . . Myrtle's accident . . . now seemed years distant. He felt that he and his excellent friend Ace Merrill finally had Them right where they wanted Them: in the palm of their collective hand.

"You bet," he said, and watched Ace slide down the wet, grassy bank beside the bridge with the blanket-wrapped parcel of dynamite held against his belly.

It was relatively dry under the bridge; not that it mattered—both the dynamite and the blasting caps had been waterproofed. Ace put his package in the elbow-crook formed by two of the struts, then attached the blasting cap to the dynamite by poking the wires—the tips were already stripped, how convenient—into one of the sticks. He twisted the big white dial of the timer to 40. It began ticking.

He crawled out and scrambled back up the slippery bank.

"Well?" Buster asked anxiously. "Will it blow, do you think?"

"It'll blow," Ace said reassuringly, and climbed into the van. He was soaked to the skin, but he didn't mind.

"What if They find it? What if They disconnect it before—"

"Dad," Ace said. "Listen a minute. Poke your head out this door and *listen.*"

Buster did. Faintly, between blasts of thunder, he thought he could hear yells and screams. Then, clearly, he heard the thin, hard crack of a pistol shot.

"Mr. Gaunt is keeping Them busy," Ace said. "He's one clever son of a bitch." He tipped a pile of cocaine into his snuff-hollow, tooted, then held his hand under Buster's nose. "Here, Dad—it's Miller Time."

Buster dipped his head and snorted.

They drove away from the bridge about seven minutes before Alan Pangborn crossed it. Underneath, the timer's black marker stood at 30.

6

Ace Merrill and Danforth Keeton—aka Buster, aka Zippy's Dad, aka Toad of Toad Hall—drove slowly up Main Street in the pouring rain like Santa and his helper, leaving little bundles here and there. State Police cars roared by them twice, but neither had any interest in what looked like just one more TV newsvan. As Ace had said, Mr. Gaunt was keeping Them busy.

They left a timer and five sticks of dynamite in the doorway of The Samuels Funeral Home. The barber shop was beside it. Ace wrapped a piece of blanket around his arm and popped his elbow through the glass pane in the door. He doubted very much if the barber shop was equipped with an alarm . . . or if the police would bother responding, even if it was. Buster handed him a freshly prepared bomb—they were using wire from one of the bench compartments to bind the timers and the blasting caps securely to the dynamite—and Ace lobbed it through the hole in the door. They watched it tumble to a stop at the foot of the #1 chair, the timer ticking down from 25.

"Won't nobody be getting a shave in *there* for a while, Dad," Ace breathed, and Buster giggled breathlessly.

They split up then, Ace tossing one bundle into Galaxia while Buster crammed another into the mouth of the bank's night-deposit slot. As they returned to the van through the slashing rain, lightning ripped across the sky. The elm toppled into Castle Stream with a rending roar. They stood on the sidewalk for a moment, staring in that direction, both of them thinking that the dynamite under the bridge had gone twenty minutes or more early, but there was no blossom of fire.

"I think it was lightning," Ace said. "Must have hit a tree. Come on."

As they pulled out, Ace driving now, Alan's station wagon passed them. In the pouring rain, neither driver noticed the other.

They drove up to Nan's. Ace broke the glass of the door with his elbow and they left the dynamite and a ticking timer, this one set at 20, just inside, near the cash register stand. As they were leaving, an incredibly bright stroke of lightning flashed, and all the streetlights went out.

"It's the power!" Buster cried happily. "The power's out! Fantastic! Let's do the Municipal Building! Let's blow it sky-high!"

"Dad, that place is crawling with cops! Didn't you see them?"

"They're chasing their own tails," Buster said impatiently. "And when these things start to go up, they're going to be chasing them twice as fast. Besides, it's dark now, and we can go in through the courthouse on the other side. The master-key opens *that* door, too."

"You've got the balls of a tiger, Dad—you know that?"

Buster smiled tightly. "So do you, Ace. So do you."

7

Alan pulled into one of the slant parking spaces in front of Needful Things, turned off the station wagon's engine, and

simply sat for a moment, staring at Mr. Gaunt's shop. The sign
in the window now read

YOU SAY HELLO
I SAY GOODBYE GOODBYE GOODBYE
I DON'T KNOW WHY YOU SAY HELLO
I SAY GOODBYE.

Lightning stuttered on and off like giant neon, giving the window the look of a blank, dead eye.

Yet a deep instinct suggested that Needful Things, while
closed and quiet, might not be empty. Mr. Gaunt could have
left town in all the confusion, yes—with the storm raging and
the cops running around like chickens with their heads cut off,
doing that would have been no problem at all. But the picture
of Mr. Gaunt which had formed in his mind on the long, wild
ride from the hospital in Bridgton was that of Batman's nem-
esis, the Joker. Alan had an idea that he was dealing with the
sort of man who would think installing a jet-powered backflow
valve in a friend's toilet the very height of humor. And would
a fellow like that—the sort of fellow who would put a tack in
your chair or stick a burning match in the sole of your shoe
just for laughs—leave before you sat down or noticed that your
socks were on fire and your pantscuffs were catching? Of course
not. What fun would that be?

I think you're still around, Alan thought. I think you want
to watch all the fun. Don't you, you son of a bitch?

He sat quite still, looking at the shop with the green awning, trying to fathom the mind of a man who would set such
a complex and mean-spirited set of events in motion. He was
concentrating far too deeply to notice that the car parked on
his left was quite old, although smoothly, almost aerodynami-
cally, designed. It was Mr. Gaunt's Tucker Talisman, in fact.

How did you do it? There's a lot I want to know, but just
that one thing will suffice for tonight. How *could* you do it?
How could you learn so much about us so fast?

Brian said Mr. Gaunt wasn't really a man at all.

In daylight Alan would have scoffed at this idea, as he had scoffed at the idea that Polly's charm might have some supernatural healing power. But tonight, cupped in the crazy palm of the gale, staring at the display window which had become a blank dead eye, the idea had its own undeniable, gloomy power. He remembered the day he had come to Needful Things with the specific intention of meeting and talking to Mr. Gaunt, and he remembered the odd sensation that had crept over him as he peered in through the window with his hands cupped at the sides of his face to reduce the glare. He had felt he was being watched, although the shop was clearly empty. And not only that; he'd felt the watcher was malign, hateful. The feeling had been so strong that for a moment he had actually mistaken his own reflection for the unpleasant (and half-transparent) face of someone else.

How strong that feeling had been . . . how very strong.

Alan found himself remembering something else—something his grandmother used to tell him when he was small: *The devil's voice is sweet to hear.*

Brian said—

How *had* Mr. Gaunt come by his knowledge? And why in God's name would he bother with a wide place in the road like Castle Rock?

—Mr. Gaunt wasn't really a man at all.

Alan suddenly leaned over and groped on the floor of the station wagon's passenger side. For a moment he thought that what he was feeling around for was gone—that it had fallen out of the car at some point during the day when the passenger door was open—and then his fingers happened on the metal curve. It had rolled underneath the seat, that was all. He fumbled it out, held it up . . . and the voice of depression, absent since he had left Sean Rusk's hospital room (or maybe it was just that things had been too busy since then for Alan to hear it), spoke up in its loud and unsettlingly merry voice.

Hi, Alan! Hello! I've been away, sorry about that, but I'm back now, okay? What you got there? Can of nuts? Nope—that's what it looks like, but that's not what it is, is it? It's the last joke Todd ever bought at the Auburn Novelty Shop, correct? A fake can of Tastee-Munch Mixed Nuts with a green snake inside—crepe-paper wrapped around a spring. And when he brought it to you with his eyes glowing and a big, goofy smile on his face, you told him to put that silly thing back, didn't you? And when his face fell, you pretended not to notice—you told him . . . let me see. What DID *you tell him?*

"That the fool and his money soon parted," Alan said dully. He turned the can around and around in his hands, looking at it, remembering Todd's face. "That's what I told him."

Ohhhh, riiiiight, the voice agreed. *How could I have forgotten a thing like that? You want to talk about mean-spirited? Jeez, Louise! Good thing you reminded me! Good thing you reminded us* BOTH, *right? Only Annie saved the day—she said to let him have it. She said . . . let me see. What* DID *she say?*

"She said it was sort of funny, that Todd was just like me, and that he'd only be young once." Alan's voice was hoarse and trembling. He had begun to cry again, and why not? Just why the fucking hell not? The old pain was back, twisting itself around his aching heart like a dirty rag.

Hurts, doesn't it? the voice of depression—that guilty, self-hating voice—asked with a sympathy Alan (the *rest* of Alan) suspected was entirely bogus. *It hurts too much, like having to live inside a country-and-western song about good love gone bad or good kids gone dead. Nothing that hurts this much can do you any good. Shove it back in the glove compartment, buddy. Forget about it. Next week, when this madness is all over, you can trade the wagon with the fake can of nuts still in it. Why not? It's the sort of cheap practical joke that would appeal only to a child, or to a man like Gaunt. Forget it. Forget—*

Alan cut the voice off in mid-rant. He hadn't known he could do that until this moment, and it was good knowledge to have, knowledge that might be useful in the future . . . if he *had* a future, that was. He looked more closely at the can, turning it this way and that, really looking at it for the first time, seeing it not as a sappy memento of his lost son but as an object which was as much a tool of misdirection as his hollow magic wand, his silk top-hat with the false bottom, or the Folding Flower Trick which still nestled beneath his watchband.

Magic—wasn't that what this was all about? It was mean-spirited magic, granted; magic calculated not to make people gasp and laugh but to turn them into angry charging bulls, but it was magic, just the same. And what was the basis of all magic? Misdirection. It was a five-foot-long snake hidden inside a can of nuts . . . or, he thought, thinking of Polly, it's a disease that looks like a cure.

He opened the car door, and when he got out into the pouring rain, he was still carrying the fake can of nuts in his left hand. Now that he had drawn back a little from the dangerous lure of sentiment, he remembered his opposition to the purchase of this thing with something like amazement. All his life he had been fascinated with magic, and of course he would have been entranced by the old snake-in-a-can-of-nuts trick as a kid. So why had he spoken to Todd in such an unfriendly way when the boy had wanted to buy it, and then pretended not to see the boy's hurt? Had it been jealousy of Todd's youth and enthusiasm? An inability to remember the wonder of simple things? What?

He didn't know. He only knew it was exactly the sort of trick a Mr. Gaunt would understand, and he wanted it with him now.

Alan bent back into the car, grabbed a flashlight from the small box of jumbled tools sitting on the rear seat, then walked past the nose of Mr. Gaunt's Tucker Talisman (still without noticing it), and passed under the deep-green awning of Needful Things.

8

Well, here I am. Here I am at last.

Alan's heart was pounding hard but steadily in his chest. In his mind, the faces of his son and his wife and Sean Rusk seemed to have combined. He glanced at the sign in the window again and then tried the door. It was locked. Overhead, the canvas awning rippled and snapped in the howling wind.

He had tucked the Tastee-Munch can into his shirt. Now he touched it with his right hand and seemed to draw some indescribable but perfectly real comfort from it.

"Okay," he muttered. "Here I come, ready or not." He reversed the flashlight and used the handle to smash a hole in the glass. He steeled himself for the wail of the burglar alarm, but it didn't come. Either Gaunt hadn't turned it on or there *was* no alarm. He reached through the jagged hole and tried the inside knob. It turned, and for the first time, Alan Pangborn stepped into Needful Things.

The smell hit him first; it was deep and still and dusty. It wasn't the smell of a new shop but of a place which had been untenanted for months or even years. Holding his gun in his right hand, he shone the flashlight around with his left. It illuminated a bare floor, bare walls, and a number of glass cases. The cases were empty, the stock was gone. Everything was blanketed by a thick fall of dust, and the dust was undisturbed by any mark.

No one's been here for a long, long time.

But how could that possibly be, when he had seen people going in and out all week long?

Because he's not a man at all. Because the devil's voice is sweet to hear.

He took two more steps, using the flashlight to cover the empty room in zones, breathing the dry museum dust which hung in the air. He looked behind him and saw, in a flash of lightning, the tracks of his own feet in the dust. He shone the light back into the store, ran it from right to left along the case which had also served Mr. Gaunt as a counter . . . and stopped.

A video-cassette recorder/player sat there, next to a Sony portable TV—one of the sporty models, round instead of square, with a case as red as a fire-engine. A cord was looped around the television. And there was something on top of the VCR. In this light it looked like a book, but Alan didn't think that was what it was.

He walked over and trained his light first on the TV. It was as thickly coated with dust as the floor and the glass cases. The cord looped around it was a short length of coaxial cable with a connector at either end. Alan moved his light to the thing on top of the VCR, the thing which wasn't a book but a video cassette in an unmarked black plastic case.

A dusty white business envelope lay beside it. Written on the front of the envelope was the message

ATTENTION SHERIFF ALAN PANGBORN.

He set his gun and his flashlight down on the glass counter, took the envelope, opened it, and pulled out the single sheet of paper inside. Then he picked up the flashlight again and trained its powerful circle of light on the short typed message.

Dear Sheriff Pangborn,
    By now you will have discovered that I am a rather special sort of businessman—the rare sort who actually *does* try to stock "something for everyone." I regret that we never were able to meet face-to-face, but I hope you'll understand that such a meeting would have been very unwise—from my standpoint, at least. Ha-ha! In any event, I have left you a little something which I believe will interest you very much. This is *not* a gift—I am not the Santa Claus type at all,

as I think you will agree—but everyone in town has assured me that you are an honorable man, and I believe you will pay the price I require. That price includes a little service . . . a service which is, in your case, more good deed than prank. I believe you will agree with me, sir.

I know you have wondered long and deeply about what happened during the last few moments of your wife and younger son's lives. I believe that all these questions will be answered shortly.

Please believe that I wish you only the best, and that I remain

Your faithful and obedient servant
Leland Gaunt

Alan put the paper down slowly. *"Bastard!"* he muttered.

He shone the light around again, and saw the VCR's cord trailing down the far side of the case and ending in a plug which lay on the floor several feet from the nearest electric socket. Which was no problem, since the power was out, anyway.

But you know what? Alan thought. I don't think that matters. I don't think it matters one little bit. I think that once I hook the appliances up and plug them in and feed that cassette to the tape-player, everything is going to work just fine. Because there's no way he could have caused the things he's caused, or know the things he knows . . . not if he's human. The devil's voice is sweet to hear, Alan, and whatever you do, you must not look at what he's left for you.

Nevertheless, he put the flashlight down again and picked up the coaxial cable. He examined it for a moment, then bent to plug it into the proper receptacle on the back of the TV. The Tastee-Munch can tried to slip out of his shirt as he did so. He caught it with one of his nimble hands before it could fall to the floor, and set it on the glass case next to the VCR.

9

Norris Ridgewick was halfway to Needful Things when he suddenly decided he would be crazy—much crazier than he had been already, and that was really going some—to tackle Leland Gaunt alone.

He pulled the microphone off its prongs. "Unit Two to Base," he said. "This is Norris, come back?"

He released the button. There was nothing but a horrid squeal of static. The heart of the storm was directly over The Rock now.

"Fuck it," he said, and turned toward the Municipal Building. Alan might be there; if not, someone would tell him where Alan was. Alan would know what to do . . . and even if he didn't, Alan would have to hear his confession: he had slashed Hugh Priest's tires and sent the man to his death simply because he, Norris Ridgewick, had wanted to own a Bazun fishing rod like his good old dad's.

He arrived at the Municipal Building while the timer under the bridge stood at 5, and parked directly behind a bright yellow van. A TV newsvan, from the look.

Norris got out in the pouring rain and ran into the Sheriff's Office to try to find Alan.

10

Polly swung the cup end of the bathroom plunger at the obscenely rearing spider, and this time it did not flinch away. Its bristly front legs clasped the shaft, and Polly's hands cried out in agony as it hauled its quivering weight onto the rubber cup.

Her grip wavered, the plunger dropped, and suddenly the spider was scrabbling up the handle like a fat man on a tightrope.

She drew in breath to scream and then its front legs dropped onto her shoulders like the arms of some scabrous dime-a-dance Lothario. Its listless ruby eyes stared into her own. Its fanged mouth dropped open and she could smell its breath—a stink of bitter spices and rotting meat.

She opened her mouth to scream. One of its legs pawed into her mouth. Rough, gruesome bristles caressed her teeth and tongue. The spider mewled eagerly.

Polly resisted her first instinct to spit the horrid, pulsing thing out. She released the plunger and grabbed the spider's leg. At the same time she bit down, using all the strength in her jaws. Something crunched like a mouthful of Life Savers, and a cold bitter taste like ancient tea filled her mouth. The spider uttered a cry of pain and tried to draw back. Bristles slid harshly through Polly's fists, but she clamped her howling hands tight around the thing's leg again before it could completely escape . . . and *twisted* it, like a woman trying to twist a drumstick off a turkey. There was a tough, gristly ripping noise. The spider uttered another slobbering cry of pain.

It tried to lunge away. Spitting out the bitter dark fluid which had filled her mouth, knowing it would be a long, long time before she was entirely rid of that taste, Polly yanked it back again. Some distant part of her was astounded at this exhibition of strength, but there was another part of her which understood it perfectly. She was afraid, she was revolted . . . but more than anything else, she was angry.

I was used, she thought incoherently. *I sold Alan's life for this! For this monster!*

The spider tried to gnash at her with its fangs, but its rear legs lost their tenuous grip on the shaft of the plunger and it would have fallen . . . if Polly had allowed it to fall.

She did not. She gripped its hot, bulging body between her forearms and squeezed. She lifted it up so it squirmed above her, its legs twitching and pawing at her upturned face. Juice and black blood began to run from its body and trickle up her arms in burning streamlets.

"NO MORE!" shrieked Polly. *"NO MORE, NO MORE, NO MORE!"*

She threw it. It struck the tiled wall behind the tub and splattered open in a clot of ichor. It hung up for a moment, pasted in place by its own innards, and then fell into the tub with a gooey thump.

Polly grabbed the bathroom plunger again and sprang at it. She began beating it as a woman might beat at a mouse with a broom, but that wasn't working. The spider only shuddered and tried to crawl away, its legs scrabbling at the rubber shower-mat with its pattern of yellow daisies. Polly pulled the plunger back, reversed it, and then rammed forward with all of her strength, using the shaft like a lance.

She caught the wretched, freakish thing dead center and impaled it. There was a grotesque punching sound, and then the spider's guts ruptured and ran out onto the shower-mat in a stinking flood. It wriggled frantically, curling its legs fruitlessly around the stake she had put in its heart . . . and then, at last, it became still.

Polly stepped back, closed her eyes, and felt the world waver. She had actually begun to faint when Alan's name exploded in her mind like a Roman candle. She curled her hands into fists and brought them together, hard, knuckles to knuckles. The pain was bright, sudden, and immense. The world came back in a cold flash.

She opened her eyes, advanced to the tub, and looked in. At first she thought there was nothing there at all. Then, beside the plunger's rubber cup, she saw the spider. It was no bigger than the nail on her pinky finger, and it was very dead.

The rest never happened at all. It was your imagination.

"The bloody fuck it *was*," Polly said in a thin, shaking voice.

But the spider wasn't the important thing. *Alan* was the important thing—Alan was in terrible danger, and *she* was the reason why. She had to find him, and do it before it was too late.

If it wasn't too late already.

She would go to the Sheriff's Office. Someone there would know where—

No, Aunt Evvie's voice spoke up in her mind. *Not there. If you go there, it really will be too late. You know where to go. You know where he is.*

Yes.

Yes, of course she did.

Polly ran for the door, and one confused thought beat at her mind like moth-wings: *Please God, don't let him buy anything. Oh God, please, please, please don't let him buy anything.*

CHAPTER TWENTY-THREE

1

The timer under Castle Stream Bridge, which had been known as the Tin Bridge to residents of The Rock since time out of mind, reached 0 at 7:38 p.m. on the night of Tuesday, October 15th, in the year of Our Lord 1991. The tiny burst of electricity which was intended to ring the bell licked across the bare wires Ace had wrapped around the terminals of the nine-volt battery which ran the gadget. The bell actually *did* begin to ring, but it—and the rest of the timer—was swallowed a split second later in a flash of light as the electricity triggered the blasting cap and the cap in turn triggered the dynamite.

Only a few people in Castle Rock mistook the dynamite blast for thunder. The thunder was heavy artillery in the sky; this was a gigantic rifleshot blast. The south end of the old bridge, which was built not of tin but of old rusty iron, lifted off the bank on a squat ball of fire. It rose perhaps ten feet into the air, becoming a gently inclined ramp, and then fell back in a bitter crunch of popping cement and the clatter-clang of flying metal. The north end of the bridge twisted loose and the whole contraption fell askew into Castle Stream, which was now in full spate. The south end came to rest on the lightning-downed elm.

On Castle Avenue, where the Catholics and the Baptists—along with nearly a dozen State Policemen—were still locked in strenuous debate, the fighting paused. All the combatants stared toward the fire-rose at the Castle Stream end of town. Albert Gendron and Phil Burgmeyer, who had been duking it out with great ferocity seconds before, now stood side by side, looking into the glare. Blood was running down the left side of Albert's face from a temple wound, and Phil's shirt was mostly torn off.

Nearby, Nan Roberts squatted atop Father Brigham like a very large (and, in her rayon waitress's uniform, very white) vulture. She had been using his hair to raise the good Father's head and slam it repeatedly into the pavement. Rev. Rose lay close by, unconscious as a result of Father Brigham's ministrations.

Henry Payton, who had lost a tooth since his arrival (not to mention any illusions he might once have held about religious harmony in America), froze in the act of pulling Tony Mislaburski off Baptist Deacon Fred Mellon.

They *all* froze, like children playing Statues.

"Jesus Christ, that was the bridge," Don Hemphill muttered.

Henry Payton decided to take advantage of the lull. He tossed Tony Mislaburski aside, cupped his hands around his wounded mouth, and bawled: *"All right, everybody! This is the police! I'm ordering you—"*

Then Nan Roberts raised her voice in a shout. She had spent many long years bawling orders into the kitchen of her diner, and she was used to being heard no matter how stiff the racket was. It was no contest; her voice overtopped Payton's easily.

"THE GODDAM CATHOLICS ARE USING DYNAMITE!" she bugled.

There were fewer participants now, but what they lacked in numbers they made up for in angry enthusiasm.

Seconds after Nan's cry, the rumble was on again, now spreading into a dozen skirmishes along a fifty-yard stretch of the rain-swept avenue.

2

Norris Ridgewick burst into the Sheriff's Office moments before the bridge went, yelling at the top of his lungs. *"Where's Sheriff Pangborn? I've got to find Sheriff P—"*

He stopped. Except for Seaton Thomas and a State cop who didn't look old enough to drink beer yet, the office was deserted.

Where the hell *was* everybody? There were, it seemed, about six thousand State Police units and other assorted vehicles parked helter-skelter outside. One of them was his own VW, which would easily have won the blue ribbon for helter-skelter, had ribbons been awarded. It was still lying on its side where Buster had tipped it.

"Jesus!" Norris cried. "Where *is* everybody?"

The State cop who didn't look old enough to drink beer yet took in Norris's uniform and then said, "There's a brawl going on upstreet somewhere—the Christians against the cannibals, or some damn thing. I'm supposed to be monitoring in dispatch, but with this storm I can't transmit or receive doodly-squat." He added morosely: "Who are you?"

"Deputy Sheriff Ridgewick."

"Well, I'm Joe Price. What kind of town have you got here anyhow, Deputy? Everyone in it has gone stone crazy."

Norris ignored him and went to Seaton Thomas. Seat's complexion was dirty gray, and he was breathing with great difficulty. One of his wrinkled hands was pressed squarely in the middle of his chest.

"Seat, where's Alan?"

"Dunno," Seat said, and looked at Norris with dull, frightened eyes. "Something bad's happening, Norris. Really bad. All over town. The phones are out, and that shouldn't be, because most of the lines are underground now. But do you know something? I'm *glad* they're out. I'm glad because I don't want to know."

"You should be in the hospital," Norris said, looking at the old man with concern.

"I should be in Kansas," Seat said drearily. "Meantime, I'm just gonna sit here and wait for it to be over. I ain't—"

The bridge blew up then, cutting him off—that great rifle-shot noise ripped the night like a claw.

"Jesus!" Norris and Joe Price cried in unison.

"Yep," Seat Thomas said in his weary, frightened, nagging, unsurprised voice, "they're going to blow up the town, I guess. I guess that comes next."

Suddenly, shockingly, the old man began to weep.

"Where's Henry Payton?" Norris shouted at Trooper Price. Price ignored him. He was running for the door to see what had blown up.

Norris spared a glance at Seaton Thomas, but Seat was staring gloomily out into space, tears rolling down his face and his hand still planted squarely in the center of his chest. Norris followed Trooper Joe Price and found him in the Municipal Building parking lot, where Norris had ticketed Buster Keeton's red Cadillac about a thousand years ago. A pillar of dying fire stood out clearly in the rainy night, and in its glow both of them could see that Castle Stream Bridge was gone. The traffic light at the far end of town had been knocked into the street.

"Mother of God," Trooper Price said in a reverent voice. "I'm sure glad this isn't *my* town." The firelight had put roses on his cheeks and embers in his eyes.

Norris's urge to locate Alan had deepened. He decided he had better get back in his cruiser and try to find Henry Payton first—if there was some sort of big brawl going on, that shouldn't be too difficult. Alan might be there, too.

He was almost across the sidewalk when a stroke of lightning showed him two figures trotting around the corner of the courthouse next to the Municipal Building. They appeared to be heading for the bright yellow newsvan. One of them he was not sure of, but the other figure—portly and a little bow-legged—was impossible to mistake. It was Danforth Keeton.

Norris Ridgewick took two steps to the right and planted his back against the brick wall at the mouth of the alley. He drew his service revolver. He raised it to shoulder level, its muzzle pointing up into the rainy sky, and screamed "halt!" at the top of his lungs.

3

Polly backed her car down the driveway, switched on the windshield wipers, and made a left turn. The pain in her hands had been joined by a deep, heavy burning in her arms, where the spider's muck had fallen on her skin. It had poisoned her somehow, and the poison seemed to be working its way steadily into her. But there was no time to worry about it now.

She was approaching the stop-sign at Laurel and Main when the bridge went up. She winced away from that massive rifleshot and stared for a moment, amazed, at the bright gout of flame which rose up from Castle Stream. For a moment she saw the gantry-like silhouette of the bridge itself, all black angles against the strenuous light, and then it was swallowed in flame.

She turned left again onto Main, in the direction of Needful Things.

4

At one time, Alan Pangborn had been a dedicated maker of home movies—he had no idea how many people he had bored to tears with jumpy films, projected on a sheet tacked to the living-room wall, of his diapered children toddling their uncertain way around the living room, of Annie giving them baths, of birthday parties, of family outings. In all these films, people waved and mugged at the camera. It was as though there were some sort of unspoken law: When someone points a movie camera at you, you must wave, or mug, or both. If you do not, you may be arrested on a charge of Second-Degree Indifference, which carries a penalty of up to ten years, said time to be spent watching endless reels of jumpy home movies.

Five years ago he had switched to a video camera, which was both cheaper and easier . . . and instead of boring people to tears for ten or fifteen minutes, which was the length of time three or four rolls of eight-millimeter film ran when spliced together, you could bore them for hours, all without even plugging in a fresh cassette.

He took this cassette out of its box and looked at it. There was no label. Okay, he thought. That's perfectly okay. I'll just have to find out what's on it for myself, won't I? His hand moved to the VCR's ON button . . . and there it hesitated.

The composite formed by Todd's and Sean's and his wife's faces retreated suddenly; it was replaced by the pallid, shocked face of Brian Rusk as Alan had seen him just this afternoon.

You look unhappy, Brian.

Yessir.

Does that mean you are *unhappy?*

Yessir—and if you turn that switch, you'll be unhappy, too. He wants you to look at it, but not because he wants to do you a favor. Mr. Gaunt doesn't DO favors. He wants to poison you, that's all. Just like he's poisoned everyone else.

Yet he *had* to look.

His fingers touched the button, caressed its smooth, square shape. He paused and looked around. Yes; Gaunt was still here. Somewhere. Alan could feel him—a heavy presence, both menacing and cajoling. He thought of the note Mr. Gaunt had left behind. *I know you have wondered long and deeply about what happened during the last few moments of your wife and younger son's lives . . .*

Don't do it, Sheriff, Brian Rusk whispered. Alan saw that pallid, hurt, pre-suicidal face looking at him from above the cooler in his bike basket, the cooler filled with the baseball cards. *Let the past sleep. It's better that way. And he lies; you KNOW he lies.*

Yes. He did. He did know that.

Yet he *had* to look.

Alan's finger pushed the button.

The small green POWER light went on at once. The VCR worked just fine, power outage or no power outage, just as Alan had known it would. He turned on the sexy red Sony and in a moment the bright white glow of Channel 3 snow lit his face with pallid light. Alan pushed the EJECT button and the VCR's cassette-carrier popped up.

Don't do it, Brian Rusk's voice whispered again, but Alan didn't listen. He carted the cassette, pushed the carrier down, and listened to the little mechanical clicks as the heads engaged the tape. Then he took a deep breath and pushed the PLAY button. The bright white snow on the screen was replaced by smooth blackness. A moment later the screen went slate-gray, and a series of numbers flashed up: 8 . . . 7 . . . 6 . . . 5 . . . 4 . . . 3 . . . 2 . . . X.

What followed was a shaky, hand-held shot of a country road. In the foreground, slightly out of focus but still readable, was a road-sign. 117, it said, but Alan didn't need it. He had driven that stretch many times, and knew it well. He recognized the grove of pines just beyond the place where the road curved—it was the grove where the Scout had fetched up, its nose crumpled around the largest tree in a jagged embrace.

But the trees in this picture showed no scars of the accident, although the scars were still visible, if you went out there and looked (he had, many times). Wonder and terror slipped silently into Alan's bones as he realized—not just from the unwounded surfaces of the trees and the curve in the road but from every configuration of the landscape and every intuition of his heart—that this videotape had been shot on the day Annie and Todd had died.

He was going to see it happen.

It was quite impossible, but it was true. He was going to see his wife and son smashed open before his very eyes.

Turn it off! Brian screamed. *Turn it off, he's a poison man and he sells poison things! Turn it off before it's too late!*

But Alan could have done this no more than he could have stilled his own heartbeat by thought alone. He was frozen, caught.

Now the camera panned jerkily to the left, up the road. For a moment there was nothing, and then there was a sun-twinkle of light. It was the Scout. The Scout was coming. The Scout was on its way to the pine tree where it and the people inside it would end forever. The Scout was approaching its terminal point on earth. It was not speeding; it was not moving erratically. There was no sign that Annie had lost control or was in danger of losing it.

Alan leaned forward beside the humming VCR, sweat trickling down his cheeks, blood beating heavily in his temples. He felt his gorge rising.

This isn't real. It's a put-up job. He had it made somehow. It's not them; there may be an actress and a young actor inside pretending *to be them, but it's not them. It can't be.*

Yet he knew it was. What else would you see in images transmitted by a VCR to a TV which wasn't plugged in but worked anyway? What else but the truth?

A lie! Brian Rusk's voice cried out, but it was distant and easily ignored. *A lie, Sheriff, a lie! A LIE!*

Now he could see the license plate on the approaching Scout. 24912 V. Annie's license plate.

Suddenly, behind the Scout, Alan saw another twinkle of light. Another car, approaching fast, closing the distance.

Outside, the Tin Bridge blew up with that monstrous rifle-crack sound. Alan didn't look in that direction, didn't even hear it. Every ounce of his concentration was fixed on the screen of the red Sony TV, where Annie and Todd were approaching the tree which stood between them and all the rest of their lives.

The car behind them was doing seventy, maybe eighty miles an hour. As the Scout approached the cameraman's position, this second car—of which there had never been any report—approached the Scout. Annie apparently saw it, too; the Scout began to speed up, but it was too little. And it was too late.

The second car was a lime-green Dodge Challenger, jacked in the back so the nose pointed at the road. Through the smoked-glass windows, one could dimly make out the roll-bar arching across the roof inside. The rear end was covered with stickers: HEARST, FUELLY, FRAM, QUAKER STATE . . . Although the tape was silent, Alan could almost hear the blast and crackle of exhaust through the straight-pipes.

"Ace!" he cried out in agonized comprehension. Ace! Ace Merrill! Revenge! Of course! Why had he never thought of it before?

The Scout passed in front of the camera, which panned right to follow. Alan had one moment when he could see inside and yes; it was Annie, the paisley scarf she had been wearing that day tied in her hair, and Todd, in his *Star Trek* tee-shirt. Todd was looking back at the car behind him. Annie was looking up into the rearview mirror. He could not see her face, but her body was leaning tensely forward in the seat, pulling her shoulder-harness taut. He had that one brief last look at them—his wife and his son—and part of him realized he did not want to see them this way if there was no hope of changing the result: he did not want to see the terror of their last moments.

But there was no going back now.

The Challenger bumped the Scout. It wasn't a hard hit, but Annie had sped up and it was hard enough. The Scout missed the curve and veered off the road and toward the grove of trees where the large pine waited.

"*NO!*" Alan shouted.

The Scout jounced into the ditch and out of it. It rocked up on two wheels, came back down, and smashed into the bole of the pine tree with a soundless crunch. A rag doll with a paisley scarf in its hair flew through the windshield, struck a tree, and bounced into the underbrush.

The lime-green Challenger stopped at the edge of the road.

The driver's door opened.

Ace Merrill got out.

He was looking toward the wreck of the Scout, now barely visible in the steam escaping its ruptured radiator, and he was laughing.

"*NO!*" Alan screamed again, and pushed the VCR over the side of the glass case with both hands. It struck the floor but didn't break and the coaxial cord was just a little too long to pull out. A line of static ran across the TV screen, but that was all. Alan could see Ace getting back into his car, still laughing, and then he grabbed the red TV, lifted it above his head as he executed a half-turn, and threw it against the wall. There was a flash of light, a hollow bang, and then nothing but the hum of the VCR with the tape still running inside. Alan dealt it a kick and it fell mercifully silent.

Get him. He lives in Mechanic Falls.

This was a new voice. It was cold and it was insane but it had its own merciless rationality. The voice of Brian Rusk was gone; now there was only this one voice, repeating the same two things over and over.

Get him. He lives in Mechanic Falls. Get him. He lives in Mechanic Falls. Get him. Get him. Get him.

Across the street there were two more of those monstrous rifleshot explosions as the barber shop and The Samuels Funeral Home blew up at almost the same instant, belching glass and fiery debris into the sky and the street. Alan took no notice.

Get him. He lives in Mechanic Falls.

He picked up the Tastee-Munch can without a thought, grabbing it only because it was something he had brought in and thus was something he should take back out. He crossed to the door, scuffing his previous trail of footprints to incomprehensibility, and left Needful Things. The explosions meant nothing to him. The jagged, burning hole in the line of buildings on the far side of Main Street meant nothing to him. The rubble of wood and glass and brick in the street meant nothing to him. Castle Rock and all the people who lived there, Polly Chalmers among them, meant nothing to him. He had an errand to do in Mechanic Falls, thirty miles from here. *That* meant something. In fact, it meant *everything*.

Alan strode around to the driver's side of the station wagon. He tossed his gun, his flashlight, and the joke can of nuts on the seat. In his mind, his hands were already around Ace Merrill's throat and starting to squeeze.

5

"HALT!" Norris screamed again. *"HALT RIGHT WHERE YOU ARE!"*

He was thinking it was a most incredibly lucky break. He was less than sixty yards from the holding cell where he intended to store Dan Keeton for safekeeping. As for the other fellow . . . well, that would depend on what the two of them had been up to, wouldn't it? They weren't exactly wearing the expressions of men who have been ministering to the sick and comforting the grief-stricken.

Trooper Price looked from Norris to the men standing by the old-fashioned board sign which read CASTLE COUNTY COURTHOUSE. Then he looked back at Norris again. Ace and Zippy's Dad looked at each other. Then both of them eased their hands downward, toward the butts of the guns which protruded over the waistbands of their pants.

Norris had pointed the barrel of his revolver skyward, as he had been taught to do in situations like this. Now, still following procedure, he clasped his right wrist in his left fist and levelled the revolver. If the books were right, they would not realize that the muzzle was pointed directly between them; each would believe Norris was aiming at him. "Move your hands away from your weapons, my friends. Do it *now!*"

Buster and his companion exchanged another glance and dropped their hands to their sides.

Norris snapped a look at the Trooper. "You," he said. "Price. Want to give me a little help here? If you're not too tired, that is."

"What are you *doing?*" Price asked. He sounded worried and unwilling to pitch in. The night's activities, with the hammering demolition of the bridge to cap them, had reduced him to bystander status. He apparently felt uncomfortable about stepping back into a more active role. Things had gotten too big too fast.

"Arresting these two boogers," Norris snapped. "What in the hell does it look like?"

"Arrest this, fellow," Ace said, and flipped Norris the bird. Buster uttered a high, yodelling laugh.

Price looked at them nervously and then returned his troubled gaze to Norris. "Uh . . . on what charge?"

Buster's friend laughed.

Norris directed his full attention back to the two men, and was alarmed to see their positions relative to each other had changed. When he had thrown down on them, they had been almost shoulder to shoulder. Now they were almost five feet apart, and still sidling.

"*Stand still!*" he bawled. They stopped and exchanged another glance. "*Move back together!*"

They only stood there in the pouring rain, hands dangling, looking at him.

"*I'm arresting them on an illegal-weapons charge to start with!*" Norris yelled furiously to Trooper Joe Price. "*Now get your thumb out of your butt and give me a help!*"

This shocked Price into action. He tried to take his own revolver out of its holster, discovered the safety strap was still on,
and began fumbling with it. He was still fumbling when the
barber shop and the funeral home blew up.

Buster, Norris, and Trooper Price all looked upstreet. Ace
did not. He had been waiting for just this golden moment. He
pulled the automatic from his belt with the speed of a Western
quick-draw artist and fired. The bullet took Norris high in the
left shoulder, clipping his lung and smashing his collarbone.
Norris had taken a step away from the brick wall when he
noticed the two men drifting apart; now he was driven back
against it. Ace fired again, chipping a crater in the brick an
inch from Norris's ear. The ricochet made a sound like a very
large, very angry insect.

"*Oh Christ!*" Trooper Price screamed, and began to labor
more enthusiastically to free the safety strap over the butt of
his gun.

"*Burn that guy, Dad!*" Ace yelled. He was grinning. He
fired at Norris again, and this third bullet tore a hot groove
in the skinny Deputy's left side as he collapsed to his knees.
Lightning flashed overhead. Incredibly, Norris could still hear
brick and wood from the latest explosions rattling down on the
street.

Trooper Price at long last managed to unsnap the strap over
his gun. He was pulling it free when a bullet from the automatic Keeton held took his head off from the eyebrows on up.
Price was hammered out of his boots and thrown against the
brick wall of the alley.

Norris raised his own gun once more. It seemed to weigh
a hundred pounds. Still holding it in both hands, he aimed at
Keeton. Buster was a clearer target than his friend. More important, Buster had just killed a cop, and that shit most definitely
did not go down in Castle Rock. They were hicks, maybe, but
not *barbarians.* Norris pulled the trigger at the same moment
Ace tried to shoot him again.

The recoil of his revolver sent Norris flying backward. Ace's bullet buzzed through empty air where his head had been half a second before. Buster Keeton also went flying backward, hands clapped to his belly. Blood poured through his fingers.

Norris lay against the brick wall near Trooper Price, panting harshly, one hand pressed against his wounded shoulder. *Christ, this has been a really lousy day,* he thought.

Ace levelled the automatic at him, then thought better of it—at least for the time being. He went to Buster instead and dropped on one knee beside him. North of them, the bank went up in a roar of fire and pulverized granite. Ace didn't even look in that direction. He moved old Dad's hands to get a better look at the wound. He was sorry this had happened. He had been getting to like old Dad pretty well.

Buster screamed. *"Oh, it hurts! Oh, it hurrrrts!"*

Ace just bet it did. Old Dad had taken a .45 slug just above his belly-button. The entrance hole was the size of a headbolt. Ace didn't have to roll him over to know the exit hole would be the size of a coffee cup, probably with chunks of old Dad's spine sticking out of it like bloody candy-canes.

"It hurrrts! HURRRRRRTS!" Buster screamed up into the rain.

"Yeah." Ace put the muzzle of the automatic against Buster's temple. "Tough luck, Dad. I'm going to give you some painkiller."

He pulled the trigger three times. Buster's body jumped and was still.

Ace got to his feet, meaning to finish the goddam Deputy—if there was anything left to finish—when a gun roared and a bullet whined through the windy air less than a foot over his head. Ace looked up and saw another cop standing just outside the Sheriff's Office door to the parking lot. This one looked older than God. He was shooting at Ace with one hand while the other pressed against his chest above his heart.

Seat Thomas's second try plowed into the earth right next to Ace, splashing muddy water on the toes of his engineer boots.

The old buzzard couldn't shoot for shit, but Ace suddenly realized he had to get the hell out of here, anyway. They had put enough dynamite in the courthouse to blow the whole building sky-high, they had set the timer for five minutes, and here he was, all but leaning against it while fucking Methuselah took potshots at him.

Let the dynamite take care of both of them.

It was time to go see Mr. Gaunt.

Ace got up and ran into the street. The old Deputy fired again, but this one wasn't even close. Ace ran behind the yellow newsvan, but made no attempt to get into it. The Chevrolet Celebrity was parked at Needful Things. It would do excellently as a getaway car. But first he intended to find Mr. Gaunt and get paid off. Surely he had *something* coming, and surely Mr. Gaunt would give it to him.

Also, he had a certain thieving Sheriff to find.

"Payback's a bitch," Ace muttered, and ran up Main Street toward Needful Things.

6

Frank Jewett was standing on the courthouse steps when he finally saw the man he had been looking for. Frank had been there for some time now, and none of the things going on in Castle Rock tonight had meant much to him. Not the screams and shouts from the direction of Castle Hill, not Danforth Keeton and some elderly Hell's Angel running down the courthouse steps about five minutes ago, not the explosions, not the most recent rattle of gunshots, this time from right around the corner in the parking lot next to the Sheriff's Office. Frank had other fish to fry and other lemons to squeeze. Frank had a personal APB out on his excellent old "friend," George T. Nelson.

And boy-howdy! At last! There was George T. Nelson himself, in the flesh, strolling by on the sidewalk below the courthouse steps! Except for the automatic pistol jammed into the waistband of George T. Nelson's Sans-A-Belt polyester slacks (and the fact that it was still raining like hell), the man might have been on his way to a picnic.

Just strolling along in the rain was Monsieur George T. Motherfucking Nelson, just breezing along with the Christing breeze, and what had the note in Frank's office said? Oh yes: *Remember, $2,000 at my house by 7:15 at the latest or you will wish you were born without a dick.* Frank glanced at his watch, saw it was closer to eight o'clock than to 7:15, and decided that didn't matter much.

He raised George T. Nelson's Spanish Llama and pointed it at the head of the son of a bitching shop teacher who had caused all his trouble.

"NELSON!" he screamed. "GEORGE NELSON! TURN AROUND AND LOOK AT ME, YOU PRICK!"

George T. Nelson wheeled around. His hand dropped toward the butt of his automatic, then fell away when he saw he was covered. He placed his hands on his hips instead and peered up the courthouse steps at Frank Jewett, who stood there with rain dripping from his nose, his chin, and the muzzle of his stolen gun.

"You going to shoot me?" George T. Nelson asked.

"You bet I am!" Frank snarled.

"Just shoot me down like a dog, huh?"

"Why not? It's what you deserve!"

To Frank's amazement, George T. Nelson was smiling and nodding. "Ayup," he said, "and that's what I'd expect from a chickenshit bastard who'd break into a friend's house and kill a defenseless little birdie. *Exactly* what I'd expect. So go ahead, you yellowbelly four-eyes fuck. Shoot me and get it over with."

Thunder bellowed overhead, but Frank didn't hear it. The bank blew up ten seconds later and he barely heard *that*. He was too busy struggling with his fury . . . and his amazement. Amazement at the gall, the bold, bare-ass *gall* of Monsieur George T. Motherfucker Nelson.

At last Frank managed to break the lock on his tongue. "Killed your bird, right! Shit on that stupid picture of your mom, right again! And what did *you* do? What did *you* do, George, besides make sure that I'll lose my job and never teach again? God, I'll be lucky not to end up in jail!" He saw the total injustice of this in a sudden black flash of comprehension; it was like rubbing vinegar into a raw scrape. "Why didn't you just come and *ask* me for money, if you needed it? Why didn't you just come and ask? *We could have worked something out, you dumb bastard!*"

"I don't know what you're talking about!" George T. Nelson shouted back. "All I know is that you're brave enough to kill teeny-tiny parakeets but you don't have balls enough to take me on in a fair fight!"

"Don't know what . . . *don't know what I'm talking about?*" Frank sputtered. The muzzle of the Llama wavered wildly back and forth. He could not believe the gall of the man below him on the sidewalk; simply could not *believe* it. To be standing there with one foot on the pavement and the other practically in eternity and to simply *go on lying* . . .

"No! I don't! Not the slightest idea!"

In the extremity of his rage, Frank Jewett regressed to the childhood response to such outrageous, baldface denial: "Liar, liar, pants on fire!"

"Coward!" George T. Nelson smartly returned. "Baby-coward! Parakeet-killer!"

"Blackmailer!"

"Loony! Put the gun away, loony! Fight me fair!"

Frank grinned down at him. "*Fair?* Fight you *fair?* What do you know about *fair?*"

George T. Nelson held up his empty hands and waggled the fingers at Frank. "More than you, it looks like."

Frank opened his mouth to reply, but nothing came out. He was temporarily silenced by George T. Nelson's empty hands.

"Go on," George T. Nelson said. "Put it away. Let's do it like they do in the Westerns, Frank. If you've got the sack for it, that is. Fastest man wins."

Frank thought: Well, why not? Just why the hell not?

He hadn't much else to live for, one way or the other, and if he did nothing else, he could show his old "friend" he wasn't a coward.

"Okay," he said, and shoved the Llama into the waistband of his own pants. He held his hands out in front of him, hovering just above the butt of the gun. "How do you want to do it, Georgie-Porgie?"

George T. Nelson was grinning. "You start down the steps," he said. "I start up. Next time the thunder goes overhead—"

"All right," Frank said. "Fine. Let's do it."

He started down the stairs. And George T. Nelson started up.

7

Polly had just spotted the green awning of Needful Things up ahead when the funeral parlor and the barber shop went up. The glare of light and the roar of sound were enormous. She saw debris burst out of the heart of the explosion like asteroids in a science fiction movie and ducked instinctively. It was well that she did; several chunks of wood and the stainless-steel lever from the side of Chair #2—Henry Gendron's chair—smashed through the windshield of her Toyota. The lever made a weird, hungry humming sound as it flew through the car and exited by way of the rear window. Broken glass whispered through the air in a widening shotgun cloud.

The Toyota, with no driver to steer it, bumped up over the curb, struck a fire hydrant, and stalled.

Polly sat up, blinking, and stared out through the hole in the windshield. She saw someone coming out of Needful Things and heading toward one of the three cars parked in front of the store. In the bright light of the fire across the street, she recognized Alan easily.

"Alan!" She yelled it, but Alan didn't turn. He moved with single-minded purpose, like a robot.

Polly shoved open the door of her car and ran toward him, screaming his name over and over. From down the street came the rapid rattle of gunfire. Alan did not turn in that direction, nor did he look at the conflagration which, only moments ago, had been the funeral parlor and the barber shop. He seemed to be locked entirely on his own interior course of action, and Polly suddenly realized that she was too late. Leland Gaunt had gotten to him. He had bought something after all, and if she didn't make it to his car before he embarked on whatever wild-goose chase it was that Gaunt was sending him on, he would simply leave . . . and God only knew what might happen then.

She ran faster.

8

"Help me," Norris said to Seaton Thomas, and slung an arm around Seat's neck. He staggered to his feet.

"I think I winged him," Seaton said. He was puffing, but his color had come back.

"Good," Norris said. His shoulder hurt like fire . . . and the pain seemed to be sinking deeper into his flesh all the time, as if seeking his heart. "Now just help me."

"You'll be all right," Seaton said. In his distress over Norris, Seat had forgotten his fear that he was, in his words, coming down with a heart attack. "Soon as I get you inside—"

"No," Norris gasped. "Cruiser."

"What?"

Norris turned his head and glared at Thomas with frantic, pain-filled eyes. "Get me in my cruiser! I have to go to Needful Things!"

Yes. The moment the words were out of his mouth, everything seemed to fall into place. Needful Things was where he had bought the Bazun fishing rod. It was the direction in which the man who had shot him had gone running. Needful Things was the place where everything had started; Needful Things was where it all must end.

Galaxia blew up, flooding Main Street with fresh glare. A Double Dragon machine rose out of the ruins, turned over twice, and landed upside down in the street with a crunch.

"Norris, you been shot—"

"Of course I've been shot!" Norris screamed. Bloody froth flew from his lips. *"Now get me in the cruiser!"*

"It's a bad idea, Norris—"

"No it's not," Norris said grimly. He turned his head and spat blood. "It's the *only* idea. Now come on. Help me."

Seat Thomas began to walk him toward Unit 2.

9

If Alan hadn't glanced into his rearview mirror before backing out into the street, he would have run Polly down, completing the evening by crushing the woman he loved under the rear wheels of his old station wagon. He did not recognize her; she was only a shape behind his car, a woman-shape outlined against the cauldron of flames on the other side of the street. He jammed on the brakes, and a moment later she was hammering at his window.

Ignoring her, Alan began to back up again. He had no time for the town's problems tonight; he had his own. Let them slaughter each other like stupid animals, if that was what they wanted to do. He was going to Mechanic Falls. He was going to get the man who had killed his wife and son in revenge for a piddling four years in the Shank.

Polly grabbed his doorhandle and was half-pulled, half-dragged, out into the debris-strewn street. She punched down on the button below the handle, her hand shrieking with pain, and the door flew open with her clinging desperately to it and her feet dragging as Alan made his reverse turn. The nose of the station wagon was pointing down Main Street. In his grief and fury, Alan had totally forgotten that there was no bridge to cross down that way anymore.

"*Alan!*" she screamed. "*Alan, stop!*"

It got through. Somehow it got through in spite of the rain, the thunder, the wind, and the heavy, hungry crackle of the fire. In spite of his compulsion.

He looked at her, and Polly's heart broke at the expression in his eyes. Alan wore the look of a man floating in the gut of a nightmare. "Polly?" he asked distantly.

"*Alan, you have to stop!*"

She wanted to let go of the doorhandle—her hands were agony—but she was afraid that if she did, he would simply drive away and leave her there in the middle of Main Street.

No . . . she *knew* he would.

"Polly, I have to go. I'm sorry you're mad at me—that you think I did something—but we'll sort it out. Only I have to g—"

"I'm not mad at you anymore, Alan. I know it wasn't you. It was *him,* playing us off against each other, like he has just about everyone else in Castle Rock. Because that's what he does. Do you understand, Alan? Are you hearing me? *Because that is what he does!* Now stop! Turn off the goddamned engine and *listen to me!*"

"I have to go, Polly," he said. His own voice seemed to be coming to him from far away. On the radio, perhaps. "But I'll be ba—"

"No you *won't!*" she cried. Suddenly she was furious with him—furious at *all* of them, all the greedy, frightened, angry, acquisitive people in this town, herself included. "No you won't, because if you leave now, *there won't be a goddam thing to come back TO!*"

The video-game parlor blew up. Debris stormed around Alan's car, parked in the middle of Main Street. Alan's talented right hand stole over, picked up the Tastee-Munch can, as if for comfort, and held it on his lap.

Polly took no notice of the explosion; she stared at Alan with her dark, pain-filled eyes.

"Polly—"

"*Look!*" she shouted suddenly, and tore open the front of her blouse. Rainwater struck the swells of her breasts and gleamed in the hollow of her throat. "Look, I took it off—the charm! It's gone! Now take yours off, Alan! *If you're a man, take yours off!*"

He was having trouble understanding her from the depths of whatever nightmare it was which held him, the nightmare Mr. Gaunt had spun around him like a poisonous cocoon . . . and in a sudden flash of insight she understood what that nightmare was. What it *must* be.

"Did he tell you what happened to Annie and Todd?" she asked softly.

His head rocked back as if she had slapped him, and Polly knew she had hit the mark.

"Of course he did. What's the one thing in all the world, the one useless thing, that you want so badly that you get it mixed up with needing it? *That's* your charm, Alan—*that's* what he's put around your neck."

She let go of the doorhandle and thrust both of her arms into the car. The glow from the domelight fell on them. The flesh was a dark, liverish red. Her arms were so badly swollen that her elbows were becoming puffy dimples.

"There was a spider inside of mine," she said softly. "'Hinky-pinky-spider, crawling up the spout. Down came the rain and washed the spider out.' Just a little spider. But it grew. It ate my pain and it grew. This is what it did before I killed it and took my pain back. I wanted so badly for the pain to be gone, Alan. That was what I wanted, but I don't *need* it to be gone. I can love you and I can love life and bear the pain all at the same time. I think the pain might even make the rest better, the way a good setting can make a diamond look better."

"Polly—"

"Of course it has poisoned me," she continued thoughtfully, "and I think the poison may kill me if something isn't done. But why not? It's fair. Hard, but fair. I bought the poison when I bought the charm. He has sold a lot of charms in his nasty little shop this last week. The bastard works fast, I'll give him that much. Hinky-pinky-spider, crawling up the spout. That's what was in mine. What's inside yours? Annie and Todd, isn't it? *Isn't* it?"

"Polly, Ace Merrill killed my wife! He killed *Todd!* He—"

"*No!*" she screamed, and seized his face in her throbbing hands. *"Listen to me! Understand me! Alan, it's not just your* LIFE, *can't you see? He makes you buy back your own sickness, and he makes you pay double! Don't you understand that yet? Don't you get it?"*

He stared at her, mouth agape . . . and then, slowly, his mouth closed. A sudden look of puzzled surprise settled on his face. "Wait," he said. "Something was wrong. Something was wrong in the tape he left me. I can't quite . . ."

"You *can,* Alan! Whatever the bastard sold you, it was wrong! Just like the name on the letter he left me was wrong."

He was really hearing her for the first time. "What letter?"

"It's not important now—if there's a later, I'll tell you then. The point is, he oversteps. I think he *always* oversteps. He's so stuffed with pride it's a wonder he doesn't explode. Alan, please try to understand: Annie is *dead,* Todd is *dead,* and if you go out chasing Ace Merrill while the town is burning down around your ears—"

A hand appeared over Polly's shoulder. A forearm encircled her neck and jerked her roughly backward. Suddenly Ace Merrill was standing behind her, holding her, pointing a gun at her, and grinning over her shoulder at Alan.

"Speak of the devil, lady," Ace said, and overhead—

10

—thunder cracked across the sky.

Frank Jewett and his good old "friend" George T. Nelson had been facing each other on the courthouse steps like a pair of strange bespectacled gunslingers for almost four minutes now, their nerves twanging like violin strings tuned into the ultimate octave.

"*Yig!*" said Frank. His hand grabbed for the automatic pistol stuck in the waistband of his pants.

"*Awk!*" said George T. Nelson, and grabbed for his own.

They drew with identical feverish grins—grins that looked like big, soundless screams—and threw down. Their fingers pressed the triggers. The two reports overlapped so perfectly that they sounded like one. Lightning flashed as the two bullets flew . . . and nicked each other in mid-flight, deflecting just enough to miss what should have been a pair of point-blank targets.

Frank Jewett felt a puff of air beside his left temple.

George T. Nelson felt a sting on the right side of his neck.

They stared at each other unbelievingly over the smoking guns.

"*Huh?*" said George T. Nelson.

"*Wha?*" said Frank Jewett.

They began to grin identical, unbelieving grins. George T. Nelson took a hesitant step up toward Frank; Frank took a hesitant step down toward George. In another moment or two they might have been embracing, their quarrel dwarfed by those two small puffs of eternity . . . but then the Municipal Building blew up with a roar that seemed to split the world in two, vaporizing them both where they stood.

11

That final explosion dwarfed all the others. Ace and Buster had planted forty sticks of dynamite in two clusters of twenty at the Municipal Building. One of these bombs had been left sitting on the judge's chair in the courtroom. Buster had insisted that they place the other on Amanda Williams's desk in the Selectmen's Wing.

"Women have no business in politics, anyway," Buster explained to Ace.

The sound of the explosion was shattering, and for a moment every window of the town's biggest building was filled with supernatural violet-orange light. Then the fire lashed out *through* the windows, *through* the doors, *through* the vents and grilles, like merciless, muscular arms. The slate roof lifted off intact like some strange gabled spaceship, rose on a cushion of fire, then shattered into a hundred thousand jagged fragments.

In the next instant the building itself blew outward in every direction, turning Lower Main Street into a hail of brick and glass where no living thing bigger than a cockroach could survive. Nineteen men and women were killed in the blast, five of them newspeople who had come to cover the escalating weirdness in Castle Rock and became part of the story instead.

State Police cars and news vehicles were thrown end over end through the air like Corgi toys. The yellow van which Mr. Gaunt had provided Ace and Buster cruised serenely up Main Street nine feet above the ground, wheels spinning, rear doors hanging by their mangled hinges, tools and timers spilling out the back. It banked to the left on a hot hurricane thermal and crash-landed in the front office of the Dostie Insurance Agency, snowplowing typewriters and file-cabinets before its mangled grille.

A shudder like an earthquake blundered through the ground. Windows shattered all over town. Weathervanes, which had been pointing steadily northeast in the prevailing wind of the thunderstorm (which was now beginning to abate, as if embarrassed by the entrance of this avatar), began to whirl crazily. Several flew right off their spindles, and the next day one would be found buried deeply in the door of the Baptist Church, like a marauding Indian's arrow.

On Castle Avenue, where the tide of battle was turning decisively in favor of the Catholics, the fighting stopped. Henry Payton stood by his cruiser, his drawn gun dangling by his right knee, and stared toward the fireball in the south. Blood trickled down his cheeks like tears. Rev. William Rose sat up, saw the monstrous glow on the horizon, and began to suspect that the end of the world had come, and that what he was looking at was Star Wormwood. Father John Brigham wandered down to him in drunken loops and staggers. His nose was bent severely to the left and his mouth was a mass of blood. He considered punting Rev. Rose's head like a football and helped him to his feet instead.

On Castle View, Andy Clutterbuck did not even look up. He sat on the front step of the Potter house, weeping and cradling his dead wife in his arms. He was still two years from the drunken plunge through the ice of Castle Lake which would kill him, but he was at the end of the last sober day of his life.

On Dell's Lane, Sally Ratcliffe was in her bedroom closet with a small, squirming Conga-line of insects descending the side-seam of her dress. She had heard what had happened to Lester, understood that she had somehow been to blame (or *believed* she understood, and in the end it came to the same thing), and had hanged herself with the tie of her terrycloth bathrobe. One of her hands was thrust deep into the pocket of her dress. Clasped in this hand was a splinter of wood. It was black with age and spongy with rot. The woodlice with which it had been infested were leaving in search of a new and more stable home. They reached the hem of Sally's dress and began marching down one dangling leg toward the floor.

Bricks whistled through the air, turning the buildings some distance away from ground-zero into what looked like the aftermath of an artillery barrage. Those closer looked like cheesegraters, or collapsed entirely.

The night roared like a lion with a poisoned spear caught in its throat.

12

Seat Thomas, who was driving the cruiser Norris Ridgewick insisted they take, felt the car's rear end rise gently, as if lifted by a giant's hand. A moment later, a storm of bricks had engulfed the car. Two or three punched through the trunk. One bonked on the roof. Another landed on the hood in a spray of brick-dust the color of old blood and slithered off the front.

"Jeezum, Norris, the whole town's blowing up!" Seat cried shrilly.

"Just drive," Norris said. He felt as if he were burning up; sweat stood out on his rosy, flushed face in big drops. He suspected that Ace had not wounded him mortally, that he had only winged him both times, but there was still something dreadfully wrong. He could feel sickness worming its way into his flesh, and his vision kept wanting to waver. He held grimly onto consciousness. As his fever grew, he became more and more certain that Alan needed him, and that if he was very lucky and very brave, he might yet be able to expiate the terrible wrong he had set in motion by slashing Hugh's tires.

Ahead of him he saw a small group of figures in the street near the green awning of Needful Things. The column of fire towering out of the ruins of the Municipal Building lit the figures in tableau, like actors on a stage. He could see Alan's station wagon, and Alan himself getting out of it. Facing him, his back turned to the cruiser in which Norris Ridgewick and Seaton Thomas were approaching, was a man with a gun. He was holding a woman in front of him like a shield. Norris couldn't see enough of the woman to make out who she was, but the man who was holding her hostage was wearing the tattered remains of a Harley-Davidson tee-shirt. He was the man who had tried to kill Norris at the Municipal Building, the man who had blown Buster Keeton's brains out. Although he'd never met him, Norris was pretty sure he'd run afoul of town bad boy Ace Merrill.

"Jeezum-crow, Norris! That's *Alan!* What's going on now?"

Whoever the guy is, he can't hear us coming, Norris thought. Not with all the other noise. If Alan doesn't look this way, doesn't tip the shitbag off—

Norris's service revolver was lying in his lap. He unrolled the passenger-side window of the cruiser and then raised the gun. Had it weighed a hundred pounds before? It weighed at least twice that now.

"Drive slow, Seat—slow as you can. And when I tap you with my foot, stop the car. Right away. Don't bother to think things over."

"With your *foot!* What do you mean, with your f—"

"Shut up, Seat," Norris said with weary kindness. "Just remember what I said."

Norris turned sideways, stuck his head and shoulders out the window, and clutched the bar which held the cruiser's roof-flashers. Slowly, laboriously, he pulled himself up and out until he was sitting in the window. His shoulder howled with agony, and fresh blood began to soak his shirt. Now they were less than thirty yards from the three people standing in the street, and he could aim directly along the roof at the man holding the woman. He couldn't shoot, at least not yet, because he would be likely to hit her as well as him. But if either of them moved . . .

It was as close as Norris dared go. He tapped Seat's leg with his foot. Seat brought the cruiser to a gentle halt in the brick-and-rubble-littered street.

Move, Norris prayed. One of you please move. I don't care which one, and it only has to be a little, but please, please move.

He did not notice the door of Needful Things open; his concentration was too fiercely focused on the man with the gun and the hostage. Nor did he see Mr. Leland Gaunt walk out of his shop and stand beneath the green awning.

13

"That money was *mine,* you bastard!" Ace shouted at Alan, "and if you want this bitch back with all her original equipment, you better tell me what the hell you did with it!"

Alan had stepped out of the station wagon. "Ace, I don't know what you're talking about."

"Wrong answer!" Ace screamed. "You know *exactly* what I'm talking about! Pop's money! In the cans! If you want the bitch, tell me what you did with it! This offer is good for a limited time only, you cocksucker!"

From the tail of his eye, Alan caught movement from below them on Main Street. It was a cruiser, and he thought it was a County unit, but he did not dare take a closer look. If Ace knew he was being blindsided, he would take Polly's life. He would do it in less time than it took to blink.

So instead he fixed his sight-line upon her face. Her dark eyes were weary and filled with pain . . . but they were not afraid.

Alan felt sanity begin to fill him again. It was funny stuff, sanity. When it was taken away, you didn't know it. You didn't feel its departure. You only really knew it when it was restored, like some rare wild bird which lived and sang within you not by decree but by choice.

"He got it wrong," he said quietly to Polly. "Gaunt got it wrong on the tape."

"What the fuck are you talking about?" Ace's voice was jagged, coked-up. He dug the muzzle of the automatic into Polly's temple.

Of all of them, only Alan saw the door of Needful Things open stealthily, and he would not have seen it if he had not directed his gaze so stringently away from the cruiser which was creeping up the street. Only Alan saw—ghostly, at the very edge of vision—the tall figure that came out, a figure dressed not in a sport-coat or a smoking jacket but in a black broadcloth coat.

A travelling coat.

In one hand Mr. Gaunt held an old-fashioned valise, the sort in which a drummer or a travelling salesman might have carried his goods and samples in days of old. It was made of hyena-hide, and it was not still. It puffed and bulged, puffed and bulged below the long white fingers which gripped its handle. And from inside, like the sound of a distant wind or the ghostly cry one hears in high-tension wires, came the faint sound of screams. Alan did not hear this horrid and unsettling sound with his ears; he seemed to hear it with his heart and in his mind.

Gaunt stood beneath the canopy where he could see both the approaching cruiser and the tableau by the station wagon, and in his eyes there was an expression of dawning irritation . . . perhaps even concern.

Alan thought: And he doesn't know that I've seen him. I'm almost sure of that. Please, God, let me be right.

14

Alan didn't answer Ace. He spoke to Polly instead, tightening his hands on the Tastee-Munch can as he did. Ace hadn't even noticed the can, it seemed, very likely because Alan had made absolutely no attempt to hide it.

"Annie wasn't wearing her seatbelt that day," Alan said to Polly. "Did I ever tell you that?"

"I . . . I don't remember, Alan."

Behind Ace, Norris Ridgewick was pulling himself laboriously out of the cruiser's window.

"That's why she went through the windshield." In just a moment I'm going to have to go for one of them, he thought. Ace or Mr. Gaunt? Which way? *Which one?* "That's what I always wondered about—why her belt wasn't buckled. She didn't even think about it, the habit was so deeply ingrained. But she didn't do it that day."

"Last chance, cop!" Ace shrieked. *"I'll take my money or this bitch! You choose!"*

Alan went on ignoring him. "But on the tape, *her belt was still buckled,*" Alan said, and suddenly he *knew.* Knowing rose in the middle of his mind like a clear silver column of flame. *"It was still buckled AND YOU FUCKED UP, MR. GAUNT!"*

Alan wheeled toward the tall figure standing beneath the green canopy eight feet away. He grasped the top of the Tastee-Munch can as he took a single large step toward Castle Rock's newest entrepreneur, and before Gaunt could do anything—before his eyes could do more than begin to widen—Alan had spun the lid off Todd's last joke, the one Annie had said to let him have because he would only be young once.

The snake sprang out, and this time it was no joke.

This time it was real.

It was only real for a few seconds, and Alan never knew if anyone else had seen it, but *Gaunt* did; of that he was absolutely sure. It was long—much longer than the crepe-paper snake that had flown out a week or so ago when he had removed the can's top in the Municipal Building parking lot after his long, solitary ride back from Portland. Its skin glowed with a shifting iridescence and its body was mottled with diamonds of red and black, like the skin of some fabulous rattler.

Its jaws opened as it struck the shoulder of Leland Gaunt's broadcloth coat, and Alan squinted against the dazzling, chromic gleam of its fangs. He saw the deadly triangular head draw back, then dart down toward Gaunt's neck. He saw Gaunt grab for it and seize it . . . but before he did, the snake's fangs sank into his flesh, not once but several times. The triangular head blurred up and down like the bobbin of a sewing machine.

Gaunt screamed—although with pain, fury, or both, Alan could not tell—and dropped the valise in order to seize the snake with both hands. Alan saw his chance and leaped forward as Gaunt held the whipping snake away from him, then hurled it to the sidewalk at his booted feet. When it landed, it was again what it had been before—nothing but a cheap novelty, five feet of spring wrapped in faded green crepe-paper, the sort of trick only a kid like Todd could truly love and only a creature like Gaunt could truly appreciate.

Blood was trickling from Gaunt's neck in tiny threads from three pairs of holes. He wiped it away absently with one of his strange, long-fingered hands as he bent to pick up his valise . . . and stopped suddenly. Bent over like that, long legs cocked, long arm reaching, he looked like a woodcut of Ichabod Crane. But what he was reaching for was no longer there. The hyena-hide valise with its gruesome, respiring sides now sat on the pavement between Alan's feet. He had taken it while Mr. Gaunt had been occupied with the snake, and he had done it with his customary speed and dexterity.

There was no doubt about Gaunt's expression now; a thunderous combination of rage, hate, and unbelieving surprise contorted his features. His upper lip curled back like a dog's muzzle, exposing the rows of jostling teeth. Now all of those teeth came to points, as if filed for the occasion.

He held his splayed hands out and hissed: *"Give it to me—it's mine!"*

Alan didn't know that Leland Gaunt had assured dozens of Castle Rock residents, from Hugh Priest to Slopey Dodd, that he hadn't the slightest interest in human souls—poor, wrinkled, diminished things that they were. If he *had* known, Alan would have laughed and pointed out that lies were Mr. Gaunt's chief stock in trade. Oh, he knew what was in the bag, all right—what was in there, screaming like powerlines in a high wind and breathing like a frightened old man on his deathbed. He knew very well.

Mr. Gaunt's lips pulled back from his teeth in a macabre grin. His horrible hands stretched out farther toward Alan.

"I'm warning you, Sheriff—don't fuck with me. I'm not a man you want to fuck with. That bag is mine, I say!"

"I don't think so, Mr. Gaunt. I have an idea that what's in there is stolen property. I think you'd better—"

Ace had been staring at Gaunt's subtle but steady transformation from businessman to monster, his mouth agape. The arm around Polly's throat had relaxed a little, and she saw her chance. She twisted her head and buried her teeth up to the gumline in Ace Merrill's wrist. Ace shoved her away without thinking, and Polly went sprawling into the street. Ace levelled the gun at her.

"Bitch!" he cried.

15

"There," Norris Ridgewick murmured gratefully.

He had rested the barrel of his service revolver along one of the flasher-bars. Now he held his breath, caught his lower lip in his teeth, and squeezed the trigger. Ace Merrill was suddenly hurled over the woman in the street—it was Polly Chalmers, and Norris had time to think he should have known—with the back of his head spreading and flying outward in clumps and clots.

Suddenly Norris felt very faint.

But he also felt very, very blessed.

16

Alan took no notice of Ace Merrill's end.

Neither did Leland Gaunt.

They faced each other, Gaunt on the sidewalk, Alan standing by his station wagon in the street with the horrible, breathing valise between his feet.

Gaunt took a deep breath and closed his eyes. Something passed over his face—a kind of shimmer. When he opened his eyes again, a semblance of the Leland Gaunt who had fooled so many people in The Rock was back—charming, urbane Mr. Gaunt. He glanced down at the paper snake lying on the sidewalk, grimaced with distaste, and kicked it into the gutter. Then he looked back at Alan and held out one hand.

"Please, Sheriff—let's not argue. The hour is late and I'm tired. You want me out of your town, and I want to go. I *will* go . . . as soon as you give me what's mine. And it *is* mine, I assure you."

"Assure and be damned. I don't believe you, my friend."

Gaunt stared at Alan with impatience and anger. "That bag and its contents belong to *me!* Don't you believe in free trade, Sheriff Pangborn? What are you, some sort of Communist? I dickered for each and every one of the things in that valise! I got them fair and square. If it's a reward you want, an emolument, a commission, a finder's fee, a dip out of the old gravyboat, whatever you want to call it, that I can understand and that I will gladly pay. But you must see that this is a *business* matter, not a legal m—"

"*You cheated!*" Polly screamed. "*You cheated and you lied and you cozened!*"

Gaunt shot her a pained glance, then looked back at Alan. "I

didn't, you know. I dealt as I always do. I show people what I
have to sell . . . and let them make up their own minds. So . . .
if you please . . ."

"I think I'll keep it," Alan said evenly. A small smile, as thin
and sharp as a rind of November ice, touched his mouth. "Let's
just call it evidence, okay?"

"I'm afraid you can't do that, Sheriff." Gaunt stepped off the
sidewalk and into the street. Small red pits of light glowed in
his eyes. "You can die, but you can't keep my property. Not if I
mean to take it. And I do." He began to walk toward Alan, the
red pinpricks in his eyes deepening. He left a boot-track in an
oatmeal-colored lump of Ace's brains as he came.

Alan felt his belly try to fold in on itself, but he didn't
move. Instead, prompted by some instinct he made no effort
to understand, he put his hands together in front of the station
wagon's left headlight. He crossed them, made a bird-shape,
and began to bend his wrists rapidly back and forth.

The sparrows are flying again, Mr. Gaunt, he thought.

A large projected shadow-bird—more hawk than sparrow
and unsettlingly *realistic* for an insubstantial shade—suddenly
flapped across the false front of Needful Things. Gaunt saw
it from the corner of his eye, whirled toward it, gasped, and
retreated again.

"Get out of town, my friend," Alan said. He rearranged his
hands and now a large shadow-dog—perhaps a Saint Bernard—
slouched across the front of You Sew and Sew in the spotlight
thrown by the station wagon's headlights. And somewhere
near—perhaps coincidentally, perhaps not—a dog began to
bark. A large one, by the sound.

Gaunt turned in that direction. He was looking slightly
harried now, and definitely off-balance.

"You're lucky I'm cutting you loose," Alan went on. "But
what would I charge you with, come to that? The theft of souls
may be covered in the legal code Brigham and Rose deal with,

but I don't think I'd find it in mine. Still, I'd advise you to go while you still can."

"*Give me my bag!*"

Alan stared at him, trying to look unbelieving and contemptuous while his heart hammered away wildly in his chest. "Don't you understand yet? Don't you get it? *You lose.* Have you forgotten how to deal with that?"

Gaunt stood looking at Alan for a long second, and then he nodded. "I knew I was wise to avoid you," he said. He almost seemed to be speaking to himself. "I knew it very well. All right. You win." He began to turn away; Alan relaxed slightly. "I'll go—"

He turned back, quick as a snake himself, so quick he made Alan look slow. His face had changed again; its human aspect was entirely gone. It was the face of a demon now, with long, deeply scored cheeks and drooping eyes that blazed with orange fire.

"—but not without my property!" he screamed, and leaped for the bag.

Somewhere—close by or a thousand miles away—Polly shrieked, "*Look out, Alan!*" but there was no time to look out; the demon, smelling like a mixture of sulphur and fried shoe-leather, was upon him. There was only time to act or time to die.

Alan passed his right hand down the inside of his left wrist, groping for the tiny elastic loop protruding from his watch-band. Part of him was announcing that this would never work, even another miracle of transmutation couldn't save him this time, because the Folding Flower Trick was used up, it was—

His thumb slipped into the loop.

The tiny paper packet snapped out.

Alan thrust his hand forward, sliding the loop free for the last time as he did so.

"*ABRACADABRA, YOU LYING FUCK!*" he cried, and what suddenly bloomed in his hand was not a bouquet of flowers but a blazing bouquet of light that lit Upper Main Street with a fabulous, shifting radiance. Yet he realized the colors rising from his fist in an incredible fountain were one color, as all the colors translated by a glass prism or a rainbow in the air are one color. He felt a jolt of power run up his arm, and for a moment he was filled with a great and incoherent ecstasy:

The white! The coming of the white!

Gaunt howled with pain and rage and fear . . . but did not back away. Perhaps it was as Alan had suggested: it had been so long since he had lost the game that he had forgotten how. He tried to dive in below the bouquet of light shimmering over Alan's closed hand, and for just a moment his fingers actually touched the handles of the valise between Alan's feet.

Suddenly a foot clad in a bedroom slipper appeared—Polly's foot. She stamped down on Gaunt's hand. *"Leave it alone!"* she screamed.

He looked up, snarling . . . and Alan jammed the fistful of radiance into his face. Mr. Gaunt gave voice to a long, gibbering wail of pain and fear and scrabbled backward with blue fire dancing in his hair. The long white fingers made one final effort to seize the handles of the valise, and this time it was Alan who stamped on them.

"I'm telling you for the last time to get out," he said in a voice he did not recognize as his own. It was too strong, too sure, too full of power. He understood he probably could not put an end to the thing which crouched before him with one cringing hand raised to shield its face from the shifting spectrum of light, but he could make it be gone. Tonight that power was his . . . if he dared to use it. If he dared to stand and be true. "And I'm telling you for the last time that you're going without this."

"They'll die without me!" the Gaunt-thing moaned. Now its hands hung between its legs; long claws clicked and clittered in the scattered debris which lay in the street. "Every single *one* of them will die without me, like plants without water in the desert. Is that what you want? *Is* it?"

Polly was with Alan then, pressed against his side.

"Yes," she said coldly. "Better that they die here and now, if that's what has to happen, than that they go with you and live. They—*we*—did some lousy things, but that price is much too high."

The Gaunt-thing hissed and shook its claws at them.

Alan picked up the bag and backed slowly into the street with Polly by his side. He raised the fountain of light-flowers so that they cast an amazing, revolving glow upon Mr. Gaunt and his Tucker Talisman. He pulled air into his chest—more air than his body had ever contained before, it seemed. And when he spoke, the words roared from him in a vast voice which was not his own. *"GO HENCE, DEMON! YOU ARE CAST OUT FROM THIS PLACE!"*

The Gaunt-thing screamed as if burned by scalding water. The green awning of Needful Things burst into flame and the show-window blew inward, its glass pulverized to diamonds. From above Alan's closed hand, bright rays of radiance—blue, red, green, orange, deep-hued violet—struck out in every direction. For a moment a tiny, exploding star seemed balanced on his fist.

The hyena-hide valise burst open with a rotted pop, and the trapped, wailing voices escaped in a vapor which was not seen but felt by all of them—Alan, Polly, Norris, Seaton.

Polly felt the hot, sinking poison in her arms and chest disappear.

The heat slowly gathering around Norris's heart dissipated.

All over Castle Rock, guns and clubs were cast down; people looked at each other with the wondering eyes of those who have awakened from a dreadful dream.

And the rain stopped.

17

Still screaming, the thing which had been Leland Gaunt hopped and scrambled across the sidewalk to the Tucker. It pulled the door open and flopped behind the wheel. The motor screamed into life. It was not the sound of any engine made by human hands. A long lick of orange fire belched from the exhaust pipe. The taillights flared and they were not red glass but ugly little eyes—the eyes of cruel imps.

Polly Chalmers screamed and turned her face against Alan's shoulder, but Alan could not turn away. Alan was doomed to see and to remember all his life what he saw, as he would remember the night's brighter marvels: the paper snake that became momentarily real, the paper flowers that had turned into a bouquet of light and a reservoir of power.

The three headlights blazed on. The Tucker backed out into the street, smoking the macadam beneath its tires to boiling goo. It screamed around in a reverse turn to the right, and although it did not touch Alan's car, the station wagon flew backward several feet just the same, as if repelled by some powerful magnet. The front end of the Talisman had begun to glow with a foggy white radiance, and beneath this glow it seemed to be changing and reforming itself.

The car *shrieked,* pointing downhill toward the boiling cauldron which had been the Municipal Building, the litter of smashed cars and vans, and the roaring stream that no bridge spanned. The engine cranked up to insane revs, souls howling in a discordant frenzy, and the bright, misty glow began to spread backward, engulfing the car.

For one single moment the Gaunt-thing looked out the drooping, melting driver's-side window at Alan, seeming to mark him forever with its red, lozenge-shaped eyes, and its mouth opened in a yawning snarl.

Then the Tucker began to roll.

It picked up speed as it went downhill, and the changes picked up speed, as well. The car melted, rearranged itself. The roof peeled backward, the shiny hubcaps grew spokes, the tires grew simultaneously higher and thinner. A form began to extrude itself from the remains of the Tucker's grille. It was a black horse with eyes as red as Mr. Gaunt's, a horse encased in a milky shroud of brightness, a horse whose hooves struck up fire from the pavement and left deep, smoking tracks impressed in the center of the street.

The Talisman had become an open buckboard with a hunchbacked dwarf sitting up high on the seat. The dwarf's boots were propped on the splashboard, and the caliph-curled toes of those boots appeared to be on fire.

And still the changes were not done. As the glowing buckboard raced toward the lower end of Main Street, the sides began to grow; a wooden roof with overhanging eaves knit itself out of that nourishing protean shroud. A window appeared. The spokes of the wheels took on ghostly flashes of color as the wheels themselves—and the hooves of the black horse—left the pavement.

The Talisman had become a buckboard; the buckboard now became a medicine-show wagon of the sort which might have crisscrossed the country a hundred years ago. There was a legend written on the side, and Alan could just make it out.

CAVEAT EMPTOR

it said.

Fifteen feet in the air and still rising, the wagon passed through the flames sprawling out from the ruins of the Municipal Building. The hooves of the black horse galloped on some invisible road in the sky, still striking off sparks of brilliant blue and orange. It rose over Castle Stream, a glowing box in the sky; it passed over the downed bridge which lay in the torrent like the skeleton of a dinosaur.

Then a raft of smoke from the burning hulk of the Municipal Building blew across Main Street, and when the smoke cleared, Leland Gaunt and his hellwagon were gone.

18

Alan walked Polly down to the cruiser which had brought Norris and Seaton upstreet from the Municipal Building. Norris was still sitting in the window, clinging to the flasher-bars. He was too weak to lower himself back inside without falling.

Alan slipped his hands around Norris's belly (not that Norris, who was built like a tent-peg, had much) and helped him to the ground.

"Norris?"

"What, Alan?" Norris was weeping.

"From now on you can change your clothes in the crapper any time you want," Alan said. "Okay?"

Norris did not seem to hear.

Alan had felt the blood soaking into his First Deputy's shirt. "How bad are you hit?"

"Not too bad. At least I don't think so. But this"—he swept his hand at the town, encompassing all the burning and all the rubble—"all this is *my* fault. Mine!"

"You're wrong," Polly said.

"You don't understand!" Norris's face was a twisted rag of grief and shame. "I'm the one who slashed Hugh Priest's tires! I set him off!"

"Yes," Polly said, "probably you did. You'll have to live with that. Just as I'm the one who set Ace Merrill off, and I'll have to live with *that*." She pointed toward where Catholics and Baptists were straggling off in different directions, unhampered by the few dazed cops who were still standing. Some of the religious warriors were walking alone; some walked together. Father Brigham appeared to be supporting Rev. Rose, and Nan

Roberts had her arm around Henry Payton's waist. "But who set *them* off, Norris? And Wilma? And Nettie? And all the others? All I can say is that if you did it all yourself, you must be a real bear for work."

Norris burst into loud, anguished sobs. "I'm just so *sorry.*"

"So am I," Polly said quietly. "My heart is broken."

Alan gave Norris and Polly a brief hug, and then leaned in the passenger window of Seat's cruiser. "How are *you* feeling, old buddy?"

"Pretty perky," Seat said. He looked, in fact, absolutely agog. Confused, but agog. "You folks look *lots* worse'n I do."

"I think we better get Norris to the hospital, Seat. If you've got room in there, we could all go."

"You bet, Alan! Climb in! Which hospital?"

"Northern Cumberland," Alan said. "There's a little boy there I want to see. I want to make sure his father got to him."

"Alan, did I see what I thought I saw? Did that fella's car turn into a wagon and go flying off into the sky?"

"I don't know, Seat," Alan said, "and I'll tell you the God's honest truth: I never *want* to know."

Henry Payton had just arrived, and now he touched Alan on the shoulder. His eyes were shocked and strange. He had the look of a man who will soon make some big changes in his way of living, his way of thinking, or both. "What happened, Alan?" he asked. "What really happened in this goddam town?"

It was Polly who answered.

"There was a sale. The biggest going-out-of-business sale you ever saw . . . but in the end, some of us decided not to buy."

Alan had opened the door and helped Norris into the front seat. Now he touched Polly's shoulder. "Come on," he said. "Let's go. Norris is hurting, and he's lost a lot of blood."

"Hey!" Henry said. "I've got a lot of questions, and—"

"Save them." Alan got in back next to Polly and closed the door. "We'll talk tomorrow, but for now I'm off-duty. In fact, I think I'm off-duty in this town forever. Be content with this—it's over. Whatever went on in Castle Rock is over."

"But—"

Alan leaned forward and tapped Seat on one bony shoulder. "Let's go," he said quietly. "And don't spare the horses."

Seat began to drive, heading up Main Street, heading north. The cruiser turned left at the fork and began to climb Castle Hill toward Castle View. As they topped the hill, Alan and Polly turned back together to look at the town, where fire bloomed like rubies. Alan felt sadness, and loss, and a strange, cheated grief.

My town, he thought. *It was my town. But not anymore. Not ever again.*

They turned to face forward again at the same instant, and ended up looking into each other's eyes instead.

"You will never know," she said softly. "What really happened to Annie and Todd that day—you will never know."

"And no longer want to," Alan Pangborn said. He kissed her cheek gently. "That belongs in the darkness. Let the darkness bear it away."

They topped the View and picked up Route 119 on the other side, and Castle Rock was gone; the darkness had borne that away, too.

YOU'VE BEEN HERE BEFORE.

Sure you have. Sure. I never forget a face.

Come on over, let me shake your hand! Tell you somethin: I recognized you by the way you walk even before I saw your face good. You couldn't have picked a better day to come back to Junction City, the nicest little town in Iowa—at least on *this* side of Ames. Go ahead, you can laugh; it was meant as a joke.

Can you sit a spell with me? Right here on this bench by the War Memorial will be fine. The sun's warm and from here we can see just about all of downtown. You want to mind the splinters, that's all; this bench has been here since Hector was a pup. Now—look over there. No, a little to your right. The building where the windows have been soaped over. That used to be Sam Peebles's office. Real-estate man, and a damned good one. Then he married Naomi Higgins from down the road in Proverbia and off they went, just like young folks almost always do these days.

That place of his stood empty for over a year—the economy's been rotten out here since all that Mideast business started—but now somebody's finally taken it over. Been lots of talk about it, too, I want to tell you. But you know how it is; in a place like Junction City, where things don't change much from one year to the next, the openin of a new store is big news. Won't be long, either, from the look of things; the last of the workmen packed up their tools and left last Friday. Now what I think is—

Who?

Oh, *her!* Why, that's Irma Skillins. She used to be the principal at Junction City High School—the first woman principal in this part of the state, I heard. She retired two years ago, and it seems like she retired from everything else at the same time—Eastern Star, Daughters of the American Revolution, the Junction City Players. She even quit the church choir, I understand. I imagine part of it's the rheumatiz—she's got it awful bad now. See the way she leans on that cane of hers? A person gets like that, I imagine they'd do just about anything to get a little relief.

Look at that! Checking that new store out pretty close, ain't she? Well, why not? She may be old, but she ain't dead, not by a long chalk. Besides, you know what they say; 'twas curiosity killed the cat, but it was satisfaction that brought him back.

Can I read the sign? You bet I can! I got glasses two years ago, but they're just for close work; my long vision has never been better. It says OPENING SOON on top, and under that, ANSWERED PRAYERS, A NEW KIND OF STORE. And the last line—wait a minute, it's a little smaller—the last line says *You won't believe your eyes!* I probably will, though. It says in Ecclesiastes that there ain't nothing new under the sun, and I pretty much hold to that. But Irma will be back. If nothing else, I imagine she'll want to get a good look at whoever it was decided to put that bright red awning over Sam Peebles's old office!

I might even have a look inside myself. I suppose most everyone in town will before everything's said and done.

Interesting name for a store, ain't it? Answered Prayers. Makes you wonder what's for sale inside.

Why, with a name like that it could be anything.

Anything at all.

October 24, 1988
January 28, 1991